The Flower Brides

D0752361

The Flower Brides

GRACE LIVINGSTON HILL

BARBOUR BOOKS

An Imprint of Barbour Publishing, Inc.

All scripture quotations are taken from the King James Version of the
Bible.

This book is a work of fiction. Names, characters, places, and incidents
are either products of the author's imagination or used fictitiously.
Any similarity to actual people, organizations, and/or events is purely
coincidental.

Published by Barbour Books, an imprint of Barbour Publishing, Inc.,
P.O. Box 719, Uhrichsville, Ohio 44683, www.barbourbooks.com

*Our mission is to publish and distribute inspirational products offering
exceptional value and biblical encouragement to the masses.*

Member of the
Evangelical Christian
Publishers Association

Printed in the United States of America.

Contents

Marigold

Chapter 1

Philadelphia, 1930s

Marigold brought the big white box into her mother's bedroom and put it on the bed. Her eyes were shining, and her lovely red-gold hair caught the sunlight and flamed gloriously, lighting up her happy brown eyes with topaz glints.

"Come, Mother, and look. I brought it home with me. I couldn't wait to have it sent up; I wanted so much to have you see it at once."

The mother came and stood beside the bed smiling, with just a bit of a troubled look in the deeps of her eyes. "It's a lovely box, anyway, satin smooth, and looks as if it ought to hold a wedding dress at least," she said wistfully.

"Yes, isn't it!" said Marigold brightly. "And to think I have a dress in the house from that wonderful shop! I never thought that would happen to me! The best part of the box to me is that magic name on the top, 'François.' I've dreamed of having that happen!"

"Dear child!" said her mother, with a sad little smile. "But, do you think it is so much better than other places that aren't so expensive? I've always thought we had some lovely things made for you here at home."

"Of course you have, you dear! I never discounted them. It's only that I wanted this one to be, well, different from anything ever. I wanted it to have a big name behind it. And then there's always some little touch that can't be achieved except by those great designers. You know that, Mother. Oh, Mother dear! Don't look so grieved. The things you've always made for me have been wonderful, and some of them much, much prettier than any I ever saw from the great dressmakers of the earth. Some of those are positively ugly, I think, and yet they do have that something about them that nobody else can quite achieve and only the knowledge-able recognize."

The mother smiled.

"I suppose so," she said with a sigh. "But go on and open your box. I'm curious to see the garment that is worth a whole hundred and fifty dollars. I hope it lives up to my idea of what it ought to be."

"I'm sure you'll think it does," said the girl with happy eagerness in her face. "It's wonderful!"

She lifted the lid slowly, such a happy light in her face that her mother was busy looking at her instead of watching for the first glimpse of the Paris garment.

Marigold put the lid down on the floor and turned back the satiny folds of tissue paper. Even the tissue paper seemed to have a rare quality. Then she stood back and watched her mother's face.

"There!" she said. "Isn't that gorgeous?"

The dress lay folded carefully, showing its lovely quality even at the first glance—rich, glistening, thick white taffeta, memories of yesterday woven into its texture and silvery finish. At the slender waistline was knotted a supple velvet sash, soft as thistledown, in deep vivid crimson, with long silken fringe at the ends, and on one shoulder was a dark, deep velvet rose to match.

Marigold's eyes were like a child's with a new doll she was exhibiting.

Mrs. Brooke caught her breath in a soft exclamation of admiration.

"It is very lovely," she said. "It looks—almost regal!" And she gave a quick glance at her daughter and then back to the dress, as if trying to harmonize them. "You've never worn that deep shade of crimson. I'm wondering—" She studied her daughter's vivid face and then turned back to the dress.

"How will it go with my red hair?" asked the girl joyously. "Wait till you see it on me. I'm some sight!"

"Your hair is not really red, Marigold, only reddish-gold," answered the mother. "It really goes with anything."

"Well, you ought to have heard the saleslady rave over the combination," laughed the girl. "She positively waxed eloquent."

"She probably wanted to sell the dress!" said the mother wisely. "But put it on. You can't always tell beforehand. Wait! Let me spread a sheet down on the floor! You mustn't run any risks with that lovely thing!"

When the sheet was spread Marigold slipped out of her little green knitted dress and into the rich, shimmering evening gown and turned excitedly to face her mother.

The mother stood studying her daughter critically.

"Yes, it's good," she assented. "I hadn't realized that you could wear that color before, but it's rather wonderful. It does something to you, makes you look as if the light of the sunset were shining on your face."

"I thought you'd like it," said the girl in satisfaction.

"Yes, it's very beautiful, and very attractive," said Mrs. Brooke. "Turn around and let me see the back."

Half shamed, the girl laughed.

"I'm afraid you won't like the back so well," she apologized, twisting her head to look over her shoulder at her mother. "It's a low back, of course, but I couldn't get any other. Everybody, simply *every*body wears them. I couldn't find one without. And really, Mother, this was the most conservative back they had!"

"Oh, *my dear*!" said her mother sorrowfully. "I couldn't think of you wearing a back like that! Your father would have objected to it seriously. He hated such nakedness. There was a woman in our congregation who used sometimes to put on an evening dress for church socials, quite out of place, of course, and he disliked it so. But even that wasn't low like this. I can hear him now comically saying: 'Mrs. Butler had her dress trimmed with real vertebrae, didn't she?'"

Marigold laughed half-heartedly.

"Oh, but Mother, that was a long while ago. He wouldn't have felt that way now. Why, you even see low sun-backs in the daytime, and on the beach, and everywhere. And nobody has evening dresses made high in the back."

"Yes, I suppose so," sighed the mother, troubled. "But couldn't we fit in a piece of real lace, or perhaps get some of the material and do something with that back?"

"Mother! How simply *dread*ful! You would take all the style away and ruin it! Everybody would be laughing at me behind my back. No, Mother dear, you'll have to get used to such things. Nobody thinks anything about backs today. What's a back, anyway? Just a back."

"Well, but backs are ugly!" said the mother, with a troubled gaze. "I don't see why they do it! And it makes me ashamed to think of my girl going around in front of a lot of people unclothed that way."

The color rolled up impatiently into Marigold's lovely cheeks. "Mother, how ridiculous! You don't realize that everybody wears such things nowadays, and nobody thinks a thing about it! If Father had been alive today, he would have had to change some of his ideas. In those days it wasn't done, but it is now. I'm sure Father wouldn't think a thing of it if he were alive today."

"I wonder—" said Mrs. Brook, with a troubled frown.

Marigold turned to face her mother again. "Mother, isn't that thin line of crimson just exquisite, falling down against the thick white silk? I think that fringe is adorable the way it falls down the skirt. You do like the dress, don't you, Mother?"

She lifted a charming face eager for approval, and her mother's anxious face relaxed.

"Yes, it is indeed beautiful, and surprisingly flattering."

But there was something in her mother's tone that did not quite satisfy Marigold.

"Mother! You don't quite like it! What is it that you don't like besides the low back? I knew you wouldn't like that, but any dress I could buy that would be suitable would have had that objection. But there's something else; come, own up! I know your tone of approval, and this isn't just hearty."

"Oh, my dear!" said the mother, with a trembling little smile. "No, child, I find nothing else to criticize. It is very beautiful and very distinguished-looking. I'm only questioning whether a quiet little Christian girl—I suppose you still call yourself that, don't you?—has the right to spend all her money on one dress that is so perishable and at most can only be worn half a dozen times. You couldn't possibly get enough others of the same quality to make up a whole wardrobe."

"Mother!" said the girl, her sweet face suddenly shadowed. "You are spoiling the whole thing! I shall never want to wear it now!"

She turned abruptly toward the window, a quick flush mounting over her fair skin to her forehead.

"My dear! I didn't mean to hurt you! But doesn't it seem too bad to spend almost everything you have in a lump sum this way? The dress is wonderful, but I'm quite sure we could have copied it and made it just as lovely. I even know how to put fringe like that on the sash. I've often done it. I'm afraid you'll be sorry afterward that the money is all gone."

"No, Mother, you don't understand. I had to have something that was as good as anybody's; that is, if I'm to go to this party at all. I have to have it for sort of 'moral support,' you know, this first time among Laurie's friends. It isn't as if they were my friends whom I have always known. Those people on the north side of the city are total strangers to me and rather inclined to be snobbish. Laurie isn't, of course, or he wouldn't be going with me. But his mother has never called or recognized me in the slightest way till now, and I feel as if I want to show her that I know what is fitting for such an occasion as well as she does. I don't want to let Laurie down. His mother is not like him. She's very aristocratic and exclusive, and I don't want Laurie to be ashamed of me. I don't want his family pitying me and saying what a shabby girl he goes with. I want his mother to see that I know how to dress just as well as she does."

"Oh, my dear! That's not a very good motive to admit to, is it? She with her millions and you with your two hundred dollars! If Laurie's mother's admiration is worth winning, I'm quite sure she would think far more of you for dressing within your means than for aping millionaires, especially since you can't keep up this style of dressing."

Marigold was silent and troubled for a moment.

"But, Mother, I shan't need to," she said with a quick-drawn breath. "It isn't in the least likely there will be more invitations like this. Besides, I can put away a little money now and then for another occasion that might come up. And, too, Mother, I'm not going beyond my means getting this one dress. Aunt Carolyn told me to spend it on something I really wanted—some luxury, something frivolous if I liked—and this is the thing I wanted with all my heart. This was only a hundred and fifty dollars, and there'll be enough left for gloves and shoes and maybe an evening wrap. Oh, Mother, you're spoiling it all! You don't understand! It's sort of an if-I-perish-I-perish state of mind I'm in. I've got to go dressed so that Laurie's mother can't criticize me, or I won't go at all. If I don't pass inspection, well, she'll never be bothered with me again, that's all; but I'm going right or not at all."

The mother sighed and studied her daughter's flushed, lovely face a moment, a compassionate look in her own eyes. "Dear! Don't look that way! In a way I do understand how you feel, of course, but I'm afraid it's not right. I'm only sorry for you that you seem to be tangled up in a situation that makes you feel you must step out of your natural way of living. You know your fortune in life has not been set by God in the environment of a millionaire's daughter. Your father was a plain minister of the Gospel, and when he was called away from earth suddenly, he had no millions, nor even thousands to leave behind. All this grandeur just doesn't seem to be consistent with your sensible life so far. But there! Don't look so sorrowful! One dress isn't going to wreck your fortune, even though it does take all you have, and perhaps the experience will be worth a good deal to you. Come, since the dress is bought we might as well enjoy it. Forget what I said and be happy."

But Marigold stood staring out the window at the bare brown trees, unseeing, her eyes filling with sudden tears.

"Oh, child!" said her mother in dismay. "You mustn't cry! You'll ruin that dress. Here! Wait, I have a handkerchief. Let me mop you up, and then for pity's sake take off the dress. We can't have it ruined before it's ever worn. That would be disastrous. I never meant to make you feel that way, dearest. Forgive me!"

As she talked, Mrs. Brooke was dabbing Marigold's eyes softly with her own handkerchief. "There! Take it off quickly before I start you off again! Wait! I'll help you!"

Marigold began to giggle hysterically as she emerged from the enveloping silk.

When the dress was hung on the softest hanger the house afforded, swinging from the rod in the open closet, and Marigold had donned her plain little knit dress again, they stood back and looked at it.

"I so wanted to have you like it!" sighed the girl as she looked at it wistfully. "It seemed to me the prettiest evening dress I had ever seen."

"But I do like it, dear. It's a gorgeous garment, the grandest I have ever laid eyes on. It wasn't a question of like; it was a question of wisdom and suitability."

"I know," said the girl, her lips quivering just a tiny bit again, "but, Mother, I thought it *was* wise and suitable. There's no question about its suitability for the occasion, Mother. I've read a number of times in the society columns the kind of clothes they wear at Mrs. Trescott's parties."

"I didn't mean suitable for Mrs. Trescott, Marigold; I meant suitable for you, a plain little girl who has to earn her living. Won't even Mrs. Trescott question the suitability of such a dress for you?"

"Well, but Mother, if I'm going there at all, oughtn't I to go right? And if I'm going with Laurie to things, I've *got* to be dressed the way he would want to see me."

The mother's brows drew together with a trouble frown again. "*Why*, Marigold? Does he mean so much to you? Dear, are you planning to marry Laurie?"

"Mother!" said Marigold, her cheeks flaming suddenly into brilliant color. "Why, *Mother*! He hasn't even asked me to—yet!"

"*Yet?* Then you're expecting him to? Dear, I hate to force your confidence, but a good deal depends on your attitude toward the question. If he does ask you, are you wanting to say yes?"

"Oh, Mother!" said the girl, with quick panic in her eyes. "I haven't got as far as that yet. I'm only having a good time."

"Well, that's what I was afraid of."

"Why, Mother, you don't think a girl should go ahead and

plan things like that, do you, not till she's been asked?"

"A girl ought to know whether she *could* love a man before she lets him go too far in falling in love with her. She has no right to lead him on if she knows she cannot care for him. You know, dear, you have been going pretty steadily with Laurie for several months now and people are beginning to couple your names and to question and to take things for granted. I only want you to know yourself. When it comes to spending a hundred and fifty dollars for one dress, it seems to me you must be pretty sure of yourself."

The dear eyes were clouded again, and this time the tears really came.

"You don't like Laurie, do you, Mother?" she charged unexpectedly, whirling around and facing her mother with beseeching eyes. "He's so merry and—*dear*, I don't see how you can help liking him!" And the tears poured down with unexpected swiftness.

"I didn't say I didn't like him, dear child!" said the mother, distressed. "Oh, I never meant to make you feel badly. I just wanted to warn you. Of course Laurie is likable. He certainly is merry—yes, and dear in his ways—I understand how you feel. But I scarcely know him well enough to judge whether he is suitable for my precious girl. He drops in here, has a pleasant word, flashes his handsome eyes, smiles charmingly, smoothes his beautiful dark hair; and he's courteous and delightful in every way for the five minutes while he is waiting for you. Then you flit off together, and hours later I hear him linger at the door a minute when he brings you back. How can I know?"

"Oh, Mother! I didn't realize! Of course you don't really know him, do you? Couldn't we ask him here to dinner some night?"

"We *could*," said the mother thoughtfully. "Are you sure he would want to come? Of course, now since his mother has invited you, it will be easier for us to invite him—*perhaps*. But, dear, I want you to face the future, be sure of every step you take, and not rush into something that will bring you sorrow after the glamour has departed."

"Mother! Isn't there any real love in the world that lasts? All glamour doesn't depart, does it?"

"There certainly is a true love that lasts, and that's what I want you to have, dear. That's why I'm daring to invade the privacy of your heart and warn you."

Marigold pondered this, perplexed. "But why are you especially worried about Laurie, Mother? When Eastman Hunter and Earle Browning used to come here a good deal, you never said anything, nor when John Potter came. You seemed to take it all perfectly naturally and counted them my good friends. You didn't probe me to see if I was going to get married right away. I wasn't so much younger than I am now. It was only a little over a year ago. Did you like any of them better than Laurie?"

"No, not as well," said the mother frankly, "but, dear, Laurie is of another class. It is always a serious question when young people of different classes try to come together. Once in a great while such a marriage is a happy one, but too often it is not. I want you to be really happy, darling!"

"Mother, I didn't think you believed in classes and aristocracy!" charged Marigold unhappily. "I thought you thought we were just as good as anybody else."

"I'm not talking about one being better than another, child. I'm thinking of the different ways of upbringing."

"Laurie has been beautifully brought up," said the girl proudly. "He has more real courtesy and culture than anybody I know."

"Yes," said the mother thoughtfully, "as far as courtesy goes, he is charming! But it isn't just courtesy and culture I mean. There are other things, things of the world. Marigold, you know yourself he has been brought up by the standards of the world, and he considers worldly things first."

"Oh, but Mother, that wouldn't make any difference with us. He always wants to do what I want. That is, *almost* always," cried the girl.

The mother smiled sadly.

"That's very nice now, dear," she said, "but would it last? And have you realized, my girl, that you yourself have let down some of your own standards since you began to go with Laurie?"

Marigold dropped her glance and flushed uneasily.

"Oh, well, not in things that really matter," she said. "I don't think it's right to be too straight-laced. I found Laurie didn't understand my attitude at all, and I didn't see that a few trifles were important. He doesn't insist on much. And anyway, what's that got to do with my new dress?"

The mother studied her a little sadly and then with a sigh said, "Well, dear, let's put it all away and just enjoy your dress. I've been looking at it while we talked, and the richness of it is growing on me. It is really distinguished-looking. The silk is a beautiful texture. It must have been especially woven for the company that made the dress. We don't get silk like that in the stores today. It's more like the quality of my grandmother's wedding dress. And I like that way the sash is tied around the waist and the line of crimson fringe falling on the heavy white. It's most unusual."

Suddenly Marigold came up behind her mother and flung her arms around her neck.

"Oh, you dear, precious mother!" she cried. "You're rare! You always did cheer me up just at the last minute when I'm ready to hate myself for something I've done. You're a good sport if there ever was one. I know you don't like that dress, not as much as you'd like to like it. You think it's all out of place for me, and perhaps you're right. At least if I had only myself to consider, I'm sure you are. But I just felt I must have it. You see, Mother, the woman who sold it to me showed me the dresses Laurie's mother and sister have ordered, and I know what I'm up against. She said this one came in after theirs were ordered, or she was sure Gwendolyn would have taken it instead of the one she got, for she had asked for white with a touch of this new red on it and was disappointed that they didn't have it. However, her own is lovely! It's pale apricot silk mesh, frilled till it looks like foam. She'll be a dream in it. She has dark hair and eyes, like Laurie's."

Mrs. Brooke watched her daughter's changing vivid expression with troubled eyes. How thoroughly intrigued her dear child was with all that belonged to Lawrence Trescott! Was her warning too late? Should she have done something about it sooner? Or was she perhaps mistaken? Could it be that this was the way her child's life was planned? Could Laurie bring Marigold the best happiness? Was he worthy of her? She could not bear that there should be heartbreak in store for her wonderful little girl.

"You're not listening to me, Mother!" charged the daughter reproachfully. "Your eyes are quite far away!"

"Oh yes, I'm listening. Apricot-colored silk mesh would be lovely on anybody. Will she wear pearls with it, I wonder?"

"No," said Marigold eagerly, "the saleswoman said she was wearing rose quartz—a long rope of rose quartz beads, with a buckle and bracelet to match. She had the buckle there. She showed it to me. It's most unusual. Strange for her, isn't it, to choose semiprecious stones when she might have real pearls! Or diamonds! But things like that are worn now instead of the real precious gems. And I can see that there's something about the depths of rose quartz that gives just the right light and sparkle to the silk mesh."

Her mother smiled whimsically. "Fortunate, isn't it, that diamonds are not necessary, or where would you be? We have only a small diamond pin and my engagement ring."

"Oh, Mother, you would suggest that I would demand

diamonds! Well, if I wanted them I might get them at the five-and-ten!" She giggled suddenly.

"Dear child!" The mother stooped and touched her lips to the fair, young forehead and tried to drive the shadows away from her own eyes. If her girl was making a mistake, at least she herself would try to act gallantly through the experience.

Oh, heavenly Father, keep my child! Guide her! Save her from sorrow! her heart prayed, even while she entered into the merry talk as they prepared the evening meal.

They were just sitting down to the table when there came a ring at the door—a boy with a special delivery letter!

"A letter from Aunt Marian," announced Marigold, coming back eagerly. "Special delivery, too. Open it quick and see if anything is the matter."

Aunt Marian was Mrs. Brooke's older sister, an invalid, who lived with her married daughter in Washington, DC.

Dear Mary (she wrote),

> *Can't you come down and spend my birthday with me? Elinor is going with her husband on a short trip to Bermuda and she hates to leave me alone, especially on my birthday. If you and Marigold could come and make me a little visit while they are gone and stay over a few more days to see them when they get back it would be wonderful. Do you realize that I haven't seen you for four years—though we're not so far apart? My heart is "just a wearyin'" for you. Can't you come? And I haven't seen Marigold since she was a wee child. It isn't right.*
>
> *I'm hurrying this off because I want you to have plenty of time to plan to come, and I shall await your answer eagerly. My birthday, you may*

*remember, is the fifth. Remember I'm sick and I'm
getting old.*

*Lovingly and eagerly,
Marian*

Marigold watched her mother as she read the letter aloud and saw the wistfulness in it.

"Mother, you ought to go!" she said vehemently when the letter was finished. "*I* can't go, of course, because that's the night of the Trescott party, but there's no reason in the world why you can't go and stay a whole week or two. It isn't right you shouldn't see more of your only sister!"

Mrs. Brooke drew a deep sigh and gave a faint little smile of negation. "I couldn't possibly afford it now, dear. It costs quite a lot to go down, even on the bus, and the rent will be due just before that. You see, having to get a new fur collar on my coat set me back a good deal this quarter, and there's no telling whether there will be any income from my few investments next month or not. Things have been terribly tied up, you know. Besides, dear, I wouldn't want to be away the day you go to that party. I want to see you dressed and ready. I want to be sure that everything is right about you, and I want to have the memory of you in your wonderful gown. Then I want to be waiting for you when you get back and hear you tell all about it. I like to see the first light in your eyes before the joy has faded and life settled down into the humdrum again."

"Oh, you dear sentimentalist!" laughed Marigold. "Those things would all keep! And as for the money, you make me ashamed. If I can afford to spend a hundred and fifty dollars for a grand gown, you certainly can afford the few dollars it costs to go down to Washington for your sister's birthday, especially when she asks you in that special way."

"No, dear, it's quite impossible!" said Mrs. Brooke firmly. "I would need a lot of new things to go down there, and I'm not going now. Perhaps in the spring I'll be able to manage it. And I know your aunt will understand—your first grand party! She will know I would need to be here! She was that way about her Elinor, too!"

"But, Mother, you make me feel very selfish."

"No, dear. You mustn't feel that way. It's all right. You let me manage this!"

And just then Laurie rushed in unexpectedly. "Come on, Mara. I've got tickets for the ice carnival. Get your skates and we'll make the first number!"

In almost no time Marigold was gone, and her mother was left alone to read her sister's letter and shed a few quiet tears on her own account. Then she sighed and thought of her girl and wondered. Was she foolish to worry this way about Marigold? Good, dear Marigold, always thinking of her and wanting everything happy for everybody.

But Marigold was off skimming on the ice at the rink, her cheeks as bright as roses, her eyes like two stars, and the red-gold hair flaming brightly as she glided along. For Laurie's arm was around her, his handsome face was looking down at her admiringly, and back at home there hung a wonderful garment from François's, ready for her appearance at the Trescott party. Life seemed good to Marigold. Why worry about anything? It was a mother's duty to worry, perhaps, but it would all come out right in the end. She was Laurie's girl, and that was all that she cared about now.

Chapter 2

That very afternoon over in the Trescott mansion, Laurie Trescott's mother was sitting at her desk with a pile of letters and papers before her, talking to her sister-in-law, Irene Trescott, who had just run in to talk over a few plans connected with the party that was to come off the next week.

Out in the hall, Maggie, a woman who was sometimes called in for an extra to supplement the regular staff of servants, was washing the baseboards and wiping up the floor after some electricians had finished the work of installing some new outlets. The door stood wide open and Maggie could hear all that went on, though she hadn't been much interested to listen until she heard a name she knew.

"Well, Adele, how are you getting on with your arrangements?" asked Irene. "Everything's going as well as all your parties do, I suppose? But say, Adele, what's all this I hear about Laurie having a little rowdy girl and you inviting her to the party? Is that true?"

"I don't know that she's a *rowdy*," said Adele, facing her sister-in-law and answering in a voice that had suddenly congealed. "I really don't know much about her except that she's respectable. Poor but respectable—at least they *say* so! She's the daughter of a deceased clergyman, I understand, without a penny to her name. Imagine it! Going around with my Laurie! And the foolish boy doesn't in the least realize what he's doing! He's just having a good time, of course, but with quite an impossible girl. Her name is Marigold Brooke! You wouldn't know her, of course. She's not in the limelight, thank goodness! Not yet, anyway, and shan't be if I can help it!"

"Then why is she invited to the party? Or isn't that so?"

"Yes, I invited her. Of course. Laurie wished it, and I didn't think it wise to argue with him. I just invited her as I would have invited any other girl he put on his list. I didn't wish to put up an opposition. Laurie is very headstrong, you know. He takes after his father in that. And if he thought I didn't want her, it would be just like him to say he wouldn't come either. He never can stand being driven; you have to humor him in everything or else you don't get anywhere."

"Well, I think you're making a very grave mistake," said Irene. "I always did think you were too easy with Laurie. However, that's not my business. But I can't understand inviting her if you don't want to foster the friendship."

"You don't know my plan, Irene. I'm doing this with a purpose. Have you never heard of the expulsive power of a new affection? They had a woman in the club the other day who talked about that. At least, maybe it was a book by that name, or something someone had said, I'm not sure which. I was making out my list of guests and didn't listen much, but I caught that phrase and thought it was a good one. I think I can make a great deal of use of it in various ways. But it especially struck me, because it is just what I'm trying to work in Laurie's case.

"Irene, have you heard who I'm having as my guest of honor? Robena DeWitte! Do you know her? Did you ever see her? Well, you've something to anticipate, then. She's the most regal girl I've ever met, perfectly stunning-looking and dresses like a queen, besides being fabulously rich. She's graceful, accomplished, athletic. She flies her own plane and is good in all sports, has the most entrancing figure, and is very clever. You've heard of her, of course. Well, she's my drawing card. With Robena there, I'm not afraid any mere preacher's daughter can get any attention from my son. I shall give her just a hint of how the land lies, and I'm quite sure she's clever enough to turn the trick. When this little simple child of a preacher that Laurie has taken on appears on the scene, she'll certainly find out where she doesn't belong! And so, I flatter myself, will my son. Laurie is very quick to see a thing when it is presented to him in the right light. Just put that poor little common child in this environment and he'll see soon enough what a mistake she is. And it will all come about in the most natural way, you see, without my having to expostulate with him at all. He'll just see he was wrong and stop going with her. There's nothing like showing up the wrong girl side by side with the right one to bring a young man to his senses!"

"Well, you're making a very grave mistake, Adele," said the sharp sister-in-law complacently. "I take it you haven't seen 'the wrong girl' as you call her. But when you do, you'll be surprised. She's a raving little beauty and no mistake, and you won't work anything on Laurie that way, mark my words, for Robena isn't in it beside Marigold Brooke."

"Do you mean you've seen her, Irene?" asked the alarmed mother. "Do you mean you know her?"

"Well, I can't be said to know her, exactly," said the woman of the world, "but I've seen her plenty, and I can't say Laurie's taste in beauty is so bad. She's Betty Lou Petrie's teacher in school, and Betty Lou is perfectly crazy about her. Every time I go over to the

Petries' I hear it. 'Miss Marigold says this,' and 'Miss Marigold says that,' and Eva Petrie says the children just think the sun rises and sets in her. And she's got the most gorgeous hair! My word! If they wanted anybody to pose for an angel's picture I should say she would be simply stunning! Robena is no match for her in beauty."

"Oh, dear me! But, Irene, not in this environment, you wouldn't think, would you? She wouldn't have the clothes, would she?"

"She's clever!" said Irene dryly. "She'd get the clothes, if she had to make them, and she'd make you like them, too! She'd wear them as if they came from Paris."

"But, how *could* she? A little country minister's daughter! A schoolteacher!"

"I tell you she's clever, and she's out to win whatever she wants!"

"Gracious, why didn't you tell me this before I invited her? I didn't have any idea it was anything like that."

"What did you think your son was, a dummy? Going with a girl who wasn't a good-looker nor a good dresser? Laurie knows the right thing when he sees it! He's nobody's dummy."

"Well, I don't think it was very kind of you not to warn me!"

"Look here, Adele, I hadn't an idea you'd do such a crazy thing as to invite Marigold to your party. I thought your line was ignoring her, and besides, you never take my advice when I give it, so why should I bother? But I will say this: if you want Laurie to walk your way, take his pocket money away. That's the only way in the world you can curb that lad. He just can't exist without money."

Maggie, out in the hall, had rubbed so hard at one spot on the baseboard that she had almost eradicated the paint, and she had knelt on her stiff rheumatic knees so long that she could hardly struggle her over-plumpness into a standing position. But she lumbered up at last, took herself reluctantly down the back stairs, and presently went her troubled way home, going over and over what she had heard and wondering if she ought to tell Miss Marigold. Dear, pretty, sweet little Miss Marigold, who always had a kind word for her and a smile and never scolded when she broke a trinket cleaning her dressing table! Mean woman, calling that pretty child a "rowdy girl." Maggie's blood boiled.

❀

Marigold, when she got home after her pleasant evening with Laurie, glimpsed her beautiful dress hanging in the closet with a throb of pride. How wonderful to own a dress like that! She would show them all that she knew how to enter their world in the right clothes, even if she was a minister's daughter and wasn't rich! How proud Laurie would be of her!

But when she turned out her light, after a hurried prayer, and crept into her bed, a thousand little demons jumped up and hopped around her, tormenting her, and driving sleep from her eyes. Why had she thought she ought to buy as expensive a dress as that, anyway? And how was she ever to enjoy the party knowing that her mother could not afford to make even a brief visit to her only sister?

In vain did she tell herself that she had to do this for Laurie's sake. The night grew long and wearisome as she argued things out that she had never questioned before. Had it been Mother's searching questions that started her off, or the fact that Mother couldn't go to her sister for a few days? She wasn't sure. She struggled to get to sleep, trying all sorts of devices to fall unawares into a doze, but all to no effect, until almost morning. Gray streaks of light staring into the windows at her and fevered thoughts chasing one another indistinctly through her excited brain blurred finally into a restless doze, a kind of waking consciousness climaxed in a terrible nightmare such as she had never had before.

She seemed to be standing on a narrow ledge high up in a great room like the library where Mother worked, a great vaulted room with a frail cornice extending along above the tiled floor, at least the height of two stories up. There was no back to the room so that she did not realize at first the dizzying heights on which she crept along. It seemed to be a task which she must accomplish, and she had at first no doubt that she could do it. But as she went on, the ledge grew narrower, and she was obliged to put out her hands and cling to the smooth wall as she edged along, a step at a time. But suddenly the task seemed impossible. The frail ledge on which she stood would now hold only one foot at a time, toe pointed straight ahead, one foot behind the other. Inching along, she could see that just a few feet ahead the ledge became still narrower and then vanished into smooth wall! What would happen when she got to the end? She *was* at the end now! She could go no farther and hope to cling up there.

Then for the first time she turned her glance downward, a hundred feet or more below her, and was frozen with horror at the dizzying height. How had she ever started out on this perilous way? Why had she come? What had been her aim? She could not tell. But here she was, and her coming there seemed somehow connected with Laurie.

And there Laurie was down below her, cheerfully walking along and talking with someone else.

She cried out to him, and her voice sounded small and inadequate. She glued her palms to the smooth wall to keep her balance. She called several times before Laurie looked up, and then he only laughed and waved and walked on.

What was the matter? Didn't he realize where she was standing? Didn't he know her peril? She cried again desperately to him, and he turned, laughing over his shoulder and waving again. "How do you like it up there?" he called and walked on, disappearing through the arches into an adjoining room. Had he gone for help, and was he trying to be cheerful to give her courage until he could bring a ladder?

But the thought of going down a ladder all that terrible distance made her head swim, and she had to turn her face to the wall again to keep from dropping down into space.

And then she tried to turn the other way, edging her feet around. She had come out there, somehow; she ought to be able to go back the same way, she thought. But the ledge was too narrow to turn her feet, and when she tried to edge them backward, she suddenly realized that the way she had come was narrower, too, since she had passed over it. She must hurry before it vanished entirely, yet she could only creep! What awful situation was she in, and how was it she had gotten there? She was paralyzed. She could not move, and any instant she might fall down into that awful space below her. Clinging to the wall with desperate hands outspread, she tried to scream but could make no sound. Struggling with all her might to call out, suddenly something seemed to snap and send her dizzily through a dim, foggy place back to herself and life again. But she found her hands and feet drenched with cold perspiration, and horror still filled her being.

At first she could not get away from the thought of her awful situation just past and had to imagine herself back on that height, edging along toward safety. She tried to think how she got there, and why, and to plan a possible way that she might have been saved if the situation had been real.

At last she sprang from the bed and dashed cold water on her face, trying to forget the fear that had possessed her. But thoughts of it lingered with her as she dressed, and back in her mind the sting of it all seemed to be that Laurie, her Laurie, had done nothing to save her. He had just walked off with a wave of his hand and a mocking call! Laurie would never have done that!

She reminded herself how careful he had been of her last night on the ice, how gentle and thoughtful he always was for her. She tried to thrill again as she had then over the tone of his voice, the touch of his hand as he led her out to skate, and the joy of motion as they swayed together around the arena. But she had been too shocked by her dream to shake off her terror yet. Was this whole thing a symbol of what her friendship with Laurie was going to be?

Nonsense. Laurie was the soul of honor. He would never leave her in dire straits. He would plan some instant relief for her. He would—and she tried to think what he would have done if it had been reality.

❀

Meantime Maggie had thought a lot about the conversation she had overheard at the Trescott house. Lying awake on her none-too-comfortable bed, which she shared with her cousin, sometime in the night she arrived at a conclusion.

"Dat child ain't gonna enjoy no party where folks feels dat-away towards her. I guess I have ta warn her!"

It wasn't her day to clean at the Brookes' apartment, but on her way to her day's work, she stopped there a little early and barged into the kitchen just as Marigold was getting her mother a cup of tea for the headache that had gripped her during the night.

" 'Scuse my buttin' in, Miss Marigold," said Maggie, looking half frightened in what she was going to do, "but is you-all goin' to dat swell party they's givin' up at Trescotts' house?"

Marigold gave her a surprised look.

"Why, I'm invited," she said with a bit of pride in her voice. "Why?"

"Well, Miss Marigold, if I was you-all I wouldn't go! I really wouldn't. 'Scuse me for buttin' in. It ain't none of my business, but I just wouldn't go!"

Marigold laughed out, her clear ringing laugh. "Why, Maggie, what funny advice! Why do you say that?"

"Well, I ain't no business ta say it, but I's just warnin' you; you-all just better not go. I always think a lot of you-all's mama, and I just thought I'd stop by and tell you. I hope you-all don't get mad, Miss Marigold, but I had ta tell you."

"Why of course not, Maggie. Thank you for your interest. But I can't see what difference it could possibly make to you whether I go or not."

"Well, I likes you-all a lot, Miss Marigold, and it ain't no fittin' place for such as you-all. I hated ta tell you, but I had ta. Mornin'! See you next Friday!" And Maggie was gone.

Marigold stood staring blankly at the back door for a minute.

"Well, of all things!" she said at last and then dropped down into a chair and laughed.

Marigold told herself that she wouldn't let the words of an old woman affect her, and she hadn't the slightest intention of staying away from the party. What would Laurie think? What would he say?

But the truth of the matter was she was not happy about it herself. Why, she did not know. When she sifted her thoughts down to the truth she found she kept seeing her mother's eyes when she had renounced all idea of going to her only sister on her birthday. But what had that to do with the party, and why should that trouble her conscience? She couldn't help it that her mother didn't have the money, could she? Of course, it did seem terrible that Mother couldn't afford to go to her sister when her daughter had been able to pay one hundred and fifty dollars for a single dress. But Mother would never have accepted any part of that money for herself. She was sure of that. It was Aunt Carolyn's gift, and she knew her mother. Aunt Carolyn had always been a little lofty about Mother. Mother would never use a penny of money Aunt Carolyn had given. Aunt Carolyn was Father's rich sister, and Mother liked to be independent. No, Mother wouldn't have heard of it that even a part of that precious two hundred should be spent on her.

So she tried her best to put away such thoughts, just as she had tried all night to get rid of that uneasy feeling about that expensive dress she had bought.

But she had her hands full, what with getting her mother to stay in bed until she had had some breakfast and swallowing a few bites herself before she got away to school. She knew her mother would go to her duties in the library despite all she could say, if she could possibly drag one foot after the other, so all she could do was to see that she had something hot to drink before she went and a hot water bag at her feet for a little while before she left.

It was just as she was going out the door that her mother called her back.

"Dear," she said weakly, "won't you please stop at the telegraph office and send a wire to your aunt Marian? I meant to go a little early and do it, but I guess you'll have more time than I will."

Marigold cast a furtive glance at the clock. She had meant to do a bit of shopping herself on the way to school—shoes and gloves and a few little accessories—but the telegram must go, of course.

"What do you want me to say, Mother?"

"Just tell her it is impossible for us to come just now; perhaps we can come later. Say I am writing."

Marigold kissed her mother and hurried away. If she took a taxi instead of the trolley, she might get in her shopping and the telegram, too.

But there were no taxis in sight, and Marigold was too excited to wait, so she walked. After all, she could walk almost as fast as a taxi in traffic.

But as she went down the familiar way, trying to word that telegram in just ten words that would say all that was necessary, somehow her thoughts got tangled up with the look in her mother's eyes when she asked her to send the telegram. Such a shame she didn't feel she could go now.

But after all, why shouldn't she go? Couldn't it be managed somehow? What nonsense that Mother should let anything keep her away from her sister when she so much wanted to go! Why she, Marigold, had seventy-five dollars in her savings account, besides the two hundred Aunt Carolyn had given her. If Mother was fussy about taking Aunt Carolyn's gift, she would give her that. Of course, she had been half planning to put that with the rest of the two hundred and get that perfectly gorgeous evening wrap of black velvet with the ermine collar, but she didn't really have to have that. A cheaper one would do. And the seventy-five would pay Mother's fare and get her some new clothes, too. Mother never bought expensive things.

Suddenly she stopped short and the color flew hotly up into her cheeks, as it all came over her how she was planning to do things in a cheap way for her mother and splurge for herself in grand style, salving her conscience by getting her mother a couple of bargain dresses and maybe a five-dollar hat. She, going to a grand party where she had no right to be, in a dress that cost a hundred and fifty dollars!

Suddenly she despised herself and then more slowly, very thoughtfully began on her way again.

It was odd how things looked at from a new angle took on an entirely different appearance. It suddenly became extremely important that Mother should go to see her sister, right now, when she had been invited and when Elinor and her husband were away and Mother could have Aunt Marian all to herself. That might not happen again in a long time. Of course, Cousin Elinor and her husband were very pleasant and would be most hospitable, but it wouldn't be quite like having her sister all to herself. And then, if she waited until she felt she could afford it, Aunt Marian might die. She was very frail! Or—Mother might die!

Marigold stared into the future with new panic in her eyes.

She had never thought that Mother might die! And if Mother died and she had it to remember that she went to that grand party wearing the price that might have given her Mother the vacation and the companionship of her only sister, how would she ever stand it afterward, no matter how much good fortune came to herself?

Her eyes blurred with sudden tears so that she failed to see a traffic light and almost walked into a car that was coming. As she stepped back, just in time, she realized that she was standing in front of François's, where she had bought her wonderful party dress, and she fairly hated the sight of it. She gave a little shiver and turned away again, but the light was still red, and she could not go on. Her eyes went back to the window where her lovely dress hung only yesterday, and now in its place a street dress was on display, the single offering in a cream-colored plate glass front.

It was a lovely suit, quiet and distinguished-looking, of a rich dark brown with a touch of sable on collar and pockets, just the kind of thing she would like to wear—well, anywhere. But, of course, it would be expensive, too, probably. She sighed as she remembered her mother had said she never could afford to complete a wardrobe that would go with the white evening gown. And here she was, her eyes still filled with tears for the thought of her mother, her heart still sore with compunction over having bought the white dress, and now turning her eyes toward more of the world's gorgeous goods put on display.

Oh, this window of François's had been her undoing! She wished she never had passed here, never had seen the white dress, never had bought it! If she was going to buy anything here in this ultrafashionable place she would be so much wiser to choose this dark suit, which she could go on wearing for months, even years. And this brown would be most attractive, too. What a fool she had been! If she could only undo it all and begin over again, how differently she would do! It was ridiculous, as Mother had said, for a poor girl who was earning her own living to buy a dress that a girl with millions would wear. It was true they could make beautiful enough things at home. And that would have taken very little of her two hundred dollars. The rest could have been used for things Mother needed! How silly that she shouldn't enjoy it, too! Aunt Carolyn had said she was to get what she really wanted. And what could she ever want more than to have Mother have some of the lovely things of life? Why, of course, that was what she wanted more than anything else. To have Mother have nice things. Mother who had planned and scrimped all her life to get her nice things, Mother who had seldom had anything nice, really lovely-nice.

Her heart suddenly beat high, and a new thought came to her. Perhaps, if she bought something else in place of it, for her mother, François's would be willing to exchange the white dress.

She turned swiftly and went into the shop, before her courage should fail her, a sharp pang of relinquishment hitting her in the heart as she entered.

The one who waited on her yesterday came swiftly toward her, and Marigold felt a throb in her throat. Now that she was here and face-to-face with making such a request her courage almost vanished. Also, it suddenly overwhelmed her to give up the dress. But she had to say something, and she lifted her head and smiled. "I've come to ask if it would be possible for me to return the dress I bought yesterday, exchange it perhaps for something else. You see, my Mother isn't quite pleased with it, and I thought I could get something she would like better."

The saleswoman's face grew cold.

"We don't usually exchange," she said haughtily, "not dresses like that. They're so apt to be soiled or mussed. Too bad your mother didn't like it. What is the matter with it? I thought it extremely smart. It seems a pity to give it up when it suits you so well. Don't you think your mother would get accustomed to it?"

36

Marigold's face flamed, and she wished she had not tried. After all, what a mess she was making of it.

"Well," she said firmly, "I don't want her to have to get used to something she doesn't like. I want to get what will please her. After all, I only had it out of the shop for a few hours."

"And it hasn't been worn?" asked the woman suspiciously. "We can't on any account exchange garments that have been worn."

"Certainly not!" said Marigold. "And you needn't bother if you feel that way. I can go elsewhere for what I want." She lifted her young chin a bit haughtily and turned to go out.

"Well, wait a moment. I'll speak to Madame," said the woman, and then she sailed away to the back of the room, disappearing for a moment.

Marigold was more perturbed than ever when she saw Madame herself approaching with the saleswoman. But there was a smile on her face as she came up to Marigold.

"Your *maman* was not please with the gown?" she said pleasantly. "Well, you know, I thought myself, a very little too sophisticate for *ma'm'selle*. It is not quite your type. I would have suggest a more ingenue style, but you seem so please!"

Marigold colored quickly and looked relieved at the same time.

"That was it," she said relieved. "Mother didn't like the low back. I was afraid of that, but I loved the dress so I hoped to win her over."

"Well, that is all right, my dear," said Madame soothingly. "We do not as usual thing exchange exclusive garments, but you so soon return, and I have only just now receive request by telephone for a gown of same type. You bring it with you?"

"No, but I can go after it." She glanced anxiously at her watch. Could she get back to the house, fold it, and return it without being late to school?

"If you can have here before eleven o'clock—well, yes, I will take back. I think I have customer who will take it."

Marigold gave another frightened glance at her watch.

"I'll go right back and get it," she said breathlessly.

She hurried out of the shop and up the street, fairly flying, her contradictory heart sinking. The dress was gone, her beautiful dress! But she was rid, at least, of the awful burden of self-reproach for having bought it.

She would not let herself think of anything as she flew back to the house, except the dress and how to fold it safely. She would take a taxi back to the shop so that she would not have to carry the big box in such a hurry. And would her mother be there still to question her?

Fortunately, Mrs. Brooke was already starting to her work at the library. She stood on the corner waiting for her bus as Marigold came up.

"Is anything the matter?" she asked anxiously.

"No," said Marigold, "I'm just going back for something that I had to have. Are you all right, Mother?"

"Yes, dear. You won't forget the telegram?"

Marigold smiled and shook her head. She was almost too out-of-breath to speak and was glad that the bus pulled up to the curb just then and her mother waved her hand and was gone. Now she could fold that dress without fear of her mother finding out. She wanted the deed to be irrevocably done before her mother knew, because she would surely suspect it was done for her sake and protest. She simply mustn't find out until it was all over.

She rushed upstairs and found her mother had covered the dress with the satiny tissue paper, and it hung there like a white ghost, so out of keeping with the plainness of the rest of the room.

Marigold gave one gasp of sorrow and renunciation, lifted down the papers carefully, and arranged then in the big box that still stood on the little table by her bed. She took down the dress, held it up for a second, taking one last look at it, and then began

38

swiftly to lay it in the wrappings, as nearly as possible as it had been wrapped at the shop, touching it tenderly, like some pretty dead thing that she was folding from her sight forever. While she did it she would not let herself think of Laurie or the party or any of her grand aspirations of yesterday. She was intent only on one thing: to see that dress safely back in the shop and its burden off her conscience. As she laid the last folds of paper carefully over the lovely silk, tucking in the last dripping crimson thread of the sash fringe and patting it down, it came to her that this was all like her dream of the night before. She had started out to walk a narrow highway, far above her own natural little sphere, and had found it too far and too high for her. She sensed vaguely that she had almost gotten to a place where disaster might have come to her soul, and now she had to get back and start over again. If she was still going to the party, or if she was not, what would happen next she could not consider now. When she got that dress back and her hundred and fifty dollars in her purse, then she could think of the next move. She had known all the time that it wasn't right for a girl in her position to spend so much for one dress.

But now she had to move so swiftly, so carefully—oh, if anything should happen to that dress before she got it safely back! Or if Madame should profess to find a tiny spot of dirt! Oh, suppose she had let a tear drop on the silk! A hundred-and-fifty-dollar tear!

She giggled as she tied the cord around the big box, slipped into her coat, grabbed her purse, and went out the door. She felt as if she were a little bit crazy, but she was getting that dress taken back! It was too good to be true. And she was doing it, without Mother having to worry about it either!

She was unprepared for the smiles that wreathed Madame's face when she got back to the shop.

"I thank you a thousand times," she said graciously. "My customer is on her way, and I had nothing to show her. She is a very wealthy woman, and very particular. She buys many garments from me. I like to please her, and I thank you for your promptness in bringing it. And now, I shall return your money—or can we serve you further?"

"Why, I cannot stop now. I have an appointment to which I must not be late. Perhaps I had better take the money now, if you don't mind. But—would you just tell me the price of the suit in the window?"

"Oh, that brown? Yes, that is lovely for you; it will just suit your type. That is now fifty dollars. If you like it, I give you a discount on it, for returning the evening dress so quickly."

"Oh!" gasped Marigold. "I—*could* you hold it until I can return this afternoon? I would want to try it on, you know."

"*Certainement!*" Madame said, smiling. "I give you an option. You come in about four to five? *Oui!* I shall keep. Good morning, *ma'moiselle!*"

Marigold found herself in the street breathless, wondering. What did it all mean? She had returned the evening dress without any trouble, and here was this wonderful suit, furred and exquisite, at such a reasonable price—that is, it was reasonable for garments at François's. But she must think it over and do some calculating before she even considered this, bargain though it was.

She cast one appraising eye at the window as she signaled a taxi. The suit was wonderful. It did not shout its price to the world, either. Her practiced eye saw at once that the material was of the best and the fur was lovely. Moreover, she knew that it was her type, a garment she could wear for several years, conservative, yet nice enough for anywhere. Only, of course, it would not do for the party!

She winced a little as she realized that the wonderful white-and-crimson gown was no longer hers.

Did that mean that she was not going to the party? That

perhaps she would be going with Mother down to Washington for Aunt Marian's birthday?

Her heart quivered and fairly turned over at that.

Or did it mean that she was to buy some little cheap evening gown, which everyone acquainted with the stores of the city could immediately price, or that she was going to slave at night making a dress for herself—or—? Or what?

Marigold didn't answer that question to herself. She got into the taxi and looked at her watch. If this taxi didn't get caught in traffic, she might make the school door by the time the last bell rang! That was important.

But what about the party?

Chapter 3

During the morning, in the intervals of work in the library, Mrs. Brooke wrote a letter to her sister, intended to supplement the telegram that she thought she had sent.

Dearest Marian:

It almost broke my heart to send you that telegram this morning, declining your wonderful invitation. I wanted to fly to you. I'm sure you know how hard it was to say no.

But, you see, my little Marigold is passing through a new experience, and how much it is going to mean in her life I do not know. For the past three years, she has been happy with a lot of young people in her church circle and in her school circle and has not seemed to think further than each day.

But for several months now, her circle has been

narrowing down more and more to those who move in a group with a certain young man, named Lawrence Trescott. His people are wealthy and worldly. I have been much worried. They neither know nor care anything about our Christ. They may attend church sometimes, I don't know, but I should judge their only reason would be a wedding or funeral, or possibly a christening.

I have not mentioned this young man to you before because I hoped the friendship meant nothing but an occasional good time, but quite lately he has singled out my little girl for his attentions, until I have come to fear for her.

There is nothing the matter with him that I know, except that he isn't of our world, and I don't think he knows much about it either, now or for eternity. But that's enough, isn't it?

Yet he's handsome, charming, seems devoted. And she? I'm afraid she's more interested than I thought.

And three days ago there came an invitation to a glamorous party at his home. My girl wants, of course, to go, and the party is on your birthday! Do you see, Marian, why I cannot leave her now? Why I must be on hand?

For I am afraid for my girl. Afraid of the letting down of standards, afraid of the worldliness into which she seems to be hurrying.

I might oppose her going, yes, but I'm not so sure that would be wise. Perhaps I should have started before it ever grew into a problem, only, of course, I didn't realize. Or perhaps I, too, was a little flattered that a handsome, wealthy, well-mannered youth

*seemed interested in my child. But I didn't stop it,
and now it is a problem. Or—is it? How I wish
I had you here to tell me and to advise. You have
piloted your one daughter into a safe harbor with a
fine husband. Oh, pray that my dear child shall not
shipwreck her happiness.*

*You will understand, won't you, Marian, and
know that it is not because I do not want to come
that I am staying at home with my child?*

*I shall be thinking of you on your birthday, and
as soon as I feel I can, I will come and see you.*

*But you will understand—as you always did
understand.*

*With a heart full of love and longing to see you,
and many birthday wishes,
Mary*

Mrs. Brooke folded the letter and addressed it. She would mail it on her way home that night. Then she put it safely into her handbag and went about her work, trying to forget her problems and her longing for things it seemed she could not have, counting up the future possibilities and wondering how long it would be before she could afford to set aside a little every month in anticipation of another chance to go to Marian.

Meantime Marigold, in her classroom, air-conditioned and furnished with all modern equipment for teaching the young mind, was trying to make clear to her class of well-dressed, well-groomed, adoring little girls the difference between adjectives and adverbs, and trying to keep her mind on what she was doing. But in spite of herself, white silk evening gowns with long velvet sashes would persist in parading up and down the aisles in range of her vision, and the grand party, which had for the past few days been the background of her thoughts, whirled nearer and nearer to her view. And now it was Laurie's smiling face that came questioning her thoughts, demanding to know why she had taken that wonderful dress back to the shop. Laurie's face as he smiled down upon her at the arena, skimming along over the crystal surface of the ice. Laurie with admiration in his eyes. How could she have so forgotten it and her longing to please him and see the surprise in his eyes when he first viewed her in that wonderful dress? Had she actually taken the dress back? She must have been crazy! Surely there would have been some way to keep that dress and send Mother to Aunt Marian's besides! There was nothing anywhere in the city that could equal that dress! She must have it! She simply must! She could not go to the party without it! As soon as this class was over, she would slip out into the hall and telephone the shop that she had changed her mind and would keep the dress! It would not do to wait until recess time. The other woman might come and buy it! She could never go to the party without that dress to give her confidence.

But when the class was over at last, a visiting mother appeared and had to be taken around on a tour of inspection. Then another class claimed her attention, and before long with a dull thud it came over her that it was almost noon and she hadn't been able to telephone yet.

And now her common sense was asserting itself again. She must not spend so much for a dress for one evening's pleasure! She must find another less expensive! And her mother must go to her sister's birthday party.

The last period in the morning was a study period in Marigold's room. She had nothing definite that had to be done, yet she must not leave the room, for it was her duty to see that the young people under her care were diligent in their work.

So she sat with pencil and paper at her desk and began to

make some plans. She wrote down a list of things her mother needed for the trip and their probable cost. She speculated on what it would cost her to buy some other less expensive dress for the party, a wrap and accessories, also the relative cost of buying material and making a dress. She added it all up and puzzled over it until her head ached. Why, oh, why did this, her first wonderful party, have to be so complicated with duty and disappointment to others?

At noontime she was frantic. She must get her lovely dress back at all costs. She would somehow manage to work a few evenings in the library or somewhere and get enough to send Mother properly provided for, too. She couldn't go to the party without that dress, and of course she must go to the party or Laurie would be offended. Although Laurie hadn't said anything about it the other night. Perhaps he didn't know yet that she had her invitation. However, she *had* to look right at that party.

So she went without her lunch and took a taxi back to the shop.

As she entered, the saleswoman who had sold the dress to her yesterday came smiling toward her.

"It's sold!" she announced cheerfully. "The customer was crazy about it the minute she saw it and it fit her all right, although I must say she didn't have as good a figure as yours. I thought it was a little snug. She's taller than you are, too, and the hem had to be let down a trifle for her. But she was tickled to death about it. She said it was just what she'd been looking for and she had begun to think she couldn't get it this side of Paris. And wasn't it wonderful you should have brought it back just in time for Madame to make that wonderful sale! She charged her more for it than she did you. She knew she wanted it so much. Don't tell her I told you that. But I'm sure she'll give you a good price on that brown suit if you want it. You came back to try it on, didn't you? Just go into the fitting room there and I'll bring it to you. Madame is out to lunch, but she'll be back before we get it on you; she never stays long."

Marigold, with her heart drooping down heavily, walked into the fitting room without a word. Her dress was gone, her beautiful dress, thrown away by her own hand. This morning it was hers, hanging in her modest closet with her plain little wardrobe. And now it was gone, to some rich, arrogant stranger, and she would never likely see nor hear of it again! She wanted to sit down on the gray upholstered chair and cry! Her lovely, lovely dress that she had discovered and paid for with her own money and rejoiced in! And now, by her own silly act, she had thrown it away! Could she ever forgive herself?

While she unfastened her plain little school dress and got ready to try on the brown one, she was staring at herself in the mirror and trying to remember what had worked on her to make her do this foolish thing. And as she looked at herself she caught a glimpse of her background—the gray velvet carpet, the ivory woodwork, and the delicate rosy tint of the walls—and suddenly it reminded her of the walls of her dream, and with strange whimsy she stood again on that narrow ledge, with the ivory and rose of the walls above her and below her the grayness of the tiled floor so far away, and only vast space between. Her heart contracted. Laurie had been down below there, somewhere, in her dream, and had deserted her; and in the dim quiet of the room beyond the arches, her mother had sat working away at her library records, while she had hung in peril on that fantastic ledge of plaster and swayed between heaven and earth!

It was all fanciful, of course, yet there was something uncanny about it, like a warning of some peril that she could not see, and suddenly she was under the power of that dream again. Whatever the feeling might be, whether of peril to her dear mother or of some danger connected with Laurie, she could not let it go unheeded. No future happiness founded on a mistake could make up for torture of soul. Well, she must be calm about it. The dress was gone, and the saleswoman was bringing the brown suit. She would try it on as if that was what she had come for, and then she would go her way back to her school, and perhaps this chaos of mind would finally subside. When she became normal again, she would try to plan for Mother and for another dress for herself, but now she was simply dazed with her various emotions. Was one dress and one party worth so much?

But when the brown suit was put on her, her mood changed again. It was lovely and sensible, a garment she could wear for years because the style was not extreme. And it was flattering. Yet what good would it do for the party? If she were going to Washington with Mother it would be ideal, but what would she do for the party?

"It's just your style, you know," said the saleswoman.

"Yes," said Marigold thoughtfully. "I like it, and I'm sure Mother will like it, but I'm not sure I should pay so much for such a suit."

"You wait till Madame comes," said the woman with a knowing wink. "I'm sure she'll make the price right. You know, it's getting late in the season now, and Madame always puts down the winter things. This is really your style. You just wait! Madame ought to be here any minute."

"Well, but I can't wait," Marigold said, smiling. "I have to be back at once. And besides, while I'd love the suit, it's an evening gown that I set out to buy, and I'm not sure how much that's going to cost."

"I'll tell you what!" said the woman in a low tone. "I'll put this aside for you, until you can run in this afternoon. Meantime, I'll be looking up something nifty for you in an evening dress at a low price and see what we can do. Do you like green? There's one that would be wonderful with your hair. It's quite simple. I'm sure it would be better for you than that sophisticated white one with that startling red sash! It's just a little importation that was ordered in blue by a customer and it came in green by mistake. It has a high back, too, and that's what you like. I think Madame would give you a good price on it. You know, the season is coming to a close, and Madame never likes to carry stock over. You come in this afternoon, and I'll see what I can do for you."

"Oh!" said Marigold, catching her breath and feeling more bewildered than ever. "Well, perhaps I will come in on my way home."

She got away at once and hurried back to school, buying an apple and a cake of chocolate at a corner grocery and eating them on her way. Perhaps by afternoon her thoughts would have straightened out and she would know what she ought to do.

Back in school, she suddenly remembered about the telegram she had not sent. She must attend to that the first thing when school was out. And what should she say? Obviously not the message that Mother had told her to send, for by this time she was thoroughly determined that, come what might, party or no party, Mother should go to Washington in time for her sister's birthday.

At last she succeeded in writing a message that pleased her.

MOTHER THINKS SHE CAN'T POSSIBLY GET
AWAY NOW, BUT I AM TRYING TO PLAN FOR HER
TO COME. WILL WIRE ANSWER LATER. LOVE,
MARIGOLD.

She sent it off with satisfaction on her way home, and as she walked on toward the shop again she felt calmer now. She had done something, anyway. She had sent that telegram, and it was up to her to plan the rest and make it a success. Mother needed some dresses. It was ages since she had had a new dress. All of her things were tastefully made, of course, but it would be so nice to take her something that was all ready to put on, something she hadn't slaved over herself. She ought to have at least two new dresses if she went on a journey, perhaps three. A nice suit to travel in, a pretty crepe for dress-up, a simple morning dress— perhaps her dark blue crepe would do for morning if she had fresh collars and cuffs.

By the time Marigold had reached the shop, it was her mother's wardrobe she was interested in, not her own. She entered in a very businesslike way and told Madame what she wanted for her mother, and Madame smiled and brought out dresses, just the things that pleased Marigold's beauty-loving soul. She could see her sweet, quiet mother arrayed in these. And suddenly it seemed to her far more desirable that her mother should be suitably dressed than that she should have an evening gown. Why, if she gave up spending a hundred and fifty dollars she could get all three of these dresses she liked so much for her mother and still have some left for other needs. Why should she have a grand party dress? She had always gotten along with very cheap little dresses and looked all right; everybody seemed to think so, anyway.

And while she hesitated, Madame spoke. "You like to take these up and let your maman to try them on? Or she, will she come down here?"

"I'm afraid she couldn't. She—is a businesswoman."

"I see. Then I send them up. Marco is driving out to deliver some dresses now. I could send them up within the hour, and you perhaps will return any in the morning that you do not keep?" She smiled. "And now, you will try on your own?"

Marigold gasped a little then. "Oh, I don't know that I could afford—that is, if I take these for Mother. You see, she does not know yet. I want her to take a little trip. She is tired."

"That is quite lovely of you, my dear. But I send these up, and you and your mother try them and see which you like. You can return what you do not wish to take. And now we see about this green dress. It was just made for you, my child. So simple! So ingenue. And only—" She lowered her voice to a whisper and named a price that almost took Marigold's breath away, it was so reasonable. Why, even if she bought all five of these dresses she would be spending less than she would have paid for that one evening gown, which somehow in the light of this simple green silk now seemed too stately and sophisticated for her. And suddenly her young soul, which had been so tried all day, seemed to have reached a quiet place where there was a solid foundation under her feet.

She went home with a springing step and prepared supper so that it would be ready when her mother got home. She called up the bus station and got schedules and rates to Washington, and she had everything ready to convince her mother that she should go.

❀

They had a great evening trying on dresses and making plans.

At first Mrs. Brooke was adamant. No, she could not think of going. No, she did not want to go, not the day of the party. She must be there to see her girl dressed in fine array.

But the mother was really relieved when she saw the green dress instead of the white one.

"It is much more fitting to you, dear, and I do like you to wear things that Christian people would consider decent. I cannot bear for you to go in for all the freaks of fashion, especially when they verge on indecency. You look so lovely in that green dress, and yet you look like my dear girl as well. I didn't feel as if I quite knew you in that other one last night. I felt as if you were being drawn into a world where neither you nor I belong, and that if you went there, you and I were going to be terribly separated."

"Well, but Mother, when one goes into the world occasionally, doesn't one have to do, at least to a certain extent, as the world does?"

"You must answer that question to your own conscience, my child," said her mother, with a troubled look. "I question whether a Christian has a right to go where he has to lower his standards."

"Oh, Mother!" exclaimed Marigold wearily. And then the telephone abruptly interrupted.

It was Laurie. He couldn't come over that evening as he had planned to take her skating again. His mother had made plans for him, some fool girl from Boston was coming and Mother expected him to take her out. It was a beastly bore, but he couldn't get out of it. He might not be able to get over the next night, either. Mother had so many plans on that seemed to require his presence, but he would see her in a day or two.

As Marigold hung up the receiver, she was graver than her usual self. What omen of peril was there in her thoughts? Had Laurie been less eager about getting to her than before? Who was this girl from Boston? Was she staying for the party? Would there be all those days without Laurie perhaps? Would he have to divide his attentions between them? She had thought of that party in terms of being Laurie's companion, and suddenly she knew she would not be, not all the time, anyway. He was the son of the house and would have to divide his attentions. And all at once she felt terribly alone and frightened at the thought of the party.

Her mother watched her anxiously as she took off the pretty green dress and hung it where last night the white one had hung.

"I'm glad you found it," Mrs. Brooke said with relief in her voice. "It is so much better for you than the other one!"

"I don't know, Mother," said Marigold in a disheartened little voice. "I'm not sure it is the right thing for such a formal party. Madame said it was, of course, but then she wanted to sell it to me. I don't feel as if it would be a moral support like the other."

"My dear, if you were thinking to go out and conquer Laurie's family on the strength of that expensive dress, you were making a very great mistake. You would have been like David in Saul's armor."

"Oh, Mother dear!" Marigold suddenly laughed out. "You surely don't liken my going to a worldly party to anything so righteous as David going out to kill a giant, do you? Aren't you getting your metaphors mixed? I though you didn't quite approve of my going to this party."

"Well I don't, child, if you must know the truth. I think you are going into a world where you do not belong and never should. I think you are getting further and further away every day from the things you have been taught, and more and more you are forgetting God and your relation to Him."

Marigold was silent. It seemed there was nothing for her to say in answer.

At last she looked up. "Well anyway, Mother, I may as well tell you what I've done. I telegraphed Aunt Marian you would be with her on her birthday. And now you've got to begin to get things in order, for I called up your supervisor at the library and told him I was worried about you, and wouldn't it be possible for you to get away for a few days' rest right away, and he said it would. He said he could spare you as well as not for a week, or even ten days if you wanted to stay so long, and it wouldn't affect your salary. He said you had sick leave that you had never taken, and he would be glad to let you go whatever day you wanted to start."

"Oh, my dear!"

But there was dismay rather than joy in the mother's eyes.

"Don't you *want* to go, Mother?"

"Yes, oh, yes, I want to go, but not now. Not with that party so near. I couldn't relax until that is over."

"Why, how silly, Mother. Can't you trust me? You don't think I'm going to run away with anybody, do you, or get into trouble?"

"I trust *you*, dear child, perfectly, but I don't trust—well—the world you are going into. I must be at home and get you ready and be there when you come back to look into your eyes. I could not be content without that. I have written your aunt. She will not expect me."

A worn gray look settled down upon Mrs. Brooke's face, and the daughter suddenly realized that she was tired out.

"There! Mother, we won't talk another word about it tonight. You are very tired. In the morning you will see things differently. Now, I'm going to put you right to bed, and you're not to think another thought about it at all tonight!"

Chapter 4

When Aunt Marian Bevan got Marigold's telegram, she wondered and looked a bit disappointed. She wanted her sister to come very much indeed, but she also wanted to see her niece whom she hadn't seen since she was an adorable little child of three. But when her sister's letter came, she looked troubled and spent an hour in prayer. She was a great one to take everything to the Lord in prayer.

About six o'clock that night, she called up a number on the telephone and talked with a very dear nephew, the son of her dead husband's brother, who from the time of his own parents' deaths had been almost like a son to her.

"Ethan," she said, "what are you doing this weekend? Don't tell me you have plans. I want you."

"If I had, dearest aunt, I'd cancel them for you," said Ethan Bevan heartily. "But I haven't a thing. What can I do for you? I was thinking of coming to call on you, for one thing, anyway. You have a birthday on the fifth, you know."

"Oh, dear lad! Did you remember that? Well, I want more than a call. I want you to come and stay the weekend with me. I'm having a party."

"Good!" came the cheery answer. "I'm with you. Your parties are always worthwhile. Who's coming? Or is that a secret?"

"No, it's not a secret, but the truth is I'm not sure who will be here. You see, Elinor and her husband have gone to Bermuda, and I'm alone except for my nurse and the servants. There's just a little hope that my sister may be able to come. I'm not sure. Do you remember her?"

"Aunt Mary? I should say I did! She used to make maple taffy for me. That was very long ago, but I always put her in my list of beloveds, just next to you. I never saw her again after she was married, did I?"

"No, she lived here in the East, and of course you and I lived mostly out West. I've never told you, have I, how glad I am that you've come east now, too?"

"Well no, but I've hoped you were as glad as I am. I'll tell you all about it when I get there. Is that all your party? That's swell! I like parties where there aren't any inharmonious elements. I shall just bask in the light of both your countenances."

"You ridiculous boy! Remember you are talking to an old woman and that my sister is just another old woman. It's not a very alluring party for a young man of your age. I had hoped that my niece, Aunt Mary's daughter, could come with my sister, but she has another party to keep her at home, so I'm disappointed. Her name is Marigold Brooke. I wanted her to come so we could get acquainted with her, but she says she can't."

"Don't worry! I'm just as satisfied. I'm fed up with girls. I just hate lipstick and red fingernails. There isn't one of them as nice as you, Aunt Marian."

"Well, but I'd hoped Marigold would turn out to be different," said the aunt. "You know, she's Aunt Mary's daughter and would be brought up differently."

"Perhaps," said the young man suspiciously, "but I doubt it. That doesn't always follow by any means these days. What a frilly name she has."

"Yes, isn't it pretty? I believe her father named her, partly for her mother whom he used to say was worth her weight in gold, or something like that—Mary-gold, you know—and partly from the color of her hair when she was little."

"Well, Mary is good enough for me," said the manly voice in a superior tone. "I'm just as pleased she's not coming. When may I arrive?"

"Just as soon as you want to come. I'll be glad to see you anytime; and, of course, if you'd like to bring someone with you—"

"No! I don't want to bring anyone with me. I'm glad to get away from everything and have a little time alone with you, Aunt Marian. And besides, I have some work to do. Engineering problems. Mind if I bring it along? I really have been looking for a quiet place in which to work. Do you mind?"

"Not in the least. You may do just as you please while you are here. And if nobody else comes, well, I shan't mind at all."

Aunt Marian hung up the receiver and picked up her sister's letter again, a little pang of disappointment still in her heart. How nice it would be to have Marigold meet Ethan. But then, if she was touched with worldliness probably he wouldn't like her. And she might not like him, he was so quiet and big and almost shy with women he didn't know. And what was Marigold like? The little sprite with the red-gold hair and the dancing eyes. Poor little girl! Was she going to have to go through trouble? Better that than go to dwell far away from God. Poor Mary! Yes, she would pray! Of course she would!

❀

Was the answer to those prayers already on its way the night before they were made, while Marigold lay wide awake for the second night and tried to think her problems through?

One thing she was resolved upon, and that was that her mother should go to see her sister on the birthday. Party or no party, that should be accomplished. She hoped to get Mother off Friday afternoon. The birthday was Saturday. The party was Saturday night. That was another thing that Mother didn't like about that party.

"It will run over into Sunday, dear. It can't help it, and that doesn't fit with your upbringing and traditions. Saturday night was always a quiet time in my old home, a time for resting and preparing for the day, which with us was especially set apart for worship."

"Mother, times have changed!" Marigold had responded almost petulantly.

"Yes, but God hasn't changed! And people have not changed, either. They are the same weak, sinful creatures they have always been, and they need God and quietness to think about Him, just as much as they ever did. And I believe God likes to have His own take time to look to Him."

She had stopped because Marigold was not listening. But Marigold had heard, and her mother's words came back to her now as she lay in the darkness and thought.

Why was it that this question of the party seemed to bother her so much these last few days? When the invitation had been received, she had had no such qualms. She was only filled with joy that she had been included in this grand event, that Laurie's mother wanted her to come and was going to include her in her list of friends at last.

She had waited a couple of days before replying to the invitation. She wanted to get used to the thought that she was going to be a part of the social life of the elite. She wanted time to think out what she should wear, time to get herself in hand and be sure of herself. She wanted above all to talk it over with Laurie. But Laurie had not said a word. He was likely taking it for granted as he did everything else, not realizing how strange she was going to feel going among his friends who were all unknown to her. Or didn't Laurie know that his mother had invited her? Perhaps that was it. Perhaps it was to be in the nature of a surprise for Laurie, and if that were so, it must mean that Laurie's mother had a kind, friendly feeling toward her.

All these things had influenced her in selecting that white dress. She wanted to do Laurie credit. But now that the white dress was gone, irrevocably, and it was even supposable that she would meet it on someone else at that very party, she felt a kind of unpreparedness which even the charming green silk could not make up for. Was that green silk all right, or should she try and get some material and make another dress even yet?

Or should she stay away entirely? Stay away and go with Mother down to Washington?

She faced the disastrous thought for the first time openly, lying there in the dark, defenseless, alone. It was quite possible that she might not be going to the party at all. If Mother wouldn't go without her, then she was determined to sacrifice everything for her mother. It was silly, perhaps, when there were other days coming, and birthdays, not the actual date, didn't count anyway. Mother and Aunt Marian could have just as good a time together if they came together next week, as this particular Saturday. But she had completely finished with that argument. She had settled it in her mind that Mother had to be there on the birthday, silly or sensible.

And now she had to face another issue.

Was it true as Mother said that she did not belong in a

worldly place like that? She was a Christian, a member of the church, and all that. She had taught a Sunday school class for several years; she believed the Bible, of course, in spite of mocking denials she had met in college. But she hadn't really been living her faith very clearly. It might even be true as Mother said that she had lowered some of her lifelong standards since she had been going with Laurie. After this party she must check up on her life and straighten out a few points with Laurie, make him understand that they didn't fit in with what she believed. But now, of course, it was too late until after this party was over. It stood in the nature of an introduction to his people and it was not her place to question manner and customs of the family where she was to be a guest. Afterward she would explain a lot of things to Laurie and turn over a new leaf as to some of his worldly amusements and ways. But now—well now, what was this new uneasiness that was prodding her very soul as she lay there trying to be complacent about her green dress and plan how to make Mother want to go without her?

Was it—it couldn't be that she was unhappy about Laurie himself. Of course, he had said he would call her up again this evening and he hadn't done it. Doubtless something had prevented him. But—ah—now she was getting down to the real sharp sting that hurt her. It was not that he hadn't called as he had said he would. It was not that he had passed her in his car as she walked along on her way home late that afternoon and he had not noticed her. That might be easily explained, and she could have a lot of fun teasing him about not recognizing his friends on the street. But it was that he had been in the company of another girl, a dashing, dark-haired girl with vivid lips and shadowed, furtive eyes full of arrogant assurance, eyes that offered and dared and were never shy nor true. And the thing that cut had been that Laurie, her Laurie, as she had come to feel he was, had been looking down into those other luring eyes with exactly the same tender, melting expression that he had often worn when he looked into her eyes.

Marigold, as she lay there in the dark, bared her soul for the first time to the truth. She let the vision of Laurie's look that she had seen and photographed clearly on her memory come out in the open while she examined it, and her honest soul had to admit that Laurie had never given her any more melting glances than he had lavished on that chic, sophisticated girl he had with him. Like a knife she let it go through her soul, as if she would see the worst, press the wound, and cut out the thing that hurt her.

And then a new thought came to her. Was this girl whom his mother had invited to be the guest of honor at the party? Was it this girl who would be her rival? She stared at the wall in the dark and saw as it were her own soul, with all its unworthy motives crying out within her for vengeance and victory. Had she really been going to that party to show them all what a winner she was? To conquer his mother and sister, and his whole social set? And her only armor that fateful dress that she no longer had? What presumption! What colossal conceit! But—could she have done it even with that dress? Would it not, as her mother had suggested, have become unwonted armor to her that would merely have embarrassed her with its unaccustomed elegance?

All her self-assurance, her self-sufficiency, her cocksureness had vanished now and left her in the dark alone there to face her situation. And suddenly she saw herself out again in that vast expanse of her dream, in that same impossible situation, with nothing before and no way behind, and a dizzying drop waiting to swallow her! And Laurie! Where was Laurie? Gone, waving his hand, and smiling into another girl's eyes!

In due time, she got hold of herself, brushed away angry, frightened tears, and tried to think what to do.

Should she go and get another dress even more regal than

the first, perhaps black velvet with startling lines and a single flashing pin of rare workmanship? No matter how much it cost, she could borrow money and pay for it in time! Should she? And try to compete with that unprincipled other girl? That she was unprincipled seemed obvious, even in the brief glimpse she had had of her. But Marigold would have to be prepared for even more than lack of principle, if she really started out to compete, to have them all at her feet, and Laurie with them. Or should she just drop out of it entirely? Did she want Laurie if he had to be won by such methods? If he did not really care for her it would be better to learn it now than when it was forever too late.

Then she tried to calm herself. She told herself that she was getting all worked up over nothing. That Laurie was only being polite to a guest and that it was her own excited state of mind that had imagined him flirting with that other girl. Probably the mother was being very friendly and really wanted to get to know her. Probably Laurie had asked her to invite her and would be terribly disappointed if she didn't come. Besides, she had finally accepted the invitation two days ago. She couldn't write another note and decline it, could she?

Over and over again she thrashed out the question. Then suddenly old Maggie's warning that morning came to her. What had old Maggie meant? Was it just a crazy notion she had gotten into her head? Or had she heard something, seen something that made her come in love to warn her? Why hadn't she questioned her? Wait, didn't Maggie say she was sometimes called in to work at the Trescotts' when they needed an extra hand?

Wearily she went on nearly all night tormenting her young soul with this and that, until the thought of the party was almost repulsive to her, and the pretty green silk she had been so pleased about that morning became a symbol of great mortification. A simple dress like that to appear at a party where everything was most formal! She couldn't wear it!

She slept a few moments at intervals but awoke quite early when the first dawn was beginning to streak the sky, and somehow a great decision had been reached. She was no longer tossed about by every thought that entered her head. She knew what she was going to do, and she would lose no time in doing it. If Laurie felt hurt about it afterward she could not help it. This surely would be a way to tell whether he really cared for her or whether he was just having a good time while it lasted.

But her face had a wan, white look as she hurried down in the morning and found her mother already getting breakfast.

"Now, Mother," she said firmly, as if she were the mother speaking to her child, "we've got a lot to do today. We're starting for Washington tomorrow afternoon as soon as I get out of school!"

Mrs. Brooke looked up at her daughter in bewilderment.

"What do you mean 'we'?" she asked. "Do you think that *if* I went I couldn't take care of myself, and you would have to take the double trip in order to take me there?"

Marigold laughed. "No, Mother dear, I know you're perfectly capable of taking care of yourself, but I was thinking of going along. I was invited, wasn't I? And I'd like to be there for Aunt Marian's birthday, too."

"My dear! That would be foolish for you to take that long ride and back again just for a couple of hours there. You would be all tired out for the party, and you would look like an old rag when you got back here. You would have to rush dressing, and there would be nobody here to help you. I certainly won't hear of it."

"Party!" said Marigold calmly. "I've given up the party. I'm not going. That is, not unless Laurie makes a terrible fuss—and I don't think he will find out in time."

"What do you mean? Have you sent your regrets?" asked Mrs. Brooke with deep anxiety in her tone. What was this that Marigold was doing, anyway? Giving up the party that she had so set her heart on, giving it up just for her? Or perhaps she was disappointed about not having the dress she wanted and would blame her mother in her heart for having disapproved of the other dress.

"I'm mailing it this morning on my way to school," she said quietly. "I'm saying that 'Miss Brooke regrets that unforeseen circumstances will prevent her accepting the kind invitation of Mrs. Daniel Trescott on Saturday evening, February the fifth.'"

"But, child! I can't let you do that just for me!"

"I'm not sure that I am doing it *just* for you, Mother dear. I've decided it is best. Now, don't you say another word. We haven't time. Perhaps sometime I'll tell you all about it, but now we've got too much to do to quibble over this and that. Have you got to go down to the library at all today? Couldn't you just call up and tell them you're not coming?"

"I certainly could not. If I am to be away, I shall have to give instructions to whoever is to take my place. They would not understand all my records. I had to leave a number of unfinished items last night, and it is important."

"All right then, you go to the library and finish there as soon as you can, and then go to Grayson's and get yourself a new pair of shoes and some pretty slippers. Yes! Don't look that way. If you don't get them for yourself I'll go and get them for you. And mind you get good ones. It doesn't pay to buy cheap ones that aren't right. If you don't get good ones, I'll make you take them back and exchange them, you know." She laughed and twinkled at her mother, being almost merry in spite of the hurt look deep in her eyes.

"But, my dear, I cannot let things go so easily. I must understand why you are doing this. If it is for me, I must positively refuse to accept so great a sacrifice."

"But, Mother, I thought that was what you wanted, wasn't it? You didn't think I belonged there, and perhaps you're right."

"Yes, I thought it must be something I had said—"

"Now look here, little Mother; why can't you let well enough alone? Perhaps my conscience or something has got working. Anyway, I've fully made up my mind."

"I'm afraid it is because I didn't quite like the white dress and you feel unhappy about the green one."

"No, it's not that. I love the green one, and I guess it is the most sensible thing. But perhaps the dress, or the lack of it, did help me to come to my senses and see that you were right. Anyway, something did, and we haven't time to argue about it. The question is, can you meet me at François's this afternoon at half past three and try on a darling little gray wool that I know you would look perfectly spiffy in?"

"Indeed, no!" said the mother firmly. "And I'm only going to keep one of those dresses you brought up earlier. I can afford to pay for that myself. I'm not going to have you spending Aunt Carolyn's money on me. She gave that to you to spend for something you wanted most and—"

"Look here, Mother," interrupted Marigold eagerly, "that's exactly it. She said I was to spend it on what I *wanted most*, and this is it. I want most in life to have you dressed right. It was a revelation to me when I saw you in those dresses yesterday, and I don't know why I haven't seen it before. My lovely mother wearing old made-overs! I'm not going to stand it any longer. I have a good-looking mother, and I intend to keep her so. It's time you had a few stylish things instead of putting them all on your renegade daughter's back. No, there's no use in the world in your talking any more about it. I'm determined. See my lips! Aren't they nice and firm? If you think you can get out of having pretty clothes by refusing to try them on, you're mistaken. I'll buy them without trying on and let them hang in the closet and go to waste if they don't fit well enough for you to wear! There! What do you think of having a bad, wild daughter like that! I'll turn modern, so I will, and boss you around a lot!" And she caught her mother in her young arms, whirled her around, and then kissed her soundly on each cheek.

The mother laughed and brushed a quick tear away.

"Dear child!" she said. "It's lovely of you to want to fix me up."

"Why?" demanded Marigold. "Haven't you done the same for me all my life? I think it's my turn now."

"But, darling, I'm afraid you'll regret this—"

"Well, I like that!" laughed the daughter. "The first unselfish impulse I ever had in my life you think I'll regret."

"Oh, my dear! I didn't mean that! You've always been unselfish. But I meant you'll regret giving up your party!"

Marigold grew sober at once.

"I wonder, will I?" she said thoughtfully. "Perhaps I'll be glad someday, who knows? But anyway, I've given it up!"

Her mother looked at her anxiously.

"Has Laurie done something?" she asked.

"Oh no. I think perhaps it's what he has not done."

Her mother was still a minute. "Perhaps he's been very busy helping his mother. You know there must be a lot to do to get ready for a grand party like this, and she would need his help."

Marigold laughed a sharp little gurgle of amusement with a tang of bitterness mingled with the mirth. "Oh, Mother mine! Do I hear you taking up for Laurie? Making excuses for him? That is too good. The idea that he would be helping his mother is also good. I don't believe it ever entered his handsome head to do that."

"Why, my dear! How could you seem to be so anxious to go around with him if you think so poorly of him as that?"

"I don't think poorly of him, Mother. I just know it wouldn't be like Laurie to help his mother. It isn't his way. They don't do that! They have a lot of servants."

"But—there would be things that her own son could help in, I should think, that nobody else could do. Oh, my dear! I feel so troubled! I cannot have you give up this party that I know you counted so much on, and I know you have done it just for me."

"Now, look here, Mother! If I want to do it for you, haven't I a right? You who did so much for me? And if it gives me more pleasure to get you some new dresses than to buy—well, anything that amount of money could have bought, aren't you willing I should be pleased? And it *does* please me, truly! Besides, Mother, I thought it was best not to go. I really did. Now please don't ask any more questions. Not now, anyhow. Sometime I'll tell you all about it. I'm testing something out, and I don't want to talk about it."

The mother gave her a quick uneasy look, her eyes lingering, troubled, half relieved yet not wholly satisfied.

"Can't you trust me—a few days at least?" said Marigold wistfully.

"Yes, I can trust you—but—?"

"No *but*s, please. We haven't time. I'm sending a telegram to Aunt Marian this morning on my way to school telling her that we will be there tomorrow night on the train that reaches Washington about ten o'clock, and we'll take a taxi right up to the house. Now, will you be good and do what I want? Will you meet me at the shop? Bring the dress along that needed the hem taken up. She'll pin it for us. She offered to. Will it bother you to carry it? Perhaps I'd better take it myself. I haven't many books this morning."

"No, you run along. It's getting late. I'll bring it."

"And you will put away all your little worries and get ready to have a good time? Have a good time getting ready, I mean?"

"Yes, I will," said the mother, smiling. "You dear child! I do hope this is not going to bring sorrow and disappointment to you."

"No!" said Marigold, her firm little lips shutting tight in resolve. "It won't. I'm going to have a grand time going on a spree with you. It's a long time since we've gone on a trip together. I don't seem to remember any since you took me last to the zoo, and how long ago was that?"

"Child!"

"It's a fact, I don't. So much has happened since—school and college and then work! Now, Mother, you won't be late coming, will you? They positively told me at the library you could go exactly when you pleased. And I've put some money in your purse. You're to use it *all*, and *not to touch* your own! Positively! I won't go on any other condition! And why don't you pay the rent now and have it out of the way? Then you won't have that to look forward to when you get home, and we can have a real relaxed time with no worries."

"All right!" The mother smiled. She was beginning to catch the spirit of holiday, too.

Well, it looked as if Mother was going to be all right. If she only didn't get balky about the dresses down at the shop. It was going to be fun after all, going off this way with Mother, giving her a real vacation. If she just could keep herself busy enough and interested enough, perhaps she wouldn't feel that sick thud at the bottom of her stomach whenever she remembered the party that she wasn't going to attend. Maybe she could forget it entirely, count it a bad dream and let it go at that.

But then, she thought, with a quick wistful catch in her breath that brought the color softly up in her cheeks, *perhaps* after all, Laurie would come over that evening and somehow straighten out the painful part of things and fix it so that she could go to the party and still take her mother to Washington, too. She wouldn't let herself reason out the possibilities. She just liked to think that there was a little alleviating possibility in the vague uncertain way of the next few days.

It might even be that Laurie would call her up at the school during the morning, after he found out that she had sent her regrets.

So she cheered herself on her way into the day.

And her mother, watching her from the window as she did every morning, said softly to herself, "Dear child! Such an unselfish girl! But I wonder what has changed her mind? There is surely something behind all this. God must be answering my prayers for her in some way I do not understand."

Chapter 5

But the day went by and there came no word from Laurie.

Mrs. Trescott had taken good care of that.

Her sister-in-law dropped by in the course of the morning.

"Well, Adele, are you all ready for the grand parade?" she asked sarcastically as she threw aside her coat and helped herself to some specimens of confectionery that had been sent up for selection.

"Mercy no!" said the harassed hostess, reaching out and choosing a luscious bit of sweet. "You can't imagine what a lot of things can come up to make trouble. Here's my new butler mad as a hatter because he's got to wait on the caterer's men tomorrow night, and threatening to leave; and Daniel Trescott saying he can't have any peace in his own house with parties, and you know yourself, Irene, we haven't had any besides my regular bridge afternoon in three weeks. I can't see why your mother didn't bring her son up better! Men are so selfish!"

"Yes?" said Irene dryly. "I suppose you're looking out that you don't repeat the trouble with Laurie."

"Indeed I am!" said Laurie's mother. "I told him only this morning that since I was taking all this trouble for him he ought at least to help me out a little with the guest of honor. Sometimes I wonder why I do things for other people. Sometimes I wish I hadn't been brought up to be so unselfish." She gave a heavy sigh and took another piece of candy.

"Oh yes?" said Irene, lifting her brows in a way that made her look exasperatingly like Laurie. Mrs. Trescott hated to think either of her children looked like the Trescotts. She wanted them to be like her family.

"Well, I'm sure I don't know why I do so much for people when they are so ungrateful. I don't know why I took all this trouble to have this party tomorrow night. I don't believe Robena is a bit grateful, either."

"Yes you do, Adele!" said Irene. "You know perfectly well that you did it to shake Laurie free from that rowdy little Marigold. By the way, has she replied to her invitation?"

"Oh yes, replied all right, jumped at the chance. 'Miss Brooke accepts with pleasure.' And then, what do you think came in just now from her? Regrets! Can you *imagine* it? After she had accepted! Now what do you make of that? Do you suppose she hadn't money to get the right kind of gown? I understand they're very poor."

"That's odd!" said Irene, struggling with a particularly sticky caramel. "No, I don't believe it's that. I tell you she's clever. She could make a dress you couldn't tell from Paris, if she wanted to. Doesn't she give any reason?"

"'A sudden change of circumstances,'" quoted the mother, lifting Marigold's note with a disdainful thumb and finger as if it might contaminate. "I declare it's discouraging, after all the trouble I've taken, and now to have her drop right out of the picture—all my work for nothing."

"I'm not so sure it isn't better for your plans," said the sister-in-law thoughtfully. "She's a clever piece and very fetching. She could put it all over that selfish beast of a Robena if she tried, although I'm not so sure but she's too well bred to try."

"What do you mean, Irene?"

"Oh, nothing at all, Adele. Wait till you see her sometime and you'll understand. Does Laurie know she isn't coming?"

"No, he doesn't, and I don't intend he shall. Not till it's too late for him to walk out on me. And don't you tell him, either! You're the only one who knows it, and if he finds out I'll know who told him."

"What if the girl herself tells him?"

"Well, I'll take good care to keep him so busy she won't have a chance. He's out now showing Robena the sights. She hasn't ever been here before, and so there's plenty to see. She's wise to the situation, too. I gave her a quiet hint, and she certainly is a good ally. She doesn't give him a minute even to call up on the telephone. We've managed so far to keep him away from it entirely, but Robena plans to follow him if the girl calls him up or anything and be around to hear what is said."

"You surely make a lot of trouble," said Irene. "She isn't the only undesirable girl around these parts, and at that I'm not so sure she is so undesirable as she might be."

"Irene! A poor minister's daughter!"

"There are worse!" said Irene, lighting a cigarette.

"Well of course, but you know my son wouldn't look at a girl like that!"

"Wouldn't he? How do you know?"

"Irene! And you can talk that way about your own nephew?"

"Why, Adele, I wasn't talking about him, I was talking about human nature. I haven't much faith in human nature, not in these days, anyway."

"But don't you think it makes any difference how a child is

born and brought up, my dear?"

"Not much!" said the sister-in-law. "I used to believe that bunk, but when I saw the way some of my friends got bravely over their training I decided there wasn't so much to it as I had been taught."

"I do wish you wouldn't utter such sentiments, Irene. It isn't respectable to say things like that!"

"Oh, very well, I take it all back; perhaps it was the fault of the upbringing after all. It didn't go more than skin deep. But I still say if you would stop trying to manage Laurie and simply take his pocket money away and make him go to work, you would have better results. However, I'm only an old maid, and I'm not supposed to know how to bring up children, though if I didn't do a better job of it than some people I know, I'd be willing to pay a fine. But what I'd like to know is: after you get Laurie pried loose from this penniless little person, how are you going to prevent his falling in love with something worse?"

"Really, Irene, I don't like the way you talk. I'm sorry I mentioned it at all. I'd rather not say anything more about it."

"Well, I'm just leaving now, anyway. Give my love to Laurie-boy; and tell him to drop in and see his young aunt someday, and I'll give him some good advice. But perhaps you'd rather not as I'm afraid I'd advise him to stick to his Marigold and get out and go to work for her."

"I certainly would rather not!" said the mother severely. "If I thought you meant all you say I certainly should be grieved about it. By the way, I wish you'd run over and take a hand at bridge some evening while Robena is here. Can't you? Say Friday evening?"

"I'm afraid not, Adele. I might contaminate your child! Besides, I can't abide that double-faced Robena, and I'm afraid I'd let her know it before the evening was over. Bye-bye! I wish you well in your campaign, but I think I see disappointment of some sort lurking around the corner for you!"

Irene put on her coat and went out smiling ironically, and Mrs. Trescott looked after her deeply annoyed.

Oh, dear me! she sighed, *why does she always have to be so unpleasant? She wears on my spirit; I'm so susceptible to moods! Now I'm all worn out. She's exactly like her brother! Always saying sarcastic things, and I'm not quite sure what she means by them! She's tired me unutterably. And in some ways Laurie is just like her. Always thinks he's entirely right. Dear me! I hope he doesn't find out his little paragon has sent regrets. If we can only get him through Saturday night, I think he will come out all right. By that time he will get over his prejudice against Robena. I can see she's making good headway. I caught his glance this morning when she came over and stood in the window with him and asked him if he wasn't going to give her a good-morning kiss, and I actually believe if I hadn't come into the room just then he would have done it. Once let him get to wooing Robena and he'll be safe from all the little penniless designers anywhere. Robena is one who knows how to hold her own.*

❀

As Irene Trescott walked down the street in the morning sunshine, she was wondering about Laurie. Would he really be won away from his pretty little schoolteacher by that bold flirt? Well, perhaps it was just as well, for he would probably break the other girl's heart if he stuck to her long enough to marry her. He never would have the courage to do it if his mother cut off his fortune or even threatened to. Irene loved her nephew, but she knew his limitations and had no illusions about him. He was a chip off the old block in more ways than one.

❀

The morning went on, and Marigold at her desk in the schoolroom was conscious of an undercurrent of excitement. Even her small pupils noticed it and thought how pretty she looked with her cheeks so red and her eyes so bright.

For somehow Marigold had become increasingly certain that Laurie was going to call up pretty soon and make everything right, and if so, all the rest would surely work out beautifully somehow. Mother would understand. Mother always did!

But the morning wore on, recess, and then noon, and no Laurie. Afternoon session closed, and no message in the office for Marigold, though she stopped and inquired on her way out.

Well, perhaps he would call later. But, of course, with guests in the house and his mother demanding things of him, possibly he couldn't get away. She probably ought to realize, too, that since he had said he might not be able to come for a day or two that he thought he had made it plain to her not to expect him. And perhaps he hadn't been noticing the replies to the invitations. Of course, that was it. It wouldn't enter his head but that she was coming. Well, it was just as well that she was going away, perhaps. She ought not to let Laurie feel too sure of her.

So she coaxed herself to put away all thoughts of Laurie and the party and enter into her mother's preparations with at least a semblance of eagerness.

She found her mother waiting on the corner, the suit box in her hand, eyeing the great show window of François's with hesitancy.

"Don't you think perhaps you had better just take these back, dear, and let us go to some cheaper place for what I want?" she asked in a troubled voice.

"Not a bit of it," said Marigold. "You like these dresses, and you're going to have them. Come on!" And she breezed her mother through the big plate glass door and introduced her to Madame, who treated her like the lady she was and thereby more than won the daughter's heart.

The shopping tour was a success from every point of view, and they had a good time every minute, both of them. There was something about Marigold today that her mother did not quite understand, something that restrained Mrs. Brooke from pro-testing against the pretty little accessories that the daughter was determined to buy for her and kept her feeling that she must play the game and give her child a good time to make up somehow for this mysterious sacrifice of the party that she still seemed so set upon. For she sensed the undertone of excitement, the firm set of the young lips, the determined sparkle in the bright eyes, and knew that underneath somewhere there was pain. Please God, it might be pain that led to something better, but still it was pain, and she must help all she could.

So they went happily through the shopping—shoes and hats and gloves—each urging some sweet little extra extravagance on the other. After all, what were a few dollars more or less if it helped her girl to go through the fire? And if it turned out that it wasn't fire after all, well, the gloves and shoes and hats would be needed sometime and were all good buys.

A roomy suitcase of airplane-luggage style and an overnight bag to match were the final purchases, and they put their smaller parcels into them and carried them home with them.

"Now," said Marigold firmly, as they got out of the bus at the corner near their home, "we are stopping at the tearoom for din-ner. No, you needn't protest. You are tired and hungry and so am I, and we have a lot to do tonight. Besides, I happen to know there isn't much in the refrigerator for dinner tonight, and I forgot to telephone the order. This is my party, and I want you to be good and enjoy it."

So Mrs. Brooke smilingly submitted again, and they had a steak and hot rolls and ice cream and coffee.

"It *is* a party!" said the mother, leaning wearily back in her chair, "and we're having a lovely time!"

She noticed as they started to walk the few steps from the tearoom at the corner to their own small apartment a few doors up the block that Marigold had suddenly quickened her step and was noticeably silent. She sensed that the child was hoping that Laurie had telephoned.

But the woman who occupied the apartment across the hall and was kind enough to answer their telephone had nothing to report, and Mrs. Brooke, with a relieved sigh, saw that Marigold set her lips in a determinedly pleasant smile and went straight to the business of unpacking their purchases and talking about the details of their trip, giving herself no chance for sadness. Brave little girl!

There was the hem to sew, and Marigold insisted on doing it herself, making her mother rest awhile. After the dress had been tried on again and pressed and pronounced perfect, Marigold insisted on getting all the little things together that they would need and partly packing them. It was after eleven o'clock when they finally got to bed. The whole evening had gone by and still no word from Laurie. Mrs. Brooke kept longing in her heart that they might get away entirely without it. If Laurie would only keep away and Marigold could have this outing without him, who knew how her eyes might be opened to see that he was not the only friend the world contained. But she dared not pray insistently for things to come out as she desired. She wanted only her child's happiness, and how was she to know which of all the possibilities was really in God's plan for her dear one? So she prayed quietly in her heart as she lay in her bed in the darkness, *Oh, Father, have Thine own way with my child! Don't let her make any terrible mistakes. Bring about Thy will in her life.*

But Marigold lay staring into the darkness and thinking of Laurie, her face burning now and again as she realized how much she had taken for granted in Laurie's friendship and how little he had really done to actually commit himself.

And then her cheeks burned again at the thought of how she had been led along, and led along, to surrender this and that standard and opinion and yield to every whim of Laurie's.

There were not so many of these, perhaps, but in the darkness amid her heart searching, desperately facing her problems, they loomed large with her conscience, her young trained conscience that used to be so tender and so sharp before she ever met Laurie.

Dear God, she prayed suddenly, her hands clasped tensely, her young heart beating wildly, *if You'll only let Laurie be* real, *if You'll only let him come back and be what I thought he was, I'll never go into another nightclub with him, never, as long as I live. I promise You!*

Then all at once it was as if God stood there and she realized what she had been doing, offering that small concession as bait to the great God to do something for her, even if it meant changing His plan for her life and Laurie's. Oh, that was a dreadful thing to do! *Please, God, forgive me! Forgive me! I ought not to have prayed that way. Oh, I'm all wrong! Please help me! I'm so unhappy!*

She soon fell into an uneasy slumber that ended in that horrid dream of the high ledge again, and she woke in great distress, crying out for fear of falling down, down into space.

"Why, what is the matter, dear child!" said her mother bending over her. "Are you in pain?"

She stared wildly at her mother, standing there in the dimness of the room. Then she tried to shake off the reality of that dream and laugh.

"I—must have had a nightmare!" she explained, rubbing her eyes. "I guess it was that piece of mince pie I didn't eat at the tearoom," she giggled. "I'm all right now, Mother, get back to bed. You'll catch cold! You haven't your robe on!" She sprang up and, taking hold of her mother's shoulders, led her back to bed, laughingly tucking her in, kissing her, and promising not to dream any more that night. The cold of her own room had somewhat dispelled the gloom of the dream, but she lay there for some time still in the power of that awful feeling that she was standing high on that ledge. If this went on she would be a nervous wreck, and that mustn't happen. She had Mother to think of. Mother mustn't be frightened. If she should get sick, what would Mother do? She had to snap out of this and do it quickly, and to that end she had to stop thinking about Laurie. If he telephoned, well and good; but if he didn't, it was just going to be something she expected, that was all. She and Mother were going off to have a good time. She must forget about the party and the beautiful dress with its crimson sash. She must come down to living in her own world and not go creeping after another where she didn't belong.

And, of course, it wasn't as if she had been *turned* out of the other one. She had turned herself out, deliberately taken back the dress she had bought and sent regrets to the party. She had her pride still with her, anyway.

With that consolation, she turned over and went to sleep again, and when the morning came was able to look fairly cheerful and even a bit excited while they ate their breakfast.

"Now, Mother, don't you get too tired," she admonished as she hurried away to school. "Everything but a few trifles is packed, and I shall be home in plenty of time to see to those. You've no dinner to make. We're getting that on the train. I'm so glad we decided to go by train instead of bus. I adore eating in the diner. And I got chairs in the Pullman, so we'll have a swell rest before we eat." She kissed her mother and hurried away, not allowing her eyes to lift and scan the road to see if a yellow roadster was hovering near, as once or twice it had done before when Laurie planned some special treat for her and wanted to make sure she would go. Laurie was out of the picture today, absolutely. She was not going to spoil her radiance by any gloom.

She was able to carry this attitude through a rather trying day and came home excitedly with a piece of news.

"What do you think, Mother," she said, bursting into the house like a child. "I have two days more vacation! Can you imagine it? And to think it should come just at this time. Isn't it wonderful? I've always wanted to have a little time to look around

Washington! Isn't it grand, Mother? I don't have to be back here till Wednesday morning."

"Wonderful!" said the mother. "But how did it happen?"

"Oh, there's something the matter with the boiler, and they've got to pull it to pieces. The workmen say they can't possibly get it done before Tuesday night."

"Well," said the mother with softly shining eyes, "this whole expedition seems to have been prepared for us in detail, as if it were a gift from heaven!"

Marigold caught her breath sharply and smiled. "Yes, doesn't it?" she said brightly.

And her mother, watching, wondered. Was this real or just put on for her benefit? It was hard to deceive mother-eyes.

But Mrs. Brooke noticed that Marigold was very particular about writing out the address and telephone number in Washington for Mrs. Waterman to give to anyone who might telephone during their absence, and most careful to call up little Johnny Masters, the paperboy, and ask him to save the daily papers for her until her return. It might be that Marigold had put aside her own wishes and was determined to give her mother all the happiness possible on this trip, but she wasn't forgetting entirely the party she was leaving behind, for she made all arrangements to read its account in the society columns, and the mother sighed softly, even while she rejoiced that her girl would not be present at that party after all. What would the future days bring? Would Laurie come after her again when the grand display was over? Would the interval only serve perhaps to bring things to a crisis? Well, it was all in the Lord's hands, and she could do nothing but trust it there.

The next two hours were full and interesting. Putting in the last little things, seeing that the apartment was all in order to leave—the note in the milk bottle for the milkman, the note for Mrs. Waterman to give the bread man. And then the taxi was at the door, and they were off. And it was so long since the two had gone on even a short journey that they were like two children when they first started.

Lying back luxuriously in the Pullman chairs, admiring furtively each other's new garments, watching the home sights disappear and new landscapes sweep into view, was most exciting.

"I'm glad you got that lovely brown suit," said Mrs. Brooke, leaning forward to speak softly to Marigold. "It is just perfect. So refined and lovely. Your father would have liked that. It seems to me the most perfect outfit a young girl could possibly have."

"I'm so glad you like it, Mother!" Marigold said, with a twinkle in her eyes. "I love it myself, and I'm glad I have it."

They were still a long time looking at the pearly colors in the evening sky, and then Mrs. Brooke, from out of a silence in which she had been watching the little sad shadows around her dear girl's eyes and mouth, suddenly spoke. "You know, my dear, you don't have to go out gunning for a husband!"

"*Mother!*" Marigold turned startled eyes toward her parent and sat up in shocked silence.

"That sounds rather crude, doesn't it, dear?" Her mother laughed. "But I've been thinking that a good many girls have an idea that the main object of living is to get married and that the whole thing is entirely up to them, therefore they must go out hunting and capture a man, *some* man, even if they can't get the one they want!"

"Mother! What have I ever done that has made you think I thought that?"

"Nothing, dear. I wasn't speaking of you just then. I was thinking of the scores of young things that come into the library. I hear them talking together. They seem to feel that it would be a calamity not to be married. I wish I had a chance to tell them that life is not a game of stagecoach in which the girl who cannot get a husband is hopelessly left out; that only a strong, true, tender, overwhelming, enduring love can make a married life bearable for more than a few days, and love like that does not come for the running after, for the brooding over, nor for clever wiles and smiles. It is God-given!"

Marigold sat startled, looking at her mother.

"What do you think I am, Mother?" she demanded indignantly. "I know you're talking to me. I can tell by the tone of your voice. I'm not trying to fall in love! Just because I wanted to go to one party, I wasn't running after anybody."

"No," said her mother gently. "I didn't think you were. But this party was a kind of crisis in your life. You've chosen to stay away from it. You say it wasn't all on my account. Therefore there must be something else behind it all. I am saying these things because if in the next few days or weeks you come to face any of these problems, I would like to have you think about what I have said. Don't make the mistake of lowering standards, of making cheap compromises and desperate maneuvers to win love, for it is not to be had at that price. Now, that's all. Come to me if ever you want me to say more on the subject."

Marigold studied her mother's face for a long time thoughtfully and then turned her gaze out the window to the deepening twilight on the snowy landscape. Finally she leaned over and patted her mother's hand. "Thank you, Mother dear, I'll store that up for future use. But for the present, I've almost made up my mind that I never shall be married at all. I think I'll just stay with you, Mother, and we'll make a nice lot of money and have a ducky little house together. But now, dear, don't you think we ought to go into the diner car and get our dinner? I'm starved myself. How about you?"

Yet though they both smiled and chatted as they sat in the diner car and enjoyed their evening meal, watching the quickly darkening landscape from the window, the brilliant cities, the quieter unlit country flashing by like a panorama, still the mother watched her girl, trying to hide her anxiety. Why had she done this thing in the first place? Was it just an impulse to please her mother, or was it something deeper? Something about Laurie? And was she going to suffer from her rash impulse during the next few days, or would the Lord mercifully deliver her from it and give something to divert?

They had a pleasant journey, and as they neared their destination and thickening clusters of lights announced a city nearby, they both felt a little ripple of excitement.

Then the dome of the capitol flashed into view, like some far heavenly city painted on the sky, and the dim specter of the Washington Monument dawned in the myriad lights. Such a lovely vision! Marigold, who scarcely remembered her earlier impressions of Washington, was breathless and bright-eyed as she looked, and then rose to leave the train.

Just as they were passing through the train gate in the wake of a porter who carried their luggage, a young man stepped up to Mrs. Brooke and spoke. "You are Mrs. Brooke, aren't you? I thought I couldn't be mistaken. I'm Ethan Bevan. Aunt Marian sent me to meet you. Perhaps you don't remember me, but I remember you."

Chapter 6

Marigold looked up annoyed. Who on earth was this stranger? Heavens! Did he belong to the household where they were to visit, and would he always be tagging along spoiling the good times they were planning to have with Aunt Marian? She stared at him in surprise.

"Why, of course I remember you, Ethan!" exclaimed Mrs. Brooke eagerly. "How wonderful to see you here! Though I must confess I wouldn't have recognized you. How nice of you to meet us! And this is my daughter, Marigold."

The young man gave a brief, casual glance at the girl and bowed. Marigold acknowledged the greeting coolly and distantly. How annoying that there had to be a young man barging into the picture to spoil their outing! Who was he, anyway? Ethan? She seemed to have heard the name before but couldn't quite place him, and she scarcely heard her mother's quick explanation: "He isn't exactly a cousin, Marigold, but he'll make a nice substitute."

Marigold walked stiffly along on the other side of her mother and said nothing, annoyed to be interrupted this way in her first sight of the city. She had no need for a cousin, real or otherwise.

But the young man did not seem to be any more anxious to be friendly than she was. He was talking with her mother, animatedly, almost as if he considered her daughter too young to be interesting. Though he didn't look so old himself, she thought, when she got a good glimpse of his face as they passed under the bright lights of the station entrance.

He put them in the backseat of a lovely, shiny car and stowed their luggage in the front seat with himself, and then they drove out into the brightness of the charmed city. Marigold was entranced with her first view and paid little attention to the young man, who was still talking with her mother.

"But I thought you lived in California," her mother was saying when she came out from her absorption enough to listen.

"I did," answered the young man. "I lived with another uncle, Uncle Norman, after Uncle Robert Bevan died and Aunt Marian came east. Then I went away to school when Uncle Norman married again; and college later, of course, and then I had a couple of years abroad. But now I've got a job that brings me east for a time, and just now it's Washington."

"And are you living with your aunt Marian?" asked Mrs. Brooke.

"Oh, no; no such luck as that! I'm boarding out in a forlorn dump near my job, worse luck! I'm only in town for a brief time. Aunt Marian thought she was going to be by herself over Sunday, and she called me up and asked if I wouldn't come out and relieve her loneliness. Then your telegram came, and she commandeered my car to come after you. I don't know but she'll send me back where I came from now that you have arrived. But I'm glad to have seen you again, anyway. You loomed large in my small life the day you made that maple taffy for me and actually let me help pull it myself. I've never forgotten it."

"You dear child!" said Mrs. Brooke feelingly. "To think you would remember that!"

Now why did Mother want to get sentimental? This was a man she was talking to, not a child. Mother always was that way, easily touched by wistfulness, sentiment! Why couldn't she see how unpleasant it would be to have this young man always around underfoot? How it would just spoil the whole lovely vacation!

Suddenly Marigold wished very much that she had kept the lovely white-and-crimson dress and stayed at home and gone to her party! If this fellow was going to be around the whole time, perhaps she would just go home in the morning, anyway, and leave Mother in Washington. Mother wouldn't mind so much after she got there, especially if this young man was so fond of her. Perhaps he would take Mother around a little and she wouldn't be missed. Then she would take her pretty green silk and go to her party after all. She had been a fool to throw all that loveliness away. Of course, she had declined the invitation, but she could call up Mrs. Trescott and explain that she had been called away but had unexpectedly been able to return, and might she come anyway? That was being a little informal, but knowing Laurie as well as she did, perhaps it would be excusable.

Just in the distance of one short brilliant city block, the thought came to her and left her breathless, smashing all her well-built resolves, blotting out utterly her vision of Laurie looking down into those languishing eyes of that other girl, and making her heart beat wildly with the daring of it.

Well, she wouldn't say anything about it tonight, of course. Let Mother enjoy her first evening to the fullest, and then along in the afternoon tomorrow spring it on her that she felt she must go back. Mother wouldn't stop her, of course. Mother was really troubled that she had given up the party, and while she would be disappointed, still Aunt Marian would be there to make her forget about it, and she would promise to telephone her the first thing the next morning.

Then the car swept into the glitter and glow of another wonderful avenue, and she caught her breath with the beauty of the lovely city.

Ethan was pointing out the places of interest. Over there was the White House, here the Treasury Building, and now they were coming into the region of the embassies. He had a pleasant voice and spoke distinctly, but it was dark and Marigold could not see his face. Anyway, Marigold was not interested in his face or in him as a person at all. She was interested in knowing about the great buildings they were passing, and she sat entranced as the vistas of the city stretched out before her delighted eyes.

When they reached the house, the young man sprang out and opened the door for them. Then he capably gathered the suitcases and escorted them into the house. Marigold didn't notice him any more than if he had been a taxi driver doing his duty.

It was a pleasant house, and they had glimpses of a wide living room with a generous fireplace, a beautiful dining room beyond, and on the other side of the hall a large library whose walls were almost literally lined with books. Cousin Elinor had married a literary man. Marigold looked around with pleased eyes on everything. She loved luxury and pretty things and had very little of either in these days. She felt that the time spent in this house was not going to be wasted by her. She hoped she would have the opportunity to curl up on that big leather couch and do some reading while she was here. Another fireplace, too! How charming!

"I think Aunt Marian is expecting you to come right upstairs," said the young man, and Marigold found herself a little jealous of the possessive way in which he said "Aunt Marian," as if she were *his* aunt and not related to them. What was he? Just an in-law by marriage!

He followed them up the stairs with the baggage, setting it down in a large room across the hall from Mrs. Bevan's room.

They found the invalid in bed, eagerly awaiting their coming.

"Take off your things and let me look at you," she said when the greetings were over. "I wanted to come downstairs to meet you, but my nurse had to go away this evening, and she thought if I was going to be carried downstairs tomorrow for a while and stay up to my birthday dinner, I'd better stay in bed tonight. So here I am, flat on my back! My, but I'm happy to see you! My heart jumped up and turned over when I got your telegram. And oh, my dear! Is that your baby-girl Marigold? Grown to be a young woman! Isn't she lovely?"

Marigold's cheeks flamed as she bent and kissed her aunt, somehow terribly conscious of the young man in the background and wishing the aunt wouldn't be quite so enthusiastic before strangers.

But when she straightened up, Ethan was gone. She heard the front door closing and wondered if that was all they were to see of him after all. Perhaps he was only on duty until he escorted them to the house. She sincerely hoped so.

But he appeared again after they had taken off their coats and hats and came back into Aunt Marian's room. He came carrying a large silver tray containing cups and a pot of hot chocolate, a bowl of whipped cream with a little silver ladle, plates of tiny chicken and lettuce sandwiches, cinnamon toast, and little frosted cakes. Such a lovely spread-out! And though they protested that they had had dinner on the train, they ate with a real relish as Ethan proved himself efficient in the art of serving them.

Marigold watched him without seeming to do so. How easy he was, how much at home, as if Aunt Marian were his own mother. He was rather good-looking, too, in a serious sort of way, had nice eyes and a pleasant smile, talked a lot of nonsense to her mother and aunt, and made himself very useful. But he looked straight through Marigold when she happened to be in his line of vision and mostly avoided her when she wasn't. That didn't bother Marigold in the least. She wasn't interested in him, she told herself. He wasn't in the least like Laurie, who was lithe and slender of build, tall and willowy, and handsome as a picture. This man was strongly built and seemed to have a kind of power about him.

Then suddenly she thought of Laurie. Had Laurie called her up after she left? Her heart gave a lurch and she almost contemplated calling up home tonight before she went to bed, if she could get a good chance when nobody was listening. Though it was late to hope to get Mrs. Waterman. She usually went to bed at nine o'clock and likely wouldn't hear the telephone. It would be better to wait until morning.

They sat up talking until midnight, Aunt Marian's eyes so happy and Mother looking as if she had just arrived in heaven. Marigold couldn't help being glad that she had come. Just to look at Mother's face was enough to make her sure she had done the right thing. But surely by tomorrow Mother would be having such a good time she wouldn't mind having her go back in time for the party!

Ethan Bevan told some very amusing stories and had them all laughing, although he didn't once look at Marigold, and she had the impression he was doing that by intention. He didn't seem to be shy, either. She couldn't quite understand it. It was more as if he weren't in the least interested in her, any more than if she had been a kitten that had come along. He just didn't take her into the picture at all. Well, that was all right. That suited her perfectly. She was free to think her own thoughts and not have to bother with him. Since he had to be there it was better that he didn't want her attention at all. He told them a little bit about the "camp" where he worked and gave an amusing anecdote or two of the boardinghouse where he stayed, eating at the same table with his men. That was interesting, and she thought more of him that he could be friendly with the workers under him. He must be a good sort after all. But likely he would go off to the camp in the morning and she would be able to go out and see the great new city on her own. Of course, her mother would want to stay with her sister, but she would slip away and look around at one or two places she had always wanted to see. The Capitol, of course, and the Library of Congress, and perhaps the Smithsonian. She hadn't an idea what a proposition she had mapped out for herself in one brief morning, but she only intended to take a causal glance and then telephone and perhaps spring it on her mother at noon that she was going to take a train at about three o'clock. That would give her plenty of time to dress and get to the party!

Then suddenly her thoughts were broken by her aunt's happy voice.

"I thought you and I would take it a little easy in the morning, Mary, and have a good talk. Marigold, of course, will want to see the city since she hasn't been here for so long, and Ethan being here makes it nice. He will take her over to the Capitol and library and any other buildings she would like to see, and show her the really interesting points in them. He knows how to do that to perfection. Elinor's husband says he is a master at giving a quick, comprehensive view of the right things without wearying one too much." She gave a swift, loving smile toward Ethan. "And then," she went on, "in the afternoon Ethan is going to take us on a drive. The doctor said I might go along if it was a pleasant day. I thought we would go out through the park, show you the new cathedral and a few other notable places, and then we would drive on to Mount Vernon and let the young folks hop out and look that over for a few minutes. Don't you think that would be pleasant? Of course, I couldn't hope to enjoy all this with you if I hadn't been able to get hold of Ethan for the day, because there is no one else here to carry me downstairs and help me into the car. But since he is so good to give us his time, I feel like a bird let loose."

Thud! Down went Marigold's plans in one blow. She looked from her aunt to her mother and back again. Their faces were radiant with anticipation. She simply couldn't dash their hopes by telling them she wouldn't be there in the afternoon. Not tonight, anyway. Perhaps in the morning she could telephone and get some word calling her home and then it wouldn't be so much of a letdown for them. Not if it came in the nature of a call from Laurie. But the morning! How was she to escape a personally conducted sight-seeing tour of Washington in the company of an unwilling guide?

She gave a quick glance at Ethan, and it did not seem to her that he looked particularly elated at the prospect, either. He must be a grouch about girls. She certainly didn't want to go with him. Well, it would be up to her to get out of it. She could likely talk with him early in the morning and tell him she had always wanted to go around Washington alone and just see what she wanted to see herself, and she wouldn't bother him to escort her. He wasn't even looking at her now, and he hadn't said that he would be charmed to take her, nor any of the conventional phrases that the ordinary gentleman would use on such an occasion. Oh, he would be glad enough to get out of it, and perhaps it could be managed without either Mother or Aunt Marian knowing that he hadn't gone along. Well, she would see.

So they went to bed at last, and Marigold intended to lie there awhile thinking about Laurie and how to plan for the next day, so that she wouldn't have to go around with Ethan Bevan. But the next thing she knew it was morning and her mother was smiling down at her and telling her she would be late for breakfast if she didn't get right up and hurry with her dressing.

It was a pleasure to get up and put on the pretty new morning dress, with its bright silk print, and go downstairs. Aunt Marian didn't come down to breakfast. She was saving her strength for the afternoon drive, she said. Ethan Bevan was very pleasant. He did the honors like a son of the house, talking gravely with her mother mostly, though he did turn his direct gaze to Marigold once when he first greeted her with a pleasant good morning.

Marigold had begun to hope that he would just ignore what had been said the night before about taking her around, but as they were getting up from the table he turned to her and said, "Now, how soon can you be ready? I'm bringing the car around to the door in ten minutes. I need to get gas. Will that be too soon for you?"

Marigold had intended waiting until her mother got upstairs so that she could deal with the matter alone, but her mother hung around and she was forced to answer.

"Oh, please don't take that trouble, Mr. Bevan. I really don't need an attendant. I'm quite used to going around places by myself and shall have a lovely time. There is no need in the world for you to take time off from more important things to personally conduct me. Just forget me, please. I shall be quite all right."

Ethan turned a surprised glance at her and studied her an instant. Then he said in his pleasant, decided voice, "You know I couldn't think of letting you go around alone. I promised Aunt Marian I'd take you, and you're not hindering me in the least from anything I have to do. I'm entirely free for the morning."

He didn't say it would be a pleasure to take her. She was glad he didn't. It made her feel that it was more of a business proposition. He was doing it because Aunt Marian had asked him to. That was easier to combat than a mere feeling of politeness.

"But truly," she said, lifting her firm little chin with a kind of finality, "I don't need you. I am quite capable of finding my way around alone and shall enjoy it—"

"I know," he said, lifting a chin just as firm as hers, "but it just can't be. Aunt Marian would worry like the dickens, you know, and you couldn't really see half as much and not as easily alone as if I went with you. I can see I'm not the most desirable companion you might have, but I'm capable, really, and I guess you'll have to put up with me for the time being as I'm all there is. I'll promise to be just as little trouble as possible. I'll be around in ten minutes and wait out in front for you." He finished with a nice grin that almost made her like him and, turning, hurried out through the hall, grabbing his coat and hat from a chair as he passed through the door.

"My dear!" said Mrs. Brooke. "That wasn't very gracious of you."

"Well, Mother, I can't see why I have to be forced into a position that neither of us wants. Can't you see he doesn't want to go? Of course, he's very polite and all that, but it must be a terrible bore to take a strange girl around sight-seeing. I know he hates it. And so do I. I shan't enjoy it at all if I have to go with him. I'd much rather go by myself. I feel as if the whole trip is being spoiled, having him here, anyway!"

"Oh, my dear!" said Mrs. Brooke, a quick shadow coming over the brightness of her face. "I don't see why you should feel that way. He really is a very fine young man with splendid ideals and standards. I cannot see why you cannot be courteous and grateful even if you don't think he is just crazy to take you out. I should think just Christian courtesy would show you that you should be gracious and sweet for these few hours and make him have as pleasant a time as you can, while he serves you as host in the place of your relatives who are absent."

Marigold stood unhappily looking down at the toes of her pretty new shoes and feeling as uncomfortable as if she were a naughty little girl being reprimanded.

"Oh, I suppose so, Mother," she said, drawing a long sigh of surrender. "Don't look that way, Mother! I'll be good. Only I thought when neither of us wanted to do it there would be some way out."

"Not courteously, dear," said her mother reproachfully.

"All right, Mother, forget it, and look happy. I'll be a good child. Go on up to Aunt Marian and have a good time. I'll try to amuse the young man if that's possible, but to tell you the truth, I think he prefers your company to mine." She finished with a wry smile.

"Child!" said her mother, with a faint answering smile. "Run along and have a really good time. You can if you are willing!"

So Marigold hurried upstairs and put on her lovely brown ensemble with its sable collar and cuffs, tucking a fetching little orange flame of a scarf around her neck for a spot of bright color under her chin. Then she went down to meet Ethan Bevan with her head up and the fire of battle in her eyes.

However, Ethan Bevan scarcely seemed to see her as he helped her into the car. His own head was up, too, and if Marigold had looked she might have seen an answering fire of battle in his eyes. Ethan Bevan, to tell the truth, hadn't much use for modern girls, and he took it for granted that Marigold was a modern girl.

So they started out on the pleasure trip with stark animosity between them, both determined to get the thing over with as quickly and creditably as possible.

"Now," said Ethan as they drove away from the house into as beautiful a morning as had ever been born, "have you anything in mind you wanted to see, or shall I just take you the ordinary round of sights?"

"Oh," said Marigold, speaking brightly but hating it all, "it isn't especially important, is it? I had thought of the Capitol, and perhaps the library or Smithsonian, but any of the other buildings will be just as good if they are nearer. I want to give you the least trouble, of course. I'm really sorry to have been forced upon your hands for the morning, but won't you please plan the trip in the way that will be pleasantest for you?"

He gave her an amused glance and studied her haughty young profile for an instant.

"All right!" he said gravely. "Only don't worry about me. I'm still new enough to the city not to be bored anywhere. There's always something of interest. Perhaps we'd better take a flying glimpse of the Capitol first and then use the time that's left in the library, or get a glimpse of the museum. I promised Aunt Marian we would be back for lunch at one o'clock, and, of course, you can't see everything in that time."

"Of course not," said Marigold in a formal, cold little tone.

"Here, for instance, is Corcoran Art Gallery," he went on, "that white marble building on your right; and over there is the War Department. A lot of interesting things in there, but you need time for it all. There's the South American Building, a fascinating place, with all sorts of exotic plants and live birds and monkeys. And over there"—he pointed off to the right and went on describing briefly the different buildings in sight, and Marigold, eager-eyed, tried to restrain her eagerness and answer calmly.

"You are a good salesman," she said coolly. "I think I shall have to take a real vacation some week and come down and go through all these places."

"It would benefit you, of course," he said and turned a corner, sweeping back to Pennsylvania Avenue. "There is the Capitol again, just ahead of us. I always enjoy this view of it. It seems so impressive and so worthy of a great country's executive building."

Thus they discoursed stiffly and seriously, touching on politics in a general, vague way, as if neither of them cared much about it or felt the burden of their country's policies. And then they reached the Capitol and went solemnly up the great white flight of stairs.

Marigold was filled with awe at her first approach to the beautiful marble structure, and she said very little, scarcely replying to her companion's remarks. As they stepped inside the main rotunda, Marigold looked up and drew a soft breath of wonder.

"I am so glad!" she said softly, as if she were speaking to herself, quite off her guard.

"Glad?" said Ethan, studying her face as if he saw it for the first time and found in it what he had not caught before.

"Glad that it is just as impressive and wonderful as I had dreamed!" she explained. She was still talking as if to herself. She had for the moment forgotten her animosity and was speaking her innermost thoughts, as she might have spoken them to her mother or anyone she knew well.

"Yes," he said gravely, "I can understand that feeling. It is good to have great things—representative things, like buildings that stand for something real—come up to one's expectations. I remember I almost dreaded to come here and see this city about which I had heard so much, fearing it would disappoint me. This is the first time you have been in Washington?"

"No, I was here when I was a child," said Marigold slowly, her eyes still studying the paintings in the dome, "but I doubt if they brought me *here*, or if they did I didn't have any idea of what I was seeing. I was probably a tired child crying to go home."

He looked at her in new interest and began to tell her what he knew of the great frescoes above them. They stood for some minutes looking up. Marigold forgot the personality of the one who was beside her and listened to what he said, her eyes wide with interest, indelibly stamping on her memory the wonderful paintings.

They roused to go on as groups of tourists came near with a guide and drove them from their position. They came presently to the hall of statuary and studied briefly the faces of the notables done in marble.

"I have an ancestor here somewhere whose name I bear, but

he is so far back I cannot tell how he is related. Where is he? Oh yes. Ethan Allen! Here he is. One of the famous Green Mountain Boys, you know, of Revolutionary times."

"Oh yes," said Marigold. "I know. Father had an old book called *Green Mountain Boys*. I loved it. It was a grand story. And what a fine face he has!"

Their talk was just then interrupted by a group of men meeting nearby and greeting one another.

"There! There's the senator from your state," whispered Ethan, touching Marigold lightly on the shoulder. "I had him pointed out to me the other day."

They lingered for a moment watching these important personages and then went on to visit the House of Representatives and catch a brief glimpse of laws in the making. Then across to the Senate for a little visit, returning to the Supreme Court room in time to see those great men walk into their places and hear the highest court opened for the day's session. It was all most fascinating to Marigold, and she would have stayed all morning, but finally Ethan asked if she was willing to go on, and they slipped quietly out and came again to the great rotunda where they had entered.

"We have been longer than I intended at this," said Ethan, glancing at his watch. "I am afraid you won't have time for much else this morning. It is almost half past twelve, and we are due back at the house again at one, you know."

"Well, I'm glad I've seen all this," said Marigold, lifting a sparkling face. "I wouldn't have missed a minute of it. Is it time we started back at once? I'm satisfied to go."

"Well, no, we have fifteen minutes left before we need actually start. How would you like to get up nearer to those paintings above us? There is scarcely time to go to another location. But perhaps you don't like to climb stairs?"

"Oh, I'd love to go. I don't mind climbing in the least."

So they started up the narrow, winding way that led nearer to the dome. And as they walked, Ethan supported the girl's arm lightly and they kept step, slowly up and up, in a great circle, until they reached the narrow gallery above, quite close to the wonderful paintings.

Marigold was not tired. She had enjoyed the rhythmic climb while Ethan told her more about those pictures of which he seemed to have made quite a study. They stood some minutes facing the outer wall, studying the blended colors of the masterpiece, thinking of the master who had stood up there on a scaffold so many years before, laying on the pigment and leaving behind his brush strokes the picture that had endured, and then Ethan looked at his watch and said, "Time's up! We must go or we'll be late. But before we go, turn around and look down at the place where you were standing a few minutes ago. It is interesting to see how small the people look from here."

Marigold turned and looked down at the marble floor below her, and suddenly the tormenting nightmare of her horrible dream descended upon her and took her by the throat, petrifying her with fear. There was the great empty space below her just as she had dreamed and she on a little ledge out there hanging over that wide awful expanse. Almost she expected to see Laurie down there somewhere waving his hand at her and asking how she liked it up there. And in imagination the ledge on which she stood grew suddenly narrower beside her and vanished into nothing. She threw up her hands with a little cry of terror and covered her face, swaying backward, and everything turned black before her eyes.

Chapter 7

There was no Laurie there to help her, but Ethan was there, and much more alert and ready than ever Laurie would have been. He sprang to catch her as her knees crumpled under her, and he lifted her in his strong arms, holding her firmly like a little child who needed comforting, holding her, turning her away from that awful space below them. He held her so for a second or two with her face against his rough tweed coat, as if by mere contact he would compel her fright to leave her, her senses to return. Then slowly, as if she had received new life from his strength, he felt her senses coming back to her and she began to tremble like a leaf.

"Oh, poor child!" he said softly, as if he were talking to himself. "I should not have brought you up here. The climb was too much for you!"

Suddenly, as if he understood better what was the matter, he turned with her still in his arms and began slowly to go down the stairs. Step by step he went, stopping now and again to look at her, until little by little she felt the assurance of his arms around her and slowly the color began to return to her face. When he next paused, her eyes fluttered open and looked into his own, the fright still there but fading slowly, as his eyes reassured her.

"It's all right now," he murmured gently, still in that same tone as one would speak to a little, frightened child. "We're almost to the lower floor. Just a few more steps and we will be down."

Surprisingly, she thrilled to the strength of the arms that were holding her and the tenseness relaxed.

She lay quite still and let the wonder of it roll over her, the relief of the end of her dream at last. Someone had saved her from that strange, maddening peril and showed her that she did not have to go on through all her life having at times to go back to the old problem of whether she would have to edge back over that ever-narrowing ledge that vanished before her feet or take the alternative of crashing down on the stone below at fearful speed and being blotted out in pain and darkness.

Gradually she ceased to tremble. And when he had reached the last step, he stopped and smiled down at her, saying pleasantly, "Now, it is all over. We are down! Are you feeling better?"

Her lashes trembled open, and she looked up at him with relief, murmuring, "Oh, I'm glad!"

The lashes swept down again, and suddenly a tear appeared beneath them and swelled out, making a pool in the violet shadows under her eyes.

"I'm so ashamed!" she murmured.

"You don't need to be," he said comfortingly. "I understand all about it. But there are some people coming this way. Are you able to stand if I hold you, or shall I just carry you out to the car this way?"

That brought her completely to herself.

"Oh, I can stand! Put me down, please!" she said in sudden panic.

He set her upon her feet and, with his own handkerchief,

dried the tears from her face. Then as the footsteps came around the partition at the foot of the stairs, he drew her arm within his own and led her out though the doors to the outer air.

"Perhaps we should have gone down in the elevator," he said, pausing in dismay as he remembered the long white steps ahead of them. "We could have walked right out of the entrance on the ground floor."

"No, I think I'll be all right now. I feel better out here in the air," said Marigold, keeping her eyes nevertheless steadily away from the long descent before her.

"Well then, take hold of that rail, and I'll support you on this side, and only look at one step at a time. We'll soon be down, and you can't possibly fall now because I'm holding you, you know."

And once again Marigold felt that thrill of strength come to her at his touch. It was silly, of course. It was just that she was unstrung, but she was glad to her soul that he was there.

And then they were down, back in the car, and she was being driven along swiftly through the streets.

He was silent for a little as he threaded his way through the noonday traffic. At last, looking shyly up at him, she spoke in low, hesitant tones.

"I don't know what you must think of me," she said. "I never did a thing like that before! It was all because of a dreadful dream I had one night, a nightmare I couldn't shake off when I woke up. I thought I was walking out on a narrow ledge above a great depth like that, and the ledge was getting narrower ahead of me. I couldn't go back, and no one down below would help me. A friend of mine just waved his hand and laughed and went away."

"I understand it perfectly," he said, turning and looking comprehendingly into her eyes. "I had it happen to me once, when I stood high above a job I was working on and something went wrong, putting me in great peril. I lost my nerve completely and was about to fall to my death. For days after the danger was past

I could not go to my job. I dared not get to that height again. Then some One very strong came and saved me from myself, and the terror all left me. I'll tell you about it sometime, but not now. You'd better stop thinking about it at once and get some sunshine in your face before you get home or your mother will be frightened. Aunt Marian will think I didn't take very good care of you."

She looked up at him gratefully. "You won't need to tell Mother?"

"No, indeed. Why frighten her? It's all over, you know."

He turned and smiled down upon her, putting one hand warmly over hers, and again that thrilling sense of his strength guarding her filled her shaken young soul with peace.

The rest of the drive was taken in silence, his hand over hers to reassure her, and when they reached the house he said with a keen look into her eyes, "Are you all right now?"

She nodded brightly. "Only ashamed."

"Forget it!" he said, grinning, and with a friendly squeeze of her hand he sprang out to open the door for her.

❈

The lunch was a merry one. Marigold, who felt shy and silent at first, rallied her forces and grew talkative, telling of all she had seen and heard. Her mother, watching anxiously, decided that she needn't worry after all. Her dear child seemed to be enjoying herself hugely. Probably the two young people had managed to get better acquainted during the morning, and Marigold wouldn't be so difficult the rest of the time.

The day was gorgeous and the drive a wonderful one. Marigold, as the new interests of the trip enthralled her, entirely forgot her eagerness to return to her home in time for the party. She had thought about it as they were starting, deciding that even if they got back as late as five o'clock, she might venture to get the six o'clock train if she still felt it wise. Three hours would bring her home at nine, and she *could* change on the train if she wanted to and take a taxi straight to the party, explaining her appearance after she got there. But anyway, she was going on that drive. She had always wanted to see Mount Vernon, and she might never have such a good chance again.

So the party and even Laurie were forgotten as they glided along beside the wide silver river, getting new visions of the fairy city that looked even more unearthly in the pearly afternoon light than it had the evening before.

Ethan had reverted to what she judged must be his normal self. Though he had put the two sisters in the backseat and placed Marigold in front with himself, he paid little attention to her, seldom talked much to her—except to point out something of interest they were passing—and made his conversation quite general, rather ignoring her. Marigold wondered at it a little and felt even somewhat mortified. He probably thought her a little fool, emotional and silly, who couldn't keep her head. All his gentleness of the morning was quite gone. He was the same indifferent stranger that he had been the night before. It was hard to take in his kindness of the morning, to remember how he had carried her down those stairs and held her so comfortingly as if she had been a little frightened child.

Well, perhaps it was just as well. She would be able more easily to put the whole incident out of her mind and her life. But anyway, she had somehow the feeling that a permanent cure for that dream had been created for her that morning, and she must always feel grateful to him for what he had done.

But the day was fine, the winter landscape a dream, the car luxurious—why not forget it all as he had suggested and just enjoy herself?

And so she tried to do just that, though now and then she would glance at his cool, impersonal countenance and feel a trifle chagrined at his indifference, even while chiding herself that she cared. She didn't care, of course; she was only trying to forget Laurie and the party, trying also to forget her mortification of the morning.

When they reached Mount Vernon they parked the car in a pleasant place, leaving the two sisters to enjoy one another's company, and went to explore the ancient landmark. Then Ethan caught her hand and said, "Come," and together they ran up the frosty drive to the old house. That bit of interlude did a good deal toward making Marigold feel more comfortable. This pleasant impersonal comradeship was much better than the solemn dignity with which he had been addressing her all afternoon. They laughed together and joked a little about the old days when knee breeches, lace ruffles, and hair ribbons were in vogue for men, and candlelight was the only illumination even in grand mansions.

After they had been over the place, hand in hand they ran down the snowy hill again, laughing like two children, and the soft color was glowing in Marigold's cheeks as they returned decorously to the car.

The two women smiled to each other as they saw them coming. It was good to them to see the young people whom they loved having a pleasant time together.

Marigold had forgotten all about going home. It was six o'clock when they reached the house, and the pleasant scents of dinner hung in the air—Aunt Marian's birthday dinner! Of course she couldn't run away from it.

Marigold hurried up to her room and slipped on the green silk. It wasn't exactly the dress for a simple home dinner, but she felt in a gala mood, and it was bright and pretty, a dress that probably would have been much too plain for the Trescott party but was not out of keeping for almost any simpler occasion.

"Mother, is this too much? I thought it would be fun to wear it once," she said as her mother entered the room.

"It's lovely!" said her mother. "Just sweet and lovely, and your aunt Marian will be pleased. Yes, wear it. It is very charming."

So Marigold went down to dinner looking like a flower with lovely green foliage around her, and Ethan stopped in the middle of a sentence and looked at her in wonder and a kind of awe.

"I've put on my party dress to do you honor, Aunt Marian," she said as she came into the room. "You won't think me silly, will you? I thought it would be fun."

"How dear of you, child!" said the aunt, looking at her with deep admiration. "I think that was a lovely thing to do, spend its freshness on a lonely old woman! But you know, I don't believe any party would enjoy it half as much as I shall. It is a beauty, isn't it, Mary? And so attractive, so simple and quaint in its style. It is charming. I feel as though I am selfish to have all this resplendence just for me. I *should* go to the telephone and call the neighbors in to meet my lovely guest."

"Well," said Ethan suddenly, "my opinion hasn't been asked, and of course it doesn't count, but I can enjoy a good thing when I see it, too, and I should say that gown was a prize. I don't remember having seen a prettier one anywhere. The only trouble with it is that it puts me in the shade. I had some tickets for the symphony concert tonight, and I had been daring to hope that Miss Brooke would honor me with her company, but now I'm afraid she will be ashamed to go with me. You see, I didn't happen to bring any glad rags along."

They all laughed at that as they sat down, and the birthday supper began, but after everybody was served, Marigold spoke up.

"I want to get this thing settled before I begin," she said. "I adore symphony concerts, and if my glad rags are going to keep me out of this one I'd better run right up now before I begin eating and change into the plainest thing I have."

Ethan looked at her and grinned, and almost she felt on a friendly footing with him again. She wondered why it was she cared so much whether he stayed friendly or not, and what it was that made him get solemn and indifferent every little while.

They had a pleasant supper and escorted the invalid upstairs in a procession, Ethan carrying her lightly as if she had been a child. Marigold found herself wondering about herself in those same arms coming down the Capitol stairs earlier in the day. He probably thought no more of it than he did of carrying his aunt now, and she must stop making so much out of a simple little thing like that. It was ridiculous to be so self-conscious. He was nothing to her, anyway. It would have been a great deal better for herself and everybody else concerned if she had stayed at home and gone to her party and not come here and acted like a silly little fool, getting all sorts of notions in her head.

She watched Ethan lay his aunt gently upon the bed and remembered how he had stood herself upon her feet and wiped her tears away with his own handkerchief. Why on earth did she have to come here and get her mind all tangled up thinking about a strange young man who was nothing in the world to her and never could be? Laurie was enough for her to worry about without her taking on another. She ought this very minute to be worrying over the fact that Laurie hadn't telephoned. It would have been just like Laurie to get an airplane from some of his friends and come after her, if he got the idea in his head. What had happened to Laurie? Oughtn't she to go right to the telephone now, while they were all busy and wouldn't notice her absence for a minute or two, and telephone Mrs. Waterman? That was an idea. She could go home even yet and get there in time for some of the party. Should she try?

But then Aunt Marian called for a game and motioned Marigold to a chair beside her.

Well, this was Aunt Marian's birthday, and she wouldn't spoil it by being absent. She would have to go to bed pretty soon. So Marigold settled down and puzzled her brain over thirty mistakes that she was supposed to find in a picture and forgot Laurie entirely.

They had a very happy hour before the nurse bustled in and shooed them all out, saying the patient really must go to bed and to sleep at once.

"Well," said Ethan, turning toward Marigold as they came out of Aunt Marian's room, "what's the answer? Am I to be favored with company to the concert, or are you ashamed of my informal dress?"

"Ashamed! Oh, my no!" said Marigold, her cheeks flaming bright with pleasure. "I was afraid it was too late."

"No, we have plenty of time. It's barely eight, and the music doesn't begin till eight thirty. Besides, we have seats and would have no trouble getting in."

"I'll be ready in just a minute," said Marigold eagerly. "But— am I too giddy-looking in this bright dress? Will you be ashamed of *me*? I could change in just a jiffy."

"Ashamed?" He grinned. "I'll be prouder than I care to own. You look like something great! I think that is a swell dress."

Marigold's cheeks grew pinker, and her eyes sparkled.

"Thank you," she said and then flew away to get her wrap.

"How about you, Aunt Mary? Wouldn't you like to go, too? I have a friend down at the office, and I'm sure I can get another ticket."

"Thank you," Mrs. Brooke said, smiling, "I'm a little tired from the drive this afternoon. I think I'd better stay and rest. Besides, I have found a lovely book I would like to read."

So the young people were off together again.

Tucked into the darkness of the car with Ethan's tall form beside her, Marigold suddenly realized that she was having a very good time indeed and doubted if she would have had a better time if she had stayed at home and gone to the party. Somehow she felt as if she knew Ethan a little better, now that he had complimented her dress. Anyway, she was resolved to have a good time this evening in spite of everything. Ethan Bevan wasn't, of course, anything to her, and after she went home she would likely never see him again; but at least for tonight, she was resolved to enjoy everything. She loved music, and if he could talk about music as well as he could talk about those paintings that morning, surely she had an enjoyable evening before her.

"I'm glad you were willing to go tonight," said Ethan suddenly, guiding his car skillfully through traffic. "I took a chance buying these tickets. I didn't know whether you cared for music or not."

"I love it!" said Marigold enthusiastically. "Only I don't have many chances to hear it. Mother and I don't go out very much. Mother is often tired. And most of the young people I know don't seem to be interested in music. They like wild parties and jazz and nightclubs and things."

"And you? Don't you go in for those things?" He studied her face keenly in the dim light of the car.

Marigold sat in a troubled silence.

"I don't know," she said slowly at last. "I've only gone once or twice, and then I felt very uncomfortable and out of place. I don't just know why. It didn't seem real."

He was still studying her. At last he said slowly, "You *would* be out of place. It wouldn't fit *you*. It *isn't* real."

She expected him to say more, but he didn't. Just drove on and sat quietly, now and then looking at her furtively.

"Well," said Marigold at last with a little lilt in her voice, "I know I'm going to enjoy it tonight. Though I may not feel quite at home—I think it will be something like the outside door of heaven."

He looked at her and smiled. "I'm glad you feel that way."

When they were in the concert hall at last and the first great strains of the opening number were thrilling through the air, Marigold tried to think over their conversation on the way, and somehow she couldn't remember much that was said, but it had left a nice, comfortable, pleasant impression, as if they were in accord.

Occasionally when something in the program especially pleased her, she glanced up at him with her eyes full of delight, and every time she found his pleasant glance upon her, evidently enjoying her pleasure. There was none of that aloofness, that disapproval, she had felt at intervals all day, and she was relieved and content.

He was enjoying the music, too. She knew it by the way his glance met hers at the most exquisite climaxes. On the way home he spoke about certain phrases, the way the woodwind instruments echoed the melody in the symphony, the technique of the solo artist, the depth of insight into the meaning of the score shown by the conductor. She listened to his comments with interest. She had never heard anyone talk of music in this way. None of Laurie's friends knew or liked any music but the weirdest jazz, and then only as an accompaniment to dancing or as a shield for their wild, hilarious conversation. She felt as if this young man regarded it almost as a holy thing, music.

Marigold was sorry when they got back to the house and she had to go to bed. She didn't want to be by herself. She was afraid she was suddenly going to realize that the party was now going on and she was missing it. But instead, when she slipped quietly in beside her sleeping mother, all the thinking she did was to wonder about the look Ethan Bevan had given her when he had said good night. Did it have withdrawal again in its quality, or was it just pleasant approval? Almost he had looked as if he were sorry to have to say good night so soon. Buy why should she care to discuss the matter with herself? Miles away at home there was a wonderful party going on now to which she had been invited and might just as well have gone! And here she was off spending her time with a young man she had never seen before and hadn't at all liked at first. One who had decidedly disapproved of her at first, too, she was sure.

Things were strange. Why was she here? She had no one to blame for it but herself. And why did she puzzle over this young man? Let him think what he chose. He had admired her dress, anyway. Or had he? Sometimes she thought he was just poking fun at her, laughing in his sleeve at her all the time. Perhaps he thought she put on that dress to charm him. Why should she want to charm him? She had Laurie. Or *did* she? Was he not perhaps even at this moment dancing with that other girl, giving that long adoring look into her eyes that Marigold knew so well and up to two days ago had considered all her own?

Oh well!

Marigold drew a deep sigh, turning softly over, and suddenly there came to her the memory of those strong arms around her that had rescued her from that terrible sense of falling and brought her to earth so safely that her fear was lost! In the memory of that, she drifted peacefully off to sleep.

❧

It was late when she awoke. Her mother had dressed and gone to eat breakfast from a tray with her sister. Marigold dressed hurriedly and went down, wondering if Ethan Bevan would be gone.

He had finished his breakfast, that was evident, for there was only one place set at the table.

As she drank her orange juice, she wondered about him. Perhaps he had gone back to his boardinghouse. It might be that she would not see him again before she left. He had said he had important things to do.

"Mr. Ethan had his breakfast early," remarked the maid as she brought the cereal and cream. "He went out to the breakfast mission, I think he said."

Breakfast mission. What might that be? Well, she would probably not need to worry anymore what he was thinking; she could go her own way now and see the city as she pleased without having to wonder whether she was pleasing his highness or not. There must be some old churches. She would look some of them up and find quaint old-time landmarks—sacred, historic places of worship. She might have asked Ethan yesterday about them, but she was glad she had not. He would have thought he had to attend her again, and he had certainly served his time at being host to her. She would just wander out and find them for herself. There must be churches all around, and certainly a lot of places she would like to see at her leisure.

She had just finished the last bite of her delicious breakfast and was about to go upstairs to see her mother and aunt before sallying forth on her voyage of discovery, when Ethan walked in at the front door and flung his hat on the hall table.

"Oh, you're down," he said casually. "I didn't know whether the household had waked up yet or not. I had to go out on an early quest. One of my men, my laborers at the job, has been absent for nearly a week, and I wanted to hunt him up. He has been off on a drunk, I suspect, for he left with his pay envelope last Saturday. I had a notion he must be about out of funds by this time, so I went the rounds of the usual rendezvous and found him at last at the Sunday morning breakfast mission. I thought he'd be about ready for that by this time. I gave him a lecture and fixed him with the mission for the day, arranged with another fellow to bring him to the job tonight, and he promised me he'd keep straight and be on hand bright and early tomorrow morning. I hope he will, but you are never sure."

"Oh, that was kind of you to go after him."

"Nothing kind about it," said Ethan gruffly. "It's my job, isn't it, to look after my fellow men? Especially those that are under me in my work. I only wish I could reach deeper down than just the surface and get their feet fixed on solid rock where they can't be moved. I'm always glad when that can be done!"

She looked at him in surprise. This was a new view of this

young man. A man as young as he to care what became of his workers!

But before she could make any remark about it, he got up suddenly and started toward the stairs; then glancing at his watch, he turned back to her and said hesitantly, almost brusquely, "I suppose you wouldn't—care—to go to church—with me, would you?" He lifted his eyes and looked straight into hers, almost piercingly. The question was like a challenge. She had a feeling that he expected her to make some excuse and get out of it, but she lifted her eyes with sudden resolve.

"Why, yes," she said gravely, "I would, very much. I was just wondering where to find a church."

He seemed almost surprised at her answer.

"But I won't be taking you to any grand church," he said, again with a challenge in his glance.

"What makes you think I want to go to a grand church?" she parried. "I'd like to go with you; that is, if I won't be in your way."

Did his eyes light up at that, or did she imagine it? And why was there something like a little song in her heart as she ran upstairs to get her hat and coat?

Chapter 8

The church to which Ethan took Marigold that morning was a plain little structure, not even in the neighborhood of handsome buildings, but the sermon was one that she would never forget, for it seemed to be a message straight from God to her own soul. Afterward she couldn't quite remember what the text or main theme of the sermon had been. It had only seemed to her as if God had been there and had been speaking directly to her.

She was very quiet all the way home. Ethan did not seem to notice. He was silent, too, perhaps watching her furtively.

Just as they came in sight of the house she spoke, thinking aloud. "I'm glad I heard that sermon. It made me think of things I had almost forgotten, things I can remember my father saying when I was a little girl and he was preaching."

"Was your father a minister?" asked Ethan in surprise. "I may have known it once, but I certainly had forgotten."

"Yes," said Marigold, looking up with dreamy memory in her eyes. "He was wonderful, and he preached real things. I was only a child, but I remember a lot of them, and I needed to have them brought back to my memory."

He gave her another surprised look, mixed, she felt, with something like tenderness.

At last, just before they reached the house, he said, "I'm very glad you felt that way. I'm always encouraged when I go to hear that man preach." And as he helped her up the steps there seemed to be somehow a bond between them that had not been there before, a kind of new sympathy. Yet he said nothing more. Just looked at her and smiled as they entered the house together.

In the afternoon they took Aunt Marian for another short drive because the day was fine and the ride to Mount Vernon had seemed to do her so much good. They wound up at a street meeting held by one of the missions in the lower part of the city. Marigold was greatly interested. She had never been to a street meeting before. She studied the faces of the young people who were conducting it, giving their simple testimonies, and reflected on the contrast between them and Laurie's crowd. Yes, she had been getting afar off from the things her dear father would have wished for her, just as her mother had hinted. She was very thoughtful after that.

They stopped for a few minutes at the breakfast mission for Ethan to see if everything was going to be all right for the worker to get back to camp that night, and then they went home and had a lovely buffet supper served in Aunt Marian's room with Ethan for waiter. They all sat awhile afterward listening to Aunt Marian's favorite preacher on the radio. By common consent they lingered with the dear invalid as long as she was allowed to stay awake, feeling that their time together was not to be long and wanting to please her as much as possible. The nurse was out, and the patient begged them to remain a little longer, saying she was not tired, but at last when they insisted that she ought to be asleep, she said, "All right. But first let's have a bit of Bible reading and a prayer! Ethan, you get my Bible."

Marigold sat down again and watched Ethan in surprise as he quietly got the Bible and sat down to read. Imagine such a request being made of Laurie! How he would laugh and jeer if anybody thought of asking him to do such a thing. A pang of troubled doubt went through her soul with the thought. Had she been brought here to watch this most unusual man and see the contrast between him and Laurie? She pushed the thought away in annoyance.

Ethan opened the Bible as if it were a familiar book. He didn't ask his aunt where he should read. He turned directly to the ninety-first psalm and read in a clear voice, as if he loved what he was reading: " 'He that dwelleth in the secret place of the most High shall abide under the shadow of the Almighty. I will say of the Lord, He is my refuge and my fortress: my God; in him will I trust. . . .' "

Somehow as he read on, Marigold felt as if he were reading the words just for her. As if in his mind, they had some special significance for her. She sat there listening, thrilled with the thought.

" 'Surely he shall deliver thee—' "

Was he trying to remind her that when earthly friends were not by to help she was not alone?

" 'Thou shalt not be afraid for the terror by night—' "

And now he did lift his eyes and look straight into hers, with a light in them that surely he meant her to read and understand. He was thinking of the dream she had told him and the terror that possessed her sometimes when she woke in the night. It could not have been plainer if he had said it in his own words, and suddenly she blushed in response. Yet it was all unobserved by the two dear women who were sitting by listening, though they would dearly have loved to have caught that look that passed between the two beloved children.

And the steady voice went on: " '. . .he shall give his angels charge over thee, to keep thee—' " It was like a benediction, and Marigold felt she never could forget it as his voice read on to the end of the psalm.

And then he knelt and prayed, such a simple, earnest petition, filled with deep thanksgiving, humble confession, heartfelt trust, and joyful praise. And this was the young man she had scorned when she came. The man she wished anywhere else but where she was to be!

She looked at him with a kind of shy awe and mingled humility as they rose from their knees, and he smiled at her again as if she were suddenly one of his closest friends. She couldn't quite understand what made the difference in his attitude, but she knew it was there and it gave her a warm feeling around her heart. That was something more than just happiness. It seemed almost as if it were something like a holy bond.

She went to sleep that night wondering about it and not realizing that she hadn't once remembered the party or Laurie all day long. It seemed as if somehow she was entering a new era in her life. She didn't question what it was to be, but she knew that she could never go back home and be the same thoughtless butterfly that she had been before. She found herself wishing wistfully that she might be with the wonderful young man and learn the secret of his sweetness and his strength. She hoped—and this was her last waking thought—that in the morning he would not again slam the door of his soul, leaving her outside. Not until she could ask him a few questions and perhaps get nearer to his Source of strength, anyway.

She hurried eagerly downstairs early the next morning, but he was gone. Gone without a word!

"Ethan was sorry he had to leave without farewells," said Aunt Marian to Marigold's mother, calling from her room as Mrs. Brooke went by her door. "Someone called him last night about a man, one of his workers, and he had to go and hunt him up. Some poor soul for whom he feels responsible. He slipped out without waking anybody. He called me just now on the phone and asked me to say how sorry he was not to be able to say good-bye. He had not intended to leave until after breakfast and was hoping to get another word with you both before he left."

Marigold, at the foot of the stairs, heard, and her heart went down with a thud of disappointment, the light out of her eyes and the brightness out of the new bright day! So! That was that! She would probably never see him again and their brief meeting would pass into the "had been" and be forgotten!

She stared blankly around her wondering what she would do with the day. Of course, she could call up Mrs. Waterman now and find out if Laurie had called, but somehow it didn't seem to matter much whether he had or not.

Then she heard her mother's footsteps coming down the stairs, and she roused to a cheerfulness that she was far from feeling. What was the matter with her, anyway? Silly thing! What difference did it make whether Ethan Bevan was there or away? He was nothing whatever to her. Two days ago she would have been glad enough to get rid of him. She ought to be glad that he went away with a pleasant smile and she didn't have to remember him as a grouch before whom she had been humiliated. He had been nice to her in the end. And he was a good man. He had helped her. She must be honest about that. And it was just sheer foolishness for her to be disappointed that he had gone without giving her a special word. What was she to him? What could she expect? She was nothing but one of his fellow mortals upon this earth who needed help. She was no more to him than that poor worker who had called him from his sleep to search him out and save him. She was just a weak sister who couldn't bear to stand somewhere high and look down, and he had carried her down and given her his strength, for the time being, to help tide her over her dismay. She firmly believed that he had given her permanent help against that obsession, and she ought to be thankful that God had given her this brief contact with one so strong and so able to help others. And now she had to go back and meet her own world alone.

But God had seen that she needed help and had sent her here to get it. He had seen that she needed to be awakened to the fact that she was getting away from the things of her childhood's faith, the standards and customs that had been so safe and wise, and He had taken this way to show her where she was drifting. Now it was up to her to use her new knowledge. Or was it? Wasn't she just as helpless alone, as if she were still standing out on that narrow ledge above the great height of peril? She couldn't get back alone, could she? She needed someone's strength to steady her until her feet were on solid ground. Some *One*, Ethan had said! How she wished she had asked him more about that experience of his own, in some of those silences yesterday. Now, probably, she would never know. But he had, at least in his reading of the psalm last night, given her a hint of where her strength was to be found. That was it. God would be her strength! She had to find out by herself how to get back to God and the things she had been forgetting so long.

"Well," said her mother suddenly, watching her intently, "what are you going to do today, dear? You have your freedom now to go about alone as you wished. What is going to be your plan?"

Marigold looked up with sudden illumination and laughed. "Oh, Mother! I'm sorry I was so unspeakably disagreeable the night we arrived. I ought to have been spanked. He was lovely. He really was wonderful, and I enjoyed all the places he took me and had a very good time. I don't know about today. Isn't there something I could do to make a happy time for you and Aunt Marian? It seems to me I've had enough enjoyment to last me a good long while."

"Well, that's sweet of you, dear, but I don't see what you could do for us, this morning at least. We haven't any car, and you couldn't carry your aunt downstairs. Whatever we do for her will have to be done in her room until Elinor and her husband get home, since she can't get downstairs."

"I could do jigsaw puzzles with her," said Marigold brightly. "I heard her say she loves them, and you know I always did like to do them."

"Yes, well, perhaps you could part of the day, toward evening. But I'm sure she won't be happy to have you cooped up all the time this lovely day. I think she would like it better if you went out somewhere awhile. She was speaking of some of the places around here she wanted you to see, to which you could walk easily. I think it would be nice if you were to go out a little while this morning, and perhaps again in the afternoon for a few minutes, and then come in and entertain her betweentimes with what you have seen."

"All right, I'll go out for a walk. I'll bring her back a new puzzle she hasn't seen, and we'll do that some of the in-betweens. But how about yourself? You've been cooped up most of the time. Why shouldn't you go out, too, or let me stay here and you go alone?"

Mrs. Brooke smiled. "You know, my dear, the best thing I can do is stay with my dear sister. We've been hungry for each other for many long years. But I'll go out with you a few minutes for a walk if you would like it. Aunt Marian was telling me about a lovely place she wants me to see, and she says it's only a few blocks from here. She says it reminds her so much of our old home when we were children. I'll walk with you there now, right after breakfast, if you'd like, and then you can be free until lunchtime to go your own way."

So they went out together, and Mrs. Brooke studied her dear child's face, wondering if the wistful look in her eyes was for

Laurie and the party she had missed.

But Marigold never mentioned the party or Laurie, either, and talked brightly of having her mother stay another two weeks after she herself went home. Talked blithely of little changes she meant to make in the apartment when they got back, new curtains they might have, to make things more cheery, and so they walked the lovely streets and came back to the house. Then Marigold started out on her lonely tour. But somehow there wasn't a great deal of spice in this independence after all. Where should she go?

Well, there was the art gallery. Ethan had said that was worth taking time to study. She would do that this morning. And then in the afternoon she would go awhile to the Smithsonian. If she ever should see Ethan again and he should ask her, which, of course, he wouldn't because he asked very few questions, she would hate to say she hadn't done anything with her precious time in Washington after he left.

So she spent the morning in the Corcoran and came back impressed with the fact that she knew very little indeed about pictures, and only a few of the great ones she had seen that morning had meant very much to her. As she entered the house, the thought did come to her that perhaps that was because her mind had been more or less on other things all the time.

She had stopped at a store long enough to purchase a fascinating jigsaw puzzle, and she and Aunt Marian worked at it until her aunt hurried her off to the Smithsonian, telling her that she would find the time all too short until four o'clock when everything belonging to the government closed.

So she started out again, wandering here and there, getting a glimpse of this and that, and wondering what Ethan would have said if he had been here with her.

And there she was again thinking about Ethan. How utterly ridiculous! Why not think about Laurie? How nice it would be if

Laurie were like Ethan, that is, like him in some things, anyway. For instance, Laurie wouldn't have stopped a minute to look at pictures or listen to classical music. He would have said it was too slow for him. He would have wanted something exciting. He never stopped to look into the history or the beauty or the reason of things. And Laurie, if she were frightened—well, Laurie in her dream had turned and waved his hand at her and then gone off laughing. It was so characteristic of his carefree nature that she couldn't quite think of his carrying her comfortingly down those stairs and wiping her tears away. Laurie hated tears. He wanted smiles and laughter and excitement. Laurie would never have read the Bible and prayed, nor gone to church! Oh, if she started out on this new life she was vaguely planning, would she have to give up Laurie? Or be continually at swords' points with him?

She began almost to dread going home. What was she going to meet when she got there? What would this strange new kind of young man she had been companioning with the last two days do if he were put into her situation?

One thing she knew, he would never give in and go the way of the world. There was something about him that showed he had distinctly given up the world as far as amusing himself was concerned. He didn't go to nightclubs, nor admire girls who went to them. He hadn't said so, but somehow she knew. And by the same token, she was sure he would never compromise with anything he had decided was not right.

She walked herself around and took in the main points of the great museum. Then she took a taxi back to her aunt's house, without ever really putting her mind on what she was seeing. In a vague way she recalled this and that, enough to mention a few things when she got back to the two who watched her and hoped she had had a good time, but all the time there had been that undertone of thought, gradually focusing in her mind into one overwhelming wish—that she might have one more chance to talk to Ethan Bevan and ask him a few of the questions that filled her with consternation as she contemplated meeting them all alone when she got home.

The idea followed her all day, grew deeper while she worked on the puzzle with her aunt and in the evening while she sat in the lovely library and tried to read a book with only half her mind while the other half turned over her problems. It stayed with her and kept her awake after she had gone to bed and met her at the break of day when she awoke. This was her last morning here. Today she must go home. If she could only talk with that young man a half hour before she went away and ask him to advise her!

And then—while she was eating an early lunch because both her mother and aunt had decreed that she must go on an earlier train than she had selected so that she would not arrive at the apartment alone late in the evening—in he walked!

Chapter 9

Marigold's heart gave a quick leap of gladness, and a light glowed in her eyes and flamed in pretty color in her cheeks.

"Hello, folks!" Ethan said casually, as if he had only gone out a few minutes before, but his level gaze was straight at Marigold, and an answering glow came into his eyes, as if he was pleased at what he had seen in hers. It was as if their two hearts had spoken to one another across the room in a look that neither quite realized.

Ethan held her gaze for a full second before he went on, still watching her earnestly. "I found out I have to run up to Philadelphia after some parts of a machine we need that are not to be had around here. I wondered if you might care to drive up with me, or would you prefer to go on the train as you planned? Don't feel you have to go with me if you would rather go some other way."

Marigold's cheeks flamed a sweet color now, and she cried out softly in delight, "Oh, I'd love to go with you! I was dreading the long trip alone."

"How kind of you to think of her," said Mrs. Brooke in relief. "I hated to have her go home alone, it seemed so desolate, and I've been making her start earlier than she had planned because I didn't want her to have to go into the apartment alone so late at night."

"Well, I can make sure she gets in all right," Ethan said. "I won't be able to stay long, though, because I have to start right back and drive nearly all night. We can't hold up our machine another day. I've telephoned ahead to have the parts ready so I won't lose time."

"Well, you could wait long enough for me to make a cup of coffee and scramble some eggs, couldn't you?" Marigold asked.

"Perhaps!" he said, with a grin like a shy boy.

In a little while, they were off into the brightness of the day and soon had left Washington behind, the road winding ahead of them in a broad white ribbon.

But it was hard for Marigold to believe that there had been that look between them, now that they were alone in the car. He had returned to his silent aloofness, and somehow Marigold didn't seem to be able to think of anything to say that would break the spell of silence. She got to thinking that perhaps he had only asked her to join him out of a sense of duty. Perhaps he hadn't wanted her to come along at all.

She sat there silently thinking it over, and then a sudden remembrance of that glowing look with which he had welcomed her acceptance of his invitation brought a degree of comfort. How silly she was! This was his nature, and why should she question it? If he didn't want to talk, let him remain quiet. He hadn't had to ask her, and he likely was friendly enough and wanted her there or he wouldn't have taken the trouble to come after her. Why be bothered by his manner? This time with him was what she had wanted, to ask him a lot of questions, why not use it? If he didn't want to answer, he could say so.

So she summoned her courage, casting a sideways glance at his pleasant, friendly face.

"There are some things I would very much like to ask you," she said in a strained young voice, almost wishing now that she had started that she hadn't begun.

"Yes?" He turned a look of quick interest toward her, and all her hesitation vanished. He was again the friend who was ready and eager to help, able and understanding.

"We were speaking of worldly amusements the other day. Nightclubs and that sort of thing. Of course, I was brought up without them, but people—sometimes Christian people—are telling me that times have changed and that everybody thinks those things are all right now. They say young people can't get along without those things. I wanted to know what you think. Is it wrong for a Christian ever to go to such things? Do you think a girl or a man could be a Christian and still do those things?"

Ethan looked at her with one of those deep, searching glances, as if he would find out through her eyes just what she thought herself before he answered. "Do you mean, do I think a person can be *saved* and still do those things? Because, yes, I suppose they can. For salvation isn't a matter of what you do yourself. It's something Christ did for you, and you have only to accept. But if you're asking about those things as the practice of a person who is saved, that's another question."

Marigold sat thoughtfully, looking into the bright landscape ahead.

"I see," she said earnestly. "But if they were considering whether they would accept the Savior as theirs, wouldn't the matter of what they had to do or not do afterward have to be considered? Wouldn't they have to be willing to renounce things if they took Christ as their Savior?"

"It doesn't say so in the Bible. It says 'Believe on the Lord Jesus Christ, and thou shalt be saved.' "

"Then you think it is all right for a Christian to be worldly sometimes, do you?" she asked with evident surprise in her tone.

"I didn't say that," he answered quickly. "I don't think those things are to be considered when one accepts the Lord Jesus as his Savior. The question is just that Jesus Christ died for your sins and is willing to take them and their penalty upon His own account instead of yours, and do you want Him to do that? If you say yes, if you accept what He has already done for you and believe fully that He has done it, then you are born again. You have a new nature born of God, and that nature does not desire the things of this world. Yet you still have that old sinning nature with you, will have as long as you live on the earth, that draws you in spite of your best resolves and makes you want to do the things that you have resolved over and over again you will never do. As long as that old nature has a chance to get on the top every little while, you haven't much chance of living the steady testimony a saved soul should live. But God has provided a way of victory for you over the old nature. He has said that if you will go the whole way with Him, even to the cross, and let the old nature be cru-cified with Him, consider it to have *died* with Him, that He will give you His own resurrection power in your life; that is, He will live His life in you on a different plane from ordinary living. Am I making it plain?"

"I think so," said Marigold thoughtfully. "You mean hand ev-erything over to Him and be willing for what He wants?"

"Yes, it amounts to that. It is believing yourself to be dead to the things of the flesh and alive unto God; it is asking Him to slay self in you so that you can honestly say, 'I am crucified with Christ: nevertheless I live; yet not I, but Christ liveth in me: and the life which I now live in the flesh I live by the faith of the Son of God, who loved me, and gave himself for me.' When you honestly say that to Him, then He can come in and fill you with Himself, and it will be no more you who is living in your body but Jesus Christ who is living your life for you. And then if He wants you to go to nightclubs and all that sort of thing, He will tell you. He'll make it very plain to you. It isn't a matter of giving up things. It's a matter of whether you are willing to *die* with Him."

"Oh," said Marigold softly, a strange illuminated look on her face, "that makes life all different, doesn't it?"

She was still trying to think it through, he saw.

"Yes," he said, looking with a great yearning upon the sweet face as she sat thinking. "It makes life very wonderful!" And there was something in his tone that showed he knew from experience the truth of what he was saying. "It puts the power of God at your command, to conquer for you the old sinful nature that is in you. It's His resurrection power."

She looked at him, perplexed. "I don't exactly understand. What is the resurrection power?"

"It is the power of God that Jesus Christ brought with Him out of the tomb when He rose from the dead. He said, 'All power is given unto me. . .go ye,' meaning that they were to go forth in that power to conquer, what of themselves they never could. They were to go out to witness for Him. That was their only commission, and you know yourself that neither they nor we could ever do much witnessing for the Lord Jesus by the lives we live in our own power. Just our own resolves and beliefs wouldn't go very far in making others accept Christ as Savior, nor even in showing them that He was the Son of God!"

"That is all new to me," said the girl earnestly. "You mean we can have Christ's own power instead of our own to live by?"

"Yes, if we are willing for this death-union with Him. He has promised, 'If we have been planted together in the likeness of his death, we shall be also in the likeness of his resurrection.' And it is just in proportion as we are willing for this death-union with Him, this daily dying with Him to the things of this world, the things of the old nature, that we shall be able to show Him to others."

They were silent for a moment while she considered that. Then Ethan spoke again. "You know self is not easily slain. It has a habit of coming to life again, self with all its old programs and ambitions and tastes and feelings and wishes. It is a case of having to be slain continually. 'For we which live (here on this earth, you know) are *always* delivered unto death for Jesus' sake, that the life also of Jesus might be made manifest in our mortal flesh.' I wonder if I have made that perfectly plain. Do you see how all this affects the question you asked me about worldly ways and amusements?"

"Oh yes, I think I do," said Marigold slowly. "That would be very wonderful living. I never dreamed that such living would be possible on this earth. I didn't know that—we could—get so close—to God—as that! But I can see that if one lived that way, those other questions wouldn't even come up at all. They would settle themselves, wouldn't they?"

"They certainly would! They certainly do!" said the young man with a ring of triumph in his voice.

She was still a long time, and then with a little sigh of troubled perplexity she said, "That would be all right for those who wanted to have Him as Savior like that; wanted to die with Him—were *willing* to. But what about those who are not willing?"

A shadow came over the brightness of his face. Was she then going so far and no farther? Had he been mistaken in her interest? Was she so entangled in the world that she could not surrender it?

He did not answer for a moment, and then he said with a sorrowful note in his voice, "Does it matter? If one isn't willing to go the whole way with the Lord Jesus, just staying away from a few nightclubs and movies isn't going to get you any nearer. There are plenty of people who don't do any of those things and yet are not saved."

There was such disappointment in his voice as he finished that she looked up and suddenly read what he had thought.

"I don't mean myself," she said quickly. "I mean somebody else. Suppose you had a friend who wanted to go to those things all the time, who couldn't see anything wrong in them."

"Is he saved?" asked Ethan quickly with a sharp note of tenseness in his voice.

"I—don't—suppose he is!" she answered with down-drooping gaze and sorrowful demeanor.

He gave her another keen, furtive glance, his lips set in stern lines.

"You mean—?" he started and hesitated.

"I mean do you think a Christian should try and stop him going? Or—should perhaps go with him sometimes, when he is insistent—and try to win him away from such things?"

"I should think the question would start farther back than that. I should think a Christian who was willing to have this death-union with Christ that we have been speaking of could not possibly make a habit of companionship with one who is an acknowledged outsider, an enemy of Christ. For you know He said, 'He that is not with me is against me.' And Christ has made it very plain that He does not want His saved ones to choose their companions from the world. A Christian lives in a different realm."

His voice was almost harsh as he said this. He would rather do almost anything than give advice to this girl on a subject like this. And she was still considering what he had said. At last she answered in a low voice, "Yes, I know. I was brought up to think that. And my mother has reminded me, too. But somehow I don't seem to come into contact with many believers nowadays. The church where we go is very worldly. And—well—I was wondering whether there was anything I could do for some worldly people I know. It isn't a question of *beginning* to go with them. I have known them for a long time. It's a question of what I might be able to do for them now, knowing them as well as I do. Should I humor them and go with them, trying to help them to get away from such things, or should I just cut loose from them entirely?"

She waited, looking at him anxiously.

His face grew suddenly tender.

"Forgive me!" he said gently. "I'm not your dictator. God Himself will guide you in such things if you will let Him. But I am quite sure that you could never win a person away from anything by doing it with him. If you come to know Christ and the power of His resurrection and the fellowship of His sufferings, and you share the likeness of His death, and He makes you know that these things are not for you, then surely you can see that you must be consistent in your life with what you believe. But I do not think you will have to ask me such a question. It will be something that Christ and you will settle together. And as far as you are concerned, if you know Him through dying with Him, your testimony will be such that the worldly people will drop you, and these things will likely drop away. You will no longer want to do them because you have better things to do, just as you don't want to play with dolls now as you probably used to do when you were a child. You will be as truly dead to these things as a person lying in a coffin would be dead to any temptation that used to lead him astray in his lifetime. That is, of course, you would unless you made it a *practice* of doing those things constantly. You cannot hold hands with the world and expect to have this death-union with Christ and the resultant resurrection power in your life."

There was a long silence while Marigold thought that over.

Once they stopped to get gas, and she watched her escort as he lifted the hood of his engine, talked a minute or two with the attendant, and then took a leaflet out and handed it to him with a smile, saying, "Good-bye, brother, I hope to see you sometime again." Marigold could see the young man standing where they had left him, curiously reading the little tract that had been given to him. What a man this was with whom she was privileged to travel! He was trying to make men everywhere see Christ! For she sensed that he had spoken of His Savior to the stranger, and that his word had been graciously received. How was it that she had not understood how fine he was when she first met him? How was it that she had even resented his presence?

Ah, she had been looking upon him merely as another young man, judging him in the worldly sense, from her own personal interest in him. She had not realized that he was an envoy from another world who might perhaps have an important message for her own soul.

What was it that made him so different from other men she knew? Well, of course it must be this death-union with Christ he had been talking about. But how had he gotten that way? How was it that he alone of all the young men she knew anywhere should be like this? Had it been through his own efforts, through some special environment, through some experience? Then she remembered.

"You promised to tell me about your experience with high places," she suddenly said. "May I know now? When you were in danger once, and how you got over it."

"Yes?" he said, looking at her sharply. "Are you sure it will not make you dizzy again to hear it so soon?"

She smiled.

"No, I think you have helped me over that place," she said. "My obsession came when I dreamed myself into a situation for which I could see no help when I woke up. I had to be continually going over and over it in my mind trying to find a way to save myself, and so the dream returned again and again. But you showed me a way out. You brought a strong arm and carried me down. You gave me the sense of being secure, anyway, even if I was in peril, and I haven't had the dream since. I don't believe it will ever bother me again. I can't thank you enough for that."

He smiled.

"I'm glad I was there!" he said with satisfaction. "Well, I'll tell you my story. It isn't long. I was in a high place on the scaffold of my biggest job, the biggest I had ever had then, and it was nearing completion. I was very proud of the work that I had done. I knew it was good work and was going to make me a degree of fame in my profession so that I might continue to go on up and do bigger things. I was rather swelled up about it, I'm afraid, *my* bridge over a great chasm, and *I* was the designer and builder!"

Marigold looked up at him in surprise. He certainly had no look of conceit about him now.

He went on: "And then, something suddenly went wrong while I was standing up there, looking up at my almost-completed job. A piece of machinery weighing tons crashed down beside me, carrying with it scaffold and stonework and flying masonry and leaving me standing there on just the slender board that was left, wavering out over an abyss, nothing to hold to, no way apparently to get back to anything tangible at all. It didn't matter then whose fault it was. I found out incidentally it had been partly mine, away back in the beginning of the job. I hadn't been as careful as I should. But that didn't concern me then. All I saw was that I was standing in an awful space between heaven and earth with no possible hope for my life, no way ever to get back to earth again, and only a few minutes, perhaps seconds, left before I, too, should crash down into the horror of debris below. All my pride, my ambition, my attainment was in ruins below me, and I dared not look down at it. I dared not look away and try to forget it, I dared not look up, and I could not plan any way to save myself! And then a man risked his life and crept out on the tottering masonry of the arch above me and let down a rope. He let it down carefully in front of my hands where I could grasp it. It had a loop in it that I could hold on to. And I stood there holding to that little loop of rope, knowing the masonry from which it hung might soon come crashing down, too, and carry me with it. Yet I had the rope, and how I clung to it! After what seemed eons more, they made a way to get down to me, and strong arms pulled me up and into safety. I won't trouble you with the details. I came out of that terrible situation knowing that one man had risked his life to save me.

"For days I lay in a dark room trying to steady my senses, knowing that I was ruined—body, mind, and soul—if I could not get away from the horror that possessed me. I never could go on a job site again. I would always have death staring me in the face if I climbed to any high place.

"Then one night as I lay tossing, unable to sleep, the Lord came to me across great space to that terrible pinnacle upon which I always seemed to be standing alone whenever I tried to sleep, came down, and, as easily as I picked you up that day, took me in His arms. He looked Me in the eyes, and He said to me, 'Ethan, you belong to Me! Don't you know it? Don't you remember that day long ago when you told your Sunday school teacher you would accept Me as your Savior? You were only a boy then, but you meant what you said, and I accepted you. You haven't thought much about Me since. You've been wandering strange paths where I can't go, and you haven't listened for My voice when I called you. But now you've found out where they lead and that they end in ruin, those paths you thought were so bright when you started out, those paths of ambition that you thought would lead you to fame.

" 'And now you think you are done, that your career is ended. But you are mistaken. You are *Mine*. You have been Mine all the time, even when you wandered so far you could not hear My voice. And I never lose my own. I've come after you, and I'm going to bring you back and let you go on in your profession, but you must walk with *Me*! It is the only safe way. No, you needn't be afraid of this horror anymore, because you are going to remember that from now on I am with you, and wherever duty calls you, I will be there and have My arm around you. I gave My life for you once, and I'm never going to let you fall. Now get up, Ethan, and go on with your work, for you and I have died together once, and we're going on to live together now and show men what the power of the resurrection in a life can do.' "

Ethan was still a minute, and then he looked down at Marigold and smiled.

"That's all," he said. "That's how it came about! I know He'll do that for you, too, if you will let Him!"

"Oh, I'd like Him to," breathed Marigold softly.

Just then they came within the city traffic, and there was no more opportunity to talk.

Chapter 10

That very afternoon Irene Trescott had stopped in at her sister-in-law's home to talk over the party. Knowing her sister-in-law as well as she did, she hadn't thought it wise to go sooner lest the reaction to the affair would not be over yet. Adele Trescott always had a lengthy spell after any social event, during which she tormented herself with all the petty details that had, to her way of thinking, gone wrong. Irene wanted to give her time to get over this before she appeared.

But she had reckoned without knowledge. Mrs. Trescott had not yet recovered.

She was sitting up in bed attired in a costly nightgown, beribboned and belaced to the utmost degree, her heavy form lolling against many pillows, a large box of sweets on the bedside stand within reach, and a couple of novels on the bed beside her.

But she was not reading. When her sister-in-law entered the room, she looked up with eyes that were swollen with weeping and dabbed futilely at her sagging cheeks and heavy lips that for once were guiltless of rouge and lipstick.

"Oh, my dear! Is it you?" she sighed heavily, her words ending in a half sob. "I wondered why you didn't come. I didn't think you would desert me in a time like this!"

Irene sat down heavily, after having helped herself to a handful of chocolates selected carefully, and settled to a siege.

"For heaven's sake, Adele! What's the matter? Haven't you recovered from the party yet? I thought you would be up and planning for another by this time," said Irene, carefully biting a fat chocolate peppermint in half and surveying the portion still in her fingers speculatively. "What's the matter now? Was the caterer's bill larger than you expected, or did Mrs. Osterman's little stepdaughter have a more expensive dress than some of your favorites?"

Adele gave her a withering look. "How can you be so trivial when you were there and know perfectly well what happened. You saw how Laurie behaved. You know he was positively under the influence of drink the whole last half of the evening. It was the most mortifying thing I ever went through. You saw what he did, went out in the street and brought in that unspeakable girl and danced with her. You don't mean to tell me that you didn't see that, Irene?"

"Well, what did you expect, Adele? You furnished the liquor, didn't you? And you were down on the girls he wanted you to invite for him, weren't you?"

"Irene! Of course, you would take up for him and go against me," whimpered the mother, putting the lace-bordered, soppy little handkerchief to her swollen eyes again. "Blaming *me*! When I did all I could. I invited the little nobody he wanted me to, and I—tried to humor him—in every way—"

"Oh certainly, you always humor him," said Irene dryly. "You can't reproach yourself about that. You humored him—in your way. But you despised the girl he was in love with, and you probably have been so cold to her in the past that she didn't care to accept your invitation when it came."

"There you go, taking Laurie's part against me! I haven't been cold to her! I haven't had anything at all to do with her! I haven't had occasion to."

"Exactly!" said Irene, licking the peppermint off her fingers. "You've been cold to her. You've ignored her. You *meant* to ignore her and freeze her out. You can't blame Laurie for his attitude last night."

"My dear! You don't know what Laurie did last night. You don't know what he said to me. His own mother!" whimpered Adele, her body shaking with her sobs.

Irene got up and went and stood at the window, looking out, where she wouldn't have to watch her sister-in-law weep. "Yes, I know. I was standing right behind him. I know what he said. He told you you had fixed it so his girl wouldn't come to the party. You hadn't been friendly and she wouldn't come, and now he was going out and get a girl from the street, any girl he could find, and bring her in and dance with her."

"He was drunk, of course," sobbed Laurie's mother. "He wouldn't have said that if he had been sober. At least he wouldn't have said it *right before people*! That was what hurt so, having people hear him say that to me. To *me*!"

"Well, you got the liquor, and you never brought him up not to drink—" reminded Irene again. "I never thought it was a good thing to drink—at least not to drink too much—and Laurie always does everything just as hard as he can."

"You're hard, Irene! You're very hard! I never *taught* Laurie to drink, and I always told him a gentleman knew how to carry his liquor. That's what my good old father used to say. He was a real Southern gentleman, and he always said a true gentleman knew how to carry his liquor! My father never was *drunk*!"

"Well, it's evident Laurie can't carry liquor. Perhaps your

father's drinking is coming out in Laurie now, in his not being able to carry it. I wouldn't blame Laurie altogether!" said Irene contemptuously.

"I suppose it's *his* father coming out in him," said the indignant mother, "not *my* father!"

"Well, it really doesn't matter, does it? What I was thinking was that if you had let Laurie have that girl that you despised so, he wouldn't have been drunk. She would have kept him from it. I happen to know she doesn't drink."

"Oh, I suppose she never had a chance, being a minister's daughter! But she would have learned quick enough. Those are the worst ones, when they've never been taught self-control."

"No, she wouldn't have touched it. She doesn't believe in it. She's that kind of a girl."

"Well, you talk as if *I* kept her away. I sent her a perfectly good invitation, didn't I? I told you about it, and I showed you her acceptance. And then she sent word she couldn't come after all—an awfully rude thing to do, *I* think, after she had once accepted. *I* think it was because she found out what kind of a party it was going to be, and she simply knew she couldn't dress up to the occasion, and so she didn't dare come."

"You're mistaken there!" said Irene in a superior tone. "I happen to know she had her dress all ready, a gorgeous dress, all bought and paid for."

"You happen to know? How could you possibly know a thing like that?" said Laurie's mother, lifting her tear-streaked face in astonishment. "Did she tell you so herself? Probably she was lying, then. Of course, she couldn't possibly afford the kind of dress one ought to wear to such a party as we had Saturday night."

"No, she wasn't lying," said Irene with satisfaction. "She didn't tell me herself, either. She isn't the kind of girl who would lie or who would speak to me about such a thing. She's *refined*, I tell you, Adele. She wouldn't consider it was my affair."

"Well then, how in the world could you possibly find out whether she had a dress fit to wear? Where would she get money to buy a proper dress?"

"Well, I'm sure I don't know where she got the money, but she had it. I don't think she stole it. I've always heard she was perfectly honest. But she bought the dress and paid a hundred and fifty dollars for it! And then when she found she couldn't come, she took it back and exchanged it for some other dresses just as handsome. In fact, she spent *more* than the hundred and fifty!"

Irene was enjoying herself heartily as she watched her sister-in-law's face filled with incredulity.

"And you say she didn't tell that extraordinary tale to you herself?" Laurie's mother had utmost contempt in her voice.

"Oh no, she didn't tell me. I haven't even seen her. No, I got my information from Rena Brownell. You remember Rena? I'm sure you do. She always used to head your list for parties till her father lost all his money and then died and left them penniless. She's working in François's gown shop, a model there. You know she has such a lovely figure."

"You don't say! Well, that explains who that model was! She tried to recognize me, but I only stared at her. I thought she looked somehow familiar. But, of course, I wasn't expecting to see anybody I knew *serving* in François's. You see, I was there last week with Robena to get a dress for Saturday night. You saw it, didn't you? That gorgeous white taffeta with the stunning scarlet velvet sash? I thought that was the most stunning dress we had present."

"Yes, I saw it," said Irene with a sardonic grin. "The irony of it all was that that was the very dress that Marigold Brooke bought and then took back because her mother didn't approve of the low back."

"You don't *mean* it, Irene!"

"Yes, I do. Rena Brownell told me all about it. She said

Madame made Robena pay two hundred for it because she knew she wanted it so much."

"And she dared do that to a friend of mine!"

"Good gracious, Adele, don't be so snobbish. Robena *bought* the dress, didn't she? She telephoned and asked for just such a dress, white with a crimson sash. I heard her myself when you were at the telephone with her. You were as sweet as honey to Madame yourself, said you'd do all sorts of things for her if she would try to get a dress like that for a friend of yours. You didn't expect Madame to do it for nothing, did you? And now you are making a fuss because you know Marigold didn't want it."

"Well, but—daring to pass off a secondhand dress on *us*!"

"Secondhand nothing! Marigold exchanged it. She only had it out of the shop a few hours. You were grateful as could be that Madame found the kind of dress you wanted. Don't be a silly fool, Adele. You know that dress was the sensation of the whole evening. If you don't believe it, go and read the society notes over again and refresh your memory. And what's more, I can tell you it would have been a still greater sensation if it had been on Marigold Brooke, instead of that stiff, awkward Robena, and you wouldn't have had half so much to regret if it had, either."

"Irene! I will not listen to any more of your ranting. You are just saying these things to make me suffer, and you know I have practically been in tears all day over this thing. My darling boy Laurie acting that way at the party, bringing in that unspeakable girl from the street and insisting on dancing with her, and letting Robena go without a partner! My darling Laurie, telling me *in front of people* that I had kept his girl away and now I could take my medicine!" And the distressed mother wept into her handkerchief again, though it already was saturated with tears and only made her whole face sloppy and desolate-looking.

"Where is Laurie now? Why didn't you tell him it wasn't true? Why didn't you show him the notes from Marigold and make him understand that it wasn't your fault?"

"Oh, I did. I tried to, but he wouldn't listen. He just went on drinking and drinking, and dancing with that one awful girl."

"Well, you've Robena to thank for that. She started him drinking. Every time I saw them together the first part of the evening she was either handing him another glass or he was handing her one. And if you ask me, I think *she* was the disgrace of the whole party, the way she carried on with that Russian-looking man that came in late. She was drunk herself! She's the one I would have been ashamed of if *I* had been in *your* place."

"Really, Irene, I don't think you are very kind. You've just taken a dislike to Robena because you know I like her. And the idea that that other girl should presume to buy a dress like that! It's absurd! It's not suitable for her position, a little schoolteacher!"

"All right, Adele! Talk that way if you want to, but if Marigold Brooke had been here wearing that sumptuous white dress with the crimson velvet sash, you would have seen something worth describing in the society columns, and you wouldn't have seen her lolling around with any foreign counts and acting crazy, either. It's my opinion that she wouldn't have remained here long if she had come. She isn't used to a drunken crowd. I thought it was disgusting the way that Robena acted. You needn't be surprised at anything your precious Laurie does if he stays around that girl long. She's enough to be the downfall of a saint, and I don't mean maybe. But if Marigold had been here, I suppose you would have somehow blamed it on her. Though you couldn't if you'd once see her face. Really, she's lovely, Adele, and if you had any sense at all about managing Laurie, you'd cultivate that girl and get her to use her influence with him to keep him away from drink. He can't stand it, and that's the truth! Where is he now, did you say?"

"I didn't say," said Mrs. Trescott severely. "But he's probably asleep. I'm sure I hope he is. And when he comes to himself, he probably won't know what it's all about. But I feel disgraced forever, having him bring in that awful, frumpy girl. Why, my dear, did you notice? I'm sure her evening gown was made of *rayon*, and her makeup was appalling."

"Well," said Irene thoughtfully, "she was pretty awful, but I don't know as you deserve any sympathy. You deliberately asked for it. I've heard Laurie myself asking you more than once to be nice to Marigold, and she really is a nice girl, even if she hasn't much money. She doesn't use any makeup at all. She doesn't need to. She has plenty of her own color, and charming taste in dress, even when she has no money and has to make her own clothes. However, as I told you, if she had been here at the party, she would have worn the white and crimson, and your precious Robena would have had to seek further for something royal enough to wear."

"I really can't credit that, Irene. A little nobody wouldn't know enough to buy a gown like that white one and wouldn't have had even a hundred and fifty dollars to say nothing of two hundred to spend on one dress. It's just some cock-and-bull story that some of those salespeople have put over on you."

"Suit yourself, Adele. I'm sorry I mentioned it. But someday you'll find out. Go down and ask Madame, if you don't believe me. She'd have to own up. I'm sick of the whole story, though I do feel sorry for you after all the trouble and time and money you spent on that party. But I must say you brought it on yourself. When you could have had a perfectly good girl for Laurie that doesn't ever drink and you *chose* to bring Robena here who drinks like a fish, I don't see that you can ask pity of anyone. Marigold *never* drinks."

"But that's not respectable either, Irene. A girl *has* to drink to a certain extent today when everybody expects it. The difference is she ought to be trained not to drink *too much*. Not to get beyond the respectable limit."

"You don't seem to have succeeded very well in training your son," said Irene coldly.

"There you go again, Irene. You've no human kindness at all. When you see how sick and nervous I am about having that awful little street girl in here. He just *picked her up*! Somebody he *never heard of* before! And *introduced* her in *my parlor*! I am ready to *drop with shame*!"

"At that he didn't pick so badly," said Irene contemptuously. "And she *wasn't* a stranger to him. He told me so."

"What do you mean!" demanded the irate mother. "He told me he was going out to pick up the first girl he met in the street just to get it back on me. He told me that right in front of everybody before he went out!" She began to weep again.

"Yes, but he didn't. He went outside and saw a girl he used to know in grammar school, Lily Trevor. She used to be a cute, smart little thing. And when he went outside and saw her coming by with somebody else to the movies, he made her come in, just to make good his word. But he knew her. She wasn't a stranger."

"What difference does it make?" sneered the outraged mother. "Everybody saw she was just a cheap little thing, beside herself with conceit because Laurie had brought her in."

"Well, if you ask me, I thought she behaved as well as the rest of them," said Irene dryly. "I think myself the gem of the whole evening was the fact that your precious Robena appeared in the dress that had been turned down by the girl you scorned. Wasn't that something you'd call 'the irony of fate'? I haven't been able to stop laughing since I heard it."

"Well, I *don't believe it*! I don't believe a *word of it*!" said the irate mother, flashing her swollen eyes as well as they would flash. "I wish you would go away and leave me to my misery. *Every*-thing has gone wrong since that awful Brooke girl came into the picture, and I believe in my soul *you* had something to do with my Laurie meeting her! Anyway, if you didn't introduce them, I'm sure you *encouraged* the relationship. You with your outrageous bourgeois tastes and your strange whims and fancies! *Gold* hair, you say. Probably *bleached*! There isn't any real gold hair today. An intriguing little fortune-seeker! And I have to have all my plans and ambitions and hard work for nothing just because Laurie has an infatuation for her. Now, if he becomes a drunkard, I shall have *you* to thank for it." And she plunged into her damp handkerchief again in new self-pity.

Irene cast a withering glance at her.

"Someday," she said cuttingly, "you'll see that girl, and then you'll know what a fool you've made of yourself, turning her down, and then you'll have to eat your words! But you're mistaken about me! I never had anything to do with Laurie meeting her. I wish I had. She's quite the decentest girl I know and would have done Laurie a world of good. But I'm sure if she knew what *he* was, she would never have anything to do with him again."

"What do you mean, Irene? What is the matter with my Laurie? Why should a little upstart nobody turn down Lawrence Trescott?"

"I mean just what you've been telling me. He drinks too much and does horrible things like bringing in strangers when he gets beside himself. *Drunk,* you said he was! But you've always given him too much money and let him have his own way. What can you expect?"

"Yes, you who have brought up so many children! Of course, you know all about it," sneered the mother.

"Well, all right. You can sneer, but you try it awhile. Take Laurie's money away and don't have so many cocktails around, and see if Laurie doesn't turn out to be something worthwhile after all—unless perhaps it's too late. Good-bye. I'm going home till you are in a pleasanter mood." Irene took off angrily, a secret gleam of triumph in her eyes to think that she had been able to find out about the white dress with the scarlet sash that everybody had raved so much about. What a pity Marigold Brooke hadn't stuck by her first acceptance and come in the dress instead of Robena! It certainly would have opened Laurie's mother's eyes to a few things. Marigold Brooke in that gorgeous array would have been a winner! Irene gave a wistful sigh. She would like to see her favorite nephew paired off with a girl like Marigold instead of a vapid creature like Robena. But, of course, Robena had money, and that was everything in the eyes of Laurie's mother. Poor Laurie!

Then she went home, and that night she sat in front of her mirror for a long time, reflecting on her own face, which was beginning to age. Not that she was old yet by any means, but she could see the flesh beginning to sag. She noted the dullness of her eyes and the threads of silver that had slipped in among her well-dyed locks. It wouldn't be long before she would look as old as poor Adele, though never quite so fat, she hoped. And life! What was it worth? What was the use of living, anyway? Just clamor and conceit and ambition, each trying to get ahead of the other, weary contests, and what did it all amount to? Why did anyone want to live? And yet there was nothing attractive in the thought of dying. One must go on with the race, the losing race, unsatisfied soul struggling with unsatisfied soul and never getting anywhere!

Marigold didn't look as if she felt that way. She was young yet. Life hadn't disappointed her and left her a piece of flotsam cast up on the edge of the stream. But it likely would. Probably Laurie would disappoint her. Someday she would find out he got drunk whenever he liked and made a fool of himself. And then where would her bright looks be? Her flame of hair would turn white, the firm pink flesh and the rounded cheek would grow fragile, and even a Marigold would begin to fade. Or would she? Irene had seen her that day, and there had been such a look about her of fadelessness and peace, as if she had a source of endless life within her that would never let the sparkle go from her lovely eyes, the prettiness from her sweet face. What was it that made Marigold so entirely content? She wished she knew the secret.

And about that time, Marigold was kneeling beside her bed giving herself utterly to her Lord, that she might know the joy of a resurrection life lived by faith in Christ, in the strength of His resurrection power.

She was not even thinking of Laurie at all.

Ethan Bevan had taken her straight home to the apartment, carrying her baggage up and turning on the lights, exactly as if he belonged there. He cast one glance around him and said with satisfaction, "This is nice. It looks like home!" And there was wistfulness in his eyes. Then he threw his hat and coat on a chair and went to work.

He brought in the milk that was left outside the door, according to the note left in the milk bottle, and the loaf of bread that lay beside it.

Marigold hurried into the kitchen and started some coffee, got out a can of baked beans, a glass jar of tongue, and another of luscious peaches.

"It isn't a very grand meal," she said, with a deprecatory look at the can opener she was holding, "but it will only take a jiffy to have it ready."

"It looks like a swell meal to me," he said happily, putting his hand around hers and gently but firmly possessing himself of the can opener. "I'll do that. That's my job," he said, and then he attacked the cans capably.

Marigold laughed happily and surrendered the cans to his ministrations. There was butter in the refrigerator and there were tins of cookies. Marigold prepared the beans with butter, molasses, salt, and pepper and a brisk bit of cooking, and they sent out a savory odor. She whisked a clean tablecloth onto the little table in the kitchenette, set the table invitingly with her mother's lovely sprigged china and silver, then she scrambled some eggs. It was all ready in no time and they were sitting down together, just the two of them, with such a pleasant sense of coziness upon them that a sudden shyness came upon Marigold. As she bowed her head while Ethan asked the blessing, she felt as if peace were descending into her heart, as if the presence of God was there with them. How wonderful to have a cheery, strong, reverent friend like this! How nice that he had been willing to stay and eat this simple meal with her.

All too soon the minutes flew away, and he looked at his watch.

"Well, time's up!" he said, with a wistful smile. "I'm glad we had this brief hour together. It's been a wonderful meal, and we've pretty well cleared the cloth and licked the platter clean, haven't we? I wish I could stay to help wash the dishes, but I guess I must go, for that fellow said the shop closed at six, and I must be there to get my package."

Then he was into his overcoat, hat in hand, and standing by the door about to leave when there came a tap on the door.

Marigold looked up in annoyance. Why did it have to come just then? Somehow that last minute seemed important. She didn't like to be interrupted. But, of course, that was silly.

She opened the door and Mrs. Waterman stood there, looking her slatternliest, her hair in crimpers and a soiled, torn dress on.

"I forgot to give you this letter," she said apologetically. "Your young man was here about noon wanting you. I told him you'd likely be here tonight, and he wrote this letter. He said he'd be back. You must excuse my looks; I'm getting ready to go out this evening."

The color flamed into Marigold's cheeks, and she stared at the woman, annoyed.

"*My* young man?" she laughed, embarrassed. "Who is *he*?"

"Why, the fellow with that swell car that comes here to take you out so much."

Marigold took the letter, her cheeks still glowing, and closed the door after the retiring neighbor. She looked down at the letter with troubled eyes. Then she looked up and saw the expression on Ethan's face. She didn't stop to analyze it. She wasn't just sure what it meant, but there was tenderness in it, she was sure of that. Suddenly she spoke from the impulse of her own need, looking down at the unopened letter, which bore her name in Laurie's large, bold handwriting.

"I'm going to need a lot of help," she said slowly. "Would— you—sometimes—pray for me?"

She lifted her lovely, worried eyes with a look that went straight to Ethan's heart.

"I surely will!" he said earnestly. "Shall we begin now?"

Right where he was, he knelt beside the chair, flinging his hat down on the floor, grasping her hand in his, and pulling her gently down beside him. Marigold knelt, her hand enfolded in that warm, strong clasp, the letter lying between them on the chair forgotten. Laurie's letter! She was not thinking about it. She was listening to the tender prayer. She felt she would never forget the words, they were so indelibly stamped on her heart. She felt as if she were brought in touch with her Savior as she heard this earnest voice pleading Christ's precious promises, claiming the resurrection power in her life, not only for herself but for her friends. She felt suddenly a strength at her command that she had never dreamed existed.

When they rose, the letter was left lying on the chair, and Marigold looked up with a radiant face. There were no words to express her feelings, but somehow she knew he understood.

Ethan stood for a moment looking gravely down at her. There was something so deep and tender in that look that it almost brought tears to her eyes, but she did her best to turn them into a smile, and the answering smile she got was something she felt she would hide away in her heart to remember.

She wanted to thank him for what he had done for her, but still the words would not come. He might be going out of her life forever, but she felt he had taught her to know the Lord Jesus and put her in touch with the resurrection power. Whatever came, she never would forget him.

Then he reached out and took her hand in a quick clasp once more.

"Good-bye," he said quietly. "I'll be praying! And—sometime—perhaps you'll let me know how things came out."

Then, before she could answer, he was gone. She heard his footsteps outside on the stairs. Would she ever see him anymore?

She went to the window, and sudden tears blinded her eyes, but she brushed them away and looked out. She could see the lights of his car down there, and now he was opening the car door. But before he swung himself into the seat, he turned and looked up, waved his hand, and she waved hers back in farewell, glad that her room lights were on and that he could see her. This was perhaps the best way of saying what she could not find words to speak.

And then the car glided away from the curb and shot down the street. The little red lights at the rear seemed to be blinking to her as it swung around a corner and onto the main road.

She turned back to the room and felt all at once most desolate. What a happy hour they had had together preparing supper and eating it in the little kitchen. How wonderful he had been, acting just as if he belonged there. It thrilled her to go over the moments of the incident.

And then, with one more wistful look down the street where he had disappeared into the fast-gathering darkness, she turned and went over to the chair where they had knelt to pray and there lay the letter! How mortifying that Mrs. Waterman had brought it just then and called Laurie "*her* young man." What must Ethan have thought? But how he had taken it all as a matter of course and entered into her vague anxiety about the future, promising to pray, kneeling right down and praying!

She thrilled again as she went over the prayer word by word, learning it like a lesson that she must not ever forget. It was some minutes before she brought her mind back to the present and realized that there was a letter to be read. How that letter would have stirred her just four or five short days ago. Even the very outside of it, sealed, as she held it now. Yet now she opened it with a divided attention, treasuring moments just past and looking into a new kind of life to which she was committed.

Chapter 11

Marigold roused to read the letter at last, with a curious aloof mind that seemed to be far removed from the writer of the letter, as if time had swept in and obliterated the little filaments of happenings that bound her interest to him.

Mara darling:

What have you been doing with yourself? I called this afternoon to make a date with you for this evening and found you away, although it is the time when you usually get home from school.

The human slat that resides across the hall informs me you will be home this evening and that you are coming alone! So much the better. We shall not have your mother to spy on us and can have a real time.

I'm coming along to get you sometime after

*seven or a little sooner, and we'll have dinner and
then do the nightclubs in a regular way, see sights
you've never seen before. We'll have some evening,
Mara my beautiful!*

*So light up the front windows for me and let
me know you are ready. I'll know by your lights
that you are waiting for me.*

Yours as ever,
Laurie

Marigold, as she read, began to grow cold around her throat
and to tremble. Somehow there was something strange about
that letter, not like Laurie! Or had it been there all the time and
she had been blind to it?

She felt like a person whose eyes had just been opened and
she was seeing "men as trees walking." She couldn't be sure of
herself and her own judgment.

But when she had read the letter over again, several things
stood out sharply. First of all was the thought that Laurie had not
mentioned the party to which she had not come, nor said a word
about his long, unexplained silence! All her anxiety and uneasiness and anxious waiting when she first got to Washington, and
he hadn't even noticed it! Far from telephoning her in trepidation
and begging her to come to the party as she had expected that
he might, offering to drive down after her perhaps, he acted as
if he had not even known she was invited. Exactly as if the party
wouldn't be counted within her world.

And next there stood out the fact that Laurie was beginning
on nightclubs again, and she was going to have to meet that question right away tonight before she had thought the matter out on
her knees. It was then she began to tremble.

And reading the letter over the third time now, like a stab in her heart there came that reference to her mother as being a spy. Laurie had never spoken of her mother's carefulness as "spying" before, and something in her rose up and resented his attitude. The whole letter didn't sound like Laurie, the Laurie she had so admired and enjoyed and loved to companion with. It was as if she were seeing a new side of him entirely.

Then it flashed upon her that she had been holding in abeyance her judgment about Laurie that had tried to force itself upon her ever since she had seen him in the company of that other girl, looking down into her eyes with the glance that Marigold had supposed was all her own.

Yet now the whole thing seemed unreal. She seemed to have grown beyond it all since she left home last Friday.

But he was coming tonight and was expecting to take her to a nightclub! What should she do?

With a quick motion, she went to the switch and turned off her lights. Laurie was going to look to her lit windows to signal to him she was at home, and there would be no lights! She was not going to any more nightclubs! That was settled. She had known in her heart while she was talking with Ethan Bevan that they would never interest her again. In fact, they never had of themselves. It was only Laurie's insistence that drew her a couple of times. She had never felt at home there. It was an alien world, and she had felt ashamed. She saw it plainly now. She had been half ashamed to be there.

She had always evaded her mother's questions as to what kind of places Laurie took her. That had hurt her conscience, too. But now she was face-to-face with the whole thing, and she knew it must be settled for all time. She had told Ethan Bevan and she had told her Lord that she wanted to die with Him. She had felt already the joy of realizing what that was to mean to her whole life. She could not compromise.

If Laurie came anyway, even though there were no lights, she would tell him plainly that she would go to no more such places with him. But she felt somehow that she did not want to have to talk it over with him tonight. She wanted to get her feet firmly fixed, to get near to her Lord. She wanted to be alone and to think over that wonderful prayer that had put her so far beyond these things of earth and made her see herself as a redeemed sinner commissioned with a message to other lost sinners. Laurie would not understand that now, probably, and she must learn the best and wisest way to say it to him.

So she sat in the dark and faced her problem. Looked at Laurie, *her* Laurie, as she had considered him for long, pleasant, thoughtless months in the past, looked him straight in the face and made herself acknowledge just where he now seemed to be lacking.

Laurie was not of her world. That was plain. Mother had said so, and her own honest self had sometimes been afraid of it. Yet she had told herself that her influence would gradually give him different ideals. Had it? Had her influence done anything to him?

Looking at the question as she sat there in the dark, she had to acknowledge that, far from bringing Laurie to see as she saw, *she* had been yielding little by little to *his* wishes, going here and there and breaking down standards that had been hers since childhood until she had come to the place where she had even once or twice questioned whether those weren't outworn standards and perhaps she wasn't doing such a dreadful thing in giving them up, if it pleased Laurie.

But now as she faced herself and her world, with that sense of God's presence in the room that had been there since Ethan's prayer, everything looked different to her, and she began to ask herself why she had wanted to please Laurie anyway?

She had had beautiful, happy times with him, oh yes; but was Laurie all she wanted in life?

She tried to bring a vision of his handsome face, his smile, his adoring eyes looking into her own, and in spite of her best efforts she could only see him looking into that other girl's eyes! Was Laurie wholly false or just fun-loving and irresponsible? And if only irresponsible, would he ever grow out of it into a strong, dependable friend, such a man as Ethan Bevan?

Her thoughts grew more and more troubled, and finally she rose and went into her own room, dark except for the arc light from the street that sent long fingers of brightness across the wall. There she dropped upon her knees and began to talk to her Lord. And when, half an hour later, Laurie pulled up at the corner of the street and slowed his high-powered car to a crawling gait, Marigold had forgotten that he might be passing. She was gazing into the face of her dying Lord and saying softly with closed eyes, "Oh, Jesus Christ, I want to be crucified with Thee, and though nevertheless I have to live here in this earthly body, I want it not to be myself that is living in me any longer, but Christ who lives my life for me; and the life that I now live in the flesh, I want to live henceforth by the faith of the Son of God who loved me and gave Himself for me."

When she got up from her knees and turned on the light she was surprised to find that it was much later than she supposed. If Laurie had come that way at all, he saw no light, and he must have gone on his way, thinking she was not yet at home.

She drew a breath of relief. The she remembered that the dishes were not washed and she had not unpacked her suitcase. She did not want to talk to Laurie tonight. She did not want to argue about nightclubs. She was tired, and she felt as if such an experience would dispel some of the glory and beauty from the talk she had had with Ethan before he left. She wanted to fix that in her memory so that its joy could never be effaced. She did not want it dulled by other experiences yet. Ethan, of course, did not belong to her, and after he felt the need of praying for her was over he would probably never think of her again; but the touching of their lives had not been for nothing. It was a sacred experience.

So she turned on her light, changed into a little cotton house dress, and went about the work of putting the kitchen to rights for the morning when she would have to hurry off to school.

The kitchen seemed to be filled with bits of pleasant memories floating about among the dishes. The bread plate she had passed to Ethan when they had almost dropped it between them; the look in his eyes when he smiled; the clean, clear ring of his laughter when she told a funny little story about her childhood; the delicate sprigged china coffee cup that he had admired and drunk from. She handled them all gently as she washed and wiped them, her face vivid with happy thoughts. She was by no means trying to think how to talk to Laurie about not going to nightclubs. That subject had a reprieve in her mind, while she gleaned every bright little memory from the brief time that Ethan had been there with her. Ethan, who had helped her to find peace and had lit the perplexity of her pathway.

Then, just as she was opening her suitcase to hang up her garments and put everything to rights, the telephone rang.

It startled her. She almost contemplated not answering it, for perhaps it was Laurie. Let him think for this one night that she had not returned. But then she thought better of it and answered the second insistent ring.

It was her mother's voice, and her heart gave a glad little extra beat, for after all, the apartment was a bit lonely. She hadn't realized that it would be so without her mother, not for just a few days.

"Oh, Mother *dear*! Yes, I'm all right. Yes, we had a lovely drive, the day was perfect. Yes, Ethan came in for a few minutes and had a bite of supper. We had fun getting it together—beans and scrambled eggs and tongue and peaches, some combination! But Ethan had to hurry, you know; the shop where he was to get those parts he went after closed at six. Yes, he has gone. Started back right away. Yes, I'm quite all right. No, I'm not going out anywhere. Just unpacking and then I'm going to bed. Be good and don't worry about me. I want you to stay all next week and get really rested up yourself. Besides, you mustn't leave Aunt Marian until Elinor gets home."

When she hung up the receiver she looked around her, and the place seemed all at once terribly empty and lonely. More than a week yet before Mother would come back! Perhaps she would accept some of those invitations from the teachers, which she had always declined before on the plea of not leaving her mother alone.

She went into the bedroom and began to hang up her dresses again, touched lightly the smooth silk of the little green dress, remembering with a thrill the evening she had worn it when Ethan had taken her to the symphony concert. What a lovely time she had had that evening! How happy she had been, and how Ethan had admired the dress! Strange for such a quiet, serious young man to notice a dress! But he really did admire that. She could see it in his eyes, and her heart quickened as she remembered his look when he said it. She gave the dress a little soft pat, shook out the folds, and put it on a hanger wistfully. She was glad she had that dress. It was a much better dress to have than the white one would have been, regal as that was. Suppose she had bought the white instead and gone to the party! It would be at the cleaner's by now very likely and never be quite as pretty and fresh again. And what further use would she ever have had for it? Oh, she was glad she had taken that white dress back!

Then the telephone rang out sharply again, and startled, she went to answer it. Had Mother forgotten to tell her something and called again? How extravagant of her!

But it was Laurie's voice this time that sounded harshly over the wire.

"Mara! Is that you at last? Well, it's high time! I've been driving back and forth, passing your place every little while, waiting to see a light, and I couldn't understand why you didn't get home. Didn't you get my note? I thought I saw a light from the back room just now, but couldn't be sure, and I didn't care to risk another conversation with that woman across the hall so I thought I'd telephone. Did you get my note or not?"

"Why yes, I got it," said Marigold, trying to think swiftly what she should say. "I—haven't been home—so long, Laurie! And—well, you see, I really couldn't go out tonight anyway."

"Why not? Your mother didn't come home with you, did she? You don't have her notions to deal with, do you?"

"Laurie! Really!" Marigold's tone was indignant. "What is the matter with you, Laurie? I never heard you talk that way before about Mother."

"Well, I'm getting about sick of having to run my affairs to suit her straight-laced ideas. I don't see why you can't break loose and do as other girls do. She's no right to tie you down this way. You don't get a chance to see anything at all of life!"

"Laurie! I don't care to talk to you if you are going to say things like that. I never heard you be rude before!"

"Oh well, forget it, Mara. I've lost my temper, I'll admit. But I'm fed up waiting around for you. Where have you been, anyway, and what have you been doing? I tried to get you all day yesterday."

"I've been away visiting in Washington," said Marigold a bit haughtily. "You didn't suppose I had nothing else to do but sit around here till you called me, did you?" She tried to end her caustic words with a laugh to take the sting out of them. It wasn't like her to be sarcastic to Laurie, and she knew it. Neither was it the way she wanted to speak to Laurie, but it had suddenly come to her sharply that Laurie had had plenty of time to call her up before she went to Washington and he hadn't explained yet why he didn't.

"That's a nice way to talk!" snarled Laurie, speaking in a tone Marigold had never heard from him before. "I've been busy. Company at the house and a lot of engagements. I came this way as soon as I could. But you certainly don't seem very glad to see me."

"Well, I haven't seen you yet!" she said, trying to force a little laugh, and then she was instantly sorry, for now perhaps he would try to visit this evening and she didn't want him to come, not so late. She hurried on: "But listen, Laurie, I wasn't finding fault. You have a right to arrange your coming when it is convenient. I was just joking."

"That sounds more like my Mara," said Laurie, somewhat mollified, yet his voice was still harsh to Marigold's ears. Somehow he did not sound like himself. "All right, baby, get your togs on and meet me down at the door in five minutes. We'll go somewhere and get some food, and then we'll make a night of it. Nothing to hinder. I've been wanting to show you for a long time what night life is really like in our little old town. Put on something bright and giddy, and touch up your features a little. I'm going to take you where they know what a pretty girl is like. I never had a chance to really take you 'out among 'em' before; your mother has always kept you so close and censored every place I wanted to go."

Something seemed suddenly to take Marigold by the throat, and a great fear and heaviness came into her heart. For a moment she didn't answer, and then she summoned a cold little threat of a voice and said, almost haughtily, "Thank you, Laurie, but I wouldn't care to go places Mother wouldn't like, and I don't think I care to know what night life is like."

"Oh, now, look here, baby, don't get stuffy! I'm not taking you places that are any harm. Your mother doesn't understand what up-to-date places are, and she just gets anxious, but tonight we can go without worrying her, see? Hurry up and get your things on. I don't want to waste any more time. I've hung around long enough waiting for you now."

There was kind of a snarl in the last words, and the whole thing wasn't like Laurie. He had never called her *baby* before, either. And he had said the word in a careless, too-intimate way, not in a gentle, tender way that would have made the word a real endearment. What could have come over Laurie? Had he been drinking? She dismissed the thought. She had only seen Laurie drink two or three times, and then just a glass of what he called "light wine." It hadn't seemed to affect him. But tonight he was talking so strangely. She was half frightened. She wished she had not answered the telephone at all.

"Listen, Laurie, I'm not going to any nightclubs anymore, either tonight or any other night! I've been thinking the matter over seriously, and I've decided it's something I don't want to do ever again."

"But you don't really know anything about nightclubs, darling," said Laurie contemptuously. "You oughtn't to decide a thing like that without knowing. I'm going to show you what a really good nightclub is tonight. Come on, baby! Hurry up and meet me at the door!"

"No!" said Marigold firmly. "I'm not going to any nightclubs, now or any other time. That's final!"

He was silent for a minute, and then his tone changed. "Now, Mara, you're not being kind to me! It's not like you to talk that way. Come on, Mara, be a good sport and come out with me. I'm lonely. You've been gone a long time. If you don't want to go to a nightclub tonight, come on and we'll go to the rink and have a skate."

"No," said Marigold, "I'm not going anywhere tonight. It's too late, and I'm tired."

Her voice trailed off almost into a sob. She felt so shocked at the change in Laurie. She felt almost afraid of him when he spoke in that voice and utterly sick at heart at the way he talked. He must be drunk or he never would be so rude. It was not at all like Laurie as she knew him in the past. He was always courteous, always laughing, never cross.

"Well then, how about tomorrow?" Laurie asked, after an ominous pause. "We'll have a good time tomorrow night. I'll meet you at the school and take you driving somewhere, and we'll get dinner and"—he hesitated for an instant—"and then go to the rink and skate!" he ended.

She finally compromised on the rink, explaining that she had things to do at home and couldn't go until evening.

After she had hung up the receiver, she turned troubled eyes across the room, wondering if she had done right to promise even for tomorrow night. Somehow she felt strangely disturbed about the whole matter. Laurie had been so different from his usual self. Was he just sore that she had not come to the party, and yet wouldn't say anything about it?

The party. Why, she had been home almost the whole evening and hadn't even thought to look at the papers that Johnny Masters had dutifully brought and Mrs. Waterman had left on the table by the door! Somehow the interest had gone out of them for her.

But she went over and picked them up, settling down in a chair and turning on the lamp beside her. She turned over the pages until she reached the society columns, and there right at the head of the page was the face of that girl she had seen with Laurie before she went to Washington! She couldn't be mistaken. There was something about the haughty, self-centered face—handsome though it was—that was stamped indelibly upon her memory.

Miss Robena DeWitte of Sandringham-Heights-on-the-Hudson, the caption beneath said. And, *Guest of honor at the exclusive entertainment given Saturday night in the Trescott mansion, Walnut Terrace and Gardingham Road, this city.*

The article describing the party occupied three columns, with minute descriptions of the outstanding gowns of what was exuberantly described as "this city's best-dressed crowd of the season." And as she read it, Marigold's face flamed scarlet to think she had been about to compete with that company of peacocks, each aiming to have the prize for the best feathers.

She glanced down the column and caught the name of Robena DeWitte once more, and read:

> *Miss DeWitte, the guest of honor, was wearing a stunning white gown of taffeta, the kind our grandmothers used to buy when silk was silk. It was closely molded to her plump form, with perfection of line such as only the great artists of the mode can attain, and girdled with a crimson sash, deep fringed, that hung to the floor. It was adorned at the shoulder with a single velvet rose of the same new crimson that is now considered so smart. One could not but see that Miss DeWitte was the center of attraction and that her gown was greatly admired. With her dark hair that was sleek like a satin cap and her long-lashed, dark eyes, she had a regal bearing that took attention from all others present whenever she moved or spoke. It was noticeable that the son of the house, young Lawrence Trescott, was her constant attendant, to the obvious annoyance of most of the other men present.*

Suddenly Marigold stood up and cast the paper from her, a look of utter disgust on her face.

Was that what she had made herself miserable about only a few days ago? Had she really wanted to compete for that sort of notoriety? For Laurie's sake, she had made herself believe, but had it not been for her own pride's sake, if she told the truth? Yes, she had wanted to prove to Laurie's mother and friends that she could be just as smartly dressed and just as beautiful as any of that crowd who had loads of money! What a little fool she had been! Actually spending a hundred and fifty dollars for a dress! But— wait! Wasn't that the same dress? White with a crimson sash!

She grabbed the paper from the floor and looked carefully at the girl's picture again. Yes, that was the same dress! She could not mistake those unusual lines, the hang of the sash, the very placing of the rose! The picture had been taken before the party just for the papers! Oh, it *must be* her dress the other girl was wearing.

She had drawn Laurie away, and then she had gone and bought her dress and worn it to the party!

Marigold flung the paper down again, threw her head back, and laughed aloud. How funny! How very, very funny!

She laughed so loud that Mrs. Waterman came across the hall and tapped at the door.

"Did you call?" she asked in a curious voice. "I thought I heard you call."

"Oh, no," said Marigold, giggling again, "I was just laughing at something—a joke—I found in the paper! I'm sorry I disturbed you."

Mrs. Waterman went back baffled. She had hoped that Marigold would tell her something about her trip or at least something about the two young men, the one at home and the one who had come home with her and then gone so soon again. Well, she was glad she had gotten that cut in, anyway, about her young man at home, to warn the poor fellow who came up with her from Washington. But why didn't he have sense enough to stay the evening when he had the chance, if he was interested in her?

Mrs. Waterman was keen for any romance, having had little of her own. She was always scenting out love stories in any young things she met.

But Marigold stopped laughing and picked up the paper

again, looking long and steadily into the eyes of the girl in the picture, trying to realize that this was the girl she had seen Laurie so absorbed with. Her rival! Could it be possible that Laurie really was interested in that vapid, selfish-looking girl? There wasn't a hint of moral character in her face.

Of course, it was only a picture, and newspaper pictures were noted for being very poor likenesses, but she had seen the girl herself. She knew!

After a long time, Marigold gathered up the newspaper, went over to the fireplace, and burned it. Then she went in and knelt by her bed and prayed.

Oh, Lord Jesus, won't You teach me what to do about Laurie? I thought I loved him, but perhaps I shouldn't. I want to be crucified with You and have Your resurrection life. I want to count myself dead to the things of this world and alive only to You. Won't You please show me the way and not let self come alive in me and make me go astray. I'm trusting You to live for me, step by step. Help me, Lord Jesus, please! I'm Yours now. Not my own anymore.

Chapter 12

Marigold slept late the next morning and had to hurry to school, with no breakfast except half a glass of milk swallowed in a hurry. It was raining, a fine, thin drizzle, and somehow the gloom of the day had entered her soul. The peace of last night seemed to have been rudely broken in upon, and she had awakened with a burden upon her. There had been no time for prayer, and her heart felt strangely depressed.

As she hurried along to school in a taxi, she tried to search into her depression and find out its cause and finally traced it back to Laurie. She had an unsatisfied feeling about having promised to go with him tonight. And yet as she thought it over, she couldn't understand why. She had been plain enough about not going to nightclubs. She had taken her stand about that. And if he was willing to go to the rink and skate for a while instead, she couldn't really in decency decline, could she? There was nothing wrong in skating. Mother hadn't ever objected to her going.

Yet again and again that vague shadow of uneasiness kept

returning. All during the morning classes it came back, filling her thoughts and making her distraught and inattentive to her class. And the children realized it, of course, and took advantage of it. Her class was a riot once or twice, and she found her temper slipping and a dazed, sick feeling coming over her. The children were restless, too, on their own account, for the long, unexpected vacation had put an unusual spirit of mischief into them.

So it was with a sigh of relief that Marigold tidied her desk at three o'clock and hurried home, puzzling over and over in her troubled mind the exact reason for her worry.

It was Laurie, of course, but what could she do about it now? She had promised to go skating with him. She couldn't call it off at the last minute. She would not know where to find him. He had never given her his telephone number. Of course, she could easily find the number of his home, but she sensed that he did not want her to call there, and she was too proud to call him, anyway.

After all, she had to see Laurie at least once more, even if it turned out that she was to break things off with him. And perhaps this outing was about as simple a way to see him as any.

So with determined lips she hurried on and went swiftly to work when she reached the apartment, setting things to rights, even doing several things that were not necessary because she could not bear to stop and think.

It was when she was dusting the living room that she suddenly spied a little leather book lying unobtrusively on the floor between the two chairs. Wondering, she stooped and picked it up, and a thrill of comfort went through her as she saw it was Ethan's pocket Testament that he carried with him everywhere. It must have fallen from his overcoat pocket. That was where he had put his hat and coat while they had been getting dinner ready last night. And it had fallen out when he put on his overcoat in such a hurry!

She held it between her two hands for a moment as if it were a talisman, as if its very contact could give her strength. How she wished he were here and she could talk all this troubled situation over with him.

But, of course, it was her own problem. In a way, no one but God could help her.

She bent her head for an instant and closed her eyes. Touching her forehead softly to the Testament, she sent up an inarticulate prayer. Then she went and sat down by the window and, opening the book, read:

> Be ye not unequally yoked together with
> unbelievers: for what fellowship hath righteousness
> with unrighteousness? and what communion hath
> light with darkness?

She paused and stared at the words, amazed. It was as if the great God had stopped to answer her questions in person, as if He had sent down through the long ages words to that little book for her to read, that afternoon, words that would fit her very situation.

She read on through the passage.

> . . .what part hath he that believeth with an
> infidel? . . .what agreement hath the temple of God
> with idols?

She paused to think. An infidel was one who did not believe in God. But perhaps this went deeper than that. It meant an unbeliever in Jesus Christ as Savior. She knew that Laurie was not a believer. He had often laughingly said he had no religion. He was not bothered with a conscience. He thought you had only one life and you ought to enjoy it as best you could, for you were "a long time dead." Strange that hadn't bothered her before. She had never counted herself an unbeliever, although she could see now that she had never before accepted Christ in His fullness, nor really understood what salvation meant until her talk with Ethan. But she had been enough of a believer to be a little shocked at Laurie's open declaration that he had no religion; that is, the first time he had said it. She remembered she had reproved him laughingly, though, and never taken it very seriously. Laurie's fine eyes laughing into hers and Laurie's high-handed way of carrying all before him, of flattering her into thinking he was making her a kind of queen, had erased any feeling of uneasiness she had had. But now suddenly it was very clear to her that Laurie was an unbeliever, quite openly, and she now was one of the Lord's own. She had surrendered her life to Christ, had asked that she might be counted as crucified with Him. She belonged to Him.

> *For ye are the temple of the living God; as God*
> *hath said, I will dwell in them, and walk in them.*

And now she had asked what she was to do in the matter of this friendship with Laurie, and this was her answer.

She was not superstitious. She had never been one who would have lightly settled questions by picking up a book and taking her guidance from the first words her eyes met. It was not like that. No, the Lord had caused this little book to be left here and had brought it to her notice just when her heart was crying for light. And here was the light in these words. The verses were marked heavily with penciled lines and had called her attention to this side of the page instead of the other. She could not help but think that the Lord had intended that, too. Things so startling as this did not just *happen*!

And now she noticed that there were penciled words written above the passage and down along the margin, very fine but clear.

This must have been written by Ethan. She wondered at the comfort that thought brought. It was as if Ethan had come into the room and was helping her to solve her problems.

To Christians! the passage was headed. She paused to think that out. Then she glanced at the writing along the margin.

You never know full privilege until you are a grown son, and a tiny line led to the last two verses of the chapter. Marigold read them eagerly.

> *Wherefore come out from among them, and be ye*
> *separate, saith the Lord, and touch not the unclean*
> *thing; and I will receive you. And will be a Father*
> *unto you, and ye shall be my sons and daughters,*
> *said the Lord Almighty.*

Could anything be plainer than that? Such separation was made a condition to experiencing sonship, to close walking in fellowship with God!

There was no longer any question in her mind. She had her answer, and she must break things off with Laurie. But strangely the thought brought no terrible sorrow as she had expected, no great wrench, only sadness for the friendship that had been so pleasant while it lasted. Could it be that she did not care for Laurie as she had shyly dreamed she did? Or was God making it easier for her by thrilling her soul with Himself and the thought of walking with the great God?

She had turned on the light to read the little book, for the dusk had been coming down, and now as she looked up when the clock struck, she saw that it was quite dark outside. Laurie would be coming soon, and she must be ready. Perhaps this was the last time she would go out with him.

She was not sure what the next step was to be or whether the break was to come suddenly or would be gradual. But she was definitely sure there was to be no more compromise and that she must somehow let him know where she stood.

Hurriedly she ate and dressed for skating. She was barely ready when she heard his horn below. He always pulled up with a flourish and plenty of horn as a greeting. And now that horn with its cheery call did something to her heart. Always she had been so happy to hear it. After all, Laurie was dear! So bright and merry and handsome. Oh, was she going to be strong enough to do this thing that she had set out to do?

It was strange that there should come words out of the past few days just at that instant: *"Surely he shall deliver thee."* She could envision Ethan's face as he read them last Sunday night in Washington. *"He shall give his angels charge over thee, to keep thee in all thy ways."*

As she went down the stairs, she had a feeling that a guard was all around her, and a new strength came to her.

But down in the car, it was not the same Laurie she knew so well. It was a scowling, haughty Laurie, with his handsome chin held up and his eyes cold and disapproving.

He was courteous as usual, rather elaborately so, but before they had even started on their way, she was made to feel like a naughty little child who had transgressed the laws of the universe unbelievably.

"What's the idea, Mara," he said haughtily, as he stepped on the gas and they dashed down the road, "all this nonsense about you won't go here and you won't go there? You never acted that way before. Has your mother been putting the squeeze on you that you don't dare to call your soul your own?"

Something constricted Marigold's throat so that for an instant she could not voice the indignant protest that came to her lips, and Laurie went right on: "You surely are old enough to know your own mind and go your own way, and no parent in these days has a right to restrict a child. Such actions are a relic of the dark ages! You have a right to see life as it is and choose for yourself what you will do and what you will not do. It is your life, not hers, and you belong to yourself!"

Suddenly, Marigold spoke.

"No," she said quietly, "you are utterly mistaken. It is not my mother who has anything to do with my decision that I will not go to nightclubs anymore. She does not even know that I go. I have never told her. But I do not like the way you speak of my mother. You never spoke of her in that way before."

"Well, as long as she minded her business and didn't interfere with what I wanted to do, I didn't mind her," said Laurie bluntly. "But when it comes to putting fool ideas into your head, I'm done with her."

"I tell you my mother has nothing whatever to do with this," said Marigold, her own tone haughty now. This was not her old cheery friend Laurie; this was a stranger, a rude, disagreeable stranger. "My mother would never dream of my going to a nightclub. I am ashamed to say I have never told her that I went with you two or three times. I did not feel happy in going. I went to please you, and I feel I was wrong."

He swept aside her explanation with an impatient motion of his hand. "If your mother didn't influence you, who did?"

Marigold spoke in a clear voice. "God did. He made me feel that it was something not consistent with Christian living. You said just now that I belonged to myself. But that is not true. I belong to the Lord Jesus Christ who bought me with His own precious blood. I know I have not been living lately as though I believed that, but I do, and I always have, and now I have come to a place where I can't go on that way any longer."

Laurie turned his handsome, steely glance toward her, searching her face as well as he could by the lights that glanced into the car from the street.

"So!" he said after his scrutiny was over. "You have turned

fanatical on me! Is that it? Well, I certainly was deceived in you. And who, may I inquire, did this to you? Some fool woman, I'll bet! If it wasn't your mother, who was it?"

"I don't like the way you talk, Laurie," she said gently. "If you are going to talk that way, I wish you would take me home. I can't listen to you when you say such things!"

"Oh, you can't, can't you? Well, you're going to listen, and you're going to like it, too, when I get done with you. I have no intention of having you spoiled. You're one of the best sports I ever went with, and I don't intend to give you up. You promised to go skating with me, and you're going! We're getting out at the rink and have the time of our life tonight, and when the evening's over, you will have learned a thing or two, and you won't be quite so old-grannyfied in your notions, either. I'll teach you how to forget you ever had a conscience and just be happy."

Marigold was silent for a moment as they dashed on. She cast a quick glance at Laurie's face, which was still cold and angry, and finally she spoke. "Certainly, I'll go and skate. I'll keep my promise to you and try to have as pleasant a time as we have had in the past, but you'll have to promise not to speak about my mother that way and not to cast contempt upon my God."

"Well, I don't believe in your God, see?" said Laurie contemptuously. "He's nothing in my young life. But as for the old girl, we'll leave her out of the matter for the time being, since she isn't in these parts just now. If you can be a good sport as you've always been, I'm willing to go on, but I won't have whining fanatics around me, and that's flat!"

Marigold, startled into horror, sat there and stared at him through the darkness. What had happened to Laurie? She had never seen him angry like this. She didn't know he had a temper. He was always so cheerful and breezy. It is true she had never crossed him before in what he wanted to do, but—something more than that must be the matter.

She did not speak until he stopped the car and left it with a valet at the rink. It seemed there was nothing she could say that would not provoke him more. Perhaps he was ashamed of himself already and would soon apologize.

Silently she walked beside him into the rink. Strains of blithe jazz music floated out to greet them along with the tang of cigarette smoke, and the chatter of young voices and laughter was in the air. But Marigold no longer felt the cheery anticipation of the evening. She was full of trouble. She looked at Laurie and saw that his eyes were over-bright and there was a feverish color in his face. There were heavy shadows under his eyes, too, and his whole manner was unnatural. She did not know what to make of it.

She let him fasten her skates as usual, but there was no happy banter; no lifted eyes full of admiration; no gentle, almost fond lifting of her foot as he laced the boots. Instead, he pulled the laces almost roughly, until she had to tell him he was making them too tight, and then he flung away from her and told her to fix it to suit herself.

Sudden tears sprang to her eyes at that, and her heart was hot with shame and wonder. What had happened to Laurie?

He lit a cigarette and swung away on his own skates while she slowly unlaced and relaced her boots. He returned just as she was ready and stood sullenly in front of her. Then, when she stood up, he caught her hands and swung away into rhythm, but it was not like his usual long, graceful swing. He kept changing his motion and tripping her up. Once she almost fell, and he caught her close to him and swung her along, so that she had no choice but to let her feet follow where he led. But he was holding her close in a way he had never done before, a way he knew she despised, when occasional bold skaters had done it, a way he had been wont to criticize himself. She struggled to get loose, but he held her fast and bent his face over, almost as if he were going to kiss her, murmuring with white set lips, "You little devil, you, I'll teach you to go religious on me!"

It was then she caught that strong whiff of his breath and knew that he had been drinking.

"Let me go!" she cried, struggling frantically against his vise-like grip. Then, suddenly she slumped, relaxing and becoming a dead weight on his hands. Her feet slid out from under her and she went down in a pitiful little heap on the ice. Laurie had to execute a number of frantic gestures to keep his own balance, while other skaters came on and piled up in a heap upon Marigold.

The spill partly sobered Laurie, and looking half ashamed, he picked her up and helped her over to the bench.

"Now," he said half savagely, "what did you do that for? You know you did it on purpose. Why did you do it?"

"Because I did not like the way you were holding me, the way you were skating. It—wasn't—respectable!" She was almost in tears. "I—didn't know you ever acted that way, Laurie! You never did before!"

"No?" he said, lowering his heavy, unhappy eyes. "Perhaps not! I was trying to teach you a few things. Trying to open your eyes to life!"

She stared at him in unspeakable horror.

"Laurie!" she said. "You *did it on purpose*? You knew how it would look to those around us, and *yet* you did it? I thought you were my friend!"

The look in her eyes scorched him deeply, but he suddenly tottered to his feet. "Oh heck!" he said. "Have we got to be tied down by little antiquated ideas of propriety? You've just spoiled this whole evening for me! I'll find a real skater who knows how to take things! Just sit here and watch us and see what you think the world cares!"

He flung away from her in a long, sweeping curve, grace

and skill in every movement; and darting in among the skaters, he came to a flashily dressed girl who was executing some startling tricks and bore her off in his arms, holding her close and looking down into her impudent face surrounded by bleached hair. A face with a tip-tilted nose and a painted mouth. He caught her around the waist with a daring leap and swung her off with him, drawing her closer and closer until she lay with her face almost against his as they glided crazily on. Everybody was watching them, and they knew it. Marigold's cheeks burned as she turned her eyes away and began hurriedly to unlace her boots. This sort of thing was not supposed to go on here. As she lifted her eyes after putting on her street shoes, she saw an attendant on skates was approaching the two. Laurie could see him coming, too, but he went right on. Laurie doing a thing like this! Oh, it was unspeakably awful. Laurie who had always been the pink of propriety. Laurie was *drunk*!

She fastened the buckles of her shoes with fingers that were numb with sorrow and shame, and then with her heart beating wildly, she slipped behind the crowd of watchers and got away out of the building while Laurie and the girl he had picked up were skating off with their backs to her.

She did not realize until she was in the trolley that she had left her skates lying on the bench with the bag she always carried them in. They were a gift from Laurie and, before this, greatly cherished. But now they did not matter. Nothing mattered but to get away, not to have to talk to him again with that awful frown upon his face, that thickness of speech so foreign to him, that roughness upon him. Actually swearing at her once! Laurie had never sworn in her presence before.

She felt cold as if she had a chill as she rode along, watching the streets anxiously, in a hurry to get home. She wanted to hide her face in her pillow and ask God to forgive her for having let Laurie lead her so far into the world that this thing could have been possible tonight. She felt as if she could never get over the shame and the humiliation of it. Laurie, bright Laurie, so devoted before! And he had scarcely spoken a friendly word to her tonight. Oh, how long had he been drinking? Was it a habit with him? How was it that she had never seen him under the influence of drink before? Could it be that because he was angry with her about the party he had deliberately taken a drink or two to show her she had no right to frustrate his plans? Oh, surely he wouldn't be as mean as that! Did liquor change men and make them into fiends like that? She had supposed that one had to be a seasoned drinker to have it make such a difference. The men she had always known would never think of drinking. Never until Laurie had taken her for the first time to a night-club had she been among people who were drinking, and never before had she been offered liquor. Of course, hers had been a guarded life. She had always known there was a world in which habitual drinking, social drinking, hard drinking went on, but it was not her world. And she had been shocked when she saw Laurie once toss off a glass of what he told her was "only a light wine." But she never knew he drank enough to get under its influence, and she felt almost stunned with the idea.

When she reached her corner and got out of the trolley, she looked around her fearfully. Laurie would likely follow her as soon as he found she was gone. She couldn't conceive of Laurie letting her go, not the Laurie she knew, and doing nothing about it. Even a little drunk he would surely follow her to be sure she had gotten safely home.

But there was no Laurie in sight, and with relief she went up to her apartment and locked herself in. She did not turn on her light at first but, flinging off her coat, threw herself on her bed and wept. The old-time happy companionship with Laurie that had been so beautiful a thing in her life was spoiled, ruined. She could never think of Laurie again, no matter what happened, without heartache. The things he had said that night, even though he was not himself, had seared their way into her heart and disillusioned her.

The tears came at first, a deluge of them, until she was worn out. And gradually her thoughts grew steadier and she could look things in the face.

She had gone out to face her problems, and the problems had become more than just the simple matter of firmly refusing to go to nightclubs. They had come swiftly to be the giving up of a lot of things that she had thought were dearest of all in life to her. And as she lay there facing facts, one by one many pleasant things of the past were torn away!

Then suddenly, as if someone had spoken the words, she heard Ethan's voice reading that psalm: *"Because he hath set his love upon me, therefore will I deliver him. . . . I will be with him in trouble."*

Was that a promise for *her*? Could she rest quietly upon it? She had handed over herself to her Lord, as crucified and risen with Him, could she not trust herself utterly to Him?

And so she fell asleep.

An hour later, her mother called again to know if she was all right, and she wakened, surprised to find herself on the outside of the bed. After she had hung up the receiver she undressed quickly and slipped back into bed, too sleepy to think about anything.

In the morning when she woke, she was startled to find it was very late. She had forgotten to wind her alarm clock and had overslept. And there was the whole thing spread out before her, all that had happened the night before!

However, she had no time to think. She would be late to school unless she hurried.

She sprang out of bed, dressed as rapidly as possible, and was about to get herself a brief breakfast when there came a tap at the door.

She opened the door quickly, thinking it was the milkman

coming for his money. Here would be another hindrance.

But when she opened the door, there stood Laurie Trescott, looking at her with stormy, miserable eyes of reproach!

Laurie! And she hadn't a possible minute in which to talk to him!

Chapter 13

Laurie's eyes were giving quick, hinted glances around the room to see if she was alone. Then they fastened on her face with heart-breaking reproach.

"So! You were here all the time!" he said hoarsely. "And I've spent the night hunting for you. Nice way to act when I take you out—run away and leave me! And I didn't know what had become of you. Had to go out and hunt for you all night!"

"You knew where to find me," said Marigold coldly. "You knew I went straight home. I have been here all night, and you didn't attempt to see if I was here. You didn't telephone."

He dropped his haggard eyes and didn't answer for a minute, and then he said, "Why did you go off and leave me like that, Mara?" There was the old imperious tone again, finding fault with her instead of asking her pardon. Her indignation rose.

"Don't you remember what you did to me, Laurie, made me ashamed of you in front of everybody? Held me as no gentleman holds a lady while skating!"

"I had no trouble in getting other girls to skate that way with me," he argued. "You're getting prudish!"

"No!" said Marigold sharply. "I'm not getting prudish. You didn't used to think such ways were nice yourself. I can't talk about it, Laurie. I've got to go to school at once. I'm going to be late as it is."

"But we've *got* to talk about it, Mara!" His voice was thin and high and full of anguish. Laurie was always dramatic, whatever he did. He stepped inside and shut the door sharply after him, leaning against it. As he stood there with the morning sunlight streaming across his face, he looked like the wreck of something beautiful, and it was as if a rough hand suddenly jarred across the girl's heartstrings. Then his voice changed and grew pitiful, reproachful again. "Mara, I came here to make everything right with you. I came here to tell you I'm going to marry you!"

Marigold gave a startled look at him, a look which took in his worn, haggard face; his bloodshot eyes; his disordered hair; his soiled, expensive linen and rumpled garments, and suddenly saw him in contrast to the Laurie she used to know. Only a few short days before, so immaculate, so handsome, so assured and splendidly overbearing! A pang shot through her heart. All the torture and revulsion of her disillusionment were in her voice as she covered her face with her hands and shuddered.

"Oh, *Laurie*!" she cried out with almost a sob in the end of her words.

He came toward her quickly, recognizing the compassion in her voice, and tried to put his arms around her, but she stepped back out of his grasp.

"No! No!" she cried. "I could *never* marry you now, Laurie!"

"Why not!" He glared at her, and she could see he was not himself yet. "I'll apologize!" he went on imperiously. "But I did it for your good, you know. I wanted to teach you what life was like, but I'll apologize again if that's what you want." He lifted his bloodshot eyes and gave her one of those pleading looks, the kind that always used to reach her heart. But Marigold steeled herself against it.

"You had been drinking, Laurie!" she said furiously. "Why don't you tell the truth?"

"Yes, I'll admit I had had a glass or two too much. It was your fault, though, you know. You went away, and I didn't have anything else. You kept me waiting the night you got home, and all into the next night. I had to do something. But I'm sober now. I've come over to ask you to marry me."

"This is no time to ask me to marry you. Besides, I would *never* marry a man who drinks! I wouldn't go through last night again for anything in the world." There was scorn in her glance.

"Now, Mara, you're exaggerating. You mustn't make too much of a small thing. I'll admit I must have been half stewed last night. I'd had a heck of a week and was all in. I took a little more than usual to carry me through. But I'm not often like that. Oh, I get lit up now and then, of course, but nothing like last night! If you'll marry me, I'll quit drinking. I swear I will!"

Marigold looked at him aghast.

"No," she said gravely. "People do not reform after they are married. I would never marry a man to reform him!"

"Now, Mara, that's not like you! You were never hard like that. You always did what I asked."

"Yes?" said Marigold with almost a sob. "I was that kind of a fool. I thought you were fine and grand and wonderful. And I thought I could respect you and that you honored me!"

"Now, Mara, all that fuss just because I got lit up a few hours—"

"Don't!" said Marigold, putting her hands over her face and shuddering again.

Again Laurie came near to her and tried to take her hands down from her face.

"There now, Mara, don't you feel bad. You love me, don't you, baby? We'll get married, and then I'll quit and everything will be all right."

Marigold jerked her hands away from him.

"Don't you *dare* to touch me!" she cried. "And don't you ever call me *baby* again! I hate it! *No,* I don't love you."

"Oh, but you do love me, Mara! I've seen it in your eyes!"

"No!" said Marigold in a hard young voice. "You are not what I thought you were. I hadn't got around to thinking about marrying yet, but if I ever do get married it will have to be to someone I can trust and respect. I couldn't marry anybody who might go off and get drunk. Never! It wouldn't be *right*!"

Laurie's face darkened. "There you go, talking fanatical stuff. What's *right*? Who's got any right to say one thing is wrong, another right?"

"God has!" said the girl, lifting a firm young chin and looking him straight in the eyes. "And if I'd known you didn't believe in right and wrong and hadn't any use for God and mothers, I never would have gone anywhere with you. I'm sorry I ever did!"

"Now, Mara!" the boy pleaded, coming toward her again. "Mara, you don't realize what you are saying. Don't you remember what good times we've had? Can't you forget this and go on from here? Come, Mara, let's go and get married and then everything will be all right!"

"No! Never!"

"Now, Mara darling, don't get that way! Don't you know you'll drive me to desperation? Wouldn't you marry me to save me? I swear I'll stop drinking when we are married. Can't you believe me? I'm sober now, and I tell you it's the only way I can quit drinking."

Marigold's face hardened. "Laurie, if you can't get sober without me, it wouldn't be long before you'd be at it again. *No!*"

"But I swear I'll drink myself to death if you don't marry me!"

"Look here, Laurie," said Marigold, suddenly turning toward him, "that's ridiculous! Anybody who could say a thing like that isn't fit to get married! And I can't talk any more about this. I've got to get to school. I'm late already."

Laurie muttered a curse at the school, but Marigold darted around the room frantically, putting on her hat, gathering up her purse and coat and gloves, while he stood with angry eyes watching her. Then as she came toward the door with the evident intention of leaving, he stood in front of her and tried to prevent her.

"Mara, my Mara, *darling*! Say you'll marry me, and I'll be all different. Everything will be as it used to be!"

"Will you please go out, Laurie? I've got to lock this door!" she said in a voice that was trembling from excitement. "Please don't talk anymore, either. It's useless!"

She stepped into the hall, and he followed. Then she locked the door and darted away.

"But wait!" he shouted after her. "I'll take you to school!"

But Marigold had reached the street and signaled a taxi that happened to be passing, and when he reached the street she was getting into it. She did not look up or wave to him, just drove away, and he stood there gazing angrily after her, his brow drawn in a heavy scowl.

And back behind her curtain, Mrs. Waterman was watching, feasting her eyes and her imagination on what had happened, getting ready a story to spread out for the pleasure of her friends who lived in the neighborhood.

But Laurie climbed slowly into his car, a look of defeat on his weakly handsome face. He drove off like a madman, whirling around the next corner so that Mrs. Waterman held her breath expecting to see the car overturn or smash into the oncoming bus. But Laurie was off to a place where he knew he could get another drink to carry him past this unpleasant memory. Marigold, the only girl he had ever really loved *almost* as much as himself, had scorned him, and he could not understand it. Scorned him though he had gone so far as to offer to marry her! That was really farther than he had intended to go when he went after her. He had only meant to hunt her up and smooth down her temper a little, he told himself. His mother would make a terrible fuss if he should marry Marigold, a girl without a cent of money. She might even go so far as to stop his allowance for a while, as she had several times threatened to do. She had been terribly tiresome ever since he brought that girl in out of the street and danced with her at her old party. Why did old people have to be so terribly stuffy? Well, he would be twenty-one in seven months now, and then he would come into some money of his own, a mere matter of two hundred and fifty thousand, of course, but it would tide him over until his father's money should come to him. And in case he married Marigold, he wouldn't have to tell anybody until he was of age. That would be just as well for Marigold, too. Her mother couldn't kick then, either. And when they got their money they could clear out and let the old folks whistle.

By the time Laurie had had a couple of good stiff drinks he felt better and started out to try to find his impromptu friend of the night before, the girl he had brought into his mother's party. He was quite well pleased with himself and his plans. He would take Lily Trevor out to lunch and maybe a spin in the park, then when Marigold's school was out he would go and get her and thrash this thing out once and for all. Marigold had to be made to understand just how far she could go. He wasn't going to have things all haywire. She had to cut out this fanatical stuff and learn to do as other girls did, and if one lesson didn't teach her, he'd give her plenty.

But Lily Trevor was working in a factory, running a silk

machine, and the rules of the factory were stiff. He couldn't even speak with her. So he went back to one of his haunts and got several more drinks to prepare him for the afternoon. He still had a haunting memory of the look in Marigold's eyes when she had scorned him, and he needed to be reinforced.

❁

Marigold had a hard day. The children were still unusually restless because of their long break the first of the week and seemed unable to settle down to serious work. The tired, troubled little teacher longed to get home and think her problems through, but there seemed no chance for that. When three o'clock came, the principal approached her apologetically with a request.

"Miss Brooke, would you mind looking after some wayward ones in my room? They are not through the work that I told them positively had to be handed in tonight or they will not be eligible for basketball next term. I've just got word that the parents of a boarding pupil who is quite ill have arrived. I must meet them and take them to the child's bedside. I really don't see what I can do but ask you kindly to stay for a little while. Would you mind? I hope they'll be through soon, but I can't give you a definite time. I'll be glad to return the favor sometime when there's something you want."

The principal smiled. She had a winning way with her. And, of course, there was nothing for Marigold to do but assent as pleasantly as she could.

So Marigold took a large bundle of papers she had to correct and went to the principal's room.

But it was after five o'clock when the last dallier had finished his work and she could dismiss him and feel free to go herself.

Wearily she closed her desk, put on her coat, and hurried out to the street, deciding that she would walk home. She needed the exercise.

But what was her annoyance when she reached the pavement to find Laurie's car parked in front of the building and Laurie himself, tall and formidable, standing on the sidewalk waiting as if he were a stern parent come to punish her?

"Oh, Laurie!" she said with a troubled note in her voice. "Why did you come here now? I told you I had nothing more to say. Please go away. I cannot go anywhere today. I have things to do at home."

"So that's the way you greet me, is it, when I've taken the trouble to come after you? You think you can turn me down just like that! Well, you can't! I'm not one to take a slap like that and do nothing about it! I'm having it out. You've got to go home, haven't you? Well, I'm taking you home, see? Get in! I'm taking you home when I get good and ready."

Never had she seen Laurie in this mood before. She looked at him in astonishment and started to back away from him, but suddenly he seized her wrist and with an iron grip pushed her toward the car. She could not free herself from him without making an outcry and drawing the attention of others to herself. And to make the matter worse, three of the teachers and several students who had been holding a school club meeting were just coming down the steps behind her, and she was painfully conscious of their nearness.

"Laurie, *please*!" she said in a low tone. "This isn't a joke. I really don't want to go with you now. I have an errand. I want to speak to one of those teachers."

She tried to stand her ground and resist him, but he held her arm like a vise and forced her around.

"I'm not joking!" he said grimly. "I came here to get you, and I'm taking you with me. Get in!" And he pushed her to the car so that she had to get in or stumble headlong. Moreover, it was the driver's seat into which she was shoved roughly, and she had to struggle under the wheel to the other side, as he forced her over, springing in after her and starting his car almost before the door was closed.

Her face flamed scarlet with anger and then turned white, and she began to tremble. What did he mean, treating her that way? Then as the car shot out into the road and he turned sternly to face her, she got a whiff of his breath, which was heavy with liquor. Laurie had been drinking again!

Chapter 14

A new kind of fear possessed Marigold now. She had had very little experience with drinkers, and so the situation was all the more startling. What was he going to do? Where was he taking her?

She tried to steady herself, casting furtive glances at his stern face as he threaded his way recklessly through traffic, dashing through lights, disregarding a possible whistle of the traffic cop, whirling around a corner and back into the highway again without reducing his speed.

Oh, what was going to happen? He could not keep this up! They would both be killed! There would surely be an accident before many minutes. She must do something to stop him. Wasn't there any way to calm him? He sat there without looking at her and driving like a madman. If she only knew how to drive! She had had a few lessons back in the days before her father died, but there had been no car after he was gone. And she did not dare trust herself even to try to stop this one, not with Laurie's hand on the wheel and Laurie looking like a crazy man, his face white with anger, his eyes wild and bloodshot. What could she do? *Oh, Father in heaven, help!*

Like an answer to her cry there came the words to her memory, words from that last morning in Washington when Ethan had read the psalm: *"Surely he shall deliver thee—"* and *"Thou shalt not be afraid—"* Those were all the words she could remember, but they calmed her frightened heart.

They were out of the city now and on the broad highway, but it was little better here. The traffic was thick, and Laurie, not satisfied with traveling along at a reasonable speed, was dashing in between cars and thundering past at a mad pace, rocking from side to side and barely escaping collisions on every hand.

"Laurie, please," Marigold managed to whisper with white lips, "*please* go a little slower. You frighten me!"

Laurie looked down at her with bright, strange eyes in which triumph sat like a demon. "Frighten you? Ha, ha! Nothing to be 'fraid of!" His speech was thick and unnatural, and suddenly he reached out an arm and thrust it around her, drawing her close to him and forcing her head down on his shoulder.

"Needn't be afraid. I'll take care of you! Nothing ever happens to me! Just lie down there and go to sleep."

Trembling with fear, she slid out from that embracing arm with loathing. She had never been so near a drunken man in her life.

"No!" she said as quietly as she could manage her voice. "I'd rather sit up! It makes me a little sick, this going so fast! Couldn't you go just a little slower, Laurie?"

But he only gave an evil grin.

"Sorry, can't 'commodate you, Mara," he said thickly. "Got a date and have to get there! But you'll feel better pretty soon, baby! Do you good, riding fast. Good for the lungs. Blows the cobwebs away!"

"But you said you were taking me home, Laurie," she pleaded, "and this isn't the way home. I'm feeling quite sick, Laurie, and I'd like to go home."

"Yes, after while," he said indifferently. "Gotta go shumwheres else first. Didn't I tell you where we're going? My mishtake! You shee, we're on our way to get married! Some wedding trip, baby! Like it now?"

Horror froze her throat. She could not speak. She could not think. Was God going to let this awful ride go on? Was He going to let them come to some terrible end? A crash, terrible injuries, or death? Was a tragedy like this coming to her dear mother to bear, all because she had been so silly and thought-less and self-willed and determined to have a good time with Laurie?

"Because he hath set his love upon me, therefore will I deliver him. . . ." The words came to her like a voice from far away, out of that quiet, happy Sunday night when Ethan had been reading God's Word. She had been longing then for something deep and sweet in her own life that would calm fears and doubts and question-ings and help her to anchor her soul, as the soul of the young man who was reading seemed anchored.

"Like that, baby?" demanded Laurie suddenly. "Like to get married?"

Her soul was one great cry for help and strength and guid-ance. What should she say? She loathed his calling her baby, but what was that in the midst of such danger? Not worth mention-ing. The ravings of a maniac who must be calmed, not excited. She roused her frightened soul to self-control and tried to speak quietly.

"Have you told your mother what you are planning to do, Laurie?" she asked as steadily as she could.

"Told the mater? I should say not, baby! She'd fall into a rage and stop my allowance, and that would never do at this

shtage of the game, shee? I've got eight bucks left in my pocket
and my 'lowance is due day after tomorrow. Never do to tell
the old lady I'm getting married. No, we'll keep it quiet awhile,
baby. By'm'by when I get my money, come of age, you know,
then we'll shrpring it on 'em. That ish, if we make it a go. If we
don't, nobody's the wiser, and what nobody knowsh won't hurt
anybody. Shee, baby?"

He cast a devilish grin at her, and she wondered with a sharp
thrust of condemnation how she had ever thought him handsome. Oh, could just a few drinks make a man into a devil like
this? Or had he been at it a long time, and she had been such an
ignoramus that she hadn't suspected it?

She shrank farther away from him into her corner.

"I'm—feeling pretty—sick," she gasped out. "Do—you—
mind—if I—don't talk—much?"

"Shick! Tough luck, baby! Thatsh a nish way to act on your
wedding trip!"

She barely suppressed a shudder at that and, putting her head
down on her hand, closed her eyes.

Oh, God! she prayed. *I'm trusting You to see me through this
somehow. Keep me quiet, and control this situation. You are stronger
than the devil. You are stronger than a drunken man. Help!*

It seemed a miracle that they were still on the road. The car tore
on amid traffic and barely escaped again and again. She began to
hope and pray for a traffic cop, but none seemed to be around. Once
there were two on motorcycles, but there was an accident ahead,
and when Laurie dashed by they were engaged in trying to control
the cars involved and did not seem to notice them until they were
well past. Once Marigold heard a shrill whistle ring out far behind
them and hoped they had been sighted and followed, but Laurie
pressed on, almost overturning the car once as he rounded a corner
at high speed. Often he sent them up in the air and bumping down
again with terrific force. But Laurie only rushed on.

It was growing dark now and beginning to snow, and Marigold's heart grew heavier. She sat silent in her corner, and almost she hoped that Laurie had forgotten she was there. If she only could contrive some way to make him stop at a service station she would try to make her escape! Just run around behind some building and disappear. Would that be possible? But she dared not ask Laurie to stop. Perhaps the car would run out of gas or something pretty soon. Perhaps there would be help somewhere.

But suddenly Laurie burst out again. "We musht be almost there! Down in Mar'land shomewhere—! You've heard of the plashe! Get married shlick and quick. Everybody doesh it. Don't cosht mush, either. Guess we c'n get by on eight bucks. If we get shtuck, I'll call up the old lady and tell her I'm bushted!"

Marigold tried to control the shudder that passed over her involuntarily, envisioning such a life as he was planning for her. *God! Oh, God! I'm Yours! I can't do anything for myself! You sent a strong one to help me down from the high place. Please come Yourself now and help me!*

It was snowing hard now, a blinding snow. The windshield-wiper was tripping back and forth on the glass, but the snow in great flakes clogged its movements and placed large, soft curtains of snow quickly and neatly over the spot they had cleared. The visibility was poor. Marigold closed her eyes. She had no longer strength left to watch the near escapes, the oncoming lights of cars that seemed about to crash into them.

And now they were coming into a town. Marigold knew it even without opening her eyes because the light through her eyelids was more continuous. Laurie was still going at a breakneck speed. It was a wonder that he did not get arrested.

Suddenly she felt the speed slowing, and then the brakes were jammed on with a shudder and the car screamed to a slower pace.

"Thish musht be the plashe," she heard Laurie say. "Nish little town. Marriage lishenshes on every street. Shee there!"

Marigold opened her eyes enough to see a sign lit with a row of electric bulbs above it, under a small sheltering roof. She could read the lettering through the fringes of her lashes.

MARRIAGE LICENSES
MINISTER!

it read, and a great fear took possession of her, more dreadful than anything she had experienced before. Was there going to be no way of escape? Would it be possible for an unprincipled man to go through with a ceremony and make it legal? *Oh, God!* What should she do?

"Nish place," said Laurie thickly. "Like to live here myself. Look, baby! *Minishter!* How 'bout that? You're so religious, I shupooshe you'll be tickled pink about that!"

Marigold continued to keep her eyes closed as if she were asleep. It seemed her only defense. If he thought she was asleep, perhaps he would let her alone a minute. Perhaps he would get out and go into the house without her. If she could only drive a car she could get away from him. The car was idling by the curb now, and Laurie was still for the moment. Would it be possible that he might fall asleep and give her a chance to slip out the door and away?

There was not any possibility that she had not conceived of during that awful ride.

But no, he was not asleep. He was reaching down into the pocket on the door of the car and getting that awful flask. Twice before he had taken a swallow, the car lurching crazily as he did it. She dared not turn her head and look, but a second later she smelled the strong odor of the liquor again. And now that the car was standing still, he was drinking deeply.

Then suddenly he held out the bottle toward her.

"Take a drink," he said foolishly. "Got plenty left for you. Shusht a drop, baby! Do you good! Take away your shicknesh! Better take a brasher. Then we'll go in and get tied."

But she steadily kept her head turned toward the corner of the car, and presently he desisted.

"Shtubborn! Thash what you are! Have a heckuva time breaking your will, but ish gotta be done! Awright, baby, you shtay here a minute, and I'll go tip off the parshun!"

Slowly and laboriously, Laurie opened the car door and got himself onto the sidewalk, slipping and sliding drunkenly in the snow as he made his way across the pavement and in at a little white gate.

Oh, God! Oh, Jesus Christ! Send me help. Send a strong One.

Marigold's heart seemed to be praying of itself, while her mind suddenly came alert.

She sat without stirring while Laurie half skated up the little path to the white house, stumbled up the two steps to the veranda, and reached out an uncertain hand to a doorbell, adding a knock on the door itself, just to make sure.

Now! Now was the time!

She cast a quick glance around to get her bearings and reached a cold, trembling hand out to the door handle. Was there a place to hide? There were lights ahead, cars coming—trucks, perhaps—she must get across before they came. It was her only chance. The headlights would show her up as she ran, but she must keep well behind Laurie's car so he could not see her. Once out, she would scream for help before she would ever let him put her back there. But—would he tell some tale, make them believe he had the right? Oh, she must not think of such things now. She must go at once. *God, my God, Jesus, my Savior, are You there? "Surely he shall deliver thee. . . ."*

The cold steel handle in her hand yielded and the door swung silently away, letting in a rush of cold air. She could feel big snow-flakes on her face.

She cast one quick glance at Laurie. The door was opening and a man in a black coat was standing inside. He would see her go if she waited an instant longer. She swung herself out into the road in the snow, struggling to keep her footing, and immediately the sharp light from an approaching car picked her out and startled her to action. She sprang across into the darkness beyond that path of light.

She was dazed from the long, hard ride, her senses were almost stupefied, but the snow stung her sharply in the face as she hurtled across to the shadows on the opposite side of the street and huddled there for an instant. Should she just crouch there somewhere and wait until the cars were past? No, for Laurie would raise an outcry as soon as he discovered her escape. She must be out of sight entirely before he found out. She darted a look toward the road, and suddenly she saw that the colored lights coming were on a bus! A bus! Oh, if she could get into a bus! It didn't matter where it was going, if she could only get away *some*where. It was coming on swiftly, but she dared not try to signal it here in front of this house where Laurie stood. She cast a glance ahead and saw that the road curved around a slanting corner. Perhaps she could get past that and manage to signal the bus, somehow.

She started ahead, slipping and stumbling as she went, but hurrying on. The snow blinded her, the sidewalk was slippery, the paving beneath the snow in places rough and uneven. Once just as she had almost made the corner, daring not to look back, she stumbled and almost went down, but a passing man reached out a hand and steadied her. She thanked him breathlessly and flew on, around the corner, past several stores whose bright lights made her shrink, and on to another corner. Now was she safe?

The bus was rounding the corner now and coming slowly

on. It was halting; it was going to stop in front of the drugstore. Would she dare run out and get in while it stood there in that bright light, or should she wait until just before it started again and make a dash for it?

She was standing in a little alleyway between two stores in the shadow, just for the moment hidden in the darkness. But there was snow on the ground behind her, and the whole world seemed too bright because of the snow. Her dark coat would show up clearly against the white background.

There were not many people in the bus, and they seemed to be asleep, their heads thrown back comfortably against the seats. The bus stopped just a little past the drugstore, the shadow of a great willow tree trunk half hiding the entrance from the sidewalk. The driver sprang out and dashed into the drugstore. He was carrying a long envelope in his hand. One passenger roused and followed him, digging in his pocket for a coin. Marigold peered out cautiously from her hiding place into the store window. The driver handed the envelope to a clerk, threw a coin down on the counter, and now he was tossing down a glass of something. The passenger had just received a pack of cigarettes and was in the act of lighting one.

Marigold gave a quick glance back to the corner from which she had come. Laurie was not in sight yet. Could she make it? Oh, if he should appear just as she came out into the light she felt that her trembling limbs would let her down in an unconscious heap on the snowy pavement. But she took a long breath and dashed across into the open door of the bus, sinking into a seat far back in the shadow, scarcely able to get her breath again, though she had run not more than five steps. Was she really out of danger yet?

Then she heard a car come thundering up the street behind the bus. Had Laurie discovered she was gone and come after her?

She shrank lower and lower into the seat and closed her eyes, turning her face into the shadow.

It seemed ages before that driver came out, and the passenger who was smoking his cigarette. She dared not open her eyes and look at them. Not until she was far away from this town. Would the driver notice that he had another passenger? She prayed fervently that he would not, at least until she was too far from the town to be let off the bus.

At last the engine started, the bus lurched forward, made a wide circle, and turned back on its tracks down the street out of which she had just fled! Her heart stopped still. To her horror, she saw the big sign MARRIAGE LICENSES loom into view. Was she caught? She couldn't jump out of that bus and run back. It was well under way now.

Marigold sank into the cushions, putting her arm on the window seat for a pillow, and turning her face so that it was entirely hidden from view, thankful that in her hasty choosing she had lit on a seat on the opposite side of the white house where Laurie had gone to arrange for their marriage.

Her heart almost stood still as the bus rumbled on down the street, expecting every minute that it would be held up and Laurie would come staggering in in search of her. What a fool she had been to get into a bus without knowing which way it was going!

She shut her eyes and did not dare look out until she was sure they had passed the place where Laurie's car had stood. Then suddenly she was seized with anxiety to look back.

The snow was coming down so thickly that she could not be sure of anything but the two blurred points of Laurie's car lights. But there seemed to be a group of dark figures standing on the sidewalk near the car. She could not tell whether one was Laurie or not, but as she looked she was sure she saw one of them jump into the car, and a moment later those two bright lights came wallowing on toward her. Was Laurie's brain clear enough to have figured out her way of escape? Certain it was that a car was following the bus in wavering lines! Was it Laurie?

Chapter 15

And while all this had been going on, down in Washington Marigold's mother was having a time of her own.

Some seventh sense vouchsafed to mothers only had told her that there was need for worry.

Three times during the evening, quite casually, she had tried to call her daughter on the telephone and had gotten no answer. She could not understand it. She was unable to think out a situation that would explain Marigold's not being in at any of her calls. And surely all three could not be blunders of a sleepy operator, because she had started calling quite early in the evening to ask Marigold for the address of a secondhand book firm that was famous for being able to ferret out old books, even out-of-print books, and produce them in short order.

But when the third call failed, she could not control her nervousness, and she said she guessed she would go to bed. Her sister watched her speculatively. She was older than Mrs. Brooke, had practically brought her up, and had learned through the years to read her face easily. She knew that her sister was worried about something.

Marigold's mother had been very surreptitious with her telephone calls. She had gone quite openly the first time and, coming back, said she guessed Marigold was out to supper with some of the other teachers. But when at nine o'clock she thought to try again, she waited until Sarah, the house servant, was talking to Mrs. Bevan about the next day's ordering. The third time she had professed to go and get a clean handkerchief, but it took longer than was necessary and Marian Bevan studied her face when she returned. She was pretty sure what the trouble was but couldn't quite think how to speak about it and so held her peace. She had a rare talent for holding her peace when many other women would have plunged in and torn away reservations and demanded an explanation. So she let her sister profess to be weary and retire to her room without asking what was the matter.

However, she did not drop the matter from her own mind but took it to her usual refuge and began to pray about it.

About two o'clock, Marigold's mother could not stand it any longer, and sure that her sister was long asleep, she crept from her room, velvet shod, and went stealthily downstairs to the telephone. Having closed all the doors possible to the upper floor, she huddled over the telephone and made a prolonged effort once more to reach her child, becoming insistent, declaring that she *knew* someone was there, perhaps asleep, and *please* to keep ringing until she got her. But all to no purpose. The operator finally grew irate and said very crossly, "Madam, they do not answer! Your number does not answer!" And at last she desisted and crept silently back upstairs, with slow worried tears trickling down her cheeks. She was almost sick with worry.

She had reached the upper hall and was cautiously moving past her sister's open door, confident that she could not possibly be heard, when her sister's voice spoke out clearly: "Mary, what is the matter? Why are you worried?"

She paused for an instant and caught her breath. Then she stepped to the dark doorway.

"Oh, my dear!" she said penitently. "Did I wake you? I'm so sorry! I just thought I would try again for Marigold. I was awake and thought I might be asleep in the morning and miss her before she goes out early to school. But I wouldn't for the world have woken you."

"You didn't wake me, dear! I haven't been asleep yet. But, Mary, why are you worried? Don't you trust Marigold? Come here and sit beside me. I've been wondering about it all evening. I saw you were worried, and I couldn't quite understand. Your dear girl seems so dependable. I thought you trusted her fully."

"Oh I do, entirely," Marigold's mother hastened to say. "I trust *her* fully. But, Marian, I do not trust all those with whom she spends time. You see, I have called her up three times before this, and always the report is that the number does not answer. I have tried to put it out of my mind, but to save me I cannot help imagining all sorts of things."

"Yes? Such as—?"

"Well, I don't know exactly. Weird things that probably wouldn't be at all likely to happen, but they happen like a flash in my mind, and then I cannot get rid of the thought."

"But you know, dear, the phone might be out of order."

"Yes, of course," said Mrs. Brooke crisply. "I've told myself that again and again. But it wasn't out of order last night."

"Oh, but there may have been a storm that tore the wires down."

"Of course!" she said, still briskly.

"But you still fear—?"

"Yes, I still think all sorts of wild things."

"Well, suppose you get them off your mind by telling them to me. What's first and greatest?"

"Well, Laurie Trescott!" said Mrs. Brooke sharply. "I don't trust him. He may have inveigled her into doing something, going somewhere—oh, I don't know where nor what, only I'm afraid. He isn't a bit discreet."

"Oh well, if that's all, don't fret. A little mess of gossip isn't pleasant, but it can't really harm her. Her friends know what she is, and perhaps it may serve to open her eyes a little. You don't think the young man would do her any real harm, do you? He's a gentleman, isn't he?"

"Y-e-s," said Marigold's mother uncertainly. "I suppose he is. I've always thought he was. He has lovely manners; he is courteous and quite charming. I sometimes think that is what has fascinated Marigold."

There was silence in the dark house. Nothing could be heard but the soft splashing of snowflakes on the window panes.

"It's snowing again," said Mary Brooke anxiously, looking toward the window where even the streetlights wore a shroud of snow. "It may be a terrible storm up at home. It's colder there than here, you know, and I think the storm is coming from the north. I've been thinking, if she's out in it, it would be so easy to have an accident. A crash! And they lying dead somewhere, and we not knowing—!"

"Mary, dear, you don't trust your heavenly Father very much, do you?"

"Oh yes I do, Marian, but when I hear those big snowflakes thud against the windowpanes, a little demon gets up on my shoulder and mocks me, and then I get to thinking how wild and reckless Laurie Trescott sometimes seems to me, and I forget I don't have to run the universe."

She tried to laugh, but the anxiety was still there beneath her smile.

"Yes, I know, dear. And He understands. 'He knoweth our frame; he remembereth that we are dust.' "

"Yes, I know. Thank you, dear!" sighed the mother. "But oh, I can't help thinking, if Laurie were only more like your Ethan, how happy I would be. Ethan is wonderful! I felt fairly envious of you when he was here. He is a charming young fellow and seems so responsible and mature for his years. But then, of course, he's a Christian, and Laurie isn't!" She sighed deeply.

"Yes, he's a rather wonderful young Christian," said his aunt warmly. "And he's a dear boy! There is none better! Yes, I could fervently wish that your dear little girl might find a friend as strong and fine as he is. But now, my dear, you must just trust this with the Lord. You must get some sleep, and in the morning you will be shown. You and I will pray, and then sleep and trust! Good night, dear!"

"I'm sorry I've kept you awake," said Mary Brooke as she stooped to kiss her sister, "but you've been a wonderful comfort, as you always were."

And then she slipped away to her room to pray for her child.

Chapter 16

Marigold sat in her dim little corner of the bus while the agony of the moments dragged by. Car after car came dashing by, a long bright stream of light that shot past and left only the dim whiteness of the snow-filled air again. The snow was dense now. She watched beneath her lashes as the windshield wipers played a mad dance together on the glass. The driver's outlook was like a half circle cut in a white blanket. Slower and slower lumbered the bus. Marigold could sense that the road was slippery. It deemed that nothing had ever gone as slowly before. A deadly contrast to the mad ride she had taken from her home. But oh, if she was followed, what chance had she at this snail's pace to get away? And how much liquor did Laurie have with him? Would he keep on drinking until it was all gone?

An hour dragged by. She stole a glance at her wristwatch, but it was too dark to tell the time accurately. She was thankful for the darkness and for the curtains of snow hung deeply at all the windows. It would not be easy through that for a driver outside to spot a traveler inside.

Marigold's sense of direction had deserted her for the moment, but after a little she had a feeling that she was not on her way to Philadelphia, and then she tried to reason it out. Of course, since they had passed by Laurie's car, going in the same direction that his car had been pointed, they were going *away* from, not *toward* Philadelphia. But *where* were they going? How could she find out? Not by questioning the driver or any one of her fellow travelers, she resolved. She must not draw attention to herself at all. She must act as if she were a perfectly normal traveler out for a chosen destination, not one who had merely taken refuge here and knew not where she was being taken.

So she lifted her eyes to the dim walls to see if there was any sign of destination anywhere posted. There at the front, above the driver's head, was a sign in colored glass, backward of course, for the benefit of the outside world. They who traveled inside were supposed to know where they were going. What a fool she had been not to read it as she stood in the alley waiting for the bus to be ready to start. But it was so clogged with snow it was impossible to be sure what it said. Was it Baltimore? She measured the space with her tired eyes, counting the letters. Yes, it must be Baltimore. Her heart leaped up. So near to Washington! How she longed to go on to her mother, fling herself down with her head in her mother's lap, and sob out the whole dreadful story! For an instant she was tempted.

But she couldn't do that, of course. She had to be in school in the morning. It would be impossible to get back in time. And it would only alarm her mother beyond anything. She would never feel safe about her again. Besides, she was no longer a child. She must keep this terrible experience to herself, at least for the present. She must think what was the best thing to be done and do it.

She was thankful that she had enough money with her to cover all necessities. She had debated that morning when dressing whether to leave in the apartment all but the change she usually carried in her purse and had decided against it. There would be no trouble about paying her fare. But if she were on her way to Baltimore, was it going to be necessary for her to go all the way? Wouldn't it be possible for her to change to another bus at some halfway stop?

Oh, but that would be to return on the same route, to go again through that awful town where she had left Laurie, where Laurie, by this time, might have raised a posse to hunt her. No, she mustn't go back that way. Better to go on and take a train from Baltimore. There were always fast trains from Baltimore to Philadelphia, weren't there? Every hour or so? She thought she remembered that. And a train would get there much quicker than a bus, especially in this storm.

She tried to calculate what time it was and came to the conclusion that it must be somewhere around eight o'clock. She had come out of the school a little after five, and they certainly must have been nearly two hours on the way. She had no means of knowing just where they had gone, nor how far she was from Baltimore now. She could only guess. It seemed ages since she had come out into the winter dusk to find Laurie waiting for her grimly beside his car. He had been out there all afternoon, perhaps, waiting, drinking at intervals while he waited, and growing more and more frenzied with impatience. She turned away from the memory with a shiver. Could she ever forget that awful afternoon? But she must get back to her planning and forget everything else. Yes, if they should reach Baltimore at, say, nine o'clock, could she make a train at nine thirty, or ten? Surely by ten. That would bring her home by midnight or a little after. She could take a taxi home and get a reasonable amount of sleep for her next day's work. She could doze on the train, too, and get a little rested.

But presently another passenger made his way up to the front of the bus and asked questions of the driver.

"What time you calculatin' ta get ta Baltimore?"

"Can't say," said the driver amusedly. "Due there at nine thirty, but at this rate it might be ten thirty 'fore we get in. Can't make any headway at all with this here snow cloggin' the atmosphere. It's as bad as a fog. And this here slippery road is just one glare. I don't dare go beyond a crawl. If you fellers was ta lean hard on the side o' this here bus she might skid inta the middle o' next week. I ain't sayin' when we'll get ta Baltimore. We'll get there sometime tonight, likely, if we have good luck, but I ain't sayin' when. Not 'nless this here snow quits, which she don't seem likely ta do at present."

Thereafter Marigold looked helplessly out the window, studying those slow-moving, lazy flakes as they came down, each one of mammoth size and thickness, and reflected how mighty were little flakes, if there were enough of them. Was it even thinkable that she might not be able to get back in time for school in the morning? And if so, how was she to explain her delay? She couldn't tell that she had been kidnapped and driven away to be married. She couldn't have them all know her private affairs. What kind of an explanation was she to give when she got home, if she was going to be later than midnight? There was Mrs. Waterman, too, always poking into her affairs and having remarks to make afterward. Well, she would just have to let that go and deal with it when the time came. Perhaps God would take care of that with all her other troubles.

So she put her head back, and before she knew it she was asleep. In the face of all that trouble and excitement she had gone to sleep!

When she awoke with a start, it was to realize that the bus had come to a halt and people were brushing by her getting out. Everybody was getting out. They were yawning and talking with a dreary, sleepy accent.

Marigold didn't realize where she was at first, until sitting up and staring around her, it suddenly all came back.

This must be Baltimore! Would there be a train soon? Oh, to be at home in her own bed asleep.

She paid her fare as she got out, handing out a ten-dollar bill. The driver seemed to understand where she got on, though she hadn't known the name of the town herself, but he told her how much it was.

When she got out, she gave a quick look around lest somehow Laurie would have followed and be waiting to take possession of her again. Would she ever get over the feeling that evening's experience had given her? Was it going to be like that awful dream?

Then she remembered. The dream had utterly gone. Strong arms had carried her away from that dream. She had a strong One with her always now, living in her; she had His power to carry her through.

With a steady step she went to the ticket window and inquired about trains. She had just missed one. The next would bring her to Philadelphia around half past three in the morning! A taxi couldn't get her to her apartment before four o'clock. What would Mrs. Waterman think? Could she possibly get in without being heard?

Her ticket bought, she stole into an obscure corner of the station restaurant where she could watch the door and ordered a bowl of soup. She was chilled and faint, and it tasted good, but she ate it hurriedly. It was not beyond possibility that Laurie might have followed down here somewhere or, having sighted her in that bus, might have been cunning enough to telephone the police to watch for her. She felt he would stop at nothing in his present state of mind, and she must run no risks. She must get home as soon as possible.

It seemed a long time to wait, and she dared not sleep. She was too nervous. She took refuge in the ladies' waiting room in a sheltered corner, scanning alertly everyone who passed through the outer waiting room and watching the clock.

When at last the train was called, she hurried out and got into a day coach, taking a seat at the rear of the car where she would not be seen and where she could keep her own watch. Now and then she would cast a glance at the window, but the world outside was a whirl of white and the windows were plastered with snow so thickly that they were perfectly opaque. She drew a long breath of relief. She was on the last lap of her journey now. She could count herself to have escaped. But she felt such an utter weariness that it seemed as if she would like to die.

Why had God let this dreadful thing happen to her? Especially just now when she was beginning to know Him in a new way. She couldn't understand it. She had asked to be shown—but wait! Wasn't that just what this had been for, that she might be shown? Quickly and definitely shown just what to do about Laurie? Well, she had the answer to her prayer. Not for anything in life would she want further fellowship with Laurie. Oh, there might be excuses for him. It might not be all his fault. Doubtless others had influenced him, and his home surroundings had not given him the background to resist drinking. But after all had been said for him, Laurie was himself to blame, of course. And even if he tried to reform, she could never trust him. She had been well taught concerning the hold that drinking has on its victims. She wanted no dealings with men who drank. She had had her lesson. She could forgive, and perhaps—she *hoped*—she could forget sometime, but she could never marry a man who thought there was no harm in taking a drink.

The experience had done something more for her also. It had shown Laurie apart from the life he led, the pleasant nothings he was doing, the vista of pleasure that his companionship always opened for her. She had seen what it would be to be bound to Laurie for life, to be in his power. She had seen him to be weak, selfish, hard, unprincipled. Of course, some of that was due to the effect of the liquor. But Laurie would never more in her eyes be the perfect creature that she had imagined.

And more than that, Laurie was not a child of God!

She had known that. She had felt when she came home that she was going to have to give him up. But she had expected sore heartbreak. And now God had shown her what he was in such a way that the heartbreak was gone!

Oh, it had been a shock when the illusions were torn away, but it had left her astonishingly whole, uninjured. There would doubtless be times when she would feel lonely and wish for a comrade to while away an idle hour with her, but just tonight she was glad to be lonely. To have that fearful ride ended and to be safe and quiet and alone. With no wild, red eyes glaring into hers; no hoarse, thick words flung at her; no madman trying to embrace her as they rode along at breakneck speed knowing not if the next moment would be the last. Oh, it was good, *good,* to have escaped, and God *had* answered her prayer and shown her without the shadow of a doubt what she ought to do—or rather what she ought *not* to do.

When they were almost to Philadelphia, she dropped off to sleep for a few minutes but started awake as the train pulled into the station.

It was still snowing hard when she got into a taxi and they drove out the familiar way. She looked at the old landmarks with welcome. Even the ugly houses that she had always disliked looked good to her. Oh, it was wonderful to be home and safe!

There was no sign of Laurie anywhere around. And now the snow would hide her footprints and perhaps Mrs. Waterman would not know how late she came in.

She slipped into the house and up the stairs with great caution and at last was safe in her own room with her door locked.

She did not turn on the light. She had a feeling that its radiance might somehow shine beneath the crack of the door and advertise her presence to Mrs. Waterman, advertise to the neighborhood that she was just now home.

Then she knelt and thanked God for saving her.

She undressed rapidly in the dark and was soon sound asleep, her little alarm clock set and ticking away beside her like a faithful watchdog on guard.

Chapter 17

Marigold awoke startled in the morning to the tune of her prompt little clock screaming at her over and over again. She didn't wake quickly enough to turn it off at its first sound as she usually did.

And then, suddenly, as she came fully awake, the whole awful night was spread before her, and she had a quick, sick feeling that all her world had gone wrong and her troubles were by no means over.

When she had tumbled into her bed at four o'clock, she could only be thankful that she was safely at home and her troubles were past. But now in the light of the morning, it came over her that she was by no means so safe and out of danger. For if Laurie were alive and not too drunk to forget, he would certainly be raving somewhere and trying to find her, perhaps still angry enough and still under the influence of liquor to be determined to pay her back for having run away from him. She recalled how angry he had been the morning after she had gone from the rink and left him. But this offense was still greater. She had deserted him on what he was pleased to consider the eve of her marriage with him.

She shuddered even here in her warm bed to think of the things he had said. And now as she lay for a minute trying to get her full senses, she realized that there was no telling what he might undertake to do that day. And if he was still in the mood he had been when she left him, it was conceivable that he might take some drastic method to punish her. Kidnap her, perhaps!

She stared across at the wall in the morning light, and grim fear came and mocked her.

Suddenly she remembered.

"Surely he shall deliver thee—" And He had delivered! He had brought her home safely. Could she not trust Him for the rest? *"Because he hath set his love upon me, therefore will I deliver him."* There was nothing she could do but go through her duty for the day and perhaps be unusually alert to keep out of Laurie's way for the future. She must trust the Lord who had brought her this far!

She slipped out of bed to her knees. A quick cry for help! Then her next act was to fling a warm bathrobe around her and call up her mother.

"Mother, dear! I was afraid you would be worrying."

How her mother's heart thrilled when she heard her voice!

"Did you call? Oh, I'm so sorry! I didn't go right home from school. I went in another direction. I expected to call you, but there was no opportunity, and when I got home it was quite late and I was afraid of waking Aunt Marian. Yes, I was out last night. I haven't time to tell you about it now, for I'm going to be late to school, I'm afraid. What? Did I have a good time? Well no, not exactly, but I guess it was rather good for me. Anyway, I'll tell you about it later. Oh yes, indeed, I'm all right. Are you? No, don't you think of coming home until Elinor and her husband get back. No, I won't hear of it. You needn't worry about me. I'll get along beautifully. Bye-bye, and I'll call you again tonight."

She gave a little shiver as she hung up. That had been hard, to talk lightly of that awful experience and not have Mother suspect. She felt she had done very well. Of course, she mustn't ever let Mother know what an awful time she had been through—at least not now. Not until it was so far in the past that there would never be any more worry about it, for her precious mother, anyway.

As she turned from the telephone, she had a sick longing to crawl back into bed and sleep, just stay there all day and sleep. But she knew she could not do that. She had a job and must get to it. She was not a child to lie in bed when she was weary.

A quick shower while the coffee prepared itself, toast made while she dressed, breakfast eaten a bite at a time as she prepared for the day.

The dress she had worn yesterday was mussed and dejected-looking after the ride in the train. A glance in the mirror showed her face looking gray and weary. She must keep up her appearance and not have everybody asking if she was sick. She slipped into a little knitted dress of bright cherry color edged narrowly with black. It was her one cherished afternoon dress and very attractive, but one must do something to brighten up a day after the night she had spent.

She hunted up her galoshes, put on her old fur coat and a gray felt hat that matched the squirrel of her coat, and started out.

Mrs. Waterman poked her head out her door across the hall as Marigold came out. "Well, upon my word! Are you here? I didn't hear you come in last night at all. Weren't you awful late? I didn't see you come home from school at all."

Marigold smiled engagingly.

"Yes, I was pretty late," she admitted brightly. "You see, I didn't come home right after school. I had to go somewhere else. And then when I started home, I got on the wrong bus and went out of my way and had a tiresome time getting back again. It was snowing very hard or I probably would have seen my mistake sooner.

But I got home all right. I'm glad I didn't disturb you coming in. Isn't it grand that it has cleared off this morning? I didn't think last night it would. I thought we were in for a blizzard."

"Yes, it is clear again. But I guess the walks are pretty bad. People haven't had time to get them shoveled yet. You better be awful careful not to get flu while your mother's away. Have you got your galoshes on? I guess at that you'll have to be careful. The snow's pretty deep."

"Well, I have a taxi coming for me, and there it comes now, I guess. Didn't he ring? I must go."

She hurried away, glad to escape further questioning, almost gleeful that she had gotten by the house gossip so easily. She put her head back and closed her eyes for a brief respite before she reached the school. How she longed to go to sleep. How was she going to get through the day, after such a night?

But the day rushed by with its round of inevitable duties, and Marigold had no time to indulge her desire to close her eyes for just a little minute. The children were filled with a fine frenzy of glee over the snow, and to control them was like trying to rein in a lot of little wild hyenas. Marigold, in desperation, finally finished the afternoon by reading them a story about a wolfhound in the far northland, until at last the bell rang, and they all rushed out to pelt one another with snow and fill the air with the melodious glee of young voices.

Then quickly, sudden fear descended upon her, the fear of what might be coming next. Just twenty-four hours ago she had started on that terrible compulsory ride. Was Laurie even now preparing some new torture to repay her for having escaped him?

It was the first time she had let herself think of Laurie all day, and now it came to her all at once to wonder what had become of him. It scarcely seemed possible that he could be alive if he kept on with his wild driving, drunk as he was. She shuddered as she glanced out an upper window from behind a curtain and searched the street all around the school. There was no sign of Laurie's car.

She called a taxi, giving instructions for it to come to the back steps at the schoolhouse, and she did not go out until she saw it arrive and had scanned the neighborhood carefully. All the way back home, she watched most carefully. Now, in a few short minutes, she would be at home, and she would lock herself in and let no one enter. She would make herself some hot soup and then she would go to sleep and sleep all night. What luxury! And yet, somehow there seemed to be a thought of terror in it all because she couldn't seem to believe that Laurie might not turn up again.

But God had protected her so far. He would see her through.

As the taxi pulled up in front of the house, she noticed an elegant limousine parked near, with a sedate chauffeur in uniform. The limousine was flashy with much chrome, and there was an air of ostentation about it as if this car were well cared for, like an overfed pet dog. But this was not Laurie's car. He never came with a chauffeur. She drew a breath of relief and hurried into the house, wondering who in the neighborhood had such stylish visitors.

But once inside the door, she encountered Mrs. Waterman, lying in wait and speaking in a penetrative, confidential whisper.

"You've got a caller!" she declared, speaking into Marigold's shrinking face and gesticulating energetically with a long bony finger. "She's a real lady!" she apostrophized. "She came in that big car out there with a chauffeur to ring the bell for her and help her out, and she's got a real chinchilla coat! What do you think of that? It's real, I know, for I had a muff of it once when I was young; my great-aunt gave it to me. She was wealthy and had all sorts of nice things and was real generous, so I know good things when I see them."

"Who is she?" Marigold managed to insert the question in a very low murmur.

"I don't know," said Mrs. Waterman. "She didn't give her name but just said she'd wait. She asked for you, and I said you'd soon be in, I guessed. So she said she'd wait, and I was real embarrassed not to have your key to let her into your apartment. I couldn't take her into mine because I'm getting ready for the paper hanger. So I just brought out my great-grandmother's rosewood chair for her to sit in, and she's up there in the hall. I thought I'd come down and let you know she was there, so you wouldn't have to go up unprepared. But I've been kind of worried because she's smoking cigarettes up there, and if she should burn a hole in that sweet old plush I'd never forgive myself for not getting her a chair from my kitchenette!"

Something cold and dreadfully foreboding gripped Marigold by the throat, but she flung away from this avalanche of words and went up to interview the interloper.

The caller had pulled the chair over by the window, and she was puffing away on a cigarette in a long ivory holder.

Marigold had rushed up the stairs breathlessly, her eyes bright with worried excitement, her cheeks suddenly grown pink. The old squirrel coat she was wearing was unfastened and showed her bright knitted dress. The jaunty old gray felt was perched like a bird of passage on her bright hair. She flashed before the astonished vision of her caller with startling unexpectedness amid the drab surroundings. She drew herself up with her best school-ma'am manner, and the afternoon sun, which had a concession of only about five minutes a day shining into that hall window, suddenly crept in and blazed forth, lighting up Marigold's face and figure, throwing her into relief against the bareness of the desolate hall.

The caller put up platinum eyeglasses and surveyed Marigold as if she had been an article offered for sale in some out-of-the-way shop that the great lady had ferreted out and descended upon.

"I am Miss Brooke," said Marigold, lifting her chin a trifle and eyeing her caller unfavorably, "did you want to see me?"

"Why yes," said the lady, "could we go somewhere and talk? I'm Mrs. Trescott. You are acquainted with my son, Lawrence Trescott."

"Yes?" said Marigold, lifting her chin still higher. There was an icy little edge to her voice, and her heart was full of fright. What now was this? Had Laurie sent his mother to upbraid her? Or had he been injured somehow and was his mother here to charge her with murder?

Marigold gave her caller one steady look, noticing that there was a mean, stubborn little twist to her chin that reminded her of Laurie, yesterday, when he was putting her into his car.

"We'll go in here," said Marigold frigidly, whirling around to unlock her door and hoping that she had not left things in too wild confusion when she hurried away so early in the morning. She felt she needed the moral support of a perfect setting. She was conscious of Mrs. Waterman listening avidly at the foot of the stairs. They could not talk in the hall.

She opened the door and escorted the lady in.

"Will you take a seat, Mrs. Trescott," she said.

Mrs. Trescott, however, was not quite ready to sit down. She was surveying the room in detail through her glasses, stooping to examine a few really lovely ornaments on the table, lifting her head to a fine old picture on the wall, and then giving minute attention to a framed photograph of Marigold's father.

It was quite evident that she was bristling with questions when Marigold came back from removing her hat and coat, but the girl faced her caller almost sternly.

"Now, Mrs. Trescott?" she said, with a really impressive manner for so young a person.

Mrs. Trescott whirled around and eased herself into a large armchair, staring at Marigold, who took a straight chair opposite her.

"You have really stunning hair, you know," she remarked irrelevantly. "I *heard* that you had."

Marigold looked at her coldly, almost sternly.

"You wanted to see me about something?" she asked again.

"Yes," said Adele Trescott, shifting her fur coat a little lower on her shoulders. "I came, you know, to say that I withdraw my opposition!"

"Opposition?" said Marigold with a perplexed air. "I was not aware that you had opposition to anything. To what were you opposed? I don't understand."

"Why, to your marrying Lawrence, my son."

Marigold's eyes suddenly flashed angrily. "But I have never had any idea of marrying Laurie, Mrs. Trescott."

"No, I suppose not," said the mother complacently. "Of course, you would scarcely expect a young man out of your class to stoop to marrying you. But as I say, I have removed my opposition, and I'm not sure but in some ways it might be a good thing. You seem to be quite presentable. And, of course, Laurie—Lawrence, I mean—has always had his own way, and I always try to humor him if I can. He's such a delicate, sensitive boy, you know."

Marigold recalled the silly, angry look on the face of the "delicate, sensitive boy" yesterday as he whirled her through the storm to an undesired wedding, and her expression froze into sternness.

"Mrs. Trescott, you are evidently under a misapprehension." She spoke icily. "Your son is not a very special friend of mine, and there is no question whatever of my marrying him, *and never will be*!"

"Ah, but there is where you are mistaken, my dear! You see, *I* am managing this affair for you now, and I have come to say that I will be very glad to have you marry Laurie! He seems fond of you, and I feel that you may be a good influence in his life."

"Mrs. Trescott, that is quite impossible! I have been out sometimes with your son in the evening, and we were friends, but recently I have come to see the matter in an entirely different light and our friendship is definitely at an end."

"Ah! But, my dear, you would not let a little lover's quarrel stand in the way of a good marriage."

Marigold was growing angry and frightened. She wished her mother would walk in. Perhaps she would. It was Friday, and she had threatened this morning in their telephone conversation to come back today. But oh, she would not like to have her walk into this awful conversation, either. This was another thing that her mother must never know. This humiliation! This awful woman! Oh, she didn't need this visit of his mother's now to show her how utterly of another world was Laurie, the Laurie that she used to call a prince!

Marigold rose and came a step toward her caller. "Mrs. Trescott, you are utterly mistaken. Laurie and I were never lovers and never will be. Laurie is not the kind of man I would wish to marry!"

"Indeed!" said the mother haughtily. "What do you mean by that? Are you casting aspersions on my son?"

"I mean that your son does not believe in the God to whom I belong, and he also thinks it is quite all right to drink. He belongs to another world than mine. I would not want to marry him."

"Oh—*God!*" laughed the mother. "Why, that is a small matter! I'm quite sure Laurie would be entirely willing to go to church sometimes with you. What more could you ask? And as for the drinking, that's the very thing I came about. Laurie is at this very minute in the hospital being treated for alcoholism. At least, I *hope* he stayed. I had him sent there. He came home quite under the influence of liquor, which I much regret, of course. A young man should know how to carry his liquor. My father always did. But Laurie had been out in a terrible storm, had a wild ride somewhere, and a collision! He broke his arm and injured his ankle and is quite under the weather. He got a bad bruise on his forehead. I feel that he narrowly escaped death. He was somewhat under the influence of liquor, of course, when it happened. So I thought it over and decided to come to you. I had heard that you had very good ideas and that your influence might be good, and I came right over to ask if you won't go over to the hospital with me now and see Laurie. Try to influence him to give up drink, at least for a little while, won't you, till he learns self-control? I felt that if you would promise to marry him just as soon as he got out of the hospital and would go and visit him every day while he has to be there, that it might have quite an effect on him."

Marigold was aghast, but she was thankful that evidently this woman did not know that she had been out with Laurie last night.

"No!" she said sharply. "I cannot do that. I do not love Laurie, and I know that even if I did, it would do no good for me to try to stop his drinking. A man does not stop drinking just for a girl! He needs some deeper urge than that. He needs God, and Laurie does not believe in God. He said so."

Marigold was holding her young head high and speaking earnestly. There was mingled pity and disgust in her eyes that gave her a look of wisdom beyond her years.

"Ah, but my dear, I haven't told you my proposition yet. You don't realize that I would make it fully worth your while. I would settle an ample allowance on you, regardless of how my son behaved, so that you would be practically independent."

"Stop!" said Marigold suddenly. "I don't want to hear you say another word! Mrs. Trescott, I am not for sale!"

"Now, don't flare up and be a foolish child! You know you will regret it by and by when you come to think it over. You don't realize that it will mean a small fortune. I would be willing to give you—"

But Marigold marched over to her.

"I wish you would please go away!" she said, her eyes flashing fire. "I don't ever want to hear another word about this. It is *disgusting*! You fill me with such shame and horror. If my father were alive, he would demand an apology for what you have said. Now go, or I shall have to call someone to escort you out."

There was a tremble of almost rage in Marigold's young voice, and Mrs. Trescott looked up astonished.

"Why, *dear me*!" she said, lifting up her eyeglasses and watching the girl, fascinated. "They didn't tell me you had a temper! But it's really quite becoming! I'm sure you would be a social success if you would make up your mind to try it. You know, we are immensely wealthy, and you could have almost anything you want."

For answer Marigold whirled around and marched into her bedroom, locking the door audibly, dropping down on her knees beside her bed and sobbing silently.

The older woman, thus left to herself, waited a minute or two, walked over and tried the door, called good-bye, then hesitating, added: "If you change your mind, just call me up. The offer still holds. Or even if you didn't want to consider marriage, if you would just come over to the hospital and try to influence him to give up drinking for a while, I would be willing to pay you well! You see, Laurie blames me for being opposed to you, and I can't endure it! My dear angel child!"

She delivered this to the door panel with a sob in the end of her words. It was always her last appeal, that sob. But when after duly waiting she got no reply, she turned and made her way out of the room and down the stairs. Marigold, holding her breath to listen, could hear Mrs. Waterman's quick steps downstairs scuttling out of the way, and then she could hear the front door close and the limousine roll away down the street.

Suddenly the ridiculous side of it all came over her and she burst into mingled laughter and sobs, her tired nerves giving way in a healthy minute or two of hysterics.

But after that had passed, she continued to kneel.

"Oh, God, my Father," she cried at last, "was I so headstrong and self-willed that You had to send me a terrible lesson like this to show me how far from Home I was getting? I see that I was. I know now that I have sinned, and I'm not worthy of all the care You have had to bring me back. Forgive and help me, dear Lord, and teach me not to seek my own way anymore. Let my life be ordered as Thou will."

Chapter 18

After her telephone conversation with Marigold that morning, Mrs. Brooke seemed more satisfied, though her sister noticed that she was more than usually quiet and thoughtful. Finally she spoke.

"You aren't quite at rest about Marigold, are you, dear?" she said at last.

Mrs. Brooke looked up thoughtfully.

"Yes, I'm at rest about her," she said slowly, "but somehow I keep on feeling that she needs me. I don't know why I should. I reason it away, and then the idea returns. If Elinor were back I think I should go home this morning, or perhaps not till this afternoon. I just feel as if I didn't want Marigold to be there another night alone. There! Now that's silly, I know, but I'm telling you the truth."

Her sister smiled. "Yes, I understand. Well, dear heart, you mustn't stay for me if you feel you ought to go! But make it this afternoon, anyway, Mary. You can get there before night if you go late this afternoon. Get there in time to take her out to dinner. Surprise her."

Mrs. Brooke pondered that. "But I don't like to leave you alone. You don't think perhaps Elinor and her husband might come tonight?"

"They might. They said they would telegraph as soon as they knew. But you needn't worry about a night or two more or less for me. I've my nurse here, and the servants. And it isn't as though we lived in the wilds. There are neighbors close at hand, and lots of friends. I'll be quite all right if you think you ought to go."

"Well, perhaps I am foolish. I don't *want* to go, Marian, you know that, for there will be no certainty when I can get back again once my vacation is over. But yet I can't settle down to feel right about leaving Marigold alone any longer. Perhaps, though, I could wait until noon and telephone her at the school. You see, this is Friday, and she might be planning something. I'd like to know just how things are with her."

Mrs. Brooke's brow was troubled, and her sister wore a sweetly concerned look also.

"What are you two ladies worrying about?" suddenly spoke Ethan Bevan, appearing from the stairs.

"Oh, Ethan! Are you here?" they both exclaimed eagerly. "How did you get in without making any noise?"

"Stealth is my middle name," said Ethan solemnly. "It's the best thing I do. I make my living at it. I just ran away from my job for a few minutes to see how my family was getting along."

"Well, I was just wishing you would come in," said Mrs. Brooke. "In fact, I had some thought of trying to call you up if I could find out your number without alarming my vigilant sister. Ethan, if I should go home this afternoon, could you come and stay with your aunt till Elinor gets home?"

Ethan studied her thoughtfully a minute.

"What's the idea, going home so soon?" he said. "I just felt it in my bones you were trying to slip away from us, and that's one of the reasons I ran over, to prevent it. I guess I could arrange to stay with Aunt Marian, if you *had* to go, but I'm here to try and persuade you differently. I just know Elinor and her husband will be disappointed to have you gone when they get back, and besides, there is your job. You'll be so much fresher for it if you stay a few more days and get a little rested. What's the idea, anyway?"

"She feels Marigold needs her," explained Aunt Marian.

An instant gravity came over Ethan's face and a reserve in his voice.

"That's different," he said gravely. "But *does* she? What makes you think so, Aunt Mary?"

"I don't know," confessed Mrs. Brooke. "I just feel so!"

"Well then, something ought to be done about it," said Ethan determinedly. "But see here, why should *you* go? I have a better plan. Why don't *I* go up and get her? She wouldn't resent it, would she? I'd promise on my honor to bring her back with me or die in the attempt, and there's always the telephone in case she balks. Besides, there are later trains on which you could go home if you had to."

"Oh, Ethan, that would be wonderful! But I couldn't think of making you all that trouble and taking you away from your job," said Mrs. Brooke.

"*Could* you, Ethan?" beamed Aunt Marian.

"I *could,* and I *will,*" said Ethan. "You see, Aunt Mary, it's Friday with my job, too. That is, Saturday is only a half day, and I could make up a lost Friday easily on Saturday. Besides, I have to go up to Philadelphia again soon, anyway. I would have to go next week at the latest, and personally I'd prefer to go today, provided I could have good company back. That's a great inducement, you know."

"Well, I know Marigold would enjoy it, too," said Mrs. Brooke gratefully. And she hoped in her heart that she was speaking the truth. If Marigold didn't enjoy the company of a wonderful young man like this, she ought to be spanked, she thought. "But I don't think we ought to let you do it," she added wistfully.

"But if he *has* to go anyway, Mary?" put in Mrs. Bevan.

"All I want to know is," said Ethan, "would it solve the situation? Or would you still feel uneasy and as if you ought to have gone? Because in that case, I'll stay with Aunt Marian and let you go."

"Yes, I think it would solve the situation," said Mrs. Brooke slowly. "I'd far rather have Marigold here this weekend than at home, and I don't see why she wouldn't jump at the chance. It would be wonderful for her and all of us."

"Wonderful for *me*!" said Aunt Marian softly.

"Then I'll go!" said Ethan, getting up with determination. "I'll have to run back to the job for a while, but I'm free at noon or a little after. I'll stop at the house and see if you've any errands you want done at home, a clean apron or anything you want to send for."

"I could get Marigold on the telephone," said Mary Brooke meditatively. "Would you like me to, so she won't plan anything else?"

He considered that an instant and then shook his head.

"No, I think I'd rather appear on the scene unannounced. She wouldn't have so much chance to think up excuses. I'll go armed with authority and tell her I have orders to bring her back. Just let it go at that. I'll get in touch with you by phone if any situation arises in which I need backing."

Then with a grin he hurried away, and the two sisters settled back to enjoy the morning. Mary Brooke kept praying that her girl wouldn't have gone and got up some precious engagement with that Laurie that would make her refuse to come to Washington. What silly, unwise creatures girls were sometimes; the Lord arranged nice plans for them, and they already had others of their own.

Then toward noon there came a telegram from Elinor:

ARRIVE HOME LATE SATURDAY NIGHT. MAKE
AUNT MARY AND MARIGOLD STAY OVER TILL
NEXT WEEK. WE WANT TO SEE THEM.

"Now that makes it just perfect!" said Mrs. Bevan. "My girl and her husband will be here, too, before you leave, and I can't imagine anything nearer to heaven on this earth." There came a lilt in her voice that had not been there before.

So the two went placidly to knitting and talking about old times. Ethan came back for a minute and went again, and the smiles on the two mothers' faces grew more radiant as the hours went slowly by, full of eager anticipation.

Even out in the kitchen there was a flutter of expectation. Delectable things were being manufactured for the next day's menu because Miss Marigold was coming back.

But secretly, as the evening drew on, Marigold's mother kept wondering, would Marigold elect to come? And supposing she didn't, how would Ethan feel about it? How could she ever apologize for her daughter's rudeness?

Oh, but she wouldn't let herself think that Marigold wouldn't come. She put the thought of Laurie and the plans he might have made to absorb Marigold right out of her mind and tried to trust it all to the Lord.

She had, however, secretly folded her garments and gotten things pretty well packed in her suitcase, in case Ethan should telephone that he couldn't find Marigold and he was going to have to return without her.

Suddenly her sister spoke.

"He wouldn't!" she said, right out of a silence.

"What?" asked Mary Brooke, looking up astonished from counting stitches.

"He wouldn't come home without Marigold," said Marian Bevan, knitting away hard on the coat that she was making for Elinor. "Isn't that what you were thinking, dear?"

"Why yes, something like that," faltered the other, "but how in the world did you know?"

"Oh, you had it written right out plainly across your forehead. You were thinking what if Ethan should come home without her. You were wondering what you would think next. But he won't. I know Ethan."

"Well, but suppose she isn't there? Suppose she's gone home with one of the teachers to supper and hasn't left any word? I should have reminded her always to leave word with Mrs. Waterman. Ethan wouldn't find her if she hadn't left any word."

"Ethan *would* find her," said Mrs. Bevan calmly. "He's clever. He would find her or he wouldn't come back till he did. And what's more, he would telephone before it was late enough for you to be anxious."

"Oh, of course," said Marigold's mother, relaxing into a smile.

"I'll tell you what we will do, Mary," said her sister. "There's nobody near enough to hear. Let's sing! The servants are down in the kitchen, and the nurse is out. It can't hurt anybody, and there's nobody to laugh at us, either. Let's sing all the old songs we used to sing when we were little girls washing the dishes. You take the alto as you always did, and I'll take the soprano. Let's begin on 'When You and I Were Young, Maggie,' and go on to 'Silver Threads among the Gold,' and 'Juanita,' and 'Bide a "Wee," ' and a lot of others."

Mary's eyes sparkled. "Oh, and 'Little Brown Church in the Vale,' too, and 'Where Is Now the Merry Party, I Remember Long Ago?' I haven't thought of them in years. Yes, let's sing!"

So the two sweet old sisters began to sing. Their voices were still good, though higher and thinner, and with a quaver here and there, but they blended out in the dear old songs they had both loved, and in between each there were old memories to be trotted out.

"Do you remember, Marian, how Randall Silver came in that day while we were singing that and asked for a piece of the chocolate cake Mother had just baked for the church supper that night? The new minister was to be installed, you know—and you *gave it to him?*"

"Yes, and how Betty Hemstead was jealous and baked a coconut cake for him the very next day, and *left the baking powder out!*"

"Yes, and Ran said it reminded him of a pancake it was so thin," contributed Mary. "How long has Ran been dead, Marian? Almost thirty years, isn't it? Seems strange we never knew his wife. They said she was sweet. But, Marian, what did Mother say when she found you'd cut her cake before she had a chance to send it down to the church? I don't remember."

"Why, she just went and made another," Marian said, smiling. "That was the deadliest punishment she could have given me. Mother working away patiently and frantically to get that cake done, when I knew she was so tired she was ready to drop. I never did that again. Mother was sweet, you know."

And then there was a space of silence during which both sisters counted stitches assiduously, brushing away surreptitious tears now and again.

Presently they drifted into more songs. Sweet old hymns now, "Softly Now the Light of Day," "Abide with Me, Fast Falls the Eventide," "How Firm a Foundation, Ye Saints of the Lord," and others, each bringing its set of memories, sweet and sad.

As they sang, they glanced from time to time at the clock ticking away on the mantel and smiled, remembering that it was Ethan Bevan, and not Laurie Trescott, who had gone after Marigold, and that God was with Ethan Bevan. At least that was what Marigold's mother thought.

Though sometimes, again, she would go over quickly in her

mind just how many things had to be put in her suitcase and where she had placed her gloves and coat and hat and purse, in case it became suddenly necessary for her to take the train home that night.

Then Marian Bevan, watching her quietly, would start another song:

> "Children of the heavenly King,
> As ye journey, sweetly sing."

It was a song their father used to love, and it brought back the picture of the family gathered at evening for family worship. They sang on through the well-remembered verses:

> "We are traveling home to God
> In the way our fathers trod;
> They are happy now, and we
> Soon their happiness shall see."

How many years it had been since they had all sung that together, those two girls and their brothers and parents, all now gone on before them to the heavenly home, except one brother in the far West whom they hadn't seen for years. Their voices choked as they went on with the other verses:

> "Fear not, brethren; joyful stand
> On the borders of your land;
> Jesus Christ, your Father's Son,
> Bids you undismayed go on."

"And now, Mary, I think you might go and turn on the porch light, don't you? They ought to be here in about fifteen minutes if they come on the same train you did."

Chapter 19

In a quiet, sparsely settled, somewhat obscure suburb of Philadelphia, in a great, massive stone building entirely surrounded by dense foliage, which was now heavily draped in snow, Laurie Trescott thrashed about on a luxurious bed and cursed his male nurse, who was really his jailor.

He had tried all the arts and cajoleries he knew, and these were many, for this was not the first time he had been confined within stone walls for a brief period. No period of confinement, however brief, was to be tolerated, Laurie felt. He had offered bribes, varying in value according as his keeper grew stubborn, regardless of the fact that he was not at present in a position to pay even the smallest. But when it became evident that his parents' bribe was greater than he could exceed, he had gone on to promises and cunning.

The man, however, into whose charge he had been put, was a knowing man and twice as big and strong as Laurie. He paid no more attention to all this than if Laurie had been a rabbit trying to cajole him.

Laurie had wearied himself by coaxing for liquor, and he was now in torment, as the effects of the liquor taken the last twenty-four hours began to wear off. He was desperate and frantic.

As he lay there thinking back over all he could remember of the time previous to his installment in this bed, gradually a grudge evolved from the vagueness, a grudge against Marigold Brooke. He wasn't just sure how she became connected with it all, but little by little some of it came back. He had offered to marry Marigold and she had declined. She had deserted him at the altar, as it were. There was a little white house in the snow and a minister. That was it. There had been a sign that said so. He was smoking a long black cigar and he needed a haircut, but he had opened the door cordially and put out a flabby hand. Laurie had told him he wanted to get married and had called to Marigold to come, and she didn't answer. He went out to get her, and she wasn't there. He didn't exactly remember what came next, only there was some snow connected with it, down his neck, and he couldn't find Marigold. Then he had jumped in his car and somebody ran into him and smashed things up. All Marigold's fault, and he'd like to get even with her. He thought hard about that, drawing his brows in a frown. He might get married to someone else. That was it. Show her she wasn't the only girl there was. That would teach her a good lesson. Next time she'd do as he said. Yes, that was it. He'd marry someone else. Now that he knew where that minister lived, he could go back. The minister wouldn't know whether he had the same girl or not. He would go and get Lily. Lily was a good sport. He remembered when she had lied once in school to keep the teacher from finding out who it was that put chewing gum all around the inside of her hat. Lily would go through with anything if she agreed to. Not that Mara had agreed. She never did anymore. She was getting stubborn. But Lily always agreed to anything he asked. Lily would marry him quick enough. He would marry Lily, and afterward he would call up Mara and tell her he was married and she had lost her chance to be a lady. *Then* she would be sorry.

The excitement of his plan kept him quiet for a few minutes, and the attendant came near with medicine. That was something to put him to sleep, and he didn't mean to go to sleep. But he opened his mouth and took in the spoonful, keeping it carefully in his cheek as he turned over to his pillow and closed his eyes as if for slumber. It was an old trick he used to do when he was a child and they gave him medicine. He simply let it run softly out of the corner of his mouth into the pillow, and that was the end of it.

He lay very still after he had pretended to swallow the medicine. He knew it was almost time for the attendant's supper downstairs and that he was anxious to have him go to sleep, so he breathed steadily and tried to snore a little. He was coming into his own rapidly now. He began to think how he was to get out. He knew all the tricks of the place. This was the old side of the building, and the windows were wooden frames, not steel sash. His room was in the end of the building, a large room on the second floor. There were no bars to the windows. It was the policy of the place to put the patients on their honor but also to reinforce that honor by plenty of alert attendants. If one played good-boy and got trusted, it was possible to slip over a trick now and then. Laurie was good at tricks. Even when he was drunk, he was canny. He had practiced tricks on his mother long years now.

But there would be the matter of clothes! His clothes were locked up. He was sure of that. And they never left keys around, no chance of that. He was now in pajamas, pink-and-blue flannel. They hadn't let him have his silk ones. Well, he would have to scout around and see what was available, but he would go, even if he had to go in pink-and-blue plaid pajamas.

He remembered he had a suit down at the tailor's being pressed. Maybe more than one, he couldn't be sure. He could get an overcoat at the tailor's, too. And there were several places he could borrow money if he once got out. He cocked one eye open toward the window and measured possibilities by the trees. That would be the window that faced toward the garages. There might be a car, or cars, out there. Once in a car, he could make it to the tailor's without detection, and after that all would be clear sailing.

The attendant was sitting very still over by the other window reading the paper. He held it so that it didn't even crackle. He was very anxious for Laurie to go to sleep.

Laurie attacked the problem of getting out, his mind getting more and more sharp.

Those windows over there. He could take several layers of blanket and press hard and they would break without much noise, supposing they were screwed in and immovable. Then he could surely break out the mullions with his whole strength, leaning against a mullion at a time. But wait! Why not the hall, openly? His experience had been that if one were bold enough he could usually get away with anything. If only that fellow would go to his supper. There! There was the signal bell!

He lay very still, and when the attendant tiptoed over to look at him, he was apparently sleeping, sodden, dead, the kind of sleep the drunkard sleeps when he is coming out of a spree. Laurie knew perfectly how to simulate it.

At last the man opened the door softly and went out. Laurie listened intently. He heard the rubber footsteps going down the hall, heard the man speak to another attendant. Then silence. There seemed to be no one along the hall. There were footsteps in the hall below, going toward the nurses' dining room. There was a faint tinkle of glass and silver. Now. He must work fast!

He flung the covers from him and peered around the room carefully, discovering his shoes in the corner over near the closet door. He stepped into them. No socks. That was immaterial.

A search of the closet brought only a long brown flannel bathrobe to view. That would do nicely in lieu of his own garments. He stepped to the door and opened it cautiously. There did not seem to be anybody around. They were a trusting lot, after all, these jailors of his. But nobody would think anything if they saw him in such informal array walking in the hall.

He closed the door silently and stalked boldly down the hall. From the bathroom window he reconnoitered. Yes, there was a car parked right down at the foot of the fire escape. If he could only get to it, he was safe.

If he had stopped to consider, he might have been too late, but he usually acted quickly. Besides, he was crazed and desperate for a drink, and this was the only way to get it.

A moment more and he was out on the fire escape, backing down rapidly, crouching so that he would not be noticeable. His arm in its sling hurt, but he did not stop. This was going to be hard on his ankle, too, but what was a little thing like an ankle when one was going to get a drink?

The last length of the fire escape was strung up from the ground, and he had to swing by his good arm and drop. The pain in his ankle was fierce for a minute and turned him sick, but he rose from the snow bank where he had fallen and, with a stealthy look around, crept over to the little roadster that was parked so near and crawled inside. He closed the door so quietly that it could not be heard in the building.

Yes, the key was in the car, and there was gas.

Boldly he backed the car out and sent it leaping down the road. Now, a minute more and he was safe!

The cold air cleared his brain, and the excitement brought the color to his pale cheeks. He did not know what a sight he was, but the car hid him well from view. He must go to the tailor's first. He threaded his way through the city, which he knew so well, avoiding traffic lights and well-known traffic cops who might take him in.

Neddie, the tailor, was a kind, obsequious little man who had pulled Laurie out of more than one scrape. Laurie pulled up in front of his modest establishment and blew his horn furiously. Neddie hastened out, recognizing the call that Laurie gave and the wave of his hand. Laurie hadn't any idea what a grotesque figure he presented, but Neddie didn't bat an eye. Laurie always paid well, and eccentric young gentlemen were not to be questioned. If they chose to travel the avenue in pink-and-blue pajamas with brown frog-fastened bathrobes and their hair standing on end, it was none of his business. He hurried out.

"Yes, Mr. Trescott, what can I do for you?"

"Why, you see, Neddie, I'm in a jam! Had an accident and lost my clothes. Got any of my suits here?"

"Yes, sir. I think so. A brown suit."

"That's it. Got an overcoat you can sell me? Something somewhere near my size? No, I don't care what color. Okay! Well, just let me come in and change, will you?"

The accommodating Neddie opened the door for the startling customer, and the pink-and-blue legs hurtled across the pavement into his shop. But it was in the neighborhood of the university dormitories. Any strange thing might happen around there and be only a bit of harmless hazing, today's freak orders to the freshmen.

Laurie vanished into a convenient cubby where he had often changed his garments in the past and soon emerged arrayed in his own suit.

"Better comb your hair," suggested Neddie, presenting him with a comb.

"Oh, that's all right," said Laurie indifferently, but he ran the comb through his crisp waves. Then Neddie helped him arrange the cheap shoddy overcoat over his arm that was in a sling, loaned him the ten dollars Laurie demanded, and Laurie marched out, a free man. Neddie knew he would lose nothing in the long run.

Laurie abandoned his appropriated car and hailed a taxi. He knew he could find Lily in half an hour at the factory when the day shift came out from work. But he must have a drink first. He stopped at one of his haunts, and after a few drinks he came out and took another taxi. It was awkward not having his own car. He wondered what had become of it.

He had no trouble in locating Lily, who hopped into the taxi proudly and rode away with him.

"We're going ta get married, Lily, see?" he said, with uncertain eyes looking sleepily into hers.

"Oh yeah?" said the girl, with a grin.

"Tha's right, Lily. We're going ta get married right away. Got any money, Lily? Because I'm in a jam. Had an accident and got my car smashed up."

"Where we going ta get married?" asked Lily, sharply sitting up and looking at him keenly.

"Oh, down in M'ryland, a place where it's easy. But we'll havta go in a train. My car's gone somewhere for repairsh."

Laurie's speech was getting thick and his eyes dreamier every minute.

"Oh, I know something better than that," said Lily, with a cunning look in her impish eyes. "I gotta friend will take us down an' we can pay him afterwards. He'd do for a witness, too! He's real accommodatin'."

"Okay! Thash so! We havta have a witnesh! Didn't think of that before."

Laurie stood uncertainly outside Lily's house while she arranged with the friend to take them down in a rattly old Ford. He shivered as he waited. The cheap overcoat was thin, and he had no socks on. But what did that matter? He was getting married in a little while to Lily. Lily was a good sport. She always did what you wanted her to. And then he was going to call up Mara and get it back on her for running off. He was going to tell her what a "mishtake" she had made. His thoughts were getting very much muddled now.

Lily put him in the backseat of the old car and let him sleep. She sat in the front with the driver and conversed with him affably. He was an old man and seemed to be somewhat related to her. Laurie found out afterward that he was her uncle. Laurie told him indefinitely where to go. But he said he knew, he'd been there before, and after a very bumpy monotonous drive, they finally arrived at the white house from which Marigold had fled only about twenty-four hours before.

When they came out, less than a half hour later, Laurie looked at her, dazed.

"What we going to do now, Lily?" he said drunkenly. "Lesh go shomewhere and get a drink!"

"No!" said Lily sharply. "You're married now, and you aren't going to drink anymore. I'm not going to have a drunken husband. I'm going to be a *lady*!"

"Shure!" said Laurie, appreciatively. "You're going to be a lady! But every lady drinksh a little. We'll go get a drink ta shelebrate!"

"No!" said Lily. "We're going home!"

"You don't shay!" said Laurie, looking at her stupidly. "Going ta your house? I've never been there."

"No," said Lily calmly, "we're going to yours. I've been there once, but I'm going now to stay!"

"You're going ta my housh?" said Laurie, tottering on his uncertain feet and looking at her as if it were something he couldn't quite comprehend. "But they won't let you in. They won't like it."

"Well, I'm going there all righty, and they're going ta like it this time, too. Get in, Laurie."

"But aren't we going ta get a drink?"

"No, you've had enough drinks. I want a sober husband. Here,

I'll get in the backseat with you, and you can put your head down on my shoulder and go to sleep. You gotta get sober before we get home."

"Okay!" said Laurie, settling down with a sigh against the convenient shoulder. "I guesh mebbe you're right."

Chapter 20

Marigold had washed her face and removed the traces of tears, and she was quietly, soberly putting the kitchen in order that her hurried breakfast had left in wild confusion when she heard the knock at her door. Her heart contracted sickly, and for an instant she contemplated not answering it. Then she reflected that it was probably the paperboy come for his money, and she hurriedly picked up her purse and went to answer the knock.

But it was not the paperboy.

An elegantly attired, carefully groomed woman of uncertain age stood before her. The very shoes she wore showed that she gave great attention to her appearance.

She was dressed in a smart suit of wool in a flattering shade of wine color, a trim hat, and a coat of the same color as her suit. It was edged heavily with what Marigold at once recognized as an expensive grade of Persian lamb. There was a flash of some bright jewels at her throat.

Marigold had never seen her before. She gave a startled

glance at her face and noticed her expression of deep discontent. Yet there was something wistful, too, about her.

"You are Marigold Brooke, aren't you?" said the visitor, and her voice marked her at once as belonging to a social class of wealth and culture.

"Why yes," said Marigold, astonished, for she thought the woman had surely made a mistake in the address.

"Well, may I come in just a minute? I won't keep you long. There is something I feel I ought to tell you."

Of course, she must ask her in. She could not have Mrs. Waterman listening to everything that was said. Marigold could hear the door across the hall shut as she closed her own door. Mrs. Waterman was having a hard time satisfying her curiosity this afternoon.

"I am Miss Trescott, Laurie's aunt," said the caller, sitting down on the edge of the couch as if she didn't mean to stay but a minute.

Marigold gave her another startled look.

"I came to tell you that you mustn't marry Laurie on any account! He's my own nephew, and of course I love him, but he's nothing but a trifler, and he drinks like a fish. Three times this last year he's been in a hospital to get cured, and every time he comes out he goes right back to it. There wouldn't be anything but sorrow if you married Laurie."

"But I have no intention of marrying Laurie!" said Marigold, her face deadly white and her eyes wide with horror. "Oh, why does *any*body think I'm going to marry him, when we just went out occasionally together? But I've found out he drinks, and I'm done with him. I—we—I don't want ever to see him again!"

"Oh, I'm so relieved!" said Irene Trescott, sinking back on the couch. "You haven't any idea how I hated to come and tell you this. But I just couldn't bear to see you hurt, you're so—so—kind of lovely and sweet, and so different from most girls nowadays.

You're much too good for Laurie. He would break your heart and spoil your life. I had to warn you."

"Oh," said Marigold humbly, "I'm just a silly girl. I wasn't thinking about getting married. Laurie was nice and pleasant. I never realized that he drank. I might have tried to stop him if I had known. I don't think I've ever been very helpful to him or anyone else. You see, I was just having a good time. I wasn't considering getting married. I really wasn't!"

"You're rather wonderful," said the older woman. "I've been watching you for some time!"

"Why, I don't think I ever saw you before!" said Marigold, wide eyed.

"No, I don't suppose you did. But I saw you, out of windows, and once in a while in a shop. Eva Petrie has spoken of you, too, and once I saw you in the other room with Betty Lou when you didn't even know I was there. I was interested because I knew Laurie knew you. I wish Laurie had been the kind of boy who could have had you for his best friend. For a while I hoped that knowing you would make a difference in him and maybe he would turn out to be worthy of a girl like you after all. But lately he's been simply awful, and I thought I had to come and warn you. I couldn't have you hurt. But now since you know, I won't trouble you anymore. I know young people hate to have older people nosing into their affairs. But I'm glad you aren't heartbroken. Laurie is fatally attractive, of course."

"Yes, he is," said Marigold sadly.

"You're sure he hasn't broken your heart? You're sure he won't be coming around and persuading you to try him again? Because you mustn't trust him! You really can't! He's undependable and irresponsible. He'll love you today and another girl tomorrow, and he'll promise not to drink and go at it again the next minute. I'm grieved over it, but it's true."

"I know!" said Marigold quietly, calmness coming to her now

like a mantle. "I've seen him with other girls. I've seen him—recently—when he had been drinking."

She lifted brave eyes and looked at her caller.

"And that's why you've given him up?"

"Why, I don't know that I ever actually counted him mine before that to give up. But after I knew, he never *could* be mine."

"And you're not going around long faced and heartbroken? You're not feeling terribly bad about it?"

"Yes, I feel bad. I feel shocked and sorrowful that Laurie was like that and not the delightful friend I had counted him, but—well—lately—just lately, I've come to know the Lord Jesus better, and He's given me something deeper in my life. It's made all other things quite pale beside Him."

Marigold gave her testimony slowly, deliberately, with a hint of triumph in the lifting of her head and a radiance in her face. Irene Trescott looked at her with a great yearning in her own eyes.

"There!" she said suddenly. "You *have* got something that other people don't have! I've thought that for some time. I wish Laurie could have it. He might have been worthy of you. I wish *I* could have it!"

"Oh, you *can*!" said Marigold with sudden yearning to help this other soul. "I wish I had known more about it when I was seeing Laurie often. I wish I had told him about it. But I don't think I'll be seeing him anymore. You see, I haven't known all this so very long myself, not in this beautiful, personal way."

"Well, I wish you'd tell me about it sometime. I need something, goodness knows! I'm terribly unhappy, and I haven't even the consolation of drink. I've seen too much of the effects of it in other lives to take that way to drown my sorrows. But I'm bored to death, and I want something. If I come to you again sometime, will you tell me about what you have? Not now, for I've a dinner engagement tonight and I must be going. And next week I'm going south for a while. But when I get back, may I come and have a talk with you?"

"Oh yes," said Marigold, suddenly shy, "I'll be so glad if I can help you."

Irene Trescott looked at her earnestly for a moment and then suddenly stooped over and kissed her cheek.

"You're sweet!" she said. "Good-bye. I'll come and see you when I get back."

As she turned to go to the door, Marigold put out her hand.

"But you don't have to wait till you get back," she said. "You can go to Him tonight and tell Him all about it, and He'll take you. He's the Son of God, and He died to take your place, shed His blood to pay the penalty of your sins, and it only takes believing that to make you His. If you just kneel down tonight and tell Him you will, it can all be settled."

Irene Trescott studied the earnest face of the girl for a moment, and then she said, "Well, I'll see! Perhaps I will."

Then she was gone.

Chapter 21

Marigold stood there, stirred, wondering, thrilled to think she had been able to tell another soul how to be saved, filled with awe at the joy it gave her.

She went slowly back to the kitchen and began to put away the dishes she had washed, pondering on the strange happenings that had come to her during this week, though it seemed far more than a week when she thought of all that had happened. It almost seemed as if she had lived a lifetime in those few short days. She gave a little shiver as she remembered where she was last night at this time. Weary, she was now, so weary and heartsick over all that experience! And yet in just one day she seemed to have come so far away from it! Laurie was put out of her life as definitely and fully as if she had never known him!

Then it came over her how very tired and sleepy she was, how much she wanted to rest and not think any more about it. As soon as she had eaten something, she would go right to bed and get rested. She would not think at all about *anything*, just ask God to take care of her, and go to sleep.

But while she was getting a piece of toast and a cup of tea made, it suddenly came over her how strange it was that she should have had these two callers in one afternoon. Both relatives of Laurie's; one asking her, *begging* her to marry Laurie, and the other warning her not to. She put back her head and laughed at the irony of it all. And then she put down her head on her arms and shed a tear or two! Until the toast began to burn, and then she put aside her thoughts and tried to eat something.

She had only taken one bite, however, when there came another knock on the door, and this time a heavier one, not a woman's knock.

She laid down the toast and gave a frightened look out into the living room. Who had come now? Not any more of Laurie's relatives, surely. Not his father! *Oh, God! Help me! I'm so tired, and I'm all alone!*

For an instant she thought about keeping still and not going to the door. She could not stand any more that night. Then the knock was repeated, a little more insistently, and it occurred to her that maybe it was somebody from the library come to ask after her mother.

She went wearily over to the door, hoping it might be just the milkman for his money. She was so tired and hungry.

She took a deep breath of a sigh, braced herself for whatever might be waiting for her, and, putting out her hand, opened the door.

For an instant she couldn't believe her eyes, for there stood Ethan Bevan! Then the joy came sweeping down upon her, and she put out her hands, both hands, and her eyes gave him welcome, even more than she knew.

"Ethan!" she said gladly. "Oh Ethan! I've needed you so much!"

Suddenly, without the slightest warning, Ethan's arms went around her, and he gathered her close to his chest.

"I love you, my little dear love," murmured Ethan, bending down to lay his face on hers.

And Marigold came into his arms like a homing bird and rested, feeling such joy as she never knew was on earth.

Suddenly the bliss of the moment was rudely broken by the sound of eager footsteps hurrying toward the door of the room across the hall.

"Oh, quick! Shut the door!" giggled Marigold, lifting her rosy face from Ethan's tweed overcoat. "She thinks she has to oversee everything."

But Ethan had already reached out one hand and closed the door behind him and now gathered Marigold into his arms again and laid his lips upon hers.

"My darling!" he murmured. "My darling Marigold!" And Marigold felt that there could be no sweeter words on earth than those.

Now Ethan Bevan had by no means come to Philadelphia with any such denouement in view. All the way up as he sat in the train, he had been calling himself a fool for having come. Marigold might not want him, might put on her aloofness that she had worn that first day in Washington when she obviously resented his presence, might have some engagement, and he might be bringing about a very embarrassing situation.

Who was he, anyway, but a stranger? They had had a few pleasant talks, and he had been able to help her to understand some truths from the Bible, for which he was thankful, but he must not presume upon that!

He remembered the letter that had lain between them on the chair as they knelt to pray. That letter had troubled him a lot, ever since he went back to Washington, until he had to pray about it and ask the Lord to take it out of his mind. Marigold had a friend, whether wisely or not, a person who had been something to her, more or less, presumably more, and he, Ethan, should play no part in her life.

There might have been a break between them, it was true, but he had promised to pray for him—that had been rather understood between them he was sure, though the man had not been mentioned openly. Still, the woman across the hall had called him "your young man," and she had said that he took Marigold out often in his car. Ethan had been trying all the week to teach his heart not to give that sick thud whenever he thought of that remark. He had been trying to pray for the unknown young man as one whom Christ loved and who might also be loved by this girl. Yet all the while Marigold's face had come dancing before his vision with the wistful look in her eyes, or with the happy look when she had been enjoying something with him in Washington. And now and again, fight against it as he would, he kept remembering the thrill of her in his arms as he carried her down those stairs in the Capitol and felt her frightened face against his shoulder. He remembered the touch of her tears on his hand as he wiped them away at the foot of the stairs.

He had prided himself on keeping away from all women, on concentrating on his job and letting the world go by, on taking his joy in sharing the Gospel here and there where souls seemed to need it. And now here, after all his resolutions, he had fallen for a girl who belonged to someone else—or so it seemed—and he was just going to make a fool of himself like any other fool. Traipsing off to get her! Making an excuse to spend a few hours with her on the train, just because his soul had been hungering for a sight of her all this week!

So he had reasoned with himself, and he told himself that he must be very distant and reserved with her. Treat her like a younger sister; help her as a Christian brother! And not for anything in the world, not under *any* circumstances, let her suspect for an instant that he had the slightest interest in her, apart from her salvation and her Christian growth.

Having given himself a set of very severe rules for a young man calling upon a girl who was practically engaged to somebody else, having trembled in his soul as he drew nearer to her home, and having braced himself with commands like the laws of the Medes and Persians to guard his soul, he had marched up those stairs, and—taken her right in his arms before even the door was closed! A fine gentleman he was! And he didn't *care*! He was happier than he had ever been in his life. And before he said anything about it, or even questioned his soul, he bent above his dear Marigold and kissed her long and sweetly and thrilled to her lips as he had thrilled to the thought of her dear self all day, whenever he couldn't keep himself from thinking of her.

But after a little while, she dropped from the weariness of her joy, dropped in his arms, and looked up with such a beatific smile that his heart was strengthened to speak plainly.

"I didn't know," he said, "whether you belonged to someone else or not. I told myself that I must wait and see, that I must not let you know my heart till I found out. And here I have walked in and taken you by storm! Can you forgive me? For oh, I do love you!"

Marigold looked up and forgot all the weariness and perplexity of the hours that had gone before and smiled her joy into his face and heart.

"And I love you!" she said softly. "I think," said Marigold—and thought she spoke the sacred truth—"I think that I have loved you ever since I looked into your eyes!"

"You certainly didn't look it!" said Ethan suddenly and kissed her again. "I'm afraid you are a dear little liar, with it all, for I could swear you did anything but love me that first day you spent in Washington."

"Well, maybe I didn't know it yet," twinkled Marigold, "but in my heart I'm sure I did, because I feel as if I had been at home with you always."

"You dear!"

Then startlingly the little clock on the mantel chimed six, and simultaneously the two absorbed lovers realized that the room was full of the odor of burnt toast and had been for some time, only they hadn't noticed it until now.

Marigold switched off the toaster, and Ethan suddenly remembered why he had come up to Philadelphia.

"Is that all the dinner you were getting for yourself?" he asked. "Is that why your cheeks looked pale and thin when I came in? They don't look so now, I'll admit, but I'm afraid you haven't been taking very good care of yourself. Do you know what I came up here for, young lady?"

"I thought perhaps you came to tell me that you loved me," said Marigold in a very small, shy voice.

"Well, yes, that's why I *wanted* to come, but ostensibly I came to take you back to Washington, and we're starting in half an hour. Can you get ready that soon?"

"Oh, Ethan! Really? How wonderful! But—why, I'll have to make supper for us first."

"We'll eat on the train. That's what I'd planned, only I didn't take into account how you were going to come and take me right into your heart with a look, you precious! Swallow that tea, and then go and get your hat on. Because I don't want to keep the two mothers waiting too long. They're expecting us. What do you have to take along? Can't I pack it? Just a toothbrush and that green dress, perhaps. I like that."

"Oh!" said Marigold, laughing breathlessly and then rushed into action.

"Oh, you don't need to wash the dishes," said Ethan. "I'll

fix this kitchen to leave. You go get ready. Don't you know I've cooked at camp?"

He held the cup and plate under the spigot and mopped them with a towel that hung on the rack. He disconnected the toaster, turned out the gas stove, put the bread into the bread box, and fastened the windows.

"There," he called to Marigold, who was wildly flinging a few necessities into her suitcase and folding the green dress and the brown suit in a scandalous hurry, "I've fixed everything to leave! We'll let the lady across the hall do the rest."

Gloves, purse, hairbrush—Marigold was thinking over the absolute necessities, too happy to care whether she had them all or not.

Ethan telephoned for a taxi while Marigold rushed over to tap at Mrs. Waterman's door.

"Oh, Mrs. Waterman," she said eagerly, "Mother has sent a friend to bring me down to Washington again for the weekend. I'm leaving right away. Would you mind telling the milkman and the bread man I shan't need any till Monday? And—what's that? The telephone? Oh no, you needn't bother to answer it. There won't be anything important, I'm sure. Just let it ring!"

Then suddenly the telephone rang out as if in protest.

Marigold rushed back to answer it.

"Hello! Who? Oh, Miss Trescott! Yes?"

"I just thought I ought to tell you before you read it in the papers," said Irene Trescott earnestly, "Laurie escaped from the hospital this afternoon and went out and got married to that girl, that Lily Trevor, and he's bringing her home. Or rather, she's bringing him home. She just telephoned and said he was pretty drunk, but they were married, and she'd see that he was all right in a few days if they would just be patient till she got him in hand. I thought you ought to know. Good-bye. And, oh

Marigold! I hope your God will *bless you!*"

"The taxi is here, Marigold," called Ethan from down in the hall.

"Coming!" said Marigold happily, her voice like a sweet song as she hastily locked the door and flew down the stairs.

Chapter 22

Oh the bliss of that brief ride to the station in the quiet darkness of the taxi—Ethan's arm stealing around her and drawing her a little closer to him; her hand in Ethan's while the lights of the city flashed by, leaving no terror in her heart; Ethan's love around her like a garment. She felt almost crowned. They sat in sweet silence and let their gladness have its way in their hearts.

In the train at last, Ethan caring for her.

"We're going right into the diner," he said as he surrendered his coat to the porter of the Pullman and tossed his hat into the rack above their chairs. "You ought to have some dinner right away. I seem to feel that you're all in." He smiled tenderly down at her.

"Not anymore!" said Marigold, giving him a bright glance.

People were coming into the car now, chattering about which chairs were theirs. Marigold felt proud of her escort. It seemed so wonderful that this was to be her lot now, a companion like this for her lifetime, and not just for a single hour or two. Oh, God had been good to her!

"I like that hat!" said Ethan as he sat opposite her in the diner presently and looked across the table admiringly. "And that pretty red dress. And the fur coat. They all suit you wonderfully."

"It's a very old coat, and quite shabby," said Marigold, looking down at it ruefully. "But I didn't dare come without it in this cold weather."

"It doesn't look shabby. It looks homey, as if it belonged. When it wears out, I shall get you another just like it. It is wonderful on you, makes you look like a princess. It's going to be great to have someone to buy pretty things for."

"Oh!" said Marigold, pink cheeked and shining eyed at the preciousness of his words.

"Tomorrow," he said, "we're going to get the prettiest ring they have in Washington!" And then he grinned at the sweet confusion of her face.

Such a happy meal, Ethan ordering almost everything on the menu and insisting on her eating. Such joy! And only last night—!

Ethan saw the shadow cross her eyes.

"You're not sorry?" he asked anxiously.

"Oh no!" she said fervently, with such a look in her eyes that he was satisfied. "I was only thinking of some dreadful things that I've escaped." And she gave a little shiver at the thought. "There are a great many things I have to tell you. I've been having a pretty hard time since I went home—!"

"Well, we'll talk them over tomorrow and get them out of the way. But don't let's spoil tonight with any shadow. You are tired. Just forget all the hard things and be happy. We'll work everything out together after this, shall we?"

"That will be wonderful!" said Marigold. "Oh, God has been so good to me! You don't realize—!"

"Don't I? Well, perhaps you'd better let me tell you how good

I think He has been to me. You don't know how hard I worked on the way up here, trying to get you out of my thoughts, because I thought there was someone else ahead of me."

"I'd better tell you all about it right away," said Marigold with sudden resolve. "Then you'll know there's nothing to worry about."

"All right, if you feel you'd like to get it out of the way. But personally, since you've told me you love me, I'm trusting you all the way, and I'm not worrying about it anymore. If any other poor fish tries to barge in, I'll take him out and whale him. But eat your supper first."

So when they went back to the Pullman, Ethan turned their chairs so they could talk together quietly without being over-heard, and Marigold told the story of her acquaintance with Laurie Trescott. But she found it to be astonishingly short after all, for the things she had thought important seemed all too trivial to waste many words upon when Ethan was so near, look-ing so strong and dependable. So when she reached the account of her last night and her terrible ride, she found it did not take long. Ethan, watching her quietly, caught more of the picture from the little shudder she gave as she described her terror and from the sudden darkening of her eyes than from the words she used. He had no trouble in filling in where she left description unfinished. He could see just what kind of a weak, attractive, selfish creature Laurie was.

"Now I *know* I will whale that fellow sometime!" he exclaimed as she finished. "*Really* whale him, I mean!" he added vehemently.

"I don't believe you need to," said Marigold thoughtfully. "He's married a terrible little creature. Married while he was drunk! I expect life will give him all the whaling he needs now. That was what that telephone message was about just as we left the apartment. Didn't I tell you? That's why I was so long coming down. Miss Trescott phoned me. She thought I ought to know before it came out in the papers."

"Who is Miss Trescott, and what did she know about it?"

"Oh," said Marigold, laughing, "that is another story. I haven't told you about my two callers yet, and why I was so long opening the door for you. I was afraid you would be another member of the family come to plead with me."

Then she told him the whole story, and he listened, a big grin growing slowly on his nice, understanding face.

"So that's what I walked in on, is it?" he said when she had finished. And then he threw his head back and laughed so heartily that some of the bored passengers at the other end of the car looked over the tops of their evening papers and wondered what those two good-looking young people had found to laugh at that was so funny; looked enviously at them when they saw the joy in their faces and thought of their own youth and bright spots that had relieved the tedium of the way.

"Well, now that's out of the way," said Ethan, when they had laughed together over the two callers. "I still think I'll whale him sometime, though I might try to help him get saved, too. He certainly needs saving, and I guess you've got a commission toward that aunt of his, too, sometime. I'm glad you got in a word about the Way before she left. You might not get another chance, you know, and she was ready for it then. You may never know the result in this life, but perhaps she'll meet you over There! And now, I guess we're getting into the city. Shall I help you on with your coat?"

And there was the dome of the dear old Capitol looming on the night sky. But now it was no longer simply the seat of her country's government, but it stood also for the memory of a great love that had come to her there!

Marigold watched it for a minute with shining eyes. Then Ethan put her into her old fur coat and buttoned it up to her chin, giving her a loving smile and a little surreptitious pat on her shoulder, utterly aware of the eyes at the other end of the car watching the pretty romance in their two faces.

❀

"I think I hear a taxi," said Aunt Marian suddenly. "Did you turn the porch light on?"

"Yes. It's on."

"Shall I go down and open the door?" asked Marigold's mother eagerly.

"No, Ethan has a key."

So they sat quite still, knitting and dropping stitches irresponsibly, as if nothing out of the ordinary was about to happen, and it seemed that the next three minutes were unconscionably long.

Then came Ethan's glad voice booming up the stairs: "I brought her, folks! I told you I would!"

Something in his voice, perhaps, kept them very quiet, waiting for them to come.

They came slowly up the stairs, his arm around her and their hands clasped, and into the room that way, standing in the doorway, looking from one to the other.

"Well, Mothers, we've discovered that we love one another," said Ethan with an exultant voice. "Do you mind?"

❀

The anticlimax came the next week when Maggie arrived one day for work lugging a big pasteboard box.

"My girl, Viola May, is gonna be married next week," she announced, with a radiant face, "an I done bring her weddin' dress along ta show you-all."

"It's somethin' grand," she said as she untied the box. "We couldn't a bought it ourselves noways. One o' their company up ta the Trosset house give it to me for takin' home her laundry ta wash. She was a mighty hateful piece herself, awful high-an'-mighty, but I gotta give her credit for bein' real generous once. She said this dress was worth a heap mor'n the work I done for her, but she didn't want the dress no more. You see, she'd spilled some kinda wine all down the front. But I took yella soap an' a piece of an ole' turkey towel, and I just washed it out. Ain't nothin' like yella soap an' water ta get stains outta things, an' it don't show no more, only a dear little bit, but I figure ta take a stitch or two on them red floaters on the sash an' catch 'em down over the spot, so Viola May can get married in it. An' then it 'curred ta me, Miss Marigold, you-all could do them stitches so much better'n I could! Would you mind? I'd stay an hour extra an' clean that there bookcase in the livin' room if you would. See! Ain't it purty? Just like some heavenly robe! I never did see such a purty dress. Never thought my child would be married in a dress like that!"

Marigold unfolded the dress and shook it out. Marigold's grand white dress with the scarlet sash! Poor crumpled dress, its velvet streamers limp and dejected, its grandeur draggled and stained and dingy with one night's frivolity!

As Marigold bent over it to put in the few stitches Maggie asked, her heart was murmuring: *Father, I thank You that You didn't let me keep this dress!*

Mystery Flowers

Chapter 1

1930s

Diana Disston stood at the window watching for the postman. Before her the wide, velvety lawn sloped to the tall hedge, which hid the highway from view. A smooth graveled driveway circled the lawn and swept down to the arched gateway where a little stone cottage, formerly the porter's lodge, nestled among the trees. It was up that driveway the postman would come.

Beside her in the wide window, just between the parting of the delicate lace curtains, stood a little table bearing a tall crystal bud vase with three pink carnations. Their fragrance filled the room. The girl turned and looked at them whimsically, an almost tender light coming into her eyes, her lips parted in a wistful smile, reminding one of a child dreaming over a fairy tale. Suddenly she stopped and took a deep breath of their fragrance, closing her eyes, and half shyly touching her lips to their fringed petals then laying her cheek softly against their delicate coolness.

Then, laughing half ashamedly, she straightened up and took another look down the road. No postman yet! She glanced at the tall old clock in the hall beyond the arched doorway. It was fully five minutes beyond the time he usually came. Why should he be so late this particular morning when she wanted especially to know just how to plan for the day? There would surely be a letter. Or if there wasn't a letter, she would know her father would be at home in an hour.

If her father was coming, she wanted to dress and be ready to meet him. Perhaps he would suggest that she should go down to the office with him, and they would have lunch somewhere together. That was what he often did when he had had to be away for a day or two and leave her alone in the house with Maggie. Lately, though, he had always seemed so busy or so absent-minded when he got back from a business trip. She puckered her brows with the worry that had disturbed her more or less ever since he had been away. Somehow he didn't seem just as he had been after her mother's death. He had been so thoughtful of her, so almost tender in his treatment of her. He understood how desolate she was without her precious mother. And, of course, he was desolate, too! Dear Father! It must be terribly, terribly lonesome for him. Such a wonderful woman for his wife, and to lose her! But, of course, Father was reticent. He never said much about his own sorrow. He was just thoughtful for her.

And yet, what was this haunting thing that troubled her? Surely it could not be business cares that worried him, for when they had sold off such a large portion of the estate, dismissed a retinue of servants, cut off a good many unnecessary expenses, and even rented the little cottage at the gateway, he had told her that all his debts were paid and they had enough to live on quite comfortably for the rest of their lives, provided, of course, they did not go into any great extravagances for a few years while his business was picking up. Investments were doing well, and there was no reason for him to worry. He had given her a larger allowance and told her to get herself some new clothes. No, it could not be money.

And yet, was it really anything? Was it not perhaps merely her own imagination? She had been so close to him during the first intensity of her sorrow that now that he was getting back into his usual habits of life she had grown too sensitive. That was it, of course, and she simply must put it out of her mind. When he came, *if* he came this morning, she would not let herself think of such a thing. She would rush out and meet him as she always had done, and she would show him how glad she was to have him back again, but she would not let him suspect that she had been worried about anything. She was silly, of course, to allow imaginings to return and make her uneasy.

She turned her eyes once more to the flowers and touched them lightly with her hand. Sweet flowers! So mysterious and lovely! Coming in such a magical way. If she only knew who dropped them, one every morning in her path just where she went down the driveway to take her daily walk. And so fresh and perfect they were! Not old ones that had stood in a vase in a warm room. Not as if they had been thrown away after having been pinned to a coat. A single, perfect bloom lying in almost the same spot every morning! It couldn't have *happened*. Not three times just alike!

And if it had, if somebody had been carrying an armful of them and it could just happen three times that one slipped out and fell right in that spot, where would the person carrying them be coming from? Where would he—they—*she* be going? That driveway belonged to the Disston house, and nobody would have any business going down it every morning. Not since the butler was gone, and the other servants, and only Maggie in the house. Of course, there was the milkman and the grocery boy, but they always came in at the back entrance, never the front, and what would milkmen and grocery men be doing with pale pink carnations early in the morning? They certainly wouldn't be throwing them away one at a time, nor dropping them carelessly. Diana reasoned that young men who delivered milk and groceries would not have so many hothouse flowers that they would be careless about them, anyway, certainly not three days in succession. What could be the explanation of the mystery? Probably it had some quite commonplace explanation, but Diana dreamily touched the petals of the flowers again and smiled. She preferred to think there was some delightful romantic magic about it. And since an explanation seemed quite out of normal expectation, why not indulge her dreams? At least it would be fun to see whether a fourth carnation lay on the drive tomorrow. If it did, there would be a real mystery, and she would have to begin investigations. But perhaps it would stop at three times, and then she could just cherish her dreams and not worry herself by the troublesome suggestion of her conscience that perhaps she ought not to have picked them up. They had lain there in the drive, fresh and sweet, demanding to be rescued from a chance passing wheel, and just in the one spot she could not possibly see from the windows of the house, because a big clump of rhododendrons spread out gorgeously and hid the road.

Well, at least she could find out one thing. She could get up very early and see that no one went down the drive from the direction of the house. Or could she? Might not the flowers have been placed in the drive before dawn? Her eyes melted into the dreaminess of speculation.

If Father came this morning, perhaps she would tell him about the flowers. Would she? Or should she take them up to her room and wait to see if another would come tomorrow morning?

Then suddenly she saw the postman carrying a single letter in his hand that he had just taken out of his pack. She sprang to the door to meet him, her eager eyes on the letter. Oh, would he be coming this morning, or would she have to wait another day or two? She sighed at the thought of continued loneliness. And then as she took the letter, recognized the handwriting, and saw how unusually thick it was, her heart sank. He could not be coming or he would not have written so long a letter!

She flung an absent-minded smile at the postman in answer to his good morning and went in with the letter in her hand.

Diana was in a peculiarly lonely position just at present. Her mother had been dead only a little over a year, and for two years before that she had been more or less of an invalid. Diana had delighted to be with her constantly, as much as her school duties would allow. She had attended a nearby college for a couple of years until the invalid needed her more and more, and so, dropping out of her classes for what at the time had seemed to be only a temporary absence, she had dropped out of the lives of her young friends and become more or less of a recluse. After her mother's death she found herself left out of the youthful merriment of which she had been a part in her high school and early college days, and without a strong desire to enter it again.

It was not that she was too shy or gloomy, it was just that the precious last days of her companionship with her beloved mother had somehow set her apart from the little world where she had moved so happily when she was a child and a growing girl, and had made her more thoughtful, more particular, perhaps, about her friendships than she might have been without the refining experience of sorrow.

Oh, there were a few of her old companions who came dutifully out to call. Some of them had even tried to drag her back into young society again. Others had written her lovely notes and sent flowers, but somehow her place among them seemed gone. They were interested in new things—some of them were married, most of the rest engaged—chattering about social affairs in which she had no part and almost no interest, and she hadn't felt eager to follow them back.

Later their mothers had called, and there had been quite a good many invitations recently. Diana had accepted some of them and found a strange distaste for the life she had once so enjoyed. The conversation seemed to her vapid, the activities sometimes almost stupid, and the excesses in which some of her former companions now indulged did not tempt her. She found herself revolted at the way some of them talked; the way they drank at their parties, just as a matter of course; and the way so many of them spoke of sacred things, lightly, flippantly. Was she growing morbid, she wondered, or was this just growing up? Certainly her old friends had changed. Perhaps they had grown up and she had just stayed a little girl. But she was twenty, and she had become rather close with death and sorrow. Still death and sorrow were not meant to sour one on life, to make one a recluse. So, from day to day she had tried to reason it out and had forced herself to go more and more among her acquaintances.

There were several of her young men friends who had begun to come to the house of late, but none of them especially interested her. They were nice boys, she told herself, some of them were quite grown up and dependable. There were even a couple who did not drink—at least not much, just politely. But she had never thought seriously about any of them. She told herself that it would make little difference to her if they all stayed away, though she smiled whimsically as she said it and realized that she would probably feel forsaken if nobody ever came. It was a significant thing that in puzzling over the carnations she had never questioned if any of them could possibly have dropped those flowers in the drive for her. It was a thought that her mind rejected when it was first presented as a solution to the pleasant mystery. There were several who might have sent flowers formally, a whole box full, but not just a single blossom dropped on her pathway daily.

So Diana came in with her letter, intending to sit down by the window and read it. Then suddenly she wanted to take it to her room. Perhaps some premonition warned her that she would want to be uninterrupted as she read, would not even want Maggie coming in for the orders of the day. As she turned back toward the hall, she paused and picked up the crystal vase, carrying it with her up to her room.

She put the vase on a table in her own pretty room, a room whose windows looked out on the same sweep of lawn and drive and nestling cottage among the trees, where she had just been watching for the postman. She sat down beside the table to read her letter, but even as she tore the envelope open, again a premonition warned her. This was such a thick letter! Was he having to stay another week and leave her alone? Her heart sank. And then she began to read.

My dear daughter:

Somehow the words seemed more formal than his usual, "Dear Di," or "Dear little girl." How silly she was. It must be true that she was growing morbid! Then she read on.

*I have something to tell you which may surprise
you, and perhaps will even shock you a little at
first, but which I hope will prove in the end to be a
great happiness to you, as it is to me.*

Diana lifted frightened eyes and looked quickly around at the familiar beauty of her own room—the sweet room that her mother had planned for her before she went away—as if to reassure herself that nothing could hurt her, nothing destroy the home and the steady things of life that the years had built up around her. She gave a little gasp and closed her eyes as if she were afraid to read on then drew a deep breath, taking in the spicy perfume of the flowers before she went on with her letter.

> *I have had this in mind for some time, and several*
> *times have thought to tell you, but the way did not*
> *open and it seemed rather a delicate subject to talk*
> *about—*

Ah! Then there was something! There had been something that had worried him. It had not been her imagination after all! Oh, was it money, in spite of what he had said? Well, if it was money, she would just be thankful that it was nothing worse. Even if both of them had to go out and do hard manual labor and be very poor, she would not care. They would have each other. She drew another deep breath and tried to take courage as she read on.

> *And so I have thought it better to write it to you*
> *before I come home that you may get used to the*
> *thought of it and be ready to be glad with me—*

Her trembling hands suddenly dropped the letter into her lap, and she relaxed in her chair. Oh, would he never come to the point? Must there be this long preamble before she knew the worst? Yes, the *worst*! She felt sure now it was going to be something terrible, or else why would he not have enjoyed telling her face-to-face? Her eyes went back to the letter.

How words could stab! She felt she never would forget the sharpness of the pain that came as she read the next words.

> *It is just this, Diana, I am going to be married*
> *again. I hope it is going to be as happy a change*
> *for you as it is for me. I have felt for a long time*

that our loneliness had been too great to endure. I
am sure I have seen this in you also. Your mother
would never have wanted us to go on alone—

Alone! Did they not have each other?

Diana steadied herself tensely to take in this awful, cataclys-mic thought. Her father was going to put another woman in her mother's place! How could he? Oh, how could he!

This *couldn't* be true! She was dreaming!

Her eyes wildly sought the letter again to extract some word of hope somewhere from what yet remained to be read.

And so, Diana, I am doing what I feel is best
both for you and for me. And now, you needn't
get excited and think I am trying to make you
accept a stranger in place of your mother, because
the best part of this is that the woman who has
honored me by promising to be my wife is more
nearly your companion than mine. She is only a
very little older than you are, and will therefore, I
hope, be most congenial to you. And we shall have a
delightful home together. I am sure that you will be
glad that she is not a stranger to you—

Diana wildly began to go over the list of their acquaintances, rejecting each one as impossible, while she swept the sudden tears away that blinded her eyes so that she could not read the rest. Then, desperately she read on.

In a sense she really belongs to us because there is a
distant relationship, though very distant, of course,
and that only by marriage. I am marrying your
mother's cousin, Helen Atherton, my dear, and I

> *hope you will rejoice with me and make her most*
> *welcome in our home and life, and that we shall all*
> *be very happy together—*

But suddenly the letter dropped from Diana's nerveless fingers and she gave a terrible, wild little cry, the tears pouring down in a torrent!

"Cousin Helen! Oh, *not* Cousin Helen!" she gasped aloud in quivering sobs, shuddering as she wept. "Oh, he can't, he *can't*—he *wouldn't* do that! My f–f–father—w–w–would–n't—do *thha–at*!"

The great house was still and only echoed back her piteous cries hollowly. Suddenly she was aware how empty the home had become—and how *dear* it was! And now her father was going to destroy this home for her forever, destroy it so fully that she would not even want to think of it or its pleasant memories because it would be so desecrated!

She staggered to her bedside and dropped down upon her knees. Not that she was thinking to pray, only that she must weep out her horror over this new calamity that had befallen her.

Kneeling there and weeping in her first abandoned grief, she seemed hardly to be able to think. "Oh, God!" she cried again and again, until it seemed that God must be there somewhere listening, though she hadn't been conscious of Him before. Yet it seemed somehow to comfort her to think that perhaps God might listen to her trouble.

There were no words in her frenzy, but scene after scene in her girlhood in which this cousin Helen had figured went whirling through her mind, as if she were presenting pictures of what happened for God to see and remember, to remind Him how unbearable a situation it would be with Cousin Helen in her mother's place.

"Oh, Father doesn't understand!" she sobbed out. "He never knew how hateful she was!"

Instance after instance of unfortunate contact unfolded before her frightened brain, beginning with little things in her childhood, too petty perhaps to notice now, since they were both grown up. She had been only a baby when Cousin Helen took her precious best doll and singed her hair all off with her curling iron. It had been a desecration of something precious to the little girl. But the fourteen-year-old cousin had laughed impishly and flung the doll aside, breaking its lovely face, and then had run away laughing.

Diana, even in the midst of her weeping, recognized that it would not be fair to judge the woman by an act of a partly grown girl. But there had been so many ugly things. Every time she had come to visit, each day had been full of trial and torture to the finely strung child.

There was the time she hid Diana's essay that she was to have read in school that afternoon. She let the whole household search for it frantically, and Diana finally had to go and read from scraps of paper on which it had been written, only to find the neat manuscript lying on her desk on her return from school with a placard beside it scrawled in Helen's most arrogant handwriting, "April Fool!" Diana had been fourteen then, and Cousin Helen old enough to know better. Cousin Helen had left for home that morning before Diana got back from school. Diana's father had taken her into the city to the train. He had missed the whole excitement about the essay. Perhaps no one had ever told him the outcome. So he didn't understand. Diana's wild thoughts glided over dozens of other unhappy times when Cousin Helen had cheerfully, almost demoniacally, committed some selfish depredation upon something Diana counted precious.

There was the affair of the green taffeta dress, Diana's first real party dress. How her mother and she had delighted in it, selecting the smooth, shimmering silk with care, having it made in the style most becoming to her slender form; how happy she had been when she tried it on the last time before the party. Mother loved it so, and she felt as she looked at herself in Mother's long mirror as if she were a child in a fairy tale. A great part of the anticipation of that party had been in the thought of the lovely dress she was to wear, her first really long dress.

And then Cousin Helen had arrived! On the very morning of the party day she had arrived. She had a way of arriving at inopportune times like that, and it always annoyed Mother. Though Mother never had said a word about it, Diana somehow knew that Mother did not enjoy Cousin Helen's visits. She wondered now—was it—could it have been that Cousin Helen so often absorbed Father's time and interest when she happened to have no other admirer near? Somehow Diana's eyes were being opened quickly to several things that had happened in the past.

But not even Cousin Helen's advent had quite dimmed the thought of that wonderful party. And so the day had slipped by in glad anticipation until it was time to dress.

Cousin Helen had gone upstairs immediately after dinner, telling them someone was coming to take her to the country club that evening for a party. She had been dressed for evening when she came down to dinner, but while Diana was in her mother's room getting something done to her hair that only Mother could rightly do, Cousin Helen had suddenly appeared in the doorway with a rustle and called out nonchalantly, "Well, folks, how do you like me? Don't I look delicious? I found this up in a closet and liked it so much better than my own that I put it on. Hope you don't mind!"

And there stood Cousin Helen in Diana's lovely green taffeta party dress, smiling impishly, her eyes showing that she had full knowledge of the confusion she was occasioning.

Diana remembered her own indignation, how she had cried out in horror: "Oh, that's my party dress! I'm going to wear it to a party tonight! You can't wear that, Cousin Helen!"

And Mother had turned quickly, the brush in her hand, and protested firmly: "I'm sorry, Helen, but you couldn't wear that—"

And Cousin Helen had just given a laugh, whirled around, and flung back: "Sorry, kitten, it's too late now. You'll have to wear something else. My boyfriend is downstairs waiting for me! Ta-ta!" and was halfway down the stairs before they could get to the door.

Mother had followed her indignantly to the head of the stairs and called down sharply, "Helen! Come back here! You *can't do* that! You really *can't*!"

But Helen only laughed and called back, "Can't I? See if I can't!" and went out the front door, slamming it after her. They could hear the sound of a motor starting before they fully comprehended what had happened. That was Cousin Helen! And Father was going to marry her!

There had been other depredations as she grew older, acts utterly disloyal to her family when she was their guest, borrowings from others, unasked, of things far more important than dresses. Diana recalled dimly discussions between her father and mother concerning intense flirtations with other women's husbands in which Cousin Helen had utterly alienated some of Mother's best friends because of her calm way of taking possession of their husbands.

Diana suddenly remembered that, most unaccountably, Father had always taken Cousin Helen's part in these discussions. He said she was only a kid and was "a cute little piece" and "a pretty child," and insisted that she had no idea she was doing anything to hurt anybody. Insisted that she was entirely guileless and only having a good time.

Even in the matter of the green taffeta he hadn't been able to see that there was anything more than an innocent prank.

"What's one dress?" he said amusedly. "Let Diana wear something else. She has plenty of clothes, hasn't she?" They couldn't seem to make him understand that she hadn't any real party dress that would be suitable for the occasion. That this had been her first really grown-up dress, and it had meant so much to her. He had smoothed her head caressingly when she had dissolved in tears and refused to go to the party at all and told her she was silly to stay at home just because she couldn't wear a certain dress. Also he had insisted that nothing should be said to Cousin Helen.

Even when Cousin Helen came home with a tear in one of the taffeta ruffles and a large spot on the front of the skirt where she had spilled ice cream, and no apology by a laugh, Father dismissed the whole matter as a trifle. Oh, had Cousin Helen even then begun to get her hands on dear Father to pull the wool over his eyes? She had that faculty whenever she chose to use it. She had never bothered to do it with Mother and herself.

There had been many times later when Cousin Helen had demanded a great deal of Father's attention. And it was all done so prettily. Father was always gallant to every woman, though he had ever been most devoted to Diana's mother. But the girl remembered now those evenings when Helen had dragged Father off to an entertainment she was bent on seeing. Diana more than once on such an occasion found her mother in her darkened room in tears. Mother said she had a headache, or something of the sort. But now Diana began to have a feeling that Cousin Helen had a lot to do with those headaches. Helen would steal a man's heart as easily as she would borrow a party dress!

And Father hadn't realized it. No, Father wasn't one of those men who enjoyed going off with other women, no matter how pretty and young they were. Father loved Mother deeply always. But now that Mother was gone—! Oh—! And now Helen made him think he ought to marry her! Oh, he mustn't! He *mustn't*! She must stop it somehow! She must save him from Cousin Helen! He didn't know! He didn't realize! She must do something about it at once. Even if she had to tell him all the little, silly, annoying

things from her childhood up, she must make him understand
what a calamity it would be if he married Cousin Helen!

She picked up the letter again and began to read once more.
She must find out if he was coming home that morning.

So she read on.

> We are to be married at once and will come right
> home for a few days before we go on a wedding
> trip. Helen feels that there are changes she will
> want made in the house and those could be made
> while we are absent—different furnishings and
> decorations. But I am writing to you now to make
> a few suggestions about our homecoming. You will
> want to have a nice dinner ready, of course, and the
> rooms in order. Perhaps Maggie will want some
> help about special cleaning. You will know how to
> look after that.
>
> But there are a few little things that you can
> do for me before I get there. Please go through my
> room and take away anything you feel might be
> annoying to Helen. Your mother's picture and any
> little things that were especially hers. Just put them
> away out of sight. You have nice tact, and I'm sure
> you will understand what to do. Helen has a very
> sensitive nature, you know, and might feel it if
> anything were left around to remind her of the
> past.
>
> Helen seems to think you would rather not
> be present at the wedding, and being a woman,
> of course, she probably knows how you would feel
> about that, so I will not suggest that you come. In
> fact, by the time this letter reaches you it would
> be too late for you to start. But I am sure you will
> understand that I have refrained wholly for your

> *sake from asking that you come. And, of course,*
> *when we get home, we'll all have good times*
> *together—!*

Diana caught her breath in a great sob. Good times! Would there ever be any good times again? A panic seized her! She must get in touch with her father right away! She must not waste another minute. She must somehow stop this terrible catastrophe that was about to happen to herself and her father!

She glanced at the letterhead to get the name of the hotel at which he was staying and hurried to the telephone. Oh, would he be there? Would she be able to talk to him if he were? What should she say? How should she begin?

Chapter 2

It was two full hours before Mr. Disston was finally located in the distant city hotel to which she telephoned, and Diana spent those two hours alternately walking the floor in desperation and flinging herself on her bed to weep her heart out, then springing up again to listen for the telephone.

During that two hours, every tantalizing deed of Cousin Helen Atherton's came back in vivid form to torture her imagination. When she finally heard her father's beloved voice over the telephone she was almost too worked up to speak.

"Oh, Father!" she cried with a great sob in her voice. "Don't, *don't* do this dreadful thing! Don't marry that terrible woman!"

"Why, Diana!" said her father sternly. "You don't realize what you are saying!"

"Yes, I do, I do! Oh, Father, I *do*! She is *terrible*! You don't know! We never told you everything. We thought it would annoy you. But Mother almost hated her. I'm sure she did!"

"Stop!" said Diana's father in a tone she never had heard

him use to her since she was a little child and had been guilty of extreme naughtiness. "Diana, I cannot believe my senses! To think that you should speak such words! To think that you should charge your lovely, sweet mother with ever having hated anybody, much less one who has often been an honored guest in our home!"

"Oh, Father! You do not understand. Helen is deceitful! She does the meanest, most underhanded things and just laughs, and you have to stand whatever she does! She doesn't care how she hurts you! She doesn't care what she ruins or how she spoils other people's plans! She often made Mother cry. And she used to take my things and wear my clothes without even asking if she might, and—"

"Oh, now, Diana," said her father in a soothing voice, "you have gotten yourself all excited over the memory of some of those childish things that happened when Helen was a mere child herself. You can't forget that foolish party dress! I know that was a little hard for you to bear, but you were a mere baby yourself, and, of course, you must realize that she is grown up now. I didn't think you had it in your sweet nature to hold a grudge so long about such a trifling thing as a dress. Of course, I expected you to be a little surprised, perhaps even somewhat startled. But I never dreamed that you would allow your lips to utter such bitter words about another fellow creature, let alone the woman you know your father is going to marry—"

But Diana's spirit was goaded again into a frenzy. "That's it, Father! You *mustn't* marry her! Oh Father, *Fath*-er, *please* don't do it! Anyway, wait until you can come home and let me tell you all about her. It isn't alone for my sake I'm asking this. It's for yours. If you knew how hateful she can be you wouldn't *want* to marry her! Why, Father dear, even before Mother was gone she tried to get you away from Mother!"

"*Diana!*" Her father's voice was angry now. "Don't attempt to say another word to me! You are beside yourself! I certainly did not foresee any such demonstration as this or I should have prepared you beforehand for what I have been contemplating for some time. I am sure when you get by yourself and have a chance to think over what you have said you will be ashamed of yourself and be quite ready to apologize. In the meantime, it is not good to talk about these things over the telephone. We won't say any more about it! Just please remember, when you come to your senses, what I have asked you to do, and if I do not find it done, and well done, as I know you *can* do it, I shall consider that you have given me a personal affront. You know, Diana, I am really making this move partly for your sake, that you may have a richer, fuller life, and it ill becomes you to carry on like this even for the first few minutes until you get used to the idea. Now, child, just go and calm yourself, do the things I have asked of you, and let us say no more about it. Certainly not over the telephone!"

"But, Father—!" Diana's voice was full of desperation. "I must talk to you. I *must* tell you something—Father, *dear*! *Won't* you come home even for a few minutes? Won't you take the next train and come to me quick? I *must* see you!"

Her father's voice was cold and displeased as he answered. It made her shiver to listen to him. "That is quite impossible, Diana! My plans are made, and I have no time to take the long journey home just now. Be sensible and forget your former little jealousies and prejudices. Believe me, we are going to have a very happy time now if you do your part."

"No! *No!*" protested Diana, the tears raining down her cheeks. "No, Father! I could never stay here in this home if you brought Helen here. I *couldn't*! And she would not want me! You'll find out! Oh Daddy, Daddy! Don't do this!"

"Diana, would you want your father to be lonely the rest of his life?" came the question after a brief pause. His tone was almost placating, gentle.

"Daddy, you wouldn't be any more lonesome than I would. We

would have each other." The tone was very sweet and pleading.

"But, little Di, you don't realize that pretty soon you'll be getting married yourself, and then where would I be?"

Diana recognized Helen's fine strategy in that argument.

"I? Getting married? Who would I marry, Daddy? There isn't anybody in the world I would rather be with than you. There isn't anybody I care for. I'll promise *never* to get married if you won't. I'll stay with you always. And we'll have such a happy home!"

The man's voice was sharp with almost a hint of sudden pain as he replied. "Diana, stop this nonsense. Get hold of your self-control and put these wild opinions out of your mind. You think you won't get married now, but you don't realize that such ideas change—"

"Oh, Father! *Father!*" sobbed Diana, feeling the utter futility of what she was trying to do. "Please don't marry her. If you must marry somebody, get somebody else, not *Helen*. I know Mother would tell you so if she were here."

"That's enough, Diana!" said the father angrily. "Your mother would be the first one to advise me to marry. In fact, we talked about that once. She did not want me to be lonely—"

"But not Helen! Oh, not Helen, Father *dear*!"

"It is time to end this discussion," said the father sternly. "I am marrying Helen tomorrow, and we'll be home the next evening for dinner. By that time I hope you will have some control over your silly feelings and be ready to meet us in the proper manner as a true daughter should do. Till then, *good-bye!*"

The receiver hung up with a click, and Diana felt her heart sinking down, down, until it seemed that she could not stand up any longer. Slowly she hung up her receiver and sank down in a chair, feeling as if the worst thing that life could ever bring had happened to her. Her own father, speaking to her in that tone! Utterly refusing to hear her pleading! Determined to bring in this separating element into their lives! It seemed too horrible to be true. Her young, frightened spirit fought and struggled within itself, rebelling utterly against what had happened.

Suddenly she heard the sound of the dining room door opening from the butler's pantry, and she knew Maggie must be coming. Swiftly, silently she rose and flew up the stairs. She did not want Maggie asking her questions. Not yet. She would have to tell her, of course, if this awful thing were really true, but not yet—not until—well, at least until she could think it out and get some degree of composure. Not until she had given her father time to think over how cruel he had been. Not until there was no more chance that he would call her up again and say he would come home and talk it over. Oh, something, *something* would surely happen to change the terrible fear into calm and peace again. It could not be that such a horrible happening could come to her, Diana Disston! It had been so hard to lose her mother, to try to get along for life with Mother gone. She had thought that she would never be able to take an interest in life again after her mother was gone. She thought that she had suffered the ultimate sorrow when death came; but now she saw there was something infinitely worse than death, and her young heart gazed into her future appalled.

But a peremptory tap on the door interrupted her sorrowful meditations. Maggie announced that the milkman had come for his money. "And what's for dinner the night, Miss Diana? We'll need ta be gettin' the orders, especially if your father is comin' the day."

Diana suddenly revived from her seclusion, summoned the self-control that had been the habit of her life before others, and answered, though with a somewhat shaky voice: "Yes, Maggie, I'll give you the money. Just a minute. And I'll be down very soon about the orders."

Maggie was a canny woman. She heard the shaky voice, and she peered keenly at Diana as the girl opened the door a crack to hand out the money.

"You'd best come at once," she said shortly. "We'll not get the best cuts o' the meat if we don't get our orders in soon."

"All right," said Diana, drawing a deep breath and trying to sound cheerful. She went to the washstand and dashed cold water over her face to erase the signs of tears.

In a few minutes she was downstairs trying to wear a nonchalant air, but the canny old servant saw through her subterfuge.

"Father won't be home today." Diana spoke slowly, steadily, as if she were addressing her own soul. "He—won't be here till—Wednesday night—!"

But suddenly her lip quivered, and without warning the tears brimmed over and rolled down her cheeks. She turned instantly away from the room and stared hard out the window, trying to hide her tears from Maggie. But it was too late. Maggie had known her since she was a child. She could not be deceived when something was troubling her bairn.

"There, there, child!" she said in sudden tenderness. "You're not ta grieve because of a couppla days. The day and the day's day will pass that quick you'll not meet it before it's gone."

But the sound of sympathy completely broke Diana's self-control, and she put her head down on the window seat and gave herself over to weeping for the moment. Then suddenly she gained control again and raised her head, fiercely brushing away the tears.

"Oh, but Maggie, you don't know the half," she said with a long, shuddering sob that shook her whole young frame. "Father's going to be married again, Maggie!"

There was an ominous silence while Maggie took in this new disaster, and a view of her kindly old face would have shown a number of emotions chasing themselves across her countenance like clouds and storm and sunshine across a summer sky. Storm first—a fury of angry clouds that the father of a girl like this and the husband of the wife he had married could be willing to put another in his dead wife's place; compassion for the girl; then a search for comfort, for sunshine in the dark view.

"Aw, but perhaps it won't be so bad, my bonnie dear!" she said pitifully. "Perhaps he'll bring you a nice, good woman who'll mother you and make it homelike again. Don't take it so hard, my dearie. Your father's a good man. Seems like he would pick a good woman. Look who he picked the first time!"

Maggie ventured a cheery little rising inflection to her voice. But the girl shook her head.

"No, Maggie, that's the worst of it. He won't. Maggie, it's Cousin Helen Atherton!"

Maggie's blue eyes blazed at Diana in amazement, and her cheeks flamed redder than their usual apple red.

"That hussy!" she exclaimed, her eyes beginning to snap. "You can't mean it, Miss Diana! Your father wouldn't do the like o' that to you!"

"It's not his fault!" sobbed Diana. "I know it's not his fault. He doesn't understand! He just doesn't know what she's like. Helen never did those horrid things when Father was around!"

Maggie's eyes held inscrutable thoughts, and her thin lips were pursed incredulously.

"Mebbe not!" she said in a noncommittal tone, though her eyes belied her tone. "Aw, but these men is that stupid when it comes ta judgin' a pretty woman, especially if she has a bright way with her and knows how ta work her eyes. Ah! But the poor man'll rue the day he ever saw her if he ties up ta that hussy! You no think you can try ta tell him, my lamb?"

"Oh, I have, I *have*, Maggie! I've just been talking to him over the telephone. I've begged him to come home and let me tell him everything, Maggie, and he was really very displeased with me. And oh, I don't know what to do!"

Maggie suddenly came over to the girl like a little protective hen, every feather bristling, to guard a chick, and laid a work-roughened hand on Diana's bright bowed head.

"There, there! You poor little lamb!" she crooned gently.

Diana suddenly turned and flung her arms around the servant's neck and put her face on her shoulder, weeping with all her might. For a moment the Scotch woman held her in her arms, her own tears falling upon the girl's head.

"There, there!" crooned the woman, patting the heaving shoulders gently. "Mebbe it won't be so bad as you think! Mebbe your father'll be able to manage her rampaging ways when he gets to know what she is!"

"No," said Diana sadly, "he won't find out." There was a hopeless ring to her voice. "You know what she is, Maggie. You know how she'll go about it. She'll tell him everything in her own way and make it appear that it is all my fault. She always did that, and now I won't have a chance in the world to make him see the truth. She's begun to pull the wool over his eyes already. She's told him I wouldn't want to be at the wedding!"

"The hussy!" breathed Maggie under her breath. "She would! But he'll find out, poor man! Give him time an' he'll see what a mistake he's made!"

"But that'll be too late!" wailed Diana.

"Mebbe not. Mebbe you won't find things so hard. You must just stand up for your rights, child, and not let her get the upper hand. Remember, you're a woman grown now!"

"But I haven't any rights here now, Maggie," said the little stricken voice of the girl. "She'll be the mistress here!"

"You've the rights of the daughter of the house!" said the servant grimly. "You mustn't forget that. You'll have to let her see that you don't mean to give up your rights as a daughter in this house. You've a right to the same place you had when your own mother was alive!"

"But I couldn't stay here, Maggie! Not with her! You know

life would be unbearable! You know what she does to everybody around her!"

"Would you let a thing like her bein' here drive you out of your own home, Miss Diana? I'm surprised at the way you're talkin'. You was here first, an' it's here you belong!"

Diana shook her head and lifted a hopeless, tear-stained face.

"You know I won't be long when she gets here, Maggie. You know what she'll do, what she always has done, just put me in the wrong at every turn. No, Maggie, I'll have to go. It's probably what she has planned."

"Aw, my lamb! I can't think that! You'll mebbe make out ta get along for a wee bit while till something turns. And you'll be gettin' married soon an' have a home of your own, you know. She can't touch you then!"

"Married!" said Diana bitterly. "Who would I marry? I don't want to marry anyone, and no one wants to marry me!"

"Don't be so sure, child!" said the woman, trying to speak brightly. "There's many a lad would be glad to if you'd give him half a chance. There's that young Tommy Watrous that's been comin' of late; what's the matter of him? He's well fixed, and what would he come for if he's not thinkin' of askin' you, my lamb?"

"Oh, Maggie!" cried Diana with a little shiver of dislike. "He's got a mouth like a fish! Would you want to wish any such fate on me as to marry him?"

"Well, child, he's not the only one. There's young Arthur McWade. I hear he's doin' very well in the law, an' he certainly is a fine, upstanding man. He 'minds me of your father sometimes, he's that grave and quiet."

"Yes," said Diana with asperity, "he's like an old man, and he's awfully set in his ways."

"But mebbe it's a good way, child, and he seems dependable. But then there's that Bobby Watkins. He seemed that disappointed when you weren't home last week. They do say he'll inherit his uncle's estate, and there's none better in these parts. He's that cheerful and witty, you must admit that, dear child."

Diana turned wearily away. "Oh, don't let's talk about marrying now, Maggie; I'm not wanting to get married. Not now, anyway. Marrying makes a lot of trouble. Oh, Maggie! How can I bear it?"

But suddenly the grocery boy arrived at the kitchen door with an order that had been given the day before, and Maggie had to answer his knock. Diana made a quick escape up the back stairs to her room again, and Maggie wisely left her alone for a little while.

But the interval, and the opportunity to speak her heart to another human being, had helped Diana so that she could face her immediate problems more sanely. And there was her father's request about putting away her mother's things! She must attend to it at once and get it over. It would be the hardest thing she had to do. She turned with swift steps and crossed the hall to her father's room, the room that had been her mother's also through all the years. How terrible it was going to be to have Cousin Helen have the right to be there in her mother's place! Her heart contracted with a sickening thud as she stood in the doorway looking across at the lovely portrait of her mother by Sargent that her father had had hung there where he could look at it in his first waking moments.

And now he was willing to have it stored away out of sight! Oh, what had Cousin Helen been able to do with him already! Ah, she would wind him around her slender little finger and give that amused smile to his tortured daughter, and that would be all!

Diana went and stood beneath the portrait and looked up into the calm, serene eyes.

"Oh Mother, Mother, *Mother*," she sobbed softly. "Do you know what is happening to Father and me? Do you *know*? And don't you care anymore? Is everything so wonderful where you are now that you don't care anymore? Or perhaps in heaven you can see so much more and understand so much more widely than we do down here that it doesn't seem as dreadful to you as it does to me. Oh, but Mother, I know you understand how I feel—"

Diana raised her arms and lifted the frame from its hanging, holding it close in her arms and looking into the painted eyes with tender yearning, her own brimming over until the tears splashed down the length of the portrait. She laid the painting down upon the bed and tenderly dabbed the tears away from it, as if their saltiness had been a desecration.

Then came the pain of the thought of putting the picture away out of sight. Must she? How could her father be willing to put her precious mother's picture away out of his room and his life, that picture of which he had been so proud, which had seemed to be such a comfort to him in the early days of his bereavement? But then, what should make him willing to bring another—and such another—into his beloved's place? Well, it was all a terrible mystery that she could not solve.

She wondered if she dared to hang the picture in her own room. How she would love to have it there, and very likely her father would love to have it there, also. It was the natural place for it now, of course. Then suddenly there came a rush of memories. The broken doll; a fragile cup lying in fragments on the hearth where Helen had thrown it in pettishness because she had spilled some of its contents on her hand and scalded it; a precious book that her mother treasured and loved to read, slashed from start to finish, every page disfigured, and Helen's only explanation: "Because I didn't like it! Because it was a silly book. It was too goody-goody!"

In sudden terror, Diana took the picture in her arms once more and carried it to her own room. If she should leave that picture around and Helen should take a dislike to it she would not hesitate to take a carving knife and slash its painted canvas as she had done the pages of her Mother's devotional book. Diana's face grew hard. Her eyes flashed. That should never happen! She would do something with the picture to make it safe.

Swiftly she went to work, laying a sheet of cardboard from among her drawing materials over the painted surface, soft cotton above that, and then wrapping the whole thing in a big old quilt and tying it securely. And where should she hide it that it could not be found? She pondered the question anxiously as she went back to the big pleasant room across the hall that had been her father and mother's all her young life. How empty it looked now with Mother's picture gone. The blank space on the wall seemed to reproach her as she entered and looked around, bringing bitter tears to her eyes again.

But there was need that she act quickly. There was much to be done, and now her work began to assume proportions that she had not realized at first.

She hid the picture back in the dark end of her closet with garment bags hanging in front of it. That would do for the present, though she was by no means satisfied with its safety. Then she went to work in good earnest, gathering out the precious things from her father's room until she was satisfied there was not a thing left to remind of her mother. She was standing in the doorway surveying the finished work. There was not even an embroidered bureau scarf nor a delicate satin pincushion to speak of the former occupant. Then suddenly she was aware of Maggie standing grimly behind her in the hall holding a broom and a dustcloth in her hands.

"I'll just finish redding up now," she said with an air of authority. "You get you to your room and rest yourself awhile."

Maggie's sandy eyelashes were wet with recently shed tears, and her lips were set thinly, defiantly, but she would do her duty to the end.

Diana turned with a start.

"Oh, thank you, Maggie," she said wearily, "that will help a lot. But I can't lie down now, I've a lot to do. I've other things to—" she hesitated ashamedly and added, "put away."

"Yes," assented Maggie, "you can't be too careful. Mind your mother's pearls! And her brooch! The diamond brooch."

Diana gave her a startled look.

"Oh!" she gasped sorrowfully. "Yes, of course. I hadn't thought."

"She'll be after the pearls," the old servant commented sagaciously. "I mind her coaxin' your mommy once ta let her wear 'em."

"She never did let her have them?" Diana asked the question half fearfully, as if she would discover a precedent that might give her courage.

"Not she!" said Maggie. "She knew her well, that Helen. The pearls would never have come back if she'd once got her hand on them."

Diana hurried away and hunted up a little chamois jewel bag in which she deposited the precious jewels, strung it on a slender chain around her neck, and dropped it inside her dress. Then with a light of battle in her eyes, she went through the house to cull out and gather into safety all precious things for which she feared.

There were a few fine paintings that had been her mother's delight, small ones done by good artists. There were some bits of statuary, a few pieces of carved ivory and crystal. They were curios associated especially with her mother. Her father would not think of them nor notice their absence if they were gone, but they might incite the new mistress of the house to destroy them if she at all suspected that they were precious to either Diana or her mother.

When Diana was through with her work the house bore a bare, severe air as if all feminine trifles were done away with forever. She stared around in dismay. How was she going to live with so much gone that had made a great part of the background of her childhood's home? And yet, they were only trifles she was carrying away, just a small basket full of pretty trifles.

Then she went to the dining room and linen closet and gathered out all the articles that were monogrammed with her mother's initials. A great deal of the silver, too, that was marked with her mother's maiden name. Mother had always said they were to be hers. So she carried them, a basket at a time, up to the attic and packed them carefully away in an old haircloth trunk, with a pile of old magazines on the top, and shoved it back under the eaves with plenty of things in front of it. At least for a few days Helen would not go searching, and it was safe there until she could talk with her father and find out his wish in the matter. Still, as she thought over each article she had packed, nearly everything really belonged to herself if she cared to claim it. She had a right to put the things where they would not be seen, a right even to take them out of the house if it became necessary.

The idea crossed her mind that she might even take a small room in a storage house and have some of her own things taken there if she found Helen was likely to make trouble. And yet, could she do that after the new mistress had once arrived?

Puzzled, troubled, weary, and perplexed, she worked, stopping for a sketchy lunch at Maggie's most earnest insistence and then back to work again.

When she went to her room after a brief meal, which Maggie described as dinner, she looked around at her own little haven with a sense of coming to a refuge. This room, at least, was her own. Here she had her things around her and here she could live her life perhaps, if she could once induce Helen to let her alone. She would try it, at least. She couldn't go away and leave her dear father. For his sake she must stay. She must endure it somehow.

She looked around miserably on her own precious things. She would have to keep her door locked, she supposed. She couldn't call a thing her own unless she did, not if Helen took a fancy to it!

The leaden horror of what had befallen her settled down upon her young soul unbearably. The tears fell once more. She was standing by her table where the little crystal vase containing the flowers stood. Their delicate color seemed to stand out in the shadows of the room and lean toward her as if to comfort her, and with sudden impulse she bent over them and laid her tear-wet face against them, her lips on their petals, her burning eyes half closed and brushing across them, their fragrance drenched with her tears. And suddenly, startlingly, they seemed to be human, their petals almost like cool living flesh, their touch like to the touch of a mother, and she buried her face once more in their sweetness and let their tenderness flow over her tired soul. Oh, if she only knew where those flowers came from. If only some unknown, pleasant friend had left them there, some friend to whom she might go and weep and tell her trouble. Their cool impersonal touch soothed her disturbed being and rested her. If there were only a friend somewhere like those flowers, who would understand and help and comfort! Perhaps God was like that! But God seemed so far away! And she didn't know God!

Chapter 3

It was early when Diana went to her bed and burrowed her face in the pillow to weep. It could not have been more than half past eight. She did not hear the doorbell ringing nor Maggie's steps along the hall as she went to open the door. Her ears were covered by the pillow.

But Maggie's hand upon her shoulder made her start up, feeling as if all her worst fears had come upon her without warning.

"It's Mr. Bobby Watkins come to call!" announced Maggie with deep satisfaction in her voice. "You're ta get up and put on your prettiest frock and go down. It'll cheer you up a bit."

"Oh, Maggie, I *can't*!" wailed Diana. "You tell him I've gone to bed. Tell him anything. Tell him I'm not feeling well if you want to. That's true."

Diana, even in the dim room lit only from the hall, was a woebegone enough young creature to touch the heart of her severest critic, and Maggie was anything but that. Her eyes were swollen, her nose was red, and her cheeks were dripping tears. But

Maggie stood her ground relentlessly. "Now, Miss Diana, that's no way to go about it. You're not ta be unkind ta the nice little man. He's come ta call, an' if you don't see him he'll be hurt! An if you've got a hard thing ta bear in the eyes of the world, you'd best take it facin' it an' not lyin' down. It's doin' you no good ta lie there an' grieve. You'll only be sick the morn's morn an' give that hussy a chance ta gloat over you. There's no point in lookin' like a ghost. Get up quick an' put on your pretty frock an' come down the stair an' meet life. Bobby's a good wee man an' he'll make you laugh, an' that's half o' bearin' things, at least in the eyes of the world."

"But, Maggie, I'm a sight!" said Diana despairingly.

"A good dash o' cold water'll mend that!" encouraged Maggie. "Where's that new frock with the big white collar? I'll get it for you while you wash up an' give your hair a bit lick."

So Maggie encouraged and urged and prodded, and finally Diana dressed and went down to her caller.

Bobby Watkins was a round-faced little man, not much taller than Diana herself. He was good-natured and kindhearted and rich, but Diana had never been especially interested in him. Now as she went down the last steps it suddenly occurred to her that here was a possible way out of her difficulty. She might marry Bobby. Bobby hadn't actually asked her to marry him, but her intuition told her that he had come very near to asking her on more than one occasion. It had been her own fault that he had not actually done so. Well, now, suppose she let him ask her, and suppose she should accept?

The thought repelled her yet forced itself upon her wrought-up consciousness, and as she entered the big living room and Bobby rose to greet her with his round, red face shining and his thick lips rolled back in a wide grin of welcome, she saw him in a new role, that of a possible husband. Could she stand it? Could she ever get used to having that bland, self-satisfied, childlike smile around her continually? Was it conceivable that she could ever grow fond of him?

She gave a little shiver of dislike as she entered the room, trying to smile in her usual way and be pleasant, conscious of her recent tears, aware suddenly of the strangeness and bareness of the room from which little homelike touches seemed to have utterly fled as the result of her activities that afternoon. She gave him her hand in greeting and winced at the grip he gave her. His hand seemed so big and powerful, so possessive!

She lifted her face, and it was good she did not know how lovely she was with that hint of tears around her lashes, the troubled light in her eyes, the flush on her cheeks left over from her weeping.

He had brought her flowers, and she was glad to withdraw her hand from his greeting and open them. Gardenias in their stiff loveliness, a lot of them. He was extravagant in his buying. She could have anything she wanted if she belonged to him! The thought stabbed her with the memory of Maggie's words that morning. But again her soul recoiled from the thought. She was in trouble and sorely needed someone to comfort her, but she could not conceive of finding comfort in Bobby's broad, plump shoulder. She couldn't even think of being willing to tell him what had happened to upset her world.

She heard the jokes he was telling as if she were far above him somewhere up by the ceiling, looking down on him and not really listening to what he was saying. His loud, boisterous laughter grated on her sensibilities and made her wish to turn and fly upstairs again and get away from the thought of him. Oh, why had Maggie put that suggestion in her mind? Bobby had been just a pleasant, rather tiresome friend before, one who didn't matter much either way. Now he seemed to have come to torment her in her misery. Why hadn't she just insisted that Maggie should go down and make some excuse for her?

But she smiled graciously and thanked Bobby for the flowers. Her lips seemed stiff with suffering and her whole face too weary to smile, but she managed it. And perhaps Bobby noticed the misty sweet look of aloofness as she sat down. Certainly he was impressed by something in her manner, for he said with a boisterous laugh, "You're certainly looking your best tonight, Di! It must be what you're wearing. That white around your shoulders is very attractive. Makes sort of an aura around you, or isn't that the right word? Perhaps *halo* is the word I mean, only that is over your head, isn't it?" And Bobby laughed as if the joke were very great indeed.

Diana sat in the chair opposite him, stiffly, with the box of gardenias in her lap, and looked at him. She tried to imagine herself confiding in him that her father was about to marry a perfectly impossible woman. She tried to imagine his blunt, embarrassed reaction to her confidence if she should attempt it and felt almost hysterical over the probable result. It was with difficulty that she controlled the sudden desire to laugh, with laughter that was near to tears.

Then she heard the telephone ringing, and she sobered suddenly, her face turning perfectly white and fear coming into her eyes. Oh, could that be her father? Had he telephoned at last? Perhaps there was relief in sight! *Oh, God! If only that could be!*

She half rose from her chair with a gesture almost as if she would fling the gardenias from her, box and all. Then she heard Maggie's faithful hurried steps in the hall, and she knew she would answer and call her. And she dropped back again with the box still in her lap, realizing that she must not appear to be anxious. So she sat with a frozen smile locked upon her pale lips, waiting in a perfect fever for Maggie to come and set her free to go and talk with her father, wildly hoping all sorts of lovely things—that her father had seen what an impossible thing he was about to try to do and had called her up to soothe her fears and tell her he had reconsidered, tell her he loved her, tell her he hadn't realized.

But the seconds went by and grew into minutes, and she heard Maggie go back to the kitchen without calling her. Oh, could it be possible that Maggie had told her father she was busy with a caller, could Maggie have dared to presume to do that? Or had she taken a message and was waiting until the caller was gone to deliver it? Oh, had she missed talking with her father? The thought was agony. She must find out. And finally she lifted miserable eyes to her guest's and interrupted a long, eager description of an accident he had suffered driving with a friend in his new car. "Bobby, excuse me just a minute. I heard the telephone ring, and I've been expecting a call from Father all day. I must see if that was he."

She rose hastily, deposited the box of flowers in her chair, and fairly flew to the kitchen.

"Was that Father calling?" she asked Maggie breathlessly.

"No, it was just some person had the wrong number," said Maggie, vexed that Diana had not trusted her. "Go you back to yon lad. I'll call you if you're wanted on the phone."

So Diana, weak from excitement and disappointment, went back to Bobby and her flowers, and presently Maggie came with a vase of water and she could busy her shaking fingers placing the flowers while Bobby talked on, dully enjoying his own conversation and feasting his eyes on the lovely girl. Bobby was having the time of his life. Diana was shying away from him as she usually did, and he wasn't perceptive enough to know she simply wasn't even listening to him.

For a new thought had occurred to Diana. Perhaps her father would come back tonight to talk it over with her. He had said he couldn't, but perhaps he had thought it over and decided to come anyway. If so, it was about time for his train, and he might arrive at any minute.

But Bobby was only flattered at the sweet attention she seemed to be giving him. That distant look in her eyes seemed to him to be real interest. A new interest that he had never been able to stir in her before. He took new heart of hope and went on to further relate an incident of his boyhood, rejoicing in the dreamy smile with which she fixed her eyes upon his face, while Diana, all tense, sat and listened for the sound of her father's step.

Then, startlingly, the doorbell rang, and Diana jumped a little and caught her breath, her eyes suddenly seeking the hall door. He had come perhaps—! He might have left his key at home by mistake. He often did that.

She started to her feet, but Bobby motioned her to sit down.

"You don't need to go," he said blandly. "Maggie is coming. I hear her."

And Diana dropped back into her chair again, weakly, now beset with a new idea. What if they were married already and had come ahead of the time planned? That would be like her father to hurry to her when he knew she was in distress. But oh, if he brought Helen—now—! Her eyes sought beseechingly the round, bland face of her caller. She would have to tell him! Father would bring his new wife in, perhaps, and introduce her. Then Bobby would tell it all over the countryside. Bobby never could keep a secret. And the world would have to know, and then all would be over. Oh, if Father would just come first and let her talk it out with him! But if he waited until they were married it would be too late!

Over and over like a chant it rang through her brain during that extended period while Maggie was walking the length of the hall to the front door. Then a breathless moment during which Bobby occupied the air with his incessant talk and she had to strain her ears to hear the low voice at the front door. Diana caught the words, "Sign here!" and her heart gave a leap. A telegram, perhaps. Her father might be calling her to come to the wedding. In which case she would go—not to the wedding but to her father—and try with all her might to get him to give up this terrible idea of marriage!

She sat with her hand on her heart and her eyes fixed fearfully upon the doorway as if she saw a ghost.

Bobby stopped in the middle of a sentence and followed her gaze, and they both saw Maggie come by the door with a large florist's box in her arms.

"Maggie!" Diana called, unable to maintain her silence any longer. But her voice was faint and frightened.

"It's just some more flowers, Miss Disston," said Maggie formally, and it must be owned a bit importantly. "Would you like me ta open them an' put them in the water?"

Then a wild idea seized Diana. Perhaps her father had sent flowers. It would comfort her greatly if he had. But, if so, she wanted to open them herself.

"No, you needn't mind, Maggie," she said, trying to put up a tone of indifference. "I have lovely flowers here enough for the present. It won't hurt them to leave them in the box."

Bobby looked at her gratefully, a sudden effulgence of joy in his round, red face. His flowers were enough for her. She was wanting him to know that she was especially pleased with his flowers. He took heart of hope and bloomed into good cheer.

"I'm glad you like them, Diana," he said in a tone of exuberance.

"They are lovely!" said Diana again, wondering just how many times she had used that phrase that evening with regard to those gardenias.

But Bobby seemed well pleased. He was not critical. He felt that suddenly fate had turned the sunny side of life to him, and he came over and pulled a chair up closer to her. "Diana, I came over very especially to ask you to go out with me Wednesday evening," he began, puffing a little in his excitement. Before this Diana had always managed to evade his invitations on one score or another, but now he meant to press his vantage while she seemed to be favorable to him. He gave her no opportunity to reply but hurried on. "I've tickets for a very fine concert in the city, and I thought we'd go in early and have dinner together. I know it is short notice, but I wasn't sure I could get tickets until tonight."

But a frightened look was coming into Diana's face. Wednesday night! That was when they were coming home—if Father really did as he had said he would!

For an instant she considered the idea of going with Bobby anyway. Even Bobby's company would be better than that awful meeting with a stepmother for the first time, and such a stepmother! Then almost instantly she knew it would not do. Her father would consider it an affront to both of them. He would never forgive it. No, she could not do that. Not the *first* night, anyway. And perhaps, perhaps there was a chance—oh, she didn't dare think of what the chance might be—but she could not pledge herself to be away until she knew. Her eyes clouded and a troubled pucker came in her brow, and instantly Bobby's face froze into disappointment. He had so often met with disappointment before, just when he had hoped to gain a little with her.

"I'm sorry, Bobby," she said, "I'm afraid Father has planned something else. . ." her voice trailed off into silence. She couldn't tell Bobby that Father was marrying Cousin Helen, not just yet anyway. It seemed too awful for words when she came to consider actually telling it. Bobby knew Cousin Helen. Bobby would be shocked, for Cousin Helen had always been rude to Bobby. She had laughed at his round face. She had laughed almost to his face! Bobby would be offended on his own account. He might not understand Diana's situation. She felt instinctively that he would not be able to appreciate her horror and sorrow, nor to tenderly comfort her, but he would be indignant that a respected neighbor like her father had married a young woman who had practically insulted him on more than one occasion, and he would be so filled with his own part in the matter that he would fail to appreciate hers. No, there would be no relief in taking on a husband, certainly not if he had to be Bobby. Oh, why did she have to consider such awful problems? Marrying! Why should marrying create such sorrow?

And then she knew that she could not tell Bobby. She must not tell anyone until all possibility that it was not true had passed. Surely yet there would be some word from her father or he would arrive on the early morning train. Never before in all her life had he failed her when he knew she was in trouble. Surely, surely he would not do this terrible thing!

Then she realized that her caller had asked her a question.

"You weren't listening!" he charged her crossly. "I asked you if I might not see your father and talk it over with him. I'm quite sure he would be willing to let me have you for Wednesday evening. You don't go out half enough. I've heard several of your friends say that. Won't you call him, Diana, and let me ask him?"

"He isn't here," said Diana. "He's not coming back till Wednesday sometime. And no, I can't reach him by telephone now, not unless he calls up. I don't know where he is tonight. But, you see, he called up this morning and—gave me directions. He's— bringing someone—a lady—home to dinner. That is, he thought he might—and, of course, you know I would have to be here."

"Not necessarily!" said Bobby, quite vexed now. "Don't you have the least idea where I could call him?"

"No," said Diana, "I don't."

"Well, will you let me know as soon as you find out whether you can go?" persisted Bobby.

"I could do that," said Diana, with a troubled look. Oh, why did she have to be bothered with Bobby now?

But at last he took himself away, having extracted a promise that she would let him know as soon as her father came home if there was any chance that she could go with him, and she drew a sigh of relief, reflecting that she could send him a note as soon as she was sure, and she meant to be sure one way or another that she could not go. She was definitely certain that marrying Bobby Watkins would be no way out for her. If she could not endure him for one short evening, how would she ever get through a lifetime in his company?

As soon as Bobby was gone, Diana flew to the box of flowers and opened them. She did not look at the flowers themselves but pulled out the little envelope and looked at the card it contained, hoping against hope that it would bear some message from her beloved father. But no, it bore the card of Arthur McWade, another of the young men who from time to time came to call upon her and occasionally asked her to some party or entertainment with them. He was a nice, kind man, but very formal in spite of his brilliant intellect. Diana always felt rather overpowered in his company.

She pulled the wax paper aside and glanced at the wealth of red roses he had sent. They were beautiful, yes, and with a deep, musky perfume. She ought to enjoy them, but somehow she had no heart tonight. She did not even bend her head to get a whiff of their perfume. They didn't interest her tonight. She drew a deep sigh and went off upstairs to her room, leaving the abandoned roses to Maggie's tender mercies. If only her father had sent them! But somehow she felt Cousin Helen's hand in all this. With keen intuition she knew that he had probably reluctantly admitted to her that his daughter was not pleased, and she had likely advised him to let her alone, promising that she, like the proverbial sheep of little Bo-Peep would soon come home wagging her tail behind her. She could almost see the naughty gleam in Cousin Helen's eye as she said it to Father. Strange, Father never seemed to understand what that sinister gleam meant. He trusted her so. That was the hopelessness of it. Helen would tell him a cheery version of anything that happened and he would trust her beyond his own daughter! How was life ever going to be endurable again?

She went into her dark room and found her way to the window that looked out across the lawn and down to the hedged highway. Off to the right she could see the twinkling lights in the stone cottage through the trees. There was a light upstairs in the gable room, and she could see someone moving around. It was pleasant to have lights in the cottage again, it had been closed so long, since they could not afford to have a servant occupying it anymore. These people were a mother and son, Maggie said. She had sent Maggie down with coffee and sandwiches the day they moved in, and Maggie had come home delighted. The people were Scotch like herself. They were from Edinburgh and knew the street where she used to live. Maggie said they were quality folks and said she wished Diana would call on the "poor wee buddy" as she called the mother. "The son, he's got some kind of a job in the city and he goes back and forth every day," Maggie had said, "and she's that lonesome, the poor wee mother! She's live a' her life in Scotland, an' it's a' quite strange here for her!" And Diana had promised and meant to go that very day had not this terrible catastrophe befallen her. But now—well, the "poor wee buddy" would have to get along as best she could in the company of her son. At least she had her son. She wasn't all alone as she, Diana, was. The thought brought a sudden gush of tears. Would she ever be able to think a continuous thought again without crying?

But then like a flash she remembered that probably that son would get married like all the rest of the benighted earth, and then where would the poor mother be? She felt a quiver of pity for the unknown mother. Oh life, life, how cruel everything was! But she had no time now to think of calling on strange, lonely people. Her heart was too heavy for comforting strangers now. Down there across the dark lawn among the trees where twinkled pleasant lights of friendly folk, how many of them all had some deep, new sorrow such as she had to bear? How many of them knew that feeling of being stricken by some happening that seemed worse than death? Oh yes, there were things in life far more bitter than death.

Diana drew nearer to the windowpane, and the little crystal vase with its three carnations swayed and would have fallen if Diana had not caught them. Some of the water splashed out, and the flowers slid out and brushed her hand as they fell. She gathered them up and laid them against her burning eyelids and then against her lips and let them once more typify comfort and understanding, as if behind them were a rare human love.

The flowers downstairs, the roses and gardenias, were richly beautiful, probably far costlier than these three single blossoms, but somehow they didn't comfort her like these mysterious flowers that had come to her so impersonally that they almost seemed like the breath of heaven, as if they might have been dropped from an angel's hands as he passed on his way to some sad heart.

If these had come from either Arthur McWade or Bobby, she knew she wouldn't want to put her lips against them. But it wasn't conceivable that either of them would have dropped them on her casual path as she had found these. She liked to think that it was without intention, just a happening, and yet the one who had dropped them had become in an indefinable sense a friend, and the only friend in whom she would care to confide her troubles.

So she laid her lips against the delicate fringes of the petals and breathed her sorrow into them.

Downstairs, Maggie had come upon the abandoned flowers and stood for a minute looking down at their rich beauty.

"Ah! Poor wee thing!" she murmured, brushing away the quick tears with the corner of her apron. Then she trotted away into the living room and glanced at the gardenias in their silver bowl in state on a polished table, abandoned also. Neither suitor could divert her from her trouble.

"Ah, poor wee thing! Poor wee thing!" she murmured again

softly as she trotted back and put the large sheaf of crimson roses in water. Strange and sad and significant that both these floral tokens had come in one evening! Then, her work done, Maggie stood with her hands on her hips surveying the flowers, and her mind reverted to a tiny crystal vase she had seen upstairs in Diana's room.

"*Those* flowers?'" she said meditatively, interrogatively. "Where did those flowers come from?" And her eyes narrowed thoughtfully.

"Ah! The poor wee thing!" she said with another sigh. "What would her bonnie mother say if she knew it?"

Chapter 4

$\mathcal{D}$own at the little stone cottage by the big iron gates, the "poor wee buddy" who was the new tenant was welcoming her son back after the day's absence.

"You're late, Gordon. I've been worried about you. I was afraid something had happened. I'm always worried when you go off on those long motor trips with someone else driving. I was sure you had had an accident. You've always been so good about telephoning when you're late."

"I know, Mother. I'm sorry. We had a flat tire away out in the country where we couldn't get word to a garage, and we had to fix it ourselves with inadequate tools. It's strange to me what risks some men take, when a few little tools would put one on the safe side. There wasn't a telephone near us, and when we got to a town if we had stopped to telephone I should have missed my bus out from the city. And I knew you'd rather I'd hurry on and catch it than have to wait up till all hours looking for me, as you always will even if I telephone."

"Yes," said the mother half sheepishly. "I like to, you know, dear son."

"Yes, I know you do," said the son, stooping and giving her an affectionate kiss, "and I ought not to find fault with you. I'd be mighty lonely if you weren't here to watch for me. I'm pretty fortunate to have a mother that likes to watch for me, I know. But say, you didn't have the forethought to save a bite of dinner for me, did you? I'm starved. We had lunch at twelve o'clock, and not a minute nor a place to stop to eat again. I just barely caught the bus as it was."

"Of course I saved the dinner, Son. You didn't think I'd forget how you love home-cooked dinners, did you? Go wash up, and I'll have it on the table by the time you get down again."

She hurried away eagerly, a soft roseleaf flush on her cheeks like a girl, her eyes alight, a glad look of relief on her face. She really had been worried. She had been so worried that she had been praying about it.

So presently her tall son returned just as she was setting a steaming silver platter down in front of his plate.

"Mother!" he exclaimed. "Chicken! Are we celebrating something tonight? And I don't believe you've eaten a bite of it! Mother! And it's all of nine o'clock! Two legs, two wings, a whole breast"—he leaned forward with the carving knife in his hand and pretended to count the members of the bird. "Why, Mother, even the neck and the back and the gizzard are here. Now, Mother, that won't do! You'll get sick going without your food so long. You've got to stop doing this way."

She smiled. "Oh, I had a cup of tea and a biscuit just to stay my stomach till you came. Besides, when you're anxious it's not so good to eat, you know."

"There you are, little Mother MacCarroll, what'n all am I going to have to do with you? And I can't help being late sometimes no matter how hard I try. Sometimes it's impossible even to telephone."

"Oh, I'll be all right," said the mother with a happy smile. "You always get home eventually, and then we have such happy times! It's worth waiting for!"

"But not worrying for, Mother dear! I thought you had faith in your heavenly Father! Why can't you trust me in His care?"

"Well, I do!" laughed the mother. "I always trust you there. I was just bearing you up in prayer."

A tender look came over the young man's face.

"And where would I be, Mother, if you didn't do that?" he said with a smile like a benediction.

He bowed his head then reverently prayed, "Lord, we thank Thee for each other, and for Thyself, and for this food which Thou has furnished us tonight."

There was chicken with dumplings, light as feathers. How she managed it none could say, unless she had an uncanny intuition just when to put them in or some trick about not uncovering the pot until they were ready to be taken out and eaten; but there they were, not a soggy one among them. And mashed potatoes, too; not sulking as mashed potatoes know how to do when they have to wait too long to be eaten. There was plenty of gravy and little white onions creamed and a quivering mound of currant jelly left over from last winter, with sugar cookies and coffee to top off. It was a supper fit for a king.

And when they had both been served and were seated enjoying everything, Gordon said, "Well, Mother, what's been going on at our estate today?"

It was a joke between them when they took this tiny, beautiful little cottage on the edge of the wide lawn that the whole was their estate, and they spoke of the people at the "mansion" house as "their family." They hadn't met any of them, of course. The cottage was rented through an agent, and the new tenants had moved in without the family in the big house even knowing they were there until they chanced to notice a light in the windows one evening and remarked about it. So for some little time they did not know who were the inmates of the house, and most assuredly did not know them except by the general term of *tenants.* All of which, however, did not hinder the tenants from being deeply interested to know who lived in the big, beautiful house and to watch everyone who came and went with eager interest and a kind of possessiveness, as one would watch the scenery around a new home to become familiar with it and grow to love it. So the MacCarrolls watched and talked over their landlord's house and felt as if they somehow had a landed right in them, and so Gordon asked his mother, "What's been going on at our estate today?"

"Well," said the mother, smiling, "not much. The little lady took her customary walk early in the day, but she came back earlier than usual, and I couldn't help thinking she had a worried look. But maybe that was just my imagination. She didn't come out again all day, though I kept a watchful eye out. I hope it wasn't because she was sick that she didn't come. I thought maybe I'd see the Scotch woman who came down the night we moved in, but never a sight of her did I get. If the little lady isn't out tomorrow, I'll maybe make an excuse to run up with some jelly and inquire after her."

"Well, that would be friendly," the son said, smiling. "Oh, you'll get to know her yet, I'm sure. No one can resist you when you once take a liking to anybody. And what did she look like this morning when she went by? Did she look pale that you should think she was ill?"

"Well, no," the mother said with a smile, carrying out the little farce they played together to keep from being lonely in this strange land to which they had come, away from their many friends. "No, I wouldn't say pale. Perhaps just a little absorbed, as if she had something on her mind. But she was pretty and bright as ever. And she was wearing a little green dress I've never seen her wear before, a sort of knit garment that made her look like a part of the woods as she came out of them, a nymph, perhaps. It was very pretty, a mossy green, with a little green cap to match, and she carried a flower in her hand."

"A flower?" said the young man. "What sort of a flower?" He seemed unusually interested in his plate as he carefully cut a delicate bit of the breast of the chicken.

"It was a pink flower," said the mother. "I couldn't quite be sure, but it looked like a carnation. A pink carnation. She held it up to her lips as she walked along, smelling it probably, and the soft pinkness of it was like the delicate rose in her cheeks. No, I don't think she looked sick at all, only—it might be a good excuse to go up to the house and ask. But perhaps it's too soon yet to try and make acquaintance. Perhaps it's better to wait and see if she'll come here. Though maybe she wouldn't think of it. Maybe she'd think people in a cottage at the gate wouldn't be the kind she would want to know."

"Well, and how do we know that she's the kind we want to know?" the son said, smiling a bit haughtily. "If she would scorn people in a porter's lodge just because they lived in a cottage, we would rather not know her, wouldn't we? Perhaps you'd better bide a wee, Mother, and give her a chance to take the initiative. Personally I'd rather not know her and think she was lovely than to get well acquainted and find out she was not. Wouldn't you?"

"Well," said the mother speculatively, "I'm not sure. Isn't that just two kinds of the same pride, after all?"

"Perhaps," said the son, with a grin. "Do you want me to understand that you are calling *me* proud, too, little Mother?"

"If the shoe fits, put it on," responded the mother quickly.

"Well, on the other hand, Mother, we're playing a great game, and I'd hate to do anything to spoil it, wouldn't you? At least until we get acquainted somewhere and have some real friends, we'd better not find out too much about the make-believe ones, had we?"

"Probably not," said the mother, passing the second cup of coffee, "but all the same I hope she comes out to walk tomorrow. I'll not feel quite easy in my mind about her if she doesn't."

The son looked up with an engaging grin.

"Mother, if this game of ours is only giving you someone else to worry about," he said with an undertone of real earnestness in his voice, "we'd better stop right here and now and think up some other form of amusement."

The mother laughed. "You silly boy. It's you who are always worrying about me. Eat your dinner and listen to the rest of my story. She had a young man caller tonight. He wasn't much to look at, too short and dumpy with a round, red face. He came before it was really dark, and he brought a big box. It looked like a florist's box. And he had a fine, big shiny car. I think perhaps he's up there yet. I haven't heard him drive out again. And then about a half hour after he came, a florist's car drove in and out again. I think he left flowers, too. He stayed about long enough. She must be pretty popular. Two boxes of flowers in one evening, don't you think?"

"It would seem that way," said the son gravely. "But Mother, Mother, I'm afraid you're getting to be a seasoned spy. You'll be telling me gossip next if I don't look out."

"Listen!" said Mrs. MacCarroll. "That must be his car now. He's staying a long time. I was at the window watching for you when he came. And it's almost eleven now. He must be some very special friend."

"Yes, probably," said Gordon MacCarroll grimly. "She'll be getting married on us next, and then what'll we do for our romance? Come, Mother, it's high time I got you to bed. No, you sit still and I'll put these things away. You've done enough for today and it's my turn. If things keep on as well as they have today, the hope is I'll be able to get you a servant to look after the heavy work."

"Oh, Gordon," she said eagerly, "tell me about your day. How did your work go?"

He told her in detail all that he had been doing and the bright prospects that seemed to be opening up before him in his chosen profession, and she listened as eagerly as any girl would have done, following his day step-by-step, watching his face as he talked. Her boy! Her precious, wonderful boy!

When they finally went upstairs, and before Gordon lit that light that Diana had seen from her window, he went and stood several minutes looking out on the grassy stretch between the cottage and the mansion and then up at the starry sky speculatively.

"Of course," he said to himself, "I suppose I'm a fool." But whether it was about his work or his mother or what, he did not say, even to himself.

Chapter 5

When Diana awoke the next morning, the first thing her eyes looked upon was the crystal vase containing the three pink carnations. A sparkle came to her face as she remembered that it was a new day and there would be the possibility of another flower waiting for her. With eagerness she sat up in her bed and reached out for the flowers, drawing a deep breath of their fragrance. Then suddenly memory came on the breath of perfume and—*bang!*—the joy went out of her heart and the large dark cloud loomed over her head again. Her father was getting married to Cousin Helen, and they would be coming back tomorrow night! Cousin Helen was coming to stay *always*!

The sorrow settled down around her once more, beyond the power of the mysterious blossoms to cheer. She looked around her room and marveled that the draperies could be so pleasant a color and the sun could shine as it had in the past when such sorrow was so near. And then she remembered several things she had planned last night to be done this morning, and she sprang up and began to dress. There was no time to waste. There were still many precious treasures to be put out of sight and packed carefully where they could not be harmed. The menu must be made out for tomorrow night's dinner; things had to be ordered. Father must be pleased, whether Helen was pleased or not. But the worst of it was to remember that if Helen was pleased that was the thing just now that would most please Father! And oh, that must go on all through life! If life was really going on under such terrible conditions. It didn't seem as if it could.

The next two days seemed eons long to Diana, and yet she kept finding so many things she needed to put away or change that they grew frantically short as Wednesday evening drew nearer and she went around breathlessly making the house over to be ready for an enemy. Hour by hour she had continued to hope for another message from her father, but none came. Evidently he was not going to risk even another conversation with her over the telephone. And yet he must know she was suffering, was fairly frantic! How could he do a thing like this to her, without at least talking it over with her and trying to reconcile her to it? Not that she could ever have been really reconciled to it, of course, but it would not have hurt so much if she could have felt that he was thinking a little about her in it all, that he had not just cast the thought of her, his only child, aside as if she didn't matter in the least. And every time she thought of him the hurt of his stern, angry tones as he had talked over the phone went through her heart again with a wrench that was actual pain. Oh, now added to all the unfairness and indignities of the past, here was this appalling loss staring her in the face. Helen was about to steal her father!

❀

The roses and the gardenias occupied the big living room and wasted their sweetness alone. Not even Maggie had time to go in and admire them. She, good woman, was intent on making the house spotless from cellar to attic before the new mistress should arrive. If this thing had to be, she would leave no slightest flaw in her work. Not at first would that hussy have a chance to find fault with her, anyway. Or, as she put it to herself, "The master shall have no cause to be ashamed of me, anyway."

The master was getting himself a new wife, and things might be so that she would be obliged to leave, but at least she would leave everything in good order.

When Diana came downstairs she found Maggie wiping off the windows in the living room.

"They were that dirty!" she said, frowning. "And I don't want the likes of her to be findin' fault right at once."

Diana winced at the thought and stood staring around the room, which looked bare and alien with so many familiar objects gone. Then suddenly as her glance went over the roses and gardenias, she remembered the carnations. This was the time she had meant to go out and try to discover just when those carnations were dropped! She would go at once before she did anything else. Of course, it might be that there were to be no more carnations, but at least she would go and see if one was there now. She would run no risk of its being picked up by anyone else. So she opened the front door and stepped out in spite of Maggie's admonition that her breakfast was already on the table.

"I'll be back in just a minute," she called, and she sped away down the drive.

"Now what can the bairn be after now?" queried Maggie of herself as she came to the window and watched Diana running swiftly as if she were going on some distinct errand with a destination.

She watched until the girl appeared in sight again and then discreetly withdrew behind a curtain until she reached the house. She was holding a flower in her hand, looking down at it with a lovely look in her face. Now where did that flower come from? Had she brought it downstairs with her? Maggie could distinctly see the flower. It was just like the others that were up in the girl's room. Where did those flowers come from? Had Diana brought them when she went on her walk yesterday? Or had some other admirer sent them? Maggie took distinct satisfaction in the flowers that had been given to the girl last night. The only thing that troubled her was Diana's seeming indifference to them. Was she really as indifferent as she seemed? All those gorgeous roses in the living room, all those stately gardenias, and yet here she was putting a mere carnation to her lips as if she loved it. There seemed some mystery here that Maggie would have solved. However, she was industriously dusting when Diana came into the house. But her eyes were wide open, and she noticed that there was no flower in sight as the girl came in. Had she hidden it in her dress?

Later, when she went up to put Diana's room to rights, she stood for a long time looking down at the crystal vase with its four pink carnations. Had her eyes deceived her? She was sure there had been only three there yesterday when she dusted. And Diana had run quickly upstairs before she came in to her breakfast.

On the whole Diana seemed more cheerful after that little run down through the grounds, and Maggie kept reverting to it all day long and turning it over in her mind.

Diana reverted to it also, wondering, feeling somehow comforted over the unknown friend who had manifested an interest in her just as trouble was coming her way. Of course, she told herself, those flowers might not have been meant for her at all. They might have been dropped for some utterly different reason or just from a happening that had no reason about it at all, by someone who never saw her or even heard of her. But it comforted her to feel that they were meant for her or even just sent from heaven now in her need. Nevertheless, silly as it was for her to make so much out of them, it gave her a thrill to remember they were up in her room waiting for her while she worked at her unpleasant task around the house, her task of obliterating all traces of her beloved mother from the home.

Down at the stone cottage Mrs. MacCarroll watched for her in vain, and when her son came home that night she had little news of the neighborhood to tell him.

"The little lady didn't take a walk today at all," she told him over the remains of yesterday's chicken, appearing now in the form of a delicate chicken pie. "I thought I spied her coming out as usual from her front door. I was upstairs making your bed and I saw her come out the door, this time without a hat, and the sun shining on her bonnie hair till it looked golden. She was walking very fast, almost running I thought, and I stopped and watched her run, she is so graceful. I watched her till she disappeared behind the group of trees, and then I went into my room thinking to see her as she came out by the gate into the street. But she didn't come out, though I watched for some time. She must have gone back another way, perhaps, or have run very fast, for when I went to the back to look out she was gone. But I sighted a blue-bird's nest in the tree just below your window. Did you know it was there? There are three dear little eggs in it, and the mother bird was sitting on the edge of the nest with ravellings of white in her bill."

"Oh," said Gordon, "so we have even nearer neighbors to watch now? That is good. You'll not be able to call on them, perhaps, but I'll warrant you'll be leaving more ravellings on the window sill for that nest. You just can't let your neighbors alone, can you, Mother?"

So the two joked away the supper hour trying to forget that there was an empty place at the table where the husband and father had sat in the old home, that would never again be filled by him on this earth. Trying to make cheer for each other while the one went out to struggle with the world and wrest a living from it and a prospect for the future and the other kept the home and marked time till in the plan of God the day of reunion should come.

❀

The day slowly wore itself away in heartbreaking nothings, and Diana, just before sunset, came to stand by her own front window and looked out at the long slant shadows on the lawn.

The sun was flashing silver signals of good night to the world on the upper windows of the stone cottage where she had seen the light the night before. The panes of glass looked like molten metal on fire. The light flashed through the trees sharply and quivered into flames again. She felt a poignant pleasure in the brilliancy of sunset and in the dear familiar scene, a pleasure akin to pain it was so sharp. All this scene that was so familiar, so dear, would it be hers very much longer? Or would Helen steal this, too, if she knew it was precious to her?

She turned and bent her head to the carnations as she was falling into the habit of doing every time she passed them. These, too, if they continued to come, Helen would somehow discover and manage to appropriate or turn into ridicule. She gathered them to her face and laid her lips among their coolness, her lips that quivered with the sorrow of what was about to come. For this day, too, had passed without any further sign from her father. And now, if he had carried out his purpose, he and Helen were undoubtedly married. How the thought wrenched her heart! She turned away suddenly to stop the tears. She dared not weep any more. She could not face tomorrow in a storm of tears. She must be adamant. She must not let Helen see how keenly she felt this whole thing. Helen would gloat over it, anyway. Helen had an uncanny way of finding out how people felt and pressing the thorn into the lacerated heart until it became unbearable.

She must not let them see her heart. There would be nobody to understand and comfort but Maggie; and if she let poor Maggie understand how she was suffering, Maggie would show her own indignation and Helen would send her out of the house in short order. Perhaps she would, anyway. Then there would be nobody to understand. For there was no hope that her father would ever understand again, not with Helen as his wife. Not as long as Helen chose to keep him blinded to her true character.

She sat down in the rosy twilight that was filling the room and tried to plan how she was to conduct herself, how to steel herself against the inevitable animosity that she would have to meet from the new mistress of the house; but in spite of herself, she found no way to plan ahead.

What she really wanted to do, of course, was to run away before they arrived. The nearer she came to their arrival, the more her heart cried out for freedom to go. But something fine in her would not let her do it. She must stand by her father even though he had not been fair to her.

The more she considered his action, the more the fact stood out that the sharpest hurt of the whole matter, outside of the stunning fact itself, was that her father had made the thing inevitable before he had even intimated to her that such a change was possible. In a matter that so deeply affected her own life and happiness she felt she had a right to have been informed at least, if not consulted, before everything was determined. In a way, it had lowered her father in her eyes, though she struggled against such a thought, that he had not had the courage to talk it over with her. He had thrust it upon her without the courtesy of allowing her to put her own case before him. It was not fair to her, and sometime surely he would know it and be ashamed. Just now he was angry; and if she should run away, he would only think that she was angry, and she was not. She was only appalled and hurt. More deeply hurt than she had ever been before in her life. Even her mother's death had not given her a hurt like this. It was as if all that her father had ever been to her had been erased, wiped out of her life and love. As if he had never been what she had thought she loved.

Diana was young and inexperienced, of course. She forgot that human nature is never perfect. She had idolized her father, and now he had done something that showed a weakness in him. She did not know that a clever woman can influence a wonderful man to do a foolish thing, under the guise of righteousness. She had no notion that Helen had subtly worked on her prey to make him believe that what they were doing was largely for the good of sweet, little, motherless Diana, and that she meant to devote her life to making her happy so that when Diana went away by and by to the home of some marvelous husband she would carry a precious memory of her home. It was good, perhaps, that she did not know all that that wily serpent of a Helen had said on different occasions to her troubled bridegroom, until she had brought him to see Diana and their life and even his own actions in a new light. It was not that he had lost his love for his precious daughter, nor that another love had superseded it. It was only that his horizon and his love had widened to take in Helen that they all might be happy together. That was what the father was thinking, and he was amazed and hurt that his child could not see how beautifully it was all going to work out for everybody.

But Diana had seen only his anger, and she was hurt to the core. Yet her conscience would not let her go away before he came. Not yet. She would stay and show him that she had done her best—if that were possible. Her best with Helen present had always been her worst in spite of her best efforts. But, anyhow, she must stay and face the battle, at least until she was utterly defeated.

So she went down the stairs to satisfy Maggie and pretend to eat something, and then endure another night before the dawning of her evil day.

That night she drowned her pillow in tears, and when she was roused by the telephone to give Bobby Watkins a decided answer to his invitation for Wednesday evening, her voice was shaky with emotion.

"I'm sorry, Bobby. I wish I could go," she said with an honest ring to her voice. If only things were not as they were, how gladly would she go anywhere with Bobby for an evening, if that could have brought back the happy past wherein she and her father lived in a charmed world of their own.

❀

Wednesday morning dawned with a cruelly bright sun. It hurt Diana as she opened her eyes and took in the glory of the morning.

The first thought that met her waking soul was that her father was married. He had taken someone in Mother's place! It hit her in the heart and between the eyes, as a blow might have done. But she winked back the tears that rushed ready for a deluge and shut her lips tightly. She just must not give way today at all or she could not go through the ordeal tonight.

She turned her eyes resolutely toward the carnations and drew a deep breath. Then the wonder came, would there be another flower this morning? How early were they put there? She would run out now, right away, and see. Perhaps she could catch the fairy at her work. She just must think of pleasant things until tonight was over or she would die. She felt as if she were bleeding in her heart. Controlled tears turned inward and drained the life, but she must not weep today.

She sprang from her bed and, dressing quickly, slipped out of the house before Maggie knew she was awake.

The dew was on the turf by the little path that skirted the edge of the driveway, and it caught the morning light and hung bright jewels on each blade of grass.

Diana could not help but feel the beauty of the day as she hurried down the road, despite her heavy heart. It was as if she were going into the secret places of the morning, to the treasury of the world's jewels, where a diamond or an amethyst or a ruby flashed out a greeting to her as she passed and sapphires nodded blue sparkles to the fire of opals.

Just this side of the group of trees that hid the cottage from view she thought she heard a stirring, and she walked softly, shyly, hesitating an instant. Was she coming upon the secret of her mysterious flowers, and did she want to be disillusioned? Did she want to discover how they came there, if perchance the donor was passing now?

On the other hand, perhaps the flowers were meant for some-one else who was missing them because she had come in before and taken them. If she went on now, would there be a clue that would destroy this bit of romance, the only hint of real romance that had so far come into her life?

Only an instant she hesitated, then her common sense as-serted itself and she went forward. If there were so sensible an explanation of all this, she had better know it now and get this nonsense out of her head. With all this trouble she was probably making too much of just a few plain carnations.

So she went on, rounding the group of shrubs that hid the place where she usually found the flowers. Then she heard the sound of a door closing at the back of the cottage. Was that a step? Probably just someone in the cottage shed that opened this way.

She paused, and her eyes sought the grass by the gravel path. Yes, there it lay, close by the walk, its face looking up from the grass. It was in the shadow, but there was a flash of jewels all about the dew. And—were those footprints in the dewy grass? They trailed away to a bare place around the roots of a tree then disappeared in a series of disconnected spots irregularly leading toward the cottage. Was it conceivable that the flowers came from the cottage? But of course not. There was only an old lady living there with her boy, Maggie had said. No young boy would go dropping flowers around for sentiment's sake, and certainly his mother wouldn't be likely to do it. Besides, those footprints were probably made by a dog not a human, and, anyway, they weren't near enough to the flower to count, unless someone stood at a distance and threw the flower there.

She stood for a moment measuring the distance with her eye, calculating how it could be done. Then she stopped, picked up the flower, and sped back to the house.

All day as she was working, doing last things, filled with anguish as she was, there still was an undertone of exultation that the flower had been there again. It seemed to be the one bright thread in the dark fabric of her life. She did not want to think about it too carefully lest sane reasoning might take it away from her. She wanted to hold on to this one little cheerful thing while she was going through these blackest hours that had ever yet come her way.

❁

They set the dinner table as soon as Diana had swallowed the few mouthfuls that made up her brief lunch. Maggie wisely saw that the best thing she could do for her young mistress was to keep her busy, and this matter of the evening meal would be the hardest of the day. It was best to get it over with since it was inevitable, so she asked in an innocent tone, "Will you be wantin' the best china tonight?" And Diana turned a startled look on her.

"Oh, not Grandmother's china!" she exclaimed in a pained voice. "Helen made fun of it once, said it looked as if it came out of the ark. Besides, Mother always said that was to be mine. Grandmother's wedding china, and not a piece broken!"

"You'll want to be packin' it up then," warned Maggie, with a grim look on her face.

"I ought to get a professional packer for that," said the girl, with a troubled look at the clock. "I wonder if there would be time to get it done today. It will be no use to do it after she comes. She'll manage to break it or sell it or something if she knows I love it."

"No need for a packer," said Maggie briskly. "Many's the set of china I've packed in my day and never a wee bit chipped. You bring me all the old newspapers from up the stairs, an' I'll have it out of the way in the whisk of a lamb's tail. There's a nice clean barrel or two down in the cellar that will be just right, and when it's away, I'll nail the head up and whisk it off in a dark corner an' she'll never know it's there."

"Oh, Maggie, you're such a comfort!" said Diana, struggling with her feelings. "But—I'm wondering—you don't suppose Father will notice that we haven't it on the table, do you? We always used it on very special occasions, you know. He might think I was insulting her by using the everyday dishes."

"He said for you to put away your mother's things that might mind his new wife of her, didn't he? Well, then he can't blame you. But anyway, he'll not notice. He'll have enough on his mind without takin' on the dishes also. Come, away with you and bring the newspapers. We'd best get the dishes out of the way first."

So Diana got the newspapers and then came back to help Maggie take the dishes down from their top shelf and carry them all down to the cellar. Maggie wiped off the cupboard shelves, put fresh papers on them, and arranged other dishes of which there were many not in daily use so that the grandmother's set was not missed. Then they went down to the cellar and Diana wrapped cups and plates under Maggie's direction, and in an incredibly short space of time the barrel was filled and rolled off into a dark corner and they came up to set the table.

"You'll not be wantin' flowers for a centerpiece?" asked Maggie.

"No!" said Diana in a bleak voice. "No flowers!"

"You could take out a few roses from the livin' room an' never be missed," she suggested speculatively, "but I wouldn't if I was you."

"No," said Diana crisply, "no flowers at all. This isn't a festive occasion. I don't feel right to make it so. It wouldn't be appreciated if I did. Let the flowers stay where they are."

"You're right," said the old servant. "You're not called upon to do more than your father suggested. She's not one would ever miss the blossoms, not if she didn't get them herself."

So the table was set with a fine new tablecloth and napkins that had never yet been monogrammed, set with formal precision and care but with no festive touches, and Diana hesitated a long time whether to set a plate for herself. Would it not be better taste to let them eat by themselves this first time? It would be much pleasanter for her not to have to be present.

But Maggie shook her head. "It's your right to be at your father's table, an' I'm sure he would consider it an unnecessary affront. He'll find out soon enough what a bitter mistake he's made without your hastenin' it."

So Diana let the place stay and went away to her room to face this new thought about the dinner. How was she going to eat dinner under the circumstances? The food would choke her. And if she didn't eat, her father would be annoyed and speak of it and Helen would laugh with that look of a naughty little devil in her eye. If she only had someone to advise her and help her through this hard time! For an instant she had a wild thought of asking Bobby Watkins to come to dinner, and then immediately she knew that would not do. For, in addition to the fact that he hated Helen and considered her very ill-bred and that Helen always made fun of him to his face, there was the fear that both her father and Helen would, of course, think that Bobby had become something more to her than just a friend, and Diana realized that that would be most repulsive to her. It would be equivalent to announcing that she was engaged to him! Inviting him that way in an intimate family party the first night her father brought his new wife home. And, of course, she didn't want them to think any such thing as that. Bobby would take such significance out of it also. No, she couldn't invite Bobby, even if she wanted him there, and she didn't.

The afternoon went all too swiftly at the last for the numberless little things that were to be done. Diana felt as if she had lived through centuries since she had received that awful letter from her father. It seemed as if she had passed through every phase of human feeling that there was. And at last she stood by the window in the living room looking out down the drive, just as she had done that morning when the letter came. But there was no crystal vase with carnations by her side. She had hidden it in her closet. Helen should not get a sight of the carnations, not if she had to burn them up. Her romance would turn into ashes if once Helen found out about it.

Diana was dressed plainly in a slim black dress with nothing to brighten it. She would not give the impression of having dressed up. She had knelt down beside her bed before she left her room and prayed to God that He would help her to behave in a right way in this new and trying situation, but it had not done her much good. She had never learned to pray in anything but a formal way, and she had no heart in her prayer now, but it seemed that she needed some help somewhere lest she overstep the bounds of justice in the present part she had to play in the tragedy that her life had become. She had no desire to do anything which would be unjust to either her father or Helen, but her love for her father and her indignation for what he had done and her hatred for Helen's ways were so mixed up in her frantic young mind that she wasn't able to discern just where was the borderline between right and wrong; so she went to God, feeling that if it were something He really cared about, He might in some mysterious way help her. That was all she knew of God.

So Diana stood in her slim black dress with big dark circles under her eyes and weary lines around her young lips and watched down the driveway for her father and her new mother to come.

It was growing dark and there were cheery little lights twinkling from the cottage through the trees. She watched them enviously. It wasn't likely that the cottage housed any such tragedy as had come to her. A mansion didn't bring happiness. How glad she had been that they had been able to keep their own big house that had been home so many dear years. But how gladly would she tonight surrender the big house and go and live in the little cottage by the gate, just she and her father together, if only they might have each other and not Helen!

And then, just as she felt tears smarting into her eyes again in spite of all her best efforts, another light flashed out from the group of trees and came rapidly on around the curve of the drive. A taxi! They had come, and now she must meet them! A panic seized upon her and she longed to flee to her room, lock her door, and refuse to come down, but she stood her ground; and the taxi came on, swept up in front of the door, and stopped. The new mistress had arrived!

Chapter 6

Gordon MacCarroll brought home a little cheap car that night and housed it in the speck of a garage that used to be a barn. There wasn't much room for anything else in the building when the little car got in, but Gordon's mother came out to admire the shabby little car and to beam upon her son with pleasure when he told her what a bargain he had made in buying it.

"There are just one or two things that need fixing up, and I know how to fix them," he said gleefully. "The fellow that sold it is going abroad, and he has no use for it anymore. He just got his orders to go and he hadn't much time to sell, so he was willing to let it go at a bargain. And now, Mother, I shan't have to be dependent on trains and buses any longer."

"Yes, but you'll be very careful, my son," said the mother, eyeing the car dubiously. "I've always felt afraid of them. Of course, I know you are a careful driver, but it's other people I'm afraid of."

"Well, Mother, I guess we can trust that to God, can't we? Aren't we as safe one place as another if we're following His guidance?"

"Yes, of course," said his mother timorously, and then more firmly, "Yes, *of course!*"

He laughed and drew her arm through his.

"Now, come in. I'm hungry as a bear, and I want to tell you the result of my day and what I'm to do tomorrow. I've got a chance at a big opportunity if I can make good. I've got to start early in the morning, however, in order to see a man before he leaves for a week's absence. I wish I could take you with me, for it's going to be a beautiful drive and I know you would enjoy it, but I can't tell how long I'll be, and I may have to go farther and be very late getting back, so I guess I won't risk it this first time. But pretty soon now we can have some good long drives together after I get this buggy tried out. There comes a taxi. They must be having guests at the great house."

"It'll maybe be the master returning," said the mother, looking toward the taxi as it came on. "The Scotch woman said he was away on business."

"Then he's brought someone home with him," said Gordon, turning to look at the car as it sped by. "There's a lady with him."

"Some relative, probably. I haven't seen any of them today. They must have been getting ready for company."

They entered the immaculate little kitchen with its pleasant scent of some sweet pastry baking, mingled with cinnamon and cooking apples.

"A baked apple dumpling, Mother, am I right?" said Gordon eagerly. "Nothing could be better. I hope you made plenty of sauce."

"Yes, there's plenty of sauce," laughed his mother, as she stopped to take out the fragrant steaming dish. "And I've made a wee salad out of some bits of chicken I saved, and there are roast potatoes. Here's the fork. Take them out, and don't forget to crack them and let out the steam."

A moment more and they were seated at their pleasant

supper table, their heads bent in thanksgiving. While up at the great house the taxi had deposited its travelers and presently went speeding by on its way back to the station.

Diana had turned from the window when she saw them get out of the car, and she stood there frozenly awaiting them. She had a strong impression now that she should go into the hall and meet them, say something, do something appropriate, but somehow she had lost the power to move. It was as if she had suddenly become petrified. The power of speech seemed to have gone, too, for when she heard her father's voice saying in vexed tones, "Well, I wonder where she is," the cry with which her heart wanted to greet him died in her throat. He seemed a stranger, an alien, and not her father whom she loved so dearly.

Then a light laugh with a sneer in the tail of it like the venom of a serpent stung her with the old deadly hatred, and she swayed and would have fallen had she not reached her hands back and clutched the windowsill with her cold, frightened fingers.

A step and they were in the doorway scanning the room, her father's eyes upon her where she stood. Her face was white with anguish, her eyes dark and tortured, her sensitive lips trembling.

He looked at her questioningly, his glance changing into sternness. Then his voice, stern and displeased, spoke: "Well? Diana, is that the way you welcome us?"

With a cry like a hurt thing, now Diana sprang forward, her eyes on her father, threw her arms around his neck, drew his face down and kissed his cheek, then buried her face on his shoulder and burst into tears, as she clung helplessly to him.

His arm stealing softly, almost gently around her in the old, familiar way upheld her for the moment and steadied her quivering shoulders that shook with her sobs.

Then that light, mocking laugh fell on her senses again, and the pain stung back into her heart.

"Oh, my word! Diana," trilled the bride in a penetrating voice that found her senses through her sobs, "are you still such a child that you have to go into hysterics? A great big girl like you to be acting like that! I should think you'd be ashamed."

The comforting arm that had held her close for an instant in such a reassuring clasp and the caressing hand that had been laid on her sorrowful young head suddenly ceased their tender contact, and her father pushed her from him as one would a naughty child.

"For heaven's sake, Diana, be a woman, can't you?'" he said in low, vexed tones that showed plainly that he was displeased that she should be laying herself open to criticism right at the start.

His words stung her into silence. She felt shamed and sick that she should have given way. She drew her quivering breath in and realized that she was alone against these two and she need no more expect her father to be on her side in anything. It had come just as she had foreseen it would, only she hadn't thought it would come so soon.

She lifted her head and stepped back, brushing the tears away with her hand and lifting a proud young chin that no longer quivered.

"I'm sorry!" she said coldly, and gave her father a look as alien as his own. Then, with sudden self-control, she added, as if they were stranger-guests, "Dinner is ready to serve whenever you wish it. Will you go upstairs first?"

"No!" said Helen decidedly. "We'll eat at once. I'm starved. We'll go upstairs after dinner. I want to give a few directions before we leave. We're not staying here tonight, you know. Come!"

Diana gave her a bleak glance, and they went out to the dining room, Helen leading the way as if she had always done so. She was still wearing her hat, and she drew her gloves off as she went.

Diana watched her take the mistress's place at the table as a matter of course, and reaching out, change the position of several dishes as if they offended her. Then she gave a quick glance at the table and a mocking smile came on her lips.

"I'm glad you didn't put out those hideous old dishes that you always considered the company set. I've always secretly wished to take those out and smash them, and now I think that will be one of the first things I'll do."

She laughed as she said it, flashing her little white teeth between her red, red lips and twinkling her eyes at her husband amusedly in the way she had of saying outrageous things and making them pass for a joke before those whom she wanted to deceive.

Mr. Disston answered her look with a grave, worried smile. It was evident he saw nothing in her words but pleasantry. But Maggie, coming in at that moment with her tray, heard and fully understood, and the red flamed into her cheeks; her blue eyes with the wet lashes of recently shed tears, angry tears, flashed fire, as much as blue kindly eyes could flash. But she shut her thin lips and went about her serving.

Diana had slipped into the third seat and was trying beneath the tablecloth to keep her trembling hands still and her lips from quivering. She found her teeth suddenly inclined to chatter, and she had to hold herself tense to keep from trembling like a leaf.

Helen, after the first taste of her fruit appetizer, gave her attention to her new stepdaughter.

"For heaven's sake, Diana, you haven't gone ascetic on us, have you?" she asked flippantly. "Why such somber garb? I don't object to black, of course. It's smart just now, but that isn't smart what you have on. It's just a dud. It isn't your type and not a bit becoming. I'll have to get at you and reconstruct your wardrobe, I see. We can't have you around looking like that."

Her father looked up and surveyed her critically.

"Yes," he said, "Diana, it does seem as if you might have dressed up a little more festively on an occasion like this." He gave her a cold look that was meant to show her how disappointed he was in her, and Diana suddenly choked and, for an instant, was on the point of fleeing to her own room.

"Don't speak to her, Stephen, she's got the jitters," laughed the new mother in an amused tone. "Let her alone till she gets her bearings. Can't you see she's all upset, just as I told you she'd be? Let's talk about something else. What time did you say that train to the shore goes? I want plenty of time to give Diana my directions after dinner."

Diana regained a semblance of calm and went on pretending to eat, and the meal dragged its slow progress to the end, the conversation a mere dialogue about trifles between her father and the new wife. Diana sat there listening and realizing more and more how utterly out of things she was intended to be from now on, hardening her heart to the thought, struggling to look as if she did not mind. Perhaps it was the knowledge that she was affording so much wicked amusement to her new stepmother that made it so much harder to bear even than she had expected.

Diana felt as if she were a long way off looking at herself, analyzing her own feelings, reasoning out things, trying to look dispassionately at the whole situation and create a philosophy about it that would make her able to live in spite of it all. She fixed her eyes on the olive dish and tried to say to herself what a beautiful dish it was, how well it set off the dark green of the olives, what handsome olives they were, anything just to keep her mind away from what was happening and get her through the ordeal until they left. Oh, she was glad, glad they were going away that night. She was tired, so tired with emotion and hard work that she could hardly hold her head up. She wanted to close her eyes, to lie down and rest from the unshed tears that hurt her so much more than if they had been shed. She wanted to get rested enough to think out what had happened to her and try to get where she could do the right thing. That was what she had prayed for, that she might do the right thing. Where was God that He had not answered her prayer?

Well, perhaps such prayers as hers had no right to be answered. Probably God hadn't time for little personal troubles.

She tried so hard to sit up and look pleasant but only succeeded in being dispassionate. Her hurt eyes looked out upon the two, the one who was so dear and the one who was not, with torture in them and met no comforting glance to help her back into a normal attitude. And when they rose to leave the table her father said in low, displeased tones, "I certainly am disappointed in you, Diana!"

It needed only those words to make Diana feel that life and happiness for her had come to an end and the only thing she could possibly hope to do was to get creditably through the rest of the evening and then crawl into a hole somewhere and die. She felt as if she had received her death blow from her father's attitude and words.

"Now, we're going upstairs!" said Helen. "Come, Diana, I want to get this over with and be on our way!"

Diana wanted to get it over with, too, so she followed silently up the stairs after the bride, who skipped up lightly as if she were enjoying herself.

"No, not in there!" she said sharply, as Diana swung the door of her father's room open and switched on the light. "I never liked that room. I'm going to take the room across the hall when I come back."

"Oh, but that is my room," said Diana quietly.

"I know," said Helen amusedly. "I have a perfectly good memory. But it's going to be my room now. I've got it all arranged. Your father and I talked it over, and we decided to give you an apartment on the third floor. Then we can take this whole floor ourselves, and you can feel more independent. We're doing the whole house over soon, anyway. And then you can arrange the third floor as you like and have a place to receive your friends and entertain as much as you like without interfering with us."

"I wouldn't care for that, Helen," said Diana with sudden spirit. "I'd rather keep my own room. Mother had it done over for me just before she died, and I feel more at home there than anywhere else."

"Oh, indeed!" laughed Helen amiably. "Well, you'll have to get used to feeling at home somewhere else, then, for that's the room I'm going to have. In fact, I'm using the whole second floor myself, so you may as well understand it. I shall have lots of guests and shall need every inch of space, so that's that. Take it or leave it as you like, but you rate the third floor."

Helen stepped across the hall and swung Diana's door open, glancing around the lovely room with satisfaction.

"You can leave this furniture and hangings just as they are. They're not so bad! I may use them entire for a guest room. It's rather a good color scheme. And you can take the furniture from your father's room up to the third floor for yourself. I never did care for it, and I suppose you'll like it for its association!" She gave another mocking smile and turned back to the other room. "That was what I wanted to tell you: you're to hire someone and have everything from here moved to the third story. You can arrange it as you like, of course. It'll be your domain for a while. You'll be getting married soon yourself, I suppose, but until then you can fix that floor to suit yourself."

Diana stood and stared at her, a frozen look upon her face, utterly appalled at the attitude the new mistress was daring to take toward her on this the very first night in the house. It seemed as if some enemy had her by the throat. She could not think of any reply that would be adequate. Her lips seemed to be sealed. Even if she knew what to say, she felt that no sound would come from her. It was as if her vocal chords were paralyzed, as if her whole being were turning to stone. Her feelings were beyond mere indignation. This thing that was being said to her was incredible. Surely her father would interfere. And yet, and yet, so well she knew this woman who had been set over her that she felt her strength draining from the tips of her fingers. She felt as if in a moment more she would lose her power to stand upright and would fall over on her face, stiff and rigid like a statue. Then, suddenly, because she must do something, she fell to laughing, a wild hysterical little giggle, ending in a real fit of laughter.

Helen gave her a startled stare then took hold of her arm and gave her a fierce shake until Diana's teeth chattered.

"Stop that!" said Helen. "You needn't think you can get your father's sympathy by any such carryings on as that. He'll see through that ruse, and you can't get your way by carrying on, no matter how many hysterics you have. And another thing. It's time you stopped kissing your father like a little girl! It's ridiculous! You! A great big girl! Besides, I don't like it!"

Diana yielded herself to the shaking, relaxing into a hall chair, the laughter ceasing as suddenly as it had begun. She lifted her hands and pressed them to her quivering lips. The tears were very near the surface, and she wanted to fend them off. She must not cry in front of Helen. That would please her more than anything else. She must not let her father hear her. There must be a way to behave that would give dignity to this humbling occasion.

Helen was watching her sharply.

"Now, if you are sane again," she said, keeping a suspicious glance on her, "I'll tell you the rest. We're going down to the shore tonight, and I expect these changes to be all made by the time I come back. I want you to oversee them, and you'd better call up a man to move things. He ought to come early in the morning. It ought not to take long. I've had my own things sent on. They may get here tomorrow by van, and they should be put right in the rooms, to save moving twice. I've marked everything, which go in the east room and which in the west. Of course, I wasn't counting on the furniture in your room being so good, but you might have what I've marked for your room put in the middle guest room. And the furniture in there you might sell to a secondhand man, unless there's something you want to save. I always hated that in the days when I visited here and had to sleep in that room. It gave me the horrors, so I'd like it to be disposed of out of my sight by the time I get back. Now, do you understand? You sit there like a sphinx and don't say a word! Have you heard anything I've said or haven't you?"

Diana summoned the stiff muscles of her throat to utter three words: "I have heard," and sat quietly watching her tormentor.

"Well, see that you carry out my orders, then," said Helen, flinging up her chin imperiously. "I want this all done and your things entirely out of the way by the time I get back! Now, do you understand?"

"I understand," said Diana again gravely, watching Helen with a steady gaze. She was mistress of herself now, and her strength was coming back to her again.

"Well then, see that you attend to everything." Helen tossed her head and laughed lightly, her laughter evidently intended to reach the hall below where Diana could hear her father entering from the front door. Helen trilled another light laugh and ran briskly down the stairs. But before she reached the last step, Diana heard her pause a moment and then turn and run back up again.

"Diana," she challenged, "were those flowers down in the living room sent to me, or did you buy them?"

"They were sent to *me* last night," answered Diana, still in that steady, grave tone.

"Oh really?" Helen's voice expressed mingled incredulity and envy.

"You can have them if you like," went on Diana in a voice

from which all expression seemed to have been extracted. "I don't care anything about them."

"Oh *really*?" said Helen again, this time with a sting in her voice. "You think I would care for your cast-off flowers? No thank you, I can get plenty of my own. And by the way, better take yours upstairs after this so there won't be any mistake."

Diana sat still and let the disagreeable words, uttered in a silvery voice for the benefit of the listener in the lower hall, roll away from her. Her whole sensitive being quivered at their impact, but she did not reply.

Then, just as the new lady of the house turned to go downstairs again, a shadow loomed below her and Maggie appeared, her countenance like a thundercloud.

"Is Miss Diana up the stair?" she demanded haughtily as if she were the mistress and the other the maid.

"I believe she is," said the new Mrs. Disston coldly. "What do you want?"

"There's a young gentleman down the stair to see her!" announced the Scotch woman.

"Oh!" said Mrs. Disston with a note of curiosity in her voice. "Well, go up and tell her." Then lightly as a feather she skipped downstairs and peered into the big living room where Bobby Watkins sat impatiently on the edge of a chair awaiting Diana.

He rose eagerly as Mrs. Disston parted the doorway curtains and faced him, and then stepped back with an exclamation of dismay.

"Oh, it's *you*, is it?" she said and then backed away from him rudely without further words.

Bobby flushed angrily and stepped out into the hall after her, but Mrs. Disston was already halfway up the stairs again.

"Diana!" she called in a clear, sweet voice that was quite audible both upstairs and down in the living room. "It's the fat one, dear. Don't keep him waiting, he's already quite impatient."

By which Diana knew that her father must have stepped outside again, for Helen would never have spoke so in front of him.

The girl's face flushed angrily, and she felt a passing pity for Bobby; therefore, she did not wait to smooth her hair nor dash cold water on her face to take away the stricken look. She rose and hurried downstairs with a set look upon her lips and a light of battle in her eyes. She would not heed the annoyances that were meant for herself, but in so far as she could she would try to make up to Bobby for the rudeness that had been dealt out to him. Oh, if her father knew what had happened, it would open his eyes. But alas, it was too late! Poor Father, when he should finally find out what sort of woman he had married!

"How did she get here again?" asked Bobby wrathfully, as Diana hurried into the room a trifle breathless.

"Sh!" she said under her breath.

"Why should I hush? She didn't hesitate to shout her opinion of me all over the house. She's a pest! Why does your father let her come here?"

"Don't, please!" said Diana hurriedly. "You—I'll have to explain. Come over to the other end of the room where we can't be overheard."

"No!" said Bobby authoritatively. "Come outside! She'd be snooping round the corner!"

"Oh, Bobby, please—!" Diana begged. "You mustn't! You don't understand!"

"No! I'm afraid I don't understand!" said Bobby arrogantly. "Even if she is your guest, that doesn't give her the right to be protected in her insolence. Come on outside!" And Bobby led Diana out the front door and down the drive.

"I've left my car out in the street," he said as he walked her away by the sheer force of his will. "We'll get in the car and talk. I didn't bring it up the drive because I wanted to find out how the land lay before I was announced to your father, if he was here. A car in the driveway always announces one's presence too quickly."

"No, Bobby," Diana stopped on the path and tried to pull her arm away, but he held her fast.

"I can't go out to your car," she said. "I have to be here now. Father has just come home, and he's going away again. I can only stay a minute to explain to you, and then I must go in. Let go of my arm, please, you are hurting me."

"Well then, stop trying to pull away!" ordered Bobby wrathfully. "I've stood your putting me off again and again, but I'm not going to stand your having to go in to that woman when I've come to visit. And besides, I've got something to tell you!"

"But you must listen to me first, Bobby!"

Diana's tone was quiet and collected. She turned and walked by his side but drew her arm away from his. "You've got to know that Helen has a right to stay at our house now. She is my father's wife!"

Diana felt as she said it that she was talking in a dream. It couldn't be true that it had really happened and she was making it known to the world! It wrenched her heart to think it, and she was not half listening to Bobby. He had stopped short in the path and was staring at her.

"Diana! You don't mean that your father has been such a fool! You're trying to put something over on me."

"It's true, Bobby," said Diana sadly, "and I wish you wouldn't talk about it. It's hard enough to bear without hearing—what you think about it."

"But, Diana, it can't be possible that your father would do a thing like that to you."

"Please don't!" said Diana wearily. "He thought he was doing the best for me. He really did. I'm sure he thought so!"

"He couldn't!" said Bobby righteously. "He simply couldn't!"

Diana pulled away, shrinking from his words as if they had been blows.

"I must go back, Bobby. I really must. My father will want me."

"Let him want awhile!" shouted Bobby arrogantly. "You come on down to that group of trees. I've got to talk to you. Let's get out of sight of the house. I've something to say, and I don't want to say it before the whole world."

"Well, for only just a minute," yielded Diana hesitantly.

He drew her swiftly along and they were soon within the shelter of the thick growth of trees that hid the stone cottage from the driveway. Diana realized as they halted that she was standing almost directly in the spot from which she had picked up the carnation that morning. She glanced down, and there a few feet from where she stood a white something caught her eye, a delicate flower face looking up to her! Was she seeing things?

She passed her hand over her weary eyes to brush imagination away and looked again. Yes, there it really was, or seemed to be! Only a frail moonbeam or two penetrated the darkness, but that was certainly a flower! Could she be mistaken? Perhaps it was only a stray bit of paper. What a fool she was! Always imagining another flower. Silly! It wasn't time for a flower to be there yet. They always must have been placed in the early morning or else they would not look so fresh. And she had already had one today. It was only paper, of course. But after Bobby was gone she would come back by herself and see! She certainly would!

"You are not listening to me!" charged Bobby savagely. "I am asking you to marry me. To go away with me now and get married, and then I can take you away from that woman! Your father is no longer to be considered. He has spoiled your home, and now I am asking you to go away with me tonight, at once! You do not need to go back for anything. I can buy you a hat and whatever else you need. Let them wonder where you are! Let them search for you if they want you. Telephone and tell them they have driven you away!"

Appalled at his torrent of words, Diana pulled away.

"Oh, don't, Bobby! I am so tired and troubled. I can't think now. I must get rested. I couldn't go away!"

"That's silly, Diana. There'll be plenty of time to rest after we're married. We can run right down to the rectory and get it over with. I'll attend to the license. I've got a friend—! I can fix that all up afterward. Then I'll take you to a hotel in the city and you can rest all you want to, and in the morning we'll go off on a honeymoon!"

He reached out and caught her two hands and pulled her close to him, folding his cushiony arms around her, his hot breath was upon her face, and his thick, moist lips suddenly pressed possessively upon hers, as if he would draw her very soul from her body in a kiss that suddenly became to her repulsive, unclean. His eyes looking into hers in the moonlight had the selfish, beastly look of a cannibal about to sate his cruel desire for human blood.

Diana shrank back in horror from the touch of his lips, but the lips followed her. She struggled and gasped and uttered a half-stifled scream. Her arms were pinioned to his chest, held in a viselike grasp of one fat hand, and the other hand was behind her head holding her lips to his as if he could not get enough. Terror and loathing filled her soul as she tried to get her hands free.

"I love you, Diana! I love you!" The hot words were breathed fiercely.

Diana managed to turn her face to the side for an instant.

"I hate you!" she gasped! "I *hate* you! If that is love, I want none of it!" And then his heavy face came down upon hers again, and he held her head so that she could not struggle free, while he kissed her again and again, pressing her close in his arms.

It was then she gave a real scream!

"Can I be of any assistance?" A voice spoke close behind her, and a strong blow came down on the inner curve of Bobby's elbow, making it fall away powerless for the instant.

"Who the devil are you?" roared Bobby, dropping his other arm from around Diana and turning to face the interloper. "What business have you got interfering?"

But Diana, free for the instant, turned and fled!

Chapter 7

Diana arrived back at the house with a face as white as chalk and eyes that were dark with terror. Her recent experience had overtopped all climaxes in her life and had almost made her forget for the time being the tragedy in her home. It seemed to her that the covering of decency had been stripped from life and love and everything worthwhile was left stark and naked. Was love like that, and could caresses turn to so hideous a thing? She never wanted to see or hear of Bobby Watkins again.

Helen stared at her as she entered the door, narrowing her eyes and searching her face.

"Why the tragedy?" she asked flippantly.

Diana ignored her remark.

"Where is my father?" she asked. Her voice was steady and grave, as if she had a serious matter on her mind.

Helen's eyes grew belligerent. "He's in the library calling up a taxi. We're going away at once, so you needn't think you're going to have time to talk with him. You might as well learn to cut out any long conferences. I don't like them. I remember how you used to do, and I don't like it, understand?"

"Oh yes?" said Diana, coolly giving her antagonist a level look and walking slowly up the stairs.

Diana went to the front window in her room and looked out into the darkness. The lights in the cottage windows glimmered in a friendly way, but Diana only shuddered as she watched them. Once it came to her to wonder who it had been that came and stood behind her and rescued her from those terrible iron-muscled arms and those fiendish, moist, fat lips? Could it have been some passerby on the street who had heard her scream? Bobby Watkins! How had she ever fancied it might be possible for her to find refuge in marriage with Bobby Watkins even to escape from her present tragic situation? To think of having him around every day, with the right to kiss her—that way! How terrible!

But her meditations were interrupted by her father's imperious knock at her door. "I've got to go now, Diana. I came up to—to—! Diana, have you nothing to say to me? You certainly have been acting in a strange way. I cannot understand it."

Diana turned and faced him, and again the sternness of his tone seemed to overwhelm her so that she could not think nor speak, and her lips and chin were trembling in her effort to control the tears. Never, never since she was a little child and had disobeyed his express command not to take the ink bottle down off the desk and had spilled ink all over Mother's new oriental rug had she ever heard her father speak to her in a tone like that. It seemed she could not bear it. It seemed that it was something irreparable!

"And so," he said, eyeing her sternly with a kind of desperation in his face, "you have nothing to say. You do not want to ask forgiveness? You do not want to say you are sorry for such rude conduct to my wife?"

His wife! How she quivered at the words! Even so soon

those words were separating them! But—*forgiveness*. What had she done? Broken down, yes, but that was his fault, not hers. He should have told her beforehand, talked it over with her and helped her to understand, allowed her to tell what she knew, not separated himself from her without a word and then tried to force this terrible relationship down her throat. She longed to cry out, "I was not rude to her, Father, you do not know. You did not hear what she said to me!" but she could only choke back a sob and turn her face away.

"So! You intend to keep it up, do you? You're not even going to kiss me good-bye?" His voice was more deeply angry than she had ever heard it before. "I thought you loved me! And you're not even going to kiss me good-bye!"

But Diana turned at that.

"I *can't*, Father! I can't *anymore*!" she burst forth sorrowfully. "She told me not to. She said I was too old to kiss my father, and she didn't like it!"

He looked at her as if he could not believe his ears.

"And have you descended as low as that, that you will lie to me to prove her in the wrong?" His voice was grieved now, incredulous.

"Father! You know better! You know I do not lie. She said it. She took me upstairs and told me that just a few minutes ago!"

He stared at her an instant more, and then his face cleared with a half-contemptuous smile. "If Helen said that, you know she said it in a joke. You know she would never mean a thing like that. You are being willfully hateful to prove your point, just because years ago you took a prejudice against her on account of that silly dress. I would rather have bought you a dozen silk dresses than to have your judgment and your sweet innocent nature warped."

"Father!" cried Diana desperately. "Go and ask her! She did say it. She was not joking. She never jokes. She means it. She was quite vexed. She said she did not like it and she wouldn't stand for it! Go and ask her. Perhaps she will be willing to tell you the truth about it."

"Are you implying that she also lies?" His voice was very stern again now.

"Oh Daddy, Daddy, dear!" Diana cried out, suddenly turning and putting her head down on the broad window seat, her shoulders shaking with suppressed sobs.

He watched her a moment, his brows knit in deep trouble, and then sighing turned away.

"Well, I cannot wait any longer for you to see your error," he said sadly. "I never thought that my child would behave like this. Well"—wistfully—"I must go."

He turned and walked sadly out of the room and down the stairs, and a moment later she heard the taxi driving away. He was gone!

She flung herself on her bed and wept until it seemed her heart was breaking. Wept until Maggie came up and tried to soothe her, bathed her face with cool water, said, "There, my lamb, my lamb," and tried in every way to hearten her.

At last the violent sobbing was over, and she could speak to the old servant.

"I can't stay here, Maggie, I can't! I can't! She wants to get rid of me. She says I'm to go upstairs...." And she poured out all the directions that the new mistress had given.

Maggie's face was full of indignation as she listened, but at last she said, "Well, my lamb, it's a sore trial I mind, put it how you will, but I'd advise you to get to your bed an' sleep the night over it, an' in the morn we'll see what to do. Now, I'll fetch you a sip o' hot milk, for you didn't eat enough o' the fine dinner we had to keep a bird alive. And do you put on your little bed gown and get you to your rest. The morn will bring you new wisdom. Bide you till the morn. Then we'll see."

Diana was worn out with excitement and emotion, and she readily fell asleep from sheer exhaustion, after the drink of hot milk. But for one in sorrow sleep does not last. It suddenly vanishes in the small hours of the night and the sufferer is left to toss and turn and see the ghosts of possibilities all go trooping by. So Diana woke. It might have been one o'clock or it might have been later, and sharply on her waking thoughts came the memory of a flower lying in the dewy grass, staring up from almost underfoot, pale with the reflection of the moon drifting through dense branches.

The flower! Oh, why had she not picked up her flower! Was it really there at all or had she dreamed it? If it was there, then that made six. There were three the morning the letter came, one yesterday morning, one this morning, and now this one tonight, if it was really a flower and not a figment of her imagination, not just a bit of paper or a fragment of fluff blown about by the wind.

Somehow her drowsy thoughts hovered around that flower without touching on her troubles. It was as if her first waking consciousness was afraid to think of all that had come upon her, as if she took refuge in thoughts of the pleasant bit of romance that seemed to be dropping into her quiet life.

More and more as she grew wider awake she longed to know whether that flower were really there. It seemed as if her only hope of riding out her troubles lay in knowing whether that had been a flower, a real flower, there in the dim shadows. If it had been a flower, she might grasp its sweetness to her heart and go on somehow working out her strange problems. Suddenly it seemed to her that she must rise and run out there and discover for herself.

Oh, she knew it wasn't a reasonable thing to do at all. The house was dark, Maggie was asleep, all the countryside was asleep. It wasn't a safe thing for her to do, either, to go down that lonely drive in the night on such a foolish errand. Her father wouldn't approve. Her mother would not have approved. Maggie would cry out and insist on going along if she knew. But Maggie didn't know. Maggie was sound asleep and snoring. And Diana knew even before she made the first actual move to rise from her bed that she was going. She must know whether that flower was there or not. If she waited until dawn, some mysterious person might come by and get it. She would never know then whether it had been there at all, and it seemed most important to know positively whether it was there now.

All the time she was flinging on garments, stepping into slippers, and throwing a long, dark silk robe around her, she was resolutely refusing to let her mind spring back and reveal to her all the sorrow and horror that was there beneath the surface of her consciousness.

When she was ready, she crept down the hall and stairs with silent tread, unfastened the door, and slid out like a wraith.

The moon was low in the west by now and was casting long, faint, weird shadows across the grass. In her dark robe with her silent tread she seemed like one of the shadows, a swiftly moving shadow as noiseless as a moth drifting along on faint, pale moonbeams.

As she approached the group of trees and was about to pass into the depth of shade they made, the memory of her experience burst back upon her with full force and she paused, frightened, looking ahead, listening. Was it conceivable that Bobby might be lingering around the place yet? She shuddered at the memory of his lips, his great possessive arms. But somehow she must go on. A power within herself was compelling her, would not be satisfied until she found the flower. And though her heart was wildly beating, she went on again. There could be no turning back. Silly! Why should she be frightened? There would be no one around at this hour, of course, and who would want to steal a silly little single cast-out flower in the grass—if there was a flower at all. She must know. So she went on.

She slipped into the depth of the darkness and stood look-ing down until her eyes grew accustomed to the blackness, and suddenly she saw it there, right at her feet, staring up at her, its fringed petals making a soft blur of light in the dimness.

With her heart beating as wildly as if she were seeing a spirit-flower, she stooped and snatched it, and then turning, fled back to the house, her white face showing like the passing of a moonbeam. For now it seemed that Bobby, with his hot breath fanning her face and his fat arms reached out to clasp her, was running with great strides just behind her and would presently win out in the race and she would be in that awful embrace again. And there would not be a stranger near at hand this time with a voice of authority to protect her.

She was like a sleepwalker in a nightmare as she ran until she reached the front door and fastened it behind her. But unlike the nightmare victim, she did reach the door before she came to herself. She stood there panting, her eyes closed, leaning back against the door for a moment's respite, trying to get her breath and courage to go on and know what life had in store for her. She seemed to know that as soon as she had mounted the stairs again and entered her room her trouble in its entirety would rush upon her, take her in its grasp, and sting her with its sorrow again. So she lingered until her breath came back and then crept softly up to her bed, with Maggie still noisily slumbering in the back bedroom with the door open wide to be near to guard her bairn if anything should trouble her.

Back in her bed again, strangely enough the evil specter of her troubles stood at bay, exorcised, perhaps, by the fragrant breath of the flower.

She did not put the carnation into the vase with the others but kept it in her hand, and it lay against her cheek on the pillow, and whether because of sheer weariness or because the flower seemed to bring something like peace upon her worn spirit, she fell asleep again.

When morning came at last she slept on until Maggie, worried about her, slipped softly in to see if all was right and found her sleeping with the flower on the pillow just touching her lips.

"Aw, the poor wee thing!" she said under her breath. "The poor wee thing! If her father could but see her now! But I doubt if he'd understand the while yet. He's that fey about the hussy! Poor silly man! He'll be that shamed when he understands! An' he'll see it yet! He's a good man, only just silly for the whiles. But I doubt it'll be too late for savin' his girlie's happiness! Poor wee thing!"

Then Maggie slipped quietly away and closed the door.

But a half hour later the sun cast a warm finger across the pillow, touching Diana's eyelids and lighting up the flower, and she awoke with a start. No bewilderings now. The whole terrible tragedy flashed across her consciousness in full force, and her mind was on duty at once informing her of what was necessary to be done. Instantly the words of her new stepmother came to her about the changes that were to be made, strong hints of what might happen to things that had grown dear to the girl through the years, and she realized that if she did not save them they would go out of her care and keeping and would be sold or destroyed ruthlessly.

And now as she lay still she saw what she had to do. Whether she stayed herself or not, those precious things of her mother's must be put in a safe place. Sometime Father would rouse to the situation and inquire for the household goods. If he was ever disillusioned, he would surely feel bad that they were gone. Moreover, many of them belonged to Diana. Both her father and mother had spoken of this often. The ancestral dishes, the portraits, a lot of things that she had packed away in inconspicuous places and had hoped were safe from the iconoclast, she now saw would be ruthlessly rooted out and sold or destroyed.

She did some swift thinking and decided that she would send them to a storage house. Even if she went away herself, she could not take them with her until she had someplace to put them, and it might take days to find the right place. It might even take weeks. She had a little money in her own checking account and could pay the storage and get along somehow if worse came to worst, but the things that were to be saved must be saved today or it would be too late. They could not be gotten out of the house after Helen came back, that was certain.

Further consideration made it plain also that the goods must be stored where they could not be traced and brought back. What Helen had not seen or noticed might not be missed, but it was certain that Grandmother's sprigged china and many other little things would be. Well, she would not telephone to the storage house from home, for that perhaps might be traceable from the itemized telephone bill. She would run down to the village, three quarters of a mile away, and telephone. She would tell them that they must come by two o'clock. That would give her time to get her own furniture ready to go.

Suddenly Diana rose and began rapidly to dress. There were no tears this morning. There was excitement, anxiety, overwhelming haste.

But just as she turned to leave her room her eye fell on the flower lying on her pillow, and she caught her breath with a great wonder in her eyes. She had jumped up so suddenly and been so absorbed in her problems that she had not noticed the flower, for it had fallen away from her face over to the other end of the pillow.

She went slowly over to the bed and touched the flower, lifted it to her face, and drew a deep breath of its perfume. It was real, then. She had thought it a dream! Then she had really gotten up and gone out on the driveway to find it! How strange! Poor little flower! It should have been in water all night! Yet it seemed almost as fresh as its mates for whom she had cared so tenderly. How did it happen that the flower was out there in the evening? Had all the others been put there at that hour? It didn't seem possible; they had been so fresh and dewy. It was a mystery flower. She could not solve it. She just knew it had been a comfort to her in this her great life sorrow.

Then like a flash she remembered all that she had to do today! She waited only to put her flower in the crystal vase with its mates, and then she hurried downstairs.

Maggie came out into the hall with an anxious face and saw that Diana had on her hat.

"You're not goin' away?" she asked fearsomely. "The breakfast is near ready an' we can talk whilst you're eatin'."

"I'm running down to the village to do some long-distance telephoning," said Diana breathlessly, glancing at the clock. "I don't want it to go on the bill for Helen to see. I'll explain it all when I get back. I won't be long."

"But couldn't you wait for a bite first?"

"No, Maggie, I must go at once. I want to get some people before they are gone to business. I'll be right back."

Diana dashed out the door and down the drive without waiting for further parley, and Maggie, with distress in her face, followed to the veranda and watched her out of sight.

"Now what's the poor wee thing got on her mind this time?" she said aloud to herself, her arms akimbo, her cheeks red with worry, her mouth in a vexed line. "It's a bad business, tormentin' the poor wee bairn. Her father is storin' up sorrow, an' him not knowin' what the little hussy is at, but the day'll come when he will. Well, he'll rue the day he ever saw that flipperty-gib."

Just then the scones sent up a smell of burning and she flew to their rescue.

"Poor wee thing, she'll be that hungry when she comes back," said Maggie as she set about preparing a more elaborate breakfast than she had planned.

As Diana went flying down the drive, her mind was busy with her plans, but her breath was coming in long, sobbing gasps. Out here in the open she felt that no one could hear her for the moment and she let herself give a long trembling moan, let the smarting tears fall for a minute or two. She felt sick and dizzy with all she had been through and with loss of sleep. She began to tremble as she neared the scene of her silent struggle last night and wondered at herself that she had dared come down there in the middle of the night—just for a flower! What was a flower, after all? It probably belonged to someone else and all the fairy romance she had woven about it was just of her imagination. Perhaps someone had plenty of these and threw them away every now and then. Yet there it had been in the middle of the night as if it dropped down from the soft moonbeams. There for her greatest need. Well, it was probably the only one she would have found this morning if she had waited. It was likely placed there every night instead of morning and the dew kept it fresh.

Then suddenly she started back, stopped, and looked down at her feet, for there lay another carnation, sweet and pink and fresh, just like all the rest. She gasped in astonishment and looked furtively around her. What could it mean? It was fully two hours before her usual time to walk that way, and yet there it lay smiling up at her.

Then she stopped and picked it up. As she touched it to her lips, the tears came rushing down again, and she sobbed softly to herself as she went on her way. It certainly was strange and uncanny, and somehow it seemed as if somebody like her mother were doing this. She almost believed for an instant that the flower actually fell from heaven at her feet. It seemed so wonderful to have it come just when she so needed comfort, and she hugged it to her lips and kissed it, sobbing softly as she hurried on. As she passed the end of the cottage and neared the street, she paused to brush away the tears. She must not cry in the street! And she must hurry on or she would perhaps miss the mover for the day, and those things *must* leave the house before Helen got back or they would never leave, that was certain.

She could hear Helen's laughter now if she should come even while they were being moved, and knew as well as if it had happened before her eyes how quickly she would have her father persuaded that it was absurd for them to go. Oh, Helen would never let the things go out of the house until she had investigated every one, that was certain. And she would save some of them for the pleasure of destroying them. No one who hadn't seen Helen work would probably believe that. If Diana had not suffered from her methods many times, perhaps she would not have believed it herself. But she was taking no chances. The things she loved would go out of the house before Helen got there if she had to drag them out one by one herself and hide them in the barn or the back meadow.

Such thoughts hurried her feet until she reached the village drugstore and went in to telephone. Even then she had to try three storage places before she found one that would promise to come that afternoon. Diana found she was trembling when she hung up the receiver.

She waited only to get a few trifling things she would need in packing, and then she hurried back.

On her way home her thoughts were leaping ahead, planning what she would do first, counting up different matters that must be attended to before the movers arrived. In imagination she took down her pictures and curtains, folded her garments into drawers and trunks, gathered out her books from the library, tabulated on her fingers the boxes and furniture stored away in attic and cellar that must not be forgotten. It seemed as if the thoughts in her mind were like bees buzzing around in confusion to be sorted out and marshaled in orderly array. She was fairly running the last lap of the way and arrived at home quite out of breath. Maggie had to draw her by sheer force to the dining room.

"Sit you down," she said, vexed. "Here have I kept breakfast waiting all this time. You cannot work on an empty stomach. Come, eat a good breakfast, or I'll not help you a stroke. Your porridge first. I do not hold with the folks that puts sour fruit juices in on an empty stomach. It heartens you to get a good fill of porridge first, nice an' hot! And there are scones to come with strawberry jam. Mind your milk, too. You cannot keep up unless you eat. I'll wager you na slept the night much. You must eat if you cannot sleep. You do not want to give her a chance to have you sick on her hands."

So Diana ate a sketchy breakfast.

"I haven't time," she protested as she hurriedly buttered a scone. "I'm sending my things away, Maggie, the things she would smash or take away. I can't leave them here for her to destroy, and I won't let her have my precious furniture that Mother got for me."

"But where will you send them, child?"

"To storage. At least for a while till I know what to do."

Maggie looked startled. "Won't that cost you a lot? You mightta sent them to my sister's house, only it's such a wee bit housie I don't mind where she could put them."

"No," said Diana firmly. "I'm not going to involve you and your sister in my troubles. She'd just go there and get them if she found out. No, Maggie, this is the best way. It doesn't cost so much, and I can get them out any time I like, of course. They'll be protected in storage and be insured. I have a little money of my own, you know. I'm quite sure this is the only way to do it."

"Then come!" said the servant determinedly. "We'll get it off your mind. I'll take down the draperies and brush them. Do you put away your pretties in the drawers."

They set to work in silence, and in due time the room that had been so sweet and homelike was reduced to bare walls and desolate furniture standing around. Even the pretty bed was wearing only its springs now, the mattress being trussed around, covered with an old sheet, and neatly tied with rope by the capable hands of Maggie.

Suddenly Diana turned around and surveyed the place, and a great desolation swept over her.

"I can't stay here, Maggie," she cried with a soft little wail in her voice. "I couldn't stand living in the third story and having her take my pretty room and put herself or her guests here, the kind of guests she always has when she has her way. Am I wicked, Maggie, that I feel I can't stay here? Not even my Mother would want me to, I'm sure. I couldn't stay and have her always putting me in the wrong before Father! It wouldn't do him any good, and it would make endless trouble. I couldn't, Maggie, could I? I *must go*!"

She bent her head, and the tears gushed out as she stood with pitiful clasped hands and let the tears splash down on the rug at her feet.

"But where would you go?" asked Maggie, lifting her face and discovering the slow tears that for some time had been coursing over her honest, sorrowful face. "What can you do, my wee birdling?"

Diana stood silent for a minute, then she lifted her face, and her eyes were dark and tragic as she looked at Maggie.

"I can make some visits!" she said bravely, drawing a deep breath. "I thought it all out on the way home. Maggie, I've got to be gone before they come home tonight. They'll likely be here for dinner, and I must be gone before they come. I couldn't meet her—*them*—again, not now with Father feeling as he does against me. I've got to go. There's Aunt Harriet, a great many miles away. I can take the sleeper at midnight and be there in the morning.

And there are those girls that invited me to house parties. They'll all be glad to have me visit them a few days each. I'll write them that I'm coming their way and will stop off a few days if it's convenient. And by that time I'll get settled in my mind and know what I want to do."

"But what if your Aunt Harriet isn't at home?" queried Maggie anxiously.

"She's always at home. She's an invalid, you know," said Diana. "She's often invited me."

"You better send her a wee wire, then, sayin' you're comin'."

"No," said Diana, "I'll just go. I can't explain things in a wire, and I haven't time for a letter."

"Aw, my wee lamb! If I only had a place of my own, I'd share it with you! I'd not let you stray around the world this way. If I only hadn't of let my sister's husband borrow my earnings to buy his house! To be sure, I'm that welcome, an' I doubt not he'd take you in, too, if I'd asked him."

"No, Maggie!" said Diana. "You're very kind, but I want to get farther away. But we mustn't stand here and talk; there's so much to do. It's almost twelve o'clock and the van will be here at two. I've all my clothes to pack. I'll take a suitcase and the big Gladstone bag, that'll be all I'll need for visiting. The rest of my things I'll pack in the bureau drawers."

They went silently to work again, like two who had just read a death warrant, speaking no words that were not necessary, furtive tears slipping down their cheeks, which each ignored.

At last the work was done, and Maggie insisted on Diana's lying down a little while on a bed she had fixed for her in the guest room.

"I'll just run down the stair an' get you a bite to eat an' a cup o' tea whilst you sleep," said Maggie.

"Oh no, Maggie," protested the girl. "I can't sleep now till it's over. Wait till the things are gone. Then we'll have lunch and rest."

"You'd best drink a sip o' tea!" admonished the woman and hurried down to get it. Then Diana sat down at her little desk where she had spent so many happy hours of her life studying and writing, and penned a letter to her father. It had to be done quickly, for the men would come and the desk must go, and she couldn't think of writing *that* letter anywhere else but at her own desk. It seemed as if another desk or another room might some-how snatch the meaning of her letter and turn it to a traitor use. She must write it here with her pen dipped in the love and agony of her heart, here in the four walls of her dismantled room be-fore they became alien walls, sheltering her enemy. And she must write it rapidly, too, because her heart might weaken if she took a long time and weighed her words too well. She would just tell briefly what were the facts.

And so with her own fountain pen that had been her father's gift on her last birthday, her initials set in green-and-gold enamel in its barrel, she wrote. Oh, she had never, never thought when he gave it to her that she would write such words as she was writing now with that cherished pen.

Chapter 8

Dear Father,

I must go away. If you knew everything, you
would fully understand and would think that
I am right. It would only make terrible trouble
for all of us if I were to stay. Things can never
be as they were before, and you would soon see it
yourself.

At first I thought I could stay until you
found this out and then I could talk it over with
you and plan for my going in the way that you
thought was best, but several things last night
showed me that that would be impossible. There
would be no way now for you and me to talk
together alone, and I could not talk it over with
Helen. So I see that I must go at once without
waiting for you to come back.

> *You need not worry about me, for I shall be visiting for a while, and I will write and let you know my plans as soon as I have had a chance to decide what I am going to do. I shall write you at your office. And meanwhile, you can just say that I am visiting friends and relatives.*
>
> *I have not taken anything with me that did not belong to me personally, except things that you yourself suggested should be put away. If I have taken too many, you can just let me know and I will have them sent back. They are in a perfectly safe place, and insured, so I hope you will think I did right about them.*
>
> *And now, dear Father, I want you to know that I love you very dearly, but I could not stay here under the circumstances. And it is too late to talk about it, so I will just say again I love you, and good-bye.*
>
> *Your little girl,*
> *Diana*

The movers arrived just as she was writing the last word, and Diana hastily sealed her letter, addressed it to her father, and swallowed the tea that Maggie had brought her. Then she went down to meet the movers and show them what things had to go.

How ruthlessly those stalwart men marshaled the few household articles, which had seemed so many only a few minutes before, and dropped them into the depths of that yawning van. Diana rushed from cellar to attic to make sure everything was gone that she had intended. Then she directed that a trunk containing part of her wardrobe should be put where it would be accessible if needed while the other things were in storage.

They stood in the doorway together, the servant and the girl, watching the big van rattle off jauntily down the drive and disappear, carrying with it a part of what had once been the furnishings of an unusually happy home. The old servant had her lips set in a grim line, and she was sniffing back a stray tear.

"Well," she said with a heavy sigh, "at least they'll be safe. An' now," she said, turning back to Diana, "come! I've got a bit lunch ready. Sit you down now an' eat. Yes, you're not to wait. It's nice an' hot, an' I'm not lettin' you leave it to get cold."

"If you'll sit down with me, Maggie," said Diana with a catch in her voice. "I can't sit down and eat alone, this last time."

"It's not the last meal in your home, bairnie," said Maggie fiercely. "I feel it in my bones the day will come when you'll be back an' happier than ever. An' it's not fittin' that a servant should eat with her mistress, but I'll bide in the room while you eat, an' we'll talk a bit."

But Diana would have it that she should eat with her.

"You're the only friend I've got left, Maggie!" she pleaded, and so the old servant reluctantly yielded and sat down, every mouthful a protest against her sense of the fitness of things.

"Maggie, I've written a letter to Father, and I want you to see that he gets it when he's alone. I don't want her to know I've written it. At least, not until he's read it. Will you give it to him?"

Maggie was silent a moment.

"I wasn't thinkin' of stayin' after you was gone, my bairn," said Maggie slowly, "but yes, I'll stay to give it to him, anyway."

"Oh, Maggie!" wailed the girl. "I'm doing you out of a job!"

"It's not you, you poor wee lamb," said the woman. "It's her. That Helen! You don't think I could stomach the likes of her, do you? I was studyin' what I should do, for I couldn't bear to leave you alone with that hussy. But I knew she an' I'd be two people from the start. We never did get along when she was only visitin',

361

and I'd never take orders from her."

"No," said Diana sadly, "I suppose you couldn't. Oh, I'm so sorry for Father! He'll miss your cooking so much!"

"It's nobody's fault but his own, poor silly man! An' he'll find out good and soon, I'm thinkin'. But I'll stay an' deliver your letter, an' I'll see she don't get her hands on it till he's read it through, so don't you worry. An' now, you better get a bit o' rest before you get back to work. Aren't you almost done?"

"No, there's quite a lot of things yet. I haven't packed my bags, and there are some boxes of letters I've got to look over and burn. I don't want her to be reading my letters." Diana sighed wearily and turned away.

As she passed the door of the living room, she looked wistfully on the piano, her mother's piano! Helen wouldn't want it and would probably try to sell it or relegate it to the attic, for Helen couldn't play. But several of her friends were musicians, or called themselves so, though the music they played was modern stuff that Diana hated. They would probably play on her mother's piano—unless Helen could coax her father to buy a new one. Oh, the piano ought to have gone with the other things to storage, but she dared not take it away without consulting her father. Well, perhaps the fact that she had not taken it would work in its favor. Perhaps Helen would simply not think about it at all.

She stepped into the living room and sat down at the instrument, touching the keys tenderly, softly, recalling how her mother had sat there playing evening after evening all during the happy years, how she had received her own first lessons there from her mother. She remembered how happy she had been when she had succeeded in playing her first little piece perfectly. How her father and mother had stood there with shining eyes watching and commending her. How that piano was connected with all the pleasant happenings of life! And now she must leave it, probably forever! The tears began to gather again, and she put her head down on the music rack and pressed her hands against her eyes. She must not cry again, it unnerved her so. And she had still much to do.

At last she gathered strength to lift her head, giving the old instrument one more caressing touch, her fingers sweeping the keys softly, tenderly. Then she closed the lid. She wished she dared lock it, but that would be only to rouse Helen's ire, and she really had no right to lock it even if she knew where the key was. She had no memory that the piano had ever been locked. So she lingered a moment more moving her hands softly over the polished surface of the case, like a last handclasp with a friend, and then she turned and quickly went upstairs.

It was almost dark when she finished with her packing and dressing. The late summer twilight seemed to come unusually soon, but Diana, looking at her watch, discovered that it was almost time for the travelers to arrive if they came on the shore train, which they would be likely to take. She could tell by the fragrance that came up from the region of the kitchen that dinner was in process of preparation. Maggie would have a good dinner for her last one in the old house.

Diana put on her hat, gathered up her coat and gloves, and stood for a moment gazing around her empty room, her room that her mother had planned for her. And now she was leaving it forever. Her glance swept its empty walls and lingered on the wide window seats where she had so often sat among cushions reading some favorite book. It had all been so dear, and now she would see it no more!

Then she saw the crystal vase with its seven lovely flowers standing alone in the other window seat, forgotten! How had she forgotten them? She must not leave those behind. They had been her comfort during this tragic hour, and there would be no more of them. Seven mystery flowers! A perfect number. No, they must not be left behind!

She took them out of the vase and dried it, found some cotton and tissue paper, and wrapping it carefully, stowed it in her bag. There was a piece of wax paper in the closet also, and she put the flowers in that. After a moment's hesitation, she slipped them, too, in the bag. There was space for them, but she felt as if she were smothering children as she laid them in.

She paused a minute thoughtfully and then suddenly searched in her suitcase for her writing case, and sitting in the window seat in the fading light, she wrote hurriedly:

Dear Flower Person,

I am going away and will not be able to come and find any more of your lovely carnations, but I had to let you know how they have helped and comforted me during a very hard time. I shall probably never know who put the flowers in my path, nor even if they were really meant for me, but I shall never forget them. Thank you and good-bye.

She slipped the note into a small envelope, addressed it "To the Flower Person," and put it in her handbag.

Then suddenly she heard the sound of a motor, and hurrying to the front window, she saw the lights of a taxi coming swiftly up the drive. They had come and she was still there!

Panic seized her. She could not meet them! She must get away! She must be gone when they entered the house, and the taxi was almost at the door! Could she make it?

She snatched up her bags, gave one last wistful frantic look around her denuded room, and fled down the hall to the back stairs.

She appeared in the kitchen like a wraith, her face white, her eyes dark with excitement.

"They've come, Maggie. Here's the letter for Father! Good-bye, you dear! And I'll write you in care of your sister!"

She flashed out of the kitchen even as the front door opened letting in the householders. She slipped swiftly across the back lawn to a wide group of shrubs, disappearing into the midst of their friendly branches. The twilight was kind and hid her going, the shrubs were thick and formed a perfect screen. Maggie had rushed after her to the kitchen door, crying out in subdued protest, "But you mustn't go away alone. I was goin' down the road with you—!"

But Diana was not there. Then Maggie realized that the next act was hers, and she was holding the letter in her hand. She hid it quickly behind the bib of her ample apron and went back to her cooking, assuming an air of indifference toward the world but keeping a weather ear open to all developments, while her heart cried out for the girl who had fled. She had meant to give her all sorts of cautions, and now it was too late! But she could not run after her. That would be to give the whole matter away.

So the master and the new mistress walked into the house and went upstairs with no one to interrupt their progress.

Helen went up the stairs like a victor who had taken a city and meant to behead the former ruler. She marched straight to the master bedroom and flung open the door. She wanted to see if her commands had been obeyed. Then she stood staring for an instant at the prim, immaculate neatness that prevailed. Dominated by the fine old walnut furniture that had belonged to its former mistress, bare only of the little feminine and artistic touches and its lovely portrait, it had a forbidding look. As she stared, a fury grew in her face not pretty to see.

"She hasn't touched it!" she said aloud in a tone meant to reach to the lower hall.

She paused an instant, head bent in a listening attitude, then she flounced around and flung open the door across the hall. There stood Diana's room stark and bare!

She made a sound such as is generally associated with the snorting of a war horse preparatory to battle. She stepped into the room and snapped on the light. Its brilliance flung out the curtainless window and penetrated the dense shrubbery that traveled more or less irregularly from the kitchen garden down the far side of the drive toward the entrance gate. Diana was slowly progressing toward the gate as she waited for the taxi to get out of sight before she made her dash across the open to the dense growth of trees that hid the cottage. So Diana knew that the secret of her moving was discovered. She had hoped to be farther away before they found it out.

Helen walked determinedly across the bare floor and flung the closet doors wide. Everything was gone, the room cleaned. Not even a box or a paper on the empty shelf!

She ran out in the hall and up the third-story stairs, with an eye that boded no good to her enemy. The light snapped on at the foot of the stairs, and Diana saw that, too, and dashed across in the twilight to the spot behind the trees, her trysting place with the flowers. But she was not thinking of the flowers now, nor looking for them. She was crouching down beneath a huge hemlock, its lacy branches brushing her face. She was parting the branches and looking back to the house. She could see a figure walking by the hall window. That would be Helen. She was looking in every room, for each window blazed out in turn. She was finding out that her new stepdaughter had not done anything she had told her to do!

Well, there was a moment's time, perhaps. The front door was still closed. Diana searched out the letter from her handbag and, stooping, laid it in the very place where the carnation had lain the night before and this morning. She caught her breath in a little sob. There would be no more carnations for her. If one lay there in the morning, she would not be there to find it! She was leaving everything, home and love and even her bit of mystery and romance.

Then she turned a quick look back to the house and saw the front door flung wide, the light streaming out, and Helen standing slim and vibrant looking out into the darkness.

Diana shrank and, catching up her bags, fled out of the gateway and down the road, pausing in the shadow of the tall hedge to wait and listen breathlessly. It was not likely that Helen would pursue her out into the darkness on foot, but yet, there was never any telling what Helen would do. It would be hard to run from pursuit and carry all that baggage, but still it could be done. However, perhaps if she saw them coming it would be better to push the bags around the hedge and come back for them later. She considered that an instant, then peering through the thick hedge she saw the light of the doorway shut off and distinctly heard the closing of the front door. Helen would likely have gone to consult Maggie, and it would take her some time to get anything out of Maggie if Maggie chose to be stupid and not understand.

Diana relaxed against the hedge and found herself terribly weary. There would be a bus along soon. If she might only sit down on the grass, lie down, close her eyes, and rest. But, of course, she couldn't. She was thankful, however, for the momentary ease against the strong resilient arms of the old hedge. She put her head back. She could almost go to sleep here. She resolutely put away from her all thoughts of what might be going on at the house behind her. She could not think of it now. She could not bear it. The tears would come if she did, and one could not get into a public bus weeping. She took a deep breath and shut her lips with determination.

Then behind her she became aware of a voice—or was it voices?—speaking low and gently—a voice, it was a voice speaking to someone. She could not hear the first words, they were very low and gentle, just behind her within that open window of the cottage. She turned instinctively and looked at the square of light that was the cottage window, screened by sheer muslin curtains moving softly in the breeze and thickly sheltered by the tall hedge. It was as safely private as a bird's nest in a tall tree. Pedestrians did not creep within the shelter of hedges as she was doing. An ordinary passerby would never have heard that voice, so reverent, so tender. She found herself soothed by the very tone.

And then the voice grew more distinct: "We thank Thee for the care of the day and for these gifts for our refreshment."

He was saying grace at the evening meal! Father used to do that while Mother was living, but of late it had become a mumbled formality. Who was this person? The voice was grave but not old. She had understood from Maggie that the woman who had taken the cottage was elderly. Perhaps after all her husband was living. Maggie had only spoken of a woman and her boy. But perhaps this was some relative having supper with them.

The voice rose again just a little so that she heard the words: "And, Lord, we would ask Thy mercy and tenderness and leading for the people up at the great house. Perhaps some of them are sad. Lord, give them comfort. Perhaps they need guidance. Do Thou send Thy light—"

And then suddenly the bus rumbled up to the curb to let off a passenger. The bus would never have stopped at all if it hadn't been for that passenger, for Diana had been back in the shadow out of sight. But now she came back to herself with a start, caught up her bags, and hurried forward into the bus. She was whirled away, but she turned wondering eyes toward the quiet cottage with its cozy light shining softly through the tall hedge and forgot entirely to look back at the home she was leaving until it was too late to see anything but the long streaks of light that streamed down across the lawn from the front windows. Her mind was wholly occupied with what she had heard. It seemed so extraordinary. She would never forget it. She said it over to herself silently, conning it like a lesson of which she must not lose one precious word. "Lord, we would ask Thy mercy and tenderness and leading for the people up at the great house. Perhaps some of them are sad. Lord, give them comfort. Perhaps they need guidance. Do Thou send Thy light—"

How she longed to know what was to have followed that half-finished sentence. Why had she not stayed to hear? Another bus would have been only a half hour longer and left plenty of time to catch her train. She glanced at her watch. Yes, she could have waited, but it was too late to go back now. It was too far to walk with her bags, and she was much too tired.

Then she said the words over again, "And, Lord, we would ask Thy mercy and tenderness and leading for the people up at the great house." Was it conceivable that the person meant the Disston house? It was the way a servant would speak of a master's family. Perhaps the reference was to some former master's family, just being tenderly remembered in prayer, the way Maggie would do. How the words throbbed and thrilled along her sore, tired heart! Here was someone who believed in God, believed that God was interested in individuals, even interested in individuals who were not especially interested in Him. Could he be speaking of God's interest in her father's house by individuals? Was it really her father's house? Of course, it might be some other house far away. But it soothed and rested Diana to think it was the house of Disston the voice meant.

She was too tired now to question why, it was just enough to have someone care, even in a quiet, impersonal way, and pray for them. Oh, how they needed praying for—that is, if prayer did any good. At least it was comforting to think that someone cared to try. She put her head back against the window frame and closed her eyes on the hot tears that tried to struggle to the lashes and squeeze through. She thought of the flowers in her bag and the prayer in her heart and was glad she had heard those few words. They helped her, anyway, even if they were not meant for her. Perhaps there was a God who cared after all, instead of just a mere impersonal Creator. If one soul could speak like that as if he knew Him, he must have had some experience to make him sure God was like that. If she ever went back to her home—it was not conceivable tonight that she would, but if she ever did—she would try to seek out the people who lived in the cottage and get to know them and see if she could find out what it was that they had that would explain the tenderness of a prayer like that.

Presently she got out her pencil and a bit of card from her handbag and wrote down the words as well as she could remember them. She must not forget that prayer. She must hide it in her heart and memory. It was like the flowers.

She went on into the city to take her train. It seemed a very long ride tonight, longer than usual. She hoped the train would be ready soon. She wanted to lie down.

She hadn't bothered to look up the time of the train. There was usually one along toward midnight going in the direction of the city where Aunt Harriet lived, an hour or two more or less either way didn't matter. She forgot that she had had no dinner and very little lunch. She was not hungry; she only wanted to lie down. She felt that she was too tired even to cry.

As she neared the city and got away more and more from thoughts of home and tragedy that made her going necessary, she began to review wearily the few arrangements she had made. She had plenty of money with her for her journey, for it just happened that her father had given her her generous allowance in cash the day he went away for his trip, and she had carelessly neglected to put it in the bank, so she had not had to take time to look after that. She had fastened part of her money inside her dress, but she had enough in her bag to pay her fare and some over. There was nothing about that to worry over. Also, she had paid a month's storage on her goods with the privilege of refund if she decided to take them out sooner. Somehow all these details seemed so unimportant. They had been merely things to fill this awful day until she was gone. None of them seemed to be of as much importance as the few words of the prayer, which she had had the privilege of hearing. How those words seemed to float around her like a sweet protection as the bus rumbled along into the city and the country was left behind.

Meanwhile, back at the great house, Helen had come rushing down the stairs, searching vainly in the rooms for Diana, hoping to find her at once while her wrath was hot. There was more satisfaction in serving wrath piping hot than after it had a chance to get lukewarm. But no Diana was to be found.

Then Helen arrived magnificently in the kitchen with all the air of a full-fledged mistress of the house.

"Maggie, where is Diana?" she demanded, with something in her voice that suggested that Maggie might have hidden her somewhere.

"She's away!" stated Maggie crustily.

"Away?" said Helen in an annoyed tone, as if it were all Maggie's fault. "Where has she gone?"

"She didn't *say!*" said Maggie, shoving the iron frying pan across the top of the stove with a great clatter.

"She didn't say!" repeated Helen in an outraged tone. "When did she go?"

"Awhile back," said Maggie laconically.

"But didn't she tell you where she was going? Didn't you ask her?"

"It was none of my business, why should I ask?" snapped Maggie.

"But didn't she say when she was coming back?"

"She didn't mention comin' back. She said she'd be payin' visits for some while."

"It was very rude of her to treat us that way. I wouldn't have thought she would have dared do that to her father."

Maggie was silent, her face very red, her deep blue eyes angry with sparks in them.

"Well, what did she do with the furniture she had taken out of her room, and—other things—that I miss, around the house?"

"I couldn't say," said Maggie in a belligerent tone. "I try to mind my own business around a place where I'm workin', Miss Helen, as much as I'm let be."

Helen looked at her haughtily.

"You will call me Mrs. Disston after this!" she said icily.

"Oh, *will* I?" said Maggie, rolling the words out with satisfaction. "I'll not be callin' you *any*thin' very long. I'm leavin' tonight after the kitchen is redd up. You can get someone to call you any name in the dictionary if you like, but I wouldn't work for the likes of you for any wages."

"I'll have Mr. Disston speak to you," said Helen furiously. "You can't leave a place like that without any notice."

"Oh, I can't, can't I? Well, I'll have you to know that I've worked in this house before you was born, an' I'll leave when I like, an' not a day later."

"You'll not get your wages, then. I'll tell Mr. Disston not to give you a cent."

"Wages or no wages, I'm goin' tonight. But the master is not like that. You don't know him very well if you think he is. The master is a silly fool sometimes, I'll admit, but he's honest! The master may be blind as a bat sometimes, but he's a good man in spite of it, an' he's honest as the day is long. I'll leave my case in the master's hands, an' wages or no wages I'm leavin' the house tonight!"

Helen gave her a baleful look and turned away furious, going in search of her husband. Maggie went on calmly preparing her dinner.

"The dinner's ready," she called after the mistress, "an you'd best eat it now unless you want to wash up afterwards. I'm not stayin' late, so you'd best come at once."

Chapter 9

Down in the stone cottage about half an hour before the taxi bearing the master and mistress of the great house reached the door and Diana made her hasty exit from the kitchen, Gordon MacCarroll arrived home from his long day's trip. He stabled his car in the old barn and came in to greet his mother.

He had been away since dawn on a longer journey than any his new connection in the business world had demanded of him yet, and he had been greatly successful. There was a light of victory in his face as he stooped to kiss his mother and a keen delight in getting home again after a hard day's work. He was tired and hungry and glad to get back where he could rest. The dinner was beginning to send out a delectable aroma from the oven where something delicious and spicy was in preparation, and the little cozy house looked good to him.

"Well, how is everything, Mother?" he asked as he went to the sink and washed his hands, wiping them on the spick-and-span roller towel. He was just like a boy with a playmate when he got home to his mother. There was a lovely comradeship between them.

But the mother's face clouded over a trifle.

"Oh, do you know, I'm afraid there's some trouble up at the great house," she said, turning from the celery she was washing and placing in a narrow crystal dish. "The little lady came by this morning just as usual, or maybe a bit earlier, and she was carrying a flower again— Isn't that curious? I wonder if they have a greenhouse up there! This is twice she's carried flowers— But, Gordon, she was *crying*!"

"Oh, Mother! You must have been mistaken!" The young man frowned and looked at her intently.

"No, I was not mistaken. I saw her quite distinctly, though she didn't see me. I had just gone out the back door to hang out the dishcloths for a good sunning, and I saw her coming through the trees. She was running along, and she stooped to pick something up—perhaps she had dropped her flower. I saw her just as she was rising from stooping over, and she bent her head down over the flower. I saw her chin tremble and then her face went down right into the flower, and she was crying hard, as if she was terribly grieved. And she caught her breath in one little sob. It sounded so piteous I wanted to rush out and put my arms around the sweet child and comfort her. But I didn't stir. I even held my breath, lest she would spy me and know I had heard, and somehow I felt that would hurt her still more to know anyone had seen her. I was behind the bushes, and I felt like a thief seeing her there when she wouldn't have wanted me to, but I couldn't get away. And even if I had closed my eyes, I couldn't help hearing that sob. The poor sweet child. I'm afraid she is in some real trouble. I've been wondering if it is connected with some of those young men we've seen driving in occasionally. Poor child without any mother! I must really try to get acquainted somehow and see if I can't win her confidence. My heart goes out to her."

The young man gave a startled look at his mother and then

turned and looked meditatively out the window. His mother was thickening the gravy for the moment. She was putting in the salt and pepper, a bit of butter, and stirring it while it bubbled smoothly over the fire. Gordon turned back and watched her.

"Did she come back again?" he asked gravely, trying to make his voice sound quite casual.

"Yes, she came back, but she had stayed away longer than usual, and she was hurrying as if she were out of breath. And then about two o'clock a big moving van came driving in and went up to the house and stayed about an hour or more. I couldn't see so well, but I went up to your window and looked out because I was troubled. I didn't know but our folks had lost all their money and were moving out. But they didn't stay long enough to move all that furniture. It might have been just some things that belonged to someone else, or that they were selling or giving away, so my mind was free about that. The van was all closed up, of course, when it came out so I couldn't tell what like things they were that were taken away."

"My word, Mother! You certainly are getting to be a nosy little neighbor, prying into other folks' business. I never knew you to be so curious before," laughed Gordon, albeit with a thoughtful look in his eyes.

"Well, it's not exactly curiosity you know, Son," protested the mother. "I just can't bear to think of that sweet, pretty little girl having to suffer. I hope it's not more money troubles. You know, that agent that rented this house to us said the owner had seen reverses and that was why he was willing to rent the cottage."

"I know." Gordon was grave again.

"But there are worse things, of course, than losing one's house and one's money," went on the mother. "I couldn't help wondering, was the child going to marry one of those men that call on her? The fat one or the gray-haired one or maybe the one with the long, thin face and foppish clothes? And maybe she just isn't happy about it. Oh, I'd like to get my arms around her and get her to let me help her a bit with her decisions. You know that van might have come to take her things away to her future home."

Gordon made a quick movement with his hand and almost knocked a cup off from the table. He caught it just in time but sent a spoon clattering on the floor.

"Oh, I say, Mother! Aren't you going a little too far with your wonderings?"

He tried to laugh, but the sober look stayed in his eyes.

"Well, perhaps I am," the mother said, smiling. "I think perhaps I am making a story out of it. Being a stranger here with not very much to do all day I can't help being interested in what's around me. Pretty soon we'll get acquainted hereabouts and then it will be different. Though I shall never be quite so much interested in any other people, I'm sure. I somehow feel they are in a sense our own folks because we're renting from them. Now, come, the dinner is ready. Let's sit down right away. I know you are good and hungry. Listen! Isn't that a taxi coming in the drive? Maybe it's a wedding after all." She laughed cheerily, but Gordon turned sharply around and looked out the kitchen window for a long time and for once forgot to help his mother put the dinner on the table.

There was a bit of delay after all with the dinner, for Mrs. MacCarroll had been so interested in telling the happenings of the day that she had forgotten to put the butter and cream on the table, and then she had to go back to the refrigerator again for pickles and jelly and to the pantry for some crackers for the soup.

Gordon so far recovered himself as to get a pitcher of water and fill the glasses, and then with another glance up at the window he remarked, "There's no sign of any festivity up at the house, Mother, only two rooms are lit up. And there! There comes the taxi going away. Perhaps her father has arrived. Didn't you say he was away?"

"Yes," said the mother. "That's probably it. Come, let's get on with the meal. I'm afraid everything will be stone cold. Ask the blessing, child, and let's forget the neighbors while we eat. Besides, I want to hear all about your day."

Then Gordon MacCarroll bowed his head and asked that blessing, which was more than a mere saying of grace, and outside the tall hedge his heartfelt petition reached to the lonely girl waiting there in the dark and was imprinted on her memory indelibly.

They had a pleasant time at their evening meal; they always did together, those two. They talked over the developments of the day and Gordon's work, and they laid their cheerful plans for the future. And then Gordon helped his mother put the kitchen to rights for the night.

"You'd better get right to bed, Son, and make up your sleep. You look dead tired. Do you have to go very early tomorrow morning?"

"No, not till eight thirty," responded the son cheerfully. "I'm due at the office in the morning to report, and the bosses don't care to wake at dawn to hear what I've done, so for once I can have a real sleep."

When Gordon had gone to his room and closed his door he stood for a long time looking out his window toward the great house. There were lights in plenty now, from the first floor to the roof, and in a kind of consternation he watched. Then it occurred to him that a single taxi wasn't likely to make a wedding, and he stood and laughed at himself. He was getting as curious as his mother. Besides, there, the lights were going out again!

But though he turned away and turned on his own light, trying to banish the thought of the little lady from the great house weeping with her lips against a flower, he could not get his mind at rest, and finally he just frankly opened his door and went down the stairs.

"I'm just running out to the garage for a minute, Mother,"

he called, and then he went out the back door. A few minutes later he came in with a small white envelope in his hand, and his mother put her head down on her pillow with a smile. What a good dear boy he was, and what blessed fortune was hers that she should have him when all the rest of her family were gone!

And about that time up at the big house the new mistress, having adroitly put Maggie in a very bad light before her husband, had slipped off upstairs to reconnoiter with a gleam of victory in her eyes. She had accomplished her purpose of driving out her stepdaughter sooner than she had hoped.

But perhaps she would not have been so sure of her victory if she could have seen the tired, troubled look on her husband's face when he came out in the kitchen to talk to Maggie and try to get her to reconsider her rash resignation. "What's this Mrs. Disston has been telling me, Maggie, that you're going to desert us? That surely can't be right. I told her I thought there must be some mistake. I told her it must be merely some little misunderstanding. You've been with us so long, Maggie, we won't know what to do without you. I never thought you would leave us."

"I wouldn't, sir, not for a minute if 'twas just yourself an' Miss Diana. I'd stick by you till there wasn't a stroke of work left in me. But it's herself I cannot abide. She an' I could never stay by in the same house. It was bad enough her visitin' when the missus was here to manage, but now, her with the airs she takes, I no can bide an' work for her."

The master's eyes grew stern.

"Nonsense, Maggie!" he said sharply. "I'm afraid Diana has been putting notions in your head. Diana is a foolish child who will get over her pettishness in a day or two and everything will be all right."

"Miss Diana didn't need to put notions in my head. I had them before she did. If you'd ever tried to get a meal in this kitchen with that limb o' Satan around you'd know without bein' told, and I'm no bidin' an' that's all there is to it. I'm only here tonight to give you the letter."

"Letter?" The father turned a grave, puzzled look on her.

Maggie fumbled in the capacious bib of her apron and finally brought out Diana's letter. "I was to give it to you where there was no one else by. She wanted you should read it by your lone. After that I've no more to do with it. I'm packin' now an' leavin' the house tonight, an' you needn't pay me the wages that's comin' to me unless you like. I'm goin' just the same."

The man took his daughter's letter with a hand that trembled and tried to make his voice stern as he searched the face of the old servant. "Maggie, have you been helping my daughter in this nonsense? Did you help her to go away? Did you put this idea in her head?"

"If you mean did I try to comfort her when I saw her grievin' her heart away an' cryin' her pretty eyes out by her lone, yes, I did. If you mean did I help her get her bit things together when she said she was goin' away, sure I did! But for puttin' the notions in her head, no! She had the notions herself, an' rightly. An' if you had not been as blind as a bat you would have seen it yourself before it was too late!"

Anger rose in the father's face, and he lifted his head haughtily, preparing a stern rebuke. But Maggie went around the room doing little last things, hanging up her dishcloths, hanging the dishpan on its hook, closing the cupboard door with a finality that seemed to have a strange foreboding, and suddenly the master of the house realized that his time might be short and he was losing another link in the chain that had made up the home life all these years. Suppose Maggie should carry out her purpose and disappear, too, and he would have lost a valuable clue to finding his foolish little girl?

"Maggie," he said, and there was almost an appeal in his voice, for somehow he began to realize that he *must* have this woman on his side, "where is my daughter?"

"She didn't tell me aught about where she was goin' save that she was on a visit. I gathered she might see some relatives an' perhaps some friends, too. I didn't ask her. I minded it was none of my business. But if you're thinkin' she'll be comin' back, you'll find yourself grandly mistaken. She'll not come back while that woman is mistress or my name's not Maggie Morrison. You brought the hussy here, an' now you'll have to abide by your own act."

"Maggie!" said Mr. Disston coldly. "You are forgetting yourself. You are presuming on your long connection in our home. I don't want to hear any more such impertinence!"

"No, I'm not forgettin' myself," said Maggie arrogantly, "I'm just statin' fact. But I'm done now, an' I'm goin' up the stair to get my bit things an' leave you. I've nothin' more to say except one thing. If you're ever alone an' need me, just send for me, an' I'll come back. But not whilst that hussy is in the house as mistress. I cannot abide her, an' I'd not sleep under the same roof with her. She's a *hussy*, an' that's all there is to it, an' you'll find it out to your own sorrow soon enough! Good-bye!" And dashing away the tears, Maggie stormed up the back stairs to her room, and the master went to his library with his letter and locked the door to read it.

And over across the lawn a young man, a stranger, knelt in the moonlight with a letter in his hand and prayed for a girl he did not know, whom the Lord had laid upon his heart.

And out through the night and the darkness, into a new country, the train was hurrying along mile after mile carrying a sorrowful girl far away from all that she knew and loved. A girl who lay with her face against a handful of pale carnations and kept them wet all night with her tears.

Anger and prayer and tears, the breath of flowers watered by bitter tears, a girl groping in terrible sorrow and darkness.

Chapter 10

The train drew into the station an hour late, and Diana, pale with weeping and the long vigil, came out into the strange station and looked around her. She had traveled often with her father but very little by herself. She was not used to looking after the details of travel, and she had never been to this city where the aunt of her mother's lived. Now that she was here she shrank inexpressibly from meeting her. She had half a mind to turn around and go back, only where could she go? She was an exile from home, a wayfarer and a stranger on the face of the earth. The realization of what it was going to mean swept over her as she followed the porter carrying her luggage, and such a wave of homesickness and heartsickness came over her that she felt she simply must drop right down there on the platform and give up.

But instead she followed the porter to the taxi stand, gave her directions clearly, and climbed into the cab, heartily wishing she had never come in search of this unknown aunt whose only contact during the years had been an occasional letter and a gift of a handkerchief or collar at Christmas. Why had she come here to her? Why hadn't she chosen one of her mother's friends and confided in her? Why hadn't she gone even to Maggie's sister's for a while as the good old servant had several times during yesterday suggested?

Oh, she knew the answers to all those questions. She had thoroughly canvassed the whole matter during the watches of the night, and it had seemed that this was the only refuge she could depend upon that was far enough to elude the indomitable Helen. So here she was, and the immediate future had to be faced.

Yet she was unable to find any help for her mind as she was whirled through one unfamiliar street after another, out into the suburbs. It was a pleasant street into which they finally turned, a bit old-fashioned, not in the least like the wide highway on which the Disston estate was situated. Well, she couldn't expect that, of course. She was an exile now and must be content with what she found.

Presently they stopped in front of a large old-fashioned house surrounded by a dismal yard containing a few scraggly trees. It looked comfortable enough but a bit neglected, as if no one had cared about it for a good many years. Diana gave a quick comprehending glance, and her heart dropped several degrees. It wasn't a pleasant outlook. Still, there was a yard, and it was not a bad neighborhood. All the houses had more or less ground around them, and there were even one or two little cottages that had almost a cheerful look. This house where she was going seemed to rather dominate the street, as if its past respectability gave it the right. Yet there was nothing really attractive and welcoming to make it seem like a refuge in her distress. It was comfortable and solid and old-fashioned, that was all.

Diana's heart beat wildly while she paid the fare and got out of the taxi to look around her. It suddenly seemed to her a very great breach of etiquette that she had sent no word ahead to announce her coming. She should at least have sent a telegram to ask if it would be convenient. Perhaps even now she should drive back to the station and telephone to ask if she might come. Yet that would seem very odd to the taxi driver. Of course, it was none of his business what she did if she paid him, yet he would be likely to think she was crazy. Well, she was here now and of course she must go on. She could say she was taking a trip and had stopped off to see her aunt. Strange it hadn't occurred to her to think of this before. She had been so taken up with her own troubles that this end of her journey had not been a consideration at all.

She walked slowly up to the house, which seemed to grow more forbidding the nearer she went. The taxi driver was following with her bags. She wished she had told him not to mind and tried to carry them herself, though they were heavy. Then she would be rid of him and could even turn back if she liked.

As she mounted the steps to the wide porch she noticed a dilapidated doll flung abandoned under a porch chair, suggesting the presence of a child. A child? The aunt had no children! She was supposed to be living alone with an old servant. But perhaps the servant had a child. A child, even the child of a servant, would bespeak a little cheer. Diana drew a deep breath and told the driver to leave the bags on the porch. Then she put out a timid hand and raised the old-fashioned knocker.

The knocker was loose and echoed through the house as if it were made of sounding boards. Diana shrank away from the door and wished again that she had not come. Then she heard footsteps coming, and she felt that frightened sinking in her heart again. What should she say? How should she explain her sudden appearance? How could she tell an unknown relative what had happened in her life. A stranger! This woman she had come to see was in reality a stranger! And now she remembered that her mother had said she never approved of her marriage to Stephen Disston. She had wanted Mother to marry an older man by the name of Eldridge who had two half-grown children by a former marriage and a handsome house across the street. That must be the Eldridge house over there, built of stone with elaborate casements and ornate columns. Suppose Mother had married him and lived there! Diana shivered at the thought and turned to meet the dowdy girl who opened the door. Then suddenly Diana didn't know what to say. Why hadn't she planned this all out?

But she summoned her senses and asked if Mrs. Whitley was in.

The girl was frankly staring Diana up and down, admiring her clothes. There was no mistaking that look, and Diana was suddenly conscious of her heavy heart beneath her chic garments. She had a feeling that presently the girl would see that heart, too, and wonder. Then the girl came to herself and answered, "No, she doesn't live here."

"Doesn't *live* here!" repeated Diana, startled. "Why, isn't this Moreland Avenue? Isn't this number 425?"

"Sure," said the girl, "but she doesn't own this place anymore. My father bought this place over a year ago."

"Oh!" Diana caught her breath. "But where did she move? Is it far away?"

"Quite a ways," said the girl complacently. "They say it takes about two hours on the bus. My father went up there once to see her about the house settlement. He said she was fixed real nice."

"Oh," said Diana, a troubled look coming into her eyes. "Do you have the address?"

"My father has. But he isn't home today. He went off fishing with a friend. He won't be home till late tonight. And my mother isn't here, either. She's gone up in the country to nurse my aunt. She's real sick. Just I and my brothers are here, and they wouldn't know the address, either. But you wouldn't have any trouble finding it. It's a *Home*, you know. One of those where you put in all the money you have and you get a nice big room to live no matter how old and sick you get. My father says her room is peachy, and she's got it fixed up lovely with what furniture she saved from this house. It's up to a place called Wynnewood. You could hire a taxi, I suppose, to take you, but it would cost an awful lot."

"Oh!" said Diana again in a growing dismay, giving a glance of trepidation around the grubby-looking front yard with a sudden relief that she didn't have to stay here, even for a day.

But—! Where *was* she going?

She turned back to the girl. "Do you know how long she has been gone from here?"

"Sure!" said the girl. "It's just a year ago last Saturday that we moved in. My father was talking about it last Sunday."

Diana gave another troubled look into nowhere. "Well—I suppose I might as well go on, then. . . The words trailed off uncertainly.

"You can come in if you want," said the girl, casting a hesitant glance at the pile of baggage.

"Oh no," said Diana quickly. There was no point in going in. "But"—she paused and looked down the road—"I'm sorry I let the taxi go until I was sure whether this was the right place."

"Oh, I can call him for you," offered the girl brightly. "He's only up the road a piece. You see, he's engaged to my cousin, and he takes every chance he can to stop at the house when he gets up this way. I can send my kid brother over to call him if you want."

"Oh, thank you!" said Diana, strangely grateful for this offer. But what was she going to do next?

The girl offered her a chair on the porch while she went to send the little brother on his errand, and Diana sat down and looked across the street at the ugly, pretentious house that her mother did not marry into all those long years ago and thought of the lovely mansion she had left last night—the rolling lawns, the groups of century-old trees, the picturesque stone cottage by the gate, and the flowers that had lain there in the shadow on the grass so mysteriously—and sudden tears sprang to her eyes.

But the girl was coming back carrying a glass of water.

"I thought perhaps you were thirsty," she said, handing over the glass and quite frankly settling herself in an old porch rocker to examine her guest. "Ted'll be back in a minute," she added. "It's only up the road a little piece."

"Is that house across the way owned by a Mr. Eldridge?" asked Diana with sudden interest.

"Why yes!" said the girl. "How did you know? Did you ever live in this town?"

"No," said Diana with a little shiver—she was glad she had never lived around here—"but my mother did for a little while. She used to tell me about some Eldridges across the road from her aunt's."

"Oh!" said the girl, giving her another speculative glance and then looking across the way to the ugly old Eldridge house, trying to harmonize house and girl. Then her eyes came back to Diana.

"He's real old," she explained, "Mr. Eldridge. He's just buried his third wife, and they say it might be he'll marry Miss Hurst, the nurse that's taking care of him. He's sick, you know, and not expecting to get well, and he's mad with all his children, so he has nobody to leave his property to. My! I wish he'd leave it to me! I'd know what to do with it." The girl's face took on a wistful look. "They say his children was all mad at him when he married this last time and tried to put him in the insane asylum, but he was too smart for them, and now he has disinherited all of them."

The girl reeled the story off as if it were a fairy tale, and Diana sat up sharply and drew a deep breath. Marrying! Marrying! It was everywhere! Why couldn't people be true to their first marriage? And here were other children suffering as she was! She felt a fellow feeling for them.

"Where are they all, the children?" she asked suddenly, wondering if their state would throw any light on her problem.

"Oh, different places, I guess. There's one daughter over in the next town teaching school; she's the oldest. They call her an old maid, and she's been teaching a good many years. The next girl married a farmer, but they're awful poor. He's got a big mortgage on his farm, and he might lose it this fall. The youngest girl ran off with a fella and they don't know where she is, and the boy's been in jail twice already."

The girl told it off as indifferently as if she were detailing the fate of a lot of squirrels, but Diana stared at the ugly old house aghast! Her life had always been so guarded! She had not realized how hard life was for many! So, she was not the only one who suffered! She had emerged out of her haven into a world where suffering and sordidness were on every hand!

"It's awful when parents get married again!" announced the girl quite irrelevantly and apathetically.

"It is!" said Diana, rising suddenly as she saw the taxi careening down the road in the distance.

"I'll help ya down with the bags," said the girl, taking up a shining suitcase admiringly. "Ted's in a hurry, I guess. It's almost train time again, and he has to be back on time or he'll lose his job."

"You've been very kind," said Diana gratefully, picking up a smaller bag and finding it taken from her hand by the grimy fingers of a ten-year-old who had likely gone after the taxi.

As the taxi swung up to the sidewalk, Diana summoned a smile and handed out a bit of money to the boy and then, shyly, gave the girl a bill.

"Just to remember me by," she said brightly and got in, thankful that she did not have to stay in that dismal spot overnight.

"Where to?" asked the driver, and Diana suddenly was brought face-to-face with her future again. Where should she go next?

"Wantta go back ta the station?" persisted the driver, thinking she had not heard him.

"Oh yes," said Diana, coming out of her daze. "Certainly."

"Which train ya takin'?" asked the driver.

"Oh, why, I have to inquire about trains. I'm not sure yet."

The young man, Ted, appeared to want to converse, but Diana answered him coolly and was glad when the station came in sight again.

"Goin' back south again?" he asked.

"That depends," said Diana sweetly, "I'm not sure yet."

Diana went and sat in the station for two long hours trying to think out what she should do. She wrote out a list of all her friends whom it would be possible for her to visit and weighed each possibility carefully, deciding at last that it would be utterly out of the question for her to visit anyone in her present state of mind. She couldn't bring herself to the telling of what had happened to her, not to mere casual acquaintances, and that was what most of her friends had become in the last three years. No, she had to get herself more in hand, get more balance, work out a philosophy of living that would keep her from shivering and bursting into tears at everything that reminded her of her calamity before she mingled again with people who thought they had a right to question her.

Having decided against any visits, she weighed, just briefly, the possibility of marrying any of the men she knew who would be likely to want to marry her and found the idea so unpleasant that she quickly put that thought away as not to be further considered.

Then what should she do?

If she had to provide a home for herself permanently, could she do it on her own small income? She would never ask her father for money since she had left his home and shelter. And if she did, she felt quite sure Helen would counsel him not to give her anything. Naturally he might think that would be a way to bring her back home, for she knew in her heart that he would miss her. No matter how much he might care for his new wife, he loved her, and naturally he would want her to return. She put her head wearily back against the station wall and thought about that. Perhaps she ought to have stayed a while just to convince him that it would not be a happy thing for anybody if she did. But no, Helen would only have made it appear that she was always at fault. It was better as it was, only what was she going to do with herself? She was not wanted anywhere, except, of course, by her father, and what would be the point in convincing him that she could not stay at home? It was too late for that now. And she was tired, oh, so deadly tired. She wished everything were at an end. Yet one couldn't jump off a bridge or wade out in a stream and drown. She had to live on and somehow go on alone! *Alone!* What a terrible word that was!

Well, she had to do it, and the sooner she started, the better. Why not begin right here in this strange town? The first thing would be to find a room somewhere. Not a boarding place. That would entail other people who had a right to inquire into one's business, and she was just now like a hurt animal that wanted to crawl away from all its kind and lick its wounds in secret.

So she checked her baggage and started out.

Chapter 11

It was almost noon, and as she passed a restaurant she realized that she could not go on long without something to eat, so she stopped and ordered a cup of coffee and toyed with a buttered roll. She drank the coffee, but somehow the food did not attract her. It was the first time in her life that she had ever eaten in a cheap restaurant, but she felt that that did not matter. Any food in any restaurant would have been as uninteresting.

Then she went on her way up one street and down another aimlessly, wondering where to begin. She had never hunted rooms in a city before. She had no idea where to look for rooming houses. Finally she bought a paper and stood on a corner studying advertisements and then went on again in search of a place to lay her head for the night.

It is safe to say that Diana never had dreamed that there were such places as some of those she saw that afternoon, following that newspaper column of advertised apartments. They were not all bad, of course. Some were really attractive, but then the price soared beyond her modest income and frightened her with the cost of life.

Her search narrowed down at last to two—one on the third floor of a walk-up rooming house, its windows overlooking the roofs in the theatrical district. An ill-smelling bathroom down the hall would have to be shared with the occupants of the entire floor. It was stifling hot and filled with the din of the city rising in a roar from the streets below. The other one was small, ornate, with built-in cupboards, cheap mirrors, and a tiny, uncertain automatic elevator to the fifth floor. A fire siren screeched all the time she was looking at it, and Diana imagined a night with the building on fire and that inadequate elevator gone below and *staying* there! Diana fled from the spot but a half hour later returned and forced herself to consider the details, because it had seemed the only approach to anything like the life to which she had been accustomed. She looked out the windows and saw an undertaking establishment across the street, a neat sign of coffins hung next door, and she fled again. Back in the station she considered both places and did some figuring and then rested her head back against the seat and closed her eyes, wishing that life was over and she did not have to consider any more possibilities. When she thought of those apartments she seemed to see herself lying alone, unknown, in a coffin.

A trainman slammed a metal sign into its frame over the station door, announcing a train back to her home city, and a great longing came over her to board it and return. Back to where she was at least known and knew her way around. Back where she could tell the sordid parts of town from the decent, respectable ones. If she must go into lodgings—and she was still determined she would not go to boarding—certainly it would be better to know what kind of place she was taking. Also, she had learned enough that afternoon to realize that she could get a room unfurnished cheaper than furnished, and by that means save the money she would be spending for storage. Also, if she was going to use her own furniture, it would cost a lot to move it here to this far city.

It suddenly seemed to her most preposterous to try to stay here, with no aunt in the vicinity and no point to the whole thing except to get as far away from Helen as possible. Surely she could hide nearer to home and not be found.

She remembered a woman's hotel in her home city where a friend had once stayed a few days. Why could she not go there for a week and look around until she found the right place?

It was growing dark. The strange noisy station seemed aloof and unfriendly. The continual coming and going of trains began to weary her inexpressibly. Oh, to be at home in her own sweet room, to lie down and sleep until she was rested, until her heart did not ache so feebly. Ah! But there was no home! The room was stark and bare and her lovely things stored in a vast storage house! She had no home anymore! It was entirely up to her now to make a place in which to stay, and she had no desire whatever, no interest in it at all. She opened her handbag to get out a hand-kerchief and the faint perfume of the carnations stole out into the sooty atmosphere of the station and carried her back on a breath to the lawn of her father's estate and the tall trees shadowing the spot where the mystery flowers had lain, and a longing filled her to go back. Perhaps this morning there had been another flower and she had not been there to find it! Perhaps another would find it! Could Helen? That would be just like Helen to steal her flowers, her few mystery flowers, after she had stolen her father and her home and everything that was worthwhile in her life. Ah! And perhaps tomorrow there would be another flower—that is, if no one else found them—but—surely by then the flower person would discover that she was gone—and that it was useless to drop any more. Would her note be found by the right one? Would it be read, and would it be understood?

What if Helen should find it? The thought seized her heart like the gripping of pain. Even there in the noisy station with the people jostling one another, she could hear that light mocking laugh that Helen would give should she find that note in the grass! Oh, why had she ever been silly enough to write that note?

Her cheeks burned red and hot at the thought. Oh, if she could only go in the night and hunt for it and find it and destroy it!

And suddenly Diana knew she was going back.

Not to her home, of course. But she must get back where she knew her way around. She must find a place somewhere where her soul belonged. She was lost, lost, lost, in a great world that knew her not nor cared. There was nobody who cared now, except her father, and he was angry at her.

She went in a sudden panic to the ticket window and asked a few questions. She bought a return ticket to her home city. She went to the lunch counter in the station and swallowed a few bites, drank a cup of coffee, and was ready, standing with her bags at her feet beside the gateway, waiting for her train, fifteen minutes before the scheduled time for its arrival.

She might have been sitting, resting on one of the station benches, for she was deadly weary, but she was too restless to rest. She had to be there, ready to go out the moment the gates were open. So she stood, tense, braced, and looking with unseeing eyes around on the vast, dusky room with its coming and going throngs. Why had she come out here? How had she hoped to find haven even with an aunt? For now she saw clearly that if the aunt had been there as she had expected, and she had been obliged to stay several days to explain her presence there at all, it would have been torture. What she wanted was to be alone in some little quiet place where she could rest and think and try to straighten out what this life meant that she was called upon to live, this life that she had no right to lay down and yet that seemed to have no solution to its problems. She had to find that out before she could go on any further. Aunts and friends or even strangers could only hinder a process like this. She must be alone to think. She must find a solution to life in order to endure it. She had always had someone to lean upon—first her darling mother and then her loving father. But now she had neither, and she had, in addition, an enemy! That was the situation. She had to work it out alone, *alone*!

The delicacy of her face, the rippling of her hair, the deep appeal of her eyes made her a noticeable figure as she stood there alone by the train gateway, surrounded by her luggage. More than one weary traveler waiting for a belated train or a wandering member of his household watched her idly as one would gaze upon a flower garden in the rain. But her eyes roved over them all restlessly, not seeing them at all.

She did not know that there were heavy lines graven in her soft face where only yesterday it was smooth and fine. She did not know that her eyes were full of anguish that anyone might read. She thought herself a quiet, patient figure, unobtrusively waiting for a train, and when she saw a slender figure rise from the bench across the room and come toward her she noticed her no more than if she had been the station janitor going around with his broom and long-handled pan to gather up the papers and the match ends.

But then the other girl paused beside her shyly, sweetly, with such a friendly look in her plain gray eyes, and spoke half hesitantly.

"I brought you this," said the other girl. "I've been reading it, and I thought perhaps it would rest you to read it, too. I could see something has hurt you. I'm sorry. I understood because I've been hurt, too. But I found something that will heal the hurt, and you will, too, if you'll read this and believe it."

She handed out a tiny printed tract, just two miniature pages. There was a look in her eyes that could not anger anyone no matter how proud.

Diana brought startled eyes down to the bit of paper the other girl held out, and a shade of the Disston pride stiffened her features. Then she turned her glance to the girl who offered it, saw the gentleness in the girl's face, and her own eyes softened.

The stranger was plainly dressed, even poorly, in the cheapest kind of garments, with a little hat that might have come from a bargain counter in the ten-cent store, and her hands were cased in cheap, ill-fitting cotton gloves; that is, one was, though the other was bare, showing that though delicately formed it was rough and hardened with work. Her shoes were shabby, and her dress of common dark cotton, ill-cut and not at all attractive. Yet there shone in the girl's face a light and joy that made her noticeable anywhere, and looking into her clear, sweet eyes, Diana could not help but trust her.

She put out her hand to take the little paper offered, and as she did so the other girl's face lit with a joy inexpressible, as if it gave her real pleasure to have the stranger accept her gift.

"What is it?" Diana asked wonderingly, looking at the paper and then up at the girl.

"It's something wonderful. I can't stay to explain. My train's called, and I have to hurry, but you read it. You trust it! It helped me, and I know it'll help you. Good-bye!" The girl started away but, pausing, turned back and said in a low, sweet voice, "I'll be praying that you'll get what I got!"

Then she was gone.

Diana watched her threading her way swiftly through the throngs, hurrying through the gate, her newspaper bundle gripped in one arm, her ticket in the other hand. One bright look she cast back and then was gone. Diana stood wondering, the little paper trembling in her hand, her thoughts utterly turned away from herself for the first time that day. This was a poor girl, hard-working, thin, and not well-fed apparently. There was a look in her eyes of suffering endured, and yet how they lit up with real joy! There was even a sparkle in her voice! Diana stood, wondering, staring at the gate where the girl had disappeared until suddenly a trainman came up and slammed open the steel gate that led to her own train and called it out, reaching out his punch to her ticket, and Diana was roused to her own situation again.

She followed the porter down the steps to the train and up into the car then down the aisle to her compartment in a sort of daze, still holding in her hand the tiny fluttering paper, gripping it as if it were something precious. And when she had paid the porter and settled down in her seat with a weary sigh of relief, she sat still holding that bit of paper, staring out the window and thinking about the look in that other girl's face.

It was not until the train was finally moving that she turned her eyes to the paper and began to read with deepening interest.

HE UNDERSTANDS!

In large letters it stood out as the title to the tiny message. Startled, she read on, as if it had been written by someone she knew and sent to her as a special message in her need. It would not have been any more startling if a telegraph boy had come through the train and handed it to her, and she had found Maggie's or her mother's name attached to it.

> *No matter what problem or sorrow is in your life today, there is Someone who understands and cares.*

That was all that was on that little front page, standing out clearly from the paper in large type, as if a voice were speaking it to her soul. Diana was almost afraid to turn the tiny page lest the spell would be broken and she would find it merely the advertisement of some trickster, some beauty parlor, or new product. Then her mind became impatient, and she turned the leaf tremblingly, so much she wanted it to be some real help for her need.

> *One reason why the Son of God came to earth and*
> *took a human body was so that He might suffer*
> *and understand and help us in our grief.*

Diana read that over twice, wondering if that could really be true and how the writer knew that. This, then, was religion, and she had been brought up to respect religion, although it had never meant anything practical to her. But these were arresting sentences, and her need was very great. Her soul seemed to be clutching for the bit of a message and seeking to draw the truth from its pages. She read on.

> *There is no kind of sorrow He does not know, even*
> *to having His beloved Father turn His back on*
> *Him for a time.*

Oh! Was that true? How had that been? Had God really turned His back on Christ? And why? There were two references below in tiny type. Diana wished she had a Bible that she might look them up. Perhaps the references would explain the statement. But how wonderful that her very situation should be described! For her father had in reality turned his back on her. She remembered that gesture of impatience when she had flung her arms around him and cried on his shoulder. How he had pushed her away and gone and stood by the mantel with his back half turned away.

The tears sprang into her eyes unbidden, and she had to dash them away before she could go on reading. It seemed to her nothing short of miraculous that this little message should have fallen into her hands tonight, of all nights, when she so much needed it, this message that exactly fitted and understood her heart's cry.

*For as He has Himself felt the pain of temptation
and trial, He is able also to help those who are
tempted and tried.*

There were more references here, and then the last little page went on in big letters again:

*In the darkest hour of your life, remember He is a
living, loving Savior.*

Then more small lines of references again. That was all. How she wished again for a Bible! She had not brought hers with her. It had never been a vital part of her life. It had not occurred to her to take it with her in her suitcase, and she could not even remember if she had packed it with the other books that were in storage. She was not sure when she had seen it last. Well, no matter, it was just a small fine-print copy, anyway, and she could surely get one anywhere. Didn't they have them in hotel rooms? It seemed to her that she remembered having seen one there the last time she and her father took a trip together. Well, when she got somewhere she would get a Bible and look up the references and see if there was really anything in it to give her comfort. She could not afford to pass by any chance, no matter how frail, of finding something to ease her pain.

She read the little tract over again slowly, before she prepared for the night. As she lay down she had a vision of that stranger girl in the station, her bright, earnest face and the words she had called back in leaving. She had promised to pray for her! What a strange thing for a stranger to do. And yet, if it were all true, perhaps that was the way the children of God ought to do with one another. Another time such interference by an utter stranger would have roused her scorn, would have repelled her. But now her heart felt strangely warmed toward another human creature who had suffered herself and therefore had rightly read her own suffering.

Finally she closed her eyes and tried to think of God as looking down on her and caring what became of her and how this matter of her life turned out.

"Oh, God," she whispered, softly like a prayer, "if You really know and care, won't You show me how to find You, for I need You very greatly."

She fell asleep at last with the little paper held tightly in her hand.

Chapter 12

About that same time Gordon MacCarroll arrived home at the cottage, put away his little car for the night, and came in to get the belated supper that his mother was keeping warm and delicious for him.

"Soup!" he said, giving a pleased sniff at the atmosphere as he entered. "Good old beef soup and plenty of potatoes and dumplings. There's nothing better than that."

"Yes," said his mother, with a pleased smile, "it's best when you don't know how long you have to wait to serve it. It always keeps well. Now, sit down right away. I know you must be starved."

"Well, all but—" said the son. "And say, I'm tired tonight! I had a lot of difficulty finding my location today and difficulty with that man after I found him, but I won out and got my contract signed, so it doesn't matter," he said as he passed his plate.

"That's good! Tell me all about it," said the mother with satisfaction, watching the light of content play over her boy's face.

So while they dallied restfully with the soup, and more soup, they talked about Gordon's business, he telling little details of the day, describing the scenery along the way he had driven, the people he had met. Gordon was a great mimic, and his mother was a good audience. She enjoyed to the full every bit of character sketch he gave and followed his delight in the woods and trees and sky effects. They were good company for one another, these two.

It was not until the delicious apple pie, delicate of crust and transparent with dripping jellied fruit, was brought in with its accompanying velvety cheese that Mrs. MacCarroll remembered.

"Oh," she said suddenly, "I've news for you about the big house. I had a caller today!"

"A caller?" said Gordon, his eyes lighting. "Someone from the village?"

"No, no one from the village yet, Son; what could you expect? We haven't been in the cottage a month yet and people haven't discovered us. Besides, we've been traveling around from one church to another on Sundays trying to find out where we belong, so people don't know where to place us yet. Another thing, too, we're among big estates, and we're neither one nor the other. We're not servants nor mansion owners, and how would anybody call on us yet till they know us?"

"Well, I don't care, Mother, only for your sake. I know you miss the hosts of friends you left in Edinburgh."

"That's all right, Gordon. I miss them, of course, but real friends like the friends of a lifetime aren't made in a day. Don't be in such a rush. I'm content."

"You're wonderful, little mother," said the son with a tender light in his eyes. "You wouldn't complain if you didn't have any friends, I know. But I do want you to have a few right away so you won't be lonely when I have to be away. But I interrupted you. Who was your caller? You don't mean to tell me it was the little lady?"

"No," the mother said, smiling and shaking her head with a flitting of sadness in her eyes. "I wish it had been. No, it was only the servant woman, Maggie, as she said I was to call her. She came to bring me the recipe for that pudding she promised the other day and to bid me good-bye. She's gone."

"You mean the whole family is moving away?" asked Gordon, with dismay in his face. "They haven't sold the house, have they?"

"No," said his mother, with a look of having more news. "No, but the woman, Maggie, is leaving. It seems there have been great doings up at our estate, and Maggie can't stand them. The master has married again and neither the daughter nor the servant like the new mistress, and they have both left, so we won't see our little lady anymore. Isn't that a pity? That must have been what she was crying about when she went by."

"You don't say!" said the young man, dropping his fork suddenly and then recovering it again and taking a long time to cut the next translucent bite of pastry.

"Yes," said his mother sympathetically as she poured another cup of coffee for Gordon. "I feel sorry for her. Maggie says she's a wonderful girl and that this new stepmother is a perfect tartar, really malicious, you know, doing mean things just for the sake of doing them and then laughing at her victim."

"Still," said the young man thoughtfully while taking a slow bite of cheese, "you can't always tell about a servant's gossip, you know. She is probably prejudiced."

"Well," said the mother, lifting her brows meditatively, "she doesn't just seem to be the ordinary servant. She's a Christian woman, I should say, and she loved her former mistress a great deal. She's been telling me about how lovely she was, and it does seem strange that a man who had such a lovely wife should have no better judgment—"

"That's it, Mother, he probably has, and this is just prejudice—"

"But, Gordon, listen, if she speaks the truth—and I think

she does, she seems like an honest woman—this new mistress is something of a freak, rather young, you know, and exercising her wiles over an older man, flattering him and torturing his daughter behind his back, yet making it appear that the girl has done it all!"

Gordon frowned. Then after a moment's thought he said, as if he was thinking it out, arguing with himself, "But this woman shouldn't have told you these things, of course! We're practically strangers, and a really loyal servant wouldn't have told the troubles of her master's home. If she isn't loyal, she probably isn't true."

"No," said the mother thoughtfully, "I don't believe that is the case with this woman. She didn't mean to tell me anything. She was quite proper when she came in with the recipe and told me most formally that she wouldn't be here again and that the young lady had sent word she couldn't make the promised call after all, as she had been obliged to go away in a hurry. But when I said it would be all right for her to come when she returned and that I would be looking forward to it, the woman turned sharply as if she were going away. And then I saw that she was crying, and I said: 'Why, is anything the matter, my dear? Isn't she coming back?' and she just stood there and sobbed silently into her handkerchief for a full minute. And then she got out the words: 'No, I'm afraid not.'

"I didn't quite know what to say, and I didn't like to ask any more questions, but in a minute she wiped her eyes and turned around and said in quite a dignified tone: 'You see, ma'am, the master is marryin' again, and my little lady feels she can't bide in the house.'

" 'Oh,' I said, 'that's too bad! But maybe she'll change her mind and come back later. Those things are hard to bear when they first happen, you know, but time heals almost everything. Maybe something will happen that they'll get to know one another better, and then perhaps she'll be glad to come back to her lovely home.' But the woman shook her head. 'No,' she said most decidedly, 'she'll not come. It was that hard for her to go, but she'll not return. She knows the woman full well already. She's her cousin three times removed, and many's the time she's suffered under a visit from her. She's a hussy, and that's true as truth! I am that shamed to be sayin' it, but it's true! It's why I'm not stayin' myself. Nobody could bide in the same house with her. She's a trollop! A wicked trollop! And I couldn't blame the poor wee bairn for leavin'.' "

The young man listened with growing sympathy.

"But doesn't her father do anything about it?" he asked sharply. "Or didn't she say anything about him?"

"Oh yes," laughed the mother, "she said plenty after she got warmed up and started. And yet you could see she was trying to be loyal to him, too. She said he was 'that fey about the hussy that he couldn't see straight.' She said he was 'a good man but blind as a bat,' and she went on to include all mankind in a general statement that all men were more or less 'feckless when it came to judgment about lassies.' "

"But what about his own daughter? Isn't she a lassie?" said Gordon, and there was a sharpness in his tone as if he were arguing with the father in question. His mother looked up with surprise in her eyes then laughed again.

"Oh, she says the father is sure the daughter will come around by and by and be as much in love with her new stepmother as he is." But Gordon did not smile. Instead, he ate his last bite of pie thoughtfully, almost seriously.

"It seems odd," he said almost savagely, "that a man who has lived his life up to the time when his daughter is grown up shouldn't be able to forget himself enough to think of her. It's selfishness, with a daughter like that. I can't help thinking he is to blame."

"But you don't know either of them," said his mother, surprised. "You can't tell what the daughter is, really. She looks very pretty seeing her go by, and very sweet, but you can't ever be sure."

"Can't I? Well, how long is it since you were saying almost the same thing about her, Mother mine?"

"Yes, I know, but still—we don't really *know!*"

"Well, just in general, then, no man has a right to bring a second mother on the scene unless his children are happy about it."

"But, Gordon, you know there are some lovely stepmothers. . ." protested his mother. "There was Aunt Genevieve! And there was Mrs. Stacey. There couldn't have been happier homes, and those children all adored those stepmothers."

"Of course there are exceptions," said Gordon. "I grant that, but they all knew and loved the stepmothers before they became their stepmothers."

"And there was Mrs. McCorkle and Mrs. Reamer and that dear Mrs. Bowman in Edinburgh."

"But the children were mere babes in all three of those cases and didn't know the difference, and besides, Mother, you know every one of those women were saints. This woman, you say, is a hussy!"

"I know"—the mother laughed—"and I can't help being sorry for the girl, Gordon. She must feel it terribly!"

"I guess they all need sympathy," said the young man, "and I suppose all the business we have with it is to pray for them."

"Yes," said his mother. "I have been praying all day—for the daughter. I can't get her out of my mind as she went by sobbing yesterday with that flower pressed close to her cheek. I can't help thinking, what if she were my little girl out in the world alone? And the world is such a very dreadful place in these days, too."

The young man did not answer. He was carefully gathering a few crumbs from the tablecloth into a neat little heap and then scattering them again. Presently the mother rose and began to gather up the dishes, and Gordon shoved back his chair and helped her. Afterward Gordon went out to the garage and walked around among the trees, thinking, and once he looked belligerently up toward the great house, studying the lit windows. The right-hand front window was all dark tonight.

But back in the library of the great house the master and the new mistress were talking. They had just returned from dinner in town because the bride had declined to prepare dinner at home and the bridegroom had declined to call up an agency in the city and have a cook and butler and a waitress sent out from town. The dishes from the breakfast that the master of the house had made—a breakfast of grapefruit, dry cereal, toast, and coffee, with soft boiled eggs, all on a tray for the bride and carried up to her room dutifully—were still lying stacked in the sink unwashed. Helen said she would ruin her hands if she should attempt to wash them, and besides, the excitement of the night before had "unfitted" her for such strenuous labor. "You wouldn't want me to wash dishes, would you, not just now when I'm supposed to be at my very best? The first few days I'm a bride? Suppose we have callers and they find me washing the dishes! My first day in the house! You wouldn't want that, would you, dear?"

She looked at him with that adoring, languishing glance that always thrilled him, the glance that had flattered the wistful growing-old part of him and made him think he was young again, and he smiled sadly, indulgently at her, looked down at the little painted fingernails, and sighed.

"No, I suppose not," he said.

"We're going out to lunch and do some shopping in the city, you said. You're going to buy that diamond clasp for me, you know, and we could just as well stay in the city for dinner and see a play or something, and then you think by that time Maggie will get over her huff, don't you? You said she was just angry and would be back?"

She lifted her liquid eyes so trustingly to his face, and he passed his hand gently over her head, thinking what a pretty child

407

she was and how sad it was that they should have anything to interfere with the perfect bliss of their homecoming. And then his heart would swell again with anger and indignation at the incredible way in which Diana, his devoted child, had taken all this, when he had really done it for her sake as much as anything else.

"Yes, I think—I hope she will be back—" he said then sighed deeply. "She's very fond of Diana, you know, and I suppose she's just angry in sympathy with her. I can't think what has come over Diana to act this way. It isn't in the least like her. I don't know but I ought to take the noon train and find her and bring her back. Things won't go right until we have an understanding. It's just as I told you, dear; Diana is hurt. I think she was hurt because we didn't insist on her coming up to the wedding. I felt that all along. You know, we've always been so close—!"

"And now you're thinking that I have come between you!" said the artful Helen, with a quiver of her red lips and a quick brimming of tears into her eyes. "You are sorry you married me! You are! You *a-a-rre!*" And soft gentle sobs and well-trained tears, not so very wet, rolled harmlessly over the smooth cheeks. Those tears and controlled sobs went to his heart like barbed darts as she had meant they should do. He had to take her in his arms then and comfort her, and assure her that he loved her above all things else, and that certainly he was not sorry that he had married her, and surely everything would come out all right as soon as Diana understood.

She let herself be comforted and swept off to the city to get the diamond clasp as a consolation prize. They had gone and stayed as she had planned, and now they had come back to a cheerless dark house, with those dirty dishes still huddled in the sink and not a scrap or sign of a repentant note or telegram from the prodigal daughter, and no Maggie in the kitchen, no prospect of anyone to get the breakfast ready for tomorrow morning. The master of the house was frantic. Nevertheless, his attitude of consolation was still required, and his role for the present was such that he must not let Helen see how frantic he was about his missing daughter.

All day Helen had kept him strained to the utmost to prove to her that she was not *superfluous*. If he sighed so much as a breath or let a distant look come into his tired eyes or let his smile droop on his lips she charged him with having to work so hard to make her think he was happy with her. And then all the day's work of reassuring her had to be done over again. He felt suddenly old and tired, and somehow condemned.

He had wanted to go and hunt for his child, but Helen had tenderly persuaded him that it was unwise, that she would only think she had the upper hand and there would be no harmony ever if she thought he was wrong and she was right. She had made the argument so plausible and so gentle, so delicately punctuated with tears and regrets that she had married him that he felt his hands utterly tied.

Time and again during the day and evening he had tried to slip away and telephone long distance to the old aunt's house where she was supposed to have gone, but always he was followed and gently questioned and urged to do the best way, just patiently wait until the prodigal returned repentant. And always he would come back with her to something she wanted to do and sit and look at her and think what a sweet, forgiving, lovely woman he had married and how amazingly wicked Diana had been to take such a silly prejudice against her. Yet underneath all the time his heart was crying out to go after Diana, have a heart-to-heart talk with her, and bring her back into the path of submission and rectitude. Why, Diana had never been like this! He was sure he could bring Diana to her senses if he only had a few minutes' talk with her.

So the harassed father and husband had gone through the house, until now they were back in the house again, the empty house, with their problems all unsolved before them, and Helen sighing and making him feel like a veritable Blue Beard in his Castle.

It was all wrong, of course. He could see it now. He should have taken Diana into his confidence. He should have had her invite Helen there or sent her to visit Helen. He should have revealed the whole matter more gradually and been near to comfort and sustain her in the first shock. Diana was merely hurt, of course. He could understand it better now since the thing was done. She evidently had had no such thought that he would ever marry again. She was a young girl, and, of course, perhaps it was perfectly natural that she should be shocked. Time did not move so rapidly with young people as it did with older ones. It seemed to him ages since the death of his first wife, and it had been so wonderful that Helen in her youth and beauty had been willing to come in and relieve the terrible loneliness that Marilla's going had made. He had always thought of it as *their* loneliness, his and Diana's, not his alone. Diana would, of course, profit by having a mother who was also young enough to be a sort of companion for her. He had deceived himself into thinking, into actually believing that Diana would be glad over the addition to the household. Her attitude had in reality been a great shock to him. Little Di whose utmost delight had always been to do his will, whose most cherished plans were ready to be flung aside for anything he had to propose. It was cataclysmic for her to rebel at anything he did or wanted. Surely this would not last! Surely she would come to herself very soon, as Helen had suggested, and return to her home and be her sweet self.

So at last he submitted to the inevitable and retired to a sleepless night, trying to persuade himself that the morrow would bring good news from the penitent. Then they could really begin to live! Then he would gently try to lead Diana and Helen to understand one another!

So the weary hours crept by but no sleep came. In the morning he looked drawn and haggard, and Helen, rousing from a late beauty sleep to take the tray he brought to her again, surveyed him with veiled vexation.

"You have no business to take things this way," she said sharply. "It makes you look old, and you can't afford that. You married me, and now it's up to you to keep young. And this toast is horribly burned! It isn't fit to eat! We've got to have some servants today or go to a hotel. I won't stand for this sort of thing!"

He winced as she said that about his looking old, and a gray look passed over his face as he turned away with a sigh and went out of the room.

Chapter 13

Diana was really too exhausted to lie awake long that night, and she fell asleep almost as soon as she lay down in her berth. But when she awoke, quite early in the morning, her first thought was of the words she had read from the little tract the stranger girl had given her in the station. It had seemed somehow to be something strong to lean upon. She hadn't grasped it yet, nor taken it for her own, but she wondered if it could be true, and her heart reached out in longing for something outside herself that would bear her up. For just now she felt as if she were going to crumple up and die just anywhere, as if she were utterly unable to think or decide any matter.

But next her whole pitiful situation flashed over her, and she realized that now in a few brief minutes she had to do something about a place to stay.

She glanced at her watch and found it had stopped in the night. She had forgotten to wind it, of course. She pulled aside the curtain and looked out. It was broad daylight, and she thought she recognized the landscape. Yes, there was the name of a town she had often heard that could not be more than an hour or so from her home city. She must hurry and get herself ready! And she must decide where she was going when she got there.

The little paper caught her eye as she was closing her suitcase. It had slipped down under the sheet. She picked it up carefully, put it into her purse, and stole a glimpse at her flowers in their soft wrappings. They still seemed to be alive. She must get them into water as soon as possible. She did not want to lose them. They were hardy little things. Only one of them was getting a bit brown around its fringes. They were all she had left of home now, dear mysterious flowers! Then she remembered the girl and her message. Mysterious flowers and mysterious messenger. Could they be connected in some way? Was God sending them both into her life? She gave the flowers a pitiful little smile and a touch like a caress, then closed her suitcase, put on her hat, and got ready to get out.

They were coming into the city now. The rows of cheap little houses, brick and wood and stucco, reminded her of the city where she had searched for a room yesterday. She shuddered as she drew a deep, courageous breath and tried to think what she must do first. She did not seem to be any nearer a decision than last night, but she must do something. She would probably have to go to the woman's hotel for a day or two, anyway.

When she got out of the train and walked through the station she looked around half frightened, almost expecting to see her father and Helen standing there waiting for her. Then she remembered they did not know where she was and took courage, glad though to take refuge in the taxi. But when she arrived at the hotel her heart failed her again, for she found that even the very cheapest room in the place was far beyond what she ought to spend in her present state of finances. She was fairly frightened to realize just how much she had spent of her small hoard in just the two or three days since she had cut herself loose from home. But she must get somewhere and rest a little and freshen up before she started on another hunt.

After breakfast and a bath, arrayed in fresh garments, she felt better and started out on foot in search of a room. If she could only find a decent room where she could use her own furniture, it would be so much more comfortable.

But a couple of hours' hunt revealed the same state of things that had been obtained in the other city she had searched. Rooms were either too expensive or in too sordid a neighborhood to seem at all possible.

As she went along the weary way from house to house she began to realize that either she must find some way to increase her income, or else she must give up her ideas of what was barely decent in the way of a residence.

Right off the start she registered a vow that she would not ask her father for money. He had made it impossible for her to stay at home and he didn't seem to see it; therefore, she would maintain herself somehow without his aid.

The matter of money had never bulked very largely in Diana's life. She knew that her mother had left her something, how much she had never bothered to inquire, or if she had ever been told, to remember. She had her allowance, which had been ample for her needs, and when she wanted anything extra, it had always been forthcoming. She knew that for a time their fortunes had been somewhat straitened, and she had not asked often for money. She seemed to have everything she wanted. But now, faced with the problem of providing shelter and food, her allowance suddenly shrank in proportion to her needs.

Many another girl with her income would have counted herself well off and made the allowance cover an amazing lot of needs, but Diana had no experience in such things and was moreover bound by the traditions of her family as to what was necessary. However, she had a lot of courage and character, and she faced the problems before her like a thoroughbred.

She spent the afternoon canvassing dreary boardinghouses and trying to conceive of herself as being one of their regular guests, but she turned from each one with a loathing that she had hard work to conceal from their hard-faced, weary keepers.

There were other boarding places, of course. She tried a few attractive ones but found them altogether beyond her price.

That night she came home with the evening papers and all day Sunday pored over the Want advertisements and columns of cheap apartments and rooms.

Three days she thus pursued her weary hunt, growing more desperate each day, until she finally located a large bare room on the third-story back of a shabby row of old brick houses in a crowded street of the old and unfashionable portion of the city. It wasn't just unfashionable; it was so far away from ever having been recognized by fashion as not to be within the awareness of those who lived on the substantial, comfortable streets now far away. It was a street where a week ago Diana would have picked her way, looking questioningly at the rows of ash cans and milk bottles, and hurried out into another block to draw a free breath again. But Diana's standards had come down a good many notches during that three-day hunt. She no longer was looking for pleasantness in surroundings or for attractiveness in a landlady or for culture in a neighborhood. The sole requirement she was determined upon now was cleanliness, and even that didn't extend to the street anymore. She wasn't sure as she entered that last door whether she would even require cleanliness in the halls or stairs, if she could just have a spot that she had a right to scrub clean herself, where she might lie down and cry her heart out and then sleep until this awful ache of weariness had left her breast and she could go out and try for a job. For now there was no more question, she must have a job or she could not live long even in this room.

Each night when she came back to the hotel there had been the slowly fading carnations, and in her purse the little tract, which she had read over more than once and pondered as she was dropping off to sleep. But though the hotel room contained the Bible she had wished for, she had been too tired and depressed to look up the references, and more and more the impression of the little tract had grown dim and left her with that lonely feeling again. Sometime when she was settled she would look into it, but she was too tired to think about it anymore now. So she slept through the nights and toiled through the days, looking alternately for rooms and jobs. She had learned to unite the two in certain neighborhoods and found each equally hopeless as to results, until she finally took that large bare room on the third-story back overlooking an alley and a row of kitchens belonging to an even shabbier row of houses on the next street. When she took the room she cast a thankful glance out the window at its dreary mate behind, whose open window sheltered a woman in dirty negligee who looked as if her every hope was gone. Diana was actually thankful that she hadn't fallen quite as low as that next row of houses and had them only to look at.

The room was not heated and had only one poor electric bulb hung from a long wire in the middle, but it was still summer and she would not need heat at present, and she would just have to manage about the light.

They told her she might have possession at once, and she called up her storage company, who promised to deliver her furniture early the next morning and refund half of the storage for the month.

The room didn't look very clean even to Diana's inexperienced eyes, and she hated to have her pretty things come into a dirty room, so she went to the corner grocery nearby, bought a bucket, a broom, a mop, a cake of soap, and a couple of dishcloths to clean it with. The woman who waited on her suggested a scrubbing brush so she bought that.

Tired as she was it was, no easy task, even if she had ever done it before, which she hadn't, to scrub that rough, dirty floor. She had to bring up the water from the floor below, and there wasn't any hot water, nor any way to heat it. In her inexperience she sloshed on the soap and water and then had a terrible time wiping it up, and as for wringing that unwieldy mop, it seemed impossible. But by the time it grew dark, she had the walls wiped down, the floor mopped up in a sort of way, the baseboards wiped off, and also the windowsills. The windows would have to wait until another time. She was too tired to drag another step. With a despairing look around in the dusk, she locked her door, toiled downstairs, and could scarcely get back to her hotel.

That night she dreamed of the girl in the station with the happy eyes who had given her the tract and awoke wondering if she were real or if that experience, too, had been a dream. She had to go to her handbag and take out the tract to straighten it all out in her mind. She was so tired she could not think and so downhearted that nothing seemed worthwhile. Was there really Someone somewhere who cared? She wished she could see that girl again and talk with her a little while.

When she got to her new abode, by morning light the room looked cleaner than she had feared. At least it had lost that musty smell. The floor had dried in streaks and the ugly wall paper showed up all its defects, and they were many. She stood in the middle of the room and looked around her and tried to imagine that this was her home now, for as long as she had money to maintain it.

She went to the window and looked out on the backyards and alley. There were two cats—a gray one with a dirty white star on its forehead and a black one with a torn ear and an ugly sneer on its weird, scrawny face—sitting tucked upon the back fence at respectable distances making faces at one another and occasionally uttering guttural threats. There was a dirty old man with a burlap bag slung over one shoulder and a long iron rod in his hand, poking around among the ash cans. Someone flung a bit of garbage over the fence, and the two cats were down in a second and after it; but a sharp little nondescript dog went like a streak from some invisible place and got there first, growling his right to the tidbit. A mere baby with tousled hair was toddling down the alley with nothing on but a diminutive shirt and mud streaks over the whiteness of its undernourished body. It was scrawnier than the cats. Two women were arguing angrily over their side fence, and an old man with crutches beside him was sitting dolefully on one pair of back steps. It was not a pleasant prospect. Even so early in the morning there were flies around, swarming over a garbage can and buzzing up in a whirl now and then as if in disagreement. Diana turned from it disconsolately with a sudden memory of the broad sweep of lawn in front of her father's home and the deep cool setting of woodland behind the house. How had her fortunes changed in these few brief hours! A few days ago she was mistress in that beautiful home that had been her mother's wedding gift from the grandfather, and now here was her fortune laid, with alley cats and garbage cans and brawling neighbors. She turned from the window with a sudden new sinking of heart and felt as if she could not stand up another minute in that bare room.

Finally she spread out the morning paper that she had brought with her and sat down on the floor, overwhelmed with the stinging tears that rushed into her eyes. Oh, would that moving van never come?

It was half past ten before it arrived, and Diana still sat there waiting when the landlady knocked at the door to announce it. She had taken out the poor little flowers from her bag and sat with them coolly against her burning eyelids, trying to imagine herself back home among the shadows on the grass picking them up one by one, and remembering how she had walked with Bobby there that night and had seen one flower and how that stranger's voice had interfered when Bobby grew offensive. She was wondering about that voice for the thousandth time and had almost lost her sense of her sordid surroundings.

But she sprang up quickly to unlock her door and saw with relief two men standing there, each with a chair in his arms.

They put the chairs down and hurried back downstairs, and Diana thanked the grim landlady and tried not to see the contemptuous glances of envy that she cast at the rich covering of the upholstery. After she had gone downstairs, Diana stood back and looked at her beloved chairs almost apologetically. If they could feel, what would they think of her for putting them into such surroundings? She felt like asking their pardon. And one was her mother's big wing chair. She could see her sitting in it now, and she put her hands softly over the covering like a caress. She was still holding the precious flowers in her hand, and she put her face down on her arms over the back of the chair and gave a little heartsick moan. It seemed as if already she had been away from her home for weeks, and the sight of the dear, familiar objects filled her with exquisite joy, almost as if they had been alive.

But the men were coming up with another load, and Diana moved the chairs where they would be out of the way and went over by the window to watch.

They had brought their arms full of small articles now that had probably been stowed in the van at the last. Diana met each object with a lingering glance of welcome and mentally began to arrange a spot where each should stand. Already the room seemed peopled, but she imagined the things stood there astonished to be brought to such a place! Yet, oh, she was glad to have them!

And now the bed was coming in sections, and two more men behind were bringing springs and mattress. How quickly they set it up and the room took on the look of habitation. Then her bureau and her desk. It was good the room was large. The landlady had said she might put her barrels of dishes in the hall by her door. She was planning to put a curtain across in front of them. Some boxes of books could go there, too.

Everything was up at last, how pitifully few when you thought of home! But they elbowed one another, and it would take some contriving to assemble them into living order.

Then men opened some boxes for her, unstrapped a trunk or two that would go in the hall eventually, and drove two or three nails to hang the few pictures she had brought. The bureau and the wardrobe filled the widest wall spaces, with the bed in the far corner, the gate-leg table in the middle. Now, when the window was washed and a curtain up, it wouldn't be so bad, and she could perhaps hang one of the superfluous curtains across that other corner and make a closet out of it.

The men stood back and surveyed it before they went.

"Ain't so bad," said one, looking from floor to ceiling.

"She wants paperin' and paintin' bad," said the other.

Then they were gone, and Diana stood alone in her new home, realizing that there was work to be done.

She took out the linen sheets, her mother's with the lovely monograms, smelling of lavender, and smooth and fine. There was another problem. Laundry! That would be yet another expense. Oh, to have Maggie along on this exile! But, of course, that was out of the question. She could never afford Maggie. She would have to learn to wash for herself. But where and how? In that terrible bathroom down a flight? Never! She shuddered at the memory of the unspeakable tin tub grimy with the dirt of the ages.

But when the bed was made, with its pretty spread that matched the curtains, when the bureau was dusted and its ruffled cover in place, a feeling of comfort began to steal into the room, and Diana looked up to the lovely portrait of her mother with thankfulness, at least, if not of joy.

The landlady came up after a time and stood looking around.

"H'm!" she remarked grimly. "I guess you're rich!"

"Oh no," said Diana quickly, "not anymore. I am really very poor, and—I'm going out to get a job. These are things from my old home."

"Ain't your mother living?"

"No," said Diana with a tremble in her voice.

Mrs. Lundy looked up to the portrait.

"That her?" she asked, taking in everything with hurried eagle eye.

"Yes," said Diana softly, trying to control the trembling of her lips.

"Well, it's plain to be seen you won't stay long," she said with a sigh of resignation. "If I'd knowed what kind you was I shouldn't uv took you. But now you're here we may as well make the best of it, only I'd oughtta uv charged you a dollar more."

"I couldn't have paid it," said Diana, lifting honest eyes.

"Well, I'm poor, too, an' I can't afford to let my rooms for nothin'. I'll want my pay good and regular."

"Of course!" said Diana, shrinking inwardly. Oh, to have to deal with coarse-grained people like this. How could she ever stand it under the same roof with a woman like that?

But the woman went away, and Diana put her things in order as best she could, washed her one window with unskilled hands, wondering how she was ever to get it clean on the outside, and finally managed to tack up her curtain temporarily. After that she lay down and took a long nap, and when she woke up it was dark. She hadn't had any lunch or dinner, but she shrank inexpressibly from going out alone in that region at night. Perhaps by and by she would grow more accustomed to the place and not be afraid. But this night, at least, she would rather go hungry than go out alone and find her way to a restaurant. There was a box of crackers on the windowsill. She would eat those and go to bed.

So, quite in the dark except for weird flickers of light that came in at the window fitfully playing over the floor now and then, she groped her way to the crackers and sat in her big chair, sadly munching them and wondering if life was always to be like this. She might have turned on the garish bulb waving disconsolately in the air above her, but she shrank inexpressibly tonight from a stark unshaded glare above the dear home things. She just couldn't bear to meet the painted eyes of her mother's portrait, here, alone, tonight.

Oh, some of those girls in dismal hall bedrooms, washing out their bits of finery and their one pair of stockings and sleeping on a hard, lumpy cot, would have thought her room a palace and her lot heavenly if they could have exchanged with Diana. But to Diana it was as if she and a few of her precious things had wandered into an alien desert land of squalor, where they were prisoners.

It was a comfort, however, the next morning to wake with familiar objects around her, and as she dressed she tried to keep back the desire for tears and just be thankful that she was in a place at last where she could have her own things, even though the place itself was anything but desirable.

After eating a few more crackers and drinking her pint of milk for which she had left an order the day before and which she found outside her door, she sat down to count her resources. There had been a few trifling expenses connected with the moving, which she had not taken into account when she calculated— fees to the men and a larger charge for the moving than she had anticipated. It had cut down her money supply tremendously, and the end of another week was approaching. If she did not get a job this week, she might have to go on starvation rations. Perhaps it would be as well to visit the bank and see if it would be possible for her to get the interest on the money her mother left to her a few days ahead of its usual time. It was customary for her father to look after such matters for her, though during his absence she had sometimes gone into the city bank herself. The bank president knew her, so it wouldn't be necessary for her to explain anything to him. He wouldn't know what had happened. And, of course, the money was hers; it was only a matter of a week to the end of the month and her usual installment. If she had been at home, she would have called him up and told him she wanted to draw a check a few days ahead of time, and that would be all there would be to it. The money was hers without question.

So, when she went out on her usual hunt that morning, she stopped at the bank with a check she had made out for a small sum more than she knew was left in her checking account. She explained to the cashier to whom she handed it and asked if it would be all right, as she wanted to use the money right away. He knew her from having seen her with her father and he met her request with courtesy.

"Just a moment, Miss Disston," he said, a trifle uncertainly. "I presume it will be quite all right, but I'll have to see."

He came back in a moment telling her that the president would like to speak with her in his office.

Diana went back with a little trepidation. Was there some cut-and-dried law that made it necessary for her to wait the five days before she could use this money that was her own?

The president met her gravely, gave her a chair, and when he had seated himself with a little more formality than usual he said, "Miss Disston, I'm very sorry, but we have received a request from your father not to pay you any more of your interest without permission from him. Being a trustee of your funds, of course, he has the right to do this. I understand he has been very much disturbed by your absence from home and has telegraphed to a number of places where he thought you might be, without finding you. He therefore has taken this method to get in touch with you. He naturally reasoned that if you had no money you would have to get in touch with him at once."

Diana sat staring at Mr. Dunham, her eyes very large and wide, and her face suddenly flaming crimson. The great man sat in his chair of authority with his elbows on its arms and the tips of his long white fingers touching one another, surveying her speculatively. He had not been prepared for the consternation that had come into her face, and he was puzzled by her sweet, quiet manner. This was no wild young thing having her fling. This looked like a conscientious girl. But he had to obey his client's orders, of course. However, he felt uncomfortable under the clear, steady gaze of her big eyes. Also, the color had receded as suddenly as it had come and left her face a dead white. There was some deep feeling behind all this. Was Disston perhaps a little hard on his child? Yet he had seemed to cherish her as the very apple of his eye. He felt almost disconcerted as she continued to sit quietly looking at him.

"I'm sorry to have to refuse your request," he said half embarrassed, "but, of course, you see how it is, and I'm sure you will accede to your father's request to go home at once and all will be right. It's probably just some little misunderstanding, and with your father's permission, we shall be glad to favor you with the advance money at any time, of course."

Still Diana did not answer. Her sweet face dropped for an instant and then lifted with a serious gaze as she half rose, steadying herself with the tips of her fingers lightly touching his desk.

Then she spoke, and her patrician chin was lifted just the least little bit with gentle dignity.

"I'm sorry to have troubled you," she said, with a fleeting distant semblance of a smile. Her voice was soft and a shade husky, but she had good control of herself.

"Not at all, not at all!" said the banker, almost cordially. "I—! You—! You understand how it is? And if you are short of funds for getting to your home from the city, why I understand there is a trifling sum, a matter of something like five dollars, perhaps, in your checking account, which you are, of course, at liberty to withdraw at any time. If you'll sit down a minute, I'll write you an order to that effect and you can make out a check and cash it at once. That will, I am sure, cover your fare to the suburbs."

Diana swept him a glance of haughtiness.

"Thank you," she said coolly, "that will not be necessary." And she walked from the room without looking at him again.

It was just as the door was swinging closed behind her that he came to himself and started forward.

"Miss Disston," he said, raising his voice, "I hope that you will go straight to your home. I assure you your father is very anxious!" He was almost shouting with the last word. But Diana was gone, and the big mahogany door had closed noiselessly.

What a fool he was! He ought to have gotten her address! Her father would blame him if she didn't go home at once. But of course she would! What was it about her that made him feel she did not intend to? He strode forward and swung the door open, looking down the passage toward the main part of the bank, but Diana was not there. There was a side entrance opposite his office door for his own private use. He opened the door and looked down the street, but there was no sign of her anywhere. How could she have gotten away so quickly? She was embarrassed, stung to the quick, of course, one could see that. He stepped into the bank and looked carefully at everyone, but she was not there. Diana was gone!

Chapter 14

At first Diana did not realize where she was going. Her only object was to get out of that bank and away from Mr. Dunham. That she was hurt to the quick was manifest in the way she walked, with long fleeing strides, and the ground seemed fairly to fly under her feet. She walked as if she were going to some direct appointment, and people watched her, turned to look after her, and marveled at her graceful movements. She made her way through a crowded street, and it seemed almost as if the crowds divided at her coming. She slid through breathlessly, crossing streets without noticing where she was, rushing on like something wound up and not able to stop.

But her mind was smarting as if a whip were lashing it. Her father had done this to her! He had stopped her money and brought her to shame before his acquaintance! His banker knew she was gone, without knowing the reason! Oh, how could she ever live this down? To her inflamed mind the whole thing grew in proportion until it seemed that the worst humiliation there could be had been put upon her. So far from feeling sorry for her, her father was only anxious to get her back and bend her to his will, wishing to punish her for having refused to try to live in the same house with Helen! Her lips were quivering as she walked, and large tears swelled out and threatened to fall; yet she held them back and went on. Her soul was bursting with sorrow. Her father had so far descended as to use her little income as a whip-lash to force her back to him.

Well, never would she go back to get money, even if she starved!

And that brought her to the next thing. She must get a job at once!

She had walked until she was breathless and weary, though she did not realize it, but suddenly she came to the end of things. A river ahead with no bridge and only a sharp turn to the left if she wanted still to go on.

She paused an instant. The river winked and beckoned to her, in bright sunny sparkles between the shipping craft and wharfs, and suddenly she came to herself and gave a sane brave little laugh. She was Diana Disston, and tragedy was not to be carried on by her. If other people did crazy things, she couldn't help it, but she could help it if she let them drive her to do more of them. Somehow she had to work this thing out, to get rid of the pain in her heart and find a way to exist, without money, if necessary, but not by doing anything wild.

There were few people around when she gave that laugh, just some men standing about the door of a warehouse, one or two lounging on steps, watching a tug slowly pulling a barge out into the river. They were not looking at her, and she gave no thought to them as she took that sharp turn to the left and walked over one block, turning back on the next street and starting toward the center of the city again.

But one man turned and looked her full in the face as she

sped by, watching her until she turned the corner and went on out of sight. He was one of those who slouched low on the step, his gaunt, ill-strung length stretched to its utmost, his gawky limbs lying absolutely relaxed, his lazy arms anchored by hands in his pockets. He had a weak chin and an irresponsible manner. It had taken the distance of a block for him to get a full recognition across to himself, and even then he wasn't quite sure. As much as he allowed his lazy mind to think, he turned the matter over once or twice and then decided it didn't matter, anyway, and went on sunning himself on the step. If she was the girl who often used to pass his mother's cottage when he was a child, what business of his was it, anyway? She wouldn't recognize Bill Sharpe, of course. It likely wasn't the same girl, and why should he care? He would have smoked a cigarette on it if he had had one to smoke, but he hadn't. That was why he was here, to see if he could pick up a job. He needed some money badly. His mother was dead and could no longer earn it for him doing fine sewing. He sat still and soon forgot that he might possibly have seen a daughter of the Disston House go by in this most unexpected place.

But Diana walked more slowly back on the next street. She was looking around her now with a purpose. She must find a job. And if she couldn't find a job within the next day or two, she might soon find herself having to move to one of these unspeakable little apartments that she was passing, for she had only two dollars and seventy-five cents between her and starvation. True, there was the five dollars the banker had suggested she might draw out at her will, but what was that? She scorned to go back and get it. At best it would keep her a very short time, and if there was a job somewhere, she must get it now.

She was keeping her eye out for signs, but there was nothing for women. Several places had a card out, BOY WANTED, and one dirty little shop had a blackboard at the door with a scrawled sign,

Man Wanted to Drive a Truck, but there was nothing for women or girls until she came into the downtown region again, and there she saw a notice in the window of a cheap little restaurant, Waitress Wanted!

Diana paused before the door and looked inside. It was the noon hour, and there was a crowd of working people, swarming in like flies, waiting behind chairs for their occupants to finish. The waitresses had highly illuminated, hard faces and untidy dresses. They were knocking about among the people with heavy trays lifted high, calling out in raucous voices for room to get by. There was a heavy odor of burned grease, fried fish, and onions floating on the air. A man with fulsome, sneering lips and little pig eyes was directing it all. Diana stood for a full minute and took it all in. Then she turned and walked wearily away. Would she have to come to that?

It was not that she felt above such work. It seemed a thing that anyone might learn to do. But to have to live in such a noisy mess and be ordered around by a loathsome man like that! Why, Bobby Watkins was a seraph compared to that man.

She allowed herself a glass of milk and one little packet of peanut butter sandwiches for her dinner that night but had hard work to finish even that. She was heartsick and could not eat. She toiled up to her third-story room afterward, too utterly weary to think. But after a few minutes lying prone across her bed, she got up desperately and went to the drawer where she had put the little tract. She must have some help somewhere or she would lose her mind!

She had bought a cheap Bible the day before as she passed a secondhand bookstore but had had no time to look at it yet. Now, as she took it out, she realized that she ought to have saved even the small sum that she had paid for it. But it was too late for such regrets. Perhaps she might even come to having to sell it again, but she wanted to find those references and write them out before it was gone. She picked up the tract and read the now familiar words:

> *One reason why the Son of God came to earth and*
> *took a human body was so that He might suffer*
> *and understand and help us in our grief. There*
> *is no kind of sorrow He does not know, even to*
> *having His beloved Father turn His back on Him*
> *for a time.*

She looked at the first reference, Psalm 22:1, and turned bewilderedly to her book. She had been so long away from any intimate contact with a Bible that the books seemed to have changed places since she last knew them. But at last she found the Psalms, and suddenly a verse caught her eye: "When my father and my mother forsake me then the Lord will take me up." What an astonishing verse for her to come upon when she was in such desperation! Her mother was gone and her father had practically forsaken her. For now as she thought over the interview in the bank, she began to see clearly the fine vindictive hand of her new stepmother in what her father had done to her. She was quite sure he would never of himself have done such a thing if Helen had not suggested it, and suggested it in such a way, fairly pursuing her victim until it was done, that he simply had to do it or rebel. Diana instinctively recognized that his marriage was too new for him to rebel yet. But at least for the time, whether he realized it or not, he had forsaken her, his daughter.

And now, was it true that there was Someone who cared about all this? She would find out. She turned back the pages to the twenty-second Psalm. But when she had found the verse she could make nothing of the desolate cry, "My God, my God, why hast thou forsaken me?" until she finally turned to the reference in Matthew: "And about the ninth hour Jesus cried with a loud voice, saying, Eli, Eli, lama sabachthani? that is to say, My God, my God, why hast thou forsaken me?"

So then Jesus was forsaken! She went back to the beginning of the chapter and read the whole story of the crucifixion. She had heard it over and over again in her childhood, of course, but it had made little impression. It had just been a story of a man who lived long ago whom she had been taught was the Savior of the world.

But now, because she realized for the first time that He was really in the position of having been forsaken by God, His Father, because He had taken upon Him the sins of the world and God could not have any fellowship with sin, she suddenly saw what had never occurred to her before, that Jesus, the Savior of the world, knew what she was going through now because *He had gone through it.* He had voluntarily accepted that separation from God, which was what His death meant, and had done it for her sake, for the sake of those He was saving.

This did not come to her all at once. It took careful reading over and over, and even then it was only a dawning comprehension. Nevertheless it was enough to fill her with wonder and a degree of belief.

At last, her mind filled with the picture of Calvary and the meaning of it as applied to herself, she found the next reference, Hebrews 2:18:

> *For in that he himself hath suffered being tempted,*
> *he is able to succor them that are tempted.*

It was as if a voice spoke to her soul from the printed page. She was so lonely and desolate that she welcomed the message with a throb of joy. It was like an assurance from heaven that there was Someone who cared after all else had failed!

She thought about it for a few minutes. Able to succor! Then

He had the power, an understanding power because He had been through the same experience. Ah! how wonderful! But—were there no qualifications that one must have to be worthy of such succor, except just to be in need? Was this for everybody? How could she be sure He would succor, even though He was able?

She turned to the next verse:

> *I will not leave you comfortless: I will come to you.*

How tenderly precious. He would come. Her father hadn't been willing to come. But this One had promised to come and bring comfort.

But wait! She still did not know whether that meant herself or not. How could she be sure? He hadn't come, had He? She had been in the direst need and He hadn't come. Wasn't there something lacking somewhere, in her case at least?

But there was one more reference. She hurriedly turned the pages. This little tract seemed so sure. Why should it be broadcast in print this way if it were not for everyone in trouble? Then she read, and it was the story of Mary going to the empty tomb to find her Lord and finding only angels:

> *And they say unto her, Woman, why weepest thou?*
> *She saith unto them, Because they have taken*
> *away my Lord, and I know not where they have*
> *laid him. And when she had thus said, she turned*
> *herself back, and saw Jesus standing, and knew not*
> *that it was Jesus.*

Diana read in astonishment. Well, what could that mean in *her* life, always supposing that this story was meant to mean something in her life? Could it be that Jesus had come to her somewhere, somehow, and she had not recognized Him? Oh, to understand, to know! But how was she to find out? She went back and read through the resurrection story, finding herself curiously interested, sympathetic with the weeping Mary, yet still perplexed, still wondering how to find Mary's Lord and whether He would be willing to be her Friend and Comforter. It all seemed so long ago, and she here alone in a new dreadful world, wherein money was withheld as well as comfort. There was no comfort it seemed. And she had never dreamed that money bulked so largely in the human equation. There had always been enough before, and she had never thought about it. But now she had to think. She must earn her way, and she was hungry! Actually hungry! But she didn't dare spend more than was absolutely necessary, and tomorrow she must get a job! Even if she had to go back to that awful restaurant, she must get one!

❁

The money was all gone, and she had actually not a cent left after the glass of milk she took for her breakfast on the morning that she did find some work.

Of course, her room was paid for the month. That was good. If she had to starve, she could at least die decently. And, of course, there were things she could sell, though she didn't know how to go about selling them, and it made her heart sink to think of it. There were the pearls! But they should be the last resort. Her mother's pearls! She laid her hand over the little chamois bag that hung around her neck beneath her dress on its tiny platinum chain and felt stronger for the contact.

" 'When my father and my mother forsake me then the Lord will take me up,'" she said softly over to herself as she started out on her desperate way. "I'll just have to trust Him, that's all. I don't know Him, but perhaps He knows me, and I'll *have* to trust He'll look out for me, for I've nobody else!"

It was just a moment later that her eye caught a glimpse of the card in the window of a small bookshop, or was it a publisher's office? She wasn't sure. But there was the neatly printed card.

GIRL WANTED
TO ADDRESS ENVELOPES
MUST WRITE WELL

She stopped short and stared. She felt somehow as if her unspoken prayer had been answered. She began to wonder if her eyes were really seeing all right. Did things really happen like that?

Then she turned and went in.

It was a neat, pleasant office with a sweet-faced elderly woman at its head and a glimpse of several nice-looking women and girls at desks in an inner room, two of them at typewriters. Farther on there was another room where she could see a gray-haired man sitting at a desk and a younger man standing by him with papers in his hand about which they seemed to be talking. She learned later that this was the editorial room.

It was all so easy. She had only to write her name and address and a sentence or two. They took her at once. She wrote a beautiful, clear hand, and her appearance was in her favor. But her heart sank when she was told that it was only a temporary job. It might last only a couple of days, or they might even get the work done by night. They were not sure. It depended upon some lists that might come in before the day was done. The pay was reckoned on the number finished each day.

Diana sat down at the desk they assigned her in the middle room and began her work. She was glad she had brought her fountain pen along in her handbag. She could work better with her own tools. Soon she was hard at it. The manager from the front office came through the room several times, stopped now and again to look over her shoulder, noticed how rapidly the finished piles of envelopes were mounting, and smiled her approval, but beyond that nothing was said to her.

At noon the office manager stepped in and told her she might take her lunch hour now, and Diana looked up with a rising color of embarrassment.

"Would you mind if I didn't go out?" she asked. "I really don't care for lunch today, and I'd like to stay and get more done, if that's all right with you."

The woman gave her a keen, swift look but told her she might stay if she preferred. "Although," she added, "I always think it's better for the girls to get out for a breath of fresh air and a little something to eat, even if it isn't much. You can, of course, bring your lunch if you prefer. There's a dressing room just up those steps to the right where you can eat it. But do as you prefer. Of course, we're anxious to get these envelopes finished as soon as possible."

"Then I'll stay," said Diana with relief. "I—had breakfast rather late, anyway," she added, and then she drove her pen rapidly on in clear, graceful writing.

The manager looked a bit troubled but turned away, and most of the workers went out by twos and threes for their noon hour. Only two others remained, and presently they went up to the dressing room with their neat little packages of lunch. One of them came down with a luscious pear in her hand and came over to Diana shyly. "My sister put two pears in my lunch box today, and I couldn't possibly eat them both. I wondered if you wouldn't like to help me out. I noticed you didn't go out to lunch, and I do hate to carry it back home again."

It was on Diana's lips to give a haughty "No thank you!" but she lifted her eyes to the girl's face and found such kindly good will that the words died on her lips and instead she smiled. After all, why should she hold herself aloof? She was a working girl now like the rest. Moreover, she was hungry, and this was true kindliness. So she reached out her hand with a sudden smile.

"Thank you!" she said heartily. "That looks wonderful!" She

ate the pear gratefully, and then wrote the faster to make up for the brief loss of time. But a strange thought came to her while she was eating. Did God send this job to her? It wasn't a very big answer to her prayer, of course, but it was something. And did He send the pear? It seemed almost irreverent to think such a thought, but there was a warming of her heart, a stealing in of a bit of comfort like a warm ray of sun. And it certainly was good to have eaten that pear, for in case the work lasted another day they likely wouldn't pay her until it was done, and there was only one cracker left in her room for dinner tonight. How long could one live and go on working without food?

But the manager came to her just before closing time and smiled.

"You've worked well, Miss Disston," she said. "It really was quite important to get off as many of these as possible. I thought perhaps you'd like your pay tonight for the day, but we'd like you to come back in the morning if you will. Some new lists have just come in by the late mail, and there is a prospect that we shall have work for you for several more days."

Diana's face lit up.

"Oh, I'm so glad," she said earnestly. "And it is good of you to let me have today's money now. I really need it."

"That's quite all right," Miss Prince said, smiling, "and I'll see you in the morning."

It wasn't a large sum of money that she carried away with her, but it meant all the difference between starvation and life. Diana went at once to a restaurant, the cheapest decent one she knew, and ate a real dinner. To be sure, its price was very small, but she chose wholesome things that would sustain life a long time. She mustn't allow herself to get so near to nothing again. She recalled the sinking feeling she had in the pit of her stomach at noon before that girl gave her the pear. And how dizzy her head had been! Sometimes she could hardly see what she was writing. One glass of milk couldn't keep one working all day. She must provide a lunch!

So while she was eating she studied the menu and, on her way out, purchased the cheapest sandwich they had and two nice red apples. Then at the little grocery near her room she bought a pint bottle of milk and a box of dry cereal. Now she was provided with food for breakfast and a lunch like the others, with an extra apple to repay her friend for the pear, and she had money left to keep her, if she was careful, for a couple of days longer. Not that she could live very expensively, of course, but she had demonstrated by this time that a fifteen-cent plate of soup and a few crackers would keep one alive for quite a length of time.

When she reached her room she put her bottle of milk in the open window with a wet cloth around it to keep it cool, stowed her sandwich in a small tin box she had, put the bag of apples beside it, and then looked around her room with a deep breath of relief. She wanted to cry, but she wouldn't. She had had her first success, and she was grateful. It wouldn't do to sit down and think from what state she had fallen, nor to sit and blame her poor father. She mustn't let herself think about her troubles or she would give way, and one couldn't work well if one cried half the night. She had tried trusting in God that morning and wonderful things had happened. She must keep on trusting.

Before Diana had left her home, in fact that last morning when she went down to the village to telephone the moving van, she had stopped at the post office and asked them to hold her mail, after that afternoon's delivery, until she should send them another address. She had even left money for forwarding second-class matter. Not that she had so much mail, but she dreaded to have anything that belonged to her fall into Helen's hands. There was Bobby Watkins, for instance. Suppose he should take it into his head to write her a voluminous letter, as he had done more than once, and try to argue with her about her attitude toward him? He had called up twice during that last day to berate her for the way she treated him going down the drive and to try to explain how much he loved her. She no longer wished to protect Bobby Watkins from Helen's mocking laughter, Bobby could take care of himself, but she couldn't bear the thought of Helen's opening letters and reading *anything* addressed to her and laughing over it as she would laugh. For she knew Helen would have no scruples against opening her letters if she chose to do so. She had seen her do it several times.

Also, there would be invitations and a few letters from her friends. Nothing that would amount to anything or that she really cared much about, but she did not want Helen reading them and destroying them.

So now that she had a job, at least for a few days, she sat down and wrote an order to the postman at home to forward her mail. The post office was not allowed to tell others her address, so she felt she was perfectly safe in doing this. Of course, by and by, she would write to her father as she had promised to do, but not until she was sure of a job that would pay for her food and room. Never should he be allowed to think that he could break her resolve by holding back her money. Her heart was full of bitterness toward him as she thought of what he had done, although there was more grief at having lost his love and her feeling that he trusted her than bitterness. And if she could have known what anxiety he was suffering about her, she would have forgotten to pity herself and would have somehow managed to get in touch with him at least to let him know she was safe. She felt that he had Helen and that was enough for him. Not for an instant did she take as sincere what the banker had said to her about his anxiety to know where she was.

His refusal to come to her when she pled with him, or to have any discussion with her before it was forever too late, was still strong in her mind. It had cut her to the heart.

So she wrote her few lines to the postmaster at home and then, because the postbox was only a block and a half down the street, she went out and mailed it. It would get there in the morning, and perhaps by tomorrow night she would have some mail. It would be more like living to be getting something of her own, even if it was nothing she cared about.

Out in the street, with its dismal half-lit shadows, she almost regretted going out but quickened her steps to a run, deposited her letter, and flew back to safety. She did not notice a lank, awkward young man slouching against a closed grocery doorway across the corner. She did not see him look up and peer across at her, nor know that he had followed her noiselessly on the other side of the street, keeping in the shadows and hiding in a deep doorway until he saw where she went in, and that later he walked by on her side of the street and studied the house, taking note of the number before he melted into darkness again and went on his unknown way.

Diana went upstairs, locked herself into her haven, and went to bed. But before she slept, she tried to pray.

"Oh, God, if You really care and have helped me today, I thank You!" she said softly into her pillow. "Oh, God, if You really do care, I would be so glad!"

Chapter 15

Diana worked in the publishing office for nearly a week, and then one morning the manager came to her just as she had begun her work for the day and asked her if she could run a typewriter. Diana looked dismayed and told her no.

"I'm sorry," said the manager. "I hoped you could. This work you have been doing is about finished. It won't last longer than today. I thought if you were a typist we could use you right along, for one of our girls is getting married next week."

"I could learn," said Diana, with a desperate look in her eyes.

The manager shook her head.

"We need experienced typists, you know," she said. "But if you will leave your address, we'll promise to send for you whenever we have any extra work that we think you could do. The editor was very much pleased with the way you took hold of things. I'm sorry," she said again with a pitying smile as she walked away.

Diana sat and worked all day, her heart as heavy as lead. She did not go out to lunch as she had been in the habit of doing.

She said she had a headache when one of the girls asked her to go with her. In reality, she was frightened. She wouldn't waste even fifteen cents to buy lunch. The money she would get tonight would not be enough to carry her many days, and here she was plunged back into the blackness of despair again, with visions of that awful restaurant in her mind. Perhaps she would have to get a job like that yet. Perhaps she wouldn't even be able to get one like that now, for likely that was gone long ago.

She received her pay envelope and the kind words of the manager that night with as brave a look as she could summon, but her feet dragged heavily as she went on her way home, and instead of stopping to get a good dinner, she bought bread and cheese and went on to her room. Why waste money on a dinner that she could not eat? Oh, why did she have to go on living? Where was the God in whom she had been trying to trust? Had He forgotten her? No one cared anymore. Her father seemed to be making no further move to try to find her. Helen doubtless had told him that she would come home when she got good and tired of wandering around without money, and likely he had believed her. *Oh, God, God, God, do You care at all? How could You care? I'm just nobody!*

The tears were in her eyes as she rounded the corner to the dismal rooming house, and all her life looked drab and dreary before her. Would there ever be anything ahead to make her feel happy again?

But as she came to the steps of the house, she saw that the door stood open and a postal delivery car was at the door.

"Here she comes!" said the landlady grimly. "Let her sign it herself. I've got too much to do to bother. I smell my dinner burning!"

Diana stared at the landlady and then at the postal delivery, and then she saw a large parcel lying on the hall chair. In the dim light permitted in that dismal place, she could not read the name clearly, but the boy was holding out a card and pencil to her.

"Sign here," he said, and he thrust the pencil into her hand.

Diana, filled with wonder, signed her name, and the boy vanished. Then she turned to take up her parcel and came face-to-face with her landlady again.

"That's from a florist's, isn't it?" she asked belligerently.

Diana gazed at her, astonished.

"I don't know what it is," she replied. "I haven't opened it yet. I wasn't expecting anything."

"Well, if you're getting that many flowers in your position, I think you oughtta be payin' more rent for your room."

Diana laughed. It struck her as remarkably original logic.

"Just how do you make that out?" She tried to say it pleasantly, trying to remember that this was only a poor, ignorant woman in a semitenement. "I couldn't really help it, could I, if someone chose to send me some flowers by mail? It wouldn't make me any better able to pay more rent, would it? Unless you think I might sell them to somebody." She laughed with a little tremble in the tail of it that gave a strange pathetic sound even to herself.

"Is he your steady, or is he just a pick-up?" asked the landlady, fixing her with a cold eye. There was a strong smell of fried potatoes and onions burning that almost stifled Diana, but she paused with her foot on the lower step of the stair and stared at the woman.

"What is a steady?" she asked, mildly interested.

"If you don't know, it ain't likely he is. Well then, I thought mebbe you wasn't so awful respectable after all as you set up to be."

"I really don't know what you mean," said Diana, almost ready to cry.

"You must be awful dumb, then. I'm askin' you if the flowers you got in that there package is from a regular sweetie you go with all the time or just from some bum you picked up at a nightclub? I like ta know what kinda character my tenants has.

This has always been counted a respectable house. It looks kinda suspicious, you havin' all that furniture and now gettin' a stack o' flowers."

Diana suddenly froze into dignity.

"Really," she said, "I'm sorry, but I can't answer any more questions. I haven't opened this package yet, and I haven't the slightest idea where it came from or what it contains. But if renting a room from you gives you a right to pry into all my private affairs, I shall certainly move out tomorrow!" And she sailed upstairs carrying her big parcel with her, and suddenly remembered as she rounded the head of the stairs and prepared to ascend the next flight that she had no job and almost no money, and if she were to move out tomorrow she could only do so by dragging her furniture to the window and flinging it out in the alley with her own hands, for she certainly couldn't pay a mover, nor rent another room, not until she got a job.

She was so filled with shame and distress by the time she reached her room that she locked the door and flung herself down on her bed without waiting to open her unexpected parcel and had a good cry all in the dark by herself. That awful old woman and her horrible room! Oh, that she might take her precious possessions and fly to the ends of the earth away from here! Anything, *any*thing would be better than this!

Then suddenly she came to herself. No, *any*thing would not be better than this! It would not be better in any way to go back home and have to live with Helen. She had come away from something infinitely worse than just an ugly room with an ignorant landlady. This was really a haven, and she must be glad for it. She must! She must ignore the poor creature downstairs and live above it all. She must have courage and trust. She would go and get a job in some little dirty restaurant if that was all there was to get. She would do anything, but she would not let circumstances conquer her. That was what Helen had thought would happen, that circumstances would be too much for her and she would come meekly home and succumb to her will, and it *should not be*! Besides, there *was* Someone who cared. She had determined to believe that little tract, and it had seemed almost as if it was so, until she lost her job. But she would not let go so soon. She would trust in the One who had suffered Himself and understood.

Suddenly she sat up and wiped her eyes, looking around her room.

She could dimly see the parcel there on the chair where she had dropped it when she came in, and all at once an overwhelming curiosity came over her to know what it was and where it came from. Of course, it couldn't be flowers. Who would send her flowers? Even Bobby Watkins didn't know her address. This was probably a parcel belonging to someone else, and it might be anything but flowers. She ought to have looked at the address carefully before she came up. Now she would likely have to drag it downstairs and take it back to the post office.

She got up and turned on her glaring bulb that, with all its unblinking blaze, barely made light enough to read by.

Yes, there was her name written clearly, but not by any hand she knew. Bobby Watkins wrote in a round, childish script as if he had never grown up. Moreover, the address was written in a different hand from the name. Ah! The address was probably in the postmaster's writing. It must have been forwarded from home, and now that she thought of it, she had not as yet received any mail since she had sent the postmaster her address. But what on earth could this be? It couldn't be anything from her father; it wasn't his writing. Nor Helen's, either. And that was a florist's label on the outside of the box. The landlady had some ground for one of her assertions at least. Well, if she found Bobby Watkins's card inside, she would throw the flowers down in the alley. Even if they were gardenias!

And what was more, if Bobby Watkins had found out where

she was, she would move tomorrow morning even if she had to go and leave her things behind her. No, she couldn't do that! She could not leave her beloved things. But she would find a way to get them out of this house at once. She would, even if she had to mortgage the job she hadn't gotten yet to move them!

With a hysterical little laugh, she picked up the parcel and tore open its wrappings.

Yes, it was a florist's box, a florist back in the home suburb!

She found her fingers trembling as she lifted the cover of the box and turned back the wax paper wrapping. Ah! A breath from a heavenly land was wafted into her face, and her weary senses drew it in with sheer delight! Suddenly the sorrows of the last two weeks dropped away from her, and a soothing perfume wrapped around her. She looked, and her eyes were wide with wonder. Carnations. Myriads of them! Her mystery flowers had come to find her!

For a moment her eyes swam with tears, and she saw the delicate seashell pink of the blossoms as if they were in a heavenly vision. She bowed her head, buried her face in their loveliness, and drew in deep breaths of their perfume. It satisfied her heartbreak and loneliness as a life-giving draught will quench a great thirst. Her heart was overflowing with tenderness. All her joy in the single flowers that she had found upon her pathway back at home rushed over her, and more. There was something deeper than mere sentimentality. It was not a fancied lover, casting admiration in her way; it was an overwhelming love offered to a soul that was starving and alone. It did not seem to matter who had sent these. It was not Bobby Watkins, she was sure of that. Bobby had no delicate, sensitive romance about him. Bobby brought his flowers himself and gloated over you while you opened them. Bobby could never forget himself long enough to drop a flower anonymously, for genuine love, one that cares to bless without receiving recognition or praise. It might be some woman, old or young—whoever it was it seemed like an angel to her now more than ever, a messenger from God.

Presently she lifted her face to search for a card, almost dreading lest she should find one, yet longing, too. She could not bear to have her delight destroyed, her illusion dispelled by cold facts. She wanted to feel that it was a gift from one who knew God.

But there was no card. Just those dear flowers, so fresh and lovely that it was almost unbelievable they had not been picked only an hour before.

When she had satisfied herself that there was no message she put her face down to the flowers again and began to talk to them softly. "You lovely things! You beautiful mystery flowers! God sent you! No matter how He got you here I am going to believe God sent you to show me that He is caring for me!"

Then softly she slipped down upon her knees, the flowers still in her arms, and with her lips against the fringes of one big blossom, she began to pray. "Oh, God, I believe You *do* care. I don't see why You would, but I *believe* You do. You wouldn't have sent me these flowers just when I needed them so badly if You didn't care a little bit. Dear God, it doesn't matter who You told to send them, I believe they came from You. And if it was anybody like Bobby Watkins You used, please don't let me find it out. Please let it seem just You unless it was somebody *dear*."

She knelt there for some time, her face among the flowers, and then as memory went back to the cool, quiet, shadowed spot where she had found those other single blossoms, slowly she began to remember. She stood once more against the tall hemlock hedge, leaning against the resilient boughs, thinking of their perfume, hugging the thought of them to her sad heart, and a voice spoke again. How long ago it seemed since she heard that voice praying. What were those words? How the days that had come between had almost blotted them out. She had written them down. What were they? Then they came flocking back like birds to her call.

"We thank Thee for the care of the day and for these gifts for our refreshment." How the words fit her own case! She paused to wonder, and then memory went on:

"And, Lord, we would ask Thy mercy and tenderness and leading for the people up at the great house."

Had that prayer been for her father's house? If it was, had it been at all answered? Mercy and tenderness and leading. Had she had those since she had left home? Would the blessings have followed her away from the house? Mercy and tenderness and leading. Perhaps there had been a degree of all. Terrible things might have happened to her. It had seemed that they did, but now she wasn't quite sure. Perhaps there was a degree of leading in it all.

"Perhaps some of them are sad," went on that unseen voice, *"Lord, give them comfort."*

Well, here were the flowers, right out of the blue, and they did seem in a degree to soothe her soul.

"Perhaps they need guidance."

Ah, didn't she?

"Do Thou send Thy light—!"

Oh, why hadn't she stayed to hear the end, stayed at any cost?

Yet the memory of the prayer was there fresh in her heart. Perhaps the answer was following her around. Perhaps these flowers had come to foreshadow some kind of light. They were comfort. Oh, for the light—!

Then at once it came to her that the light might be found in her little tract and in the Bible to which it had directed her. Was that possible? If she would diligently seek, would she find the light and some way out of this dark maze in which she had lost her way?

If she only could find the person whose voice had uttered that prayer! How many questions she would ask him! Perhaps in some church there would be a minister who was like that one. If she went the rounds of all the churches, she might find one to whom she would dare go and seek advice. But no—that would not do. She would see old friends, perhaps; they would ask her uncomfortable questions. She could not face the old world in which she had moved. She would seem to be criticizing her father; yet she could not explain her absence from home in any other way. No, she could not go searching among the churches. But she would search in her Bible, and now that the flowers were here they would help her. They would comfort her. She was beginning to have assurance in her heart that God cared. Dear flowers, dear mystery flowers!

Her job was gone, but she had the flowers! The flowers would rest her, and tomorrow she could go out and get herself a job!

The morning brought her letters, just a few, and her heart leaped up. Perhaps there would be one to explain the flowers! And yet she almost dreaded lest there would be. If it should be that they came from some commonplace source, would it destroy her newfound faith that God cared?

She hurried back upstairs to read them before she went out. If she sat down in the hall to do so, that terrible landlady would come out and question her again. She was so glad that she had met the postman just at the door.

Two of the letters proved to be bills for small purchases made at the little local stores at home. One was an advertisement of an entertainment to be given in the village, one was a brief and disagreeable note from Bobby Watkins asserting that it was high time she apologized for her strange actions the night he called, and the fourth was a short note from an old schoolmate who lived in a suburb of the city.

Edith Maythorn had never known Diana in her home surroundings, only in college. Her home, until a few months ago, had been in a far city from which she had occasionally written Diana, who for a short time had been her roommate. She had only recently come to this city to live and was not acquainted with Diana's circle of friends. The letter was an invitation to spend the weekend with her at her new home and attend a small house party among whom were two girls who had been in college with them. When Diana read it first she shrank away from the thought of attending such a festivity. Then it occurred to her that these people did not know her circumstances at all and were not likely to come into touch with her old friends. Why not go? It was only over Sunday, and as others were to be present there would be little time for intimate talks with questionings. Why couldn't she go and get a little breath of real living again? She had plenty of pretty clothes, and no one need know that she was contemplating taking a job in a cheap restaurant. None of these girls frequented restaurants of that sort. Why not just have a little relief from the strain of sorrow and loneliness? Incidentally, she would save money on her meals for two days, and that meant a great deal. Her cheeks burned as she remembered what sordid thoughts and impulses had come to move her now. But it was an item worth considering. And, of course, it was supposable that sometime in the future she might again be in a position to ask Edith to visit her somewhere, somehow. Monday morning she could quietly say good-bye and drift out of Edith's ken again and that would be that, but it would give her a much-needed rest and wholesome food without cost.

As she hurried down the street in search of that job, she was weighing the possibilities, pro and con. Of course, if she went she should call up and accept. Yet suppose she found a job and had to go on duty at once? Well, in that case she would just have to call it off, of course.

But strangely enough she came on a little eating place late in the afternoon that wanted a waitress to come on Monday morning. It wasn't a cheerful place, nor overly clean, and the food as she swept the room with a comprehensive glance did not look attractive, but she was deadly tired, and it was a job. Perhaps she could do better later. It gave her such a panicky feeling to have no job and her money melting like snow on a hot day that she was ready to take anything no matter how unattractive. She would have her board here and an infinitesimal wage, together with tips—how her soul loathed the thought of them—but she was in no situation to be fussy about such matters. She took the place, dropped into a chair by a vacant table to eat an unattractive sandwich and drink a cup of tea, and then she went to the telephone with sudden resolve and called up Edith. She would go to Edith's house party and have one day of friendliness and enough to eat before she started at her obnoxious job in that odious little restaurant. The girls needn't even know that she had left home. Edith knew only that her mother was dead, and if she told her that she had been away when her invitation came, that would be excuse enough for her delay in replying.

So she called her friend and found an eager, welcoming voice at the other end of the line, which warmed her heart and helped her to keep her resolve not to think about that awful restaurant until Monday morning.

As she unlocked her door, the breath of the carnations met her, and she felt a sudden reluctance to leave them. But it was too late now; she had given her word that she would come, and she could wear a good big sheaf of the flowers and put the rest safely in their box sprinkled and find them quite fresh and nice on her return.

So she hurried with her dressing, put some of her prettiest things in her overnight bag, fastened on some flowers, and departed.

It was dark as she went out the door, and she hurried a little as she noticed a skulking figure across the road in the shadows. Diana found it hard to get used to her surroundings and was just the least little bit afraid every time she went out into the dark, ugly street alone at night. She wished she had gotten started earlier. Well, she was off for a whole day, and she wouldn't remember that Monday was coming and she would have to serve smelly meals to a throng of coarse people. She would try to feel happy like other girls just for one day at least. After that she would have to disappear, drop out of sight. Her job would claim her inexorably. She must remember that in talking with whomever she met tonight; she must be exceedingly hazy about her future. She had engagements that would keep her away from home indefinitely—that would be a good explanation to give—and she wasn't quite sure where she would be, but the home address would reach her.

She drew a breath of relief as she settled this matter in her mind and climbed into the nearest bus that would land her at her friend's new home. She did not notice the man who stealthily slipped into the crowded bus behind her and kept in the shadow with his hat brim down, nor notice that when she got out, he dropped off into the darkness also. She even approached him a moment later as he stood in the shadow of a hedge and asked which way the numbers ran on that street and where would be number 372. He pointed indefinitely off to his right and shuffled away in the darkness like a wraith. She went on her way, presently finding that he had been wrong in his direction, but arriving at her destination safely in spite of it and meeting a warm and eager welcome.

Just for one day she would forget!

Chapter 16

That same evening at the Disston mansion a party was going on. It was not of the master's bidding, but he was there figuring in the capacity of happy bridegroom, albeit with a weary look and a heavy heart. If Diana had started out to punish her father for what he had done, she could have taken no quicker or more effective way. Though Diana would have been aghast if she had known how heartbroken he was. Diana was only hurt. She never dreamed what her going would do to her undemonstrative father.

Secretly for several days he had been going about silently, cautiously as a sleuth, while his wife was off somewhere shopping, playfully resenting the pressing business he professed to have.

He had telegraphed to Aunt Harriet, and when he found no trace of his missing daughter, even though he carefully hunted out and telephoned a number of friends, he was really frightened.

Then he had tried to find Diana's list of correspondents, but all Diana's personal belongings were gone. He had contacted every person he could think of to find out if she was visiting them, doing it cautiously and skillfully lest they should discover that her own father did not know her whereabouts, just a casual telephone message to know if she were calling there, because he wished to speak to her about an important matter, but nothing came of it. He had written scores of letters, some addressed to her friends in various places and some to herself in their care, but had found no trace of her. He could not eat nor sleep as the days went by and there was still no word from her. His imagination pictured her in all sorts of predicaments and perils, until it seemed to him that he would lose his mind.

Through all this Helen watched him warily, a little amused twinkle in her eyes and a sweetly sympathetic note in her voice. At last, having possessed herself cleverly of the facts about how much money Diana likely had with her and how much more she could get hold of without applying to her father, she asked just how much power the father had over Diana's inheritance. Then she suggested cautiously, almost deprecatingly, as if she did not wish to intrude into affairs not her own, that her husband cut off his daughter's income for a time. That would bring her back in a short time she felt sure. Ah, she went about it all in a masterly way, hesitating and yet insistent, making it quite plain that Diana must eventually apply to him for money. And the poor man caught at the suggestion as a drowning man might catch at a straw. Indeed, he insisted on telephoning his banker at once, though it was quite late at night when Helen suggested it.

The banker had been surprised, a little shocked, Mr. Disston felt. He did not try to explain except to say that Diana had gone away visiting and had not chosen to say where she was. He was taking this method of finding her. "You know young people today are getting a little highhanded and independent," he added as his sole explanation. But it had hurt him to say such a thing about his girl, who had never been anything but docile and loving to him before in her life, and he had suffered acutely ever since. He had waited all day with tense body and agonizing mind. His little girl, Diana! What would her mother think of him for having gotten Diana into a position like this?

He had heard nothing from the banker until late in the afternoon, and he had not been able to settle down to just waiting for some word. But the word when it came did not give him much comfort. Mr. Dunham reported that Diana had just been in to see him about getting some of her next month's money ahead of time, and when she heard that her father had cut off her allowance had walked out like a thoroughbred with her chin in the air, without even cashing the few dollars that remained in her own account though he told her there would be no objection to that.

"I think she'll come around pretty soon, I really do, Mr. Disston," added his friend, the banker. "I hated like sin to tell her what you said I should, too. Pretty little kid. Real thoroughbred! But, of course, I was certain when she got up to leave my office that she meant to go right home. I never had a question until I saw her turn and walk out, and then something in her manner made me uneasy. I got to thinking over what she had said, and I realized she hadn't actually *said* she was going home at all, just walked out on me and left me to think what I would. Then I went to the door to see if she cashed her check, and she wasn't there. She must have gone out the side door opposite my office, I guess, but when I looked out that, she wasn't in sight anywhere. You say she hasn't come yet? Oh, but I'm sure she will soon. Sorry, no, I didn't think to ask her address. I tell you I supposed, of course, she meant to go right home. But I'm sure she'll turn up tonight or tomorrow. I wouldn't worry if I were you. She looks as if she could take care of herself. And, of course, she's proud. She wouldn't be your daughter if she wasn't."

"That's the trouble," said the father anxiously. "I'm afraid she'll never come back for money, not if she starves to death. She's terribly proud. Just what did you say to her?"

"Well now, look here, Disston, *I* didn't think this up," said the banker. "I said to her just what you asked me to say!" And the banker went carefully over again the conversation he had had with Diana. But somehow Diana's father shrank from the words as if they had been blows dealt upon his own heart, for now suddenly he saw how they must have seemed to Diana, and he wondered why he had been willing to send her a word like that. Why hadn't he known how those words would hurt her? Yet when Helen had suggested them, the whole thing sounded so right and reasonable and kind! And now it seemed so brutal! The father hung up the receiver at last and sat back groaning in spirit. Then he remembered his position as host at a party and hastily slipped out into the other room and took up his duties again, aware subconsciously of Helen's dissatisfied eyes watching him, aware that some of the guests were looking at him and Helen, comparing their ages and wondering how she came to marry him. Of course, this lovely house—and he could see them look about upon the luxury, which even in these few days since Helen had come there to reign had become almost garish. He felt very old indeed that night.

The evening finished disturbingly for the master of the house. Some of the guests were too hilarious for his liking. Helen, too, was more boisterous than he had ever seen her before, her face a sparkle of pleasure and interest, in contrast to his own haughty expression. He looked around at the guests Helen had assembled and decided that he didn't like any of them. He would introduce Helen to his friends, of course, and gradually wean her from such companions. Poor child, she had not had a mother or father to guide her for years, and, of course, she wasn't wise in discerning character. But she would listen to him. She always had.

But when the last guests had left and they turned back to the quiet of the home again, Helen made the first attack.

"Well, and is that the way you are going to treat my friends when I have a party?" she asked in a biting voice. "If I had supposed you were going to act like an old grouch, I certainly wouldn't have invited them. What do you suppose they thought of you?"

He turned upon her with dignity. He had meant to be very tender in his remonstrance with her, but her stinging tones roused his tormented spirit.

"I didn't like the people you had here!" he said sternly. "They were coarse and ill-bred. They are not the kind of people with whom I want my wife to associate!"

"Oh really?" said Helen petulantly. "So you are going to hide your own behavior behind a grievance, are you? Well that won't get you anywhere. You remember you told me I might have a party, and you gave me permission to have it just as I wanted it. You said you didn't care who I invited, and now you're objecting. If you think that is being fair, I don't. As to my friends, if you don't like them you know what you can do, don't you? Just stay away from my parties! For I give you my word I'm not going to give up my friends! All the people I know are like that, high-spirited and free and easy."

"Then it's high time you knew another class of people," said Mr. Disston sternly. Then his voice softened a trifle. "I suppose you haven't always had the opportunity to know the right kind of people, dear, but now that you are my wife I shall want you to know my friends and move in the best circles. It's your right as my wife."

"Indeed!" said Helen, flashing her beautiful eyes. "I prefer to move in circles of my own choosing. I'm not an old fogy yet, if you are, and I want to see a little fun and life. I don't want to sit by the fire in beautiful domesticity and go to bed at nine o'clock. If that's your idea of married bliss, you can count me out!" And Helen flounced out of the room and upstairs, closing and locking the door to their room.

Then the master of the house turned out all the lights and locked himself into the dark library and sat down by himself and groaned in spirit. Was this the married bliss he had expected to have? He sat there until the morning dawned. He then came to breakfast alone and was told his wife did not wish to be disturbed, so he went his way to the office in deep sadness of heart.

❀

To Diana it was almost like entering heaven from the darkness of the pit to enter that bright home of luxury. It was as if some magic had touched her with a fairy wand and she were Cinderella at the party.

The door swung wide, and well-trained servants took charge of her suitcase and overnight bag. She was led to a chamber bright with airy organdy hangings and frills of delicate lace and ribbon, costly trifles scattered everywhere with lavish hand. Softly shaded lamps of unusual design, a picture or two that caught the eye, just a lovely homelike room. It almost took Diana's breath away, that first glimpse; it reminded her of her own sweet home, a little more lavish, perhaps, but still with the touches that spoke of taste and culture and plenty.

As Diana entered she had a swift vision of Mrs. Lundy's rooming house and the third-story back where her own treasured furnishings were waiting. The contrast brought quick tears to her eyes. Oh, if she might just take them and go home again to the place that had always been home to her!

Then came Edith rushing with open arms to greet her. Edith in bright rosy garments and her hair done in the latest thrill, jewels sparkling around her neck and wrists.

It was delightful to have to hurry and get dressed for dinner and put away all unpleasant thoughts. That was what she had resolved to do—not to think of her own troubles, neither past nor future. It would be the only way she could possibly get through this evening without everybody knowing that she was in some great trouble. And that must never happen. She simply must carry this off and never let anyone, even Edith, suspect.

So Diana put on a diaphanous dress of delicate green, almost the shade of the taffeta of years ago that Helen had so gracelessly borrowed. It was a color that Diana's mother had loved on her, and the dress was one she had ordered during her illness, with loving eagerness to have her girl go out among her friends.

While she was getting into it, she was recalling little things her mother had said about the dress and how it became her. Precious things, but she put them away in her heart, for the tears were too near the surface to trust such thoughts and she must hurry. Edith had said that dinner was about to be served.

She looked at herself in the mirror when she was ready, startled to see herself looking so well. She had been through so much during the past two weeks that it seemed to her that her brow must be seamed with care and her eyes dull with weeping.

But the excitement of the moment had brought a soft flush to her cheeks and a sparkle to her eyes, and she scarcely knew herself. As a last thought she remembered her flowers and took them from their wax paper wrappings, fastening a lovely mass of them at her shoulder, then turning her face toward them and touching her lips to their fringes caressingly. Dear flowers. They seemed somehow to give her a kind of moral support—or background, perhaps it was background. They had come from home, somewhere, somehow. When she looked at them she could think of the tall pines standing guard among cool shadows and a single blossom smiling up at her from the dewy grass. It seemed as if those flowers acted as ballast to keep her soul steady during these hours that were before her, as if just touching them with her cheek, breathing in their perfume, would calm her and give her courage if it all seemed too much for her.

Edith came back for her, and they went down the wide, deeply carpeted stair together, their arms around one another as they used to do when they were schoolgirls.

"How darling you look!" gushed Edith, and Diana for an

instant felt warmed in her soul. This was going to be pleasant after all, meeting Edith and being in things again.

Then came the other three girls whom she had known in college, and Diana began to revive in spirit. A little smile lurked in the corner of her mouth as inwardly she compared herself to a wet kitten that had been out in the storm and had crept in to find food and comfort and a place by the fire.

Edith's mother was pleasant. She accepted Diana as one of them and called her by her first name as if she had been with them always. Diana liked it and was glad she had come. No one said anything about Diana's home or her condition in life. They were all talking brightly about trifling things, laughing a good deal, cheery. Oh, it was good to be there! To get a few hours cessation from the awful loneliness and incipient fear of the future and dread of the past!

Some young men arrived after dinner, and Diana liked them all well enough. There wasn't one among them like Bobby Watkins. But she couldn't quite imagine any of them dropping a single flower in the grass day after day. Her mysterious donor was probably only a woman. But no, she would not limit those spirit flowers to any earthly means. As long as she could, she would think of them as having come straight from God. It might be that God had somewhere a young knight who would love a lonely girl and woo her with flowers, but she did not know such a one. She could please herself by thinking of it all as romance in the form of a fairy tale, but she felt a growing conviction that behind it all was God, calling to her, trying to let her know He cared, and the belief comforted her.

The young men flocked around her as they did to the other girls. She did not feel left out. One especially seemed drawn to her, Jerry Lange. He called her Diana as soon as they were introduced.

"Diana, you for mine!" he said engagingly as they paired off for the fun of the evening.

And Diana liked it. Yet as the evening went forward in the usual amusements, she had a feeling that they were just children, playing at life, not really in earnest at all, and she alone of them all had grown up. What they were doing so eagerly soon palled on her. Was that what trouble and loneliness did to your soul, made it suddenly grow old and satiated? Though she had never had a great deal of frivolity in her life, yet it seemed so trifling now. She thought of her dreary, crowded third-floor room in the unkempt street. She thought of the restaurant where she was going to work on Monday. She thought of her home, now her home no longer, and then strangely she thought of God. Was He caring for her, here, now in the midst of this bright laughing scene? Was He standing unseen behind her here and caring? What a strange thought that was to come into the midst of her outing!

She looked around at them all. She looked into Jerry's laughing eyes as he tried to tell her how he had just been waiting all his life to find her and called her "beautiful" and "darling" in the parlance of the day, laughing and giving her charming courtesy that didn't, of course, mean a thing. Just fun. And she wondered if Jerry knew God. If God cared for all these here. Of course He did, for that verse had said, "God so loved the world." Nobody could claim to be left out of that. God was caring for them, but they—were *they*—? No, they were obviously not conscious of Him. Not at the moment, anyway. And it was altogether likely that none of them ever thought of God at all. They were all as she had been before her trouble came.

She wondered idly as she watched the handsome youth beside her, talking brilliant nonsense to her, what would be his reaction if she could ask him about it? What, for instance, would he say if she were to ask, "Do you know God, Jerry?" Of course, she would not do it, but she could almost feel the chill silence that would ensue for an instant, the blank surprise with which he would look at her. But it would not be for long, likely. He would have ready some flippant reply, some brightly funny answer, and suddenly she knew she would not want to hear it. It would hurt her sense of reverence for the Lord who cared for her. What had happened to her? It couldn't be all merely sorrow that had done this. But if it was, it had certainly done something definite to her. She never used to think about God before, any more than they did. But now she realized that she had become God-conscious.

She was glad when they turned from the games and the dancing, for she somehow felt very little interest in them, and voted to go for a drive in the big convertible that one of the young men had brought. They put down the top of the car, for there was moonlight, and besides, the night was unusually warm. All eight of them piled into the car noisily, and Jerry sat by Diana and tried to hold her hand. She had some trouble to keep it to herself, for now and again he would catch it up impulsively as though they were children at play. But on the whole the ride was a lovely experience, crowded cheerily together under the white flood of moonlight, flashing out through the city streets, rushing traffic lights, barely missing pedestrians and smaller cars, and sweeping out a wide silver road into less populated regions. The sultriness of the evening was gone.

As the soft summer breeze played in Diana's hair, it seemed pleasant to have Jerry beside her, saying bright nothings, seeing to it that she was supplied with candy and that her wrap was adjusted when the breeze grew a bit chilly as they swept into the countryside. This was the life she was born to, good fellowship and fun and friendships like this. This would have been hers as a matter of course if her mother had lived. They had often talked about how she would go out to parties and enjoy herself when her school days were over. And then—they had never been over! They had just stopped!

All at once Diana realized that the road they were traveling was familiar. Her heart stood still. They were on the highway that led directly to her home! Oh, why had she come to this party? Why had she come on this drive? She nestled her frightened face down into the knot of fringed blossoms on her shoulder as if they would somehow help her through. She felt herself growing weak with the thought of the nearness of the spot that had always been the dearest on earth to her.

Then she tried to rally her forces. None of this crowd knew where she lived, except Edith, and it was to her only a name, only a postal address, she had never been there. She perhaps did not even know where they were. She had only so recently come to the city and was not familiar with the roads.

Diana felt as if she must do something to still the wild beating of her heart lest the others should hear it. How silly she was, she told herself. Even if Edith recognized the place and spoke of it, she need only be quiet. It was not likely they would ask her questions. She could just act as if it were a matter of course. If Edith should suddenly cry out as they passed the town and she saw the name somewhere, "Why, Di, isn't this where you live?" she could just say, "Yes, it isn't far from here," and be very vague about it. Would she be able to keep her voice steady to say that, she wondered?

And now they were rushing through the village. The lights were bright along the way. The village shops were blazing with display windows. There was the electric shop with its big white refrigerators and ranges and lamps. There was the post office and the drugstore. There was that new florist's shop, the window filled with gorgeous blossoms with tall tropical ferns in the background. Her flowers had come from there. Her heart gave a wild little thrill, and she put her face down close to them, her lips upon them, as if she would hush their very perfume lest it should call attention to where they came from.

And now they were passing the bank with the name of the

town in large stone letters across its white front, a floodlight bringing it out like a picture. It was a beautiful building, and it was new. The town was proud of it. But Diana trembled as they shot by it and then drew a breath of relief as they passed on up the wide avenue into the region of high hedges and estates. In a moment more her home would be in sight! Could she get by it without sobbing?

There, there it was, its whiteness gleaming against the dim green of the dark pines in the background. She wanted to close her eyes until they were by, but Jerry was looking down into them and he would ask her why she was doing it, "beautiful?" if she did. No, she must keep them open and smile back to what he was saying, though she hadn't heard a word of it. She must laugh and not seem to be interested in anything along the way. Soon it would all be past, and none of them would know that it had taken the heart out of her to pass that way, so near to home and Father and not know what was going on, not have him know that she was there! Oh, why had she come to this party?

Then suddenly one of the girls cried out, "Oh, see that lovely mansion, boys and girls, isn't it just ideal? See the way that lawn curves up to the terrace! And aren't those pines simply ducky behind there. I'll bet they have a swimming pool and a sunken garden behind it. My, I'd like to go there and visit. Pity we haven't any friends around here to scrape acquaintance with whoever lives there. Where is this, anyway? I want to remember it."

Diana dropped her face down lower and held her breath. Now it would come! Somebody would be sure to know the name of the suburb and there would be an outcry, and Edith would say, "Why, Diana, isn't this where—?"

She could see the lights of her home now, flung out like a banner to challenge the moonlight on the lawn. She could identify each light. The front door was flung wide, just as it had been the night she went away. And was that Helen standing in the doorway talking to a man?—not her father, she could see that, he was too short for her father.

But then the hedge and a group of trees swept in and hid the house from view for an instant, and the identity of the place had not yet been discovered. Oh, would they never get by? Why were they slowing up?

Here was the stone cottage at last, dear little stone cottage where she heard that prayer. She gave it a hungry, fleeting glance, and then looked again, for the door was suddenly flung open and a young man came and stood in the entrance looking out. She looked again. Could that be the man who had prayed? How she wished she knew!

Then as if in answer to her wish, their car suddenly swept up to the curve and stopped dead with a startling abruptness, and Diana's heart simply stood still. What, oh, what was going to happen now, and what should she do? Jump out and run away?

Her frightened heart seemed to be beating in her ears like a drum, and she dared not look up. Why was she so frightened? Nothing was going to happen. Nobody was looking at her. Or, were they? Perhaps they had somehow gotten a message from her father and were taking her home for a joke! Oh—!

Then the driver called out and broke the awful spell that held her.

"Hey, brother, which way to Windham Road?"

The young man in the doorway came down the step and stood in the moonlight answering. His voice had a pleasant accent. "Straight on two miles and turn to your left. Filling station on the corner. You can't miss it."

"Thanks a lot!" said the youth who was driving. Then he shot on down the road so that it seemed they had scarcely paused.

It was all over as quickly as that, and the white mansion with its grassy slope and its background of dark pines was gone, gone the little cottage with the tall young man in the doorway. But the voice that had answered their question lingered in Diana's heart.

For that was the voice that had prayed, *"And, Lord, we would ask Thy mercy and tenderness and leading for the people up at the great house. Perhaps some of them are sad. Lord, give them comfort. Perhaps they need guidance. Do Thou send Thy light—"*

What a prayer! And how its accents came back with the sound of that voice. That voice so strangely familiar! Where had she heard it before? *Had* she really heard it before the prayer, or only in her dreams? And his face as he stood there in the moonlight, a fine face, strong and trustworthy and yet tender—a face that matched the voice! It thrilled her to think of his face as he stood there in the moonlight looking at them all so interestedly and speaking with that pleasant voice. Who was he? Where did he come from? Was he just a visitor there?

And suddenly she knew where she had heard that voice before! It was the voice that had spoken in the darkness when Bobby Watkins—

"What is it, beautiful? What are you thinking about? I've asked you the same question three times and you haven't heard it yet!"

"Oh, did you?" she said, rousing with a little laugh that somehow seemed to have a new lilt in it. "Do excuse me! Ask it again. I was so taken up with the beauty of the night that everything else was just a dream!"

He asked his question and she answered it superficially, keeping up her end of the cheerful banter skillfully, with only half of her mind upon it, for deep down in her heart she was hugging to herself the thought that she had seen the man who had prayed for her house. And was it conceivable that he was still praying for them, and was she possibly included in that prayer? How she wished that sometime she might meet him and ask him some of those throbbing questions that had been roused in her mind by the little tract given to her in the railway station and her reading of the Bible!

There was more cheerful banter as they swept on through the moonlight; singing, too, rollicking songs, love songs; and shouting out of their youth and high spirits. It was all like a dream after that to Diana. She went through everything, smilingly gracious, yet pleasantly distraught.

They stopped by the wayside and had ice cream. Then they went back to the city house again and sang more songs and played more games, but at last it was over, and in the small hours of Sunday morning Diana found herself alone in the lovely guest room lying in the cool darkness dropping off to sleep, with one sweet carnation lying against her cheek on the pillow and the sound of a voice praying, a voice that soon blended with her dreams and prayed for her by name with great gentleness. And so she drifted off to sleep.

Chapter 17

Diana went back to her hot third-story room in the city early Monday morning before the rest of the weekend party was awake.

She had had much fuss to prevent their taking her wherever she was going and had to resort to strategy to keep them from knowing her present place of residence. She was utterly aghast at the thought of Jerry or any of the others escorting her to her train, for she had told them she had an engagement for the day in another part of the city. So in the very early morning, quite before any of the servants were stirring in the great beautiful house, except perhaps a sleepy cook down in the kitchen, she arose, wrote a hasty note, slipped it under Edith's door, and went silently down the velvet-shod stairs and out of the house without disturbing anyone.

The note said:

Dear Edith,

I'm dreadfully sorry to run away this way

*without seeing you again, but in thinking
it over I find I must get another change of
garments before I go on my way for the day's
engagement, so I'm just running off without
waking you. I know you will forgive me. And
I shall hope to see you again soon. I'm not just
sure where I shall be the rest of the summer, but
if I ever do get home again I hope I can have
the pleasure of a visit from you. I've had such a
lovely time! Thank you for asking me.*

Lovingly,
Diana

So Diana had slipped around the corner from the house and waited in the next street for the bus, while the morning dawned in rosy glory and most of the city was still sleeping.

Diana had gone through the Sabbath as in a pleasant dream, taking as little part as possible in the hilarity and fun that was the atmosphere of the gathering, smiling sweetly at everybody, but in reality not absorbed in what went on.

The young men had arrived again early in the day, and Jerry was as devoted as ever but failed to get the overwhelming interest from this girl that was actually accorded him everywhere. Diana was a nice, good comrade, but she seemed somehow remote. He couldn't quite understand it. He looked for an engagement ring, but there was none. And perhaps her attitude only intrigued him the more, for he was most devoted all the day and evening and quite insisted that she let him come with his car in the morning and drive her home. She had succeeded in putting him off at last by saying her plans were not fully made yet, she wasn't sure just what time she would be going, and so he said good night with a warning that he would be back early the next day to be ready for whatever plan she made.

So Diana escaped them all and went to the rooming house to change from her festive garments into the plainest black dress she owned.

She had ripped off the only pretense at decoration it had and cut the sleeves to the elbow, with just a plain hem, but even so she had a stylish look as she surveyed herself in the mirror before leaving for her day's work. Even when she enveloped herself in the big white apron she had brought, she looked a thing apart from that restaurant. Not a ring on her finger, not even a string of beads around her neck nor a pin at her throat to fasten the plain white collar, yet there were "lines" unmistakable to the simple dress that showed it well cut and tailored. There was a trimness to her plain black pumps and a delicacy of face and figure that showed she was not the usual waitress in a cheap restaurant.

Even her watch had to be left in her room. It was a pretty toy, platinum set with diamonds around its face and in the delicate links of the bracelet. It would never do to pass ham and cabbage and baked beans with such a wristwatch. She would be suspected at once, as well as being a prey for thieves.

So she locked her watch into her bureau and went her way through the noisy waking streets, dreading what was before her yet not thinking about it as much as she had expected, for in her mind there lingered the memory of a voice, a strong face with wonderful eyes, and a prayer that seemed following her out into this new unknown world, which she was to enter today.

And then she prayed to herself before she left her room, a little, trembling prayer, shyly, as if the man who had once prayed for her were there before God with her and listening to what she said. Just a shy claiming of God's guidance, an affirmation that she was trusting, and then, after a pause, an "I thank you!" She didn't say for what, but in her heart it was that she had seen the one who had prayed that night and whose words had lingered all these days in her heart. It seemed to her that the earth did not reel quite as much under her untried way as it had on Saturday, nor was the way quite as dark and empty and long since she knew there was a man like that and he had prayed for her, even just once.

So she entered her new world and was suddenly faced with all its sordidness anew.

The other waitresses were coming in, yawning, heavy eyed, loud voiced, discontented. She heard them telling one another where they had been the night before and how late they had been up. She heard their half-finished confidences, their bitter laughter; their faces wore heavy makeup, their garments were cheap but gaudy; and most of them had dark circles of unhappiness and exhaustion under their eyes. Looking at them, it suddenly occurred to Diana that these were all a part of God's world as much as she was, that He must love them, since He died for all, and the thought was startling. It made her look at them from a new standpoint, so that their commonness and coarseness and lack of culture did not stand out to her gaze as they otherwise would have done. They were dear to her God; she must not turn from them as her natural instincts would have had her do!

But those girls had no such common bond to bind them to her. They looked at her with hostile eyes. She was an intruder from another world. She had once been rich, they could see that from the very way she wore her clothes, from her walk, and from the delicacy of her lovely hands that showed no sign of having worked. They called all such girls snobs and hated them. They resolved to make it too hard for her so that she would have to leave and make room for one of their own kind. They began at once, drawing away from her and whispering with furtive eyes upon her, aloof and cold.

It had not occurred to her that she would have to have much to do with the other waitresses, but she found at the start that she was somewhat dependent upon them. She approached one girl, the least disagreeable-looking one of the lot, and asked where she should put her hat. And the girl shrugged her shoulders with a wink at the others and said, "Ask the boss! I ain't got time to show ya." Diana stepped back bewildered, feeling as if she had been slapped in the face.

Later she discovered that her very voice was an offense to these girls who had very little education. Most of them had left school to go to work even before the law allowed.

She approached the boss for information and found a beetling brow and an ugly jaw. He scarcely glanced at her.

"Ask one o' the girls," he growled. "I ain't got time! Here you, Lily, you show this new number the cloak room. Mame, what'cha standin' round for? Don'tcha see that customer over ta the corner? Get a hustle on ya. There's plenty other girls if ya don't find it convenient ta work today!"

The girl gave a frightened glance and started toward the table over in the corner where the waiting customer sat, and Diana learned a startling lesson. She stood a second waiting uncertainly for the Lily girl to show her the cloak room, but Lily had hunched her shoulders and vanished into the kitchen.

Diana shrank from asking any of the others who so obviously considered her an intruder. Then she saw another girl hurrying in out of breath, taking her hat off as she came. She resolved to follow her and ask no questions.

"Hey you, Ruby! This is a pretty time a day ta be comin' ta work!" roared the manager.

"Oh, is it late?" panted the girl, turning and almost colliding with Diana. "I—you see—my grandmother was sick!"

"Yeah? Yer grandmother again! Ain't it so? Ya can't put that over on me! Don't let it happen again!" he snapped. "Get a hustle on! Make it snappy!"

Diana shrank into the shadows of the back of the room and disappeared after Ruby. Perhaps Ruby would be kinder than the rest. She might ask her what to do.

But Ruby had slung her hat on a hook and dashed out again tying on her apron, and Diana perceived that she had better do the same. As she went out she reflected that she couldn't have that terrible man roaring her name out everywhere. What should she do? Take another name? Her middle name was Dart. She had registered as Miss Dart. But apparently that man would never call her Miss Dart. Well, let him call her Jane.

Her decision was none too soon, for he met her at the door of the cloak room with a card and pencil.

"Write yer name an' address," he commanded, "an' be quick about it! Then take a tray an' get ta work! There's a customer comin' in now. The menu's on the wall, but some of 'em can't read. Ya'll have ta memorize it as ya go. Getta hustle on! And don't bother me with questions. Use yer head!" He glanced at the card and added, "Jane!"

Diana gave him one quick, startled look, caught up a tray from the frame beside her, and went over to the table in the corner.

The man sitting there was rough and uncouth. He had a deep, stubby growth of hair on his face, and his eyes were bleared and fierce-looking. She glanced away toward the menu on the wall as she approached him and then turned beside the table to see his hateful eyes fixed upon her. She controlled a little shiver of horror and forced herself to look at him steadily and impersonally, and suddenly that same question came to her again. Did God love this man, too? Did He die for him? What a strange world she had come into! She had never questioned that before about anyone. The people she had known had been on the same social level with herself, and her contacts had been carefully guarded. She had never thought about people like this, and here she was serving them! But why should she resent them? The Son of God died for them!

But his first words and his offensive glance made her shudder again.

"You a new un, ain't ye?'" he said, and his voice was offensive also.

She gave him a frightened glance.

"I beg your pardon," she said with the least little bit of haughtiness in her voice.

"Whatcha beggin' my pardon for?" His eyes narrowed and seemed to be boring into her soul like gimlets. She gave a swift glance toward the manager and saw him watching her with an amused grin on his ugly, thick face, and instantly she rallied. Here was her testing. She must not fail.

"Will you have ham and eggs, sausages, or liver?" she asked in a voice that sounded even to herself as if it came from very far away.

"H'm! Snooty, are ye?" said the man contemptuously. "Well, make it hot cakes an' sausage with plenty o' syrup and a pot o' coffee, an' *scram*, for I'm in a hurry!"

Diana didn't know what *scram* meant, but she fairly flew, lifting her tray above the mulling crowd of customers that was beginning to pour into the miserable little eating place now in numbers too many for the accommodations, lifting her highborn chin a bit haughtily. She was here to serve, and if she lost her job, she would have to get another, perhaps worse than this. If God had died for all these dreadful people and loved her, too, He could surely protect her. And, of course, mere words or looks could not really hurt her. She had read something in her Bible the other day about being kept by the power of God through faith unto salvation. She hadn't known what it meant at the time, but now a dim vision of what it might mean came to her. She couldn't see any keeping hand nor any guiding hand. It all had to be done by faith, faith that God loved her, had sent His beloved Son to die for her, and had thought her soul worth saving. It was therefore inconceivable, since all that was true, that He would let her be lost in any way, since He was all-powerful, all-seeing, and *cared*!

While she was waiting for the hot cakes and preparing the tray as she saw the other girls do, she was thinking these things, and a memory of the man last night standing in the bright doorway of the little stone cottage by the home gate came to her. It lifted her out of her fright and gave her a kind of peace to think that a man like that had been praying for her. She liked to think that perhaps he was doing it now.

Inside the breast of her plain black dress she had pinned a single carnation, as a kind of talisman. Its breath stole up faintly like the far fragrance of another world and comforted her.

The manager was watching her. When she brought her tray back so swiftly, he seemed surprised. She was not clumsy as some of those other girls had been at the start. Her fingers were deft and worked quickly. As soon as she had learned where the knives and forks and spoons were kept and where to fill the glasses with water, her tray was arranged by the time the food was ready, and she carried it without slopping the coffee, too, not that the manager cared so much about that, however.

Before the day was over, the manager had learned that even though she was "classy" she seemed to have a better mind for her work than some of the others. Moreover, she didn't dally, and there wasn't a lazy hair on her attractive brown head. The manager decided he liked her, and he saw to it that she had a chair at a table when she ate her swift meals. The other girls noticed this and hated her for it. The manager knew that she was worth more than some of the others when she got in training, and he called her for some of his best customers, "Jane! Take that number, Jane!" and the other girls would pause and cast malevolent glances. He was giving her some of the people who gave the biggest tips, and they hated her more. They talked about it as they passed one another or when they lingered at the counter waiting for their orders.

"Next he'll be takin' her out to a movie," they whispered, "an' what'll Gwendolyn think o' that?"

But Diana went on her swift way not noticing either them or him, intent only on doing her work and not getting fired, though she was weary and footsore, with aching arms unused to lifting heavy trays and a tired back that rebelled at the unusual strain put upon it. At lunch she ate a small portion of the unattractive greasy food that was given to her, but when dinnertime came she was too tired to swallow but a few mouthfuls. The long, hurried hours were telling on her. Would the day never be done? And there would be other days, succeeding one another, day after day, working like this for her existence. And there was no end ahead. It would go on and on and on, unless God did something about it, for she had no home anymore, only that room that she must keep or be put out on the street!

She was on her way out at last when the manager stood up from his table where he was counting a heap of small change and tapped her on the shoulder.

"You done purty good, Jane, for a first try."

She thanked him wearily and, with his words of commendation in her ears, went on her way.

The breath of her flowers smote across her consciousness as she entered her room. Poor flowers, condemned to brighten this dim room alone. Yet the very consciousness that they were here in this quiet place that was all hers made it possible for her to keep on through the day. She stopped to caress them, and the healing balm of them as always soothed her. But she was too weary even to think about them tonight. She flung off her garments and got into bed, drowsing even in the act. She had never before known what it was to be so tired, and the blessedness of sleep came down upon her like a curtain. She roused only to wind her alarm clock, mindful even in the weariness of the ugly warnings those other girls had received at being even a second tardy.

Morning came with the sharp, insistent shriek of the little imp of a clock by her side, and she roused to the bitterness of her new life, languid, sore in heart and muscle, then dragged herself up to go through another day like the first one. Was it humanly possible for her to keep this up? Her gains through tips the first day had been so pitifully little, less than a dollar all told, and the starvation wage would not come until the week was up. That was the whip her new employer held over the heads of his help. Of course, she had food, such as it was, but no appetite for it. It seemed to her sick senses as if it was something that her soul had wallowed in for centuries when she came to eat that food. Its strong, greasy, scorched aroma had filled her lungs and nostrils until they were sated. Why should anyone want to eat, anyway? Why should they have to?

Even Sunday brought only half-day relief, for the arrangement was that the girls took turns getting a full Sunday off. Jane was told that hers would come in four weeks, as she was a newcomer and must wait her turn. In consternation she looked forward to four steady weeks of this toil, broken only by that half-day once in seven! And when the seventh day came and she reached her room, she had no wish but to lie down and sleep again. She did not even stop to caress her drooping flowers. What did it matter? Someone had cared to send them, but she was too far gone in weariness to give them the attention they demanded. Well, they were dying and she would soon be dead, too, perhaps.

She had tried to read her Bible nights when she came home but found herself so utterly fatigued that she could not take in the meaning of the words. She was gradually comprehending the life a large part of the world was living, and she wondered if God cared. Did He truly care? Oh, she wanted to believe it, but somehow that first Sunday afternoon after she became a waitress in that awful restaurant she could not quite feel sure anymore. She was just sick with weariness. Perhaps, later, she would become accustomed to such hard work and wouldn't mind it so much, she told herself as she put her head down upon the pillow that first Sunday afternoon without the ceremony of undressing and was immediately drenched with sleep.

It was Mrs. Lundy who wakened her, just at early evening, knocking on her door. She had a large box in her arms, and she was quite insistent. "These here come last night, but you wasn't in yet. I told Lottie to bring 'em up when she heard you come in, but she didn't bother, and when I come up this mornin' you was gone. I guess it's more flowers. Say, he must be a regular guy, sendin' 'em once a week."

Flowers? Diana looked up with her sleep-laden eyes. Her heart leaped up, and she came awake at once, a soft color stealing into her pale cheeks. The flowers! They had come again! Not just once, but at regular intervals, just as they had been at home, only now by boxes instead of by blossoms! Wonder of wonders! And she had doubted her God's caring!

Of course, the Bible said nothing at all about God's sending carnations to show His loving care, but somehow in spite of common sense those spirit-flowers seemed connected in some way with God.

"I said he must be a regular guy, sendin' 'em once a week!" repeated the landlady, looking at her curiously.

"Oh, yes," said Diana, a light coming into her eyes. "Yes, it does seem that way, doesn't it?" And she swept an upward glance at the curious old woman with a smile that suddenly wiped away all the weariness from her face. "Yes, it does!" she lilted. "He must be!"

"Well, if he's such a swell feller, why doesn't he come across an' give you enough to pay your rent on time?"

"Oh," said Diana quickly, apologetically, a flush coming to her cheeks. "I have it right here, Mrs. Lundy. I meant to give it to you last night but it was so late, and your room seemed to be dark—and I was so tired—!"

Mrs. Lundy, with a mollified manner, swept her another curious glance.

"Seem like if he can afford to send a lotta flowers like that he might do somepin' to keep you from workin' so hard!"

Diana cast her a superior smile from a cool distance.

"But, you see, I wouldn't let anyone do that, Mrs. Lundy!" she said proudly.

"Oh!" said the woman significantly, and then after a pause, "Well, some does that way, o' course, but I say it don't pay to be too pertikelar in these days! You gotta live, you know!"

"I'm not so sure," said Diana, counting out the change, and Mrs. Lundy went on her way.

Then Diana locked her door and turned back to her box, thoroughly awake now, her cheeks flaming crimson, her breath coming quickly as if she had been running, and her eyes starry bright.

They had come again! Her mysterious flowers. She did not care where they came from, they had come. God had let them come. Perhaps she would never find out who sent them, but she knew they came from God.

She opened the box and suddenly saw a white envelope bearing her name, lying right on the top of the wax paper that veiled the flowers, and her breath almost stopped. She sat back staring at it for a full minute before she put out her hand to touch it.

Was that the same handwriting that had been on the outside of the first box? No, it wasn't! She reached down in the corner and picked up the first box where she had hidden it behind the bureau. No, it was a different hand! It was a fine, clear, strong hand. A man's hand? Or—could it be a woman's? No, not possibly, and yet some women—nowadays—wrote in quite a masculine way. But the woman, if it was a woman, who would conceive the idea of putting flowers in the way of a troubled girl would never be one who would write a masculine hand. It wasn't thinkable.

These thoughts raced through her brain while she sat staring at the envelope, quite forgetful of the flowers whose perfume reached delicately out to enwrap her soul again.

How silly she was to sit here staring when she had only to open that envelope and the secret would be revealed, likely, the mystery solved. Yet she dreaded knowing the truth, now that it seemed within her grasp. She could not bear to have her one little romance stripped of its mystery and brought out in the open commonplace of day.

Then at once she could stand it no longer, and she opened the envelope with trembling hands and read what was within:

Dear Flower Girl,

I found your precious note. I am glad the flowers helped.

That was all! No name signed, no address or date or anything!

And the mystery was still unsolved, yet very precious, but now there was a definite person connected with them, with a real intention of sending them.

She arose with her flowers, knelt as before, and thanked God for sending them. Then she arranged them in a lovely jar and sat down before them to enjoy their beauty and fragrance and think over and over again the words of that message.

"I found your precious note." Precious—! It thrilled her just to think it over. Precious! Somebody cared! God cared, at least. And

He must have let *somebody* else care, too, but not in any foolish way. In a wonderfully tender way, with more of heaven than earth in its quality.

Flowers! *Precious* flowers!

Chapter 18

At the Disston mansion the servants had reigned for a week only, ordering what they liked and keeping high carnival. Helen had not bothered to look up their references. She said they were smart-looking and knew their way around. She wanted them because they had served in fashionable circles, or professed to have done so. But when she chose to insist upon weekends at the shore or mountains and spoke of whole weeks away, with the house running and ready for immediate occupancy, they looked forward to time on their hands and carte blanche to do as they liked. If the master of the house protested at such waste, Helen silenced him at once with the suggestion that Diana might choose to come home at any time, and he wouldn't want her to find a closed house, would he? And the master said no more.

He was more and more worried about Diana, waiting daily, expectantly, for word from her, which did not arrive, depressed beyond rallying after the mail would come and still no word.

He and Helen had come home at his insistence. He must look

after his business, he said. And, indeed, it had been sadly neglected, his mind being on other things. There were plenty of things about his business to worry about if he had only chosen to remember it.

They came home about the middle of the morning just after the mail had arrived, and then trouble descended upon them.

Helen looked up brightly from her sheaf of letters and invitations.

"Listen!" she cried, an open letter in her hand. "Max Copley has invited us to a house party! It's to be the end of this week. Isn't that swanky? I must get a couple of new dresses for it. I might go in town this afternoon and look around."

"No!" said her husband sharply. "Not with any idea of going to a party at *that* man's house. I want nothing to do with him or any crowd in which he moves. He isn't fit for you to speak to!"

"Oh really?" said Helen, with lifted brows. "Now that poisonous mind and tongue of yours is going to give another exhibition, is it? What a veritable old crab you are getting to be, and so soon after we are married! Well, I supposed it wouldn't last, but I didn't think you would change so soon. However, do as you like for yourself. I'm *going*! Get me? You can't tie *me* down to your age!"

The gray look that was getting to be habitual on Mr. Disston's face suddenly descended.

"Not my age, perhaps, Helen, but to my station at least, surely."

"No, not to your station, either, not if you are determined to live in a past generation. I'm stepping out, and you can go with me or stay behind for all I care. It's entirely up to you, darling. But you can't tie me down, for I won't be tied! And I'm going into town to get a few new clothes! I'd like some money, if you don't mind. You'd better give it to me now so I won't be delayed about it after lunch. I want to get an early start."

A still grayer look came over Mr. Disston's face.

"I'm sorry," he said after an instant's hesitation. "I can't give you any now. In fact, I'm afraid I can't give you any more till the first of the month. We've been spending a good deal more than usual, and I find I am running a little short." He said it in an apologetic tone, but Helen's face flushed red.

"Really?" she said with a touch of scorn on her lips. "Well, you certainly have gone to the end of your resources in a hurry. We haven't been doing very much for a honeymoon. Just a few weekends."

"We've been to the best hotels always, and you've wanted all the extras. Besides, we've had a great deal of company. You've no idea how that adds up. Of course, you haven't had much experience in housekeeping yet."

"Oh, I suppose your model daughter would have done better!" flashed Helen angrily.

"I didn't say that, Helen," said Mr. Disston sadly, "but, of course, those new servants you got did bring the bills up a great deal. I was rather appalled at the bills. They all came to the office yesterday. And coming just now when business is at the very lowest ebb it makes it pretty hard."

Helen stared at him with vexed eyes and then flounced up from her chair, letting fall a sheaf of letters to the floor, and went and looked out the window.

"Oh well," she said, still offended, "of course, I can always charge things, but I hate to be hampered this way. When you are married you naturally consider that you can have a few things the way they ought to be. Well"—with a sigh—"never mind, I can charge things."

Disston glanced up with a look in his eyes that was almost frightened.

"No, Helen, please don't do that, either. I've had several insistent letters from the places where you have been buying. It seems you have already been charging things, and I thought I had given you money enough in all reason for the things you said you wanted to buy."

"Oh, my goodness!" snapped Helen. "Have I got to be watched and spied on? I hate a spy! And I hate a tightfisted man. I supposed, of course, you wanted your wife to appear as well as she could. I only got what I absolutely had to have."

"Helen, you distress me, dear. Come and sit down, and let me explain to you."

"You distress me, too," said Helen bitterly. But she came and sat down.

"Well, it's just this way. I don't want to trouble you with my business affairs any more than is necessary, but just this last week a situation has arisen which makes it necessary that I save every penny possible, for a short time at least. You will remember that I have been much away from the office during the past month, and it seems a number of critical situations arose during my absence that had to be met by my subordinates. They did the best they knew, but it was not what I would have done if I had been there, and therefore things have got into a serious tangle. Of course, I am hoping that I shall be able to right matters soon, and all will yet go well, but just for the present, until I tell you further, I shall have to ask you to spend just as little as possible. You must know that this is mortifying to me, just after our marriage, to have to say this to you, but I am sure you will cooperate with me in this matter until we have clear sailing before us again."

He looked at her wistfully, but she regarded him stonily.

"I suppose," she said in a hard voice, "that what is really the case is that you have made such a fool of yourself over this matter of Diana's going away that you aren't fit to put your mind on your business. Oh, you needn't talk to me. I have eyes. I can see. You care far more for Diana than you ever did for me. I ought never to have married you. I might have known you were too old to give up your life habits!"

And suddenly Helen let fall two enormous, well-calculated

tears straight down into her lap and splash on her diamond engagement ring, which twinkled at her troubled husband enormously and expensively and reminded him that it was not yet paid for, as also were several other things that Helen had lately acquired at her own insistence.

"There, there, child!" he said, coming over to her and laying his hand upon her head, as he might have done to Diana. "I didn't mean to trouble you. I'm sorry. I'm only asking you to be a little careful, for a few weeks at least, till I can get things in hand again. You know I do not want to spoil your pleasure—"

"Oh yes you do!" sobbed Helen adroitly. "And I'm not a child! I'm a grown woman, and I know what I want, and you said you were going to make me happy!"

"My dear! I certainly want to make you happy. Just as far as I am able. And I confidently expect soon to have everything in shape so that our good income will be assured again. Come, Helen, be reasonable—I can't give you anything more just now."

"But now is when I need it," pouted Helen. "Why can't you put a mortgage on this house, then, and get some more money? People do that. I know they do. Max was telling that his house is mortgaged up to its full value. Or why can't we sell the old thing? I just hate it, anyway. I want a house over on the west side where all my friends live. There's a darling house over there we could buy for a little more than the value of this. In fact, I've already got a buyer for you!"

Helen's tears were forgotten now, and her impish smile bloomed out like April sunshine. "He's a friend of Max's, and he's coming out sometime today or tomorrow to look at it."

Her eyes were bright with the few recent tears, her cheeks a lovely rose. She had a mischievous beauty all her own, and her troubled husband looked at her hopelessly, a stern weariness overspreading his face, with a kind of gentleness around his eyes, as when one tries to explain serious matters to a lovely child.

"My dear," he said, "that would be quite impossible."

"There! I thought you'd say that!" stormed Helen, stamping a costly little shoe and biting her lips until the tears appeared on the horizon again.

"Well, my dear, it is impossible. This house cannot be sold nor mortgaged, either."

"Just why, I'd like to know?" demanded Helen, whirling upon him, a fierce light in her eyes. "That's silly! Of course it can. Any house can be sold or mortgaged. Why can't this? I've always hated this house, and I won't live in it. I *won't*, do you hear me? Not another day! Won't you sell it for me?"

She suddenly dropped into her sweetest wheedling tones.

"I cannot," said Stephen Disston. "Helen, this house is not my own."

"Not your own? Have you already sold it or mortgaged it, then?" she asked, looking with startled eyes at him. "You have done that and did not tell me?"

"No, I have not," he said sadly. "I have no right either to sell or mortgage it. This house belongs to Diana. Her mother left it to her!"

"To Diana!" cried Helen indignantly. "The perfect idea! If that is true, how do you happen to be occupying it?"

"I have the right of residence during my lifetime," said Stephen Disston gravely.

Helen stared for a minute, and then her shrewd eyes narrowed on her husband's face once more.

"But how could Diana live in a house like this without money?" she asked contemptuously. "If you refused her money, she could not keep it up."

"Diana has money," said her father quietly. "She has enough to keep this place and live in comfort here. She will come of age in a few weeks now."

There was silence while Helen took this in.

"But you are her trustee and guardian," said Helen with assurance. "You could easily persuade her to sell this house."

"No," said Diana's father, "that is one of the provisions of the will, that the house shall not be sold during Diana's lifetime. If she has children, it will pass on to them."

Helen's brows grew black.

"That's a raw deal for you!" she said icily. "A nice thing for Marilla to do to you."

"It was my wish!" said Stephen Disston quietly. "I knew that the house was given to Marilla with that idea in mind, of making it a family homestead from one generation to another."

There was an ominous silence in the room for several minutes, and then Helen whirled around from the window with one of her lightning changes of mood.

"Well, then let's get out of it!" she said. "You couldn't hire me to stay here any longer. You knew what you were bringing me into when you married me, now you've got to do something about it. Come on, let's pack and go to the city to a hotel. We'll stay there till we can find a new house. If this is Diana's, that's probably why she left, till we got out."

"No, Diana is not like that!" said her father sadly. "Besides, Diana does not yet know that the house is hers. Her mother did not want her to know until she came of age."

Helen turned and faced him, giving him a long, significant look, and then said, "Oh-h-h-h-*oh*!" with lifted brows. Then after a minute she added, "Then you *could* do something about it. Right now you could, before she comes of age, and you owe it to me to do it, too! Those things can always be managed. A good lawyer will find a way out of it, and Diana will never make a fuss about it anyway. *I* know Diana! You can just tell her that it seemed best for you to sell, you had a good chance. I think I can make this man that wants to buy pay a little more, enough to get the other house I want. I'm sure I can."

Mr. Disston rose and faced his wife, amazed consternation on his face.

"Helen!" he said sternly, holding her glance with his eyes, and said no more, but it was as if he had said, "Get thee behind me, Satan!"

Helen faced him unflinchingly, but her own eyes narrowed for an instant and grew shifty. Then came one of those sudden changes. She was a little innocent thing misjudged.

"Now, what have I said? What can I have done?" she quivered like a hurt child. "Wouldn't that be perfectly proper for you to do if you thought it was best for Diana? But anyway, I only meant it for a joke, and you took it seriously."

Stephen Disston was an honorable man. It went deep to have his wife suggest something dishonorable, and it was some time before Helen could finally convince him, or partly convince him, that she had meant nothing dishonorable by her suggestion.

But having at last won him back to his usual gentle self, she went upstairs with averted face and furtive eyes in which there dwelt a degree of triumph. She had won him over to say that he would take her away, at least for a few days. He would have to go to the office perhaps every morning and stay all day, but she could do what she pleased. So she hurried upstairs to pack.

As they drove away from the house late that afternoon, Stephen Disston turned his eyes regretfully back to his home and sighed. Then he looked at his wife apprehensively. He dared not even sigh in these days, things were in such a precarious state. He spoke quickly to cover his sigh. "You will remember what I said about spending money, dear, won't you? It really means a lot to our future."

"I'll try," said Helen meekly, though there was a sullen gleam in her eyes. "It's awfully hard to meet that, though, right at the beginning of my married life when everybody thinks I've done so well. I didn't suppose when I married you that I would have to go on scrimping all the rest of my days."

Her red lips were pouted prettily, and Stephen Disston foresaw another bout of weeping and complaint, so he hastened to say, "I hope it won't be for long, dear. I hope soon to get things straightened out. If we could just find Diana and my mind were free, I am sure I could easily work things out."

"There it goes again!" sobbed Helen suddenly. "You don't care for me. You only want Diana! It's nothing to you that I am here with you all the time, giving my youth to keep your days happy! You just want Diana. And that's what I told you would happen! I told you you would tire of me and want to make her happy! I told you she would resent my coming! But you said, no, no, it would be all right and we would all be happy together! You don't c-c-care for me anymore!"

Stephen Disston cast a distracted glance toward the taxi driver and another out the window at the people they were passing on the street, for Helen's voice was high and shrill, and her sobs were unmistakable.

"Darling!" he said with quick eagerness. "Don't do that! You know that is not true. You know that you are very dear to me!" And even as he put out his hand to lay it on hers he was suddenly filled with a great question, whether what he was saying was strictly true. Was she, after all, so dear as he had thought?

He put the idea from him at once. He was an honorable man. But it hung around and haunted him, made him unnatural in his efforts to soothe Helen. He groaned within himself at the new trouble that beset him. Would he never get this thing straightened out, this hasty marriage that he now saw Helen herself had really persuaded him into? Oh, if he had only taken a little more time and talked it over with Diana, he would have been assured of her usually sweet cooperation. He should have talked everything thoroughly over in a reasonable way with them both. With everybody cooperating, surely things would have gone all right!

It seemed to Stephen Disston that it was a hundred miles into the city, but he finally managed to placate Helen in plenty of time for her to get out of the taxi and into the hotel in radiant form. Helen never showed her tears afterward, and that was a thing that came to puzzle her husband in thinking it over.

She made him take her to a concert and was charming all that evening, and irresistible the next morning when she pled with him to stay with her, to take her down to the stores and let the old business go. She knew he wouldn't stay. In fact, it would have greatly upset her plans if he had, but she created an impression that she was inconsolable without him. Then as soon as he was gone, she flew around frantically to get ready to go out.

She made a careful study of the business directory of the telephone book, and then she went down a little back street in the lower part of the city and made a few purchases. Returning to the hotel, she changed her garments, stowed her purchases in a soft blue tooled leather bag that was capacious yet artistic to carry, and went out again, a look of impishness dancing in her eyes, her face all a-sparkle with determination.

Down in his office Stephen Disston was opening his mail, scanning eagerly every letter, hoping that there might be one from Diana, sighing as he laid each one aside, only half taking in its message. But suddenly his thoughts were brought to a sharp focus by a letter that involved a large sum of money owing him, which he had hoped was soon to be paid. The letter said there was no immediate hope of getting anything out of it. If that were literally true, then it spelled ruin for the Disston business, an old and respected firm originally started by Stephen Disston's father and later continued by the three sons. The other two sons had died within the past ten years, leaving Stephen Disston the sole remaining member of the firm.

He had thought that the business was on a solid foundation until a year before, but even then he had made hasty retrenchments and had sold off some of his land, which was by his wife's will left to him, clearing all indebtedness and giving a fair outlook for the future. This contract, which involved so much money, had seemed no risk at all, but the man who had guaranteed it, a lifelong friend in whom he trusted, had been killed in an accident a few months ago, and his profligate son was managing his affairs. The result was that a small technicality that under the father's regime would have been entirely safe had proved a loophole through which the unscrupulous son had slipped and taken with him the money that would have meant security to the Disston business! The result was crushing.

Stephen Disston lifted a ghastly face from the letter he held in a trembling hand and stared across his office at the blank wall, and for a moment everything in the room reeled.

Chapter 19

*L*ittle by little he took in his situation and what it was going to mean, not only in the business world but also in his home. *Home!* Did he have a home anymore? Of course, there was a place there in the old house that was Diana's where he might stay all the rest of his days, but could he, with Helen? He was bound to Helen now, and how was he going to support her? And what of Diana, his precious daughter? Oh, what a fool he had been! If only this blow had come before he involved Helen also.

If it had been only himself and Diana, how simple it all would have been. He could perhaps have enough to pay off his debts. There were not many. He had been careful until lately. And then Diana would have had enough and to spare for them both.

But feeling as she did about Helen, and as Helen was growing to feel about Diana, he couldn't, of course, let Diana do anything for them. And what was going to become of—*everybody?*

He put his head down on his desk and groaned aloud.

Ten minutes later his secretary coming in roused him to

actualities, and he realized that there was much to be done and necessity of haste in the doing. He must not let everything slip from lax hands without making some attempt to rescue part, at least, of what was his own. He sent for his lawyer, and they spent the morning together going over everything. He dictated sharp, crisp sentences to his secretary and concentrated on his business as he had not done for two months. His lawyer looked at him with eyes of admiration. He was rallying splendidly to the situation. If anything could pull the old Disston firm through this crisis, this attitude on the part of its head would. He roused himself to keep up a state of good cheer and started so many little side lines of battlements to fight the coming disaster that Stephen Disston was cheered and given heart of hope. Of course, time would tell whether all their work was in vain or not, but in the meantime it was good to feel a little hope, since they must go on and do these things whether they succeeded or not. And so with his lips in a firm line of determination and his eyes stern, Stephen Disston faced the facts and took the reins in his hands. He must drive through or all was lost, and that he would not consider— not yet, at any rate.

And for all the rest of that day it is safe to say he did not once think of the unscrupulous sprite of a woman he had married, not even while he was eating a hurried lunch he had sent up to his office while he worked.

It was a strenuous day. Drastic measures had to be taken, daring methods adopted, innumerable telephone calls made, telegrams sent, sheafs of letters written. The lawyer stuck by him like the friend he had always been, and they worked until the world outside the office grew dark. Then the lawyer rose.

"There, Steve," he said, rubbing a large capable hand over a weary, kindly face, "I guess that's about all we can do today. Now we've just got to wait and see the result of this. We ought to be hearing from these things about day after tomorrow. And, in the meantime, let's go home to dinner."

Then Stephen Disston suddenly remembered that he had no home but a hotel tonight, and nobody he dared confide in when he got there. He must adjust a smile and keep it on for the evening. He thought with a stab of pain of the daughter who had left him. Where, oh, where was Diana? Diana who always knew when her father was troubled. She never bothered with questions but crept near and slipped a quiet hand in his and smiled her comfort. Oh, how had he allowed himself to do anything to alienate Diana?

But when he got to the hotel, weary and sick at heart, he found a note from Helen. She had gone to Max Copley's apartment to help him plan for his house party, and she demanded that he follow her as soon as he arrived. Helen in that man's apartment, planning follies for a party! He frowned and sighed and sat down with his head in his hands. How were the troubles multiplying around him! He seemed to himself like one caught in a net from which it was hopeless to try to escape. Helen in that disgusting man's apartment, and he had no power to keep her away! Of course, she couldn't realize what he was, but why wouldn't she listen to him, her husband? Why wouldn't she take his word for it that the man wasn't a fit associate?

And now she was demanding that he come also. Three times this had happened already and twice he had yielded and gone, only to find that his presence was scarcely noticed by the crowd, least of all by Helen, who was wholly taken up with the others and expected him to find his own amusement. He had gone to protect her by his presence, but he had found that his presence did not protect her from the things to which he objected. He told himself that, of course, she was innocent and did not in the least realize what kind of people these were with whom she was finding her amusement. He had planned to give her other and better amusements and wean her from these people, but he found to his dismay that she did not enjoy the things he planned for her and was only eager to get back to her crowd again.

And Diana was gone, dear Diana, and there seemed no way at all to get in touch with her. What should he do? His life was going into a slump—financially, socially, domestically—and there was no way out.

So he put his head down and groaned.

He would not go after Helen this time. Let her stay until she realized what she had done. He would wait here for her return. It did no good to go.

He felt old and tired. He was hungry, too, though he did not realize that. It was long after dinnertime, but he did now know it. He was trying to think back over his past life and see just where it was that he had gotten off the beaten track, just where he had diverged from the path that he had trod so successfully all the years until now. Money gone, daughter gone, wife gone, home gone—was there anything more missing? Yes, his religion seemed gone, too.

He recalled how he always used to have family worship in the old days when Marilla was living. How they went to church together and tried to order their lives in a Christian manner. He was a Christian man, respected, for a long time a deacon in his church—where, how, had he gotten away?

Suddenly he slipped down upon his knees and prayed aloud: "Oh, God! I'm a sinner! Set me right. Show me what to do."

A long time he knelt, and then he rose and dropped into the big chair again. Helen found him sitting there with his face bowed into his hands and a look of utter dejection upon him.

She stood poised in the doorway for a moment surveying him with narrowed eyes, and then she closed the door behind her and swept to the other end of the room, assuming her battle array.

"I love the way you leave me to run around alone!" she said sweetly, tapping her hand on the arm of the chair. "And you needn't think you can sit and mope and get away with it, either. We might as well have this out now as any time. When I leave a note for you to meet me somewhere I expect you to do it, see? I don't like being deserted that way, and it certainly is too early in our married life for you to act like an old grouch."

Stephen Disston lifted his haggard face.

"Helen," he said in a weary, husky voice, "you'll have to understand that I cannot have anything to do with that man, and I do not want you to be seen with him, much less go to his apartment. I am grieved to the heart that you should persist in this. I have explained to you that the man is not fit for you to wipe your shoes on. If it is necessary for me to go into details, I can do it, but I wish you would take my word for it. You are young and innocent and have no idea what kind of a man this Copley is—!"

He was interrupted by an impish chuckle. "Oh, I like that! I don't know what Max is, don't I? Ask Max that one. Ask him if I don't know all about him, and see what he says. So, I'm innocent, am I? Well that's a good one."

She laughed immoderately and then suddenly sobered and put on a haughty dignity. "My dear, you certainly are rare! You think I am a babe in arms like your little Diana. But remember that I was left alone at a tender age and had to rub elbows with the world. I am beginning to suspect that I really am wiser in the wisdom of the world than even you, who seem to think you know all there is to know of evil. However, you might as well understand right now that I know my crowd from A to Z, and I like them just as they are, and I intend to stick to them. And what's more, if you want to keep me you'll have to like them, too, *and like them a lot*! For we are going to run around with them from now on."

"Never!" said Disston sternly, rising and pacing up and down the room. "*Never!*"

"We're going to Max Copley's house party at the end of

this week," went on his wife calmly, just as if he had not spoken, "and then early next week we're going on a yachting party with Max's friend Count De Briscka. He invited us informally today, and he's sending a written invitation tonight lest you would stand on ceremony. The yacht is one of the finest on the water; it cost a mint of money and is perfectly spiffy. Its name is *Lotus Blossom*. Isn't that precious? Everybody I know is crazy for an invitation. If it hadn't been that we are Max's most intimate friends we wouldn't have been invited, but he's just crazy about Max. And do you know, Max says if you get close to the Count he'll put you on to some good investments that will pull your fortunes back into line and make you rich in no time, richer than you've ever been before. Max says—"

"*Helen!* Have you been talking my affairs over with that viper?"

"Why, of course I have," pouted Helen. "Why not? Max has made some awfully good plays on the market lately, and I knew he would give me some pretty good hints. I was awfully down, you know, because of what you told me this morning, and so I suppose he saw I was blue, and he naturally asked me what was the matter, so of course I had to tell him. And his answer was to call up Count De Briscka, and a half hour later he came in and we had such a jolly time, and he gave the invitation before we had been talking five minutes. Max says that's what he does when he wants to show the crowd a good time, just invites them over and calls up the Count, and the Count always takes the hint and invites them on a yachting trip. He says the Count likes it. So you see, darling, it's quite up to you to change your ideas and get to liking my crowd. For that's who I'm hanging around with the rest of the summer."

"Never!" said Disston severely. "Never! Helen, I don't know how to express myself in suitable words to show you my disgust and dislike of these people. Never would I consent to dining with them again or attending their parties or going on any trips whatsoever with them. Most certainly I will not accept any invitations from any of them, and you will not do so, either, not with my consent."

"Oh, dear me, darling," laughed Helen amusedly, "that's just too bad! Because, you see, I've already accepted, and I intend to go! If you won't go with me, why then, tra-la, Max always has plenty of interesting friends for me to pair off with."

She looked at him archly with a significant smile, but she met a grave, sad expression that had almost disillusionment in it. He looked at her steadily for a moment and then said, "You cannot do a thing like that, Helen, and remain on a friendly footing with me. You cannot go to a party like either of those you are proposing without bringing disgrace on my family. Those men who have invited you are notorious drinkers and gamblers. In a fashionable way, I admit, but nevertheless a disgraceful way, and I cannot allow you to get your good name and mine besmirched by having anything more to do with them. I shall have to ask you to refrain from further friendliness with them."

Helen looked at him with angry eyes for an instant, and then her eyes began to dance with impishness.

"Oh, isn't that too bad!" she said with a giddy little laugh, and then she turned and flounced off into the bedroom and locked the door.

All night Stephen Disston sat bowed in that big armchair in the sitting room of his hotel suite, his face in his hands, his soul borne down by heaviness; while a few miles away in the suburb that had been his home for years policemen and firemen and friends and neighbors were keeping the telephone lines hot with calls, trying to locate him, to tell him that his house was on fire. They even found his old friend the lawyer, with whom he had spent the day, but he could give them no clue to his whereabouts.

Chapter 20

That afternoon Gordon MacCarroll had reached home in the early twilight and found his mother out in the driveway sniffing the air and looking up toward the great house.

"What in the world are you doing, Mother?" he called out, stopping his car by the garage and jumping out.

"Why, Gordon, I've been smelling smoke all the afternoon. At first I thought it was someone's bonfire, but I couldn't locate it, and the last half hour it has been growing stronger. It seemed to come from the back of the house, so I looked up toward the big house, and I thought I saw a thin wisp of smoke against the sky coming from that far corner. It worried me a little because the caretaker hasn't been around today at all. I thought maybe some tramps had been tampering with the wood pile back of the house."

"Maybe the family have come home and built a fire in the fireplace to get rid of the dampness," suggested Gordon.

"No, the family didn't come home," said his mother positively.

"I've been sitting right by the window almost all day sewing. I wanted to finish my dress. Even when I ate lunch I brought a plate to my little sewing table and ate while I sewed. The new Mrs. Disston came about half-past twelve for a while, but she didn't stay. She arrived on the bus and walked up the drive, and in about three quarters of an hour she came back again and stood out there on the street waiting for the next bus. There hasn't been anybody else here all day."

"Are you sure you would have noticed?"

"Yes, I'm positive. I was watching. You see, when she arrived first she had a blue leather bag over her arm, with some bulky packages in it, as if she had been shopping, and I thought perhaps they were coming back to stay and she had been to market. But when she came out again and went away she hadn't anything in her hand but her purse. I suppose I noticed the bag because it was exactly like that one that Cousin Lucy brought back from her Mediterranean trip. Do you remember that? You admired it so much. It was soft blue kid tooled in gold. I know you said it would make a wonderful cover for a Bible. And when I saw her go in I couldn't help noticing it because it was exactly like Lucy's.

"So, of course, I kept looking up that way to see if there were any signs of her, and pretty soon she came out with just her purse. I was hoping she had come to stay, and maybe all of them would come. You know, I always feel sort of responsible for that house when they are all away. It's so far back from the street none of the other neighbors can see it very well. I though she might only have gone to market. But she didn't come back. And about an hour ago I smelled the smoke getting stronger, and just now I thought I saw a sort of a glow in those windows over on the left, as if there were a fire in the room. She surely wouldn't go off and leave an open fire in the house, would she?"

Gordon's eyes went quickly to the windows his mother indicated.

"I'd better take a look," he said. "It's probably only a bonfire at the back. Maybe the caretaker came a back way or something, but I'll feel better if I just run up and see. You stay out here where you can see the end of the house. If it's anything serious, I'll come out and wave, and you can telephone for the fire company, but I don't think it's anything."

Gordon walked rapidly up the drive and disappeared around the end of the house. But only an instant later he appeared again waving his arms wildly. His mother waved back and turned running into the house to call the fire engine.

Gordon hurried back to see what he could do before the firemen arrived. He found a door into the tool house ajar and, looking in, discovered the garden hose.

The smoke was pouring out of an open cellar window, and flames were beginning to lick up like hungry tongues out of two of the windows at the back. The whole back corner of the house seemed to be involved, all the way to the roof, for wisps and feathers of smoke and flames were darting out of an upper window, tentatively, as if they were searching out the best place to really take hold and devastate. He hadn't arrived an instant too soon.

It looked to MacCarroll as if it had been a slow fire, perhaps started by a match or cigarette, smoldering through rags or rubbish in the cellar until it gained a footing. Then, creeping upward, it must have made a passage for itself and had only now begun to leap upward.

But there was no time for thought. Gordon dashed out of the tool house dragging the garden hose then searched blindly through the smoke, which was becoming dense now, for the outlet. Finally he succeeded in locating it, screwed on the hose, and turned on the water.

But it was such an inadequate little stream that poured out after he had done all he could. He turned it to its utmost and played it upon the house, but even in the minute it had taken to get the water started, the fire seemed to have gained the ascendancy. It had crept underneath and roared up the wall of a small annex, perhaps a laundry or out-kitchen, and now the flames were feathering upward from the roof, cutting it in half, and roaring in triumph. It would not take long to reduce the annex to ashes if this could not be stopped. And meantime, the main house was in grave danger. The flames were shooting out now through one corner of the roof. Would the fire company never get here?

There was another water outlet the other side of the back porch. Gordon wished there were two of him. There was a large bucket standing under it. He could draw water and throw it on where it would prevent the spread of the fire, if he could only fix up something to hold this hose so that it could work while he was working elsewhere.

But even while he was casting about in his mind what to do his mother appeared and took the hose from him.

"I'll hold this, Gordon. Do you see what else is to be done? The fire company is on the way, and I've telephoned the neighbors. Here's the ax, too, I though you might need it."

So the two worked valiantly, breathlessly, on the fire that had now leaped up into a mighty conflagration, threatening to devastate the whole house.

Neighbors came running across the fields now, and cars dashed up the drive and parked on the lawn to make room for the fire engine. And then the fire company arrived, with chemicals and a big hose running back down the drive to a hydrant in the street.

A neighbor volunteered to try to reach the owner by telephone. The police arrived and took a hand also, and the fire roared high and reached forth arms of flame greedy to envelop the whole back of the house and one end, licking out now and then tentatively around the corner to the beautiful white front with its fine lacework of vines.

As soon as the firemen arrived, Mrs. MacCarroll went home and made coffee in a large white preserving kettle. It was near dinnertime, and the chances were that some of the men would be working there for hours yet. Some of them, at least, would have to stay around and be sure that all was safe, even if they succeeded in saving the main part of the house. So she went to work quietly to help in the only way she could see herself of any use. She spread bread and sliced ham and made a lot of nice sandwiches, and putting them in wax paper in a basket, she packed another basket with cups and saucers. Then taking the kettle of coffee herself, she got a couple of boys from the rabble drifting up the drive to carry the baskets, and so she established refreshments for the firemen over by the tool house.

Gordon MacCarroll was in the thick of the fight all the way through. It was a volunteer fire company, and they were glad to get such efficient help, though everyone was so busy during the worst of it that no one had time to question who was working and who was not. So it happened that when the fire was finally under control, it was Gordon who climbed down into the cellar first, stepping knee deep in water. He was in utter darkness except for his flashlight, which peered through the smoke and murk sending a sharp, inadequate ray cutting the gloom and locating stairs, chimneys, and charred doors to storerooms and preserve closets. It was Gordon who lifted a dripping something floating on the water, turned his flashlight on it for a brief second, and then flung it far up the cellar stairs into the corner of the top landing out of sight. He came up out of the cellar window a few minutes later with a thoughtful look upon his face and his lips closed firmly.

"All safe below!" he said cryptically. He didn't mention what he suspected. There wouldn't be an investigation until the water had gone out.

That night, quite late, he came home and took a bath and ate his supper. His mother hovered around and saw that he had all that was needful and a good deal that was not. She did not talk. She was a wise woman and noticed how tired his eyes looked, how his cheek was bruised where the big hose had hit him when it was flung out by a careless amateur, and how his hands were torn and bleeding. He had worked hard and been in dangerous places, she knew, but she was too well trained to notice a little thing like that. Only one question she asked when he came in. "Is it all safe for the night now, or will you have to go back?"

"All safe!" he answered. "They've left a couple of watchmen there for the night."

Then she brought his dinner, hot and tasty, and he fell to eating. But when he had reached the cherry pie he took one bite then looked up. "Mother, what color did you say that bag was? Blue? With gold stampings?"

"Yes!" said his mother, with a startled look on her face. "Gordon! You've found it!" It was rather a statement than a question.

He didn't look up. He didn't answer.

"It was down in the cellar!" his mother said with conviction. "That means—" She shut her lips on the rest of the sentence.

Then after another silence he answered that half question. "Not necessarily, Mother."

The next silence was longer until she asked, "Did anybody else see it, Son?"

He shook his head.

"And did you—leave it—put it—*hide* it?"

"No," he said, "I wasn't sure I should. I flung it to the top of the stairs. It won't mean much there. Perhaps—in the morning— But there may be no opportunity. There wasn't time then to do more than I did. Perhaps, after all, it may not be significant."

❦

Mr. Disston did not get the word until he reached his office the next morning, where he had gone very early, before Helen had shown any sign of being awake. He did not wish to wait around to be scorned and scoffed at. Helen must understand that he meant what he said. There was no point in repeating his words or in staying to argue further. There was a point at which dignity must stand. If he had been at home, it would have been different. In his own place he could speak with more force, but this was not his home. So he went down to his office.

The elevator boy was just going on when he arrived.

"Did they get you last night?" he asked.

"Get me?" asked Stephen Disston in a weary voice. Something had got him very badly. Was there more?

"Yeah. They said your phone rang an' rang, and your secretary was wild to know if you was in the building, but I told 'em I took you down. Then a lawyer man called and wanted to talk to me. He asked did I know just what time it was you left and whether you come back last night at all, and I said you hadn't when I quit at six o'clock."

A sudden thought came of Diana. Perhaps it had been Diana. Perhaps something had happened to Diana. Then all the other worries suddenly melted away and Diana became the only anxiety in the world. Oh, if he could only find Diana and know she was safe!

It was after nine when word finally came over the phone about the house being on fire, and his heart seemed so heavy he could hardly drag himself up out of his chair after he hung up the receiver.

"It's all out, that is, some's smoking yet," said the fireman who called, "but you better come out and see whatcha want done. We had a watchman on the job all night, but the burned place oughtta be closed up for safety if you ain't comin' home to stay. Yep, we got on the job right soon, but if it hadn't been for the party that lives in that there stone house at the gate she woulda gone up in smoke before we ever heard. Yep. That's him, tall, curly hair! He helped plenty. All by his lonesome till we got there! An' he done good work, too. Yep! You better come out soon as you can. So long!"

When Stephen Disston arrived at his home he found Gordon MacCarroll just starting up the drive. He had gone early to his own office and then driven back by way of home to make sure that all was well at the scene of the fire. He looked relieved when he saw the man of the house coming behind him.

"Oh, I'm glad you've come, Mr. Disston," he said, turning around and walking up with him. "I felt as if I ought to hang around and see that there was an adequate guard until you were here to give orders. You see, the house is practically open to the public, and it seems impossible to keep the rabble away. The children have been swarming all around. I got in and locked a few doors so they can't get in far, but I certainly am glad you've come. Here are the keys I took. This one fits the door where the most damage has been done, servants' dining room, perhaps, and that opens into the hall."

Disston thanked him gravely and took the keys. "They tell me you rendered swift and marvelous assistance. The fire chief said you practically saved the house."

"Oh, I did very little," said Gordon lightly. "I'm only sorry I didn't get home sooner. Mother had been smelling smoke for an hour. By the time I got here there was a glow in some of the windows. I found her out in the driveway looking up toward the house. She didn't know whether anybody was at home or not. She said your wife went in about noon, but didn't stay long."

"Oh!" said the master of the house, turning startled eyes on his tenant. And then a forced, "Oh yes. She—we—were away—last night!" But his face wore a confused, troubled look. "How—do you think—that is, what is your opinion of how—where—the fire started?"

"In the cellar," said Gordon quickly. "It almost looked as if it had been *started*, though you can't tell surely till the water subsides. Had you any servants you had reason to distrust?"

Stephen Disston turned his tired eyes on the young man.

"Yes," he said, "there were some new servants. We didn't keep them long, but I don't see what object they would have in setting fire to the house. They were quite adequately paid. They knew we were going away for a time—" He walked on thoughtfully, his eyes upon the ground as if he were studying it over.

"What made you think it was started?"

"Well, there seemed to be a pile of debris over in the corner where the fire raged the hottest, as if things had been piled up there, and there were a few rags floating on the water that evidently had been too far away to ignite and were soaked in kerosene. But the corner looked as if combustibles had been piled up where the flame would easily reach the beams of the first floor. That was what actually happened, I think; the fire evidently was a slow one, but by the time it reached the corner it had gathered force enough to eat through the floor and run right up the wall."

The master of the house turned another startled gaze upon Gordon and they walked the rest of the way in silence.

"We'll go in the front door," said Disston as they reached the terrace. "I'd rather see the worst before I face the rabble out there."

"Shall I just wait outside?" offered Gordon.

"No! Come! I'm glad to have you with me!"

Gordon thought to himself that he had often hoped to see the inside of the great house sometime but had not expected to enter under such circumstances.

Disston unlocked the door, and they stepped into the beautiful hallway with its wide staircase and lovely vistas of rooms on either side.

"Oh, I'm glad this part didn't get hurt!" he said with quick eager exclamation.

"Yes!" sighed Disston, as if the sight of it were very dear indeed.

They walked through to the kitchen, and the master went to

the cellar door and fitted in the key. Then Gordon remembered the blue bag and wished he had left it in a corner of the cellar. But perhaps it would not be noticed!

Disston unlocked the door and swung it wide, and the morning sun from a big window over the kitchen sink flooded across the landing. There lay the blue kid bag, its lovely gold tooling stained and spotted with water and grime from the fire! Disston saw it and stared as if he had seen a ghost.

Gordon tried to look away, but he caught a glimpse of the man's face, and it was pale as death. His eyes were staring wildly.

"What is that?" he asked huskily. "How—how did that—get here?" He was too distraught to realize that he was showing his emotion before this stranger.

"It was floating on the top of the water," explained Gordon, trying to speak in a matter-of-fact way, as if he saw nothing out of the ordinary in the occurrence. Perhaps this was, after all, the best way to let Mr. Disston know without making it appear that it had any particular significance to him. He had been so troubled whether he should tell about finding the bag or not, and now here it was made plain and easy for him.

Stephen Disston stooped and picked up the bag by its dripping leather strings and held it a moment looking at it closely. Then, as if his conscience drove him and he were not in the least aware of the presence of another, he felt it then turned out upon the floor what it contained and stood there staring at it. Gordon could not help seeing what was there.

Then Stephen Disston came awake and looked up in consternation at his companion.

But Gordon stooped and picked them up.

A piece of tinder, a wire coil, a couple of candles, and a box of matches! And the whole smelled unmistakably of kerosene.

He put them carefully into the bag as if he were not noticing what they were and handed the bag over to the master of the house.

"You'll want to put those away out of sight, won't you? At least for the present? No need to have reporters poking around trying to find leads for headlines."

He tried to say it carelessly, as if it were not a thing that mattered so much. Then his eyes met the unhappy eyes of Disston, and he saw the other fully understood. His face was still very white.

"Thank you," said Disston. "I'll take your advice—for the present—at least until I understand what this means."

A newspaper lay on the kitchen table, and Gordon proffered it.

"Wrap it in that and put it away somewhere till things clear up a little."

"You're being very kind," said Disston, visibly getting his emotions in hand.

"Not at all," said Gordon. "I wish there was something really worthwhile that I could do for you."

"You have done a great deal," said Disston slowly, "and—I shall not forget it."

Their eyes met, and a smile of friendliness flashed between them. Then Disston silently unlocked the door that led to the scene of ruin, and they stood for a few minutes studying the probably course of the fire.

"This wall ought to be closed up at once," said Gordon. "When the police leave it will be practically impossible to keep out the swarm of small boys and curious people."

"Yes," sighed Mr. Disston, looking around with a hopeless sadness in his eyes. "I suppose I ought to send for a carpenter at once."

"I was going to suggest," said Gordon thoughtfully, "that there are some boards out there in the tool house. If you are willing, I could bring them in and nail them up over the largest break in the wall. That would do temporarily until you have time to get your mind on what should be done."

"Oh, I couldn't think of troubling you anymore," protested Disston.

"Nonsense," said Gordon eagerly. "We're neighbors, you know, and besides, my mother and I have taken a deep interest in our landlord's house." He smiled a deep, warm smile that comforted the heart of the sorrowful landlord. "You'd do the same for me, I'll warrant, if I were in trouble."

"I'm not sure I would know how," said the elder man humbly. "But where is this lumber you speak of? I ought to know, of course, but I've never had much time to look after the details about the house. If I could just get this place closed to curious eyes for the time being, it certainly would be a great help."

They went together to the tool house and brought back planks, Gordon handling them capably and taking the heavier part of the labor.

"Now," he said, when they had enough of the planks to cover the large gap in the wall that the fire had made, "I wonder if you happen to be able to locate a hammer and some nails? I think I saw a ladder in the cellar stairway. It won't take long to make this secure."

He went capably to work, and in a very short time the room that had been gutted by fire was closed to the eyes of the countryside, who continued to straggle about all day to look and wonder and say who they thought had done it or how it had caught on fire.

"Now," said Gordon, coming down from the ladder after driving the last nail, "you'll come down to the cottage and have a bite of lunch with me, won't you? You look white and tired. I'm sure you need it. Yes, come, I'm sure Mother will have something ready."

So, comforted by the friendly smile and the insistent hand upon his arm, Stephen Disston walked down to the stone cottage with his tenant and they had lunch together. Such a comfortable, quite lunch in that sweet little home wherein there seemed to be no perplexities nor hates nor problems. Such a home as he used to have before Marilla went away. Yes, and even afterward when he and Diana comforted one another together. Would life ever unsnarl itself and things go right again? Who had started that fire? And was that bag Helen's? Could that be the one he had seen lying across the end of the couch the night before last in the hotel? Or wait—wasn't it really Diana's, the one that someone sent her from abroad? How had Helen gotten it? And where, oh, *where* was Diana?

"Your daughter is not at home just now?" Mrs. MacCarroll was asking him pleasantly. "I thought she was such a sweet girl. I miss her going by."

Diana's father looked up with a heavy sigh.

"No, she is not at home!" he said with infinite sadness in his eyes and voice.

Where, oh, *where* was Diana? If he could only find Diana!

Chapter 21

Diana had been working hard in her restaurant, day after day. Sometimes it seemed to her that she had been there a year serving uncouth people. Sometimes it seemed to her as if almost all of them were animals, just animals feeding, with no resemblance to humanity at all, at least not to the lovely refined humanity that she knew. She shuddered as she crept wearily into her bed at night at the thought of another day that would rush upon her oh-so speedily in the midst of her heavy sleep and drag her back to her duties again.

And her pay was so pitifully small, her tips so trifling and scarce. People of the sort she served had not much to spare for tips, greedy, hard-eyed people, all but those few who appraised her eyes, her hair, her smile, her figure, and gave only when they could win her notice. From those she shrank most of all. Some were half drunk when they came in. How she loathed them! It was only through trying to remember that God must care for them, too, that Christ died for them, that she could make herself wait upon them.

How the days loomed ahead of her, each one worse than the last! How she dreaded each one as she went forth and came home so deadly tired that she could take no comfort in the quietness and peace of even that little third-story back.

The only oasis in the dreariness of her life was the box of carnations. Twice they had come on Saturday nights. Would they come again? The hope of them made one little sweet thing to look forward to. Somehow her heart rested down on those mystery flowers as if they were part of her religion, and as if they came fresh each week from God to let her know He cared. Her faith grew little by little as she breathed in their spicy breath. They were such frail, lovely things, and yet so sturdy and healthy and long-lived. For each installment had lived and glowed and been beautiful until the next arrived. And it comforted her sometimes on her hardest days to think of them back there in her little high, lonely room glowing and waiting for her, a rosy breath of love and sympathy, from someone, whom she would probably never know except vaguely as God's messenger.

It had been a hard day, harder than usual, because it was a holiday and Saturday again. There had been a tougher lot of people in the restaurant than usual. The place had been crowded from early morning on, and Diana had been greatly rushed. Moreover, some of the other girls, who had never really recovered from their resentment at her finer ways, had made it more than usually uncomfortable for her, maliciously upsetting her tray when it was all ready to take to a customer in a hurry, spilling a glass of water over the food she had prepared to take to another, tripping her as she passed with a heavy tray lifted high above her head and almost bringing her down among broken dishes. It was not their fault that she had been able to avert the catastrophe by an almost superhuman effort and recover her balance with only a broken plate and the loss of an order—which, of course, she would have to pay for. She discovered as the day went on that she had also wrenched her back, and her head was throbbing wildly. By three o'clock in the afternoon she suddenly began to feel that she actually could not go on any longer. Her feet were aching in sympathy with her back and head, and a great despair was surging over her soul. She was being beaten, beaten by this job. She could not go on any longer. Yet she knew she must or give up utterly. Because if she lost this job, where would she turn for another? Beaten! What could she do? Would she go home? Never! The thought of Helen still loomed as a positive barrier. There was no relief there. And if she gave up her job and was sick in the bargain, where would she go? Who would take care of her? Suppose she had a fever? She was burning up now. It probably was a fever. Would they take her to a charity hospital? Well, there might be even worse fates than that. Perhaps she would die, and then she would be out of it all. If God cared for her, then she would go to be with Him!

In the wildness and flurry of the sordid atmosphere, the thought of going to God seemed only a thought of quietness and peace. Nothing else seemed to matter if He cared enough just to set her free from all these worries of the world into which she had wandered, where there were no open doors to go back to home and safety and peace.

It was in this state of mind, and while she lingered an instant standing by a shelf in the kitchen, trying to swallow a cup of weak coffee that was not even hot, that she heard her name shouted by the manager.

"Jane! Here! Customer calling for you, Jane! Make it snappy!"

Her hand trembled as she set down the distasteful cup hastily, caught up her tray, and hurried away, praying as she had of late fallen into the habit of doing, *Oh, God, help me to get through this once more.*

She was almost up to the table the manager had indicated before she realized who the customer was that had called for her.

It was a man who had been there three times before that week. He was a large sensuous brute, with thick lips and a cruel face. She remembered his fulsome flattery the first time he had come in; his little pig-eyes upon her had seemed to soil her very soul. She had avoided waiting upon him several times since that first experience. But now it was too late for that, and she had been ordered by the manager to wait upon him.

She gathered all her dignity and went forward, a shudder of horror passing over her slender shoulders in spite of her best efforts, and when she reached him she found that he was drunk!

Frightened, she paused, keeping the table between them, but he reached out a burly arm and grasped her wrist, trying to draw her nearer.

"Come over here, sweetie," he demanded in a loud tone that everybody in the room could hear! "I need sympathy! That's why I sent for you, Jane! Come clost an' tell me whatcha got ta eat—!"

But Diana, more frightened than she had ever been in her life, struggled with all her might to get her wrist free from that terrible grasp, and suddenly she felt a stout arm around her waist and a familiar voice towering over her.

"Hey you, Mortie Matzan, you lay off my gal! She's *my* sweetie, an' I don't want nobody else buttin' in. Scram there! Hear what I say? This dame is mine. Ain't you, sweetheart!"

The voice was not loud on account of the roomful of customers, but the manager's hideous face loomed over her in a possessive leer that almost took her senses away.

Diana gave one terrified sound like a wounded animal, and tearing herself loose from the hateful arm, she suddenly raised a glass of water from the table before her and flung it full in the proprietor's face. The glass, falling heavily down on the drunken man's foot, brought a howl from him to add to the confusion. But Diana was not there to see. She was madly dashing down the room toward the kitchen, colliding with another waitress in the doorway, leaving a shower of tray and dishes in her wake, flying through the kitchen and out the open door into the alley at the back, barely escaping a fall over the big garbage can that stood in her way. She rounded the corner into the alley, went blindly up one street and down another, through any alley that presented itself in her way, only so that it lay in the general direction of her own little third-story room.

It was only about two o'clock, and there were people all around her everywhere, but she dared not look behind her. It seemed to her that the whole restaurant—proprietor, employees, customers, drunk and sober—must be following. She did not remember that she had left her hat and jacket. Even her purse was of no concern to her now. They were in her locker and she wore the key around her neck, but she would never go back for them, not if she starved to death. There was only fifty cents in the purse, anyway, and what was fifty cents now?

She was panting and frightened, more frightened than she had ever been in her life before, and the tears were rolling down her cheeks, though she did not know it. She turned at last into her own street and fled up the block like a shadow.

She did not see the shabby form that lurked across the street in the narrow arched court between two houses, all unsuspected, watching for her arrival. Having nothing to do for the time being, and having a hunch it might be useful, he had stationed himself there to discover if possible her comings and goings; and now she came so startlingly, flying through the street hatless and fairly flinging herself at the door with the key in her trembling hand, that he had to look carefully to be sure it was really she. He had never seen her before without a hat on, not since she had been a little girl in school, but there was something about her lithe way of running, even in her fright, that made him sure of her. And so he stood there watching until she had disappeared from sight and the grim door had slammed behind her. Then he slowly disengaged himself from the shadows of the archway and slithered down the street and around the corner, skulking close to the houses, skirting the block until he disappeared into the alley behind the house that she had entered. There he took up his stand to watch for a possible vision of a girl in the third-story back window.

But Diana was lying facedown across her bed weeping her heart out, and he presently slipped away to refresh himself with a glass of something heartening. It was not the first time he had watched in the alley under that window.

❊

Earlier in the day Stephen Disston had gone in desperation to his bank and had it out with the bank president. He had spent three lonely nights in the damaged house with no word from his recalcitrant wife and three grilling days in his office waiting for results that did not come, and there had been ample opportunity to think about his lost child. There had come no encouragement as yet from the private detective whom he had hired several days ago to hunt for Diana, and he was almost in despair. But he gained nothing by his anxious questioning of the bank president except an added load of anxiety. And finally Mr. Dunham, growing weary of the interview in the midst of his busy morning, had politely suggested to his friend that the best way to find his daughter was to page her on the radio. The idea was shocking to Diana's father. It seemed as if he would be descending among the criminals of the world to seek her. As if Diana had run away and gotten married or done some sensational thing that should not be blazoned to the world. But the more he walked around the city and saw the lurking humanity on every hand, with faces of might-be criminals, the more his tormented soul entertained the thought that something terrible must have happened to Diana or she never would have kept this long continued silence. It did not occur to him to wonder what her reaction had been to his withdrawal of her money. That seemed a simple matter. He did not realize how it had stunned her to have her beloved father take such drastic action against her. What did occur to him, and worried him beyond expression, was the fact that she had no money. He was a man who had had money all his life and plenty of it, and he could not conceive it possible that his daughter out in the world alone could get along without it. He had been entirely convinced when Helen suggested it that Diana would come home at once when she found she had nothing with which to buy food and shelter.

But Diana had not come home! What had she done? Had something terrible befallen her? He could think of no friends or relatives with whom she might have taken refuge whom he had not already questioned, and now it seemed to him that he should go crazy if there was not some immediate way of finding her. And added to all the strain and worry he had dreamed for three nights in succession now, alone in that house where he had lived so happily with his first wife, that Marilla had come to him and stood beside his bed looking at him with mournful eyes and had reproached him. "Stephen, what have you done with our little girl?" Just that question and then she would vanish with his sleep and leave him to the long, wakeful hours before the dawn.

Back in his office alone again after the interview with the banker he thought of his advice and at last surrendered to the idea. He would trail his pride of family in the dust and descend to broadcast his anxiety. If that was the only way to find Diana he would try that. He would leave no stone unturned.

And now he wondered that he had waited so long, and he sat with trembling fingers, writing feverishly, the words that were to go on the air: "Paging Miss Diana Disston, who left her father's house several weeks ago to visit relatives and has not been heard from for ten days. When last seen in this city she was dressed in—" The hurried pen paused and the father tried to conjure up a vision of his sweet, young daughter, the blinding tears filling his eyes and falling on the page as he recalled her, straight and slender in her dark dress. His description after all was vague, not helped much by the banker who had given mainly his impression of her lovely eyes shadowed by sorrow, her noble bearing, and her proud little chin. No, one couldn't put those things on the air, not even to find Diana!

But a few minutes later that afternoon, just after Diana had fled the restaurant in the noisy little plebeian street, an announcer startled suddenly into the midst of a musical comedy program of the afternoon: "Paging Miss Diana Disston, five feet two inches, slender, dark hair and eyes, weighing one hundred and ten pounds, dressed in black—"

The voice of the announcer boomed out solemnly as though he were pronouncing a requiem on the dead. One more unfortunate dead! And Stephen Disston sat in the far corner of the stuffy recreation room of a strange downtown hotel where he had never been before and knew nobody, and listened. His hat was drawn down over his eyes and his open paper flung up in front of his face. He listened while the blood crept shamedly up into his haggard face, suffusing it with a kind of purple shadow, and then receded, leaving his face white and drawn. To think it was his daughter, his little Diana, whose precious name was being called out that way to the world! And it was his own act, his hasty words, his refusal to listen to her pleadings that had sent her from home and him.

Several miles away across the city in an uptown apartment where a throng of Helen's friends were gathered playing bridge with the radio going full blast to drown their quarrels, Helen heard the words boom out and looked up with a laugh, saw no one was noticing, and hurried to turn the dial to another number. But on her way back to her seat she laughed. With no apparent reason she laughed immoderately. But no one looked at her curiously. It was a free and easy party, and no one thought anything was strange. The stranger, the better! They were combing life for thrills. It was the thing to do.

Edith Maythorn and a few of her friends spending a pleasant afternoon together heard it and looked up at one another, startled.

"Oh, that's not our Diana," said Edith carelessly after listening for a minute. "She was here just a short time ago, and besides, she never wears black, not that I ever saw. But isn't that strange? Two people of that unusual name. I'll have to telephone Diana about it. Won't she be amused? That's almost as funny as when my brother Jimmy saw his name in the papers as having won in a prize fight!" They chattered on and presently forgot all about it.

Standing at a bar in a fashionable hotel, Jerry Lange heard it as he tossed down a cocktail and paused thoughtfully. Diana Disston! Where had he heard that name? Wasn't that what they called that quiet little girl at Maythorn's? But it was probably not the same name after all. He never remembered names very well. He always thought of her as "beautiful," somehow. Of course, it wouldn't be the same name. Still you couldn't tell these days. Things were happening! So he ordered another highball and tossed it down and went on his way whistling.

Mrs. MacCarroll heard it as she sat darning Gordon's socks and setting neat patches in partly worn garments. She heard it and, gathering up her work, stuffed it into her sewing basket summarily and went to the window to look out up to the great house. Oh, poor, poor man! What was coming now? And where was the sweet little girl? Had something awful happened to her?

Maggie, in her sister's neat parlor entertaining the baby while her sister went to the store for a spool of thread, heard and went to the window again and again hoping her sister would return. Hussy or no hussy, she must go to the master as soon as Mary came to care for the child. And Diana! Poor wee thing, where was she, and night coming on again? Maggie's cheeks grew redder than their wont with excitement, and her blue eyes were drenched with tears as she stood by the window looking out and wiping her eyes with the corner of her neat white apron.

And down in the cellar of the miserable roomhouse where the scum of the city found refuge, Bill Sharpe sat at a sloppy wooden table, guiltless of even an oilcloth cover, and slowly drank a glass of vile beer while a cheap radio over in the darkness whined out whatever came along on the air. His eyes narrowed cunningly as he listened, put down his glass, and stared at the corner from which the sound came. He sat listening to the end of the announcement. Then lifting his glass he gulped the rest of the beer and wiped his mouth on his ragged sleeve as he slunk off from the table with a motion between a slouch and stealth and vanished up the cellar steps.

Down the dirty street to a dirty little shop with dusty windows, where children bought all-day suckers for a cent and their elders found salacious literature, he went. He purchased a sheet of paper and an envelope for two cents and stole away to a shelter he knew down by the river where a box would afford all the writing desk he needed, and there in the late afternoon he wrote out a communication, brief and to the point. He needed no study or thought to distort the spelling almost beyond recognition, for he came by bad spelling naturally. And while he wrote with his stub of a pencil on the cheap paper that was by no means fresh, did he have a vision perhaps of a little girl with brown curls and golden lights in her brown eyes, wearing a fresh white dress, sitting at a far desk in the same room at school with him? For a few days only it was, until he graduated backward into the grade below, and she passed on out of his horizon entirely.

The note when it was finished read:

> *Yor doter is huld fer ransom. Putt fifty thousand dolers under the big stun in yor springe howse tanite an she will cum bake tanite otherwiz she*

*will be kilt. Don't tel tha perlise ore yor lif wil not
be wuth 6 pents.*

Yors DESPRIT

He addressed the letter and stole away out of the precinct, and just before the sun set he emerged cautiously from the woods around the little creek that ran below the garden at the big house. Stealthily he approached from shrub to shrub until he stood hidden behind the bushes that fringed the top of the terrace, and from there he reached out a ragged arm with one quick motion and hung the letter by a dirty string to the doorknob. Then he melted back into the shadows and was gone, and not even Mother MacCarroll, keeping her steady vigil from window to window, caught a glimpse of him.

A few minutes later Stephen Disston swung himself stiffly off the bus and walked slowly up the drive. He walked like an old man, with his head bent down, and Mother MacCarroll watched him from the window and longed to run out and try to comfort him, only she felt that perhaps he would not like it, so she stood there at the window watching him and praying for him. Poor sad, lonely man! And where could the new wife be? Had Maggie been mistaken perhaps? Maybe there wasn't any new wife after all.

She watched him until he reached the front door. There was just light enough for her to make him out standing there fumbling with the lock. How long it took him to open the front door! Then the telephone rang, and she had to go.

It was only a wrong number, and she was soon back; but she couldn't see the master of the house anymore, and the door was shut. He had probably gone in and the light would spring up in a moment. She had watched him for three nights now and it always did, but though she watched for five minutes there came no light, and—was it imagination or was there something dark lying on the white steps?

Imagination, of course. She had better go about her business instead of watching her neighbors. But poor man, poor man!

So she turned around and flashed on her own lights, hurrying to get dinner ready. Gordon would be coming home hungry soon, and she wasn't ready. She had been daydreaming for the last hour. But she cast an anxious glance out the window now and then and there was no light in the great house!

Chapter 22

$\mathcal{D}$iana lay upon her bed and wept her heart out, wept until exhausted nature took revenge and sleep fell down upon her. Just a locking of her tired senses in oblivion for a little time, a fitful sleep wherein the terrors of the day were for a moment forgotten. Then suddenly somebody slammed up a window across the alley and loud angry voices broke her quiet release, mingled with a sudden sharp whine of two radios of different themes. The usual suppertime pandemonium had broken loose on the neighborhood, and Diana, not used to it at this hour, awoke with a start and sat up looking around her.

Then it all came back like a flash what had happened to her, and she sat there shuddering with chill and fright as memory furnished each scene of the day with vivid flashes.

But the brief respite had done her good, nevertheless, and she was able to think now more connectedly. She told herself that her door was locked and no harm could come to her. She must calm herself and try to think her way out.

Her job was gone forever, of course. And she was glad, *glad*! It would have been wrong to give it up, just for sheer weariness, but this had been something she could not stand, not even if she starved to death! So now she might rejoice.

But quickly there came the fear that that awful man might follow her, that manager! He had her address, and there was no telling what right an employer had over his employees who left without a week's notice. Perhaps there was some law by which she could be made to go back to finish out her month! Well, she wouldn't! Never! Not if she had to lie down and die, she wouldn't! But perhaps she ought to get out of here and disappear where he couldn't find her! Could she do that without money? It would cost a lot to move, especially if she put her goods in storage again. Storage would have to be paid in advance. And then where would she go? How would she live? Boarding was out of the question, anything she could afford. Afford? She laughed. She couldn't afford anything. She had barely enough hidden away in her trunk to pay Mrs. Lundy, and this week's wages would never be paid now because she would never go back for them. They were due tonight, but the manager would be so much wealthier. Even her fifty cents in her purse was gone. And her hat. Well, of course it didn't matter about the hat. But what was she going to do now? Her way seemed blocked on every hand. And where would she find another place as cheap and tolerable as Mrs. Lundy's? It was bad enough, but there were others worse, and she shuddered at the thought of going out to hunt one, and another job! Oh, did God care?

Suddenly she slipped down upon her knees beside the bed and began to pray. "Oh, God! I'm yours. You died for me and I believe it, and I'm Yours. I take You as my Savior. Nobody else seems to care for me. Will You take care of me? I can't take care of myself. I don't know how. I've tried, and I've made a miserable failure. Now I'm going to trust You to look after me, to show me what to do. Guide me, please. Give me that light that other prayer spoke of. Please, I've nobody else, and I'm leaving me with You!"

It was not like any prayer she had been taught, but she got up with a strange feeling of peace upon her. She had taken her trouble to God, and He would show her what to do. She was going to trust it with Him.

She stood for a moment looking around her room, wondering how the Light would come, and then she went to work. She was not going to be afraid anymore. But she must get ready for whatever might be coming.

Almost feverishly she began to put her things away in trunk and bureau drawers, just as if she had received definite word that she was moving. She gathered her pictures and small trinkets together and packed them carefully. She took down her garments from the closet and folded them into her trunk. Her fingers flew silently, rapidly, and in a short time her pretty room was stripped of its decorations. Quite definitely she locked them up, leaving out such things as she would need to wear away. She almost laughed at herself while she did it. Where was she going? She did not know. But at least she would be ready.

There were tears on her cheeks while she worked, yet they were no more conquering her, and the weariness of the day had passed away in the excitement of the moment. She wondered, was it just her own spirit that had worked herself up to this pitch of a false peace, or was it really God who was there helping her?

She paused beside the vase that held her carnations of a week. Their edges were brown now, and they would soon be gone. It was Saturday night, and no more had come. Was it too late? Were they perhaps downstairs as they had been once before? Should she go and see? She paused with her hand almost out to the door and then decided against it. She dreaded going out of that room again until she knew what to do. If the flowers were down there they would keep as they had done before. She hoped they would not come after she was gone. If they were God's flowers He wouldn't send them too late!

Then she smiled at herself again. Was she losing her good sense, talking fairy tales to herself? Perhaps it was dear old Maggie who had sent them. Perhaps it had somehow been Maggie all the time. But anyhow, it was God.

Suddenly she knew that she was very hungry. She had scarcely eaten anything all day. She ought to go out and get dinner. But to go down and out into the darkness of the street again tonight after all that had happened seemed an awful undertaking. No, she would rather stay hungry. She had taken off her old working dress and slipped into the one she had left out, but the outside world seemed too beset with enemies lurking in the dark.

She went over to the tin cracker box on her windowsill where she kept her supplies. There were only two small salt crackers left in it and a tiny piece of cheese less than an inch square. Well, she would eat those. That would be plenty. She took the box and turned away from the window, and as she did so her profile was silhouetted for an instant delicately on the white window shade. And down in the alley a shadowy form looking up caught the vision and slid like a gaunt rat to a drugstore not far away. He slunk unobserved into the telephone booth and called a number. As soon as he recognized the voice at the other end of the line he spoke guardedly. "It's okay by me now for the machine, Spike! Park her on the dark side the street. Say ten minutes to a half hour. S'long, buddy! I'll be seein' ya!"

But up in her quiet room Diana sat sadly and ate her frugal meal, the dying flowers beside her on a little table, their withering beauty seeming to mock her, yet she closed her eyes on the tears that would persist in rolling down her cheeks and kept saying over and over to herself: "I will believe! *I will* believe!"

❀

Back in the stone cottage Mrs. MacCarroll had dinner started so that it could be served at a moment's notice, but Gordon had not come. It was growing duskier all the time, and she kept going to the back window and gazing uneasily toward the great house, for still there was no light, and still she seemed to fancy there was something dark and bulky lying on the steps. That was purely fancy she told herself. She could not possibly see so far in this failing light. She had almost reached the point in her uneasiness where she was ready to venture up the dark drive alone, just to still her fears, when Gordon arrived.

"Oh, Son, I'm so glad you've come!" she cried out with relief.

"Why, Mother! You surely weren't frightened about me tonight, were you? It's not late."

"No, not about you, Gordon," she said with a catch in her breath, "but I've been worried about things in the great house. Do you know—did you hear? No, of course you didn't. You don't get anywhere near a radio, do you?"

"Well no, not exactly," laughed Gordon. "I have more important things to do than listen to the radio, though I'm glad you've got one to while away the hours with. But what's happened at the great house?"

"Why, Gordon, the little lady's been paged on the radio!"

"What?"

"Yes, this afternoon. It said how tall she was and how she was dressed, and the color of her hair and eyes, but it didn't say what a lovely smile she has, nor how she walks like a feather in the breeze, nor any of the things that would make folks really know her when they saw her. But it made my heart stand still with horror to think what may have happened to her, dear child! I couldn't help thinking what if she had been my child how worried I would be! And I thought of her poor father and wondered where he was. He's come through a hard place to be willing to broadcast his troubles to the world! For he's a proud man. You could see that just to look at him. And while I was pitying him he came walking in the drive. He'd got off the bus and almost fallen as he got out, and he looked old and sick. I almost ran out to offer him a cup of tea, and then I thought perhaps he wouldn't like it just now. Perhaps he'd rather suffer alone. So I let him go on by. But I watched for him to go in the house. I saw him get to the door and reach over as if he was putting the key in the lock, and just then the telephone rang. And when I came back he wasn't there anymore, and there seemed to be something bulky and dark lying on the step—only, of course, that must have been imagination. It was beginning to get dark, and I don't trust my eyes anymore. But I've watched and watched and there hasn't been a light yet."

Gordon's eyes were fixed on his mother's face with a disturbed, startled expression in them.

"I'll go right up and see, Mother," he said.

"Take your flashlight along and signal me if you want me to come," she called after him as he turned toward the door.

"Oh, it won't be anything like that!" said the young man as if he were trying to convince himself. "But I'll take it. It might come in handy." She could see that he was worried, though he was trying to laugh it off to calm her fears.

She stood by the window, watching him disappear into the darkness of the driveway, and then, before the sound of his footsteps had scarcely died away, there came a tap on the door, the back door. How strange! She hurried to open it, and there stood Maggie in her Sunday best, her blue eyes red and blurred with tears, her best hat awry because she had put it on so hastily, and her Scotch tongue fairly tumbling over itself in an attempt to talk while she was still out of breath from hurrying so fast.

"I hope I didn't fright ye," she burst out, panting. "I glimpsed the light in the kitchen an' guessed ye would be here. I'm that worried about the master's family I had ta come an' see. Did ye happen ta be listenin' in on the radio? Did ye hear them callin' for the little lady?"

"Yes, I did," said Mrs. MacCarroll. "And I've been worried ever since. But don't you know where she is? I thought she promised to write you."

"Yes, she did, but I've had never a word yet," said the old servant. "I was worried, but I thought, of course, she'd write to her father. Now it must be he's never heard neither. I wonder if he's up at the house. It seems ta be dark. I thought I'd just step in an' see if you'd heard aught? It goes sour against me ta be seen there if the new mistress is home, but I'd go if I thought I could help the master any. You don't happen to have noticed if he went in?"

"Yes," Mrs. MacCarroll said in an anxious voice. "I saw Mr. Disston go up the drive over half an hour ago, and I've been waiting ever since to see a light in the house, but there isn't any yet, and my son just came so I sent him up to see if anything was the matter and—there! There he is now waving his flashlight! I promised to come right up if he gave the signal. You'd better come with me—!"

The two hurried out the door and up the drive, walking so fast they could scarcely talk.

"Is—the—*hussy* home?" puffed Maggie, taking two little quick steps to Mrs. MacCarroll's one longer one.

"No, I don't think so," said the older woman quietly. "I saw her go up the drive several days ago, but she came back within the hour and took a bus off. I haven't seen her since."

"That's good!" said Maggie fervently, puffing along.

"There! There's a light!" said Mrs. MacCarroll, hurrying on the faster as a light streamed out from the open front door.

They rounded the drive beyond the last group of shrubbery and saw a dark form lying across the top step in front of the door.

"Oh, it's him!" cried Maggie with tears in her voice. "It's the poor master! Oh, I knew I should never have left him ta that hussy's care. I should have bided whatever she said. I mighta knowed she'd soon hang herself if I'd give her the rope. Oh, the poor man. The poor silly man! An' I promised his first wife I'd look after him well."

It was a kind of croon she uttered as she brisked along panting, talking more to herself than to her companion.

As they came up to the steps Gordon was lifting Mr. Disston in his arms.

"He's had a fall," he explained to his mother. "I wish we knew who their doctor is. No—I think he's only fainted. His pulse is weak, but it's there."

"It's Dr. Brownell," panted Maggie. "I'll just run in an' phone him!"

"This is Maggie, their old servant," explained Mrs. MacCarroll.

"That's good!" breathed Gordon as he lifted the older man and bore him inside the house.

"Lay him on the couch in the library," said Maggie, capably swinging open the door and plumping up the pillows. Then she pattered away to the telephone in the hall. Mrs. MacCarroll entered the kitchen and brought water, and Maggie, coming away from the telephone, hurried to the medicine closet for medicine.

"He's comin' at once!" she reported a moment later as she came puffing back with aromatic ammonia, her hat awry, her cheeks blazing red with excitement. There were still traces of tears on her cheeks.

Their efforts were presently rewarded by a long drawn sigh from the sick man, and fluttering eyelids opened vaguely upon them.

The two women retreated to the shadows of the hallway, leaving Gordon only for him to see.

"You're feeling better now, Mr. Disston?" said Gordon in his quiet voice of assurance. "You got a bit dizzy, didn't you? I'm glad

I was here. Take another sip of this water. That will help. The doctor will be here soon, and in a minute or two we'll have a cup of tea for you. I suspect you didn't take much time for lunch today and got a bit faint, but we'll soon have you fixed up."

Stephen Disston looked at him gravely for an instant and tried to smile. Maggie hurried away for the cup of tea, and Mrs. MacCarroll was preparing a tray, knowing instinctively where to find the tea things.

"Ach! The poor man!" said Maggie, brushing away another stray tear. "I just knew that feckless hussy would never give him the proper food."

"I wouldn't try to get up just yet, Mr. Disston," Gordon was saying, putting out a protesting hand. "The doctor will soon be here. He is on his way. Unless you would rather I carry you up to your bed? I can easily do that if you will like to be in bed before he gets here."

"Oh, no," protested Stephen Disston, making another ineffectual effort to rise and falling back again, "I must get right up! There is need for haste!" And he lifted a crumpled paper held tight in his hand! "This—" he said and looked at Gordon with anguished eyes. "I've just had a letter— What time is it?" And his eyes sought the clock.

"It's not late," said Gordon cheerfully, "but if I were you I wouldn't try to do another thing tonight. Just rest. What is it you have to do? Couldn't I do it?"

Disston's troubled eyes fixed on his face for an instant, and then he groaned.

"No," he said despairingly, "you couldn't! Nobody could! I don't see how I can do it myself, but I've *got* to *somehow*. I can't let them murder my little girl!"

"What?" said Gordon in a horrified tone. "What can you mean? Nobody is going to do anything like that!"

"They're threatening to," said the sick man tonelessly. "They've kidnapped her and are holding her for ransom! They want fifty thousand dollars put under the stone in the spring house tonight—see!" And he lifted the paper again.

With horror clutching at his heart Gordon took the ransom note and read it.

Could this be possible? His heart went up in an instant prayer for needed strength and guidance. He needed to know what to say to this anguished father. And after an instant his voice was steady, and he spoke.

"That may not be genuine, you know," he said in a quiet businesslike tone. "And even if it is there will be a way to protect her."

"But I haven't any money to put out there under the stone!" His voice was piteous. "And I don't know where I can get any! I was going to telephone my bank president, but I'm afraid it's too late to catch him now. He always—goes away—over weekends. And I'm not sure—he would do it for me—even if I got him. My—money is—*gone*! I'm on the verge of *bankruptcy*!"

"Well, God isn't!" said Gordon with assurance. "You lie there and pray to Him, and I'll see what can be done. Where did you find this note?"

"Tied to the doorknob as I was trying to fit in the key. I stopped to read it, and I must have got dizzy! I fell and struck my head." He put his hand up feebly and Gordon, looking, found a lump and a gash where the blood was seeping out and matting the hair.

"So you have! Well, we'll soon look after that." Gordon motioned to his mother, who came in just then. "Mother, we need some water and clean cloths. I wonder if you could rustle them together. Tea! That's good. That will hearten you, Mr. Disston. Let me give you a few teaspoonfuls before you try to talk anymore."

"But I must get up!" said the sick man. "The time is going! I cannot stop to drink tea."

"Look here, Mr. Disston, will you trust me with this thing?

I'll do my best. I'll do whatever you want done if you know what that is, but anyhow, I'll do something. I'll search for your daughter as if she were my—sister," he added. "Now, drink this tea!"

He slipped his arm under the man's head and lifted him slightly so that he could drink from the cup he held.

Stephen Disston drank and looked at his young comforter with his heart in his eyes.

"You have been a good friend to me. I shall never forget it," he murmured. "But I could not let you undertake all this for me. But, oh, I don't know what to do! Where can I get the money? I never thought I would get to a place where I would have *nothing*, no means to rescue my child!"

He covered his face with his hands for an instant, and then making a supreme effort he raised himself to a sitting posture and tried to rise to his feet. But suddenly he dropped back again, his face growing white.

"I *can't*—do—it—!" he said, and then, "but—I—*must*!"

He tried to rise once more, but Gordon caught him and made him lie down again.

"Now look here, friend," said Gordon, "you'll only complicate matters if you lose consciousness again. We *need you* if we are going to clear this thing up. I take it you have had no time to call the police?"

"Do you think—I should? The letter warns against that, you know."

"I think the police are better fitted to cope with a thing like this than you and I are, and the quicker they know about it, the quicker they can do something. I think they should be the ones to deal with the matter of what is put under a stone—if any."

"Perhaps you're right," said the sad voice, and the lids dropped over tortured eyes.

"Does Maggie know where that stone is located?"

The man opened his eyes again. "Is Maggie here? Oh, that is

good! Yes, she knows. You can trust her absolutely."

"I thought so. Well, I'll have an interview with the police. Shall I take the letter? And then I'm going out to find your daughter! You be resting—and praying!" he added.

A hopeless look swept over the face of the sick man.

"You can't find her," he said despairingly. "I've had one of the best detectives in the state out hunting her for three weeks, and there isn't a trace of her."

"That's all right. I'm asking the Lord to lead me to her. Will you ask Him, too? You know Him, don't you?"

Disston nodded diffidently as if he were embarrassed. "I haven't been—much—along that line lately!"

"Then get back to Him," said the young man cheerfully. "Your strength is in Him, you know. There comes the doctor! Is there anything else I should know?"

Gordon gave a brief explanation to the doctor of how he had found the sick man, and the doctor looked troubled.

"He has a rather serious heart complication," he said in a low tone. "A shock like that is bad. We should have a nurse, and I'll stay here tonight as much as possible. Can you stay?"

"I have to go out for a little while on an errand for Mr. Disston," explained Gordon. "I'll be back as soon as possible."

"That's good. We may need you. If we could only get hold of Diana that would be the best medicine possible," said the doctor anxiously.

"I'm going out to get her!" said the young man with assurance.

"Maggie's got a nice little bite of supper for you," whispered Gordon's mother as he came down from the bedroom where they had carried the sick man.

"Sorry, Mother, but I can't stop now. I'm going after the little lady. You and Maggie will have to carry on here till I get back. We've sent for a nurse, and she ought to be here soon. Mother, Mr. Disston had a note saying his daughter is being held for ransom. I'm taking it to the police; some of them may be here soon, probably not in uniform. Where is Maggie?"

"Here!" said Maggie from the shadows.

"Well, Maggie, can you show the police where there would be a stone in the spring house where ransom money could be put? They'll want to know."

"I can, sir!" said Maggie eagerly from out of a shower of anxious tears.

"Well, that's all. Don't get frightened, and *pray*! All the time!"

"That we will, sir," said Maggie, with a strong look in her blue eyes.

"But won't you take just a bite, Gordon?" urged his mother.

"No time, Mother dear!" He smiled at her. "Plenty of time to eat afterward."

He walked briskly away into the night, and his mother heard the little car cough and start on its way.

The night went on, and all was quiet in the great house. The nurse arrived and fell into her place in the scheme of things; several policemen arrived silently and entered the house rubber shod. They conversed very little. They peered out into the darkness in the direction of the spring house and prepared a neat bundle. They asked Maggie a few keen questions, and she answered them as keenly. Presently one of them was missing, and a shadow drifted out behind the house as if he had been a wraith. By and by another one was missing from the dark room at the back of the house where they had chosen to sit, and then another, until there were only two left inside on guard. At their direction all but the lights in the sickroom were extinguished, and Mrs. MacCarroll and Maggie sat side by side on the couch in the dark living room, silently, praying, and visualizing what might be happening off in the vague distance where Gordon MacCarroll had gone. And Gordon's mother tried to keep her fears back, tried to rest her faith on the almighty God, and did succeed in keeping back the tears. *Oh, God, keep him. Don't let him do anything rash! You've always guarded us. Keep us now! Raise up the sick, Father, and help Gordon to find the little lady.* Over and over she prayed.

So they sat there and listened with ears attuned to the darkness outside and the meadows down behind the spring house. That would be where the kidnappers would creep sometime in the night to get their money. They wondered what had been demanded and whether the father had had enough, and what was it that the grim policemen had wrapped up in a little bundle. They were glad of the presence of those silent policemen. It made it easier to breathe.

The hours crept slowly by, silent save for the moaning of the sick man overhead.

And sometimes Mother MacCarroll would glance out the window down across the lawn to where her own little kitchen glowed and take heart of hope. Gordon had left that light burning for her. It seemed to reassure her.

Chapter 23

Diana had just finished her second cracker when she heard footsteps coming up the stairs. She sat staring at the door. It was locked she knew, but the thought of the manager of the restaurant came to her. He could break down the door as easily as he would crush an eggshell if he cared to. Of course, she was crazy to think of him. He wouldn't leave the restaurant and come after her, but if he should, what should she do? She had no one, *no one* to protect her.

Then like a flash came a verse that she had read only that morning before she went out to her work: *The eternal God is thy refuge, and underneath are the everlasting arms.*

That was it. She must trust in that. *God, help, help!* she cried out in her heart even as the tap sounded on the door.

She hesitated a moment and then said, "Who is it, please?" Her voice sounded frightened even to herself, and she was suddenly conscious of her eyes that were heavy with weeping.

"It's me!" said Mrs. Lundy, and there was a pleased sound to her voice, not like her usual gruff tones.

Diana snapped off the bright light and went to the door.

There stood Mrs. Lundy with a big box in her arms.

"Well, they've come again!" she announced triumphantly, "and he's a *regular* guy. He bring 'em himself. You ain't gone to bed, have you? 'Cause you better get yourself togged out in your best. He's down there in the parlor waitin' for you, and he seemed like he was in a hurry."

Diana's eyes were filled with quick fear again.

"I don't understand what you mean, Mrs. Lundy. There is nobody who would come to call upon me here or bring me flowers. Those flowers that came in the past were from my old home."

"Well, here they are, anyhow, and he's downstairs. And if I was you I wouldn't keep him waitin' very long. He's some classy guy, he is. I says to my daughter as I come through the kitchen on my way up, to see the meat didn't burn, I says, 'Tilly, I always said that third-story back was different, and now I know it.'"

"But really, Mrs. Lundy," said Diana, drawing back and brushing away the dampness from her eyelashes, "I don't in the least know who this is, and I'm afraid there's some mistake."

"Well, have it your own way," said the landlady grumpily. "It's your mistake, not mine, anyway. And I must say I don't see the point of you keeping on saying you don't know him. I got eyes in my head, ain't I? Whether you know him or not, you march down there and settle it with him! I gotta cook my meat!" And Mrs. Lundy deposited the box on the floor with a thump and sailed away downstairs.

With her heart palpitating like a trip hammer Diana picked up the box. With excited fingers she tore open the wrappings, lifted the cover, and that heavenly fragrance of spicy sweetness wafted through the room.

The flowers had come again! The mystery flowers. God sent them every time in her need! But now must she go down there and have the mystery and beauty torn from them by having the giver turn out to be somebody she didn't like?

She dashed cold water on her face, smoothed her hair, and then with sudden impulse she scooped the flowers from their box and took them in her arms, carrying them in a sheaf before her to shield her.

Downstairs the doorbell was pealing through the house once more, and Mrs. Lundy ungraciously left her meat again to answer it. She eyed the creature with disdain who slid inside before she could stop him. His hair was unkempt, his face and hands were dirty, and his clothes were ragged. Mrs. Lundy herself was not beyond being untidy, but this creature was of another world than even hers.

"What you want?" She frowned at him.

He blinked in the flickering light of the hall like a creature at bay and demanded, "I wantta see the party on the third floor back."

"Whatcha want her for?" demanded the landlady.

"That's my business!" he growled.

"Awwright, you can stand there. She's comin' down in a minute!"

The man lifted his little unholy eyes toward the stairs, his mouth stretched in a diabolical grin that showed the spaces between the rotten teeth where some were missing, and he kept one hand in the pocket of his tattered coat.

Diana came down slowly, rounding the head of the stairs on the second floor, her flowers before her.

"God! Take care of me!" she breathed as she stood a minute dreading to go on. Then it occurred to her that the manager of the cheap little restaurant where she had worked would never bring her gorgeous, expensive flowers, and she had really nothing to fear in that way. It must, of course, be one of her old friends who had found out where she was and had taken this tactful way to show her homage.

So she gathered courage and continued on, dreading most of all to have the romance taken from her lovely spirit-flowers. Well, whatever came she would always say that God sent them, anyway.

The cringing man at the foot gazed up at her for an instant, his hand gripping that something inside his pocket. Then he lowered his head with a Uriah Heep motion and spoke in a whine.

"You're Diana Disston!" he charged as if it were a crime.

Diana stopped, startled, new fear coming into her eyes, her heart suddenly sinking. Was this creature the sender of her wonderful mystery flowers? Her arms grew suddenly heavy, like lead, and the flowers slid from her grasp and fell in a heap before her on the step. Her knees were weak. She felt as if she were going to sink down with the flowers. But she must not give way. She must not!

"I useta go ta school with you. You remember me?"

"*No!*" said Diana from a throat that was dry and lips that were trembling. "*No!*" She tried to scream it, but the sound was only an anguished whisper.

"My mother useta sew fer your mother," he whined on. "I got her outside now in a taxi. She's on her way to the hospital fer an operation, an' she wants ta see ya. She's got somepin' ta tell ya ta yer advantage. 'Cause she may die, that's why she wants ta tell ya. You come out ta the taxi an' talk ta her."

Diana gripped the stair railing and tried to back away. She must not fall! She *must not*! Oh, if Mrs. Lundy would only come, or somebody.

"But I *don't know* you!" she pled with that note of fright in her voice. "I *can't* go out there now!"

"I'll teach ya ta know me!" said the man, low menace in his voice now, and whipped out an ugly gun, pointing it up at her. "You scram down here right quick! Make it snappy. I ain't waitin' round any longer, see? Come on or I'll shoot the pretty feet out from under ya! Keep yer trap shut an' come on or ya'll be a dead un!"

Diana stood there powerless to move, and when she tried to scream no sound came from her frightened lips.

Then suddenly from the dim recesses of the unlit parlor, without warning, the legs of one of Mrs. Lundy's parlor chairs crashed down upon the man's wrist, his hand fell limp at his side, and his gun dropped to the floor and went off with a loud reverberation.

Simultaneously the kitchen door at the end of the hall swung open and a big burly policeman, Mrs. Lundy's brother who had dropped in for a bite to eat, came stalking out from the kitchen, a big wedge of apple pie in one hand and an ugly gun in the other.

Now the best thing the creature in the hall could do was to run, and he had taken care that the door was unlatched before he began his performance, so he proceeded to put himself into action. Like a rat he turned and would have been gone into the shadows of the street but the policeman, even while he stuffed the last gigantic mouthful of pie inside his enormous mouth, brought his gun into action with a tiny motion no more than a turn of a wrist, and a bullet went neatly into the foot of the intruder. With a howl he dropped at the foot of the stairs as the policeman came forward with a mighty stride and grasped the little human rat by the back of his ragged collar.

Then turning around to the young man who stood in between the flowered chenille curtains of the parlor doorway, the man of the law said, "Good work, buddy! I don't know who you are, but you certainly did lam him one just in the nick of time, and if you should ever want ta get on the police force I'll write ya a recommend."

"Thank you, brother," said Gordon MacCarroll, coming out into the brightness of the hall and looking down sternly at the cringing, whining creature on the floor. "I'm not applying just now, but I'll take it as a favor if you'll see that this man is fingerprinted. I think he's connected with a kidnapping, and if I'm not mistaken it was about to take place. Please don't let him get away till you hear from me."

"I'll not let him get away," swaggered the policeman. "We got him fingerprinted already. We got plenty on him without no kidnappin' as far as that goes, but we'll hold him alrighty. I been layin' fer this bird fer three weeks, an' he slipped me every time. Now I'm goin' ta keep him."

He snapped the handcuffs around the man's wrists, swung the door open easily, put his piercing whistle to his lips, and an instant later a car rolled up to the door. Strong hands lifted the crippled prisoner into it.

The door closed on this scene, leaving a huddled audience of open-mouthed Lundy relatives in the kitchen door, commenting with satisfaction on how "Uncle Bill gave the bum his medicine." Then they suddenly melted away and there were only Diana, sitting white and shaken on the stairs with her big sheaf of carnations at her feet, and Gordon MacCarroll, standing stern and relieved between the chenille curtains.

"I ask your pardon," he said, looking toward the drooping girl. "There didn't seem to be any other way."

"Oh, thank you!" said Diana, struggling with the silly tears which, now that the danger was over, seemed to insist upon raining down her cheeks. "I—was—so frightened!"

"Well, you needn't be frightened anymore," said Gordon with a lilt in his voice. "I've come for you! But—I'm forgetting—you don't know me any better than you did the other fellow."

"Oh yes I do!" cried Diana, her eyes shining through the tears. "You are the man from the stone cottage. You prayed for me once—at least I hope the prayer was meant for me. I've carried it with me ever since the night I went away. And I saw you again when we drove up to ask the way somewhere—"

"That's nice!" said Gordon, suddenly smiling, a light coming into his eyes. "That makes it a lot easier. Because I've come for you, and I'd like you to come as quickly as possible. I don't want to frighten you, but your father is sick and is calling for you. I promised him I would bring you at once. Can you trust me to take you home?"

Diana's eyes were wide with consternation. "My father is sick? Oh, what is the matter?"

"Suppose I tell you on the way. We haven't any time to waste. Your father is in great anxiety about you. Every added minute is torture for him."

Diana turned and fairly flew up the stairs.

She was back in a couple of minutes. She had grabbed her suitcase, which was all packed for going somewhere, taken her hat and her purse in hand, and come. Gordon had gathered up the flowers, and she took them from him as one takes something very precious.

"My father is sick!" she explained breathlessly to Mrs. Lundy, who stood in the kitchen door staring. "I'll be back!"

The big policeman was at the door when they went outside, and Gordon paused to say a few words in a low tone and hand him a telephone number he had written on a card. Then he put Diana into the car and they started away.

Diana sat there tense, the flowers clasped in her arms, her face white with anxiety like a little ghost above the blossoms.

"Now, please, tell me about Father," she implored.

"Your father had some sort of a collapse this evening following a shock. He fell and cut his head. I do not know just how serious it is. I understand there is a heart complication. But the doctor felt it was important I should bring you as soon as possible."

His voice was tender and sympathetic.

"Shock!" said Diana, with trembling lips. "What kind of a shock?"

"He found a note tied to his doorknob this afternoon saying that you were being held for ransom and would be murdered if a large sum of money was not forthcoming tonight."

"Oh, how dreadful!"

"He seems to have fainted and fallen. He was unconscious when I got there."

"Oh, you saw him fall?"

"No, but Mother had watched him go up the drive. She felt so sorry for him. It was just after the radio announcement that you were missing."

"*Radio?*" said Diana in bewilderment.

"Didn't you know your father had you paged on the radio?"

"Oh *no*!" said the girl, shrinking back in horror. "Oh, poor Father!" There was the breath of a sob in her voice.

"He had been under a terrible strain, of course, had employed a private detective with no results, and was desperate about you, you know."

"Oh! And did your mother see him fall?"

"No, it was growing dusk, but she saw him standing at the door, and then he seemed to disappear. And she watched for a light to appear in the house, but none came, so when I got home a few minutes later she sent me up to see if all was well. I found him lying on the steps with a cut in his head. Mother came up and an old servant of yours named Maggie who had heard the radio call, and we got him into the house. Your Maggie called your doctor. The doctor got a nurse."

"And—was Father—?"

"Yes, he was conscious. He tried to get up. Said he must do something about the ransom, but I persuaded him to put it into the hands of the police and told him I would go and get you."

"But how did you know where I was?"

"I didn't."

"Then how did you think that you could find me?"

"God knew where you were." He said it reverently and added, after an instant, "And my flowers knew!"

"Oh!" said Diana with awe in her voice. Then after a moment

of silence: "But how could you send the flowers in the first place if you didn't know my address?"

"I called up the florist on the telephone and told him you were away and I hadn't your present address but would like to send you some flowers occasionally, incognito, if he could get them through the mail to you, special delivery. Of course, the post office isn't allowed to give out addresses, but they themselves will put on the address. He said he could get the flowers to you. He had a brother-in-law in the post office who would fix it up and rush the flowers through. Of course, your receipted special delivery cards came back to the florist in due time, but he couldn't send them to me because he didn't know who I was, though he always told me when I telephoned again that they had come. But that didn't do me any good tonight, of course, so I just prayed all the way to the florist's, and when I walked in I said, 'Have my flowers gone yet?'

"He knew my voice, and he looked up apologetically and said, 'No, I'm sorry, but I'm just getting ready to drive into the city and take them. I was off to a funeral, and my son forgot to take them to the mail. But here they are, already done up and addressed.' He shoved the box over to me, and there was the address written plainly; the way was made plain for me. So I told him that was all right and that I was calling on you tonight and would take them in this time myself. That was easy, you see."

"Do you always get answered like that when you pray?" asked Diana in wonder.

"The answers are not always alike," said the young man thoughtfully. "I always know there'll be an answer if I pray in the right way, with faith, with a yielded will, with a desire to be led."

Diana was still for a long moment after that. Then she said earnestly, "You've taken a great deal of trouble for me." And then after a pause, with her lips down among the flowers, quite irrelevantly, "I should have brought the box for these. They will get all crushed. But I was so excited I didn't think of it."

"That's all right," said Gordon, a jubilant note in his voice, "they have accomplished their purpose, haven't they?"

"What do you mean?" she asked.

"Why, they served to introduce us. I was half afraid I might have trouble getting you to go with me after I got there. I brought these along hoping you would understand and not be afraid of me."

"Oh!" she said thoughtfully. "I suppose they did. I suppose I would have been afraid of you after what happened with that awful creature. You know, I couldn't see you very well, down in the shadow of those curtains. And I'd only seen you once or twice in the dark."

He gave her a quick, startled look.

"But do you know?" she went on gravely. "It's just come to me who that man was. It must have been Bill Sharpe. His mother did plain sewing. He was a bad boy and ran away several times. That's all that I know about him. But I am sure his mother is dead. She died two years ago. I remember the charitable organization that gathered money to bury her. I never heard what became of the son. But now I am sure that was him!" She drew a deep breath of horror like a shudder and closed her eyes.

"Oh! If it hadn't been for you I might have been killed!" she went on. "How can I ever thank you for what you have done for me!"

"Don't try, please!" He smiled.

They were getting near to home now, and Diana, glancing out, shrank back into the car again. Presently she asked in a small, scared voice.

"Was my father's wife—there?"

"Oh!" he said. "Why, no, I don't think she was. I didn't see her anywhere. At least—she hadn't come when I left. And—I don't think anybody remembered her! We should have sent word to her, shouldn't we? But, of course, we didn't know where to send it, and your father said nothing about her. He was only concerned about you."

"Oh!" said Diana gratefully. It soothed her soul to know her father cared for her.

"Would you know where she is?" asked MacCarroll.

"No!" said Diana quickly, a little sharply. "I went away because—that is, I thought it would be best— She is— We don't—!"

"I understand," said the young man, deep sympathy in his voice. "It must have been very hard for you."

Diana tried to answer, but she choked over the words, and all she succeeded in saying was, "It was."

"But perhaps—I was wrong—" she added a moment afterward. "I didn't think my father—would feel it so! I should have written him, anyway!"

"Well, I wouldn't worry over that now," he said gently.

They were turning in at the big gateway, and Diana sat very still as they swept up the drive among the trees. They were passing the spot where Diana had found her flowers, over there between the pine trees.

"I wish—" she said softly, hesitantly, her eyes dropped to the flowers in her lap, "that you would tell me why you did it! Why you put—those flowers—there—in the first place!"

It was Gordon's turn to be silent now, and they were just coming around the last curve to the house as he answered gravely, tenderly, "Because I love you!"

He stopped the car then and went around to open the door for Diana, and as he took her hand to help her out he said earnestly, "May I tell you about it sometime?"

"Oh—*yes*—!" The answer was almost a whisper, but then suddenly they were aware that the front door of the mansion had swung open and a silent, dark figure was standing there looking at them.

Gordon lifted her suitcase out and took her in. There was only a dim light in the hallway, and the door closed almost at once and silently.

"Better get that car away safe somewhere, brother," advised the policeman. "We don't want any means for our man to make a getaway in case he turns up."

"Nothing yet?" asked Gordon.

"Not yet, though it's still early. We've got our men pretty well planted where they won't be discovered, I think."

"Well, I've a notion perhaps he's been hindered," said Gordon, "though, of course, there may be two of them, or even more. I'll run my car back and lock it, and then I'll tell you about it."

But just then the nurse called down from the dimness of the upper hall. "Is that Mr. MacCarroll? Mr. Disston wants to see him *right away!*"

"That's all right," said the officer, "I'll guard your car till you come. He's been asking all the evening if you were back yet."

Diana stood helplessly in her own home looking around her in the dimness. It seemed to her that years had intervened since she was here. The dim light, the presence of the quiet officers, the strange voice of the nurse, the possibility of Helen's presence, all made her feel as if she must turn and flee. Then Gordon MacCarroll smiled down upon her and took her hand.

"Come," he said, "shall we go up?"

It was Maggie who met them on the stair landing and took the sheaf of carnations from her.

"I'll put them in water," she said, like a caress, and Diana smiled and yielded them up, knowing they would be safe.

Then Gordon led Diana into her father's room and up to the bedside.

"I've brought her, Mr. Disston," he said, as if he had just been in the next room for her.

"You've *brought* her?" The sick man gripped the young hand

in his, a great light coming into his face. "Is this really—my daughter—?" He peered through the shadows of the darkened room. "Turn up the light, Nurse. Is this you, Diana, or am I dreaming?"

Diana stooped over and kissed his forehead. "Yes, Father dear! I'm really here!"

"And—you won't go away—again?" he asked anxiously.

"Not as long as you want me here, Father!"

"I shall always want you here," he said wistfully. "But—you won't vanish while I am asleep! You won't let anybody murder you?"

"No," laughed Diana tenderly, kneeling beside him with her arm around his shoulder, her hand touching his cheek in the old familiar way.

"Ah!" he said slowly, feasting his eyes upon her face for a moment. "Now I can go to sleep! I've needed sleep for so long, but I couldn't sleep. Now I can!"

Gordon had slipped away. Diana could hear the car with the sound muffled, coasting slowly down the drive, and she knelt there beside her father's bed, his hand gripping hers, his love around her, reconciliation—home—love—! It was sweet! Her own eyelids dropped. She was asleep with her cheek on her father's pillow.

The nurse touched her on her shoulder lightly.

"You could go to your own room now," she said. "He is really asleep at last. This will do him a great deal of good. I'll call you if he wakens, but I don't think he will."

Maggie had prepared one of the guest rooms for her. Her flowers were there in a large crystal vase, filling the room with fragrance. Maggie had laid out her robe and turned down the covers.

Gordon MacCarroll came to the head of the stairs and whispered that he was downstairs with the policemen and she need not feel afraid. She was to go to sleep, and he gave her a smile that shot through her heart like sweet fire.

She fell asleep almost at once with the light of that smile in her heart and the memory of those low-spoken words, *"Because I love you!"*

Sometime in the night there was a disturbance out below the spring house, and several shots were fired. There were muffled sounds of stealthy feet, the clang of a police car off in the distance, and one more human rat stayed in his depredations! But the father and daughter slept on and heard nothing of it.

Chapter 24

It was Gordon MacCarroll who met the reporters from the press the next morning and answered their questions in a quiet, steady voice. He said that Mr. Disston had had a slight fall the day before and was feeling a little under the weather this morning, so was not able to come down and see them, but he would be grateful for as little publicity as possible. Yes, it was true he had announced the fact over the radio that his daughter was missing. In these days of dreadful happenings perhaps he had been over-anxious when he did not hear from her for a few days and was not sure where she had gone. But it was all right now. His daughter was at home and safe. She had merely started out to visit some relatives and friends and did not realize that her father would be anxious. Yes, it was true that some beings of the underworld had taken advantage of the radio announcement to send a note to Mr. Disston demanding ransom money, but the police had been prompt in rounding them up and putting them where they could not menace others.

It was all most courteous and quiet, and somehow the reporters found themselves bowed away with a rather prosaic story instead of the thrilling tale they had expected to extract.

One reporter, it is true, asked a few questions about the new Mrs. Disston. Wasn't there some trouble between her and Mr. Disston's daughter? He told them calmly that Mrs. Disston was away for a few days with friends. No, Mr. Disston's illness was not such as would warrant her coming back immediately, especially as the daughter was here now. Mrs. Disston would doubtless return very soon.

It was a quiet, peaceful Sunday, with Maggie making a nice dinner in the kitchen and preparing a tempting tray for the invalid; with the nurse coming and going silently; with Diana sitting near her father's side, her flowers on the chest at the foot of his bed where he could see them; and with the consciousness that Gordon MacCarroll was downstairs with an officer of the law, just to make sure there were no more criminals waiting around.

It was a time when Diana could rest at last and not even think, though there were pleasant things to consider, she realized later, when she was rested.

Monday Gordon had to go to his business, but he returned twice during the day to see if all was well and came home early at night to get the latest news, which his mother had gathered from Maggie.

Maggie, in all her Scotch righteousness, had met the reporters all day and stood for her family in great shape. A reporter would have had to cross her dead body before he could ever get by into the house, and curious neighbors went away baffled beyond belief.

There was just the quiet and peace that was needed for the invalid, and Diana basked in it and marveled that she was here after her days of sorrow and hard work.

The doctor came and went quietly, studied his patient, and seemed pleased with his progress, yet warned them not to let him have the slightest bit of excitement or extra exertion.

But Stephen Disston seemed content just to lie still and watch his daughter going about the room, bringing her vase of carnations for him to see, and sitting where he could see her with a book or a bit of sewing or just sitting with her hands resting in her lap. But there was a sadness in the smile upon his face that the doctor hoped would disappear as the result of the shock passed.

They would not let him talk, nor let Diana talk much to him. The doctor had warned her about speaking of their separation or the kidnapping incident, so there was nothing to do but wait upon him and smile, sit quietly and love him.

It was Tuesday afternoon that they sat thus, keeping quiet company with one another while the nurse took her afternoon walk.

There had been no news from Helen, not even a telephone message, though she must have seen something in the papers if she was not otherwise too occupied. But Helen was not much given to reading even newspapers. They had not been thinking of her. Perhaps for the time she was entirely forgotten, as if she had no connection with their scheme of things.

It was then, just when she was least expected, that she came.

Of course, it was because she had a key that she was able to enter the house and evade the watchful Maggie. Even then she got no farther than the foot of the stairs without a challenge.

Maggie, bearing a big spoon from which she had just wiped yellow batter with a capable forefinger, and from which a large drop of yellow batter was about to fall, swung open the door to the butler's pantry and stood like a glowering nemesis in her way.

"An' where were *you*?" she demanded. "It's high time you put in an appearance! But you're not to go up the stair till the doctor gives you permission! The master's had a fall an' a bad turn with his heart, an' he's not to be excited. You'd best ask the nurse if you can go up!"

Helen stood there for an instant looking at the masterful Maggie then put out a bejeweled hand and gave her a push backward, a push right in her ample chest that sent her entirely off her balance. Then with a laugh she ran lightly up the stairs.

She appeared in the doorway of her husband's room and stood there an instant taking in the situation. Diana was sitting quietly with her back to the door, a book in her lap, and a smile on her face. Stephen Disston was dozing upon his pillow. They looked complete enough without her. There was a mirror across from Diana that showed the sweet look upon her face, that look that Helen always had hated.

She saw the sheaf of flowers near the bed, and she glimpsed through the window the nurse returning from her walk.

She stood poised an instant longer, studying her husband's face with her own hard, beautiful eyes, and then she laughed, that bright, heartless laugh.

Diana started, lifted her eyes swiftly to the mirror, and met the amused contempt in the eyes of her father's wife! One instant their glances held, and then Helen whirled around and went lightly down the hall, her laugh trailing delicately behind her. Down the stairs she went and put her head in at the kitchen door.

"I'm going on a cruise," she announced blithely. "You can tell them if they inquire. I'm not sure how long I'll be gone. They're getting along gloriously without me, and I never was much good in a sickroom. I hate it! Just tell them I'm on the yacht *Lotus Blossom*. Mr. Disston will understand."

She was gone before Maggie could recover her breath to reply, and Maggie dashed after her, trying to walk lightly for the master's sake yet hurrying with all her sturdy might.

But when she finally arrived outside with the door closed behind her, Helen was far down the walk, breezing along like a bit of thistledown, and when Maggie flung herself down the path after her to give her a piece of her mind and let her know how it would look to the world if she went away with the master sick, Helen only turned and flung back that childish laugh and skipped on.

When Maggie, all puffed and speechless, arrived at the gate, Helen was climbing into the bus and, turning, gave a mocking smile and a wave of her hand as she rode away.

Maggie, unable to believe her eyes, stood staring after the bus, an eloquent look on her loyal red countenance. A few seconds later she burst in upon Mrs. MacCarroll, all tears and anger and out of breath.

"Never mind, Maggie," said Mrs. MacCarroll soothingly. "You know the Lord can take care of her. Just leave it to Him. He'll teach her in His own way. You can't!"

"I suppose you're right," said Maggie, snuffing back the tears, "an' I'm an old fool to grieve, but it's a sad thing for the likes of a young hussy like that to carry on lightly when her good man is lying sick."

"Well, I wouldn't say anything about it now, not unless he asks. Maybe he didn't see her."

"I'm thinkin' he didn't!" said Maggie. "I heard only her silly laughter, like a fool!"

"Well, leave it to the Lord. He'll bring it all out right in His own time and way."

So Maggie went back to finish her cake, and nobody said a word about the new mistress of the house. For Diana had looked quickly at her father when that laugh rang out and saw to her joy that he slept on and did not mention Helen's coming, wondering as the calm days went by if nobody else had seen her at all, wondering if perhaps she hadn't been dreaming herself.

❃

One evening Gordon came up to see Mr. Disston for a few minutes. The sick man had had a good day and seemed brighter than since his fall, but still the doctor would not let him try to get up.

They talked pleasantly on everyday topics, a bit of politics, the brighter outlook of the money market, the prophecy of a noted economist that things were looking up. Then Gordon turned toward Diana, who sat quietly on the other side of the bed listening.

"Have you been out today?" he asked.

"Why no," she said, with a smile and a little shiver of dread. "No, I don't think I've been out of the house since I came back. I'm so glad to get here that I don't want to leave it."

"Well, that won't do. We'll be having you sick next. Suppose we take a little walk now and catch the end of the sunset and a bit of the moonrise? Don't you think she should have a little exercise, Mr. Disston?"

"Yes, go, dear!" her father said, smiling. "I'm going to turn in now anyway, for I feel as if I might be able to really sleep tonight."

She kissed him good night, and the two young people went downstairs and out into the "quiet colored end of evening." Diana suddenly felt breathless. It was the first time she had been alone with Gordon since he brought her home, and it suddenly became a momentous occasion. *Why?* she wondered. She had never felt like this before. It was probably because she had been through so many terrible experiences and then been shut up in the house so long. She was just excited, she told herself. She tried not to let herself remember that sometime he was going to tell her about those mystery flowers, why he had sent them, *"Because I love you!"* She had been telling herself that there was some other explanation to those words than the ordinary meaning when a young man says them to a girl. She had been telling herself that those were spirit-flowers and there was something above the earthly about their coming. She had fondly believed that she was thoroughly sane and sensible about the view her thoughts had taken of the whole thing, yet now this thrill of joy! Had all her fancied sanity been false?

So they strolled out into the evening with braided colors

changing in the sky all around them and the soft perfume of growing things in the air.

Gordon purposely led her around the house to the view of the meadows in the back with the spring house nestling its white stone walls by the brook and the darkening woods standing majestic beyond. And just below them the garden, huddling in groups of dying colors, like devoted worshippers before the glory of the clouds. The breath of mignonette was there. Late pansies and forget-me-nots in close borders, the white of stately lilies towering above tall spikes of larkspurs, flocks of Canterbury bells, pink and white foxgloves, all bowed saintly heads at vespers. It was a lovely scene, and the young man wanted the girl to lose that sense of horror that must be connected in her mind with the spring house. In the colored evening light, with flowers around and the brightness of the sunset on its white vine-clad walls, and with Gordon MacCarroll's strong hand slipped protectingly within her arm, the spring house was forever robbed of its atmosphere of horror that Diana had felt since the night she came home. She would never again dread to look out toward it even in the evening.

And as the colors in the end of evening settled into purple and pearl and gray, they wandered slowly, reluctantly away from the hauntingly lovely garden wrapped in prayer; on through the shrubbery around the house to the drive, and so down across the drive to the tall plumy pines that grouped themselves behind the stone cottage.

They were walking across the grass now, their footsteps muffled by the turf and their step in unison. They had been talking of many things, and Diana thrilled to find that Gordon knew and loved the same poems and books and pictures that were her especial delight. How wonderful to have a friend—yes, she could dare to call him friend surely—who enjoyed reading. Not one of the young men in her crowd of friends had cared for reading anything but trash. They scarcely took time to read that.

But now as they entered within the seclusion of the trees, suddenly Diana saw at her feet a starry flower!

Another carnation!

"Oh!" she cried and stopped before it.

Then she looked up into Gordon's face with wonder and delight and, stooping, reached out both hands to gather up the flower tenderly and draw it close to her face.

Gordon stood looking down at her, a great reverence in his eyes.

She rose and looked at him again, a wonderful look, starry even through the dusk.

"You have put this here again!" she acknowledged. "How wonderful of you! And you brought me out here to find it!"

He slid his arm within hers again. They took another step or two, and there deeper in seclusion was another flower—and another—and another—a whole armful of carnations, it seemed like dozens and dozens of them, scattered broadcast there in the quiet luminous dark, with the stars beginning to look down from the sky.

He stopped beside her and helped her gather them up, and then as she stood breathless with them clasped in her arms he came and stood before her and, looking into her eyes, he said, "And now, may I tell you about my love for you?"

He took both her hands as she held the flowers and looked down at her as if she were the most precious thing in the world. And Diana thrilled to the wonder of his voice and, looking up, said with grave solemnity, "But how could you possibly love me when you didn't know me? When you never even saw me yet?"

"Oh, but I had," said Gordon tenderly. "I had watched you day after day. Do you know where I saw you first? Right here in this spot where we are standing, kneeling down and picking something out of the grass. I found out afterward that it was violets you were picking, for after you were gone I went out and searched and found one you had missed. I have it now pressed in the pages of my Bible over a very precious verse."

"But where could you have been? I didn't see you anywhere," said Diana.

"No, you wouldn't. I was up in the window of my room reading my Bible, and I looked up and saw you. Then when you were gone I knelt beside the window to pray, and I prayed for you. Afterward I went out and found the violet. And every morning after that I watched you come for the violets till they were almost gone. Then I was afraid you might not come there anymore, and I would miss you. So I thought of putting a flower there to see if you would find it. It was so I began to leave a flower each day for you. And each day I prayed for you, that you might know Him, my Lord, and be guarded and guided. And each day as I watched you and prayed for you my love for you grew until I suddenly knew it was a great overwhelming thing that was going to shut out the possibility of my ever loving any other woman. And I realized that you might never care for me. In fact, it even might be that I would never get to know you well enough to tell you of my love. I am not a wealthy man, and you are a girl brought up to luxury. There were all sorts of obstacles. Yet I couldn't help be glad, for I knew there was something far more precious in loving you even this way than to have a daily companionship with any other woman. So I laid it before God and went on praying for you. The flowers were my only way of telling you, and you had not put them away from you. You had accepted them."

He paused and looked down at her with question and deep hunger in his eyes.

Diana stood with her face slightly averted and spoke slowly. "You don't know how precious they were! You don't know how much I needed them just then! Oh, it is all so very wonderful. I can see now why your prayer followed me everywhere and drew me in spite of myself to God."

His hands were warm upon hers. His eyes were filled with wonder.

"But how could you possibly know that I was praying for you?" he asked. "You spoke of that before. I wondered about it."

"I heard you," she said quietly. "It was the night I went away. I had meant to be gone when Father brought her—his wife—home but they came before I expected them, and I had to slip out of the back door and hide behind the shrubbery. I was afraid they might follow me and stop me. I got down to the gate and stood out on the pavement over beyond your house, close to the hedge, waiting for the bus to come. And suddenly I heard a voice behind me praying. I did not know who you were, nor that you belonged in the cottage then. Nobody had told me except that a woman and her son had taken it. For some reason I thought the son was only a boy. But when I heard that prayer I knew it was the voice of the one who had protected me when I was terribly frightened. I thought perhaps it was a visitor at the cottage. But you were praying for *me*—at least I hoped that I was included. I hoped that our house was the one you meant when you spoke of the 'great' house, and I carried that prayer with me, for oh, how we needed it! 'Lord, we would ask Thy mercy and tenderness and leading for the people up at the great house,' you said. 'Perhaps some of them are sad. Lord, give them comfort. Perhaps they need guidance. Do Thou send Thy light—!' And then the bus came along, and I felt I had to get into it. But all the way to the city I kept saying those words over and over so that I wouldn't forget them, and when I got into the train I wrote them down. And I kept wishing I had stayed and heard the rest, even if I did get caught! Sometimes it seemed that I could not stand it because I had not heard the rest of that prayer. I almost got out of the bus and went back, only I had my suitcase to carry and I knew the prayer would be over by the time I got back. And then I was a little afraid that perhaps I might hear something more that would show it was not our house after all that you were praying for, and I felt as if I could not stand that. *I needed it so!*"

Her voice quivered, and suddenly his arms went around her and he drew her close, flowers and all, and laid his face down upon her soft hair.

"Darling!" he whispered.

She quivered in his arms and was still, and then she lifted her face to his and whispered back softly, shyly, "Dear flower-person—!"

He laid his lips upon hers and drew her closer, and heaven itself seemed to come down and enfold them.

"I love you!" he told her in tones that thrilled her. "Can it be that you love me? So soon?"

"I think I've loved you since the first flower," she said, smiling through the darkness. "I called them spirit-flowers and told myself God had sent them, but I loved and dreamed about whoever sent them. And—your prayer—God answered it! He sent me light to guide me, just as you prayed."

She told him about the girl in the station and the tract that had helped her and how she had begun to pray for herself, and he breathed a glad "Thank God!"

They had so many things to tell! There were times she had been saved from perils. There was the escape from the kidnappers. There was the way she looked when she came down the stairs in Mrs. Lundy's rooming house with the carnations held in her arms—! There was a great deal for him to tell her about that. And suddenly they realized it was growing late.

"The dew has been falling for a long time, and your feet must be drenched!" said Gordon. "This is a pretty way for me to begin to take care of you!"

But they were loath to leave the sacred place where their love had first found root, and it was some minutes before they walked slowly up the drive and entered the house, their hands clinging together until the very threshold was reached. They had said good night down among the pines, but their fingers gave a last lingering pressure as they entered decorously.

Maggie was waiting for them discreetly in the back of the hall and came forward and took the carnations to be put in water quite as if it were a common thing for young men and maidens to go out at midnight and gather carnations in the moonlight.

"There's a telegram for your father," Maggie said in a whisper, indicating a yellow envelope on the hall table.

Chapter 25

Diana and Gordon discussed whether it should be opened and decided to do so. It might be something about the kidnapping, in which case he probably wouldn't have to see it at all. But it might be something important that should be attended to at once. In any event, they must know what it was before they dared show it to him, for the doctor had warned them so much about exciting him.

So Diana opened it carefully and read. It was dated from the yacht *Lotus Blossom*, and it consisted of just ten words.

> HAVING A GLORIOUS TIME. DON'T YOU WISH
> YOU HAD COME?

Diana looked up at her beloved with startled eyes.

"It's from Helen!" she said. "She's off on a yachting cruise. What shall I do about telling him?"

"Let it drift a day or two," advised Gordon. "It will work out somehow. We'll pray about it."

She gave him a smile of wonder and awe as she put the message back in its envelope.

"I am sure that life is going to be wonderful and different now," she said, looking up at him. "You make everything seem different. But oh, poor dear Father! How is he going to get well and strong with a wife like that?"

"Leave that to the heavenly Father, too. Just trust it with Him! He'll have a way of working it out someday. Be patient!"

Maggie, lingering in the back hall, filling a vase with the carnations, kept sharp ears open to the low whispers and keen eyes furtively on the two. She was not unaware of the starriness of her bonnie lassie's eyes, and her own lingered with approval upon Gordon's strong, pleasant face and fine height and build. Here was a man worthy of her wonderful girl!

And when he was gone and Diana had gone up to her room Maggie went and stood before the hall table looking down at the yellow envelope with eyes that could almost penetrate the paper, so keen they were of understanding, and then she said in a very inaudible whisper, more like a hiss: "The *hussy*!"

❀

Two days later Mr. Disston was so much better that the nurse said he could sit up against three pillows for a little while and might have the paper to read for a few minutes.

They had given him the telegram the day before, and he had read it without comment and cast it carelessly on the table, whence it floated to the floor. Maggie, when she came in to "redd up," as she said, gathered it up and had the satisfaction at last of knowing the exact words of the message that she had read before by thought transference, or whatever it was that helped her to unravel the secrets of those around her.

So the nurse plumped up the pillows, and Stephen Disston sat up against them with the morning paper.

He thought he wanted very much to see what the stock market was doing, for his lawyer friend had been in to see him for a few minutes the day before and had brought encouraging news, but he let his eyes wander over the first page of the paper before he opened to the commercial pages, and there in large letters heading one column was the announcement:

YACHT *LOTUS BLOSSOM* SINKS IN
MID-OCEAN
WITH ALL ON BOARD!

There were definite details about the owner of the yacht, its description, its history, speed, etc., and the accident by which the catastrophe arrived, also a lengthy discussion of why the SOS did not bring neighboring ships in time, but Stephen Disston did not read them, neither did he turn over to the commercial pages at all that morning. When the nurse came back she found him lying back on his pillows with his eyes closed and the paper on his lap. She told him it was time for his orange juice and his morning nap and went to prepare the orange juice. But when Diana came in a moment later her father handed her the paper and pointed to the headlines.

"Diana, I want you to know that you were right and I was wrong," he said sadly. "It is terrible when God has to send tragedies like that to teach a man sense!"

"Oh, Father!" said Diana, looking at him with terrified eyes. "Don't say that! I was wrong! I know I was all wrong! Dear, *dear* Father! Can you ever forgive *me* for forcing a tragedy?"

"Dear, dear child!" said her father, laying his hand tenderly on her head as she knelt beside his bed. "I thank God that he saved *you*."

They did not talk further about the tragedy, and Diana watched her father all that day, dreading a reaction when he should realize the blow that had fallen upon him. But though he was quiet and grave, he did not seem greatly depressed.

"It is better so, little Di," he told her that night when she came to kiss him good night, and he recognized in her added tenderness an attempt at sympathy. "It is a terrible thing to have come but, Diana, if she had lived she would not have been happy with me. I found that out."

That evening she talked it over with Gordon.

"Didn't I tell you that God would work it out in His own way?" he said gently.

"Yes, work it out," said Diana, thoughtfully, sadly. "He's worked it out for *us*, of course, and made the way easy for Father and me. But I've been thinking about Helen. Gordon, I never thought about people that way before, until after I was saved. But I keep thinking that Jesus died to save Helen as much as He did to save me. God loved Helen and sent His Son to die in *her* place, too, and I'm quite sure she never thought anything about it. I'm quite sure she wasn't saved. Gordon, I keep thinking that I did wrong to go away. I should have stayed here even if it was hard. I don't know that I could have done anything about helping her to be saved, though, because I didn't know Christ as my Savior myself then, but there might have been a way. But now I'm practically sure she must be lost. And I can't think of her laughing to God! I don't think she laughed when that boat went down! I know she was frightened! Poor Helen!"

Gordon put his arms around her gently and drew her head to his shoulder.

"I know, little girl," he said, "but you can't tell what may have happened between her soul and God at the last minute, even in the twinkling of an eye. It does not take time to believe on Jesus Christ. I know it seems a terrible mystery, but we can safely trust our God to do right. You have seen your wrong and confessed it, now believe that it is forgiven and put away."

"Oh, do you think so?" she said, turning eager, longing eyes on her beloved. "Oh, I hope she is saved. I used to hate her, but now I hope she is saved. Since I have learned that Jesus loved everybody enough to die for them I can love her, too. And I don't want her to be lost!"

❀

Two days later was Diana's twenty-first birthday.

Gordon and Diana went together to Stephen Disston's room to tell him of their love for each other.

Mr. Disston was feeling decidedly better. The nurse had a surprise for them. Mr. Disston was sitting up in a chair beside the little bedside table, clothed in dressing gown and slippers, and smilingly ready to receive them.

And when Gordon had told him, Stephen Disston looked at them both lovingly and said, "There isn't a man in the world I know or have ever seen that I would as soon trust my girl with as you, Gordon MacCarroll. And it is not only that I trust you, I love you myself, for you have been like a son to me in my deepest trouble. And if it had not been for you perhaps I should never have had my little girl back again. I can truly receive you as my beloved son, and no 'in-law' about it."

Diana's eyes were starrier than ever as she looked toward her Gordon and touched to her lips a white rose bud, one of a new flock that he had brought her that morning for a birthday token.

They stayed on in sweet converse for an hour, and then as the nurse was heard to approach and Mr. Disston knew it was time for his morning rest he reached out his hand to a folded paper that lay on the table and handed it to Diana.

"Here, Diana, is a birthday gift from your own mother. She planned before she left us that you should be given this house with a sufficient fortune to keep it up and give you a good income all your life, on your twenty-first birthday."

Diana's cheeks grew pink with bewilderment and joy. "Oh,

Father! But I thought this house was yours."

"No, Diana! It never has been. Your mother's mother gave it to her as a wedding gift with the understanding that it was to be an ancestral home and passed to your children after your death."

Diana looked toward Gordon with sparkling eyes but was surprised to see a new gravity upon him.

"I did not know that I had presumed to ask the hand of an heiress," he said with troubled voice. "I thought you told me that you were bankrupt, Mr. Disston."

"And so I did," said Diana's father, with a sad little smile. "And so I was—although my lawyer told me yesterday that things are coming out better than we had feared and that it will not be as bad as that. I can pay all my debts and have a small income for myself. But this should make no difference to you, Gordon. Money should not enter into the scheme of things when two people love one another. It's only something for which to be thankful when God chooses to send more than you asked."

Then Diana lifted her head proudly. "Gordon, have you forgotten that you saved my life? Isn't that more than money? Don't I owe you all I have? Please don't feel that this house and money could put even a faintest cloud between us two."

She lifted her sweet eyes to his pleadingly, and he stooped and kissed her reverently.

"I won't, sweetheart. Only—well, I'm glad I didn't know it till afterward," he said with a merry twinkle.

Half an hour later as they came out from the sickroom where the nurse was bustling about with reprimand in her countenance, to hurry her patient back to bed for a rest, Gordon said, "What about your room over in that terrible place where I found you, dear? Oughtn't you to do something about that? You said you had some furniture there."

"Yes," said Diana, "I have some of my most precious possessions over there, my mother's picture for one, and I know Father would want that back in his room. I telephoned Mrs. Lundy last night that I would be over tomorrow to pay her and see about taking my things away. I telephoned the movers, too."

"Well, I'll fix it up to go with you. I think if I do a few things this afternoon while you are resting I can get off tomorrow and stay till you come away."

"Oh, you don't need to do that, Gordon," protested Diana. "I shan't have to do much. The movers are perfectly capable, and, you know, it isn't as if I didn't know my way around there," she laughed.

"That's all right, sweetheart; you may know your way around, but I'm not trusting you alone in that terrible neighborhood again. God has put the responsibility on me now, and I intend to care for you to the best of my ability. And how about taking Mrs. Lundy a box of bright flowers to go in her plush parlor just by way of farewell?"

"Lovely," said Diana, twinkling. "But they will have to be bright flowers, not spirit-flowers. The spirit-flowers are mine. My dear mystery flowers!"

White Orchids

Chapter 1

1930s

The light flashed red, and Camilla jammed on her brakes. The shabby little roadster came to a frightened, screeching stop just as a large truck came smashing down the crossroad, full power, striking the little car with a mighty impact, neatly removing a wheel and sending the car spinning straight into the air in a series of somersaults. It landed in the opposite ditch with crumpled fenders, broken bumpers, a twisted axle, and a fatal injury to its internal organs.

Behind the roadster a big shining car had stopped just in time, and a good-looking young man in evening dress and a rich fur-trimmed overcoat stepped out into the road and came over to see the wreck. He was tall, with a nice face, a firm mouth, and pleasant eyes. Just now they were filled with concern as he peered across the ditch into the darkness where the shabby little broken car lay upside down.

The driver of the truck lay across the road with a broken leg, only partly sobered.

Camilla lay huddled inside the little broken roadster, stunned from the shock, unable for the moment to cope with the happening.

"Anybody hurt?" asked the young man from the sedan in a voice that matched his fine face. The traffic cop was approaching excitedly from across the road.

"They sure oughtta be!" said the officer. "Truck driver is drunk as a fish, don't know what it's all about! Fool girl driving a junker! She tried to pass my light, didya see her? They all do. Girls think they can get by with anything!"

"But she stopped the instant the light went red. I was right behind her, and I saw. Didn't you see her? Didn't you hear her brakes?"

"Oh yeah? Sure! I heard! I hear everything! All the same, she was tryin' ta get by, an' now she's probably done for herself! Well, it happens every day, an' I gotta get her outta here. Traffic gettin' all balled up!"

He turned his flashlight onto the dark little crumpled car, and the young man caught a glimpse of a white face and a huddled slender form.

The door was jammed shut, and it was some seconds before their united efforts got it open. The stalwart policeman lifted out the girl with strong, accustomed movements. These things happen every day! Just another fool girl! He poised her on his arm and looked around for a place to lay her until the ambulance came.

"Put her in the backseat of my car!" said the young man graciously. "It's too cold and wet to lay her down by the roadside."

There was a genuineness about him that even the hurried traffic cop respected, and that in spite of the gardenia in his lapel.

"Aw right!" said the officer, with an eye already across the road, dealing with the drunken driver. He turned and took a step toward the big, beautiful car.

It was then Camilla opened her eyes and came to an understanding of things. Her eyes were large and dark, and her hair, which had fallen down around her face, was like fine spun gold.

"I'm—all right!" she murmured breathlessly. "Put me down, please—! I'll be all right! I can stand."

She slid to her feet, steadying herself with her hand on the officer's arm, and looked around her, dazed. She felt for her hat, which had fallen on the ground, and the young man from the sedan picked it up and handed it to her.

"Thank you," she said, taking an uncertain step toward her car, blinking her eyes to discern its dark, unshapely outlines in the ditch.

She looked at it dazedly and swayed, almost falling. The young man put out a steadying arm.

"I'm all right," she said again, straining her eyes toward her car. "If you'll just please—help me to get my car back—on the road—" She gasped out the words, struggling desperately now to stop trembling.

"Can't be done, lady!" said the policeman. "That car has traveled its last road! It ain't nothin' but a bunch o' junk now!"

Camilla's big troubled eyes looked in horror at the officer and then turned to the young man with an appeal in her young, frightened eyes that instantly enlisted his sympathy.

"Oh, but it's got to go!" she said desperately. "I've got to get on. I'm in a great hurry!"

"So I saw, lady, afore you decided ta put on yer brakes. Yer brakes are no good, anyhow. Guess ya ain't had yer car inspected yet, hev ya? Them brakes would never get by an inspector. Ef ya hadn't a ben in such a hurry, ya mighta been goin' on by this time instead o' bein' all but killed yerself, an' yer car dead entirely."

The officer eyed her coldly. Now that she wasn't dead it was his business to rub in the lesson she was learning.

"But it must go!" said Camilla frantically. "Please try to set it up for me! This is an emergency! I think it will go! It—always does—!" she urged hopefully. "It's old, but it always comes back again—and goes on!"

"Well, it won't never do that again, lady!" said the officer dryly. "What's yer name an' *ad*dress? I gotta have them before ya can go anywheres," he added, getting out a pencil and notebook.

"Oh, but I must go!" added Camilla. "I can't wait for *anything*! My mother is dying, and the doctor sent me to his office for some medicine that she needs at once!"

"Sorry, lady, but y'll havta go some other way. That car won't carry nobody nowhere! An' I gotta have yer *ad*dress 'fore I can let ya go."

"But what shall I do? I must get that medicine!"

Camilla was trembling from head to foot now, her lips trembling, too, and tears of which she was wholly unaware were streaming down her cheeks.

The young man from the sedan stepped closer and took off his hat deferentially.

"I will take you wherever you need to go," he said politely. "My car will travel as fast as any."

Camilla lifted terrified eyes to his face; liked his clean-cut jaw and the lean, pleasant line of his cheek; gave a comprehensive glance at the expensive car behind her; glanced back into his eyes; and knew she could trust him.

"But—it is a long way—" she said with shaking voice. "It must be almost seven miles from here! And—I have to get back again right away to the city with the medicine!"

"That's all right with me!" said the young man pleasantly. "Just step back here. Wouldn't you like to lie down in the backseat? You were pretty well shaken up, you know."

"No, I'm all right," she said eagerly. "Let's go quick! Every minute counts. My mother is dying. This medicine is the only hope!"

"I gotta have that *ad*dress, lady. I can't let ya go without that *ad*dress!" said the policeman insistently.

The young man watched her as she gave the address. Camilla Chrystie, and a street he did not know down in the lower part of the city. He studied her trim, slender young figure, her refined, delicate profile.

"I ought to do something about my car, but I mustn't stop now," said Camilla breathlessly as the stranger helped her into his car.

"Look after that car, will you, Officer, till I can get back and see to it?" said the young man, tossing a bill across to the officer behind Camilla's back.

When they were safely out of the thick of it he turned to Camilla, noting her strained, white face and the horrible anxiety that burned in her dark brown eyes.

"Now," said the young man pleasantly, "my name's Wainwright, Jeffrey Wainwright. Which way do we go?"

She gave him brief, crisp directions, as if she had learned them by heart.

"You're very kind. I ought not to let you, I'm afraid. I'm probably hindering you a lot. But—you know what your mother is to you. There is nobody like your mother, and"—with a quiver of her breath—"and—she's all I have in the world!"

"Of course!" said Wainwright with tender understanding in his tone, although he did not know. The conjured picture of his own mother showed her as he knew she probably was at that moment, elaborately gowned and playing bridge with a placid fierceness that was habitual to her. She had never been very close to him. He had known his nurses and his governesses, and later his tutors, better than his mother. Yet there was something wistful in his glance as he furtively watched the lovely girl by his side.

"We must get back to her as soon as possible," he added, speeding up his car.

"I can't ever thank you enough!" quavered Camilla.

"Don't try, please. I'm just glad to be doing something worthwhile for once."

"But I'm probably keeping you from some important engagement," she said, coming out of her own troubles for an instant and giving a quick comprehensive glance at his handsome face, his immaculate evening attire, and the white gardenia in his buttonhole.

Wainwright stared ahead for an instant silently, then answered her deliberately, thoughtfully. "No, I don't think it was important. In fact, it wasn't really an engagement at all, and I shouldn't be surprised if it turns out to be a good thing that you have kept me from it!"

Camilla stared at him, perplexed, faintly perceiving that there were problems and crises in other lives as well as her own.

"I am sure," she said contritely, "that I am taking you far out of your way."

"On the contrary," said Wainwright, "you are taking me in exactly the direction I was thinking of going before I saw your car."

"Oh," moaned Camilla, "but you are having to take me away back again!"

"But you see, my way leads back also," smiled the young man playfully, hoping to relieve the girl's evident strain. "And you know, it is odd, but somehow since decisions about the evening are taken out of my hands for a time, I am strangely relieved. I wasn't at all certain about what I ought to do before, but now I am. And I don't think I ever before had a chance to help save somebody's life. I somehow think we're going to win out, don't you?"

The girl's eyes in her white face were startling as they looked at him through the darkness.

"Oh, I hope—! I—I've been praying—all the way!"

Wainwright gave her a sudden quick glance.

"Well, I've never done much praying myself," he said almost embarrassed, "but I'll drive and you pray! Perhaps it'll take them both. But we are out to win. Let's set our minds to that. Now, is this were we turn?"

They drove on silently for some distance, sitting alertly, watching the road. Wainwright gave her a furtive glance now and then.

"Why don't you lean back and relax?" he asked suddenly. "You've had a shock, and you need to rest."

But Camilla remained tense.

"Oh, I can't rest now," she said with a catch in her breath like a suppressed sob. "I must get back to Mother!"

"But we'll get back just as quickly if you relax, you know," he reminded her sympathetically. "It seems hard that you should have had to come away at such a time. I can't understand how the doctor allowed you to do it! There surely must have been someone else to go. I should think he would have gone himself or sent a special messenger."

"He couldn't," said Camilla, lifting her strained face to his. "He couldn't leave my mother. And there wasn't anybody else who could be trusted to go. You see, his office is locked, and there was nobody at home to find the medicine and the instruments he wanted. He had to tell me exactly how to find everything he wanted. He is a very wonderful doctor. He saved my mother's life once before, you see. He ought to have been called sooner. She wouldn't let me send for him at first. She thought she was soon going to be better, and she felt we ought not to get in his debt again. He has always been so kind."

Wainwright considered that. There were people in the world then, well-educated, cultured people, who couldn't afford a doctor when they were desperately ill!

"But there surely must have been somebody else in the house he could have trusted without taking you away from your mother when she was so ill," he protested.

"No, there wasn't anybody in the house but a woman who rooms on the floor above us. She's staying there to help the doctor if he needs anything while I am gone. She can bring hot water and answer the telephone if I have to call him."

There was desperation in the girl's voice again, and he pressed harder on the gas pedal and drove fast, but he could see her white eyes watching every bit of the way.

"This is the street!" she announced at last. "It's in the middle of the next block, the fourth house on the right-hand side."

"But there's no light in the house!" said Wainwright as they drew up to the curb. "Is there nobody there at all?"

"No," said Camilla breathlessly, "the doctor's assistant won't be back until midnight, and his family is away in the south for a few weeks."

"Well, you're not going in there alone, that's certain!" said Wainwright in a firm voice, as if he had been used to protecting this girl for years.

But Camilla was not waiting for protection. Before the car had fully come to a halt she was out, fairly flying up the steps of the house, and was fitting a key into the lock of the door. As Wainwright followed her, he was relieved to see a dignified bronze sign on the house. The girl hadn't made a mistake in the house, then. It was a doctor's office.

Camilla's excited fingers had just succeeded in getting the key into the keyhole as he arrived, and putting his hand over hers, he turned the key and threw open the door.

"The switch is at the right hand!" said Camilla crisply. "The first three buttons he said would light the hall and offices."

Wainwright found the switch and instantly a spacious hall and doors to the left appeared, and Camilla drew a free breath.

"It's all right!" she said eagerly. "I was afraid I might have made a mistake in the house or something. But there's his wife's picture on the desk and his little girl and boy on the wall. And there's the package on his desk where he said it would be. You see, it's some special medicine he had sent away for that might have come after he left this morning. He wasn't quite sure it had arrived."

Her voice choked with excitement, and Wainwright looked at her, for the first time seeing her face clearly by the bright light and realizing that she was lovely.

"Is that all you had to get?" he asked, giving a quick interested glance around the office that gave so many evidences of culture and refinement.

"No," said Camilla, "there's a leather case, a black leather case, on the desk in the back room or perhaps on the floor by the desk. I'm to bring that. And a big bottle on the highest shelf of the cabinet in the other room. If it isn't there it may have been put on the inner closet shelf. He may have to be with Mother all night and not have time to get back to his office before he goes to an operation."

There was a quick catch in her breath at the thought of the possibilities the night might bring forth, but she controlled herself bravely.

They found the bottle and the case without any trouble.

"Now, do we go?" asked Wainwright.

"No," said Camilla, "I'm to call up first, to make sure there is nothing else he needs."

Her eyes grew suddenly dark with anxiety, and her hand trembled as she reached for the telephone.

Wainwright watched her again with admiration. The delicate flush that had been on her face as she hunted for the bottle and case had drained away, and her face was white with anguish again as she waited for the doctor's voice.

"It's Camilla, Dr. Willis," she said with that catch like a sob in her voice again. "How is she?"

Wainwright, as he stood near her, could hear the quiet voice of the doctor.

"No worse, Camilla. I think her pulse is a trifle steadier. Did you find everything?"

"Yes, everything."

"Well, hurry back. I hate to think of you driving all that way and going into an empty house alone!"

"But I'm not alone," said Camilla shyly, with the shadow of a smile on her lips. "I found a—a kind friend on the way who came with me!" Her eyes sought Wainwright's gratefully. He smiled back at her, and somehow comradeship seemed suddenly to be cemented between them. It was so odd! Two strangers who never expected to meet again after that evening and yet they seemed somehow well acquainted all at once.

When they had turned out the lights and locked the door, Wainwright drew her arm through his possessive, comforting grasp as they walked back to the car.

When he put her into the car she sat back with a breath of relief.

"She's no worse!" she said, looking up at him radiantly as he took the wheel again, and now that he knew how she really looked in the light, it seemed a lovely glimpse of her inner self.

"Isn't that great!" he breathed fervently in almost the same tone of rejoicing she had used. Being glad with someone gave him a new thrill. He had seldom been called upon to experience unselfish joy. In his world you got and you gave mostly for your own pleasure. Now it seemed that he was touching deeper, more vital matters. Sin and danger and trifling with doom could give thrills. He had hovered near enough to each one to understand. But this was new and sweet. He looked at her almost tenderly through the darkness, and then he laid his hand gently for just an instant over her small, gloved one.

"I'm so glad for you!" he said gravely.

"Thank you," she said brightly. "You've been just wonderful! I don't know how I should have gone through this awful evening without you."

Then she was silent a minute, thoughtful.

"Was that all true, what the policeman said about my car?" she asked presently. There was a hint of anxiety in her voice, yet her manner was strong, controlled, practical, ready to accept the worst quietly.

"Well, it's hard to say exactly," he answered with a quick reserve in his voice. "It did look rather badly beaten up, didn't it? But usually a good mechanic can do something with almost any car, you know." He tried to say it cheerfully, although his better sense told him that the little car was beyond help. "Suppose we wait for daylight and expert advice before we try to think about it."

Camilla sighed. "Yes, but expert advice costs a great deal, and I simply couldn't afford anything just now, I'm afraid. I shall want to use every cent to make Mother comfortable."

"Of course!" he seconded her heartily. "But your insurance will cover all that, you know. You had insurance, of course, didn't you?"

"No," said Camilla sadly. "I couldn't. I bought the car for fifty dollars, and it took all I had saved to get the licenses and one secondhand tire it needed." She ended with a brave little attempt at a laugh.

He was appalled at such details, but he did not let her know it. "Oh well, it will be up to the owner of the truck, anyway," he said with more assurance than he felt. "Sometimes, of course, they try to slide out of such moral obligations, but you let me handle this. I'll make it a point to call upon him tomorrow and put the thing before him in the right light. Don't you worry."

"Oh, but I couldn't let you do anything more!" said Camilla in a frightened voice. "You have already done more than any stranger could possibly be expected to do."

"Is that the way you rate me?" he said reproachfully with a twinkle in his voice. "Only a stranger, after we've gone on an errand like this? I thought we were friends now."

Camilla gave him another look in the darkness, of mingled pleasure and surprise.

"You have certainly taken more trouble than any friend I have would have taken," she said earnestly. "The truth is, I haven't many friends in this city. We haven't been here long, only about nine months. I haven't had time to make friends."

"Then you'll let me count as a friend?" he asked gravely. "At least until your mother gets well and you have time to look me over?"

He smiled down at her through the darkness, and she felt a comforting sense of being taken care of in a sort of brotherly way.

"You certainly do not need any special looking over," said Camilla gravely, "after the way you have befriended me tonight."

There was a weary strain in her tone that made him look anxiously at her. It occurred to him that perhaps she had been more hurt in the collision than she would own.

"Are you sure you are all right?" he asked earnestly.

"Oh yes," she said, rousing again and putting on that forced attention she had worn since they started on their errand.

"Well, we'll get you home as quickly as possible," he said, and he began to question her as to where her street was located.

He purposely avoided the scene of the accident and took a shortcut, for fortunately, he know the city well. He tried to talk cheerfully as he furtively watched her droop in her corner. It was all too evident that she had been keeping up on her nerve, and now that her errand was almost completed she was beginning to feel the reaction.

It was with great relief that he presently drew up at the house she indicated and helped her out, following her with the case and bottle. She took the little package of medicine and fairly flew up the steps and into the house.

Chapter 2

It was a small, high, old-fashioned brick house with white marble steps of a long-ago vintage, in an unfashionable quarter of the city, invaded now by business on every hand. The other houses on either side and across from it bore signs in the windows: VACANCIES, APARTMENTS TO LET, BOARDING. It was a sordid, dreary street. But Wainwright did not wait to examine the surroundings. He hurried into the house, finding a strange anxiety at his own heart for the sick mother whom he had never seen.

The hall was of the dark, narrow type with steep stairs mounting straight up to a darker hall above. It seemed gloomy beyond description. But at the right, one half of a double door stood open, and there the gloom ceased, for the room into which it opened was surprisingly cozy and homelike. Soft lamplight, rosily shaded, played over some handsome pieces of old furniture and a good picture or two on the walls. A soft-toned rug covered the floor. There was even a speck of a fireplace with a log smoldering flickeringly and an easy chair placed beside it. And there were low bookshelves running across the room on either side of the fireplace and bits of good bric-a-brac here and there on the top shelf. It looked a pleasant place to live.

Between the front windows was a long old-fashioned mirror in a quaint gilt frame, and in that he saw reflected the room beyond, which in the parlance of other days would have been called a back parlor.

The double doors between the rooms were open, and he caught a glimpse of a wide old-fashioned bed, too large for the room, and a delicate face on the pillow, framed in silver-white hair. It was a face strangely sweet and filled with a great peace. He held his breath. Was she dead already? He could see Camilla touching her lips to the white brow with a caress as soft as a breath and then dropping quietly to her knees beside the bed. The doctor stood there with his back to the door, his hand on the frail wrist of the sick woman.

Wainwright hesitated in the hall, wondering whether it would be intrusion to step inside the front room and put down the doctor's case and bottle.

Then the doctor turned and saw him, his quick eye noting what he carried, and he stepped quietly out into the hall.

"What more can I do here?" asked Wainwright in a low tone, handing over the doctor's case. "I'm at your service as long as I can help."

The doctor gave him a keen glance.

"Thank you," he said. "I'll be glad to accept that offer. We need a nurse at once. Could you go and bring her? I don't want Camilla to leave her mother again. I can't tell how things are coming out yet. Besides, that woman who rooms upstairs is so incapable, she can't even boil water."

"I'll go," said Wainwright quickly. "Have you one in mind, or do I hunt one up?"

"Miss York," said the doctor briefly. "I phoned. She's free.

She'll be ready when you get there. Here's the address."

"All right," said Wainwright, taking the slip of paper the doctor handed him. "But before I go I must tell you, for I'm afraid Miss Chrystie won't think of it— You'd better look her over a little. She's been in a bad accident. Her car was all smashed up. She's very brave. She insists she's all right, but she's just keeping up on her nerve."

The doctor gave him a quick look.

"You don't say!" he exclaimed. "I somehow felt I ought not to let her go alone."

"She didn't get far alone," said the young man. "I happened along and saw it all. We picked her up for dead, but she snapped out of it wonderfully and was only anxious to get on with her errand. I'm afraid, though, that she's about all in, with the shock and anxiety together."

He gave the details briefly and then went out after the nurse.

It was not a long trip, and the nurse was waiting when he reached her lodgings, so they were soon back at the house again.

Camilla was lying on the couch in the front room when they entered the house; her eyes were closed and her face was wan and white. But her eyes flew open as they came in, and she sat up at once.

Wainwright went toward her and gently pushed her back to the pillow again.

"Please!" he said in a whisper. "You'll need your strength, you know. You must save yourself. Here's Miss York. She'll attend to everything. And I'm here to help her as long as I'm needed. I'm a friend tonight, you know." And his face lit up with a sweet, gentle smile. Camilla felt again that sense of being protected and cared for in a peculiar way.

"But I must get a room ready for her," said Camilla anxiously as she yielded to his persuasive hand and lay still on her pillow.

"I can do that," asserted Wainwright firmly, as though he were quite accustomed to getting rooms ready for people. "What you need is a little rest or there'll be two patients here instead of one. That wouldn't be so good, you know."

He smiled again with a flash of his perfect teeth, and she succumbed.

"But you don't know where things are," said Camilla weakly, with a worried pucker on her white brow.

"I can learn, can't I? Where were you planning to put her?"

"Oh, I don't know," said Camilla in a troubled voice. "She'll have to have the dining room, I suppose. We'll eat in the kitchen. I wasn't planning. I didn't know she was coming. Oh, why did you bring her here? She will be so crowded here! We really haven't a need for a nurse now I am back."

"It was the doctor's orders. I only went after her," said Wainwright serenely. "He had already phoned for her before we got back. He thought you ought not to be alone when he has to leave. He said there ought to be someone here who knows what to do in an emergency."

"Oh!" said Camilla with a little sharp breath like a moan, paling at the word *emergency.*

"Of course, there may not be any emergency. We hope there won't be," went on Wainwright with a calm, steady voice and another quieting smile, "but it is always best to provide against one, you know. Now, could you just tell me what needs doing and where to find things? You must promise to lie still and wait till I come for instructions and not get up and run around, or I'll have to lock you in here till we have things in order."

There was a twinkle in his eye as he said it, but somehow his firm chin looked as if he really might do it if he were disobeyed. Camilla resigned herself, for the moment at least.

"Well, there's a cot in the third-story back storeroom. There's an eiderdown quilt there and two blankets. A pillow, too."

She glanced at his immaculate evening attire and gave a little moan.

"Oh, you oughtn't to be doing things like that! Not with that beautiful coat on!" She put her hands together with a little helpless motion. "Oh, please! It distresses me!"

"My coat will come off," said Wainwright, with a grin, and quickly whipped off, first his handsome overcoat, then his formal evening coat.

She had to smile, he was so like a nice big boy, oblivious to the whiteness of his shirt front.

"Now," he said, "that's better! Keep that expression on till I get back. I'm all set for the storeroom on the third floor!"

The words were very low. They did not penetrate to the sickroom, although the door was open. Turning swiftly, he went up the stairs with an incredibly soft tread. Even the creaky stairs were unbelievably silent under his careful strides. It was not long before he was moving down again, bearing a light cot under one arm and an eiderdown quilt in the other.

She was standing in the hall when he returned, holding clean sheets, blankets, and a pillow in a case, which she had taken from the shelves in the hall closet. She motioned him to follow her to the dining room and walked lightly as a feather.

He followed her quietly, but when he had put down the cot and taken the bedclothing from her, laying it on the table, he stopped and picked her up in his arms, as if she had been a blanket, and bore her back to the couch in the front room.

"You are a naughty child!" he whispered. "You must be good, or I shall be forced to stay here and hold you down."

She looked up and saw a pleasant grin upon his face, but there was something in his eyes and the firm mouth that made her lie back again and relax.

"I'm really quite all right," she protested.

He stopped and whispered softly in her ear.

"If you will not do it for yourself, won't you do it for her sake?" He motioned with his head toward the sickroom.

This had an instant effect in the look of fear that came into her eyes. Then after an instant's quiet she said, "If you'll just let me get up and make that bed, then I can rest."

"I can make beds!" he declared earnestly. "I went to military school and learned how!" He grinned, and she succumbed.

He slipped off his shoes and disappeared into the dining room. She heard soft little swishing sounds of a hand on the smooth sheets, but for the most part it was very still. Only the creak of a board in the floor now and then. She raised her head and tried to look through her mother's room into the dining room to the left. She could see the foot of the cot and a hand tucking the blanket in with military precision, a nice, white, well-groomed hand that did not look as if it had made up a bed in many a day. Then she heard soft footsteps and lay down quickly lest he would return and find her disobeying orders.

The doctor was speaking to the nurse in low professional growls. The nurse on her rubber-shod feet went swiftly to the kitchen. Camilla could hear running water. Wainwright had gone out into the kitchen. She could hear him talking softly to the nurse. Then the doctor went out and the nurse came back. Camilla lay there staring up at the ceiling, glancing now and then into the dimness of her mother's room, longing to be in there watching the doctor's face to know just what he was thinking at every passing minute about the possibilities of fear or hope.

Wainwright came back presently. His hair was tossed up over his forehead and again she thought how much he looked like a nice boy.

He stopped and murmured to her like a friend of years. "I'm going out to the drugstore for something the doctor wants. I won't be gone long. I'll phone about your car and see that it's cared for. The doctor wants you to lie still unless he calls you. He says you must rest so you can help the nurse when he has to go. I'll be back very soon and do anything that's needed."

She tried to protest, but he stepped into his shoes, swung on his beautiful overcoat over his vest, and was gone before she could do so. She lay there, still staring at the empty doorway where he had stood for an instant before he closed the front door so carefully after him. Then she turned her gaze back to the room, to the handsome evening coat that lay slumped across a chair as if it were perfectly at home. She thought of the strange happenings of the evening, like a dream, with a great fear standing grimly in the background and Wainwright like a strong angel dominating everything. She thought how strange it was for his coat to be lying there across their shabby little armchair; he a stranger from another world than theirs! How kind he was! How like a tried friend! And he was an absolute stranger. She didn't know a thing about him except his name, a name she had never heard before! What would her mother say to it all? Would she live to know about it?

Then fear came back and held her heart again until it quivered, and she prayed an agonized, wordless prayer.

She must have closed her eyes while she prayed, for when she opened them again it was with a sense of a strong breath of air from outdoors having blown in her face. The light was turned out in the front room where she lay, and it seemed a long time afterward. But when she looked in a fright toward her mother's room she could see the nurse coming with a glass in her hand, and then she sensed Wainwright standing near her looking down at her. Their eyes met in the dimness of the room, and he smiled. He had a kind look in his eyes, and he stooped over her and put two fingers gently on her wrist for a moment.

"Oh yes." She stirred softly and tried to rise. "I am quite rested now! I must go to Mother! And you should go home and get some sleep. You have been so good!"

He shook his head and stooped to speak in her ear. "Your mother is resting comfortably now. The doctor thinks there has been a shade of improvement. I'm staying awhile out there in the hall. If you want me, just give a soft little cough and I'll come. And don't worry about your car. They're taking care of it. It's gone to a garage."

He drifted away like one of the shadows in the room. She stared around her and wondered if he, too, had been a dream. Then she noticed the big chair was gone and his evening coat was slung across the top of the piano as if it had been a day laborer's coat. Still marveling, between wakefulness and sleeping, she fell asleep. She did not even hear the milk wagons when they began their rounds nor the bread wagons a little later when they went *clop, clop, clopping* down the icy street. It was broad daylight when she woke with a start and heard the water running in the kitchen sink. She threw aside the coverings and got up quickly, thoroughly awake now and alive to duty and anxiety.

She hurried out into the hall softly with a fearsome glance toward her mother's room where the shades were drawn, keeping out the brightness of the morning. She could not see into the dim darkness of the room; her eyes were not yet accustomed to the light of day.

She wondered as she crossed the room how her shoes came to be off and where they were, and then she came into the dimness of the hall and saw Wainwright slumped down in the old Morris chair, his overcoat around him and his hair tossed back in disorder. He was asleep, and his face looked white and tired and boyish. He had stayed all night! How wonderful! But what an obligation to have to a stranger!

But before she could pass him, he had roused and caught her hand as she would have gone by.

"Good morning!" he whispered. "Are you all right, Camilla?" He did not seem to speak her name as if he felt himself a stranger.

She caught her breath softly.

"I'm fine," she answered, "but—my mother! How is she? Oh,

I *shouldn't* have gone to sleep!"

"She's better!" he said with a light of eagerness in his eyes almost as if she might have been *his* mother. "Sleep was just what you should have done. Come out in the kitchen where we can talk."

He took her hand and led her through the dining room, and she did not realize that they were walking hand in hand until they came sharply upon the nurse washing a cup and plate. But she did not seem to think it strange. She said good morning in a businesslike tone and then, "Well, your mother is better, Miss Chrystie!"

"Oh!" Camilla caught her breath and closed her eyes for an instant, a light coming into her face. "Could I go to her?"

"No, she's sleeping quite naturally now, and the doctor said she shouldn't be disturbed. He's gone to another operation, and he'll be back again in about two hours to see how we're getting on."

"Oh, I should have been here to get him some breakfast!" said Camilla, aghast.

"Oh no you shouldn't!" said the nurse capably. "I made him some coffee and toast and scrambled him some eggs. Now you can get yourself and Mr. Wainwright some breakfast. I've had all I want. Mr. Wainwright has been invaluable. I don't know what we should have done without him."

Camilla turned to Wainwright with gratitude and apology in her eyes. "Oh, how terrible for me to sleep through everything and you, a stranger, doing it all."

Wainwright ran his fingers through his hair and turned around on her sharply, blinking at her through big, blue, pleasant eyes.

"What did you say I was, young lady?" he asked, catching hold of her wrists and looking her straight in the eyes.

Camilla, her heart suddenly light, looked up with a shamedly sweet smile on her white young face.

"I said you were a—*friend*," she said shyly.

He gave her hand a quick warm clasp.

"Thank you for those kind words!" he said. "Remember, I'm a young fellow taking his tests and mighty anxious to pass muster."

Then he let her go, but not without another look that seemed somehow to cement a friendship that she knew no way to prevent.

It was when they were sitting across from each other at the white enameled kitchen table eating scrambled eggs and drinking coffee together cozily that she summoned words again to protest gratefully all he had done for her and to deplore the fact that he had been up all night.

"This isn't the first time I've eaten in a kitchen at an early hour in the morning," he said gravely. "I've often danced all night and ended up with scrambled eggs in the morning, but I can't say they ever tasted so good as these do. And I can tell you truly that I've had more satisfaction out of this night than I ever had out of any of those other nights. I'm so very glad your mother is better!"

She looked at him, startled as his words gave her evidence of even more differences between them than she had envisioned. Yes, of course he would belong to a world like that! A fashionable world, with all it stood for today! His coat might have told her that, and the gardenia in his buttonhole. There was a strange little uneasy twinge as she took that in and put it away for future thought.

And yet, it was all the more wonderful that he had stayed and been so fine and worked so hard when he came of an entirely different world! She would not let his kindness and friendship for that one night be spoiled or discounted in the least by any differences there might be in their worlds. Whatever he was or had been or was to be, he had been great last night, and had a right to be called a friend.

He even helped her wipe their few dishes, as if he had been

her playmate from childhood. She knew it couldn't last, of course. It would be over like a dream—with this difference: it was a dream that she never would forget.

When he went away at last, after the doctor had returned and pronounced the mother out of immediate danger, he had his overcoat well buttoned up to hide his evening attire. But he came back immediately from his car with a big, long, white box in his hand and a nice grin on his face.

Camilla, from the window, had been watching him away and hurried to the door as she saw him return.

"Won't you relieve me of these flowers?" he asked, with a funny, wry smile. "The occasion for them is past, and I wouldn't know how to dispose of them. Perhaps your mother will enjoy them."

"Oh," said Camilla, with a conscience-stricken look. "I've kept you from so much!" And then as the box was put in her hands she said, "And somebody has been missing you, and missing these, and wondering! I do hope you telephoned and explained."

She lifted her eyes and saw a strange, puzzled look on his face.

"No," he said thoughtfully, "I didn't explain. I don't know that I shall. And I wasn't sure that I was going to use those flowers when I bought them. I think it was a good thing that I didn't!"

Then with a smile he was gone.

Camilla watched his car glide out from the curb where it had stood through the night, saw his lifted hand in adieu, and turned back to the house with wonder in her eyes and a thoughtful countenance. She went out to the kitchen with the big box to be alone and think this out.

But when she opened the box there were large white orchids! And suddenly her problem was complicated by the vision of a third person, the girl for whom these strange white flowers had been bought! What was she? Who was she? His friend? His sweetheart? His wife perhaps!

The distance between her world and the world of the stranger who had befriended her in her need was widening fast, and daylight was upon her. There was no more time for dreams.

Then suddenly the nurse called her, and she left the white flowers in water hastily drawn in the bread bowl and went to meet the doctor.

White orchids in a yellow bread bowl!

Chapter 3

Jeffrey Wainwright drove out into the morning, back into the commonplace of his life, and remembered what had happened a little more than fifteen hours ago, before the accident.

He had been driving away from Stephanie Varrell's apartment to which he had just brought her home from a matinee they had been attending that afternoon, and as he turned the corner and glanced back down the street, something in the swing of a figure approaching from the other direction brought a familiar wrath to his consciousness. Was that his old enemy, Myles Meredith? It certainly was. No other man could walk like that, with that insolent swagger, described in Jeffrey Wainwright's imaginative language as "walking delicately." How he despised him! Not because he was, in a way, a rival for Stephanie Varrell's smiles, for Wainwright had an honest, fair mind, and liked to play the game squarely and take his medicine if things didn't go his way. But the man was a sneak, a snake in disguise, a double-crosser, an unprincipled cad. In fact, there wasn't a word in Wainwright's vocabulary of despicable adjectives that he hadn't at some time used in reference to Meredith, either in his own mind or to Stephanie, and once to Meredith himself.

Wainwright was on his way home to dress for a dinner Stephanie was giving that night, and he had supposed himself to be in a hurry, but he brought his car to an abrupt stop on the crossing and watched Myles Meredith swing on affectedly down the street to the door of the big apartment house, which sheltered Stephanie's charming abode, and enter.

For a second he sat there, staring at the empty space on the sidewalk that Meredith had just vacated. Then he became aware of an automobile horn blowing viciously just behind him and a traffic officer's whistle not far away, and he started his car with a sudden jerk that sent it shooting down the street at a frantic pace. His usually nice, pleasant face was a study in frowns.

What was this villain doing here? He had supposed him to be on his way to Europe. He was to have sailed last Friday! Sneak! Had he dared to return after the affair of last week? And would Stephanie receive him, knowing he had been criminally involved with a girl of notorious character? Fool he had been, that he had not stayed around to watch if she sent him away. If Stephanie let him hang around her after what had happened, he was done with her!

And yet, she was the girl he had about decided to marry!

Well, he must get this thing cleared up before he went any further! He would go back and find out if Meredith was there, and if so, he would demand that Stephanie choose between them.

He was so angry that he turned corners on two wheels and pulled up speedily before the big apartment house again.

There was no sign of Meredith in either direction. He had not had time as yet to get far away. Likely he was just coming down in the elevator, if Stephanie had refused to see him. But he found himself doubting whether Stephanie would do that. Stephanie loved to trifle with dangerous things.

He decided to stay there for a few minutes and wait for Meredith. This was as good a time as any for a showdown. He could dress quickly afterward. What matter if he was late when so important a circumstance was in the balance?

So he drew up to the curb and waited, with his frowning gaze fixed upon the entrance from which he had just a few minutes ago come out so happily.

Perhaps it was the thought of his own evening garb, which he was expecting to assume hastily, that recalled the glimmer of white shirt front between the richly furred lapels of Myles Meredith's top coat. Myles Meredith, then, was dressed for the evening and had been unfastening the outer coat as he entered the apartment house door, as if he was sure of an entrance and was going in to stay.

Could it be possible that Myles Meredith was invited to Stephanie's dinner? Or had even dared to call her up and ask if he might call? Either possibility was an insult to Stephanie, whom Jeffrey Wainwright wanted with all his heart to respect. Surely, surely, after all she knew, after all she had promised him, Stephanie would not involve herself again with that contemptible creature!

He waited for ten long minutes, and still there was no sign of Meredith. Then he went into the office of the apartment house, sought out a booth, and telephoned up to Stephanie's apartment.

He was told that Miss Varrell was busy just now and not able to come to the telephone. He might leave a message or call later, but at his insistence, he finally heard her slow drawl mingled with annoyance.

"For sweet pity's sake, Jeff, what can be the matter with you? You haven't been away from here ten minutes. You can't have reached home yet. Have you been in a smash-up or anything?"

Wainwright's tone was hard and insistent as he demanded to

know: "Is Meredith there with you, Stephanie?"

There was an instant's silence. Evidently she had not expected that question. Her voice was vexed as she replied.

"Why in the world should you ask that, Jeff?" She was stalling for time to think. He could feel her hesitation over the wire.

"Because I saw him going in there just as I turned the corner!" said Wainwright. There was a grim indignation in his tone.

"Well," said Stephanie, adopting her haughtiest tones full of resentment, "and suppose he is? What is that to you? Haven't I a right to have anyone call at my apartment? Is it your business to spy on me?"

"You told me that Meredith sailed for Europe last Friday!" he accused her.

"Well, so he did. At least he went on board the ship, but he found a message delaying him another week. Really, Jeff, you are most trying. You promised me that you would go home and dress and get back as soon as possible. Please hurry! You'll delay everything if you don't get back when I asked you."

"Is that bounder going to be at your dinner, Stephanie?" The grim voice was not to be placated.

"Jeff, you are simply *impossible*! What right have you to hold up my dinner while you ask tiresome questions?"

"The right of a man who has asked you to marry him and who won't do it again until he knows where he stands."

"That's not enough to make you the censor of my list of dinner guests!" she said angrily. "I invite whom I will to my apartment. We're not married yet, remember. The question is merely under consideration. I'm sure you're not doing much just now to help your side of the case."

"Your list of dinner guests!" repeated Wainwright thoughtfully, ignoring her last remark. "Then he is an invited guest! Not a chance, unexpected caller! Then you knew this afternoon that he was coming?" His voice was accusatory, condemning.

"Well, suppose I did?" said the woman, vexed. "What is that to you?"

"A good deal!" said Wainwright. "I like to know how far I can trust my friends. Thanks for letting me know in time!"

"What do you mean 'in time,' Jeff? You certainly aren't going to stage a scene at my dinner, are you?"

"No," said Wainwright coldly with finality in his voice, "I shall not be there!"

"Infant!" she cried furiously. "Jealous infant—that's what you are! Just because poor Mylo was held up a day or two, you are fussing. I declare, I didn't know you were such a child!"

"This is not a matter of jealousy, Stephanie! You know my reasons. You know he is not fit to be around you. You know what he is, and yet you ask him to one of your most intimate affairs!"

"Oh, nonsense! Don't be so extravagant in your denunciation! How hard men are on one another! Of course Mylo isn't an angel, but I like him. I always have. I asked him. Yes, I asked him because he is good company. I like to have him around. It doesn't matter to me what he has done, nor what he is. I enjoy an evening in his company."

"Then you'll not mind dispensing with mine, of course!" said Wainwright.

"Oh, you child, you!" mocked the girl with a forced laugh. "You know you haven't the slightest intention of staying away. You know you would come just out of curiosity, if for nothing else, to see what Myles Meredith is up to next. Go home, Jeff darling, as fast as you can, get dressed, and hurry back. Don't let's have any more child's play about it. You're going to sit beside me, you know." Her tone was low and insinuating, as if she wished to guard it from being heard by a possible listener. "And remember"—there was intimate caressing in the tone now, like patting a small boy on the back after reproof—"remember, white orchids, darling!"

As Jeffrey Wainwright reviewed that conversation on the way through the next morning's traffic, it seemed to him that he was reading it or dreaming it about someone else. It couldn't be that he, Jeffrey Wainwright, had been sap enough after that, knowing that Myles Meredith was there with her, waiting for that dinner, to go on home and get dressed and actually plan to go back to that dinner.

Oh, he remembered that he was undecided about it. He had raged within himself that he wouldn't go a step, that she deserved to be let severely alone until she came around and saw how she was treating him, decided to do half a dozen different things instead of going to Stephanie Varrell's dinner.

But then he had reflected that that course would only please Meredith. It would only leave the coast clear for Meredith to play the lover to Stephanie. It would leave himself a prey to his angry imagination. He should at least be there and block the fellow's plans, sit at the feast and show his disapproval, courteously, of course, so that only his hostess should understand.

Yet even so, she would have triumphed! Had she not told him he would not stay away for anything? Had she not challenged him to stay away if he dared? The real way to show her would be to stay away, of course, and he would do it!

A dozen times he had changed his mind until he was ready to go. Nor did he hasten in his preparation. If he was late, it would not matter. It rather pleased him to keep her waiting. To make her think he was not coming.

No, he would not go, he told himself. Of course he would not go. He fairly despised himself for his hesitancy.

And after all that vacillating, he had gone and bought those white orchids.

"*Infant!*" Yes, infant! She had been right to call him that! In the clearness of the morning it seemed impossible that he should have been contemplating, even for a moment, going to that dinner with the man whom he despised and whom Stephanie not so long ago had promised to strike off her list of acquaintances.

Well, he had stayed away. Quite without his own planning. The matter had been taken out of his hands. Although he was dressed and ready and on his way with his white orchids in the backseat of his car, he had been stopped on the road and sent in an entirely different direction. And the strangest thing about it all was that he had not once thought about it the whole night through.

His mind went slowly back over his experiences since the shabby little car in front of him had suddenly stopped with screeching brakes that did not brake and the big gas truck had come roaring down upon it and sent it whirling in the air to roll over in the ditch.

He felt again that thrill of horror as he looked down into the crumpled little car and saw that white, unconscious face of the girl, certain that she must be dead. The thrill of relief when he found she was still alive; his overpowering pity for her when she turned that desperate look upon him and told him her mother was dying and she must go for the medicine.

As he looked back upon it all, he could not remember a single thought of wonder of what Stephanie thought about his absence or what Meredith was doing. By the light of day neither seemed to matter.

He had been close to vital matters. He had been watching and waiting all night while a battle between life and death went on, and for the time being, at least, life had been victorious. As he thought it over now, he wouldn't have missed that experience for all the dinners, no, nor for all the Stephanies in the world. The night seemed to have been a sort of eye-opener that had made a number of things plain to him. For one thing, he had seen life from another side, the side of suffering and unselfishness, sorrow and pain, and bravery. Beside it, even granting that Camilla and her little unconscious mother had not been interesting in themselves, his life of play, courting emotions of various sorts, seemed the merest trifling. Child's play, that was all.

Oh, he would come back to it, he knew. One smile from Stephanie would lure him as it always did these last two years; one frown would twist itself in his soul like a sword, and he would be under the same tyranny as before. Only, for this one time, matters had been overruled and taken out of his hands, and he had been a part of another world. Just now he wasn't anxious to get back to Stephanie. What she thought and felt did not seem so much to concern him as what he was going to be able to do about Camilla's poor little crumpled car.

He experienced a distinct satisfaction in the thought that whatever harm had been done by his absence last night was done already and beyond his power and that a few more hours could not make any difference. For once he had been saved from bowing to Stephanie's outrageous whims and fancies. For once he would see what would happen now that he had defied her. If she turned from him forever, well, it was not his fault, and there would be some peace at least in knowing that the tortuous problem was settled and over with. If he had to suffer afterward—well, he would have had to suffer one way or the other eventually, he supposed. At least he felt more self-respect this morning than he would have felt if he had gone to Stephanie's dinner in company with Myles Meredith.

Now that he had taken this step, unbeknownst to himself, now that the white orchids were in the safekeeping of another girl, a girl with clear, true eyes, a girl who was not out to play the game that most of womankind were playing, he might as well let things alone for a while, keep away from Stephanie, and just see what would come. He certainly would never have a better opportunity to test her. And if she wasn't true at heart—well, he didn't want her, did he? Even in spite of her glamour and her beauty, in spite of her poise and her smart dressing and her ability to thrill and amuse?

In the small watches of the night, while the son of one of the comparatively few multimillionaires who had not lost their millions in the depression had sat in a shabby Morris chair listening to the quiet movements of the nurse and the doctor in the sickroom and to the soft breathing of the exhausted girl in the front room, he had thought out a plan of action. It was one of the things that had kept him from thinking long of Stephanie and Meredith and his wasted white orchids.

It gradually became plain to his mind that this other girl, Camilla, would never let him fix up that car for her and pay for it himself. He realized that this plain little house with its shabby air of gentility had a pride of its own, and he began to suspect that that pride had even more self-respect and genuine honesty in it than even the vaunted pride of the House of Wainwright.

And yet, on the other hand, he saw with a new insight, gained from the experiences of the evening, that life for Camilla without that staunch little car was going to be 100 percent harder in the future than it had been in the past. And he knew by the dark circles under her tired eyes, by the whiteness of her face, and by the slenderness of her graceful body that it had been hard enough in the past without the deprivation of that little old friendly car that always got up and went on after every hard knock. He determined that that car must get up even this time and go on. Yes, if he had to learn how and repair it himself!

He didn't know how all this was to be accomplished, but he first determined that it should be and then worked it out in his mind. The truck driver with the broken leg must be made to help, not by money, perhaps, though it might take money to coerce him, but he must be made to own the truth, that the accident had been his fault.

So when morning came he hunted up his traffic policeman

and had an interview. Then he went to the hospital where the drunken truck driver with the broken leg had been taken.

The truck driver proved amenable to reason as expressed in dollars, and later Jeffrey sought the office of the company that employed him and discovered there a powerful acquaintance well disposed toward the family of Wainwright. A few words with his lawyer, a magic little paper for Camilla to sign, and the matter was arranged. He had been prepared to shoulder the thing himself, if necessary, only he had a strong feeling that it would be rather hard to put it over without making the keen-eyed girl suspicious, and he was sure she would never let him pay for having her car repaired. She would extract the knowledge of the exact sum from him somehow and pay it back through the years. So he was greatly relieved that the company had shouldered a goodly share of the expense and done it graciously, and he would not have to resort to deception. It was much the easier way, and he was a young man who preferred to be honest, all things being equal.

So he drove to the garage where he had ordered Camilla's car to be taken and had a long talk with the mechanic. It took a good deal of persuading, and a good deal of assurance, to make that honest mechanic admit that that little old battered, crumpled car could be renewed bit by bit in its entirety, using the one fender that remained intact, parts of the tired old engine, and the cushions—yes, the worn old cushions that would make it look like its old self again, yet supplying new parts enough to give renewed youth. Yes, the mechanic finally admitted, it would be possible, if one had unlimited money to spend and were fool enough to spend it that way. But he openly declared that no one would be fool enough for that.

Jeffrey Wainwright finally convinced the mechanic that he was that one and only fool in the world who was fool enough to want that little dead car brought to life and made to look like itself again, except for the "touching up," which an innocent driver would feel was absolutely necessary for a car that had been in a smash-up.

The mechanic, in wonder, finally folded away a bill of such denomination that he patted his pocket with awe to make sure it was real and agreed to go at the repairs that very afternoon.

"And now," said Jeffrey Wainwright to himself, "that's that, and I'd better get a bite to eat and then go back and tell her."

Of course, he could have telephoned, but somehow it seemed a trivial matter about which to cause the blatant ringing of that noisy little telephone so near the sickroom. And anyway, he had not stayed all night in the anxious household without being eager to learn if all was going as well as when he left.

So he took a quick lunch at an unfamiliar counter, not in the least like the places where his fastidious soul delighted to dine, and drove back to the shabby brick house on Vesey Street.

Camilla was in the kitchen making broth, and there was a flush on her cheeks and a light of hope in her eyes.

"She's better!" she greeted Jeffrey Wainwright as he came softly in like an old friend without waiting to knock, just tried the door and tiptoed in until he found her.

"Oh, that's good!" he said, laying a hand each side of her two that she had clasped in her eagerness and looking into her tired, sweet eyes. For just an instant he felt as if he were going to lean over and kiss her eager trembling lips, and then suddenly he knew he mustn't. Knew quite well that would spoil it all, this lovely impersonal friendship that had only existed a day. Knew also that there were other things as well as her attitude toward such a thing that should restrain him, and he took his hands down gently from hers, deciding he was a bit lightheaded from staying up all night.

"Yes, the doctor says it is wonderful. He says she reacted marvelously to that medicine that we brought. He says if she had been without it much longer he couldn't have answered for the consequences. And oh, if it hadn't been for you I would never have been able to get it here in time! I shall never get done thanking you!"

His glance melted into her own eager one, and he felt a warm glow around his heart. He couldn't at the time recall that he had ever before in his life done anything that was worth such thanks. It was good! Better than all the banter of his frivolous playtime world.

Then presently he told her about the car and watched a soft pink flush of relief steal up into her cheeks and a glow of contentment into her eyes.

"Oh, God has been very good to me!" she breathed softly. "I have been wondering all day how I was going to get along without that poor little old car. I never would have been able to pay even for a very little repair. And I'm quite sure there must have been a lot to do on it. As I remember it lying down there in the ditch, it seems to me now that it must have needed a lot. I've been remembering what that policeman said about it and trying to make up my mind that I would have to get along without it. You must have waved a magic wand! And to think it's going to be repaired without cost! It seems too good to be true!"

The glow in her eyes fully repaid Wainwright for all the trouble he had taken that morning. He hung around and tried to find something else he might do to help, but there seemed to be little left except to mail a letter for the nurse. Yet still he stayed. He watched Camilla arrange the tray daintily for her mother, the broth in a thin old china cup. He found it hard to tear himself away. Somehow this little shabby house had come to have a deep and vital interest for him, just because he had been passing through a crisis with its inmates. He waited in the kitchen while Camilla took the tray to her mother and ventured shyly to steal a glance through the crack of the door at Camilla in the dimness of the sickroom sitting on a low stool beside the bed feeding the invalid. He noticed the soft hair fallen over her forehead and the delicate outline of feature, caught a glimpse of the face upon the pillow framed in white hair, saw a feeble smile on the sick woman's lips, and felt his heartstrings pull with a new kind of joy as if somehow she belonged to him. He wondered vaguely if that was the kind of joy a doctor felt when he was able to pull a patient out of the jaws of death. He wasn't a doctor, and he had had but a very slight hand in the recovery of this woman, yet he felt a distinct sense of triumph that she was better, a distinct joy in sympathy with her sweet daughter.

He knew in the back of his mind, of course, that this was only a temporary contact; that this little shabby house was entirely out of his world, and he would presently pass back to his own environment. But just for the time he was deeply intrigued, and his heart was touched. The interests and hopes and desires of these people, this mother and daughter, had become his own interests. Passing interests seldom went so deep with him.

So he lingered and watched the glow in the girl's happy face when she came tiptoeing back to the kitchen with her tray and reported that Mother took all the broth, and seemed to like it, and that she had dropped to sleep again.

When he finally tore himself away, he promised that he would return that night about the time the doctor usually arrived and be on hand to run any possible errands and see what report the doctor gave of his patient. He drove home happily, thinking about a basket of fruit that he would take with him when he went back, planning what it should contain.

At home there was a note on his desk in his valet's handwriting. Miss Varrell had called him three times during his absence, and the telephone was ringing madly even as he read the note. This was doubtless Stephanie again. With a frown he took down the receiver and answered. Now there would be a long argument, and he hated arguments. Stephanie was not attractive when she was angry.

Chapter 4

About that time, down in the barbershop of one of the more exclusive hotels of the city, Myles Meredith, in the hands of his own special attendant whom he always demanded when he was in the city, was being polished off for the day and gathering items of news especially interesting to him. Jean knew his man, always kept choice bits of gossip for his ears, and produced them tactfully at the right moment. He was a man who made it his business to know all about his customers and produce what they wanted in the most casual and discreet manner.

Jean had skillfully succeeded in discovering where his customer had been dining the evening before, had made his little joke about the lateness of the morning hour in connection with the revelries of last night, and then, just as if it were an afterthought and not a carefully thought-out plan, he remarked, "Monsieur Jeffrey Wainwright did not dine with Monsieur and the Mademoiselle Stephanie Varrell last evening."

Meredith gave him a quick furtive glance.

"And what makes you say that, Jean?" he asked suspiciously. Meredith accepted all confidences and gave none. Jean understood his man perfectly.

"Oh, I just happened to see him halting under a traffic light, headed out of the city, with a very attractive lady by his side."

Meredith gave the man another keen glance and his voice took on a shade of interest—but not too much interest.

"A lady?" said Meredith. "Who was it? Not the platinum star from the Lyric last night?"

"No, no!" said Jean, selecting a bottle from his array of beautifiers and giving it a professional shake. "No, no, quite different to little Madame Shirley. It was a—what shall I say?—more patrician face. Veri delicate. Veri lovely. Veri aristocratic!" Jean's tone waxed eloquent. "Monsieur Wainwright seemed most interested, the brief glimpse I got. I wondered! He was always so—what shall I say?—devoted to Mademoiselle Varrell. But all things change, *n'est-ce pas*? But I wonder—!"

"Yes, all things change, Jean, including fair ladies. Isn't that true, Jean?" said Meredith, with a sinister gleam in his half-closed eyes. "What other news have you, Jean?"

A few minutes later Meredith betook himself to a telephone booth and called up his hostess of the night before. "That you, Stef? Morning, baby! How about taking lunch with me this noon? What's that? Where? Oh, your choice this time. And by the way, I happened on some news of your missing guest last night. He wasn't eating his heart out as you fondly supposed. His technique is rather sudden, it appears. He attached a most attractive lady, I understand, and went off in her company instead of coming to your party. Now will you believe what I tell you next time?"

❧

Back in the shabby old Chrystie house happiness was returning fast. Although Camilla had had to ask time off from her job and knew she was being docked on her salary for every day she took;

although the nurse's salary was mounting up minute by minute and Camilla didn't see how she was ever going to pay it; even though the coal in the cellar was almost gone and last month's bill had not been paid yet; even though the tiny bank account was all but overdrawn, she felt a song in her heart. For was not her mother growing better moment by moment? And her car was as by a miracle being repaired without charge! Oh, there were many things to be thankful for.

There were a few bruises from her accident last night that were developing, but they were trifles, just enough to make her realize how she had been saved from death, or crippling, which might have been worse than death. So her heart sang softly as she went about the little apartment putting everything in as lovely order as it was possible to do with an invalid and a trained nurse to be considered.

When, at the earnest command of the nurse, she finally lay down in the late afternoon to rest, her mind dwelt on the kind friend who had been sent to help her out in her trouble, and she breathed a little thankful prayer for him, too, and began to try to think of ways she might show him her gratitude.

The white orchids were in a lovely crystal bowl now, a relic of the prosperous past, and filled the little front room with their distinctive grandeur and loveliness. Camilla gave a thought of wonder to the one for whom they had been originally intended. Was she a girl he loved? Or a woman he honored? His mother, perhaps?

No, it would not have been his mother. He distinctly said the occasion for the flowers had passed and he didn't know what to do with them. Mothers were always there, if they were there at all. If his mother was away he would have sent them from the florist's. No, these flowers had been for a girl. They must have been for a girl, and he had been going to take them to her, take her out somewhere perhaps, or maybe just call upon her.

Camilla worked it all out carefully in her mind, and looking at the stately flowers, her intuition warned her that she must not let her thoughts get fastened upon this interesting stranger, for he surely must belong to someone else in a world that was not hers.

Yet those lovely white blossoms haunted her thoughts and tormented her conscience so that she finally got up softly so the nurse would not be disturbed from her nap and moved them into her mother's room where she could see them if she wakened. They were her orchids, anyway.

Then she went back to her couch and resolutely put out of her mind all thought of the stranger. He was a dream. She must not think about him.

It was the next morning while Camilla was carefully giving her mother spoonfuls of orange juice that her mother's eyes suddenly fastened upon the orchids.

"Camilla!" she said with a startled note in her feeble voice. "Where did those come from? You didn't *buy* them—did you?"

"Oh, no," said Camilla, trying to hide her confusion with a low laugh. Fool that she was! Why hadn't she known her mother would question her about them, and how was she to explain without alarming her? The whole story of the accident and her wild evening ride were wrapped up in the innocent presence of those flowers. White orchids did not bloom on every corner around that shabby little brick house, and, of course, her mother would be keen enough to think it all out and wonder why! Camilla's mother was a great one to scent alarm.

"Oh, no, I didn't buy them," laughed Camilla, draining the last drop of orange juice from the glass into the spoon. "Imagine me getting reckless enough to spend money on white orchids, of all flowers, this season of the year. No, Mother dear, they were sent to you."

"Sent—to *me!*" said the mother in wonder. "Who would—who that I know, *could?*" She turned large, troubled eyes on her daughter. It was not easy to put anything over on even a sick mother of Camilla.

Camilla had been thinking fast.

"Yes," she said cheerily, "but you don't know him. That's the fun of it. Not yet, that is. Maybe he'll come around again someday, though, and you can thank him. He is the man who went after the medicine the doctor needed the night you were sick. His name is Wainwright."

"Is he one of the men in your office?"

"Oh, no!" said Camilla with relief. "I don't really know much about him myself, but he's very nice and kind. He brought the flowers in from his car after he had been on an errand for the doctor and said perhaps you could enjoy them when you began to get better."

Mrs. Chrystie's face relaxed into a smile.

"How kind! A stranger!" she said, and she turned and looked at the lovely flowers.

Then, when Camilla leaned over to kiss her forehead, she smiled again and said, "Dear child! I've always wanted things like that—for you!"

Camilla's answer was another kiss, and she hurried out of the room. She didn't want her mother to see her face. She would ask more questions, perhaps, that would be hard to answer, and the daughter felt she would rather wait until her mother was really strong again before she was interrogated about the strange young man who had taken her to a lonely suburb and gone with her into an empty house. All that would be quite against her mother's code for a respectable girl, and, of course, her mother would not understand how very sick she had been and what the necessity was.

But the very next day Wainwright arrived in the late afternoon with a luscious basket of fruit.

Mrs. Chrystie was decidedly better and feeling quite bright.

Her ear was keen, and she asked the nurse if that was the young man who had sent her the orchids. The nurse replied that it was.

"I want to see him!" she demanded with a gleam of real interest in her eyes.

"I'm afraid it will tire you," said the nurse hesitantly.

"Oh, I won't talk except to thank him. He needn't stay but a minute!"

So the nurse stepped into the hall where Camilla was talking to Wainwright in low tones and announced that the invalid wanted to see him for just a second.

Wainwright eagerly followed her into the sickroom. Camilla, in trepidation, lingered in the doorway, afraid for what he might say.

But she needn't have worried. Wainwright knew his way around the world exceedingly well. He gave her mother one of his pleasant grins, said a few graceful phrases, declared he was coming to see her again when she was well enough to talk longer, and took himself away from the house. He seemed to have a fine inner sense that if he lingered around in the kitchen with Camilla, now that her mother was alive to the world again, it might excite her wonder and perhaps make trouble for Camilla.

Camilla watched him wistfully as he took his leave. What a fine, kindly, friendly person he was! What would it be to have a real friend like him! In spite of the sentinels of caution she had set about her heart to watch her every thought, his brief call had left a warm, happy feeling.

He called up the next day to say that he was going to be away for a few days and he wanted to ask how Mrs. Chrystie was before he left.

"Mother has invited some friends to our place up in the mountains, and she seems to think I've got to go and help her out," he explained. "I'm not especially keen on it, though the winter sports are always interesting, but I guess it's got to be done.

Mother sort of depends on me to look after things."

Camilla thanked him for calling and felt a flow of pleasure that he had cared to inquire for her mother, reflecting how few of the young men she knew would have taken the trouble, when they had so many other delightful interests, to call up and find out about an elderly woman who was practically a stranger. But she discovered that the world seemed lonelier when she had hung up the receiver, just because she knew he could not be expected to run in anymore.

"Yes," she told herself, standing by the tiny kitchen window and looking out on the neighbor's ash cans where shabby little sparrows fluttered noisily about trying to find a peck or two of crumbs among the trash. "Yes, you're a fool! Just like other girls! Just because a man has been kind for a few days you let yourself get interested in him! Just because he has an engaging smile. He doesn't care a pin for you beyond a passing interest, and it wouldn't do you a smidgen of good if he did, because he is not of your world. You know that, and yet you let yourself miss him. Well, it's a good thing he's gone, if you've got to be a fool!"

Nevertheless, when the nurse went out a few days later and brought in the evening paper, Camilla's eye caught at once among the illustrations on the last page, a large picture of a glorified log cabin flanked by stately pines, looking out over a snowy hillside where young people in smart sports attire were enjoying themselves, some on snowshoes, some on skis, and some skating around the glittering frozen lake in the distance. The caption beneath the picture stated that the Wainwrights were giving a house party at "The Antlers," their winter estate, and described the various sports available to their guests. Her heart gave a little lurch and her eyes grew wistful as she studied the picture. What fun it would be to be included in such a party! That was his world! He belonged there! Playtime and leisure and plenty of money to carry out whatever whim came into his head. His kindness to her and her mother had only been the carrying out of a very lovely one of his whims, of course, and she certainly had no need to quarrel with that. What might have happened to her mother and herself if he had not been there and been disposed to help?

There was a figure in the center foreground that suddenly she knew was him as she studied it. It was something about the pose of his tall splendid body, the heavy lock of dark hair that hung over his fine forehead—or was it his smile that flashed out even from those tiny graven lines that identified him?

He was bending at the back of a long sled, as if to kneel behind a load of girls and young men already seated on the sled at the top of the hill. One hand was on the shoulder of the girl just ahead of him, and she was smiling, as if at something he said.

Camilla's heart gave another lurch, this time of envy. Oh, to be a girl on that sled, about to glide down that long white hill, that even a newspaper photo gave hint of its smooth, glittering whiteness and the joviality in the very atmosphere of the shining day. He was going down that hill behind that other laughing girl, and instinctively she knew the girl must feel safe and happy, because he was there looking after her.

Suddenly Camilla straightened up away from the paper, gave it a quick decided fold that hid the picture, and snapped out into the kitchen to prepare her mother's broth. Fool! Here she was mooning again over other people's happiness! It was in another world he walked, and God had given her a way to walk of her own. If He had chosen quiet ways of service and hard work instead of continual playtime, what need had she to complain? He had also given her a faith that upheld her and a hope that she would not surrender for all the world had to offer. And had He not given her back her precious mother from the edge of the grave? God knew best. Whatever He gave was right!

She smiled a tender little smile, and then she went about the kitchen singing:

"God's way is the best way,
Tho' I may not see
Why sorrows and trials
Oft gather 'round me.

He ever is seeking
My gold to refine,
So humbly I trust Him,
My Savior divine.

God's way is the best way,
God's way is the right way,
I'll trust in Him always,
He knoweth the best."

The invalid in the other room heard her, and a smile of content grew softly on her lips, peace on her brow.

The nurse hovering about the patient said, as she patted the pillows into comfortable billows, "You've got a wonderful daughter, Mrs. Chrystie."

And the mother, with another smile, answered, "Haven't I?"

"Yes, there's many a girl would be fretting over the everyday ills, but she's taken worry like a soldier." The nurse had reserve in her tone. She did not say that she knew how much personal deprivation Camilla had taken that she might provide the better for her mother. A nurse grows wise to see the inner workings of a family where she is employed and learns not to seem to see everything.

The next day Camilla went back to her job in the office.

It was the nurse who planned it.

"There's no reason why you shouldn't go back," she said to Camilla. "I haven't another case for two weeks, and unless an emergency comes in, I really haven't any cause to go back to my boarding place. I'd just love to stay here with your mother without any pay until I'm called. She's lovely, and I'd like to be near her. And there really isn't much to be done for her anymore. In another day or two she'll be going around as usual. All you want is somebody here to just watch her a little and see that she doesn't overdo. So if you want to board me for being here with her till I have to go, I'd really like to do it. It's kind of a solitary place where I board, and I'm sometimes lonesome. Besides, if I'm here I shan't have to pay my board."

Camilla compromised on half-salary to be paid in small installments, as she could, and went thankfully back to her job in the office.

When Jeffrey Wainwright got back to the city he came by almost immediately and was disappointed to find that Camilla was not at home.

"She's gone back to her job," explained Miss York, as if he would understand what a cause of thanksgiving that would be.

Wainwright looked perplexed.

"Job?" he said vaguely and then instantly recovered himself, remembering that to this nurse he was an old friend of Camilla's who presumably knew all about her affairs. "Oh, yes, *job*," he repeated. "Of course she would be expected to, wouldn't she? I hadn't realized that her mother was well enough for her to leave yet."

"Oh, she had to," the nurse explained, "or she would have lost it, of course, and in these times jobs aren't so easy to replace, you know."

He didn't know. He had read about that in the papers, of course, but he didn't really *know*, and he stared at her with his nice troubled eyes and floundered about in his thoughts like one who was beyond his depth.

"But Mrs. Chrystie is better," went on Miss York, "much, much better. She doesn't really need me anymore. I'm just staying here for company till I'm called to my next case. Wouldn't you like to come in and see her? She spoke about you just this morning and wondered if you would ever come to see her again. She did appreciate those orchids so much that you sent her, and she said she never really half thanked you."

So Wainwright went in and met Camilla's mother, clothed now in a simple little gray housedress, silvery like her hair, and quite in her right mind. She was sitting by the window in the Morris chair where Wainwright had once spent the night, darning a tan silk stocking with delicate little stitches, and she welcomed him graciously and with as much poise as his own mother might have welcomed one of her own set.

So he sat down and talked with her, feeling at home with her at once, she looked so much like a mature Camilla. And Camilla's mother sweetly and keenly proceeded to find out all about him without letting him know that she was doing so.

He followed her lead, telling her all about the winter sports and the hunting on the estate. He had brought with him a present of some venison, which he had shot himself, and this made a good opening for the conversation. So when Camilla came in a few minutes earlier than usual and the cross examination was over, Camilla's mother had a fairly good picture in her mind of the snow-clad hills, the frozen lake, and the whole round of winter sports in which he had been indulging. She had, too, a fairly good idea of the log palace with its huge stone fireplaces, its rustic galleries, its large living room furnished with lavish simplicity, and its almost unlimited capacity for entertaining guests. With her own uncanny perception she had visualized Mrs. Wainwright loftily presiding over the bright throng she had gathered under her wide-spreading roof. A cold, hard, tyrannical, self-centered woman she judged her, just from the few sentences about her that had come from the lips of her son. She had even discovered the name of the great fashionable church with which the house of Wainwright had a vague affiliation, and she had almost as good an idea of Jeffrey Wainwright's birth and breeding and the influences that had surrounded him during his childhood as if it had been carefully indexed and cataloged for her.

Camilla came in, all rosy and brisk from the crisp outside air. A few snowflakes were falling outside, and some had lingered on her little brown hat and had melted on her cheeks and taken away the pallor that he remembered before he went away.

She had let herself in with her key and came upon them before they were aware. She stood still in astonishment and, with a quick leap of her unconquered heart, saw him talking with her mother. Saw the wonderful smile she remembered so vividly and had tried so hard to forget during the past two weeks. Saw the nice curves of it around his pleasant mouth, the flash of his perfect teeth, the light in his eyes as he became aware of her presence. Something leaped within her that she could not control, a gladness and a thrill that frightened her, it was so adverse to her own careful self-control. This was his charm, the charm of the world. This was the kind of man that made one breathlessly happy just to have him here. And this was dangerous, dangerous to a girl who was a fool like herself, whose heart would make more of the occurrence than it had any right to make.

There was that in the touch of his hand, too, that took all her practical good sense away, and she had to steady herself to make herself quietly withdraw her hand in a reasonable time.

"I'm glad to see you again!" he said, and stood holding her hand until she withdrew it, looking down into her eyes.

She had to think hard to envision that pictured scene on the snowy hillside with the girl on the sled looking adoringly up into his eyes, to make her turn her own away. This was doubtless just his way, the way he spoke and looked at all girls, and he was just calling on a girl he had befriended to see if all was well with her. He was not of her world. She must keep remembering that.

There was a cool, clear, little edge on her voice as she responded, mindful of his exceeding kindness to a stranger in the street yet not presuming in the least upon the friendliness he had given so lavishly afterward.

She sat down a bit formally with a pleasant smile on her face and tried to look as impersonal as a cucumber, and all the while her heart was thumping in the most jubilant way and crying out until she thought he would hear her, "He has come back! He has come back!"

"You fool!" said her practical, sensible self. "They always come back until they are tired of it, don't they? And anyway, even if he has come back, he does not belong to your world!"

But what was this he was saying?

"I wonder if I may take you out tomorrow evening?" he was asking. "You can spare her for a few hours now, can't you, Mrs. Chrystie?" He gave Camilla's mother a vivid look.

"Oh, that's kind of you," Camilla heard her own voice replying as her jubilant heart sunk low, "but I couldn't possibly be spared. You see, Miss York is going away—"

"Not until the day after tomorrow!" broke in the diplomatic nurse, who had been delightedly hovering nearby. "You can go just as well as not, Miss Chrystie. It will do you good. You've been so tied down here and in the office, you need a bit of change."

"But—I may have to work late at the office tomorrow night," said Camilla in a frightened tone, turning appealing eyes to her mother. "I really don't think I ought to promise. And I'm quite all right. I'm fine now that Mother is improving so fast."

"But it won't hurt you to have a change," said the young man, studying her face with a puzzled expression. Had he been mistaken? Didn't she really *want* to go with him? "I could pick you up at your office if you have to work late, you know, and then we'd go somewhere and have some dinner, and—well, I'm not just sure yet. I haven't been back long enough in the city to look up the attractions." He smiled with that clear, admiring, speculative look. He thought how different she was from Stephanie Varrell when she declined an invitation. And then it struck him that in some ways she resembled Stephanie. Somehow he didn't like the thought, and he didn't quite know why. He realized, too, that the idea would make Stephanie tremendously angry.

But Camilla was looking up with troubled eyes now.

"I really don't think I should go," she said, and she turned toward her mother as if to seek an excuse there.

"She means," explained her mother gently, "that she hasn't any festive garments for going out in the evening."

Camilla's cheeks were rosy red now, but she faced the young man bravely and tried to smile. It was as good an excuse as any, she thought, although it hadn't occurred to her yet. Her mind had been filled with a deeper matter altogether.

Wainwright studied her with a dawning understanding in his eyes.

"She looks very nice now," he said with a satisfied grin. "What's the matter with what you are wearing now? Plenty of people wear street clothes in the evening."

Camilla looked down at herself and considered. Then she looked up.

"You couldn't possibly think I look all right this way." She grinned back a challenge. "I've seen you in evening dress, you remember, and I'm positive you know better."

His eyes sobered.

"No, really," he said gravely, "I like you the way you are. It's not clothes I want to take out, it's you." There was something in the way he looked at her, reverently almost, that made her catch her breath and took all excuses away. She felt all her resolutions slipping and turned her troubled eyes toward her mother again.

But her mother was smiling. "Well, if Mr. Wainwright doesn't mind your being a bit shabby, why don't you go, dear? I think you should. I'd like to have you have a little relaxation after the hard time you've been through. Yes, go, Camilla! It will please me."

After that there seemed nothing more that Camilla could say, except to thank the young man, all the time aware of the flutter of joy in her heart.

"Well, just for this one time," she told herself. "But don't count on it. He's not your kind, and you'll probably find it out tomorrow night, so don't *dare* be glad!"

"That's great!" said Wainwright. "Then shall I call for you at the office? What time? Or do you have to come home first? I could stop for you any time you say and bring you home and then wait for you till you were ready?"

"Oh no," said Camilla hastily, "I wouldn't know just when I would be through. At least—well, it might happen I would be early, you know. I'd better just come home as usual. I'll do my best not to be late."

"Very well, then, shall we say half past seven, or would eight be better?" Camilla perceived that his ideas of dinner hours were different from her own, also. Eight o'clock for dinner! Somehow the whole occasion frightened her.

When he was gone her mother watched her silently as she went about putting her hat and coat away, watched her with puzzled eyes. She felt her mother's eyes upon her now and then while they were eating dinner, the simple little dinner that Miss York had prepared.

Chapter 5

Afterward when the dishes were washed and put away and Miss York had gone out for a brisk evening walk, Camilla came into the living room where her mother sat.

"Why didn't you want to go, Camilla?" she asked. "Was it just because of clothes?"

"Partly," said Camilla evasively.

Camilla was quite still a minute, and then she said slowly, "I'm not just sure, Mother."

Her mother considered that for a little and then asked, "How long have you known Mr. Wainwright, dear?"

Camilla was standing by the ugly little painted iron mantel, leaning her head over, looking down into the fire on the hearth. The flickering flames rested and shimmered over her gold hair and showed the big soft waves as they swept around her shapely young head. Her voice was hesitant and almost shamed as she spoke. "Not long, Mother. Only since the night you were sick."

"Is he a friend of the doctor's? Did the doctor introduce him?"

"No, Mother. Nobody introduced him. At least—he introduced himself."

"You mean, Camilla, that he is someone down at your office?"

"No, Mother. He is no one that I ever knew before. He was just a stranger who came to help me the night you were so sick, when the doctor had to send me to his house for medicine in a hurry—there was no one else—and my car wouldn't work—at least it got—it had—something the matter with it." Camilla was talking fast now, trying to cover her confusion, trying to make her story unalarming, feeling her way along word by word. "It wouldn't *go*," she added, "and I didn't know what in the world to do! The doctor had told me that every minute counted, and this man—Mr. Wainwright—was right behind me and saw I was—in difficulty—and he got out and offered to take me to where I was going in his car."

Camilla drew a breath of relief and looked up to see her mother's startled face.

"You mean," said her mother, after a pause, thoughtfully, "that you got into a stranger's car, that you rode out to a suburb with a man you had never met before?"

"I had to, Mother," said Camilla, feeling again the desperation that had been hers the night of the accident. "You don't understand! It meant your life, Mother! I couldn't wait to find somebody I had been introduced to."

Her mother was silent, pondering.

"Of course," she said quietly, "I understand there are times when one does not stand on ceremony. Go on, Camilla, what was the rest?"

"He took me to the doctor's, we got the medicine and came back, then he went and got Miss York, and after that he stayed all night and helped the doctor, went on errands for him. He was wonderful, Mother! He is a gentleman!"

"I can see that, Camilla," said her mother thoughtfully. "But why then do you not want to go to dinner with him, since he really seems to want you to?"

Camilla was still a long time, then she lifted her golden head and looked straight at her mother and said stormily, "Because, Mother, he doesn't belong to my world. He wears gardenias on his lapel and has house parties at an estate and—well, he is—different."

"You mean he belongs to *the* world?" asked her mother. "You mean you would not have the same ideas and beliefs and standards, Camilla?"

"Yes," said the girl a bit sadly, "that's it."

After another long pause her mother asked, "Do you dislike him, Camilla? Because if you do, of course it's not too late to ask him to excuse you."

"Oh no!" said Camilla rosily. "Oh no, Mother, I don't dislike him."

"Then, child, surely one dinner in his company is not going to harm you. There is always a chance that you may have been sent to witness, you know."

Camilla was very silent, looking into the fire for a long time, wondering what it would be like to try to witness of Jesus Christ before a young man of the world.

"Mother, I'm not sure I could," she faltered at last. "I wouldn't know how to talk to a man of the world, I'm sure."

"Witnessing is not always given by words, dear."

"I know," said Camilla with a sigh, "but I think it's more likely this is some kind of a testing of me, rather than a chance to witness."

"It might be both, you know, dear."

Camilla thought about that, too, and her mother watched her tenderly and finally said in a brisker tone, "Now, dear, let's think about the clothes question and have that out of the way. You'll need a new hat and some shoes. You know, these are the really important things about an outfit. You can likely find them cheap this time of year, and your black crepe will be quite all right if you have the right accessories. I'm glad your coat is black. Black is always good-looking, and the lines of both your dress and coat are good. They are well cut. You'll be able to get out and buy the hat and shoes at your lunch hour, won't you?"

"Not *possibly*!" said Camilla, whirling around with decision. "There isn't a cent to spare for finery, or even for necessity just now. I'll go as I am or I'll not go at all. If I have to mortgage the future to buy a new hat and shoes for this occasion, nothing doing!"

"You mustn't talk that way, darling child. A little hat would probably be very cheap at this time of year, and you ought to have shoes."

"Any price would not be cheap for me just now when you need so many things to help you get your strength. Positively, I will not spend a cent! But don't worry. Aren't there some pieces of black transparent velvet somewhere? Up in that drawer in the storeroom? I thought so. I'll make a ducky little velvet hat and put my rhinestone pin on it. Just you wait! It won't take long, just a twist here, and fold there, and it'll be done. And as for shoes, Mother dear, a smudge of ink on that worn spot in the toe, and the old black satin shoes will be all right. I'll shine up the silver buckles, too, and look as brave as any lady present."

Camilla ran upstairs for the velvet and her mother brushed away a tear and sighed, "Dear child!" under her breath, and then sat and looked into the fire and wondered whether she was doing right to let her precious child go out even for one evening with a total stranger, no matter how harmless he looked.

Camilla was back very soon, the square of supple velvet in her hand and the two little shabby satin shoes with their tarnished silver buckles tucked under her arm. Her face was interested and eager.

"I found it, Mother dear," she chirruped, "and there's plenty."

So she set to work with pins and scissors, standing before the long mirror and draping the velvet around her head, and presently had evolved a charming little hat so like a distinctive imported one she had seen in a shop window that one could scarcely have told them apart. Set on her golden hair, the bright little pin glittering perkily over the right eye, the effect was most becoming. Her mother was both satisfied and delighted. Then Camilla set to work on the shoes, inking the shabby places and polishing up the buckles.

By the time Miss York came back from her walk, the problem of Camilla's attire for the next evening was fairly solved.

"Put them all on, Camilla," commanded her mother, "and let Miss York get the effect. She goes around a good deal among stylish people. She'll know if there is anything wrong about you."

So Camilla donned her plain black silk crepe that she had bought at a bargain and already, in a pinch, worn several times to the office when her other dress was being cleaned or mended. She put on her rejuvenated satin shoes and the saucy little black velvet hat and stood up to be surveyed.

Miss York looked her over carefully and pronounced everything perfect.

"I can't see a thing wrong with you," she said with satisfaction, letting her eyes rest in admiration on the lovely golden head crowned with the chic little hat. "You wear your clothes so well, Camilla, that's half of it, of course. It isn't every girl with expensive clothes who can wear them so well. You have a fine form, and that dress has really good lines. As for the hat, it is delightful. You couldn't have a prettier one. All you need is a string of beads to finish you off. Haven't you got some?"

"Why yes, your pearls, Camilla. Get them. They're only cheap ones, of course, but they have a really good color," said her mother.

"I'm sorry, Mother, but they need restringing. I broke them

the last time I wore them, and I just haven't had time since to restring them."

"I'll do it in the morning!" said Miss York briskly. "I'll have lots of time. I can run out to the shop around the corner and get a bead needle and thread, and they will be all ready for you when you come back to dress. Now, what coat are you going to wear?"

Camilla drew a deep breath of determination and set her lips firmly.

"Just my black, everyday one," she said with a proud little tilt of her chin. "Lucky thing it's black. It will go with the rest of the things and perhaps won't be noticed. I never liked it very well, but it will have to pass muster. It's clean and it fits well, and the silver fox collar is rather good yet. I might comb it out a little."

"Put it on!" ordered her mother.

Camilla put it on and surveyed herself in the long mirror. She really looked very stylish and pretty.

"It's very good!" said the nurse. "I was going to offer you mine, but I'm larger than you, and it wouldn't fit you so well. You look very smart all in black!"

"Yes, Camilla, you look all right!" said her mother in a pleased tone.

Suddenly they came to their senses and realized that it was getting late. They hustled the invalid off to bed summarily, and Camilla hung up her dress and laid the little hat in the bureau drawer with a comfortable feeling that she was as ready for to-morrow night's festivity as she could be under the circumstances. When she finally lay down for the night on her bed in the front room, she was too excited and pleased to reproach herself with any questions of whether she ought to be going with Wainwright or not. It was settled now that she was going and too late to bring the matter up again. It might be the one and only time she would ever go anywhere with him—probably would be—but she was going this one time and going to enjoy it as much as possible. She might never see him again, perhaps, but she was going to have this one evening. She sent up a prayer that she might keep her witness true and stand her testing, if either was in question.

All the next day Camilla worked with a subdued excitement upon her. Not since her father died, their lovely home and practically all their money had gone through the failure of his partner, and they had moved to this strange city had Camilla been out for the evening with a young man. She could not but be thrilled by the thought, though she worked hard and left no duty undone.

Twice in the elevator that day she met the elderly typist with gray bobbed hair and too youthful lipstick who worked down the hall.

"What's the matter with you today, Miss Chrystie?" she asked the second time they met. "You look as if you'd made your fortune overnight. I never saw your cheeks look so pink. Is it a new kind of rouge?"

But Camilla only laughed.

"I am happy, Miss Townsend. My mother is so much better than she was!"

"Humph!" said Miss Townsend jealously, still eyeing her with suspicion. She had neither beauty nor youth nor living mother, sick or well. She doubted if that was sufficient reason for such a look of radiance and such a lilt in a voice.

All day the mother thought about her child, thrilling at the simple pleasure in store for her and yet praying for her often silently when she was alone, wondering if she had done right to encourage her going. *Oh, God, keep her! He is such an attractive-looking man! Don't let any sorrow come to her through this! If I have made a mistake, overrule it, undo it, prevent it, dear Lord, for Thy name's sake!*

Miss York was as eager over the hastily assembled outfit as was Camilla's mother. As soon as the few dishes were out of the way and Mrs. Chrystie dressed for the day, she hurried out to the little utility shop around the corner for the bead needle and cord. She came back with more than a cord. She had bought a pair of soft white gloves.

"I looked through her things and saw she hadn't any white ones," she apologized as she displayed them to the pleased mother, "so I bought these for her. I wanted to have some part in this. I hope they fit. She told me the other night she wore sixes."

"Yes, that's her number," said the mother. "She'll be so pleased."

"She's a dear girl!" said Miss York by and by, after she had finished stringing the beads. "One just loves to do things for her!"

"She is a dear child!" agreed the mother with a smile.

"And Mr. Wainwright seems so nice," Miss York rambled on. "I liked him the minute I saw him." Then after a pause, "Are they engaged?"

"Oh, no!" said Camilla's mother in quick alarm. "He's a comparatively new friend, in fact, almost a stranger."

"Well, I didn't know. He seemed so careful of her that first night I came, and then the white orchids and all. I sort of hoped they were. He seems so dependable. I like a girl like your daughter to get the right man. It's such a gamble, getting husbands, you know. I've often been glad I hadn't any. Going about the way I do, I see a lot, of course."

"Yes, you must," said Mrs. Chrystie reservedly. "There are a good many sad things in the world for a nurse to see, aren't there?"

"I should say there are!" said Miss York with emphasis. "The more I go about and see, the more I'm glad I'm free and single. Still, when it comes to a pretty girl like Camilla, I'd sort of like to see her get a good man to take care of her. She's so sweet and kind and tries so hard to take care of everybody that the world is apt to take advantage of her. And then Mr. Wainwright is so good-looking!"

"Looks are not always dependable," said Mrs. Chrystie with gravity.

"That's so, they aren't," said Miss York. "I learned that lesson under sad circumstances when I was a good deal younger than I am today. Now, Mrs. Chrystie, will you have your beef broth? It's almost twelve o'clock."

So the day sped by, and Camilla arrived at home half an hour ahead of schedule, her cheeks glowing and her eyes bright with excitement.

"There is a box here from the florist's for you," said Miss York, appearing in the dining room door, carrying a chubby, square white box.

"Flowers!" gasped Camilla, casting a half-frightened glance toward her smiling mother.

"Yes, isn't that nice, dear! Open them quick. I want to see if they'll go with your outfit!"

Camilla gave a little excited laugh.

"Almost anything would do that, wouldn't it? Weeds, even!" she giggled nervously.

Then she undid the string and took off the cover, folding back the wax paper.

"Mother!" she said, lifting her dark eyes lit with wonder. "Mother! They're white orchids!"

"How lovely!" said her mother with satisfaction in her voice.

"But, Mother, what—what shall I do with them?"

"Why of course you'll wear them, Camilla," said the nurse. "He expects you to wear them."

"But, wear white orchids—*me*, wear white orchids, just to go out to dinner? And with those old clothes! Oh, Mother, isn't it funny?" And Camilla suddenly sat down in a chair with the box on her lap and laughed hysterically.

"No," said her mother, "it isn't a bit funny. It's very lovely. The flowers will have just the touch you needed. White orchids, two-dollar pearls, and new white gloves. Your dress is only the background. You are going to look very nice!" There was deep satisfaction in the mother's tone.

But Camilla suddenly sobered down.

"Gloves!" she said. "I forgot all about gloves. I haven't any that are fit to wear!"

"No, but Miss York didn't forget them," said the mother, with a pleased twinkle in her eye. "Just go look on my bed where Miss York has spread all your things out and see what she bought for you."

Camilla put her orchids down on the couch and flew into her mother's bedroom.

"Oh, Miss York, you *dear*!" She came flying back with the gloves in her hand and flung her arms around the pleased nurse's neck, giving her a hug and kiss on her embarrassed red cheek. "You shouldn't have done it, of course, but I'm so pleased!" she said. "Such lovely, soft gloves!"

"Look! She's put down her wonderful flowers to rave over my poor little gloves!" said Miss York, rubbing the mist out of her eyes.

And then Camilla flew back to her orchids and stood in awe before them, her cheeks rosy again.

"But come," said her mother presently, "you mustn't spend so much time mooning over your things. This isn't Christmas. You're going out to dinner, child, and the time is flying."

"But I'm having such a good time now," said Camilla. "I don't really need to go out to dinner."

Laughing, she went away to get ready, and her mother hung over the lovely, strange flowers that seemed almost human and prayed again. *Oh, God, keep my child! Let no harm come to her through this venture.*

Camilla looked very lovely when she was ready. The cheap little black crepe dress was really very well cut for a "bargain" garment. The long-suffering satin shoes looked quite respectable now with their beautiful bright buckles. The pearls shone as lustrous around the slender white neck as if they had been real, and the sheen of the burnished gold hair was wonderful under the smart little velvet cap.

She fitted on her new gloves proudly, and Miss York stood in the doorway watching eagerly, as pleased as if she really belonged to this sweet girl.

"And now your orchids!" she said.

"Oh, must I really wear them?" said Camilla, standing over them with that look of awe on her face again. "It seems almost like presumption to wear things like that. As if I should put on a diamond tiara! Or an ermine wrap!"

"Nonsense, child!" her mother said, smiling. "They are God's flowers. They don't belong exclusively to the social world, even if society has taken them up as about the finest thing in flowers. God made them!"

"Of course!" said Camilla, lifting them up with that look of awe still in her eyes. "But knowing how the world rates them, I am afraid I'm going to be terribly self-conscious."

"How silly!" laughed Mrs. Chrystie indulgently. "You didn't steal them. Wear them gladly. They are yours. You have a right to them."

"You look like a million dollars!" said Miss York as she helped Camilla to fasten the beautiful corsage in place.

"That's what I'm afraid of," said Camilla with a little nervous laugh. "Million-dollar orchids and a five-and-ten outfit!"

"It's not like that at all, child," said her mother quickly. "You really look very lovely, and quiet and refined in the bargain. I am perfectly satisfied with your outfit."

"Then it must be all right, precious Mother," said Camilla, stooping to kiss her mother's forehead and hide a sudden feeling of tears.

"It couldn't be better!" said Miss York wistfully, watching the look of love between mother and daughter.

"But what would it all be without gloves?" laughed Camilla, suddenly giving the nurse another kiss.

And just then the doorbell rang.

Chapter 6

*L*ate that afternoon Stephanie Varrell had called up Jeffrey Wainwright's private telephone. She had been calling all day more or less, ever since she had read the morning papers that came up on her breakfast tray, but this time she got him.

Her eyes were narrowed and speculative as she settled back in an easy chair with a triumphant look on her face and prepared to talk with him. She was dressed most becomingly. She had been ready all afternoon for him to call on her, and he had not come. There was a hint of alarm, too, in her manner, though it did not manifest itself in her voice, which was honey-sweet as she recognized his.

"Oh, Jeff!" she said in soft tones. "It is really you at last! I read in the paper this morning that you were back from your hunting trip, and I've cancelled two delightful engagements and been looking for you to call."

"Oh, hullo, Stephanie!" said Wainwright. "How are you? Yes, I got back yesterday afternoon, but I've been busy all day. Meant to look you up sometime pretty soon, you know. How have you been?"

"Oh, fine!" said Stephanie, with an angry toss of her chin. "Haven't had time to miss you at all, but now that you're home you can take me out tonight and we'll have a good old talk. I've plenty to tell you!"

"Sorry," said Wainwright, "not tonight. I have another engagement tonight. I can't make it tomorrow morning, either. I've promised Dad to go over some important papers with him and can't tell how long it may take."

"Oh!" said Stephanie coldly, her chin going up again, her eyes smoldering. An engagement! With whom? A date with his dad! That sounded improbable. Was he still sore about Myles Meredith? He needed to be brought down a peg or two, perhaps.

"Well, what a pity!" she drawled as if it mattered very little. "I can't say tomorrow morning or afternoon either, for that matter. Every minute is taken. Nothing I can change! And tomorrow evening—I have a partial dinner engagement."

She waited for him to suggest her calling it off, but he answered quite casually and pleasantly, "Sorry. Well, I'll be seeing you soon!"

"Oh, very well!" said Stephanie in honey-sweet tones, her eyes snapping dull-gold fire as she hung up the receiver.

Wainwright waited a moment, hesitated with his hand on the instrument to call her back, then laughed and hung up.

"A little longer wait won't do her any harm!" he said thoughtfully. "I've got to get my bearings before I go back to her!"

Then Stephanie rose, slammed down the instrument on its stand, put on her war paint, and set herself in battle array.

Stephanie had unusual eyes. Her hair was rather lighter than Camilla's, lighter gold and more unnatural, but her eyes were a peculiar red-gold where Camilla's were dark brown, flecked with golden lights, like a topaz. Wainwright had always thought of

Stephanie's eyes as being like a jacinth stone, because of their almost orange lights that could soften and lure and thrill with a look. Yet when she was angry they contracted to tiny pinpoints, and then their orange became dull gold in color and not good to see.

Wainwright was thinking about those eyes now as he hung up the receiver. He knew the siren was angry now, knew it by sharp experience in the past, knew it by the very honey-sweetness of her voice, knew just exactly how those jacinth eyes were looking, with gold fire playing through them, and suddenly he remembered another pair of eyes, framed around by golden hair, eyes whose deep brown depths were the very essence of truth, whose golden lights reflected clearness of vision, unselfishness of living.

He stood there for a full minute with that telephone in his hand thinking about those two pairs of beautiful eyes, startled at his own thoughts. Was it possible that he had always been afraid of something in Stephanie's eyes, those eyes that had first attracted him to her? Was that why he had never yet actually been at peace about sharing his life with her?

And tonight he was going out with the other girl. Just a plain little girl he had picked up in the dark by accident. What was he doing, anyway? Well, perhaps tonight would tell him. He had seen her so far only under the extremity of her mother's illness. She had seemed lovely. Even after an absence of two weeks, she had stirred him. Could it be that it was her likeness to Stephanie that interested him? Could it be that she reminded him of the girl he thought he loved? He must go carefully. He must not confuse two personalities. Life was a strange mix-up. Two girls who had some of the same charm might yet be very different.

When Wainwright entered the little Chrystie living room and saw Camilla ready and waiting for him, wearing his flowers, he paused in amazement, wondering if his eyes had not misinformed him. To his eyes, she was garbed as smartly as any girl in his own circle of friends. The effect was charming, and even the watchful mother and nurse with jealous eyes fixed on his face were satisfied with the distinct admiration they found in his expression.

She has a truly distinguished air about her! thought Wainwright as he smiled upon her.

"You're looking wonderful tonight!" was what he said in low, admiring tones that pleased, while it frightened a trifle, the watchful mother.

He helped her into the car with deference just as he might have helped that girl on the sled in the newspaper. And now that she was started out into the night, with Wainwright still looking at her with that deep, admiring glance, which she felt even in the dark little street, she was just a bit apprehensive.

She was going out of her world into his, just the edge of it, probably, but she wondered why she had consented.

Then he spoke.

"I thought you said you had nothing to wear," he reproached.

"It's still true," said Camilla, laughing. "I haven't a new thing on except the gloves, and they were a present from Miss York. This is the very same dress and coat I wore yesterday to the office, and the hat I made out of a piece of black velvet I had. It's your wonderful flowers that have glorified my old garments. White orchids would glorify anything."

"On you, perhaps!" He spoke in low, reverent tones. He was filled with admiration. "Did I understand you to say that you *made* your hat?"

"Yes," said Camilla humbly. Somehow she wanted him to know the worst about her as she entered his world for a brief glimpse. She wanted no illusions.

"But I didn't know that—ordinary—that is to say—girls could make hats. Not hats like that. It looks to me quite charming!"

"Almost anybody can make things if they *have* to," said Camilla. "I saw one in a shop window the other day and admired it, and when I found this velvet I just twisted it up like the other one as nearly as I could remember. I'm glad you like it."

"I certainly do!" he said fervently. "You must be very clever."

"Oh, no!" laughed Camilla. "It's just that I've usually had to contrive things or go without them. You can't think how wonderful it is to me to be wearing real orchids. I never dreamed of having any, and it seems to me almost as if I had stolen into some other girl's place."

Wainwright looked at her, startled, and remembered how Stephanie had commanded him to bring her white orchids. He had never taken Stephanie white orchids. Somehow they didn't seem to belong to her. But on this girl the white orchids seemed regal. Even with what she called her shabby garments.

He answered her slowly, after a pause.

"No," he said, deliberately, "you haven't. I've never given any other girl white orchids. I almost did once, but—I'm glad I didn't!"

She caught her breath over that and wondered with a throb in her throat just what he meant by it. His saying it had thrilled her, it seemed so very beautiful and sincere. But she must remember that she was out in the world for only this one evening.

She couldn't think what to answer to that, and they rode along in silence for a long time, but it didn't matter. He didn't seem to mind. It was as if they had known one another for a long, long time, almost as if they had grown up together and understood each what the other was thinking. She couldn't understand why that should be. And it was a pity, because he was not of her world. She was sure he was not, and she must not forget it. She kept reminding herself over and over all the evening, saying it like a charm that she must repeat to keep her safe.

When the lights of the more crowded part of the city came into view, it seemed like Fairyland. She had been out very little in that part of the city at night and had not realized how beautiful it was, the millions of multicolored lights flashing on and off like many Christmases massed into one. It seemed as if this display was something Wainwright had ordered for her special delight, though, of course, she knew better. But she would never forget it. It would be always associated with her going out with him for the first time, and with the orchids, and that feeling she had of being well dressed and having his approval. It put her very much at her ease.

Yet she was a bit frightened again when they stopped before an imposing place that she recognized as one of the haunts of the rich and favored. Yesterday evening at this time she would have protested, have begged him to take her to some quieter place for dinner, but the orchids and his admiration had given her confidence, and she found herself entering the spacious dining room with only a little quickening of her natural heartbeats.

A person in uniform had taken his car away; uniformed servants bowed deferentially and gave her looks of approval as she entered on Wainwright's arm. Long mirrors were everywhere she looked, and they reflected a girl with gold hair in a fetching velvet hat, a girl she did not recognize at first as herself. Well, if that was the way she looked to his world, all right, she could hide behind that other girl for the evening and just have a good time. It wasn't her plain little self at all, but if he was satisfied, she needn't worry. And she certainly did look, at least from a distance, as well as most of the people she saw. Of course, there were some with low-backed dresses and ermine capes and glittering things in their hair, but there were plenty, too, in street garb, as he had said. It made her feel quite comfortable and ready to enjoy her outing.

As they passed among the tables, here and there people spoke to him and cast courteous, inquiring glances at her. The headwaiter was leading them to a far, quiet table, as if they were especially invited, expected guests. He had arranged about that beforehand, of course. It was all so strange, just for herself! Yet she rather enjoyed the whole thing, this masquerading harmlessly as a girl she was not and never could be. Just a costume and an escort, and there she was.

Wainwright even paused beside one table where an elderly opulent couple sat, an old man with white wavy hair and florid complexion and a stunning woman in black velvet and diamonds, and introduced her.

"Aunt Fan, Uncle Warren, I want you to know my friend, Miss Chrystie. Mr. and Mrs. Warren Wainwright, Camilla!"

There it was again! He had called her by her first name, as easily as if he had always done it. And these were his rich relatives, and they would wonder what poor little church mouse he had found and befriended. But because of those orchids and the quite composed glimpse she caught of herself in a far mirror, she found herself smiling and speaking quite easily to the imposing couple. And they were very cordial to her. But, of course, they were only looking at his orchids and didn't realize how really plain and insignificant she was.

"You have an inferiority complex!" she told herself. "You have it badly. Stop it! You are God's child, and it doesn't matter what anybody thinks!"

But that little old inferiority complex attended her nevertheless, slinking in to be on hand whenever she lost sight of real values and other-worldliness.

So Camilla sat down at a table, lovely with linen and lace and silver and crystal and flowers, and looked around her at the vast gorgeous room, took in the quiet air of refinement and beauty, the softly shaded candles, the flowers, the perfume, the soft tinkling of a fountain somewhere beyond a bower, and then the wonderful stringed music that broke upon her senses like soothing balm on a tired heart, and she felt as if she had almost reached heaven.

Wainwright carried her through the intricacies of ordering with the skill of a connoisseur and then sat back quietly with a pleased smile, his eyes meeting hers with a sweet intimacy that thrilled her.

"I'm glad Aunt Fan and Uncle Warren were here. They're grand old sports. I was proud to have them meet you," he said happily.

Camilla felt a glow of pleasure. He was not ashamed of her, then. And, of course, a young man took different girls out to dinner. There was nothing so very personal in being taken out to dinner, she must remember that. She was just one of his friends, at least for tonight.

"And now, Camilla," he said, watching the lovely expression of her eyes as she lifted them to his, "don't you think it is about time you began calling me Jeffrey? I've been calling you by your first name right along, and you slide around impersonally without calling me anything."

Camilla answered him with a level gaze, smiling a little, thinking rapidly. Was this going to take her too far? Nonsense! She could be sensible and friendly with him as well as with the boys who had grown up with her at home. God's standards did not include primness.

"After a man has slept in your own hall in an old Morris chair," she giggled to herself, "and carried down an army cot and a down comforter in his shirt sleeves, it is really absurd to stand on ceremony with him." And then she said steadily, with a friendly smile, "All right, Jeffrey, if you like."

The waiter came back then and handed Wainwright a menu card, saying something to him in an unintelligible tone. Wainwright looked at the card then looked up at Camilla.

"We didn't order anything to drink," he said. "What wines will you have? Champagne?"

Bang! Down came something hard and icy into her heart, knocking her faint and dizzy. He drank then. Of course! All fashionable society drank. One read of it on every hand, but she hadn't thought of that as one of the questions she would have to meet tonight. Somehow she hadn't connected it with Jeffrey Wainwright!

Camilla came from a long line of Prohibition ancestors, reaching away back before the Civil War time. Her principles were ingrained in her very nature, and here suddenly was a terrible reminder of the wide gulf that was fixed between her world and his.

Even while she heard her own voice, clear and quiet, saying, "No wine, thank you!" she felt her heart sinking down, down, and down, and her very lips grew white.

She knew he wouldn't understand her feelings. She didn't intend he should ever know how she was feeling, but she suddenly knew in her own heart that, in spite of all her careful warnings of herself, here she was thinking so much of this dear, bright, handsome fellow across from her, that it was like a knife in her heart to know of this gulf between herself and him. And it wasn't as if it was anything that could be bridged over, either, like ill manners or poor taste in clothes or lack of culture. It was something that had to do with moral standards, and it wouldn't be right for her to change, and it wasn't in the least likely that he ever would.

She heard him quietly dismissing the thought.

"No wine, waiter." Just as if it had been butter or soup he was talking about. He did not question her decision nor seem surprised. He did not order any for himself. He was a perfect gentleman. He just went on quietly talking as if nothing at all cataclysmic had happened. She was so thankful for that.

And yet he must have seen her sudden quietness. Could he guess how she felt?

He did not offer her cigarettes. She was glad of that. She noticed now that many women all around them were smoking. Yet he did not smoke himself. She wondered if that was just his politeness. He surely was not different from his world. And this was his world. She could never have realized it so definitely if she had not come here with him tonight.

He studied her quietly, with pleasant eyes, talked easily of music, books, and lovely things that she knew and enjoyed, and presently her color came back and a portion of her pleasure, but the light was gone from her eyes, and he missed it. He was trying to understand just what had happened.

But he did not talk about it. He put her at ease again. He began telling her about different people in the room, who and what they were. There was a famous broker from Wall Street. Across at the next table was a great oil magnate. That woman with the Titian hair and emeralds was a noted actress. Her companion was a famous artist. Just across the room were three authors. Those three women down the room to the right were daughters of multi-millionaires whose names were known all over the world.

Camilla studied them all and grew more and more silent, troubled, almost. The gulf between her and her handsome, courteous playmate was widening minute by minute. When she went out of this room and went home it would be the end, a sort of sweet dream that turned into a nightmare. And she cared! Oh, shame! Camilla cared so much! And it wasn't his fault. He had been perfectly nice and friendly and impersonal. Oh, he hadn't an idea what he was doing to her little trembling, unsophisticated self. And the worst of it was she had had plenty of warning in her own soul.

Oh, she would get over it by and by, of course. She had to. But now, tonight, it hurt so! If she only could have had this one whole evening unspoiled. But, of course, it had to be this way or she would have gone on getting deeper all the time into an acquaintance that did not, should not, belong in her life.

They were waiting for the dessert now, and she had grown very silent. She saw the great room in a blur. She watched the figures of men and women dancing a little way down the room where there was a clearer space. The women were beautifully gowned. Most of them had no backs to their dresses. They sparkled with jewels, though many dancers were just in street clothes like her own. Her eyes followed them, scarcely seeing them, quiet, troubled.

He thought how very lovely she was and tried to break the spell of quietness that had come over her, to find out what were her thoughts, her lovely thoughts behind his flowers that she wore so well. It was then he asked her if she would like to dance.

"No, thank you," she said and seemed to shrink as she lifted her honest eyes to his. "No, I don't dance. Oh, I oughtn't to have come here!" There was almost a cry in her tone, although it was very low. No one else could have heard it.

"You see," she tried to explain, "I don't belong to your world! I ought to have stayed in my own. I knew it. It is not just a difference in clothes, not only a difference between rich and poor. It is that we belong to different worlds!"

"That isn't so!" he said earnestly. "Anyone can see at a glance that you are to the manor born—the way you walk, your tone of voice, the way you carry yourself, like an empress. There is grace in every movement, refinement in everything you do and say. I will not admit that we are of different worlds."

Camilla looked at him thoughtfully.

"I'll admit," she said slowly, "that my people were educated, refined, and used to having cultured friends and lovely things around them, but it isn't just a matter of that. Yes, I was well born even as the world reckons, but it's more than that. It's a matter of standards." She hesitated, and her golden lashes went low upon her flushed cheeks. "It's a matter of beliefs—and of literally different worlds. You see—I've been born again!"

He stared at her for an instant in a kind of consternation. He did not know what she meant. He wanted to understand, but what she said conveyed nothing to him. Born again!

Just then there was a disturbance over by the door. Some new people were coming in, a bit noisily for the formality of the stately place, and all eyes were turning toward the door. The music had died away at the end of a lovely number, and there was a sudden silence that brought every eye around to see what was happening.

Camilla, too, turned her eyes to the door, and Jeffrey Wainwright looked also and gave a startled exclamation, a very low one, but audible enough for Camilla to hear.

Among the little knot of new arrivals at the doorway, two people stood out. A dark, frowning young man with an arrogant manner and an imperious glance and a girl with gold hair and jacinth eyes. A girl in black velvet, cut high in the front and low in the back, a gorgeous string of large pearls around her neck. She had just taken off a marvelous ermine cape that reached to the floor and handed it to her escort, and there she stood, staring over the room with hurrying, piercing eyes, looking for someone. She was wearing orchids, too, but they were green ones, strange, weird wraiths like gnomes of flowers, and Camilla watched her, startled.

The man who was with her was searching the room, too, with unhappy, restless eyes.

"Look! Your double!" said Myles Meredith to Stephanie. "Where did he rake her up?"

Stephanie turned her head in the direction he was looking. Her jacinth eyes became stormy, her red mouth, painted to ghastliness, grew sardonic.

"Come!" she said. "We will go there!" She pointed to a table just vacated, quite near to where Jeffrey Wainwright and Camilla sat. And suddenly Camilla knew that this was the worst moment of all.

They came straight on, those two, with their eyes on her escort, and Camilla, giving him a quick, fleeting look, saw that he had regained his poise and his quiet grace.

"Hello, Jeff!" said Stephanie, nodding to Wainwright

carelessly. She turned her head slowly toward Camilla and gave her a stare of contempt then swept on, giving Wainwright no chance to make the introduction he had intended.

Wainwright followed her with an astonished glance and then turned deliberately away. Camilla could see that he was deeply annoyed, but he did not glance again at those other two.

"It's just as well," he said in a low tone to Camilla. "I shouldn't care to introduce that man to anyone. Shall we go, Camilla?"

Camilla rose and managed somehow to get herself out of that place. She was somewhat reassured by the visions of herself in those many mirrors all around. They startled her, they looked so much like the other girl. She could feel the other girl's eyes upon her as she went. She could feel the fire and the hate in her glance; yet she knew she maintained her own poise. She owed that to her escort.

"And now," said Wainwright when they were out of it all and waiting for the car, "what shall we do next? Would you like to hear some more music, or would you enjoy a good ice hockey game at the arena? We'll be in plenty of time for the second game, and there are some exhibition skaters there tonight."

"Oh!" said Camilla, breathless, "oughtn't we to go home? Isn't it very late?"

"No, it's early yet. Aren't you having a good time, Camilla? You aren't tired yet, are you?"

He looked down at her with his charming smile, and Camilla looked up with another. She couldn't help it. There was something in his smile that melted down all her fortifications.

"No, I'm not tired," said Camilla, struggling to find words that were true. "It's been—wonderful!"

"Well, suppose we go to the arena and get something entirely different, just to freshen us up a bit."

All the way to the arena he talked brightly of interesting things. It wasn't far. He did not touch on what they had been saying when the disturbance occurred. Camilla was grateful to him for that. Somehow she did not want to go back to it. She had a feeling it was a closed incident.

All through the hockey game and through the solo skating that came between the rounds of the game, he kept her interested and happy. The joy of the first part of the evening had returned, to a certain extent. It was not quite the same; it was a more subdued joy, like the sweetness of a pleasant farewell, but she was grateful for it. It was going to be a pleasant ending to a wonderful experience. She was glad not to have had it end when they left the restaurant after that other girl came in.

Camilla loved the skating and the hockey game. It filled her with a new interest, and during intermissions Jeffrey told her about the winter sports up at their estate in the mountains. He said he would like to take her there sometime; he knew she would enjoy it. Camilla smiled back at him, just as if she were not sure she would never get there, and said she was sure she would.

At last the evening was over and he took her home, his gracious, lovely manner just the same, his attractiveness and strength and the flash of his smile, even the way his voice said "Camilla," were all hers, just as they had been when they started early in the evening. Just as if Camilla didn't know in her heart that this was the end.

And he hadn't yet referred once to what she had said.

Then, just as Camilla gave him her key to let him unlock the door for her, he took both of her hands in his and pressed them gently.

"Camilla," he said, "you're a great friend, and I'm glad I've found you; and someday pretty soon, when we can get time and a quiet place without too many people around, I want to talk more about what you were saying when we were interrupted."

And right there on her own doorstep, with all the little, sordid, shabby brick houses up and down the street asleep, and not a soul in sight either way, he suddenly laid his lips on her trembling ones and kissed her.

"Good night, little girl!"

He unlocked the door for her and swung it softly open, for they had agreed to be quiet lest they waken her mother, and Camilla said a faltering, little, frightened good night and slipped inside the door, closing it softly behind her.

He was gone. She could hear his car driving away! And his kiss was burning on her lips!

Oh, Camilla! Camilla! What had she done? Let him kiss her and said not a word. Yes, and yielded her lips to his!

It was sweet, but it must be the end! Absolutely the end!

Chapter 7

Camilla locked the door silently and stole into the front room, stepping out of her satin shoes at once so that she should not disturb her mother and the nurse, although if she had only known it, both of them were wide awake and had been for the last hour, awaiting her coming. But each for the sake of the other lay quite still. The mother could not sleep because she had gone in imagination through every detail of the evening with her beloved child. She had lain almost without stirring because she did not want the nurse to scold her and give her hot milk or a tablet to make her sleep. She was enjoying every minute of this outing for her daughter who had so little to take her out of the round of hard work.

The nurse had gone to bed early and lain very quiet for her patient's sake, but she, too, had been renewing her youth, full of excitement over the beautiful young girl and the man who had not only unusual attraction but wealth and charm besides. It seemed like a real romance to Eleanor York, and she lay there planning it out as if it had been a storybook she was reading.

So the two left at home were by no means asleep when Camilla came in and went about her preparations for bed with as few movements as possible.

Perhaps it would have been better for all three if Camilla had frankly wakened them and gushed a little bit about her evening. Certainly it would have taken her own mind from the things that disturbed her.

But she slid into her bed that stood waiting for her with its covers carefully turned back, flung the covers over her with one movement, and lay rigid, her conscience already beginning to grill her with the details of the evening, hauling out and displaying before her every disturbing element, until she felt like writhing.

Beginning with that kiss, that sweet, burning kiss that lingered hauntingly upon her lips, her mind traveled backward over each moment she had been away, sensing the preciousness of it all, even while she rejected it as something she must not have for her own.

Then back again from the moment she had left her home, down through each little thing; how clearly it was impressed upon her mind. Wainwright's smile, the way his eyes had searched hers when he asked a question, the way their thoughts had seemed to travel together, the way they understood each other, his easy grace as he helped her out of the car and led her to the table, his pleasant compliments. Were they genuine, or did he say those things to every girl? She could not believe they were not genuine, not just for herself alone.

Ah! But there was that other girl! That girl with the jeweled gold hair and the mocking red lips who had called him "Jeff" and stared at her so insolently! The iron went deep into her soul as she thought of her! And there were all the other things that made up his world: the wine, the dance, and all the carefree frivolity that constituted the difference between his world and hers; the huge gulf fixed that might not be crossed; the gulf between Life and Death, light and darkness, unalterable and eternal. That he would ever accept the Life she possessed seemed as improbable as that a camel should go through the eye of a needle.

Yet how gentle he had been with her on the way home. Almost as if he understood that something had been a shock to her. Of course, he had blamed it on the way the other girl had acted. He wouldn't have understood the other even if she tried to tell him. It was a spiritual thing and had to be spiritually discerned.

Yet he had a wonderfully fine human understanding and sympathy. She felt that instinctively, and she warmed to the remembrance of his manner toward her on the way home, and then— that kiss! If anyone had told her earlier in the day that she would have allowed a young man to kiss her, unrebuked, a strange young man at that, one to whom she had never really been even introduced, she would have been angry indeed. Yet, as the memory of that kiss came back to her, she could not seem to be indignant. It had not been given flippantly nor roughly. It had been reverent. Utterly so. It had not even seemed a liberty. And yet if some other girl had tried to explain such a thing away, Camilla would have curled a lip of scorn at her. No, according to her own confessed standards it was wrong; and yet, when she thought of it, in spite of all her theories and beliefs, even in spite of facts, she felt as if that kiss had been a sort of benediction, a tribute laid at the feet of her womanhood. It had been so reverent, so gentle. There had been nothing wanton about it.

Was this the thing they called falling in love, and was she after all her careful teaching, after her most heartfelt convictions, to lose her head and become engulfed in a love affair with a man who did not belong to her world? No, no, no! A thousand times no! This must be the end. She would tell him so. She must make him understand!

But perhaps he, too, felt that this was the end. Perhaps that had been the real meaning of that kiss, a kind of wistful, sorrowful farewell. For he must see that she was not of his class, no matter how much he might say or think about her being to the manor born. He could see she was unsophisticated. He must understand that there could be nothing more between them than the friendliness which had been that first night when he went out of his way to help her in distress.

Beating this over and over in her mind, she sank at last to sleep, with the hope that somehow the tangle would unravel and all would yet be simple and normal with her as it always had been. But in the night there came a dream, which carried on all the joy of her evening and none of the fears, and when she awoke in the morning it was with a tender memory of his lips upon hers that made her glad in her secret heart that she had had that one beautiful moment when he had said good night to her. It would be something to remember all through the years if love came never nearer to her than it had last night. It would be a way to be sure what love might be between two souls who were rightly mated.

But it was late when she awoke, and she could see the eagerness in the eyes of the two who had so willingly helped her to be ready last night. She knew that somehow she must give them their reward of joy in her outing, for they had done all in their power to make her happy. This might be the end of things for her, but they deserved their bit of description, their glimpse of the excitement and beauty of it all.

So while she dressed and hurriedly ate a few bites to satisfy their anxiety for her, she gave vivid word pictures of her evening, omitting all that had troubled her and omitting that precious kiss at the end. She gave them a fair sense of her own excitement and joy in the scene; she even managed a few bright, funny descriptions of people she had seen; and she described Wainwright's uncle and aunt gravely and briefly, made plain their cordiality and friendliness, until she found Miss York's eyes fixed on her in eager speculation and her mother's eyes filled with mingled pride and anxiety.

So Camilla made much of the gorgeousness of the famous restaurant, spoke of how stylish she felt with her new gloves, and thanked Miss York for putting her orchids in water on the table where she could see them while she ate. But she utterly refused to wear them to the office.

"No," she said decidedly. "They don't belong down there, and I don't wish to give false impressions."

Then with a good-bye to Miss York, who was to leave that afternoon, and an earnest invitation for her to come back and visit them whenever she could, she kissed her mother and was gone.

She felt as she walked to the nearest trolley-car line that she had suddenly grown a great deal older since last evening. It was a relief, too, to be away from the dear, kind eyes that loved her and searched her face so keenly.

Nevertheless, as she went her way into another part of the city and threaded through traffic from one car line to another and then to a bus, she found she was hugging to herself every pleasant thing that had happened last night, every look and tone and smile and kindly word. Wainwright had told her that her car would be ready in a couple of days, and she realized what a wonderful thing he had done for her in looking after the repairs on that. She was sure if it had been left to her own engineering she would never have had that little old car again. But he had assured her it would be good as new. And to think he had arranged it for her so that she would not have to pay a cent! Well, that was something to let her heart sing about, anyway, even if she must not let herself think about the young man.

And she mustn't! She had got to conquer this thing! She looked into the pleasant sunny morning and drew a deep breath, forced a smile, and decided that she was just going to be happy and not worry about anything. Think of her mother who was well again! Able to help clear off the table that morning! Think how her car would soon be repaired, which would carry her so much more quickly, yes, and cheaply, too, to her office! Think that she had a job to go to and with careful economy a prospect of paying both nurse and doctor before long! Think that there were orchids still at home! No, she must not think about those darling orchids! They would inevitably lead to other thoughts, which must be taboo for her or she would presently find herself in deep waters like any other silly girl!

Yet when she finally arrived at her office, just in time, and went to hang up her coat and hat, she found her heart singing, singing, singing! Why? Silly heart that would sing in spite of depression and thoughts she must not think!

That night her mother asked a lot of questions, and she answered them glibly. She had been schooling herself all day and did very well, even under those keen, loving eyes.

"And what did you think of the young man, Camilla, after spending a whole evening in his company?" asked the mother at last, watching the sweet, transparent face of the girl.

"Oh, just what I thought of him before!" answered Camilla with a trifling little laugh. "Charming, of course! Mother, it does make a difference to be brought up with lovely things around you. I'm sure it does. He is so much more gracious and courteous than most of the men in the office, for instance! But then, of course, he belongs to a different world."

Camilla caught up the tray full of dishes and hurried back into the kitchen, feeling that she had done very well under inspection.

When she came back for the rest, her mother went on. "You still feel that, do you, Camilla?" There was just the hint of a little sigh at the end of the words and the girl caught it. She was sensitive to her mother's very thoughts.

"Oh yes." She laughed lightly again. "I knew that at once when I first met him. But—" She paused for some casual ending to her sentence. "It is nice to know him. It is broadening, don't you think, Mother, to have at least one really cultured friend outside the family?"

Her mother smiled at the glib way she spoke of him, so formally, as if he were some kind of a specimen. She knew she had not gotten down to the heart of the matter yet, but she was wise enough to say nothing more about it.

"I suppose it is," she agreed with a smile. "Well, child, dear, don't lose your heart to him!" But she said it with the least hint of another sigh. It would be nice to have a friend for Camilla like that one who was fine and right in every way, a real true man—if he was all that! She dreaded the thought that she might be called away from earth someday soon and Camilla be left alone. She knew she had been very near the borderland in her last illness.

But Camilla, even while she was finishing the dishes and putting back into place the articles of furniture and bedding that had been rearranged to accommodate the nurse during her mother's illness, found her heart on the alert for a step at the door or a tap on the old iron knocker, and caught herself looking wistfully toward the telephone for a ring that did not come. He had said when he parted from her that he would be seeing her soon. Yet the first night and the second night passed with no sign from him, not even a phone call, and then indeed her heart began to sink. She hated herself for the feeling, but it was there, a sorrow that he had not come. A deep-seated conviction that he would not come. That it had really been the end!

But when she reached home the third evening and opened the front door, a subtle fragrance greeted her at the very threshold—the perfume of hothouse roses! Her heart leaped up with hope. Was it hope or joy? She didn't stop to analyze it. She went at once to the source of that fragrance, the big bowl of golden roses on the little mahogany stand in the front room, like a bee to the honey, and buried her face in their sweetness.

Glad, glad, glad! Yes, it was joy! Pure joy!

Her mother came in a moment later, a knife and spoon in her hand and a smudge of flour on her cheek.

"Too bad you couldn't have got home early tonight," she said with a lilt in her voice. "He's been gone only about ten minutes. He stayed as late as he dared. He had to catch a train! But he's left a note for you."

"A note?"

Camilla accepted it as if it had been gold and treasures. She dropped down just where she was without taking off her hat or coat and read it, a glow on her cheeks and a tumult in her heart. Her mother watched her furtively from the hall, lingering with a wistful smile upon her face, trying to read the heart of her girl through the flush on her cheek and the glint in her eyes.

Dear Camilla:

I'm sorry to have missed you. I've been hungering for a long talk ever since I left you, but I had to help Dad with some important business, and now Mother's had a bad case of bronchitis and has been ordered south at once. Dad can't get away yet so Mother has commandeered me. I hope to return in a few days but can't be sure how soon. Meantime, keep in mind what we were talking about, and don't forget me.

Yours,
Jeff
Your car will be back tomorrow sometime.

Camilla sat still, studying that note, trying to subdue the surge of happiness that went over her, trying to act casual, trying to feel casual. Now, just what was there in that note to make her feel so glad, so light and relieved? It was a perfectly commonplace note, wasn't it? Anybody might have written it to anyone else?

And yet all the heaviness of the past three days was lifted. Why? Well, he hadn't forgotten her, and she had fully persuaded herself that he had, and at least to him this wasn't the end—not yet. That in itself was a song of thanksgiving. For since she had made up her mind that it was the end, there seemed to be many reasons why she wanted to see him again. For one thing, she wanted to be sure that he did not think less of her because she had allowed that sweet kiss. She wanted to look into his face and read what he had meant by it. Not that she was at all in doubt about the impossibility of any further growth of their friendship, but that she wanted to read fineness and cleanness of purpose in his face and always be able to think well of him when she remembered him.

Presently she looked up and caught a glimpse of her mother's questioning face, and her own broke into a smile. "Did he come in, Mother?"

"Yes, and waited three-quarters of an hour. We had a nice talk together. He has great charm."

"Yes," said Camilla dreamily, going over to the roses and burying her face in their sweetness again, closing her eyes while she drew in a long, delicious breath. "Yes, he has charm. I suppose all people of the world have charm, haven't they, Mother? I haven't met so many of them, you know."

"No!" said the mother sharply. "Not all of them. In fact, I have known many who had none. Their money and position seemed to have made them hard and sharp and disagreeable. Is the letter about your car?" Mrs. Chrystie hesitated, her eyes on the paper held close in her daughter's hand. Was her precious girl in danger? If she could only see that folded note she might be able to read between the lines.

Camilla opened her note again and read it over, the color coming softly into her cheeks. Then with a lingering smile she suddenly held it out to her mother.

"It's nothing, Mother," she said with her most casual air.

"Read it if you like! Just a friendly apology because he couldn't come down yesterday or day before as he promised, to—tell me about the car."

Her mother gave her a steady look then read the note slowly, while Camilla hurried about singing a soft little excited song, trying to seem disinterested.

But her mother came straight to the point. "What had you been talking about, Camilla, that he wants you to keep in mind?"

"Oh," said Camilla, airily, her cheeks growing a trifle redder, "just, why—as nearly as I can remember, something about being to the manor born!"

Her mother looked at her thoughtfully for a moment.

"Oh!" she said, and she handed the note back.

They were very happy that night eating supper together, the first supper the mother had cooked, for Miss York had made up several dishes that would last for a day or two until the invalid was used to being quite on her own again.

"Everything tastes so good, Mother!" said Camilla, looking up with happy eyes.

Somehow it seemed as if she had had a reprieve. She didn't have to keep her conscience constantly awatch over her thoughts. He was away at least for a few days, and she might get rested and think it over at her leisure. And just for this evening, at least, she meant to enjoy home and Mother.

Her mother brought the roses and set them in the middle of the table as they sat down, and there they were in their beauty to remind of the giver.

They had a cheery meal and a happy time putting the kitchen in order, and the mother wisely said no more about the young man. But after the lights were out she did much praying. It was a situation that she did not feel herself able to judge aright, so she prayed for guidance that her girl might not be tempted into anything that would bring her sorrow.

It was the next day that the little old reconstructed car came shining home in a new coat of paint and looking as if it were brand-new throughout. And when the wondering girl started its engine, it purred as silkily as if it were finer than it had been originally.

A few days later life settled down into the old routine. The roses had faded, and Camilla was becoming accustomed to the newness of her old car. The accident and all that had followed it had been softened into the semblance of a dream, and except that she could not look at her mother without continually giving thanks for her renewed strength, all things seemed as they were before her mother's illness. Even Wainwright had become for the time being only a dream-hero who had appeared to relieve her necessity and then vanished into oblivion, and she was able to forget him hours together and sometimes to go to sleep without recalling his farewell. She congratulated herself that she had come back to sanity.

She did not see a taxi containing a handsome, dark, foreign-looking man following her little car home one night. She noticed him no more than anyone else in traffic. She did not notice the same man hovering in her street the next morning when she left for the office, nor notice another taxi following her to her parking place and the same man trailing her to the office door. She was wholly unconscious of it all and settled to her work as usual that winter morning, thankful that she had a warm woolen dress that was respectable without having to buy a new one before the doctor and nurse were paid. She looked down at herself proudly, smoothed the skirt, and noticed how well the blouse looked in spite of home cleaning and blocking, and then she settled down at her desk and to work, steadily refusing to let her mind even hint at the thought that time was going on and Wainwright might be coming home soon. It wasn't a thought she had a right to think, and she wasn't going to allow it. She was proud of herself for having conquered her foolish interest in a passing stranger.

Chapter 8

It happened just after her employer had come through from his private office and gone down in the elevator for his lunch hour. Marietta Pratt, the other girl who occupied the desk opposite Camilla's, had gone to lunch also. Camilla had chosen to let her go first today because of some letters she wanted to finish for the afternoon mail. She was trying to have them ready for Mr. Whitlock to sign when he came back from lunch.

She was working away like a whirlwind, her mind intent on what she was doing, her fingers flying over the typewriter keys with a skill and rapidity beautiful to watch. She had a feeling that she could work better when the other girl was gone, because she was a fidgeter and a fusser, always coming over and interrupting to ask a question.

Suddenly as Camilla worked she became aware of the presence of someone in the room and, looking up, startled, she saw a girl standing in the open door, her hand still upon its knob, looking at her with scorn and anger. A girl with gold hair, ghastly red lips in a chalk-white face, and eyes that seemed to be strange, evil, red-gold stones, yet stones that could pulsate and flame with a kind of hidden fire.

Camilla, even as a child, had always been strangely calm in a time of crisis, so now, even as she took in the identity of this other girl and realized that she had come to wreak some kind of vengeance upon herself, the startled look went out of her eyes and her face became a well-controlled mask filled only with a polite business inquiry. Her hands had half dropped, poised over the keyboard of her machine, and her expression showed no sign of recognition. The intruder was nothing more to her apparently than any other stranger who might have chanced to come to the office on business.

She looked up and waited an instant, as if expecting the visitor to speak, but the other girl only stared at her speculatively, appraisingly, still scornfully, with white fury in her gaze.

Camilla lifted her lovely chin a trifle, with a pride she had received by inheritance, and let her eyes coolly appraise the visitor. Then she spoke in a tone as of one in authority.

"Did you wish to see Mr. Whitlock?" she asked, and her voice carried all the generations of cultured, educated people who had been her forebears. "He has gone out to lunch. He will not be back until half past two."

The beauty stared indignantly.

"No, I didn't come to see Mr. Whitlock nor anybody else but you!" she said haughtily. "And you needn't think you can hide behind anyone. I came here to talk to you, and I mean to do it."

"Why, certainly," said Camilla courteously, whirling around from her typewriter and facing the stranger. "Won't you sit down? I'm sure I don't know why I should wish to hide from you."

"Well, you probably will before I get done with you," said Stephanie Varrell vehemently, "and you needn't put on that sanctimonious look. I've had a hard enough time finding you, and you needn't think I'll let you off easily, either. I've had to employ three men and a taxi two days to locate you, but I did it! I've come to tell you where to get off, and you probably know what that means. If you don't heed what I'm going to tell you I'll find ways to put you out of the running somehow."

Camilla found herself growing very angry indeed, and her ancestral courage rose as the other girl grew more and more insolent. She was a trifle white around her lips, and her eyes grew dark and unsmiling, but otherwise there was no change in her appearance.

"Wouldn't it be a good thing if you were to explain what this is all about?" she asked quietly.

"Oh, you're terribly innocent, aren't you? You don't need any explanation. I know your kind. A girl of your type doesn't pick up the son of a millionaire and make him take her to the place where I saw you last week with Jeff Wainwright without knowing just what it's all about."

Camilla was thankful that she was not a blushing girl. She could fairly well depend upon herself to grow perhaps whiter in an emergency but not red, and now, though her heart gave a sudden lurch and seemed to turn right over in her angry young breast, she kept her poise and looked steadily into the eye of the other girl, who had taken out a gold cigarette case, lit a cigarette, and was puffing it furiously at her foe.

"I don't understand you," said Camilla coolly. "It is quite a common circumstance, isn't it, for a girl to go out to dinner with a friend?"

"*Friend?*" sneered the other girl. "You call him a friend, do you? That's preposterous! I wonder what he would say if he could hear you? A man doesn't make a friend out of every girl he plays around with! And don't fancy he'll ever marry you. He's not the marrying kind. And besides all that, a man like that doesn't seek a wife in the laboring class. You are not of his class. You are just a low-down working girl!"

Stephanie's voice was like the hiss of a serpent.

Camilla was very angry indeed now. She wanted to rise and strike this insolent girl in the face. She wanted to scream and cry out at the insults that were being flung at her. She knew that both tears and hysterical laughter were hovering very near the surface, and she was holding her emotions back by the mere force of her will. She hoped her voice did not tremble as she answered calmly.

"I really hadn't considered marrying him!" She took a deep breath, to steady herself. "You see," she went on, "you are quite right about our not being of the same class. But you are mistaken about my being so terribly low born. It so happens that though I am working at present I really belong to royalty, and you know, perhaps, that it is not permitted that royalty should marry outside of royalty."

There was just a little ring of triumph in the clear voice as Camilla gathered strength with her words. There was also a light in her eyes that somehow startled her visitor and made her pause in her angry torrent of insolence. Camilla was certain of herself and did not seem at all quelled by the taunts that had been flung at her. Camilla had a poise that the other girl had never known.

Stephanie Varrell surveyed her contemptuously, amazed that this mere fragment of the working classes should dare to stand out against her and smile in a superior way and answer back. Royalty! Could it be that there was some mistake?

"Royalty!" she sneered, looking her over from the tip of her shabby little brown shoes to the top of her perfectly groomed golden head. Camilla was always exquisitely dainty, even in her working hours. She had lovely hands most carefully cared for. Her nails were not stained red nor allowed to grow long and pointed like claws. They were artistically lovely hands, fascinating to watch. Camilla was neat and trim and stylish, too, even in the little brown knit dress, the work of her mother's hands, that had served a long term of wear and still had time ahead. Camilla was a lady, and the other girl could not help seeing it. Just for the moment she was baffled. She looked as an angry bull might have looked when presented with a bunch of clover instead of the red rag he had been charging.

"Royalty? Are you then a foreigner?" As if that accounted for it.

"Yes," said Camilla, with a bell-like quality in her voice. "Yes, I am a foreigner. I don't belong here." She sounded as if she were proud of the fact.

"Oh," said Stephanie, "one of those little defunct nations, I suppose, that you find it hard to locate on the map?"

"Oh no," said Camilla lightly, "none of those. You won't find it on your map. My citizenship is in heaven. And now, don't you think we've said about enough? I really can't spare any more time to talk. I have work to do"—with a glance at the clock—"and I must get back to it at once. You will excuse me, I'm sure." And she swung her chair around to her typewriter and began to make her fingers fly rapidly over the keys, blindly writing whatever came into her head.

Stephanie Varrell stared at her for an instant incredulously, then she said in a shocked tone, "You must be crazy!"

But Camilla did not answer. She went right on writing, the click of her typewriter keys filling the silence eloquently.

Stephanie Varrell watched her, her face gradually hardening into anger again.

"You think you're very smart, don't you?" she mocked. "But all the same, you'll find out that it's dangerous to interfere with what belongs to me. Jeff Wainwright is mine, and I'm not going to have other girls playing around with him! Understand? If you happen to transgress again, you'll find yourself out of a job quicker than you can think. I happen to know Mr. Whitlock well, and I have ways of making people do what I say. You'll find that out, too, if you choose to ignore this warning, royalty or no royalty!"

The high shrill voice ceased, and Stephanie Varrell walked out of the office and slammed the door viciously. But Camilla kept on making her fingers fly over those keys blindly until she heard the elevator stop, its doors open and shut, and move on down. Then she rose and flew to the dark little cloakroom where she kept her wraps and, burying her face in the sleeve of her old black coat, burst into tears, sobbing as if her heart would break. They were almost silent tears, however, for she did not know what minute the other secretary would come back, and very soon she was able to control herself. That was a hard thing about being a working girl—she hadn't leisure even to weep!

Yet afterward she knew it was better so, for if she had cried long her mother would have noticed it when she went home. Mothers always saw through everything. But Mother mustn't know about this. It would kill Mother to know that anybody had dared talk to her that way.

She hurried to the washroom and dashed cold water on her eyes, and by the time Marietta Pratt returned, she seemed to be her sweet little self again, perhaps a little dewy around the eyes, but all right otherwise. She was ready to leave as the other girl came in and gave even her sharp eyes little chance to inspect her fellow worker. But Camilla, as she walked down the hall to the elevator, had a feeling that she was leaving a conversation behind in that room that would somehow get across to Marietta. How terrible it would be if conversations had a way of making themselves perpetuated and audible to others. It almost seemed as if she ought to have opened the windows and let some of those dreadful words out. She shivered as she stepped into the elevator, and the elevator boy grinned at her sympathetically and said, "Cold day!" Camilla gave him a wan smile through lips that were stiff with the shock of what she had just passed through. She was thankful that her recent caller's words were not rolling down the big stone corridors of the building in audible form for the world to hear!

It seemed to her as she walked out into the bright winter day as if the very sunshine hurt her and the keen air went through her. Humiliation was upon her the like of which she had never dreamed that any well-meaning person could suffer! To have been dragged down into such a mortifying situation! To have been forced to listen to such charges! To have been the target of such insolence, such implications!

She walked down the street and past the restaurant where she usually took her lunch without even noticing it. She was not hungry. She only wanted to get out away somewhere and try to get her bearings once more. She wanted to get calm. But as she walked her mind fairly seethed with indignation. Everything that other girl said came back again and shouted itself at her until it seemed to her the passersby must hear, and every step of the way she was thinking of something clever she might have said in answer. Her cheeks were burning red and her eyes were flashing with a great light, but it was not a light of humility. It was a light of pride and anger.

Presently she found herself in a small park where a few chilly sparrows hopped noisily about. She sat down on a windswept bench and tried to keep warm. It seemed as if her limbs were too tired to bear her farther. And then she felt the tears stinging into her eyes again. This would not do. She must not cry here where passersby could see her. Somebody would presently be offering help. She sat up straight and stared into the distance, and it was just then she remembered the haven of her soul and began to pray.

Oh, God! Oh, God! But when she tried to go on she found it was in words somewhat similar to the cursing psalms. Ah! Was there something wrong in her own heart? Surely this terrible experience that had come upon her was not in any way her fault! Or was it? Was there some lingering doubt in her mind about her own conduct? No, not really. She had not sought that young man. He had come out of the darkness to help her. He had insisted on staying by her and helping. He had come back of his own accord, without invitation. He had sent her flowers. There wasn't anything she could have done about it without being rude and ungrateful. Of course, she didn't have to go to that dinner with him, but her mother had approved and Miss York had thought it was wonderful, a chance for her to have a little innocent relaxation. No, it was something more than that that was troubling her. It was that kiss that she had allowed, no, in which she knew she had participated. Just the yielding of her lips, just the answering sweetness to his, a kiss that had seemed so reverent. Yet now she so loathed herself for having allowed it and having cherished it in her memory afterward. The man was likely engaged to this terrible girl, and yet he went around kissing other girls!

That other girl was beautiful. If she was his, why didn't he stay with her? Oh, it was a sickening world, all topsy-turvy. You couldn't trust anybody but God and your own mother. And perhaps even Mother had been wrong in thinking it was right for her to go to dinner with a stranger. And yet he hadn't seemed like a stranger. Oh, what should she do? How was she ever to look herself in the face again, how endure the thought of that session with that awful girl? How ever respect herself again?

Well, it was what came of trying to go with people of the world. It was all right so long as he was just helping her out of trouble, being kind and nice, but she ought to have made it stop at that. She knew what he was, of course. It was well enough to excuse herself by saying she mustn't misjudge a stranger. That was only an excuse. His very dress and manner marked him of another world than hers, and she knew in her heart, even if her mother didn't know, that he was not in her class. Well, she had her lesson now. Never would she forget the humiliation through which she had passed.

She put her head down on her hand and closed her eyes and tried to pray, but she found so much indignation in her heart that the prayer was choked.

She began to think over what she had said. She was glad, at least, that she had claimed her heavenly citizenship, her kinship to the royal family of God. And yet, she began to wonder whether even that had pleased God. She had done it in pride and anger, not for His glory. She remembered the words, "But God forbid that I should glory, save in the cross of our Lord Jesus Christ, by whom the world is crucified unto me, and I unto the world."

She hadn't been crucified to the world while she was getting off those smart sentences about belonging to royalty. She had been trying to show off, to say something that would startle that insolent girl. If she had been entirely crucified to the world—dead with Christ, and in this death-union with Him entering into His risen life, His resurrection power—mere words could not have hurt.

And now, indeed, a crimson color of shame rolled into her cheeks. Now she was honestly facing facts. She had boasted of her heavenly citizenship just as the world might boast. She had not boasted of the great salvation that had come to her life. She had said nothing of the fact that she had been a sinner saved by an infinitely loving Savior. She hadn't boasted of the cross of her Lord Jesus Christ, which had put her into the royal family. She had boasted in an earthly way and tried to make that girl think she was great in the earthly sense.

The wind grew suddenly sharp and cut through her thin coat, making her shiver. The sunshine faded to drab, and the day seemed overcast. There were even worse things than having a girl of the world class her with common flirts and women of the street. It was worse in the eyes of God, yes, and in her own eyes now that she realized it, to have swaggered and boasted of her heavenly lineage as if it were some inherent good in herself that gave her the right to claim such glorious kinship with the Most High.

That was the bitterest hour that Camilla had ever passed, sitting there looking into her own heart and seeing no superiority in it whatsoever. Robbed of her own spiritual conceit, robbed of her budding joy in her friendship with a man whom she had, of course, idealized—she saw that, too, now—robbed of a certain family pride, which had helped her out many and many a time when the going was hard and rough, she was just plain, shamed Camilla Chrystie with nothing to boast about at all, save that the Lord Jesus Christ had shed His precious blood on Calvary to redeem her.

Suddenly she was recalled to the fact that it was freezing, that the deep-toned bell of the big clock on the city hall was striking two o'clock and she was due back at the office at one thirty! The letters, the important letters, were not finished!

She rose hastily and walked on feet that were numb with cold and excitement, almost ran back to her office, and arrived, breathless.

"Well, I'll say you had plenty lunch!" said Marietta Pratt, shifting her gum to the other side of her jaw and inspecting Camilla's chilly, anxious face. "Whad'ya do? Have a heavy date?"

"No," said Camilla sharply, "I—it was something—I had to do. I didn't have any lunch at all. I thought I'd get back sooner. You didn't by any chance get your letters finished, did you? I wanted to get them all off by three. Hasn't Mr. Whitlock come back yet?"

Marietta, who had improved the time in the absence of Camilla and the chief by reading a library book full of murder thrills and mystery, furtively slid the volume under some papers in her desk drawer and whirled around to her typewriter.

"Naw, he ain't come in yet. He phoned ta say he'd be late. Some conference he's got on. Naw, I didn't get my letters all done yet. I'm workin' on 'em now. I didn't know there was any hurry. Say, whyn't you go on out an' get some lunch now? He won't be back fer a while, an' I'll tell him you're comin' right back."

"Thanks, no," said Camilla wearily, "I've got to get this work done and off." She sat down at her typewriter, and her fingers fairly flew. It was good to get to work again, good not to have to think, just to do the mechanical, routine work and forget her humiliation. She ignored the empty feeling in her stomach and the dizziness in her head. She wrote like a mad machine running away from its driver.

Along toward four o'clock Marietta paused in her own machinations, gave a languid chew or two to her gum while she surveyed her companion, and then said commiseratingly, "You don't look sa good! You better go out 'n get a good strong cup o' coffee! That'll set ya up. It don't do ta go 'thout meals, not's hard's you work!"

"Oh, I'm all right," said Camilla briskly. "I've just got a little headache, that's all."

"Ef I was you, I'd go home. I would. Like as not Mr. Whitlock'll never come back this afternoon 'tall. He'd never know. I won't tell."

Marietta did want to find out who did the murder in her book, and if Camilla went home there would be nothing to stop her reading. But Camilla only shook her head and smiled vaguely.

"No," she said, "I've got to finish my work. I'm quite all right." And she typed on, faster than ever, and poor Marietta was forced to work, too.

As a matter of fact, Camilla stayed at the office later than usual that night, for Mr. Whitlock came rushing in a little before five with two very important letters he wanted answered that night, and Camilla had to take dictation for another half hour and then wait to type the letters and mail them.

But Camilla was glad. She had an excuse to give her mother for her great weariness. Mother always noticed when there was anything the matter.

So at last Camilla's long day was done and she was free to take her car from the parking space and go home. She wended her way carefully through traffic, reminded sharply of that other night not so long ago when she had started on that wild trip for the doctor and had met with disaster and found a friend. Suddenly a kind of faintness swept over her. She must not count him as a friend anymore. She would never think of him as a friend without remembering the words of that disgusting girl. Those words had swept away from her in one brief instant all the pleasant comfort of his friendship. It reared a wall of unknown possibilities. It made him out a creature of whims and fancies whom it was not safe to trust.

Not that she had expected to continue the comradeship anymore now that the incident was past, not that she had ever counted on anything more than friendship, but to have to feel that any thought venturing in his direction must be forbidden seemed like snatching away a pleasant perfume, a lovely flower. It placed all that she thought she had on a sordid basis.

Her face flamed in the dark as she thought of it again, and then she knew by the imminence of tears that she positively must not think of this or she would be sure to cry as soon as she reached home and then Mother would be distressed, and she could not tell Mother. Mother would be shocked and horrified. Mother would feel that her very respectability had been assailed, her family insulted, her young maidenhood outraged. Mother was that way. She belonged to the age where those things mattered so much. If Mother had been a man and a Southerner she would have considered the experience of the morning reasonable grounds to send a challenge to her assailant. Quiveringly, she smiled a sad little smile over the folly and futility of pride. Her vigil in the park had showed her deeper things than mere pride.

And behind it all was that kiss! The kiss that she had wanted to feel was a holy thing, a thing not of the flesh, but a spiritual thing, yet that in the light of present events would probably not prove to be so if it were brought out into the open. Camilla did not mean that it should be brought out into the open. Between herself and God she would ask forgiveness for her part in it, for her leniency with it, her pitiful eagerness and thrill over it. Then she would put it away as a thing that was dead, a thing that had no right to be, and ask God to blot it out of her life. But never would she bring it out to the light of day and examine it. If it were real, it was too precious to be handled lightly. Since it could not be, why suffer anymore? She had learned her lesson, which was probably the reason it all had happened.

Chapter 9

Camilla put her car in the shabby little garage and went in as briskly and casually as possible.

"Sorry I had to be late," she said as she saw the anxious look on her mother's face. "I should have telephoned, but I kept thinking I would get away in a few minutes, and I didn't realize the time."

"Oh, my dear!" said the gentle voice. "Have you had to work so late? That's inhuman! Couldn't you have promised to come down a little earlier in the morning and do the extra work? You look so tired!"

"No, it had to get off in the night mail. Yes, I am a little tired." Camilla pressed her hand to her temples. "And I've got one of the miserable, mean old headaches in my eyes. But don't worry. I'll be all right when I get some dinner and a good night's rest. You know this doesn't happen often, Mother dear!" She gathered her frail little mother into her arms hungrily and kissed her soft, warm cheeks. She had her mother, anyway. She mustn't worry about other things. What did anything else matter when Mother was well again?

She summoned a fairly bright smile and sat down. She did not see how she was going to eat a mouthful, but yet she had to for Mother's sake. And then everything was so good that presently she found herself enjoying every mouthful.

"It's all so good, so delicious!" she said like a child who had been lost somewhere in a barren wasteland and had just gotten home where it was safe and comfortable. The day behind her seemed so wild and the way so hard.

"I'm glad I didn't make potpie after all," said her mother contentedly, watching her eat. "I was going to make potpie first, because you like it so much, but I changed to biscuits instead. I thought maybe you'd be late, and the potpie won't wait, you know. It has to be eaten right out of the pot or it falls and is heavy as lead."

"These biscuits are wonderful!" murmured the girl happily, thinking that perhaps after all the day had been but a bad dream and life was going to be livable again. She and her mother together was enough to be happy without others.

But later, when everything was in order in the kitchen, the table set for breakfast, the light out, Mother asleep, and Camilla in her bed in the front room, then came the memories in a wild flock like so many cormorants and sat around her on the dim shapes of the chairs and tables and other furniture in the dark room. They shouted out taunting and arrogant words at her until she felt that she would scream aloud and her mother would be sure to hear and demand to know the whole story. She thought she would never get to sleep. The night was going, the morning would come, and she would be unfit to go to the office. Oh, what should she do?

But sleep did come after all, and she awoke, startled to find the new day full of sunshine and her troubles not quite as heavy upon her as the night before. At least she was able to look forward to going back to the office without quite so much dread. The young woman with the gold hair would not likely haunt her steps the rest of her days. And since Wainwright was in Florida it wasn't reasonable to suppose that the girl would make her any more trouble, at least until his return.

So she went back to her office with her mind intent on her work, determined to keep so busy that she would have no opportunity to think any more about the matter. It was an incident of the past and that was all. Probably the young man would have forgotten all about her by the time he came back.

So she tried to cheer herself into contentment and forget the things that troubled her.

But now something new loomed on her stormy horizon. Mr. Whitlock, usually so quiet and courteous, so staid and dignified, came into the office with a frown on his face.

"I am looking for a letter," he said after he had searched through his desk and looked carefully over the letters in the letter tray. "It should have come in yesterday afternoon. Miss Chrystie, are you sure you did not see it? It was from Cleveland. The firm you wrote last week, you remember? They promised me an answer not later than yesterday. Are you *quite sure* nothing came? You put all the mail in my usual letter tray? You are *sure?*"

He looked at Camilla with almost an accusatory gleam in his eyes. It was evident that he was greatly excited.

Camilla told him she was sure the letter had not come. She got up from her work and went over to help him hunt, although she was positive no such letter had arrived. He kept insisting that it must surely be there somewhere, perhaps had fallen into an open drawer or the wastebasket.

At last he turned toward Marietta, who had been placidly polishing her typewriter, and told her in no very uncertain terms that she was wasting her time and that she should have been at her typing long ago. He spoke more sharply than either of the girls had ever heard him speak before.

He sat down at his desk and wrote out several telegrams for Camilla to send off. Then he had a couple of stormy conversations over the telephone, and finally, in going over to the rack where his hat and overcoat hung, his anxious eyes still searching for the letter, which he was sure must have come and been carelessly mislaid, he spied Marietta's ubiquitous novel sticking out of the lower drawer of her desk.

"What's that?" he snapped sharply.

"It's—it's just a book," said Marietta, with a frightened look in her eyes. "Just a liberry book."

"What's it doing here in the office?" he asked sharply, eyeing the girl, who drooped under his gaze and dropped her eyelashes over her startled eyes. "Is that what you're doing while you're supposed to be working for me? Is that why my work doesn't get done on time? You are reading novels betweentimes? Your mind is on some mystery story or other instead of on your work?"

"Oh no, sir!" Marietta hastened to explain glibly. "I just brought it along to leave at the liberry on my way home. It's just a—a book—my stepmother borrowed!"

He looked the girl keenly in the eyes.

"Don't try to lie to me!" he said dryly. "Pick up that book and take it in the cloakroom, and don't bring any more novels into this office!"

Then he went out, slamming the door hard behind him.

"What's eatin' the poor egg?" said Marietta as the man went out. She looked suspiciously toward Camilla as if she ought to be able to explain the mystery. But Camilla went right on working.

"He's the crankiest old thing I ever saw," finished Marietta, with an ugly frown. "He told me yesterday morning before you came in that he didn't know as he'd want me after this month was over. He wasn't sure but he was going to make an entire change in the office force. Did he say anything to you?"

"No," said Camilla, trying to keep her voice from trembling, "he has scarcely spoken to me for a week. Something must have gone exceedingly wrong in his affairs."

"I'll say!" said the girl shortly, and then most unexpectedly she banged her head down on her machine and began to cry with great shaking sobs.

Camilla looked at her an instant in consternation, and then she summoned voice to speak.

"Don't feel bad, Marietta," she said. "Maybe he's only got indigestion."

"Indigestion, nothing!" gurgled out Marietta. "He means it! I'm sure he does. He's got something on his mind. I been knowing it fer some time. He's made me do every last thing over twice for three whole days. And I've just b-b-begun ta buy a fur-r-r coat!"

"Oh, well, I wouldn't worry," said Camilla with a secret qualm for herself. "There will be other jobs."

"Not ef yer laid off. Not in these days!" said Marietta firmly, sitting up, mopping her wet eyes and getting out her lipstick and tiny mirror to repair damage in her facial landscape. "I heard when I came here he was kinda odd, but he was so nice at first I thought they had the wrong dope, but now I guess they were right. Anyhow, I don't know what I'll do. I'm buyin' it on installments."

"Well," said Camilla, trying to smile for the other girl's sake, "there's always something that can be done."

"Mebbe fer you, but not fer me," said the other girl dejectedly. "You're lucky! You c'n always get by. You work hard and know your job. And besides all that, you're a good-looker. Good-lookers always get by."

"Oh, no!" said Camilla sorrowfully. "Sometimes they get into worse trouble than the others. But, Marietta, looks don't have anything to do with it. If you do your work well, you'll be sure to get a position. If he turns us both away we'll go out together and hunt a double job. How about it?"

Marietta looked up in amazement.

"You mean that? Say! You're great! I really believe you'd do it. I knew the minute I laid eyes on you, you were different from the common run. I couldn't make out what made it, till I sighted you readin' that little Testament the other day, and then I knew. You're a Christian, aren't you? A real one, I mean, not just a bread-and-butter one, nor a whited-sepulcher kind. Well, I'm real pleased you said that, even ef you don't ever have to do it, and I don't expect you will. You're too good-lookin' ta get the go-by! He'll never let you go, even ef he didn't like your work, which he does. But I'm pleased ta know there is one girl in these days that's an out an' out Christian."

Camilla was thoughtful a long time after that. Of course, this might be the beginning of the end, and she must be prepared for it, but there was something that touched her in this girl's speech, and presently she said, "Marietta, aren't you a Christian?"

Marietta laughed.

"Not me!" she said derisively. "I'm the devil! You oughtta see me at home. I live with my stepmother, and she's some hotshot. She dresses up like all good night and goes out ta parties and plays bridge and never gets me a thing. I wouldn't stay with her a day ef it wasn't fer my kid stepbrother. He's a cripple, an' I can't bear ta leave him alone with her. She never loved him much, an' after he was hurt and his back began to grow crooked, seems as though she just hates the sight of him. I gotta stick by an' bring a little fun inta his life, ur I'd been gone from home long ago."

"Oh, Marietta!" said Camilla with instant sympathy. "Isn't that too bad! I wish I could do something to help. But—doesn't your father care for him?"

"He's dead!" said Marietta sadly. "Yes, he liked Ted, and useta hold him in his lap an' bring him toys and nice things ta eat when he could get by with it, but my stepmother, she didn't like it much. She just hates *me*! She'd send me flying now ef it weren't that I take Ted out Sundays and leave her free ta go. She's flighty, ya know. She wasn't more'n five years older 'n I when Dad married her. He told me that was the mistake of his life. He thought she'd be good company for me. Good night! 'Zif I'd want her company! Why, I ain't had a decent good time, ner no pretty clothes since my own mother died, an' I can't scarcely remember that! Not until I got this job. An' now ef I lose it I don't know what I'll do. I'm 'fraid she'll go an' put Ted in a home ur somethin', an' that'll kill him, poor kid!"

Marietta was sobbing again, and Camilla's heart was deeply touched. After all, there were deeper trials than her own. She might lose her job, but she still had her dear mother, and God would somehow provide for them. He always had.

So she laid aside her own fears and tried to comfort Marietta. And on her way home she was planning how she might invite Marietta out to see her some weekend, perhaps let her bring the little boy along and give him a really happy time.

She told her mother about Marietta that evening while they were eating their dinner, and Mrs. Chrystie was interested and sympathetic as always with anybody in distress and ready to plan to give the little cripple boy a good time.

"I'll make some cookies tomorrow, Camilla," she said, "and I'll make some funny shapes, a dog and a cat and a man, with currants for eyes, the way I used to for you when you were little. Children always like them. I saw the old cutters the other day when I was looking on the top shelf for a pan I needed. I'll make a little bag full for him, and you can take them to the sister. And can't you find one of your old books that you can lend him or give him?"

"Why yes," said Camilla brightly, and she went hunting up in the attic for old books and toys. She got so interested in getting things together that she forgot her own troubles for a while. Not once during the evening did she think of Wainwright or the girl with the jacinth eyes, and even her fears for her job were only dim forebodings now and then hovering on the margin of her mind.

But on the way down to the office the next morning she remembered what Marietta had said and felt again that dread for herself. What if she should lose her job now, while they were still in debt and Mother by no means out from under the doctor's care? Oh, what could she do? Where could she go for another job? Now, in these times, when jobs were almost impossible to find?

Then she remembered that God knew all about it. He had her life planned out for her. He knew her, and nothing was hidden from Him. She had been reading that verse in her Bible that very morning. He had planned everything in her life from the foundation of the world, and she need not be afraid. There would be a way out of this, the very way that He had planned!

Mr. Whitlock was in the office when Camilla arrived. He gave her a curt nod in answer to her good morning and went on with his writing. Camilla, as she went to the cloakroom to put away her things, felt her heart sinking. This day was going to be like yesterday, or more so. Any moment now she might be blamed for something; any moment she might be dismissed!

Marietta looked frightened when she came in and hid the paper package she was carrying under her arm. But Mr. Whitlock did not even look up or notice her entrance. He was very intent on his own affairs. Marietta hung up her things and hurriedly went to work.

Mr. Whitlock stayed at his desk until the mail came and then, with a set grim look on his face, went out. Marietta worked more steadily than usual, and Camilla saw no book around. She did a fair amount of work and seemed anxious to let Camilla know how much she had accomplished, though she did not interrupt her as much as usual.

At noon Camilla produced the book and a few simple puzzles she had found in the attic and asked Marietta if she thought Ted would like them, and Marietta was overjoyed. She also told her about the cookies her mother was making for him, and actual tears came to the homely girl's eyes.

"Say, now, isn't that wonderful!" she exclaimed. "My, how lucky you are to have a mother like that! My, ef I had a mother, I'd do just everything she said! Say, I guess that's one thing that makes you different from the other girls, isn't it, having a mother like that? My! I'd like ta see her sometime! But she wouldn't approve of me! Me, I'm a devil! That's what my stepmother calls me!"

Camilla wanted to say something kind and comforting to the girl who seemed so forlorn and lonely, but just then they heard Mr. Whitlock's quick, impatient steps coming down the hall. Marietta scuttled into the cloakroom with the things Camilla had given her, hid them, and was back working away at her machine with unusual diligence when he finally reached the door and entered.

Chapter 10

For the rest of that week matters at the office were exceedingly strained. Mr. Whitlock came and went, scarcely looking at either of his secretaries, saying nothing except what was absolutely necessary, smiling not at all, and each day found Camilla's hopes going down lower than the day before. It seemed to her as if she should scream if this kept up much longer.

Then one morning the letter from Cleveland came and things relaxed a little. There was obvious relief in Mr. Whitlock's face as he read it, and his tone was more like his old self, gracious, courteous, reserved, as he dictated the answer. Camilla thought she understood partly what had been troubling him, and she drew a free breath and took heart of hope.

Marietta, child of emotion, on the other hand, unbound from the lease of fear once more, lapsed into her novel on the slightest pretext. Not the same novel by this time, of course, but another of like thrilling interest, and at once her rate of production dropped again. Marietta bounded up from her temporary grinding industry as a bird let loose and tried to be chummy and friendly with her dignified employer, just to reassure herself that the strain was all over.

But Camilla could not so soon forget her anxiety, and she redoubled her efforts to be letter-perfect in every way in her work.

Yet as things grew brighter again at the office and her fears began to drop away, her thoughts went back to dreaming again, and she could not keep Wainwright out of her mind. Would she never get this thing conquered, or was it just that she had been under so much strain that her thoughts sought naturally the only little incident in her monotonous life that had given a bit of a thrill?

Then she would recall bit by bit the incident of Stephanie Varrell's visit and her hateful insinuations until her pride would rise and put the whole matter out of mind.

Sometimes it seemed to her that she just must tell her mother everything. There was no one but her mother who could help to take the sting out of the whole affair and make her see things sanely and be able to laugh at it all, rather than to brood over it.

But still she could not bring herself to put it upon her mother, for in spite of all she would say, and the way she would smile over it and say it was not worth worrying over, she knew it would be a mortification to her mother that the girl had dared to come to her that way.

And also, Camilla hesitated just because she didn't want her mother to lose her beautiful faith in Wainwright. She wanted her to go on admiring him, as she could not admire him perhaps if she knew of his friendship with such a girl as Miss Varrell—if she knew of the kiss that he had given her own daughter!

So Camilla closed her lips on the whole affair and did her best to close her heart and her mind to it also.

She was just congratulating herself that she had put it all behind her and had not thought of it for one whole day when

Marietta Pratt came to her one morning with a page from the society news of the night before.

"Say," she said with a grin, "whatcha putting over on us? Have you got a double, or do ya take a plane an' fly down ta Palm Beach weekends, ur what? Mebbe it's only weekends, but here ya are as plain as day."

She spread the page across Camilla's desk, and there, occupying the larger portion of the upper half of the sheet, was a full-length picture of the golden-haired beauty who had visited her in that office only a short week before! And by her side, tall, easy, grinning in his own adorable way, stood Jeffrey Wainwright! They were attired in bathing suits, the lady's white and most abbreviated. Camilla did not need to read the names below, for the eyes of Jeffrey Wainwright looked into hers with his own friendly confidence and gave her heart a terrible thrust. She knew the girl also, immediately, in spite of the fact that the expression on her face was far from being the same one she had worn the last time she saw her.

The caption below, though Camilla tried not to read it, went deep into her consciousness and undid all the careful control of a week: "Two who are often seen together on the beach" it said. "millionaire's son and noted beauty. Jeffrey Judson Wainwright, son of Robert Wainwright of the famous Wainwright Consolidated Corporation, seen on the beach in America's greatest winter playground with Stephanie Varrell, former stage star and divorced wife of Harold Varrell of California. Rumor has it that the two are engaged, though there is a famous foreign actor who seems to be second in the running, if one may judge by appearance."

Camilla turned sharply away after getting the first line, but Marietta read it aloud, rolling each syllable like a sweet morsel under her tongue and kept on reading it after Mr. Whitlock entered.

"Look, Mr. Whitlock," she called out familiarly, holding up the picture, nothing daunted by his entrance, "isn't that fer all the world like Camilla Chrystie? I'd swear it was her if I didn't know she'd been here all week."

Mr. Whitlock, with his habitual gravity, looked down at the picture and then cast a quick look at Camilla, seeming to take in her delicacy and loveliness for the first time.

"Why yes, it does resemble Miss Chrystie," he said, and Camilla saw him glace over the paragraph below the picture. But she took good care to be hard at work when he glanced up at her again. She was glad that he made no further comment.

The day went forward busily like other days and no more was said about the picture, but Camilla was strangely shaken. Somehow she could not put the thought of it away. Here was all her work to be done over again. It seemed she hadn't forgotten the charming stranger at all nor the girl who carried venom under her tongue. She had to be seeing them all day running around in bathing suits together. She had to see that nice straight grin on his fine features and the possessive, cocky smile in the other girl's eyes as she looked up at him in the picture. How it all made her anger rise, and she felt more than ever her own helplessness. How she began to wish she had never seen either of them! How she loathed herself!

She stayed late in the office that afternoon after the others had gone. Somehow her work had lagged and she had not accomplished all that she knew she ought. It was better now that her employer and Marietta were gone.

She was still working away at her typewriter when Mr. Whitlock returned and unlocked his desk to find some papers he needed. When he had locked it again he lingered and hesitated, looking toward her.

"You needn't finish those letters tonight," he said graciously. "There is no great haste. If they get off by eleven tomorrow, they will be in plenty of time."

Camilla looked up, surprised at his kindliness. He was a man of few words.

"Thank you," she said with a weary little smile. "I'm on the last one. And tomorrow's work will be coming on. I'd rather finish each day in itself whenever possible."

"You're very faithful," he said gravely. "Suppose when you are done we go out and get some dinner together."

Camilla looked up, surprised.

"Thank you," she said gratefully, "but I couldn't. My mother hasn't been very well, you know, and I don't leave her alone evenings yet if I can help it."

"I see," said the man pleasantly, noticing the delicacy of her features and the golden sheen of her hair where the light over her desk fell full upon it. "You shouldn't, of course. Some other time perhaps."

He said no more, and Camilla went on with her work.

When she had finished her last letter she closed her desk for the night, put on her coat, and paused just an instant beside her employer's desk to say a deferential good night.

He looked up and said good night, and suddenly his face broke into a smile. It occurred to her that she had never before seen him smile, except gravely when there were strangers in the office. It made his face most attractive. The smile lit up his eyes. He had nice eyes. Who was it they made her think of? Someone she liked?

She was puzzling over it as she went out and down the hall and while she stood waiting for the elevator. Nice eyes! And his voice had been kind and friendly! The echo of his good night seemed to follow her and be even yet ringing quietly in the marble hall. And here she had been worrying for a whole week lest she might be going to lose her job! It comforted her that he had gone out of his way to be nice to her, asking her to go out to dinner with him. It made her position more assured in these uncertain times. And, of course, he was a friend of the Barrons in her hometown. It was only decent that he should show her a little friendliness after the letter of introduction Mr. Barron had written for her. Well, he had nice eyes, whoever it was that he looked like when he smiled!

Then suddenly she knew. Jeffrey Wainwright! Was she always to be thinking of him every minute? How ridiculous! Mr. Whitlock didn't resemble him in the least, of course, and something in her inmost soul resented the idea that she had thought so for a minute. Well, she must be going crazy to have such an obsession about Wainwright. She must snap out of it at once. It was a good thing that he had gone away when he had. A good thing that she was busy and could put him out of her mind!

Then she reverted pleasantly to Mr. Whitlock's invitation and his kindly smile. Well, here at least was something nice she could tell her mother. Mother would appreciate a thing like that, and she would never have an idea how fearful she had been all the week lest she might lose her job.

But when she reached home that night she found her mother in quite a flutter over a crate of luscious oranges and grapefruit that had arrived that afternoon with Jeffrey Wainwright's card enclosed, and Camilla was so filled with mingled delight and dismay that she forgot all about Whitlock's invitation. For a few minutes her heart got beyond all bounds and exulted. He hadn't forgotten them after all!

She went about putting away her coat and then came and looked at the wonderful golden spheres, so much more beautiful than any they could buy in the north, and her eyes shone and her cheeks glowed with more than the glow of the crisp air of the evening through which she had been driving.

"And he sent them to *me*," said her mother, shyly smiling. "Wasn't it lovely of him? Did you notice the marking? Though, of course, they were really meant for you."

"Not a bit of it!" said Camilla, with her chin up in a moment. "There was no reason whatever for him to send anything to me. It was just beautiful of him to send them to you. And I certainly am glad he had such good sense. You know, you are really the one he admires. He sent his first orchids to you. But how did you get the crate open?"

She watched her mother's eager face as she answered and was glad, glad, even though this was going to upset again all her fine self-discipline of the past week.

"Why, I made the deliveryman open it for me and gave him ten cents extra. And, Camilla, there were some real live orange blossoms wrapped in the wet gray moss stuck down among them. Go look at them. I put some of them on the table. Aren't they wonderful! Smell them. I remember that fragrance. Your father took me down to Florida once when we were first married, and we boarded for a whole week across the road from an orange grove. It's such a spicy odor. There is nothing else like it. I can remember how I felt about it. I used to lie in the hammock on the porch and listen to the mockingbirds singing and the whispering winds in those tall pines, and smell those orange blossoms, and think that heaven must be almost like that. It didn't seem as if there could be anything better in this world, anyway."

Camilla, to hide the tears that insisted upon stinging into her eyes, bent her tired young head and kissed her mother.

"You're a dear poet!" she said breathlessly. "Yes, the fragrance is wonderful indeed. Some day when I get rich I'll take you down there again, and we'll spend a whole winter smelling them. Now, I must wash my hands and face. They are just filthy!" And she slipped away to the bathroom to stop those tired tears and get some color into her face before her mother should have leisure to inspect her.

"He meant them for you, of course," said her mother as they sat down to the table where the nice little supper was set out so invitingly.

"Oh, no!" said Camilla quickly. "Mother, you must get that idea completely out of your head. Please, Mother, that young man has no more idea of doing anything for me than the president of these United States has. You don't realize who he is. I've been seeing his name in the papers. Mother, he's the son of the head of that great Wainwright Corporation that we hear so much about. He's rich as Croesus and is only tossing some golden guilders to a little beggar girl whom he picked up by the way when she was in trouble. It was nice of him to remember you. He must be unusual to remember even a dear sick lady like my precious mother, even a lady who resembles a very costly cameo. Mother, don't get notions in your head. He's just being *nice*, and I'll say that was *very* nice. And nicer still that he sent them to you instead of to me, for now I won't be put to the trouble of writing him a letter of thanks. *You'll* have to do it, and I'm *glad*!"

"Well," said the mother eagerly, "I'll do it! Of course I'll do it. I'll love to do it! I think he's wonderful, and I'll tell him so. He may be rich, and he may be playing, but he doesn't forget kindness, and that's a great thing in this busy world."

"Oh yes," said Camilla with worldly wisdom, as if she were the elder, "only, Mother dear, don't get notions about him, for you'll only have to get over them if you do. We likely shan't see him again. He doesn't belong to our world."

Her mother gave her a quick, keen look.

"It is all God's world, Camilla," said her mother softly.

"Yes, but we're not all God's children," said Camilla, almost wearily. "Only in the sense that God made us. You taught me that yourself, Mother. You said we were not God's children till we were born again."

"How do you know he is not born again, child?" said the mother after a thoughtful pause.

"I'm sure he's not," said Camilla with a deep breath. Oh, must she be probed this way forever? "That is, I'm pretty sure," she added. "He didn't speak like it."

"We can pray for him," said the mother softly.

"Yes, we can pray," sighed the girl, as if just now she had very little faith to pray for a man like that, "but—we aren't in his class. But, anyhow, these oranges are great, aren't they? And wouldn't it be nice to send half a dozen to Miss York?"

"Send her a dozen," said the mother eagerly, and then she forgot to probe farther.

And then Miss York herself came walking in.

"Just for a glimpse of you two," she said wistfully. "Somehow you seem more like home folks than anybody I've met since Mother died."

They had a nice cheery little talk and a good laugh over some of the funny things that happened in the new household where Miss York was nursing, and Camilla forgot her troubles for the time until they were at work packing the basket of fruit for the nurse to take with her.

"Put a spray of orange blossoms in," called the mother from the other room.

"No, no, don't waste orange blossoms on me!" said Nurse York, stooping over to smell them. "I'm out of the running for orange blossoms at my age. All omens have failed on me. Keep them all for Camilla. They belong to her. I always said it wasn't but a step from orchids to orange blossoms, and it looks as if it had proved right again."

Then suddenly weary Camilla flushed crimson.

"Don't! Please!" she said sharply and hurried out to the kitchen to get a few more oranges and hide her tortured face.

She was back again in a minute, though, trying to laugh it off.

"You're all wrong," she explained with an elaborate smile on her face. "The orange blossoms and the oranges were sent to Mother, not me, and perhaps you'll recall that the most of the orchids were Mother's."

"Oh yeah?" said Miss York with a very good imitation of a small boy with his tongue in his cheek.

"Well, you can laugh," said Camilla seriously, "but really, you are all wrong, and you'll just have to put aside all your silly romantic notions, for I have it on very good authority that the young man you are talking about is as good as engaged to another girl."

Camilla brought out the words clearly, as if she were reading a lesson on her own soul. Her mother eyed her keenly, but Miss York only said, "Is that so!" mockingly, as though she had inside information and were enjoying her own thoughts.

Camilla went and got her purse and paid the nurse her monthly stipend that had been agreed upon between them. She did it with satisfaction. Come what would, her debts were that much smaller, anyway.

Camilla did not expect to sleep much that night. She had intended to take out her troubles when her mother was asleep and look them over carefully and pray about them, but when morning came she found that instead she had fallen asleep almost the minute her head touched the pillow and with only the briefest kind of a prayer, though she was so much in need of one.

Chapter 11

Mr. Whitlock was in the office when Camilla got there the next morning. He looked up with his pleasant new smile of greeting, and Camilla went happily to her desk and began to get ready for the day's work.

Suddenly her employer spoke in a pleasant, friendly tone.

"How about going to lunch with me this noon, Miss Chrystie?" he asked. "There's a matter about the office that I would like to talk over with you. Some changes that I'm thinking of making to which I would like to get your reaction. I thought we might find a quiet place where we could talk it over while we eat?"

His manner was gravely quiet, though there was still that friendly light in his eyes, and Camilla could not help feeling pleased, although she had no special desire to go out to lunch with Mr. Whitlock. Still, this was more or less a matter of her job, she supposed, and of course she would go. She probably ought to be pleased that he thought it worthwhile to consult her about the office. At least it would keep her thoughts from other things.

"Thank you," she said. "I shall be glad to go."

It suddenly occurred to her that this would be something more she could tell her mother and that she had been so full of interest in the oranges that she had forgotten last night to say anything of the day's happenings.

"Very well," said Whitlock, "I'll arrange to be here at the office for you at one o'clock."

And just then Marietta came in.

Whitlock sat still at his desk writing for several minutes more while Marietta was taking off her coat in a leisurely way. Her scare was a thing of the past, and she had fully recovered her spirits. The door of the cloakroom was open wide, and she was watching Mr. Whitlock, wondering if he were in a good mood and if she dared to ask for the afternoon off so she could take Ted to the movies.

But just as she was about to come out to her desk she saw Mr. Whitlock, with an envelope in his hand, step over to her desk. He laid it down beside her machine and immediately took his hat and coat and went out of the room.

With a dart of sudden fear in her eyes she went out and snatched up the envelope, which she saw was addressed to herself. She tore it open frantically and read with growing horror in her face.

Camilla was writing away at top speed, trying to get a lot done before she went out to lunch, in case she should be detained beyond her usual time. She didn't want to have to stay late again that night, for she knew her mother would be uneasy having her late two nights in succession. But there was something so weird and heartbroken in the sound that Marietta gave forth that Camilla had to turn around and see what was the matter.

There stood Marietta with the letter in her hand, consternation in her homely, stubby young face, and a check lying at her feet.

"I'm fired!" she cried in a tone something between a wail and a squeak. "I'm *fired*! And I promised last night to take Ted to the circus! And now I can't even pay for my fur coat!"

Camilla couldn't help but smile over the order in which Marietta's woes had culminated in her mind; the circus and the moment would always come before other considerations with Marietta.

"I'm fired! Can you beat it?" asserted Marietta, as if it were something almost beyond her comprehension.

"Oh, Marietta!" cried Camilla sympathetically, "not *really*?" And suddenly Camilla took in the full possibilities, which might involve her also. Her heart began to sink. And here she had been congratulating herself on the fact that she was invited out to lunch with her employer to be consulted about office affairs and was therefore immune to this danger! How did she know but this would be his polite way of breaking the news to her, a little less abruptly than the method he had used with Marietta because she had been introduced by an old friend and was from his home-town? That was probably it! He was taking her out and explaining to her why he had to make changes in his office force! Consternation spread over her face also, but she managed a tender look of commiseration for Marietta.

"Oh, Marietta, I'm so sorry!" she said as she saw the big tears begin to rain down the poor girl's face.

"You aren't fired, too, are ya?" Marietta paused in her grief to inquire sobbingly. " 'Cause if you are I'm gonta tell him what I think of him. You aren't, are ya?"

"Not yet," said Camilla bravely, trying to manage a wan smile, "but I'll probably come next. But anyway, I'll do all I can to help you get another job, whether I'm dismissed or not."

"Say—you're—all—r-r-right!" sobbed Marietta. "I'll—always re-remember—you—saying that! But—maybe you won't get fired. Mebbe he means ta make you do all your work and mine, too!" she blubbered noisily. "He's mebbe cutting down on expenses like everybody else, an' he's keeping you 'cause you're the most ef-f-f-ficient! Oh, I know you are! I never was m-m-much—g-g-good!"

"Don't talk that way, Marietta. I'm sure if you would just put your mind to it you could be as efficient as anybody."

"Oh, I know," said Marietta hopelessly, "that's what they told me the last place I worked. But some days I just *can't*! Life is so awful dull, just working! I havta have some excitement! I can't help thinkin' of other things besides just work. If I didn't I'd *die*! I haven't got dates and fellas like other girls! I'm not good-looking like you are. Nobody cares a hang about me!"

"Oh, don't say that, Marietta!" said Camilla pityingly. "I'm sure little Ted is fond of you."

"Oh yes, poor kid!" said Marietta hopelessly. "But what's he? And he wouldn't care a hang, either, if he had another soul in the world to turn to. He wouldn't look at me if his mother paid any attention to him."

"Oh yes he would," consoled Camilla. "Children aren't like that; they respond with love when love comes to them, I'm sure, and you've given him love. He must love you."

"Oh, well, he's the only one anyhow. There isn't another soul in the wide world cares about me."

"Yes," said Camilla softly, thoughtfully, "there is another One who cares a great deal! He cares so much that He came down here to die for you. He loves you more than even a mother could love!"

Marietta stared at her.

"Whaddya mean?" she asked, getting out her handkerchief to mop her face.

"I mean the Lord Jesus Christ. Marietta, He really loves you and takes account of every single thing in your life."

Marietta's expression was incredulity, and a deep gloom settled down over her homely face.

"Then what does He let me lose my job for, if He loves me so much? Why did He let that happen?" she asked belligerently. "Naw, you can't make me believe that bunk! Look at all the rotten times I've had. If He cares, why would He let all that come to me?"

"Perhaps to make you listen to Him," said Camilla thoughtfully.

Marietta turned to her fellow worker—her swollen tear-stained face on which the cheap makeup was badly streaked—and stared.

"Listen to Him? What in the world can you mean?"

Camilla spoke eagerly.

"You know, God speaks to every one of us. He wants to make us hear His voice, and sometimes when everything is going beautifully and we're having a good time, we just won't listen. We never even think of Him! I think very likely that is often why He has to take everything away from us for a while, so we can hear His voice in our hearts."

Marietta looked at her in bewilderment.

"But what would He want of us?"

"He wants us to love Him! He wants our companionship and love!"

Marietta shook her head.

"Not me!" she said decidedly. "He wouldn't want me! Nobody wants me. I'm not good-looking, and I'm not good. I'm a devil, I tell ya, a little devil! Why, Camilla Chrystie, I'm a *sinner!*"

"Yes," said Camilla sweetly, "but we're all that, and Jesus said He came not to call the righteous, but sinners to repentance."

"Aw! Sinner nothing. Everybody ain't the same kind of a sinner. You don't know what I mean by sin! Why, I've lied, and I've stolen—I stole some money off my stepmother once ta get a box of candy fer little Ted when she had slapped him! And I've hated! I've hated her so hard I could have killed her ef I'd had a chance, yes, and been glad of it! Oh, you don't know what a sinner I've been! He wouldn't want me except ta punish me, and I s'pose that's what He's doing now."

"But you don't understand, Marietta; single sins don't make us sinners, they only *prove* we're sinners. We sin *because* we're sinners. There is only one sin, anyway, that can keep you from God, and that is unbelief, refusing God's Son as your Savior."

Marietta was silent, almost thoughtful for a long minute, staring at Camilla.

"I'd believe all righty ef He'd just give me back my job!"

Camilla shook her head.

"We can't make conditions with God. We've got to take His conditions. He says belief must come first, belief accepts salvation. Why, if you know somebody loves you, you're not afraid to trust them to do their best for you. And God's best for you may be a great deal better than anything you have dreamed of for yourself."

Marietta looked uncertainly at Camilla and slowly sat down in her chair, staring off into space sorrowfully.

"I can't see it," she said, shaking her head hopelessly.

"You don't have to see it," said Camilla. "You just have to trust Him and let Him prove it to you."

Camilla leaned over and picked up the check from the floor, laying it in Marietta's lap. Marietta looked down at it with a long quivering sigh.

"He's paid me for the whole month," she said sadly, fingering the check. "I s'pose that's the last money I'll get the feel of for many a day! He says I can leave tamorra morning ef I want! But gosh! What'll I do?"

Bang went her head down on her typewriter again, and she began to cry afresh.

Camilla went over and patted her rough, crimped head gently. She felt very pitiful toward her. She almost forgot that she herself might be presently in the same predicament.

"Come, dear," she said suddenly, stooping over and smoothing Marietta's stiff locks away from her hot forehead, "let's get back to work. This won't make things any better. We've got to finish up this day's work honorably, whatever comes!"

"Not me!" said Marietta, looking up with flashing eyes. "I'll not do another stroke for the old snake!"

"Oh yes you will, Marietta. You'd only be justifying his dismissal if you do that. Come, let's get to work and see who will finish first."

Suddenly Camilla followed an impulse and, stooping over, kissed Marietta's hot forehead gently.

Marietta stared back.

"What did you do that for?" she asked, fixing Camilla with her dark, haunted eyes.

"Why, I guess because I loved you and felt sorry for you," said Camilla with sudden surprise at herself.

"You couldn't!" said Marietta. "That's impossible for you to love me! Why should you love me?"

"Why, I guess it's because you are dear to my Lord Jesus," said Camilla, taking knowledge of her heart and realizing that she was speaking the truth. This unattractive girl had suddenly become surprisingly dear to her. "Whatever is dear to my Lord is dear to me!"

Marietta considered that a moment, and then she said, speaking slowly, with a kind of awe in her voice, "Well, if you really mean that, and you want me to, then I guess I've gotta do what you said. But I don't know's I know how ta do it."

"You just tell Him so!" said Camilla, with a sudden joy in her heart that drove out all her fears and perplexities and put her in touch with another world.

"You mean pray?" asked Marietta, embarrassed. "Right here? Now?"

Camilla nodded.

Down went Marietta's head on her machine again, and there was silence. Then in a moment more she lifted her face with a kind of shamed look on it, and yet a deep relief.

"I did!" she said almost sheepishly, as if she were playing a child's game.

"Good!" said Camilla. "And I've prayed, too! Now, let's get to work and make up for lost time!"

For a couple of hours the two machines clattered away without interruption, and Camilla knew by the sound that Marietta was really doing her best. Then suddenly they heard Mr. Whitlock's steps coming down the hall, and for an instant both girls held their breath and fell to trembling. Then Camilla realized that her strength was in her Lord and she must go on working. He would take care of whatever was to come.

But Mr. Whitlock gave no sign that he had noticed them. He took his mail and read it and then called Camilla to take dictation.

Camilla was glad to notice that Marietta did not stop for even the lifting of an eyelash but went steadily on with her work. She gave her a furtive glance once, while Mr. Whitlock was looking in his drawer for a paper he wanted enclosed in a certain letter, and saw that Marietta's eyes were still red and her face badly streaked with makeup that had been much smeared during her weeping, but she was evidently set to do her best, for that one morning at least.

It was exactly twelve o'clock when Mr. Whitlock finished dictation, closed his desk, and said briskly, "That will be all this morning, Miss Chrystie!"

Then he swung his chair around toward Marietta's corner.

"You might go to lunch now, Miss Pratt," he said in his usual curt office voice. "Miss Chrystie will have some copy ready for you by the time you return. I'd like you to do one hundred individual copies using the addresses in this list. Miss Chrystie will go to lunch as soon as she has the copy ready for you, and if she hasn't returned when you get here, you'll find full directions on your desk. I want this work done, finished, by four o'clock sharp!"

"Yessir!" said Marietta meekly, casting a frightened glance at Camilla. She got her hat and coat and hurried out. Camilla wondered if perhaps she would not bother to return.

Whitlock gathered up some papers and went out without any further word, and Camilla wondered if he had already forgotten about taking her to lunch. However, it was only twelve. But his brusque manner to Marietta made her uneasy.

She snapped a new sheet of paper into her machine and went on with her work, trying to keep her mind from worrying about the coming interview. Praying for strength to bear whatever it should be. Praying, too, for poor Marietta.

She had scarcely finished the copy for Marietta when the door swung open and Mr. Whitlock entered, gave a quick glance around the room, then came over to her desk. There was that friendly smile again, that disturbing smile that seemed more intimate with her than he really was. That smile that reminded her of another man who didn't resemble him in the least and yet who could smile deep down into her soul. Oh, was she always to be tormented by this vision, and just because of an unfortunate kiss? She must somehow manage to get rid of this obsession and see nothing but Mr. Whitlock in that smile, and not another's eyes smiling through his. Besides, this was business and might prove pretty important business at that. She must put her mind upon it. Perhaps it would mean promotion, a larger salary, if she conducted this interview wisely, or it might mean losing her job if she did not. She was pretty well convinced, however, that it meant the latter.

"Are you ready?" he asked in his friendly tone, so different from the one he had used all the morning that Camilla smiled in relief.

"Yes, just a moment till I arrange these papers for Marietta," she answered.

He held the door open for her deferentially, and again she was struck with a memory of Wainwright. Were all cultured men alike in the way they attended a lady, the way they held open a door? That was it, of course. She was remembering how Wainwright had done everything. Until Wainwright came it had been so long since she had been attended anywhere by a gentleman that she had forgotten the feel of it, and now she was just remembering how nice it was to be taken care of. That was all. It wasn't Wainwright she was remembering; it was culture and good times and all that belonged to just ordinary social intercourse. She had been too much apart from people, too much filled with her own problems, and now just this little bit of social life, going out to lunch with her employer for a business talk to save time, was getting entirely out of perspective. Well, she must snap out of this. She might be going out to get her dismissal, and if so, she must have her wits about her and take it with her head up.

Chapter 12

Jeffrey Wainwright was writing a letter.

The room where he sat looked out on a sunlit sea, and the breeze that came in the window and wafted the delicate curtains was laden with the mingled perfume of many flowers. On a tray at his hand a cooling drink frostily invited him and a big dish of tropical fruit stood on a table not far away.

Down below, beyond the terraces of the hotel, there were fountains playing, and tall palm trees waved their graceful fingers above mosaic walks and tiled pools. Off in the distance one could see the beach already dotted with eager bathers, some lying like porpoises, well browned in the gleaming sand. Farther on were the tennis courts where a couple of world-renowned champions were to play a match game that afternoon, and farther inland some of the best of fairways awaited his attention. Cars shot here and there on the hard, smooth roads; cheerful voices called to one another; bright garments attracted the eye; birds sang unearthly sweet carols; slow gulls floated lazily over a summer sea, hovered and floated again; little ships like toys lay in the harbor or floated afar on the blue—whether sea or sky, who could say?—and merry youth awaited and grew impatient. Yet Jeffrey Wainwright sat in his room writing a letter to Camilla. Camilla, who was driving away on her typewriter at mad speed, trying to forget him and suffering as only a girl can suffer who sees all the things she wants one by one drifting away from her.

A uniformed servant with a silver tray tapped at the door and delivered a note and a telegram, and waited deferentially for the young man to read them. He tore open the telegram and read the message: CAN'T POSSIBLY GET DOWN THERE THIS MONTH. YOU'LL HAVE TO CARRY ON A LITTLE LONGER. DAD. Then he took up the note and glanced at its unintelligible, scrawled summons. He knew it was a summons without reading its particular form and threw it carelessly down on the table.

"That's all right, Tyler," he said to the waiting servant. "No answer."

"Excuse me, Mister Wainwright," said the boy. "Miss Varrell said I was not to come down without an answer."

"All right, Tyler," he said with a frown, "then tell her I can't come at present. Tell her not to wait for me. Tell her to go on without me."

The servant left, and Wainwright went back to his letter. "Dear Camilla," he wrote, and then he paused to look distantly at the sea and conjure up the vision of Camilla. And every time he almost got sight of her off there against the blue, she turned into Stephanie, with her jacinth eyes, imperious smile, and red, red lips. Camilla's eyes were deep, deep brown, and her lips were touched with rose as they should be, not painted vivid fleshly red like a bleeding gash. Yet every time he tried to think the vision through and get a flash of Camilla herself, Stephanie came jarring through. It was like trying to sing a sweet new tune that yet had some notes of an old outworn one that would keep coming in and making discord. Why could he not see her face? It was almost as if Camilla were only a figment of his imagination. Yet she had haunted his thoughts until he sat down to write to her, and now she would not seem real to him.

Dear Camilla. He looked at the words and poised his pen. There were things in his heart that he knew he must not write. Things that were not yet in words, not even consciously in thoughts, but yet he had to write to her.

He wanted to write and let her know that there was a good reason why he did not come to her, but very likely she had not noticed that he had not. He had no reason to think she would care one way or the other. No reason except that there was something between them, an unspoken something that passed in that kiss he had given her. When he thought of it, he had to close his eyes, it seemed so holy to him. It seemed to mark a time in his life, an epoch that could never be forgotten, a something like a pledge from him to her, and yet he did not exactly know what that pledge was, only that it was a pledge, and he meant to keep it.

If he closed his eyes from looking at the sea to see her lovely face and her golden hair against the blue, he could feel again the thrill of that kiss, like no kiss he had ever given or received before. It made all other kisses seem common and unclean. This was something quite holy and apart. It was not only a pledge, a tie, between him and the girl to whom he had given it, but it went deeper; it pledged something far beyond, something spiritual that he could not understand. It was as if a door had opened when his lips touched hers and he had seen in a far and lovely place where things were not all as they were in the rest of this sordid earth. Where everything had meaning and life was a greater thing than most men saw; it reached deeper and farther and had no end.

He understood that there were things for him to learn, though he did not know what they were. They were vaguely associated with words that she had spoken, though he could not always remember the phrases she had used. He only knew there was something she had that he must have.

All that was most vague and sometimes greatly disturbing, because he did not know what to do about it. Obviously it was his part to find out, but how? Yet he had to let her know that he had not forgotten.

And sometimes he wondered if the girl understood all this. If that kiss and pledge had meant as much to her as to himself. Or had she long ago forgotten, even as other girls forgot? No, she was not like that. She did not have jacinth eyes. He was glad that her eyes were brown and deeply true, and sometime he would have a chance to tell her all about this that was in his soul, which he could not express in words. But now, he must write her, nevertheless.

She had said she was not of his world. So much he remembered, and it had stricken him with its possibilities. Very well, there was a story like that in mythology. A maiden of the sea and a man who was of the earth? Or was it the other way around? He could not remember. They had somehow come together because they really belonged together, wasn't that it? Had the man plunged into the sea? Or the maiden? Somehow they had found each other. It had meant the death of one to his own environment, but he had gained infinitely! Well then, he would somehow become a part of her world. He would find a way. What was that she had said that night before they were interrupted—a strange phrase, be "born again"? Was that it? How would one be born again?

And so he lingered, looking at the sea, holding his pen over the paper, and asking age-old questions of himself that he could not answer any more than the rich young ruler of old who found the price too great.

Yet one thing worked out of that long hour of thought, perhaps deeper thought than he had ever given to any one subject before, and that was that he must find this thing, whatever it was, that would make him of her world; and not alone for her sake, but for something even deeper, some so far unsuspected longing in his own breast that demanded it of him and would not otherwise be satisfied.

Out of the chaos of that lovely hour, and that bright illusive head against the sea with deep, sweet eyes, he drew one clear thought. This thing he sought was not being sought for her, not even for love of her, though he knew he loved her, but was being sought for its own sake, because she had made him see that it was the only thing in the universe worthwhile. It was better than herself. It was enough in itself even without her, and it was not to be sought just for her sake but for its own sake and for his sake.

When he came to that point, where he was sure of his own heart about that, his pen was free and he could write.

It was only a little commonplace letter that he felt he had any right to write, but the words came quick and hot from his pen, and his face lit with a new kind of joy.

Dear Camilla,

You can't think how annoyed I am that things have shaped themselves so that I cannot come home and see you. There are questions I must ask you and things that I would understand, and I cannot find their answer anywhere down here, but I am not free to leave yet, for Dad can't come. And now Mother has taken a notion that I must go on a camping spree with my kid brother down in the Everglades. The scoutmaster is a stranger to us, and she can't feel safe unless I go along. It's fishing and hunting and a little exploring perhaps, just the thing a kid brother is crazy about, so I've promised to go for a day or two and see that it's all right. Then as soon as I can get away I'm coming north again, and I want to see you as soon as I can. I want to understand what you were saying when we parted. Perhaps you'll remember what I mean. Please don't forget.

Your friend,
Jeff

Jeffrey was humming a bright little tune when he came down in the elevator with his letter. To the girl with the jacinth eyes and the red-gold hair who sat in the opposite reception room with an open, unread book in her lap and watched the elevators all the afternoon as a cat might watch for a mouse, he looked most disconcertingly handsome in his sports attire and that strange light in his eyes that so set him apart from other young men—from her. She could not understand that light in his eyes. He did not used to have it. It was a new development, and she wanted to find its source.

She saw the letter in his hand, watched him jealously as he went over to the desk and dropped it in the mailbox. Then he walked out to the terrace and stood surveying the beach from afar.

But she did not go out to him at once. Instead, she stole to a window where she could watch him from behind a curtain and waited until he turned his footsteps down toward the beach. Then, watching her opportunity, she went over to the desk and dropped a letter into the mail slot in the counter, and slowly, casually walked away. The letter was only an advertisement of a dress shop and had been opened. Suddenly she stopped, opened her book, looked hastily through its leaves, and then turned back to the desk.

"Oh, Billy," she said sweetly, addressing the clerk behind

the desk in her husky, drawling tone, "I've made a mistake and dropped an open letter into the box along with another. Get the box out for me, that's a dear, and let me find it?"

Bill came all smiles to do her bidding. She had known he would. When she spoke in that tone, with that kind of a smile, all male population everywhere came running.

Billy reached under the counter and pulled out the mailbox that stood on a shelf under the counter, setting it up on the top for her inspection.

"It must be right on top," she said, peering in speculatively and sighting Jeffrey Wainwright's handwriting at once just below her own letter.

"There it is!" she caroled, and then she reached in her hand.

Just then a gruff old gentleman came up and demanded his key.

Billy turned alertly to take it from its hook, and Stephanie skillfully slid her own letter over Jeff's and picked both up at once, holding them firmly together so that they looked like one. She hadn't hoped for such a break as this. She had merely hoped to be able to see to whom that letter was addressed.

"Thanks awfully, Billy. You've saved me a lot of embarrassment," she said with a twinkle, as the good-natured clerk turned back and slid the mailbox down into its niche again.

Then slowly, innocently, Stephanie walked away from the desk, laying the letters carefully in her book as she ran for the elevator and rose to her room with the stolen letter safe in her possession.

Half an hour afterward she appeared on the beach in a becoming bathing suit and with narrowed eyes called a cheerful greeting to Jeff as he strolled by, still trying to conjure brown eyes and gold hair against a summer sea.

But the letter that had taken so long to write lay in little flecks of ashes in a jeweled ashtray, and the beautiful young vixen with jacinth eyes sat far into the night watching the curl of those ashes and gloating over them and over the girl who would wait forever for a letter that would not come.

But the jacinth eyes were smoldering with thought and were not satisfied. There was something behind all this. A casual letter like that, and yet something had somehow changed him. She was not sure she wanted him for herself exclusively—at least she was not sure she wanted to be his exclusively—but she did not want another girl to have him. What had those two been talking about when he left her? That was what she had to find out. That was what she would find out one day. Without that secret, she was powerless to conquer him.

In the early dawn of the tropical morning, just as the sun was beginning to tinge the sea with celestial colors and cause the world to resemble the Holy City let down out of heaven from God, Jeff stole forth from his room clad in a hunting outfit.

He went down to join his kid brother and the campers at a little rendezvous beside the sea, beyond the confines of the world where Stephanie Varrell moved. So he disappeared from the life of the great playground into an odd new playground of his own, seeking something whose name he did not know and conjuring, with the thought of a kiss, a bright head with eyes of brown.

Chapter 13

Camilla went out of the office and down the marble hall in company with her employer, a sudden constriction in her heart. What might the next hour bring forth? But there was one thing to which she was resolved. If there was a chance at all, she would put in a good word for poor Marietta. She would take her own medicine as well as she could. But she would tell her employer just what a proposition Marietta was up against. If he had a heart at all he would be affected. Perhaps the story of little crippled Ted would reach him. Of course, she knew that Marietta was by no means a model secretary, but perhaps she would do better if he would take her back and give her another trial. At least she would put in a word for her, if it seemed at all practical.

Whitlock put her in his luxurious car and threaded his way gravely through traffic, out to one of the older parts of town where quiet culture still reigned for three or four ancient blocks and vague, quaint footprints of aristocracy were visible in massive stone walls—the flute of a column, the grill of a gate or a balcony.

Camilla looked around her in surprise. She did not know where she was. She lifted a quick, questioning glance to her escort's face.

He was smiling down at her, almost as if she were something he had found and captured, a butterfly or a strange bird, out of the sunshine. "I'm taking you to a quaint old place that I love," he said in answer to her questioning look. "I felt you would appreciate it. Have you ever been here before?"

"No," she said wonderingly, "where is this?"

"Hampden Row," he answered, pleased at her interest, "and this is the old Warrington Inn. This is where the elite of fifty years ago used to come for their dignified social life. It happens that business, in its ebb and flow, has left these four blocks here high and dry, just as they used to be. A strange twist of circumstances has kept the march of progress from touching a finger to these fine old buildings. Fortunes have been offered for the land they are built upon, but the unusual phrasing of a will has so far prevented the original estate from being divided, and the absence of an heir, whose heirs in turn cannot be traced, protects them. Meantime, those who are in on the secret can enjoy the quaint old-time place and its ways. I thought you might be one of those who could appreciate this."

Camilla was intrigued at once. She had forgotten for the time being her troubles and perplexities and gave attention to this quiet oasis in the midst of the whirl and noise of the city traffic.

They entered the old Warrington Inn with its mellowed oak beams and its huge stone fireplace, its quaint interiors and vistas, and its spacious air of the dignity of other days, and immediately Camilla felt a quiet peace descend upon her.

"Oh," she said softly to her escort, "how my mother would love this!"

"We'll bring her here sometime!" said Whitlock instantly. "I would enjoy bringing her here!"

"Oh, you must excuse me!" said Camilla, with flaming cheeks. "I didn't realize what I was saying. I didn't mean to hint!"

"Of course you didn't!" Whitlock's eyes were wearing that pleasant smile, and he looked down into her troubled brown eyes. "I really mean it. I would love to bring her here. How soon will she be able to come?"

"Oh, I don't know," evaded Camilla. "Several weeks, I'm sure. She hasn't been out yet. You are very kind, but you mustn't trouble yourself. I can bring her around to see it sometime in the spring when she is able to go out. I have my little car, you know. And Mother would be terribly distressed at my going around hinting things. I really didn't realize. I was just talking to myself."

"Don't worry!" he laughed. "I'm glad you did. It rather lets me into the group, doesn't it? I must do myself the honor of calling upon your mother!"

Camilla looked distressed and rather dismayed.

"I'm afraid you won't feel it much honor," she said, frankly embarrassed, "not when you see the little old grubby house where we live."

"I am quite sure the house is being greatly honored by the people who are condescending to live in it," he said gracefully, and Camilla looked up to see a different Mr. Whitlock from any she had known before. The stiffness and dignity, the brusque manner and sharp glance were gone, and in their place were all the graces of a courteous, genial gentleman. Not that he had been discourteous before, but this was a new kind of courtesy. Social courtesy.

He saw to the ordering in the easiest way, suggesting unusual dishes that were in order when the inn was built, delectable old-fashioned things. And then he began to tell the history of the inn, of famous occurrences in its time, noted men and women who had been its frequenters, incidents, brief stories of this one and that, until Camilla could see them seated at the various tables in their strange, old-fashioned garb. And as she ate her delicious meal she felt as if she were in a fairy story. Mr. Whitlock was certainly a fascinating conversationalist. But why was he wasting it all on her, just his secretary?

Suddenly she came to herself and glanced furtively at her watch.

"Oh!" she exclaimed. "Mr. Whitlock! Do you know what time it is? My lunch hour was over long ago!"

"I have been boring you!" he said quickly. "I'm sorry!"

"Oh no, you haven't bored me at all," said Camilla eagerly. "It was delightful! You made me entirely forget that I am an employee, not a guest, and that we came here to talk business. And you haven't said a word about the business."

His eyes studied her, and she could see that he was pleased that she had enjoyed herself.

"But you're not an employee. You're my guest today. And as for the business, that can wait. I was only going to ask you what you thought about Marietta. *Is* she hopeless, or do you think she could be trained? Consider your answer with deliberation, for if she has to be trained, the training will largely fall upon you, I'm afraid."

"*I* train her? Oh, I wouldn't know how!" said Camilla, "and I don't believe she'd take it from me."

"She would if I told her," said the man, watching the play of lights on the girl's face. "You see, it's this way. I've had the offer of a Miss Townsend from the Fortescu office. She's already trained and quite efficient, I understand, but—well, I don't like the style of bob she wears for her age."

Camilla couldn't help laughing and enjoyed the answering twinkle in her employer's eyes. Then she grew more serious. This, then, was what all this pleasant afternoon had meant. He had brought her here to put it up to her whether he should dismiss herself and Marietta and put Miss Townsend in their place. For, of course, Miss Townsend was an old hand and would be more efficient than both of them put together. Mr. Whitlock had taken this way to soften the dismissal. Her heart sank deep and missed a beat or two, but she tried to summon her courage and self-respect. If she was to pass out of the office this way, by all means, let it be done bravely!

"You mean," she said, trying to steady her voice and look the man coolly in the eye, "that you would take Miss Townsend in our place? I should think that there was no question about what would be best *for you*. Miss Townsend is most efficient and would certainly be worth both of us put together."

"Where do you get that 'our place'? You surely don't think I'm going to let anyone take *your* place, do you?" He gave her a deep, pleasant look, as if they had been close friends a long time, and Camilla's tired heart gave a leap of relief. Then he didn't mean to dismiss her after all. The relief was so great that it almost hurt.

But after the pain was gone there was a perplexity in the back of her mind. A little bewilderment over that look he had given her, as if perhaps he were looking to her for more than she realized. But the thought did not come out in the open in so many words. It simply remained there, a little uncomfortable impression. Yet when she tried to analyze it she laughed at herself. Truly, she was making mountains out of mole hills. There could have been nothing but a belated interest in his eyes. His conscience had probably troubled him that he had not more definitely looked after her before this, a friend of friends from his hometown, and now he was trying to show her that he had a real personal interest in her. That was the way with busy people; they didn't quite realize what impression they were making. Well, she was glad and relieved that she was not going to have to hunt another job in such hard times!

But what she said was, "You're very kind, Mr. Whitlock, and of course that relieves me a lot. It wouldn't be easy for me to lose my job just now when Mother has been so ill and there have been so many extra expenses. Still, I wouldn't want you to feel that you had to keep me if you could get somebody that would do your work better. And, of course, I know it would easily be possible. I haven't had long experience as Miss Townsend has."

"Well, I don't want anybody better than you are at present, so you can forget that." He smiled graciously, watching the play of expression on Camilla's speaking face. If she had only known it, he was wondering how it was that he had never noticed before how lovely she was. "But I was thinking about Marietta. Do you think you could do anything with her, or shall we let her go? In fact, I practically dismissed her this morning, told her she could go tomorrow morning if she wanted to hunt another job. Then I began to think it might be better to consult you."

There was something delicately flattering in his tone, but Camilla was thinking of the woebegone Marietta who had been weeping all over her makeup that morning, and it came to her that perhaps, after all, there might be a way to help her.

"She's having a hard time," said Camilla speculatively. "Did you know about her home life?"

"Mercy, no! I don't know a thing about her except that she's the worst I ever tried. She seems to me a mess. I don't know why I question keeping her at all, except that I thought I would consult your wishes before I made any definite changes."

"You are very considerate," said Camilla gratefully, "but I think it should be what you need, not what I want. However, personally, I'd be very glad if you could see your way clear to keep Marietta. I feel dreadfully sorry for her. She's never had half a chance, if what she tells me is true. She has a flighty young step-mother who hates her and a little crippled stepbrother whom she adores, and apparently she's the only one who cares for him. I don't know whether I could do anything to help her or not, but I'd be glad to try if you think she wouldn't resent it. I certainly think it is going to be terribly hard for her if she loses her job now."

"You don't say!" said Whitlock thoughtfully. "I never thought of her as having any background at all. Of course, I'm not running a philanthropic organization, but if you are willing to give her a few hints, I might give her another try. I'll have a talk with her when I go back. But one of the worst things about her is her appearance. I suppose perhaps she can't help that, but she's so untidy, and she chews gum continually, and she tries to be so familiar, even when there are people in the office. It's her idea of being chummy, I suppose, but it doesn't make for a good office appearance."

"I see what you mean," said Camilla thoughtfully, not noticing his glances of admiration. "I'll be glad to try, at least. I'm sorry for her."

"Well," said Whitlock, "I'll give her a chance, of course, if you say so. Now, I suppose we ought to go back. I have an appointment with a representative of that Brooklyn firm in half an hour. This has been a real rest to get away from business."

"It's been delightful," said Camilla, rousing to her duty. "I've enjoyed the place and the lunch, and I've very much enjoyed your conversation. It has peopled this wonderful room with characters and made me forget all my perplexities."

"I'm sorry you have perplexities," said the man in such a gentle tone that she looked up surprised and then summoned a proud little smile.

"Oh, they're not as great as they might be," she said lightly. "In fact, when I think of Marietta's life, I feel I ought not to call them perplexities. It's awfully fine of you to be willing to try her again. I'll do my very best to make her a success."

All the way back to the office Whitlock was his genial, pleasant self, nothing of the employer about him, but when he swung open the office door his reserved manner returned upon him.

They heard poor Marietta's typewriter clicking away as they approached the room, and she sat there stolidly working as they stood for an instant in the doorway. Then she looked up with a start, not having heard them coming, and her face was wet with tears. She certainly was not a prepossessing figure as she sat there plodding away at her work, a goodly pile of finished letters lying on the desk beside her. Her face was still streaked with makeup and her hair was uncrimped and sticking out grotesquely around her head. Camilla's heart sank for her as she noticed how little like the model secretary she looked.

Whitlock stood there a moment considering her, and then he hung up hat and coat and sat down at his desk, watching her.

Camilla went to the cloakroom with her own things and came quietly back to her desk and began to work at some envelopes she was addressing.

"Miss Pratt," said Whitlock in his cold, brusque tone, and Marietta jumped and turned toward him, sweeping off an avalanche of typed pages with her arm. She stopped in great confusion to pick them up, saying "Yessir?" but her voice was choked with suppressed emotion.

"I've been talking with Miss Chrystie about you," said Whitlock when Marietta had replaced the papers and turned once more toward him.

"Yessir!" said Marietta in a hopeless tone.

"Miss Chrystie suggests that I give you another chance. Would you like to stay and try it again?"

"Oh—!" said Marietta, with a quiver of her lip, looking at him as if she could not believe her ears. "Yessir!" she said with a quick little breath almost like a sob.

"Would you be willing to take suggestions and act upon them, Miss Pratt?"

"Oh— *Yessir!*" said Marietta in an excited tone, her syllables fairly tumbling over one another.

"Up to the present time, Miss Pratt," went on Whitlock, his tone brusque and critical, "you have been most unsatisfactory in three ways, I might say in every way. In your work, which has been erratic and slouching in appearance, and slower than any office should tolerate; in your appearance, which is both unattractive and untidy; and in your manner, which is often uncouth and bold. If you are willing to try to change these things, I am willing to give you another chance. If you will take Miss Chrystie's suggestions and be more like her there might be some hope for you."

"Yessir," said Marietta, giving him a wild, wistful look. Then suddenly dropping her head down on her machine, she sobbed out, "But I can't never be like her. I haven't got her looks!" And then her stubby shoulders shook with sobs.

Whitlock looked distressed at the effect of his words, but he cleared his throat and tried to speak above her weeping.

"I was not expecting you to perform miracles," he said kindly. "I merely want a neat, efficient worker who knows how to act and how to dress and when not to speak. Suppose you talk it over with Miss Chrystie after your work is done and see what you think you can do. Perhaps you'd both like to go into the inner office for a few minutes. I'm expecting a man right now, and it won't do to have you weeping all over the place."

Marietta rose hastily and went into the little back office, which was used mostly for the storage of supplies, and Camilla, following, found her sitting on a pile of typewriter paper, shaking with suppressed sobs.

"Come, dear," said Camilla, putting her hand hesitantly on the bowed head. "Let's snap out of this. We can't do anything if we give up at the start."

"We!" said Marietta, looking up. "It was you made him say this, and I'll never forget it of you. But it isn't any good. He'll never keep me. I can't ever be like you."

"Hush, Marietta, that man has come, and he'll hear you. You don't want to finish yourself before we begin, do you? Slip quietly into the washroom there and wash your face. Wash it hard and get all that lipstick and rouge off."

"But I haven't any more to put on," said Marietta remorsefully. "I left my makeup bag at home."

"That's where you'd better keep it then, if you want to please Mr. Whitlock. He doesn't want you to look like an actress. He just wants you neat."

"But I've got an awful sallow complexion," sighed Marietta.

When Marietta came out of the washroom she had a clean, subdued look, like a little wet hen that had been in the suds much against her will. Her hair was draggled around her face and in wet strands around her neck. Her eyes were swollen badly, but the streaks on her cheeks were gone and her mouth had assumed its normal shape and lost its ghastly cupid's bow.

"I don't see how this is going to help," she wailed. "I look awful."

"Where's your comb, Marietta?" said Camilla.

Marietta produced a small, broken affair with several teeth missing.

"Sit down in that chair," ordered Camilla.

Marietta submitted herself to the other girl, and Camilla combed the recalcitrant locks until they were fairly smooth. They were not very clean, and Camilla shrank from contact with them, but she was determined to do her best for Marietta. She couldn't do much with such hair in a few minutes, but she managed to subdue it to neatness, at least, and tucked the ends in, using three of her own hairpins. Such hair would never make a pretty bob, and it did seem almost hopeless.

"You're coming home with me tonight," said Camilla as she finished her task. "I'm going to show you another way to do your hair, if you'll let me."

"Oh, will you?" said Marietta eagerly. "Say! That's wonderful! I never could make my hair look like anything."

"Well, we'll find a way," said Camilla, surveying the stubborn locks dubiously. "Now, Marietta, run back to the washroom and wash those spots off the front of your dress. That dress needs cleaning if you want to come up to Mr. Whitlock's standards."

"Oh, I know," said the girl, "but the sleeve's ripped halfway out of the only other good one I have, and I didn't have time ta mend it. Neither I didn't have money ta send this ta the cleaner."

"Clean it yourself! That's easy enough. I'll show you some splendid cleaning liquid I have. And then, you know, soap and water will do a whole lot if you just take a little care."

"Oh, my land!" said Marietta, aghast. "You'd be an awful trouble to yourself."

"Why, yes certainly, Marietta, if you want to keep your job. You don't know what a difference little things like that make. If you only hadn't started to buy that fur coat! You know, you really need a good, well-fitting office dress."

"I was gonta get a figured crepe with two flounces going diagonal on the skirt and puffed elbow sleeves. It has red-and-white flowers on it, and it's only five ninety-eight!" said Marietta eagerly.

"But you know that's not the kind of dress to wear to the office. You need a quiet, dark dress, with a white collar. Dark blue would be good for you. And you don't want flounces; you need a simple dress and underthings that will make it fit well. You might have to pay more than that. How much have you paid down on your coat?"

"Five dollars," said the girl, "and I'm to pay two-fifty every week. It's coney, white with a big collar! It's swell!"

"But, Marietta, you don't need a white fur coat unless you are going to parties and operas. And coney is nothing but rabbit and won't wear a season. Why don't you just drop it, Marietta, and use the money as you get it to buy a few very well-cut dresses of good quality, that will give the right appearance for the office. That is really what you care for, isn't it?"

Marietta's eyes got large with disappointment.

"But I like pretty clothes," she said with something like a wail in her voice.

"Yes, of course," said Camilla wisely, "but they must be suitable for the place and time in which you wear them, or they are not pretty. You haven't any place to wear a white fur coat, nor dresses with diagonal flounces. And elbow sleeves are not fit for the office, except perhaps in very hot weather in cotton material. You know, to wear a cheap party dress to work in is not good taste and does not make a good impression. It sets you down as third-class right away. Mr. Whitlock wants girls in his office who look their part, well dressed and efficient, not cheap little frowsy girls who don't know any better than to wear dressy frocks to work in."

Marietta stared at her sorrowfully.

"All right," she said at last, "I'll give up the coat, but it was awful pretty, and I don't guess I'll ever get another chance for a fur coat. And all that good five dollars gone!"

"Well, you certainly couldn't have kept the coat if you lost your job. And if you keep your job and get to be the right kind of secretary, someday you might be able to buy a squirrel coat if you need it, who knows?"

"My!" said Marietta. "I never thought of that! You think of a lot of things, don't you? I like you an awful lot. I guess I'll try ta do what you say, though I don't know anybody else I'd do it for."

"All right!" said Camilla. "Then I'll help you all I can! Now, come on in the other office, and let's get these letters off. It's half past three. We have a half hour. How many more have you to type?"

"Only ten more. I'd uv had them all done ef you'd been another ten minutes."

"Good work! Are they letter-perfect? Are you sure?"

"Yep, I went over each one as I finished it."

"All right, I'll fold them and stamp them for you while you finish the rest. But say, Marietta, if I were you, I wouldn't say 'yep.'

It isn't being done by office girls who get on. It doesn't matter with me, of course, but it's always best to keep in practice even when it doesn't matter. You don't mind my telling you, do you?"

"Nop— No, I mean," said the girl. "I want ta get right ef I can. But say, don't I look awful plain with my hair this way?"

"Not in the least," said Camilla. "And we'll fix it better tonight. Come, let's hurry!"

Mr. Whitlock did not return that afternoon. Instead, he telephoned Camilla and seemed pleased that the letters had gone out. Marietta was listening. Her eyes shone when she heard his tone of commendation. She drew a sigh of relief as she started away from the office in Camilla's company.

"My it's nice ta have a girlfriend!" she said with satisfaction, and Camilla's heart stood aghast at the thought. She was wondering how many unpleasant things this helping of Marietta was going to let her in for? Well, she was the Lord's servant. She couldn't refuse an obvious duty like trying to help Marietta keep her job, even if it wasn't going to be the pleasantest thing in the world.

"What'll your mother say, me coming home with you like this?" Marietta asked as Camilla opened the door with her key.

"She'll be glad to see you," said Camilla, thanking her stars that she had such a mother upon whom she could count in emergencies.

"Mother, I've brought Marietta home with me for supper," sang out Camilla as she entered the tiny hall.

"Now isn't that nice!" answered Mother Chrystie at once, appearing in the dining room door. "I'm so glad I decided to make potpie. I thought maybe we'd have company tonight! I'm delighted to meet you, Marietta. Camilla has told me about you. Now, get your things off quickly, girls. The potpie is all ready to be served."

Marietta was shy and embarrassed at the table, but her eyes were shining. She watched the loving looks between mother and daughter hungrily, and once she said, "My, I wish I had a home like this! I never tasted potpie before. My stepmother doesn't know how to cook very well."

She helped with the dishes, and afterward Camilla took her in the bathroom and taught her how to shampoo her hair and then how to curl it softly and loosely around her face and how to coax the long stiff locks into a neat little knot. Camilla hunted up an organdy collar she had made recently and told Marietta to mend the sleeve of her other dress and wear the new collar next day. Marietta vowed eternal loyalty to her and declared she'd try to do everything she was told. Mrs. Chrystie gave her a bag of cookies for Ted, and so Marietta went happily home at last, wearing her hair in an almost becoming style and holding the new collar and cookies tenderly.

"Thus endeth the first lesson!" laughed Camilla as she finally shut the door after her guest and sank wearily into a big chair. "Mother, I don't know what you'll think of me, but I had to undertake her reformation. She was about to lose her job."

"Dear child!" said her mother understandingly. "I'm glad you did it, though I can see that it's not going to be all rest and pleasure for you. But it's a heavenly thing to do, and I think the angels watching you love it that you are doing it."

"The angels?"

"Yes," said her mother brightly, "didn't you know, we have an audience all the time, we Christians? I was just reading about it this morning, how we are made a spectacle for the world and for angels. And it seems that word *angels* includes bad ones, too, demons who are watching the Christians' walk. Yes, I'm glad you did this, dear, and if there's any way I can help, I will. Poor, homely, lonely girl! But you know, Camilla, she didn't look so bad when you got her hair fixed. She really didn't."

When Camilla, weary with the day, crept into her bed, it came to her suddenly that she hadn't had time to think about

Wainwright and Stephanie Varrell all day long. Then, just as she was falling to sleep, there came that sharp, sweet memory of a kiss that seemed like a dream that had never been.

❀

The next few days were interesting for Camilla. Mr. Whitlock was suddenly called to New York on business, and he left with only a few hurried directions and a promise to call her up later and find out what was in the mail. He was gone before Marietta arrived at the office, which was a good thing, perhaps, for Marietta had not been quite such a success with the arrangement of her hair as Camilla had hoped, and it had to be done over again. But Camilla fixed her up and began to stimulate her to work and see what she could accomplish while Mr. Whitlock was away, to surprise him.

This was perhaps the very stimulus Marietta needed, for she was still a child in many ways and was greatly intrigued by the idea of surprising and pleasing her employer.

Camilla, moreover, was pleased that he had entrusted her with his affairs during his absence and took pride in having everything move on as if he had been there, and even Marietta caught the spirit and tried to act brisk and businesslike when anyone came in.

She brought no more novels to the office to read. She was too anxious to work every minute and get the pile of typing done that had been assigned to her.

And then Saturday afternoon Camilla took part of her precious half-holiday and went shopping with Marietta, to help her find just the right things. Mr. Whitlock was returning Monday morning, and Marietta was determined to get some new clothes before he arrived.

By this time she was getting fairly skillful at managing her unruly hair, and even in her ill-fitting, unsuitable clothes, she looked much subdued. Camilla hoped that with the purchase of a few much-needed garments, Mr. Whitlock could not help but see a change even in so short a time. So the shopping expedition was planned, and Marietta was almost too excited to work all Saturday morning.

They went to Camilla's house with their packages, and Marietta dressed up in her new dress, a trim dark blue with white collar and cuffs. Miss York came in, was introduced, and approvingly entered into the scheme of things without having to be told what it was all about. And before Marietta left she slipped in her bag a sheet of paper on which was written in the nurse's clear handwriting a few rules for bathing and breathing, exercise and diet, that Miss York told Marietta would greatly improve the complexion she was deploring. Taking it altogether, Camilla was quite satisfied about her protégée, and it was with much eagerness that she anticipated Monday morning and the return of Mr. Whitlock. She hadn't done anything in a long time that was so interesting as fixing up poor, little homely Marietta Pratt. At least, not anything real. She kept telling herself now that her contact with Wainwright had not been real, only a sort of fairy tale, and fairy tales never came true. They were only to dream about. And dreaming like that wasn't at all wholesome, so Camilla entered into the redemption of Marietta Pratt—physical, intellectual, and spiritual—with all her heart. She wanted to keep from thinking. She wanted to keep from dreaming.

Chapter 14

John Saxon was a fine, earnest young man who was taking a year off from his medical studies to earn some much-needed money to complete his course.

He had been offered the opportunity to take in charge a dozen young boys whose parents or guardians had either no time or inclination to look after them themselves. Two of the boys were not strong enough to stand the northern winters; therefore, Florida had been selected as the scene of his activities, and more especially because Florida was a sort of native land to John Saxon and he knew well all its possibilities.

It was to this group of unfortunately wealthy youngsters that young Sam Wainwright had attached himself, and he refused to be separated from them. And when, in the well-planned and educative program of John Saxon, this young company were to move down into the Everglades for a hiking-camping-fishing-exploring trip, Sam Wainwright went into the particular kind of gloom that he knew how to create, until his mother consented that he should accompany them, provided John Saxon would take him on and would also allow his elder brother to be one of the company.

Having thus gained consent, young Sam became forthwith so angelic for the next two days before the expedition was to leave that he almost overdid the matter and got his mother to worrying about him lest he was going to die. So it was with the greatest difficulty that he finally made his departure.

John Saxon had not cared overmuch for the idea, it is true, of having an elder brother along who would likely be superior and try to interfere, but the extra money that was offered, which would hasten the time he should be able to go back to the work he was eager to do, made him yield.

The two young men had not seen one another until the morning that they were to start. All the arrangements had been conducted by young Sam, and naturally the two approached one another with a thoroughly developed case of prejudice on either side.

Looked at from the standpoint of an outsider, they were not unlike. Both were young and strong and good-looking. Perhaps Wainwright had an inch or two of height in his favor, and on the other hand John Saxon had several lines of experience in his fine, strong face that were yet to be developed in Jeffrey Wainwright's. Yet they seemed well matched as they met on the beach in the pearly dawn of that tropical winter morning and measured swords with their eyes as they shook hands. "Soft!" Saxon was saying to himself, just because he had never seen a face before with such an easygoing, happy smile that at the same time concealed strong character, character that had not been severely tried as yet, but still strong character.

"Tough?" said Jeffrey to himself with a question mark, and somehow was not convinced of that. This man did not quite fit any of the types of men he knew.

There was a certain gravity behind the sparkle in Jeffrey's eyes that John Saxon could not help liking, and Jeffrey on his part was not long in discovering strength and authority, with a certain grave sweetness, in Saxon. So they started on their way, bristling with question marks concerning each other.

But in the mind of young Sam, there were no question marks. He thought his big brother was the greatest thing that ever happened, and he thought that John Saxon was the next greatest.

The sun shot a crimson rim above the opal sea and tinged the waves with ruddy gold, and strange colors gleamed and leaped in the sparkle of the waves. The sand grew alight with color, and little eager white birds with pink kid feet went hopping here and there along the rim of the waves to catch the sand crabs without wetting their feet. A big white gull sailed out over the waves looking down for fish and then circled back and settled down on a pile that stood out in the sea a few yards, surveying the strange group with their khaki outfits and paraphernalia. Strange, changing groups this wise bird saw at different times along this coast since it had been fashionable to winter in Florida, but it made no difference to him. The sea was there and did not change, and he wore the same cut of white feather coat from generation to generation, so why bother about mere humans?

Saxon gave Jeffrey a quick, firm grasp of the hand as he looked into his eyes, said "Wainwright!" just to acknowledge his presence, and showed neither joy nor sorrow over the fact that he was going with them, and Jeffrey was left to the company of the sea and his own thoughts while the small army was forming for the line of march. Then, when they were drawn up in line, there were a few questions.

"Everybody gone over the list?" All hands were raised.

"Everybody got every article on the list?" All hands again.

The young captain let his eyes sweep the row and acknowledged with a faint shadow of a grin the fact that Jeffrey had raised his hand both times, as if he were one of the boys. The stranger was perhaps going to be game after all. Nothing haughty about him so far.

"About face!"

Jeffrey obeyed the order. He was standing at the end of the line.

"Forward march!"

Jeffrey fell in step with the rest. At least he knew enough for that.

"By twos, march!"

This brought Jeffrey marching with the youngest boy in the crowd, one Carlin de Harte by name, and a little devil by inheritance, if he might be judged by his actions.

Carlin was the son of divorced parents and had been shunted off on others wherever it seemed easiest to bring him up. He was a recent addition and had not yet learned self-discipline. The young chief eyed the combination doubtfully. He had not expected the son of the millionaire bond king to choose to walk as one of the boys.

But Jeffrey looked down with a friendly wink at Carlin, and Carlin looked up with sudden respect when he saw how tall Jeffrey was, and grinned. Suddenly John Saxon knew that Jeffrey was going to be an asset instead of a pain in the neck.

The way led at first along the silver-gilt beach of the opening day, and Jeffrey Wainwright drew in deep breaths of the clean sea air and rejoiced in the emptiness of the beach. They had it practically all to themselves except for the kid-footed bird, catching crabs, and an old fisherman out in a dory.

When they had gotten so far from human habitation that they couldn't see anything but sand and sea and palms and pines, and everybody was wondering what came next, Saxon called a halt and set his young minions to work, gathering sticks, unpacking a hamper, making a fire, and setting up a contrivance for cooking. Each boy had his job and knew what was expected of him. They went at it like trained ants, hurrying around excitedly.

Jeffrey dropped down upon the sand and watched for a while, surprised at the efficiency of his young brother. But when Saxon passed, he stood and saluted.

"Say, Captain, what's my job?" he asked with a grin.

Saxon measured his height admiringly but answered with a reserved smile.

"Guest, I think," he said, "or maybe critic, whichever would suit you best." There was still smile enough about Saxon's lips to keep the remark from being an offense, but Jeffrey watched him sharply.

"Nothing doing," he said quietly. "If that's all the place you've got for me, I'm afraid I shall have to walk all the way back alone."

Saxon took his measure again and relaxed his lips.

"All right, if you really want to work. I thought you just came along to protect your brother."

Jeffrey looked him in the eye.

"I came along because my mother insisted Sam shouldn't come without me, but I'm staying because I like it—and because I like *you*!" he added with a genuine ring to his voice. "If I go back, I shall leave my brother in your care and tell my mother there's no cause to worry. But I'm staying on if you let me have a part, because I like you, and I think it's great!"

Saxon put out his hand and grasped Jeffrey's in a hearty clasp.

"All right, brother," he said with a new light in his eyes, "there are two of us! Suppose we open the milk bottles and fill the cups. I was going to do that myself, but I've plenty besides, and I'll see to assigning you a regular place when we're on our way again. I think you're going to be a big help. You've already subdued our worst particular little devil. If this keeps up, we shall have him a model child before the trip is over."

Jeffrey felt a warm glow around his heart as he watched this other young man, with his strong, clear-cut features, his crisp, brown, curly hair, and his very blue eyes that had dancing lights in them and yet could look sternly at a misbehaving charge or scorn a casual multimillionaire's son. It all intrigued Jeffrey immensely, and he felt the thrill of a new admiration. He was not going to be bored on this expedition. It was going to be interesting.

Stephanie Varrell would have been amazed to see him pouring milk into tin cups and cutting bread, distributing butter, and heaping up the tin plates with the second helping of baked beans and frankfurters. She did not know how he had served his apprenticeship at washing dishes in a tiny apartment kitchen with her rival. She did not even know yet that he had disappeared from the playground where last night she had tried and failed to inveigle him to walk in the moonlight with her. She was having her breakfast in bed about the time of this midmorning repast that was served so many miles away from her, down the beach.

The way led inland later in the day, after a dip in the sea and a romp on the beach and then a rest on the sand. Inland, among the palms and the taller pines, which now were draped more thickly with the long gray moss. Other, stranger trees appeared also, and the way grew wild and picturesque. Strange blossoms peered up at them from the ground; strange, lovely, weird ones peered down at them from the branches above their heads. Orchids! Those were orchids! Green orchids with almost human faces!

Jeffrey thought of white orchids with gold hair and deep brown eyes, and her way of holding aloof in another world.

The way led through dense tropical undergrowth, where lovely vines trailed across and barred the way with strong yet gentle hands and yellow jasmine filled the air with heavenly perfume. More orchids looking down in stranger color combinations looked more like humans than the first ones. And Jeffrey thought of a girl with dark eyes and wished she were beside him, and wondered if it would be at all possible to pack a box with these wonderful orchids and hope to get them to her before they died?

Glimpses of wild creatures they had, of deer and little beings of the forest. A bright eye, the whisk of a tail, a stirring leaf, and they were out of sight. Glimpses of serpents, slithering along their native haunts, big copperheads and rattlers. Once they stopped to take a lesson on snakes, on what to do in case of being attacked and how to render first aid. A large copperhead lay coiled below them in a little hollow by a log while they were listening, and Jeffrey marveled at the skill of the young teacher in controlling the harum-scarum boys in order to give them the most out of his teaching. And then, just as if he had been trained for the act, the big creature uncoiled his lengths and slid away beneath the undergrowth, and the boys stepped back with eyes large with a new understanding, more ready to meet possible danger, less cocksure of their own little human might pitted against real deadly peril.

Their eyes grew wise and sharp, looking for the signs of enemy life about them, learning to know the names of the growing things they passed. How much the young leader knew, and how well he told it without seeming to be trying to impart knowledge! No wonder his price was large and it was difficult to get opportunity to join his groups.

A stream developed later in the day as they climbed over fallen logs. The stream in time led to a lake, clear, sparkling, like a jewel in the forest, and here canoes awaited them, and they saw their first Indian guide.

Almost in awe they took their places as ordered and sat quiet, full of deep satisfaction, too weary to disobey.

They touched in a little while upon a shore and saw not far away a huge alligator lying dormant, partly out of the water. Storybook life was becoming real to these boys.

There were crude accommodations for camping, and a fire was all ready to start near the shore. Two old Indians muttered unintelligible phrases to the young leader, and presently the tired boys were eating a supper of fish from the lake cooked over the fire, bread that they had brought with them, and fruit, oranges that had been sent on ahead.

It was suddenly dark before they had finished, and they had only the light of the fire to eat by when they got to the oranges. Just as if somebody had touched a button and the light went out, so the sun had dropped down out of sight and left not a vestige of gleam behind. That was Florida.

John Saxon had been collecting pine knots before this happened, and now he stuck several in the fire until they caught, then set them here and there in buckets of sand.

They washed their dishes in lake water, looking furtively toward the place where the alligator basked, and then sat round the fire while the moon rose, a mammoth moon, from behind the forest across the lake. John Saxon, reclining near one of the pine knot torches, took a little book from his pocket and read how a man of the Pharisees, one Nicodemus, came to Jesus by night and asked Him the way of salvation, and He answered, "Except a man be born again, he cannot see the kingdom of God."

Jeffrey Wainwright, wearier than he ever remembered having been before yet greatly charmed with this weird, strange place of stillness and night, had been watching the scene indifferently. He was thinking that for once this wise, magnetic leader had made a great mistake in trying to do any reading with those tired boys after a day's march and excitement. Studying the strong, fine face of the other young man, he fell to wondering how he'd gotten that way, anyway. He was not listening intently until he heard that phrase, "born again," and suddenly he sat up sharply and began to listen.

On through that simple story he listened, through those matchless words that have reached round the world in every language and reached down through the ages from God for everybody: "For God so loved the world, that he gave his only begotten Son, that whosoever believeth in him should not perish, but have everlasting life. For God sent not his Son into the world to condemn the world; but that the world through him might be saved."

He listed to the condemnation that comes through refusing the light. Only a few verses, but so impressive, there with that moon looking down; the glinting silver of the lake ahead; and the black, still darkness of the forest shutting in, where the firelight flickered solemnly and a far, strange bird let forth a weird night cry. He could see that even the weary boys were impressed and liked it all. Their leader had hold enough upon them for that, after a long day's march!

The little book was closed and stuck back in John Saxon's pocket, and his voice suddenly started a chorus:

"I know a fount where sins are washed away!
 I know a place where night is turned to day!
Burdens are lifted, blind eyes made to see,
 There's a wonder-working power in the blood of
 Calvary!"

The rich tones died away, and the leader's head bent reverently. "Lord, we're glad You love us and understand us all. We're glad we can come to You for forgiveness of our sins, for cleansing, for strength by the way, and wisdom. And now tonight we come for rest, for blessing, for protection through the night. We ask it in the name of Jesus Christ our Savior."

It was very still when the prayer was over, and for an instant no boy stirred. Then Saxon said in his ordinary voice, "Now, boys, every man to his cot. Five minutes to get ready and five to get quiet!"

Jeffrey lay on his hard cot that was too short for his length and felt a great peace settle down upon him. Outside the pine knots sputtered and flared, and the fire flickered and flamed up when the old Indian watchman fed it with more pine knots, and the silver moon shone on, but there was quiet in the camp.

His brother Sam was in the next tent, but in the cot beside him little Carlin de Harte reached out a timid hand and touched Jeff.

"You don't think God would let that alligator get in our tent, do you? Nor the old long snake?" he whispered.

Then Jeffrey's hand came out and clasped the lean, young hand of the child and held it warmly.

"No, kid, I don't think he would!" said Jeffrey. "You go to sleep now, and I'll help God watch!"

The boy sighed contentedly, and soon his regular breathing told Jeffrey that his fears were over for that night. But Jeffrey lay thinking of the words he had been hearing and of Camilla and what she had said about being born again. Was this what she had meant, and was it something that came to you or did you have to go out after it? He would listen and see if he could find out, for this was what he had come questing for. And presently Jeffrey, too, was sleeping.

Chapter 15

Back at the fashionable resort that Jeffrey Wainwright had left that morning, Stephanie Varrell patrolled the beach in vain, in vain questioned this one and that one if they had seen him that morning. She searched the golf course, the tennis courts, and even the airport, and put the bellboys and desk clerks through a regular inquisition to discover whether he had left yet, but she found out nothing at all about the disappearance of the heir of the house of Wainwright.

At last, when everything else had failed, she approached Jeff's dignified mother, who was sitting with her knitting on the wide veranda talking quietly with two of her friends. She assumed a honeyed smile and said, "Pardon me, Mrs. Wainwright, I'm sorry to interrupt, but we've an expedition on for this afternoon, and we're anxious to find Jeff. Of course he's included, and we can't seem to place him. Could you give us an idea where to look?"

Mrs. Wainwright looked up when she had finished counting her stitches and studied Stephanie up and down, much as

Stephanie might have looked at another whom she considered beneath her notice, and then said coldly, "My son is away today."

"Oh really!" said Stephanie in well-assumed surprise. "He didn't mention any such thing last night when I talked with him. Could you tell me when you expect him back?"

"I couldn't say," said Jeffrey's mother, her voice still colder and more disapproving. "He may be away several days or even longer. He wasn't sure when he left!"

"Oh!" said Stephanie, a pretty dismay in her voice but with a mean gleam in her jacinth eyes. "He—hasn't gone back north yet, has he? Oh, I hope not."

Again Mrs. Wainwright favored her with another cool scrutiny.

"Well, not *yet*!" she admitted with a slight shrug of her shoulders. "But, of course, he's liable to be called back almost any time. You'd better not base any of your plans on his movements, for he's a very uncertain quantity at present." And she turned with a haughty little laugh addressed to her two friends, as if the unsought interview was now terminated.

Stephanie stood wistfully for a moment, posing in the attitude of bewildered disappointment, and then with a narrowing of her jacinth eyes and a slight, almost imperceptible shrug of her own pretty shoulders, she walked away.

She went to the farthest corner of the hotel patio she could find, which was on the sea side, and stared out into the sparkling blue for a few minutes, her thoughts growing more intense as her slender brows drew into a deep frown. Then she rose hastily and made her way to the telephone booths, calling up her lawyer in New York.

She had to wait a long time before he could be located, but at last she heard his voice, and she spoke haughtily. "Mr. Glyndon, I want you to go out and purchase a piece of real estate for me! I want it no matter what it costs, and I want the matter attended to today. I want to get it without fail at once, and you needn't wait to communicate with me and tell me it isn't worth buying at any price, for I know that now. But it's worth *anything to me*, anything I have to pay. I have private reasons for wanting it, and I don't care whether it is a good buy or not. Do you get me?"

Mr. Glyndon got her. He had had dealings with her before and knew what to expect unless he did her bidding. "Where is the property?"

Stephanie gave him the address that had been on Jeff's letter that she had burned in her ashtray. "And listen, Mr. Glyndon, there are tenants in that house, and I want them to vacate immediately. Offer them any kind of a bonus you have to get out at once. I want the house vacant by the end of the week. See? Even if you have to *move* them."

Mr. Glyndon tried to protest, but Stephanie was firm.

"It isn't as if it wasn't my own money, Mr. Glyndon," reminded Stephanie, "nor as if I didn't have enough to do what I want with it. Buy it today, please, and telegraph me tonight how you came out. But you've *got* to come out, understand? Good-bye, Mr. Glyndon."

Stephanie left the telephone booth with a gleam of danger to somebody in her jacinth eyes and, donning her most daring bathing suit, went down to the beach to captivate some new and interesting admirer in the interim.

❁

When Mr. Whitlock got back to the office Monday morning a new Marietta was already there, her typewriter burnished for action, a large, neat pile of finished typing lying in regular order on the end of her desk, and she herself seated at work upon some routine typing that was always on hand to fill in between special work.

She looked up as he entered, and he looked her straight in the face but did not know her. He stood there staring for a second, hesitating, about to ask her what she was doing there, when Camilla came in from the cloakroom and handed her a paper. "There it is, Marietta. I must have dropped it in the closet Saturday."

Then Camilla saw Mr. Whitlock and gave him a pleasant good morning, almost breaking down with laughter at the astonished look on his face. His expression fully repaid her for her hard work in getting Marietta into shape.

He smiled with that nice light in his eyes when he spoke to Camilla, and then he turned back to Marietta.

"Ah, Miss Pratt," he said pleasantly, "I see you have been acting on some of my suggestions. And I'm glad to see you've got the work done. That's going to help out a lot, for I've got a busy day before me, and I want those letters to get off at once."

A little later he came over to Camilla's desk, and after giving her several directions about the work that morning, he said in a low tone that could not be heard over Marietta's industrious clicking, "Good work! I'm delighted! I didn't think it could be done!"

Camilla smiled understandingly.

At noon he sent Marietta out for her lunch, and when she was gone he said to Camilla, "How about a little relaxation tomorrow night after all your strenuous labors?"

She turned around quickly and met that engaging smile again.

"I have tickets for the symphony concert, and I thought perhaps you'd enjoy going. Could you arrange to get someone to stay with your mother for the evening?"

Camilla's eyes sparkled. She hadn't heard any real music in so long. "Oh, I'd love it! I'll try. Can I tell you tomorrow morning? I'd have to call up a friend, and I'm not sure I can get her till tonight."

"Oh, certainly," said Whitlock, and in a moment more he went out of the office.

❧

Camilla went to her concert, and Miss York came and stayed with her mother. It proved a pleasant evening for them all, and

Camilla went about for days humming bits of melody that she loved. Whitlock had been delightful company, proving to have a fair knowledge of music himself, at least enough for intelligent appreciation. Camilla enjoyed the concert, although it must be confessed that her thoughts were a bit distracted when she happened to look toward the boxes and the elite circle where the social leaders sat. The beautiful women, their sumptuous dresses, the flash of a jewel, the deferential bend of an escort's head to his lady's word, all brought back the memory of that one poor little entry of hers into the great world of wealth and stabbed her with the sharpness of pain to remember certain thrilling incidents that had been treasured and that she thought she had buried too deep for return. Yet here they were again, rearing their heads and mocking at her. Little phrases of Jeffrey Wainwright's, the way he held her coat for her, the way he bent to listen to her slightest word. Just foolish nothings that had no meaning, and yet they haunted her memory and would not give her peace even here in this wonderful music hall amid such heavenly surroundings.

She was thankful that she did not have to do much talking. The music made that impossible, and she could close her eyes to all else and just listen.

During the intermission they went out to walk in the green room, and Whitlock pointed out some notable musicians among the throng. It was all very pleasant, only Camilla could not keep her mind from that other outing and that other escort who had made such a happy time for her.

She roused herself to be entertaining and succeeded in bringing a goodly number of those intimate smiles to the face of her employer.

The next day was a busy one, and Whitlock was away on business. Camilla was sorry not to have the opportunity of again telling him how much she had enjoyed the evening but glad in a way to have the time to think it over unhindered by his personality, which, while very pleasant, sometimes troubled her a little by its very possessiveness. It might be good for her resolves to have someone absorbing her time, but somehow it tortured a certain kind of loyalty in her, which she could not forget. Not that she was in love with *anybody*, of course, she told herself, only that she didn't want her thoughts to be "all mixed up," as she expressed it.

Chapter 16

Marietta was going along nicely, learning some new principle every day, and really doing credit to her teacher, whom she still adored. Camilla went home that night feeling that she had earned a pleasant, quiet evening with her mother and was planning to tell her all about the concert and the different people she had seen, who they were, what they wore, and how they looked.

But the moment she entered the house she felt somehow that something had happened, and when she saw her mother's gentle face, with traces of tears on her carefully wiped eyes and that look of covert anxiety, she knew that it had.

"What is it, Mother?" she cried, aghast. "You are not feeling sick again, are you?"

"Oh no, dear." Her mother managed a smile. "I'm feeling fine!"

"Then it doesn't matter what else happens," said Camilla with a breath of relief. "Go on, tell me what it is!"

"Oh, it really doesn't matter, dear! It isn't anything very terrible, and, of course, it's all in the Father's will, somehow. It's only that we've got to leave this house! Right away! This week, I guess!"

"But we *can't*!" said Camilla, aghast. "They couldn't do that to us! We have our lease. The year isn't up yet. They can't put us out!"

"No, dear, perhaps not, but I guess we've got to go, anyway. You see, the house is sold—"

"But the lease provides for that very possibility," said Camilla insistently. "I'll ask Mr. Whitlock about it. I'm sure they can't put us out."

"But you see, dear—it makes a great difference to them, and they have offered to move us and give us a bonus if we'll get out this week!"

"How much?" demanded Camilla, her firm little lips set in a thin line of resistance.

"Well, it's a good deal, dear. You see, I told them it was impossible, and they kept on offering more and more until the man said he would refund all the past nine months' rent since we moved in. I really hadn't the conscience to keep on saying no, so I told him we would think it over and let him know in the morning. But he seemed to think there would be other ways of getting us out that we might not like so well if we turned it down, so I really think we better go, dear!"

"But how can we? *This week?*" said Camilla in consternation, sitting down weakly on a kitchen chair.

"There'll be a way, dear, if we are meant to go," said her mother, smiling. "Come, let's eat our supper now, and then afterward we can talk it over. You can't tell what you can do until you try."

"This week!" said Camilla again. "How can we? Why, Mother, I can't possibly get off work to hunt a house until Saturday. Not that Mr. Whitlock wouldn't let me off if I would ask him, for he's very kind, but I couldn't be spared, I really couldn't. There is so much to be done!"

"Well," said her mother thoughtfully, "then I guess I'll have to hunt a house." She laughed. "You know, this isn't the most ideal place to live after all, and it isn't in the least likely we shall ever have an offer like this one again, nine months' rent back and our moving free! I thought perhaps we ought to try to get out tonight, lest he should change his mind by morning."

"It is wonderful, isn't it, Mother? It doesn't seem real," said Camilla thoughtfully. "And, of course, we have wanted to get away from this noisy little street before spring comes, but to have it sprung at us this way, I don't see how we're going to manage! If it were only spring, we could jump in the car and drive around and look up something."

"There are papers," said her mother hopefully. "I bought two off the little fellow next door who sells them. I've been looking through the For Rents, and I've marked several. There are some that look very promising."

"How much?" asked Camilla practically.

"Why, they don't give the price," said the mother, looking troubled, "but several said 'low price' or 'reasonable' and some of them sounded very nice indeed. There was one, a flat, that looked interesting, and two bungalows out on the edge of town. That wouldn't be bad for summer, if it wasn't too long a drive for you."

"There are so many things to consider," said Camilla, her eyes full of new trouble, and she sighed.

"If we only had more time!" she said. "Where are those papers? Perhaps there are some advertisements we could telephone about."

"Yes, a couple gave numbers. But let's wait till we have finished the dishes and go at it quietly. You mustn't get all tired and excited after your hard day at the office."

"Oh, I'm not tired," said Camilla. "It wasn't an especially hard day. And anybody would be excited to have to move overnight, as it were. What day did he say we must be out?"

"He gave us a week at the outside before he 'took other

measures', as he put it, but offered fifty dollars more for every day short of that."

Camilla looked at her, startled.

"Well, at least we could afford to pay a little higher rent than we are paying here, then! And things aren't quite so high now as they were when we moved here. That back rent would pay off the doctor and Miss York, too, and we could start fresh. That would be wonderful, wouldn't it?"

"Why, of course!" said her mother cheerfully. "Here, you put the things away in the refrigerator, and I'll wash the dishes. Then we can get to work. It occurred to me to telephone Miss York. She gets about so much, she might hear of something."

"I would hate to bother her till we are located," said Camilla proudly.

"That wouldn't be bothering her. She might just happen to know of something. Child, that's pride, and there isn't a bit of sense to it!"

"All right, Mother! Now, go in the other room and get your papers while I put the dishes away."

"Well," said her mother meekly, "all right, only I telephoned Miss York this afternoon, and she's coming over this evening to talk it over with us. I thought she had a right to know in a crisis like this. She's been so interested in us and was so lovely when I was sick."

Camilla laughed with a relieved note.

"Well, I'm glad she's coming," she owned, "and it will be fun to tell her we can pay her everything."

"Be careful," said her mother, "don't talk too much about pay. She's been just lovely, and you mustn't hurt her."

"No, I won't, Mother dear," said Camilla, stooping to snatch a kiss as she passed with her hands full of plates and cups, "only it will be so good to feel that the debts are paid! But what about the woman upstairs? She hasn't paid us for three weeks, do you realize that? Maybe we'll have trouble with her."

"No," said Mrs. Chrystie with the air of a child confessing her faults one by one, "I've fixed that all up with her. I told her that if she would move out tomorrow we would let the back rent go, and she's gone out to her married daughter's now to find out if she can have a room there for the rest of the winter. It seems she's lost her job and doesn't know when she can pay, so I think she was really relieved."

"But perhaps she's got a disagreeable son-in-law who won't have her," suggested Camilla.

"No, she says he's very nice and has often asked her to come there and live, but she likes to be independent."

"Well, that's a help, anyway. Because even if we stayed here and she didn't pay her rent, what would we have done?"

"Yes, I know," said the mother thoughtfully.

"But, Mother, even if we had a place to go, it might take several days to get a mover. They have to be engaged beforehand."

There was a wise twinkle in her mother's eye in answer to that.

"No, you see, I thought of that, and I asked Mrs. Pryor next door if she knew of a good mover. She told me of one right in the next street. She's known him a long time and says he's very honest and careful, so I telephoned him; he came over at noon and looked over what we have and said he could move it after five o'clock any day this week, tomorrow if we found a place!"

"Tomorrow!" gasped Camilla. "That would be utterly impossible!"

"I don't see why, Camilla," said Mrs. Chrystie calmly. "I've thought it all out, and I can't see wasting the offer of fifty dollars a day. Why, Camilla, if the house was on fire, we'd get out on the sidewalk inside of half an hour, and we'd probably save a good part of our things at that. And surely with a good mover we could do it in a day! And it doesn't seem reasonable for us to lose fifty dollars a day wasting time looking for a house. We can surely find something right away."

"But, Mother, how do you know that fifty dollars a day is a genuine offer? The man may be a fraud and just trying to get us out of the house and home for his own interest. I think we ought to find out more about it before we do anything about hunting a house."

"Well," said her mother with another twinkle, "you know, I thought that, too, so I called up the bank and asked Mr. Baker, and it seems the man is a noted lawyer and anything he says he'll make good. He offered to put the money in our bank in Mr. Baker's hands to be delivered to us as soon as we moved."

Suddenly Camilla sat down and looked at her mother with new respect, and then she began to laugh.

"Well, Mother," she said with admiration, "it seems you are able to run our affairs better than I am, and here I was counting myself the manager of the family! Why, it wouldn't have occurred to me to do all those things, and you've got everything practically arranged."

"Yes," said the mother, smiling, "your father taught me to be very careful about such matters, and staying here all day alone, I had time to think it all out. But you're not to discount your own ability, Camilla. I've been proud of you, managing everything so well while I was sick. And I've been glad just to lie back and have everything fixed for me. But I still can do my share occasionally when it's necessary, and I thought today, till you came back, it was necessary to act at once, so I acted."

"Well, Mother, what else have you done?"

"Oh, not much else, except to call up one or two real estate offices and get a list of houses and apartments for rent. Silcox around on Tenth Street sent a boy around with a list of places with descriptions and prices. I told him about what we could pay. Of course, some of them were more than I said. But you can look them over. You'll know locations better than I. I thought Miss York could help in that also. Three agents told me of apartments and gave me descriptions over the telephone. So, you see, I've been busy. The lists are over on the desk, and there are three places that can be seen this evening!"

"Well, I should say you've been working pretty efficiently," said Camilla meekly, gathering up the lists and sitting down to study them.

"Then I folded up some of our clothes from the closets and put them in the bureau drawers, and packed some of the photographs and vases and things around these rooms in the old carved chest there."

"Mother!" said Camilla, aghast. "Do you want to get sick again? I just know you are too tired!"

"Oh no, I've been enjoying myself!" said Mrs. Chrystie. "I didn't do much. Just little things that took time and care. I've really been sitting down all day. And it's been such a pleasure to get some things done so that you wouldn't have so much. There! That's the doorbell! That will be Miss York! Or perhaps Mr. Glyndon. He said he would come back either this evening or early tomorrow morning to get our answer."

"Glyndon?" said Camilla, startled. Things were moving so fast she felt as if she were tied to a runaway horse.

"Yes, he's the man who represents the new owner of the house. He's the lawyer."

Camilla was convinced at first sight of the lawyer that he meant business, and more so when he went away leaving a check in her hands that was a goodly advance on the sum he had promised to pay when they were out of the house.

Miss York had come in while he was there and slipped through to the kitchen until he should be gone, then she returned, her face full of interest.

"Well, isn't this nice!" she said, beaming on them. "I've been so hoping you could get out of this street before warm weather comes, and now it's all planned for you!"

"Now we're going to be able to pay all our debts!" said Camilla, rejoicing. "But how on earth we're going to get out in a week is more than I can understand, for I simply can't get off from the office any day till five, and one can't do much at lunch hour, even without eating."

"Get out?" said Miss York. "Why, of course you'll get out. I don't see why you can't be out of here by tomorrow night! There's nothing to hinder!"

"My dear!" said Camilla, protesting. "We haven't even an idea where we can find a house, and how can we move till the house is cleaned. You ought to have seen this house before we cleaned it! It was simply filthy!"

"Nonsense!" said Miss York. "In the first place, you don't need to take a dirty place. There are plenty of apartments and even little houses that are perfectly new. Yes, and prices aren't so bad, either. Besides, even if you have to pay a little more than you do here, you are making enough to cover it. The quicker you get out, the better. What we need to do is find something tonight! It's two minutes to eight now"—she consulted her watch—"before ten, Camilla, you and I ought to find something, and tomorrow morning Jinny Wilcox, the woman who does my washing, can go right to work cleaning the bedrooms. If you have a clean place to sleep by night, that is all that's necessary. You can do the rest after you get in. It won't be such ideal moving as having the whole house cleaned ahead of time, but what's a little thing like that when you are getting fifty dollars a day for tumbling in?"

"But Mother! She'll work too hard, Miss York!" said Camilla in distress.

"Mother'll have to be reasonable," said the nurse, with a look at her former patient that meant business. "We'll make out a program for Mother, and she'll have to take her oath to stick to it, or we'll put her to bed in a hospital until the moving is all over."

"Oh, I'll be good," promised Mrs. Chrystie. "I really will."

"Very well, then," said the nurse. "I'll write out the program for you before I go back. My patient's sister is staying with her tonight, so I don't have to go back till I get ready, and we can have the time of our lives. Now, first, have you any idea where you *want* to move?"

"Only where we can afford it, and not too far from my office," said Camilla. "Mother telephoned a lot of real estate offices and got a list of places, but I don't have an idea where most of them are."

"Let me see them! I haven't been nursing so long in this city without knowing a whole lot about locations."

Camilla handed over the lists, and Miss York looked them over.

"You don't want any on that list," she said, giving the first paper back to Camilla. "That's down in the slummy-slums. Vine Street is a tough neighborhood as far down as that, and Third Street isn't much better. It's unhealthy down there in more senses than one, and noisy. Besides, it wouldn't be safe for you, Camilla, going out at night. Garner Street might do, but it's terribly noisy. Victrolas and radios have the night, and brawls now and then. I nursed down there. Here, this one is better. It isn't fashionable there, but it's respectable. Still, it's desolate. Rows of red bricks like this, only a little larger, but they face a vast foundry across the street, and the noise is intolerable all day long."

Camilla ran her eye down the prices on the discarded list hopelessly. If these houses cost so much, how could they afford anything better?

"Ah! Here is one, Park Circle. That's all right, if it isn't opposite the schoolhouse! And now here, this last paper is much more possible. Would you think Brentwood was too far out, Camilla? I think you could make it in a half hour mornings. It's not in the city limits and there are not such high taxes, so the rent seems to be reasonable. These two say 'yard.' Would you like that?"

"Oh, I'd like a yard!" said Mrs. Chrystie wistfully.

"And here is one with a sleeping porch. And two apartments in the east part of the city that might be good."

Miss York was checking them off rapidly with her pencil.

"Here are three that look pretty good," she said. "How about it, Camilla? Can't you and I take the car and run around to these? They aren't so far away, and we ought to do all three in a little over an hour."

"*Tonight?*" said Camilla, wide eyed. "Why, yes, if you have the time."

"All the time there is," said Miss York. "Get your hat on. But before you go, here's an idea. How would you like to take a bit larger place and rent me a room, or even two? I'm a bit crowded where I am, and the woman's married daughter is coming home with her family. Her husband's lost his job. No telling how long they will be there, and she needs all the room there is and then some. She told me about it last night. Said she hated to send me away, but she didn't see how she was going to spare the room after they come. So I've got to be looking around, and if you think I wouldn't be a nuisance, maybe we could work out something together that would be nicer and a little bit cheaper than we could get separately?"

"Oh, that would be wonderful!" said Camilla with relief. "You'd like that, wouldn't you, Mother?"

"I certainly would," said Mrs. Chrystie. "But you'd never want to live in a plain little house such as we would have to take."

"It doesn't matter about plainness," said Miss York, "and I wouldn't want anything better than you have. Of course, certain neighborhoods are better for me than others, but we could easily find the right thing if you'd be willing to have me around. I've been paying—" She launched into details, showing that she had thought things out carefully. "If I took two rooms, I'd expect to pay more, of course, and it would be worth it to me to be with people I like. You know, there's nothing like feeling at home, and I haven't had much home in my life. Now, come on, Camilla. There's one other place I have in mind if you don't find these what you want. We'll go see it. It's a lovely location—nice, plain, substantial neighborhood, little separate cottages with a central heating plant. I don't know what they rent for, but I heard since the depression they've put the rent down. I never saw the inside of them, but the outside is most attractive. Now, Mother Chrystie, will you be good and rest while we're gone?"

"I'll be good," said Mrs. Chrystie, "but I'm going to sit in front of the desk and put my papers in order for tomorrow. It isn't hard work. I'll lie down if I feel tired."

"Well, we'll trust you. You're on your honor, you know. If you get sick beforehand, it's all off. We can't move!" declared Miss York.

So Camilla and Miss York got into the little car and started out house hunting.

It was ten o'clock before they returned, but in their eyes was a look of satisfaction almost as if they had conquered the world.

"Well, we found a place," said Miss York triumphantly. "Tell her about it, Camilla, while I heat up what coffee was left. Camilla needs something; she's too excited to sleep."

"Oh, Mother!" said Camilla, "I really believe we have found a nice place. Anyway, it will do for a while till we can look around. There doesn't seem to be anything the matter with it at all.

"It's one of those little bungalow-cottages Miss York was telling about, out in Brentwood, all on one floor and an attic in the peak of the roof for storage. It's really darling. The rooms are fairly large, with plenty of windows. It's really a little duck of a house, although the floors are pine and the porch isn't bigger than a pocket handkerchief. But there's a small yard and a big tree, and there's space at the back of the house to hang up clothes. And,

Mother, just think of it, central heating! No furnace to tend, and no coal to buy! We went next door and asked the people there about it and they say it's very satisfactory, always plenty of heat, and you can turn it off when it gets too hot."

"Why, that is wonderful!" said the mother. "I'm sure I shall like it. Is it located all right for Miss York, and is there a nice room for her? I think the tenant is the best part about this arrangement."

"So do I!" said Camilla with a sigh of relief. "It will be so nice to have her coming home to us sometimes! The only thing I'm afraid of is that she's doing this to help us out."

"Just listen to her, Mother Chrystie; she'd even begrudge me the chance to do a little good deed now and then if I got the chance. But as it happens, this time the rooms in this house are a lot better than where I am now, larger and lighter, and the closet is twice as big. There's a closet in every room, all good-sized, and one in the hall. Did you notice that, Camilla?"

"Yes, and a linen closet in the hall, and a towel closet in the bathroom."

"It sounds too good to be true," said Mrs. Chrystie. "I've kept the extra linen in a box under my bed so long I don't know that I'd remember to use a linen closet if I had one. I don't feel that I deserve so much luxury. I'm afraid I've sometimes grumbled at our close quarters."

"Never where anybody could hear you, I'm sure!" said Nurse York. "What I'm afraid of is that I'm not good enough to live in the house with such wonderful people as you are. Ever since I've been here to nurse I've called you folks 'white orchid' people. It just seems to fit you. There are people who remind me of violets, they are so shy; and some are tiger lilies; and some are like weeds, just no account at all; but you folks always seemed to me like royalty in flowers, heavenly royalty at that."

"Mother, she's a poet, not a nurse!" cried Camilla, laughing.

"Talking poetry like that. I don't know as we shall be able to live up to her. But I think she's got her metaphors mixed somehow. Seems to me, I've heard that orchids are parasites."

"There, Camilla, you've said enough!" said Miss York severely. "You go up to the third floor and get done whatever you have to do for the movers tomorrow while I get Lady Chrystie to bed. Then I'm coming up and get you, so you better hurry. It's going to be my special care to look after you two and see that you keep your health!"

"She's going to be awfully bossy, Mother," laughed back Camilla as she mounted the stairs with her arms full of garments to pack in the trunk up in the attic.

Two hours later she lay in her bed trying to memorize a list of things she must remember to do before she left for the office in the morning. It seemed incredible that this time tomorrow night they would be in another house. It wasn't going to be impossible after all to move in one day. But what a tower of strength Miss York was! And Jinny Wilcox was going to be another tower she was sure, from the brief glimpse she had of her friendly face when they stopped to arrange with her about the cleaning.

So, without any memory of her former troubles and perplexities, she dropped away to sleep.

Chapter 17

It was hard to tear herself away in the morning. How interesting it would be to stay and look after everything. There seemed to be so many little things she ought to do before she went. Maybe she had been wrong not to ask Mr. Whitlock to let her off for the day. Then she remembered that he might be still away and that he had been most anxious for certain matters to be finished at once. No, she couldn't trust Marietta to look after it all, not yet! So with a sigh, she hurried away.

"Just remember, dear, that I still have my right mind," said her mother, smiling as she kissed her good-bye. "I won't let anybody steal our furniture nor throw the dishes out the window!"

"Well, but Mother, you've been sick!"

"Yes, but I'm not sick now, and anyway, I'm not going to move the furniture personally. Now hurry along. You're going to be late! And don't think about this end of things till five o'clock!"

Camilla had no difficulty in controlling her thoughts that day, however, for she was overwhelmed with work and responsibility, and there was no time, either, for wondering how her mother and the mover would be getting on without her or for dreaming back into the brief past that had haunted her so long.

To begin with, Marietta telephoned that her stepmother had been taken very sick that morning. "And I gotta stand by, see, till the doctor gets here! I don't wantta, but I gotta! 'Cause she might die, see, and I wouldn't want it ta be my fault, even ef she hasn't been nice ta me."

"Why, of course!" said Camilla briskly. "You must stay there if you are needed. Have you sent for the doctor? Couldn't you get a district nurse to come? Can I do anything for you?"

"No, thanks! I guess she'll be awright. But she's carrying on something awful. Little Ted is all curled up on the couch looking white and sick. He's frightened, hearing his mother scream. I don't know what she's got. I guess it's her appendix. That's what the woman next door says she thinks it is. So ef you can get along without me this morning, I'll try and get there at noon. Ef I can't, I'll let ya know."

"All right, Marietta," said Camilla, with a sinking of heart. How things were thickening. What a day! And she ought to be at home this minute looking after the moving! It seemed as if everything was all awry. She bowed her head over the telephone for a minute in despair.

"Well," she reminded herself, "Mother always says that when things seem to be in a tangle to us it's just that God is executing an especially intricate and marvelous pattern in our lives, and we must be pliable in His hands, so as not to hinder. Lord, have Thy way with me today!"

She lifted her head, put down the telephone, and went back to her work. She would just rest on that and go ahead.

Many people came into the office that morning, questions came up for her to decide quickly, the telephone rang almost continually, and finally Mr. Whitlock telephoned that he would not be able to get back until late in the afternoon.

Her voice was clear and steady as she answered his questions and gave him the messages that had been left for him, writing down his directions carefully. She did not tell him that Marietta was not there. That would not help matters any and would only exasperate him with Marietta. She did not tell him that there had been no time for lunch and she was going to have a cup of coffee and a sandwich sent up from the restaurant nearby as soon as she could find time to telephone for it. She did not tell him that she was moving that day and ought to be at home. She just went steadily ahead and did her best. Determined to let her Lord have His way in her for that one day at least and not get flurried about it. And she was greatly relieved and surprised to discover as the day went on that she was not as tired as usual, in spite of it all. There was something restful in remembering that the day was not her responsibility. She had but to go ahead and leave the working out of things with God.

When intervals of quiet from telephone and patrons came her fingers flew on the typewriter keys. She discovered presently that she was really making progress with the day's work in spite of the many hindrances. Her heart was at rest, and she hadn't time to think of dreams or disappointments. Oh, if she could just keep this heart-rest all the time, how wonderful it would be!

Marietta came in breathless about two o'clock and found Camilla working away so hard that she did not see her enter, writing and taking a bite of her sandwich now and then between pages.

"You poor thing!" said Marietta self-reproachfully. "You been here all alone all day? You didn't have a chance to get any lunch? You go now and get a real good meal, and I'll stay till five. They've taken her to the hospital. It was the appendix, and they think they've got to operate right off. She's awful scared. I felt real sorry for her. I left Ted with a neighbor. Poor kid, he's scared stiff! If I had known Whittie wasn't here I'd have brought Ted along, but I guess Whittie wouldn't stand for a child in the office, would he?"

"I'm afraid not," Camilla said, smiling. "Poor child! I'm sorry he has to stay alone. I'd tell you to take him down to Mother this afternoon, but we're moving today and there wouldn't be any place for him yet."

"Moving!" cried Marietta. "Then you oughtta be home yerself. You go now, and I'll stay here. Ted's all right for this afternoon. He's got some picture papers to read. He likes ta read. You go, and I can do everything. I'll be real careful."

"Thank you, Marietta," Camilla said, "that's nice of you, but I couldn't. There are some messages I have to give people and things that have to be decided when I hear what they say. Mr. Whitlock called up. He won't be in till four forty-five, and I'd like to have the work up to the mark. If you think it's all right for you to stay, suppose you get to work on those circulars and fold and address them. I'm staying right here till five. We mustn't stop to talk. I hope your stepmother will get through all right, and afterward perhaps there'll be some way I can help. Now, let's get to work!" And Camilla's fingers went flying on.

Mr. Whitlock came rushing in, looking tired and worn, about ten minutes to five. He cast his eyes anxiously over his desk and looked relieved when he saw the pile of letters awaiting his signature.

"You got them all done?" he said pleasantly. "Well, that's great. Miss Pratt must be improving greatly. I was thinking I might have to ask you to stay overtime and finish them. It is most important they should go out tonight, for I find someone else is bidding for the same contract."

"You don't need to give me any credit," said Marietta earnestly. "I couldn't come till about two o'clock. My stepmother was awful sick, and I couldn't leave her till they took her to the hospital. Camilla was here all alone most of the day, and she had a lot done before I got here."

Mr. Whitlock raised his eyebrows at Camilla.

"Oh, I'm sorry!" he said. "Why didn't you tell me when I telephoned? I'd have let the rest of the business go till next week."

"Oh, I got along all right," said Camilla, "and Miss Pratt is mistaken about her work. She's been wonderful this afternoon. She did all that pile herself. And she must have been tired, too. She's been up nearly all night with her stepmother and came down here just as soon as they took her away."

Mr. Whitlock cast a kindly glance toward Marietta. "Well, that was great, Miss Pratt! I appreciate that. If I had known about it I would have told you not to come, even if the work had to go out to a public secretary for once."

"Thank you," said Marietta, blushing scarlet over the unexpected praise and kindness, "but I'm all right. I guess I can get along now. And ef you don't mind, I'd liketa make up this lost day on Saturday afternoons."

"Oh, that's all right, Miss Pratt," said the employer kindly. "You don't need to make that up. You have a right to an emergency now and then, and you've been doing unusually good work the last week. I appreciate the change in your appearance, too."

Then he turned to Camilla.

"You are moving?" he asked. "Isn't that rather sudden, Miss Chrystie?"

"Yes," said Camilla. "The house was sold quite suddenly, and they offered to move us if we would vacate at once, so we thought it would be to our advantage."

"Well, I'm very sorry that you should have had to be here all day."

"It's quite all right," said Camilla. "We haven't so much to move. I did a good deal last night. The movers will do the rest."

"Well, you must go at once!" he said, glancing at the clock and taking some papers from his pocket. "It must have been hard for you today."

"It's been all right," said Camilla brightly, "and they don't expect me till half-past five. I've plenty of time to finish this letter and take some dictation for tomorrow morning before I go."

Camilla could see that this decision relieved her employer very much, though he was gracious about it. So she insisted on finishing the important matters before she left. Marietta, too, stuck faithfully by, working with her homely young face in an earnest frown and her pudgy fingers pounding away on her machine.

It was almost six o'clock when all three finally went down in the elevator together, Whitlock hurrying off to meet a man and take him to dinner.

Camilla was relieved that he did not offer to go with her and help. Somehow, though he was kind, she did not want him coming into the dilemma of their moving. On the way to the house she tried to reason it out, knowing in the back of her mind that if it had been Wainwright she would have been not only relieved but overjoyed. And yet Mr. Whitlock had been most kind and considerate and would have been the natural one to help if he had offered, which, of course, he couldn't do with a dinner engagement on hand. She could sense that these were strenuous times in the office and that he was hard pressed, and she felt all the more obligated to be on hand early and get off those letters he had dictated just now. They should go in the nine o'clock mail, and she would see that they did, even if she had to leave a little earlier than usual to accomplish it.

She had meant to telephone home before driving there, to see if the movers had started away yet with the first load, but she didn't want to do it in front of Mr. Whitlock and Marietta, so she drove home as fast as traffic would allow.

She found the movers just about to leave with the first load.

"Very well, then, Mother, I'll go right along with them. Can I trust you to lie down while I'm gone? No, you're not to go yet till there's a place for you to go right to bed. Have you had anything to eat?"

"Oh yes," said her mother, smiling. "I ate at five o'clock, and I've got the thermos bottle full of hot soup for you. Will you eat it before you go or take it with you?"

"Why, I'll take it with me. That's wonderful! I'll eat it while I'm telling them where to put things. Now, can I trust you to stay right there on the couch till I get back and not lift a finger?"

"What is there left to do?" asked the mother. "But really, I don't see why I shouldn't go along now. I could rest on a chair until you got things fixed to your satisfaction, you know."

"But you wouldn't, I'm afraid."

"Yes, I would. I'd rest much better if I was right there and the journey over."

"All right, but isn't there anything more here to be done?"

"Not a thing!" said Mrs. Chrystie proudly. "Mrs. Pryor is coming in after the last load is gone to sweep all the rooms. Mr. Glyndon said that was all we need to do. He said the new owner would look after all the rest."

"Well, that's wonderful!" said Camilla, with a troubled look around to think that all this had been accomplished without her supervision. "All right, Mother, where's your coat and hat? It's pretty cold out."

"Oh, I thought you'd say that, so I got out my old fur coat before the trunks left, and I've filled a hot water bottle and wrapped it in a blanket. I thought I might as well fuss over myself as to have you and Miss York do it."

"Well, you have been good," commended Camilla, laughing. "Have you got galoshes on? The pavements are icy, you know."

"Oh yes, I saved them out, too. Now let's get going. Those men want to get done."

So, for the first time since her illness, Mrs. Chrystie went out into the winter world again.

"It's going to snow," she announced as she stepped into the car and sat down. "No, don't worry about me, I'm quite all right.

I lay down three times today, and I haven't done a thing the last hour but tell the men which things to take in the first load."

Camilla wrapped her mother warmly, put the hot water bag at her feet, and started on, the big van coming close behind.

"Now," said Camilla, "this is the first time you've been out and you mustn't talk in the cold air. Just rest back and relax."

"All right," said her mother, but her bright eyes were watching the streets as they went along, and once when Camilla looked at her anxiously her mother smiled at her happily, almost like a child.

"Having a nice ride, Millie, darling!" she said.

"You dear!" said Camilla, with a throb of thankfulness at her heart, "I believe you're enjoying this."

"Why surely," said her mother. "Who wouldn't, after all these weeks in the house?"

"Well, I hope you like the house," said the daughter.

"Why, of course I'll like it! Whatever it is, I'll like it. Didn't it bring you money enough to get that debt off your mind, and didn't our Father send it in time for our need? Why shouldn't I like it? I'd like it just because He sends it, even if I *didn't* like it!"

Camilla laughed outright with a child's sudden delight. "Mother! That's lovely! Do you know, I believe when we get settled I'm just going to take a day off sometime and be thankful for the kind of mother I have. I don't believe I ever before realized what a wonderful inheritance I have, having a mother who can take hard things that way. I wish I had such a wonderful trust as you have. I believe that's what has kept you so young-looking in spite of all that you have been through."

"Yes," said her mother thoughtfully, "I guess that has helped me through. Trusting. I couldn't have got through in my own strength, I know that. Why, Camilla, you're stopping. This can't be the house, is it? It's all lit up. Do you have to ask the way or something?"

"No," said Camilla, "I don't have to ask the way, and this is the house, but I don't understand its being lit up, unless Jinny is still there."

"But, Daughter, this is a very pretty little house!"

"Oh, I'm glad it seems nice to you. Now, you sit still, Mother, till I get a chair or something taken in for you to sit on."

"No," said Mrs. Chrystie, "I want to go in with you now. I can sit on the stairs for a while till a chair comes. Or aren't there any stairs? A box, then. For pity's sake, don't baby me now. Can't you see I'm running over with curiosity?"

Camilla laughed and let her have her way, taking her arm and carefully leading her where the walk was icy. But when they went up the steps, the front door suddenly swung open and a wide path of light poured out, and Miss York, with a big white apron over her uniform and a towel pinned over her hair, appeared in the doorway.

"Welcome home!" she cried, bowing low before them, ushering them inside and shutting the door. "Why, it's warm as toast!" said Mrs. Chrystie, looking around admiringly, "and you say there's no furnace to bother with. That will be wonderful!"

Camilla and her mother walked through the rooms with Miss York bringing up the rear. It seemed so wonderful that this was their new home.

In just no time at all they had Mrs. Chrystie established in a big chair in the living room, and the movers were putting up the beds and spreading down the rugs under Camilla's direction. It didn't take long. And Miss York, with uncanny accuracy, found the sheets and blankets and was making up the bed, while Camilla ate her soup and gave directions to the movers. Incredibly, the house began to be like home with each piece of furniture that came in.

Miss York stayed with Mrs. Chrystie when Camilla went back with the movers to get the last load and close up the house, and soon her former patient was tucked snugly into bed with the light turned out.

"Now, you're to go to sleep at once!" she ordered, "or we shan't let you get up at all tomorrow, and I'll have to give up my job and come and nurse you."

With that threat she closed the door and tiptoed away to prowl around and see what she could do to make the house more livable.

She found two big baskets of dishes wrapped in newspapers and set to work putting them on the cabinet shelves, putting away knives and forks and spoons in the drawers. The kitchen utensils had come in with the first load, also, and before Camilla returned Nurse York had the kitchen in fair order, as far as things that had arrived, for Mrs. Chrystie, with careful foresight, had sent in the first load what would be needed first.

Back at the old home Camilla telephoned Mr. Glyndon according to previous arrangement, and before long he arrived, paid the movers, and gave Camilla a check for the rest of the money promised. She stood looking at the check in a kind of daze. It seemed so strange to her that so suddenly she had been lifted out of the appalling debt that had hung over her and threatened to engulf her and been put into ease and freedom, with a better house to live in, and for her mother the companionship at times of Miss York. She hadn't known how she was going to get along, and now it was all fixed. Of course, she wasn't rolling in wealth yet, but it seemed luxury just to be out of debt and have the rent ahead for a few months so that she could have a chance to lay up a little for a time of emergency. How good God had been to her!

Then as she heard the movers coming back to get another piece of furniture, she folded the check quickly, put it in her purse, and hurried off upstairs to make sure that nothing had been forgotten.

As she came downstairs again and looked down upon the emptiness and desolation in the little front hall, a sudden sadness came over her. Something brought back that night that her mother was so very sick and Wainwright had proved such a tower of strength.

There was nothing left down there now in the living room but a few chairs and the old piano. She could seem to see Wainwright's evening coat lying across the top. And the old Morris chair! She remembered how she had found him that next morning, asleep in the Morris chair in the hall, his long dark lashes lying on his cheeks, his beautiful hair tossed back in disorder from his handsome forehead. How good and dear he had looked to her! And the orchids! Beautiful, delicate creatures! And his pleasant grin! It gave her a distinct pang to realize that she would never likely see him again. He would never appear at the door of this house and ask for her! And he wouldn't know where else to look for her!

Suddenly she was appalled to think that she was so absolutely cutting herself off from him and there wasn't any way she could leave a clue to herself. Her mother had duly written her note of thanks for the oranges but there had come no answer, and she had no excuse for writing again. And even if she had, she wouldn't, of course. No, he was gone into the unknown world of people, even as he had come, and he would never be in her life again. And it was right that it should be so! But oh, how it hurt! For there still was that sharp, sweet memory of the kiss he had given her, the kiss that seemed to seal something precious between them. To think that she, Camilla Chrystie, should have to have a memory of such a thing, a kiss that could still burn and humiliate, and yet could be so precious! She, who had always prided herself on her carefulness where men were concerned, her cool reticence, and her ability to protect herself.

And suddenly she realized that she had been counting on his

coming back sometime in spite of it all. And God, knowing that, had cut her off from any such possibility! God was helping her against her own weakness. Well, she should be thankful that she was going away where she would not be constantly reminded of him. How unheard of! Just a few days with a stranger and something had come into her life of which she could not rid herself! She *must*! She *would*!

When she finally locked the door and handed the key to Mr. Glyndon she felt as if she were shutting the door on one of the brightest experiences of her life, and she was rather glad that Mr. Glyndon was there, saying courteous things about regretting he had had to hurry her and hoping the new home would be all right. There really wasn't any time to be sentimental about leaving that doorstep, that sordid little grimy doorstep where Wainwright and she had stood together a few short weeks before, and she was glad with a kind of moral approval that it was so.

Back in her car again, speeding ahead of the moving van, she reflected on life. Why did one young man have to get such a hold on her thoughts above all other young men she had ever met? Was it just the halo of romance, meeting him in the street in the dark that way and having his help in her time of need? Was it because of his wealth and position, his personal attraction, his courteous manner, his white orchids?

Why, for instance, couldn't she be as interested in Mr. Whitlock? He was good-looking, too. He probably had plenty of wealth and social position, if one knew the whole story. And he certainly was courteous and a delightful escort. Perhaps he wouldn't ask her to go out with him anymore, but if he did she ought to be glad to put some new thoughts and experiences into her mind. That was probably the problem—she had been too much to herself. She just worked too hard and never went anywhere. That must be why the first fascinating stranger held her thoughts so long and so exclusively.

Well, the new home in the new place might give her new friends and erase morbid longings for something that was never really hers.

So she arrived at the new house and realized that she was terribly tired. Such a long day with so many responsibilities. She just must stop thinking about herself and give herself to the duties before her. She had to direct the placing of all the rest of the things before she could think of getting to bed. And there was the kitchen. She ought to get things in shape for a breakfast.

So she drove into the tiny corrugated iron garage at the back of the tiny lot and shut her car in for the night, thankful that there was a garage and she didn't have to leave the car with its new paint out in the open, for it looked as if there was going to be more snow.

But when she opened the door, there was Miss York still holding the fort and the dishes in shining rows on the shelves. A sense of comfort and peace came upon her.

"I brought over my electric toaster," said Miss York, indicating her arrangements on the shelf of the cabinet. "You can make toast in no time in the morning, and you're not to get up any earlier than usual. Jinny is coming over in the morning to work and see that your mother doesn't. I found the bread box had a loaf of bread in it, and I hunted the coffee. Also, the woman next door put a note in her milk bottle to ask her milkman to leave you some cream in the morning. I started some oatmeal, and it will keep cooking a little all night on the pilot light in that double boiler. If that isn't breakfast enough for you the first morning you can get more in the city."

For answer Camilla flung her arms around Miss York's neck and gave her a kiss.

"You dear angel-guardian!" she cried. "What should we have done without you?"

"There, there, now, no sob-stuff!" said the nurse, turning pink at the caress. "Hurry up and get done with those movers so I can tuck you into bed before I go."

"But it's almost eleven o'clock. You ought to go home at once! I don't like you running around so late alone."

The nurse stared and then laughed.

"Don't you know I've been used to taking care of myself for thirty years? Don't you worry about me."

"Well, if you're going to worry about me," declared Camilla, "then I'm going to worry about you. Come now, please put your hat on and go, and I'll promise, honor bright, to get into bed the minute the movers are gone."

The movers were not long in getting the last load placed. They had their pay and were anxious to get home to their beds. But Miss York managed to stay around until they were gone. She was used to having her way.

So presently Camilla found herself sinking away to sleep and feeling like a traveler just set sail upon new seas toward strange unexplored lands.

Chapter 18

Stephanie Varrell was reading a telegram just received from her lawyer.

She sat on the end veranda of the hotel that looked off toward the sea, but she did not see the water. On her face was the smile of the cat who has just licked the cream off the pan of milk or the frosting off the sponge cake. The telegram read as follows:

> HAVE OPPORTUNITY TO SELL AT GOOD
> ADVANCE THE PROPERTY ON VESEY STREET
> ACQUIRED FOR YOU LAST WEEK AT YOUR
> SUGGESTION. TENANTS MOVING OUT
> TODAY. CITY GAS COMPANY OFFERS GREAT
> INDUCEMENT IF SALE CAN BE COMPLETED
> AT ONCE. THEY ARE PUTTING UP NEW PLANT
> IN SAME BLOCK AND WISH TO ACQUIRE THE
> WHOLE UNBROKEN. THEY ARE TEARING DOWN

AND REBUILDING. TIME A FACTOR. CAN GET
UNUSUAL PRICE IF YOU ARE WILLING TO SELL.
CHANCES ARE THEY WOULD BE ABLE TO GET
BUILDING CONDEMNED AND COMMANDEER
IT AT THEIR OWN PRICE, IF YOU REFUSE NOW.
WIRE INSTRUCTIONS IMMEDIATELY.

R. R. GLYNDON

Stephanie read it through several times carefully, the cat-and-cream expression still on her face. Then she took her little gold pencil out of her purse and wrote rapidly on the back of the telegram:

AM WILLING TO SELL ON CONDITION THE
BUILDING IS TORN DOWN AT ONCE, THIS WEEK
IF POSSIBLE. OTHERWISE NOTHING DOING.
ULTIMATUM!

S. VARRELL

When Mr. Glyndon received that message, he smiled, amused.

"The divine Stephanie must hate somebody pretty badly just now," he said to himself.

Stephanie had sent that message on its way and then had left the view of the leaping, dancing, golden sea and searched diligently until she had discovered Jeff's mother in one of her usual knitting haunts in the windless corner where her carefully sculpted hairdo would not be disturbed. Stephanie dropped down to exclaim over the beauty of the knitting she was doing.

Madame Wainwright gave her a keen glance and ignored her, and presently Stephanie, in honeyed words, asked about Jeff.

"He's having a wonderful time, isn't he?" she gushed. "They

say that trip is great if you can stand the insects and the serpents."

"There are a good many kinds of insects—and serpents," remarked Jeffrey Wainwright's mother dryly, but gave no further information.

"But I thought he told me he had to be back in the north before this," lied Stephanie, with narrowed jacinth eyes on her victim.

"Perhaps he did," said Jeffrey's mother calmly. "He probably changed his plans."

"He went with his younger brother, didn't he? I don't blame you for being nervous about the little fellow down in an awful place like that, although it must be perfectly fascinating."

"He went because he chose to," said Mrs. Wainwright calmly, beginning to count her stitches. "There was no reason why I should be nervous about Sam. He's quite capable of looking out for himself, even if there hadn't been a competent man in charge of the boys."

"Then you think Jeffrey may return in time for the tennis tournament Saturday?" cunningly asked the girl. "It would be too bad for him to miss that. He's practically a champion now, isn't he?"

"I really don't know what my son's plans are, Miss Varrell," said Jeffrey's mother coldly.

"But at least you don't think he'll go back north yet, do you?" persisted the girl.

"That will depend entirely on whether his father needs him," said the woman haughtily. "Excuse me, I've got to count these stitches again. I think I've made a mistake."

But Stephanie had found out what she wanted. Jeff hadn't gone back north yet, that was pretty sure. She had been afraid he had slipped away home already, but she had taken a chance and caught his mother unaware. Women like Mrs. Wainwright could evade, but they didn't deliberately lie. Jeffrey was still in the

South, and if Mr. Glyndon did his duty, there would be no house left on Vesey Street when Jeffrey got back home. She walked to the other end of the veranda and looked off to sea, and her jacinth eyes glinted gold with triumph. She would win out for a few more days anyway, perhaps. She meant to crush that other gold-haired, deep-eyed girl like an eggshell under her foot if she got in her way again. And perhaps the longer Jeff stayed in the forest, the quicker he would forget the other girl and whatever it was she said to him that night they had all met.

Meantime, there were other pleasant things she could do besides worry over her hates and desires. There were other fish in the sea as good as those that had been caught, or nearly caught, and she was pretty sure that Jeff was safe for a time. Why not enjoy herself?

So she garbed herself scantily and dropped down to the beach with her best golden lure.

❀

Twenty-four hours later workmen arrived at 125 Vesey Street and began to roll up the tin roof of the little old shabby house like a scroll; unbrick its wall; pull out its windows like old teeth; and tear up the cheap, worn floors and the two stubby wooden steps where Camilla had stood to say good night to Jeffrey Wainwright the last time she saw him. And surely if intangible things can haunt, the ghost of that kiss he laid upon her lips that night must have fled the neighborhood in utter rout.

So trifling souls, even those with jacinth eyes, are sometimes used to mold history and change destinies. This time the whims of a spoiled girl with a heart full of hate for anything that came in her way, even unwittingly, decided a much-debated question of whether the city gas company should expand on its south side or on its north side. It was a question of which block they could soonest get possession, and Stephanie Varrell's cryptic telegram swung the balance.

Chapter 19

It was late in the afternoon in camp. The boys had just come in with the fish they had been catching that day, a fine lot of silvery, shining fellows. They were proud of the day's catch. A certain detachment of the company was cleaning the fish down by the water, and the low-swinging sun made ruby paths across the lake, making the tall pines stand out almost black against the glow. Another detachment was making the fire and getting the mess plates out on the crude table. Still a third was preparing the corn bread; washing lettuce; and getting out the butter, salt, pepper, and other condiments. There was a huge pile of oranges in the center of the table for dessert.

John Saxon, after giving his orders to the young workers, had swung himself in a hammock stretched between two coconut palms, and Wainwright, more weary with the day's march than he cared to own, dropped silently into another hammock and lay still with his eyes closed and his arms stretched above his head.

He was thinking how good it was merely to lie still, how pleasant the smell of jasmine and the odor of the frying fish that was beginning to mingle with the perfume of the flowers. How hungry he was. He couldn't remember ever having been as hungry in his life before. It was good to be tired and hungry and to anticipate plain food so eagerly. The very smoke from the pine fire was restful and pleasant.

If he looked out across the blood-red path on the water there was a strange picture, quiet, restful; the slipping away of the sun so silently. And presently, while they ate, it would be gone without notice, and they would be left to finish by the firelight.

He opened his eyes now and then and watched the progress downward of the ball of fire that was the sun. There were no gold lights in it now to remind him of golden hair, but there was a quiet darkness in the shadows of the woods that made him think of her eyes, darkly troubled when she had said she was not of his world.

What had she meant? The old question back again as soon as he had nothing else to occupy his mind! She was right, too, he was beginning to realize. Before this he had always thought of only one world, with workers to make it go smoothly. Now he saw there were other worlds, each different. Each complete in itself. Yet somehow he suspected that somewhere there must be a point of contact. And it was that point of contact he was out to find.

He turned his eyes toward John Saxon, lying there in his hammock, one arm swung up over his head, the damp brown curls snapping back from his bronzed forehead, his face so strong and yet so sweet sometimes, and so stern and almost forbidding at other times.

John Saxon was of another world from him also. Was he perhaps of Camilla's world? he asked himself. Perhaps. Was there no bridge? No bridge but that strange, inscrutable sentence, "ye must be born again," that Saxon had read that first night in the woods?

He lay watching the other man between the half-open lashes of his eyes. He had come to love and admire him during the few days they had been wandering in this strange tropical world together with these kids. Yet always at night when the Bible was read and he heard the strong tender voice in prayer, John Saxon seemed like another man, a man he only half understood. The best part of him seemed hidden behind a mystery that he could not penetrate.

And why was he so interested in that little worn Testament he carried everywhere, even fishing, and brought out on any occasion? He wished he dared ask him. Somehow he had not yet come to the point where he felt free enough to do so.

Suddenly Jeff followed an impulse and spoke, quietly, in a voice that could not be heard by the boys at work.

"John—"

They had come so far in friendship as to call one another John and Jeff.

"I wish you'd tell me what it means to be born again."

John looked up with a quick light of joy in his eyes, his face kindling with that strange tenderness that Jeff had seen there before several times and wondered at. It was almost as if John had recognized in him a kinship, which he had not before suspected.

"I guess the best way to understand that," he said thoughtfully, "is to think what it meant to be born into this world the first time. You did not exist in this world, you know, until you received the life of your parents. Then you were born and became a citizen of this world, gradually growing in the knowledge and privileges of it."

Jeff was watching him eagerly, weighing every word.

"In the same way," went on John, "you do not exist so far as the spiritual world is concerned until you receive the life of God. Then He says you are born spiritually and can begin to grow in the knowledge and blessings of the spiritual world."

Jeffrey was almost breathless with eagerness to grasp every word as he heard again that distinction between "worlds" that Camilla had mentioned.

He sat up in the hammock and put both feet on the ground, his arms widespread, grasping the meshes of the hammock.

Then Camilla had not meant just the difference between wealth and poverty, between social position and the lack of it! He had been sure all along that there was a deeper meaning to her words than he understood!

"How does one receive the life of God?" he asked earnestly, his eyes looking straight into John Saxon's eyes. "A child in coming into the world has no say in the matter."

"No," said John, "a child of this world is born at the will of its parents, but a child of God is born by willingly accepting the gift of God's life. To do that you must first realize that you need it—that you are a sinner, helpless to make yourself fit for God's presence, deserving nothing but His righteous judgment of eternal banishment from Him. If you don't want that banishment, that separation forever from God, if you do want to be with Him and be like Him, you will accept the gift He offers in undeserved kindness—the gift of eternal life, which He purchased for you by shedding the life-blood of His own Son instead of yours."

John's voice was full of awe and wonder as he added, "He paid that much for me, too!"

There was silence then for a long minute while Jeffrey studied his friend's strong face, a trifle puzzled perhaps. He couldn't quite see what John could have done that should make him so deserving of eternal punishment. His own thoughtless life, filled utterly with his own pleasant self, fulfilling its wishes, nothing very bad, perhaps, but still a life lived apart from God, *might* deserve punishment, though he had never considered the matter before, having always felt that he was a pretty good sort of fellow as the world went. But John Saxon. What could he have done to feel himself such a sinner that the redemption of himself should bring such awe and adoration into his face? There must be more to this than appeared on the surface, and Jeffrey felt himself to be a babe in this new study in which he had engaged.

He was about to ask a question about this matter of being such a terrible sinner when you hadn't done anything much at all, when suddenly the boys came whooping over to announce supper ready and to drag John from his hammock like so many officers of the law. Little Carlin came to Jeff, too, and slid a grubby little skinny paw into his own confidingly, pulling him up and over to the table.

Jeff put a strong arm around the slender shoulders of the little, loveless child, gave him one of his warmest smiles, and called him "little pard!"

Jeff was more than usually quiet during the evening. He joined to a certain extent in the games the boys were playing, but John noticed that he was deeply thoughtful, and when at last the camp was quiet for the night, John came and sat down beside Jeff. He was reclining by the fire, gazing deep into the night where a tired late moon was making ragged ripples of silver in the blackness of the lacquered lake.

"What's perplexing you, brother?" said John, sliding down beside him cross-legged in the sand and picking up a small stick, which he began to break into tiny splinters and throw one by one upon the fire.

"I can't quite see this sin business," said Jeff, looking up gratefully. "Now, you, I can't understand that look in your eyes when you spoke of a great price having saved you. You were never a great sinner, I'd wager that! And I, while I'm no gilded saint, of course—I've had a good time and not worried much, but I've been as good as the average, I'm sure, and a lot better than most. I've been clean and fairly unselfish! Where does the sin come in?"

Then did John Saxon unfold to him the story of sin, beginning in heaven when it was first found in Lucifer, son of the morning, the brightest angel of heaven, when pride made him want to be worshipped like the Most High.

John took out his flashlight and read snatches here and there from his Bible as he talked, until Jeff heard the whole amazing story of sin in heaven and on earth, causing the fall of man.

Jeff had never heard it before. Any phrases or references to a devil, or to the fall of man, he had always taken as foolish, whimsical language, and he had never stopped to question what might have been their origin. He listened with deep attention, asking now and then a question.

"And since then," finished John, "everyone is born with a dead spiritual nature and cannot see the kingdom of God until he is born again."

It was very still all around except for the snapping of the flickering fire and the far call of some night bird. Presently, John took up the story again, of the love of God for fallen man, and told in clear, descriptive words of the shedding of blood that was necessary to satisfy God's justice and vindicate his righteousness.

"There you have the story," he said. "It's not lying and stealing and murder, nor even uncleanness that makes us sinners. Those are only the result of our being sinners. It's turning away from a love like that! But a sinner can be made righteous in the sight of God by accepting Christ's death as his own. Do you understand now how we are all sinners and have come short of the glory which God intended for us when He made us?"

"I think I do!" said Jeff reverently, slowly, sorrowfully. "I never saw that before. I've been greatly guilty. I've lived utterly for myself—cleanly, morally, cheerfully, kindly, perhaps, but utterly forgetful of God. I think you've led me to what I came out to these woods to find. I knew there was something I had to find before I went back."

"Praise the Lord!" said John softly.

A little later the two bowed their heads beside the fire and prayed together. Perhaps the angels on the ramparts of heaven whispered together, "Behold he prayeth!"

Chapter 20

It had been snowing hard all day, white, heavy flakes, and when Camilla came downstairs from the office she paused in the doorway in dismay. She hadn't realized that the snow would be so deep. She was glad she had worn galoshes, although she had hesitated about doing so, for when she started from home there seemed to be only a few lazy flakes and she thought the storm would not last.

She stood there a minute wondering if she kept close to the buildings whether the snow was deep enough to get inside her galoshes, and then just as she was about to plunge in she heard a step behind her and a hand was laid on her arm.

She turned around, startled, and there stood Mr. Whitlock with his nice protective look, smiling down into her eyes.

"How are you going to get home?" he asked, as if he were responsible for her welfare.

"Oh, I have my car around at the garage. It isn't far," she answered gallantly.

"Well, I'll take you to the garage, then," he said. "My car is parked just outside here. I knew I wouldn't be upstairs long, and it's too stormy to go around much without it. I can't have you getting pneumonia, you know." And he gave her another of those pleasant smiles that were so almost possessive.

"Oh, thank you," she said with relief. "That will help a lot. But I have galoshes, you know."

"I'm afraid they won't do much good in this depth of snow. Here, where's the janitor of this building? Joe, where are you? Joe, just get a shovel and run out a footpath to my car, won't you? You ought to keep this walk clear, you know."

"Yes, sir," said Joe, "I was just going out again, sir. Seems like I can't keep up with this snow, nohow."

So Camilla walked dry-shod to her employer's car and was taken to her garage.

"Have you chains on your car?" asked Whitlock.

"Why, no, I've never really needed them. I guess I'll be all right. I drive very carefully."

"Put some chains on that car!" ordered Whitlock to the man at the garage, and then he insisted on paying for them himself, although Camilla protested.

"That's all right," he said. "It's to my interest, you know, that you should be protected. You'll need them in the morning, if you don't now. And I think I'll just drive along with you a ways and see that you get through all right. This is some weather. Are your windshield wipers in good order?"

When they were ready to start Whitlock said he would go ahead with his heavier car and break the way in case there were streets where no traffic had been, and so in spite of all that Camilla could say, he escorted her to her door, made her get out at the house, lifted her across the deep drift by the steps, and himself put her car in the garage. Then he came in for just a moment, he said just to meet her mother.

But Mrs. Chrystie had been worrying all the afternoon about how Camilla was going to get home, and she was so grateful for Mr. Whitlock's escort that she insisted he should stay for dinner. So he stayed.

Camilla went flying around in the kitchen helping her mother to get the dinner on the table and wishing in her heart that Mr. Whitlock's first visit to their home could have been under more favorable circumstances. Somehow she didn't feel as free with him as she had with Jeffrey Wainwright. There was something rather formal and dignified about Mr. Whitlock. She recalled the quiet dignity of the old inn, the perfect service, the immaculate table. Of course, Mother's table was always exquisitely clean and lovely, but it happened this night that there was a darn in the fine old tablecloth right where it would show. It seemed too bad when Mother did have lovely things put away that she could have put on if there had been time. But dinner was all ready and could not wait. Camilla did manage to place a lovely doily of beautiful drawn work and set her mother's little fern on it, but there were no flowers for the table, none of the accessories that Whitlock gave the impression of being so particular about. She did get out some of the best napkins, however, and put a dish in front of the darn, and it had to go at that.

Whitlock was very pleasant. He seemed to enjoy the home cooking and took second helpings. He enjoyed the homemade bread, the little white creamed onions, and the pumpkin pie for dessert. He praised the coffee, too, and said few people knew how to make good coffee.

When the meal was over, however, he did not go into the kitchen to help with the dishes as Wainwright had done. Camilla gave him no opportunity. She shut the door sharply and decidedly on the dining room and kitchen and led both mother and guest firmly into the living room. Somehow she didn't want Mr. Whitlock to help in that intimate way. It didn't seem fitting.

However, he showed no desire to help. He seemed to take it as a matter of course that they were done with dishes for the night, and he sat for a couple of hours talking with Camilla and her mother, most interestingly, telling incidents of a trip abroad, describing pictures and statuary he had seen, giving details of his visits to historic places of interest.

It was almost like attending a delightful lecture, and both Camilla and her mother enjoyed it, yet when he rose to go a little before ten o'clock, Camilla felt relieved. It had somehow been a strain, for while he was there it seemed as if every flaw and crudity of the little house stood out like a sore thumb.

"Well, he's very nice," commented her mother as they watched through the snow-blurred window and saw him drive away. "I'm glad you have a good clean-minded man like that to work for. It makes me feel safer about you when you are away. It certainly was kind of him to come all the way out here to protect you."

"I didn't need protection," laughed Camilla, "and I was scared to death to have him stay to dinner lest it was hash night. How did you happen to have chicken tonight, Mother dear? It isn't a gala night. I never expect chicken except on a holiday."

"Well, the egg man brought it," said her mother, smiling, "and the day was so snowy and forlorn, I thought we'd have a little good cheer. It didn't cost much. And besides, Miss York telephoned earlier in the day that she thought she might get off tonight and take dinner with us, but about five she called again and said the snow was so deep she guessed she wouldn't venture."

"She'd have had to walk," mused Camilla, "and the snow is almost a foot deep. It's a good thing we got moved before this blizzard came."

"Yes, isn't it? We have a great deal to be thankful for."

Then after a minute of silence, while Camilla was gathering up the dishes and making quick work of clearing up the table, her mother said, "Camilla, where does this Mr. Whitlock live? In a hotel? Or has he family? He isn't married, is he?"

"Why, no, I think not," said Camilla, looking startled. "No, of course not!" she said. "He certainly wouldn't be taking me out to dinner and to a concert, would he, if he was married?"

"Some men do such things," said Mrs. Chrystie thoughtfully, "but I remember the people at home spoke well of him. And he seems a fine, quiet sort of man. He was very interesting, wasn't he? I enjoyed his description of those cathedrals."

"Yes, he can talk well. And now I remember hearing him say that he lives at his club. It's one of the best ones downtown. I forget the name."

"Well, he seemed like a lonely man to me," said Mrs. Chrystie, "and once he spoke of his mother's death as being quite recent after a lingering illness. He's probably one of those men who have devoted themselves to an invalid mother, just as my girl is beginning to have to do for me."

"Mother! Don't talk that way!" said Camilla, with troubled eyes. "You're not an invalid anymore, and I'd rather be devoted to you than to anyone in the world!"

"You're a dear child!" said her mother, laughing. "But I'm glad you've got such a kind employer. He's really much younger than you led me to suppose."

"Young?" said Camilla, with a dreamy look. "Why, Mother, his hair is gray all around the edges!"

"You don't like him much, do you, Camilla?"

"Why, of course I like him!" said Camilla. "Why shouldn't I? I'm not in love with him, if that's what you mean. I doubt if I shall ever love anyone that way. Mother, why will you persist in thinking every man that speaks to me wants to marry me?"

"Oh, child!" said her mother in a shocked tone. "I don't! What a thing to say! But I do want to know all about anyone who shows you the least attention, of course, and I do want you to have some nice friends of your own kind."

"Well, he isn't my kind," said Camilla quite crossly. "He's much older than I am. Oh, he's nice and interesting, all right. He doesn't bore me, if that's what you mean. He talks of books and art and music and is quite intellectual, but I don't know that he's of my world any more than anybody else I know."

"He spoke of a church which he attends," said her mother speculatively.

"Everyone that goes to church nowadays isn't a Christian, by any means," said Camilla as she turned out the kitchen light.

"No, of course that's true," agreed her mother.

❦

Camilla got up early the next morning, wrapped herself in warm garments, and went out with the old snow shovel. It had stopped snowing, but the sky was still lowering. She attacked the front walk and the path to the house. Luckily they were short or she could not have managed them, for the snow was heavy and deeply packed. But she cleared the walks, made a shovel-wide path to the garage, and came in with glowing cheeks to breakfast.

"I'm glad it's stopped snowing," said her mother. "I shouldn't have let you go to the office if it hadn't."

"Mr. Whitlock said I was not to come if it was still storming," said Camilla. "He's really very kind."

"Yes, he is," said her mother. "But I wish you'd telephone me when you get to town. I'd feel a great deal better about you."

Camilla promised and went away happily.

Mr. Whitlock was in the office when she got there. He looked up from his desk to welcome her with somehow a freer, more intimate air about him than he had ever worn before. Marietta hadn't come in yet.

He greeted her pleasantly and then added, "You have a very interesting mother, Miss Chrystie. I enjoyed my chat with her very much. I shall avail myself of your invitation and repeat my visit of last night often if I may."

They were casual words, lightly spoken, but something warned Camilla that they had a deeper significance than was on the surface. It was as if he were preparing the way for an intimacy, and it came as something she was not sure she wanted. He was her employer, and it seemed fitting that she should keep him as such and not make a friend out of him. The memory of it hung around her all the morning unpleasantly, yet when she thought it over frankly, she couldn't understand why she should feel that way. She couldn't go around alone all her life and never go anywhere nor see nor hear anything, and if Mr. Whitlock was the key to a little recreation, she ought to be glad that he was willing to take her places and call often to see her, making the home life cheerful for Mother also.

When she searched her mind for a reason for her hesitance to take Mr. Whitlock into their home circle, she found that deep in her heart there was a reluctance to have anybody blot out the memory of Jeffrey Wainwright and the few beautiful days when he had come in among them. And when she realized this she became suddenly most cordial to Whitlock, who developed an interest in her home and relatives and asked questions about her father and where and how she was brought up. If Whitlock came often to the house and they grew close, perhaps in time she would get over this insane habit of returning to the thought of the young man who seemed to have obsessed her with his brilliant personality. Maybe she could get interested in Mr. Whitlock and forget Wainwright. Of course, Mr. Whitlock was good-looking, even if he did have a bit of silver in his hair. And he had nice, kind eyes when he was not thinking about business.

So Camilla answered him cordially, and presently there grew up a kind of intimacy between them, comfortably friendly, yet such as could easily be set aside when business hours came.

But before long the look in Whitlock's eyes when he turned them toward Camilla had something more than just friendship in them, and Marietta was quick to see it and react.

"Gee!" she said one afternoon after he had gone out. "He's got an awful crush on you, hasn't he? Gee, ef he'd look at me with that 'drink-ta-me-only' look in his eyes, I'd fall in my tracks. I positively would!"

"Oh, for pity's sake, Marietta, don't talk that way!" said Camilla sharply. "What a silly idea! You see, he knows a lot of my father's old friends, and he's just being kind to me for their sakes."

"Oh yeah?" said Marietta, with a grin. "I heard that old 'friend-of-my-father's' line before. He's got it bad! Me, I know the signs! I haven't been watching other folks get courted all these years for nothing! You're too innocent! That's what gets me. You never use one bit a 'come-hither' at all—though you got plenty you could use ef you was a mindta—and they come rushing ta yer feet. Oh, I haven't got any feeling about it, Camilla. I never expect ta have anybody taking me anyplace, but I liketa see you have it. I do honest. I just love you, and I wanta have you have anything you want."

"You dear thing!" said Camilla, trying to put away the annoyance she felt. "You'll have attention yet, sometime. But don't get notions about me, please. And by the way, Mother's making some more gingerbread men for Ted tomorrow. You might tell him, if you like."

"Say, that's great!" said Marietta, flushing eagerly. "Ted will be awfully pleased. And say, I meant ta tell you yesterday, only Mr. Whitlock was here all day, how I been reading the Testament you gave ta Ted, and he loves it. And my stepmother listens, too, sometimes. You know, she's back from the hospital now and can't do much all day but just lie still. She's a lot different since she was so sick. I guess she was scared, and sometimes she's real kind to Ted, talks kind of motherlike to him. Gee, that gets me. I don't care what she does to me, just so she's good to him. And he seems so pleased, poor kid!"

"Oh, I'm so glad!" said Camilla. "You know, Marietta, it may be the Lord has put you right in that hard place to lead both your stepmother and little brother to know Jesus."

"I was wondering about that," said Marietta. "Do you suppose He'd trust me ta do a thing like that? Ef I thought I could, gee, that would make up for me being so plain and homely. I'd like ta try."

"I certainly think you may be just put there for that very thing," said Camilla eagerly. "And don't you know, Marietta, one can grow beautiful by being with the Lord Jesus every day and trying to please Him? If you let Him live in you, there is a beauty of soul that will shine through—the beauty of the Lord Jesus living in you and moving you to every thought and action. You can live Jesus; even when you have no words you can speak so that people will listen. They can't help listening to your life."

So the days went by, and Marietta grew in the finer things of the Spirit and in the knowledge of God's Word. And Camilla worked hard, praying to God to conquer for her the longings and desires that were not of Him.

And Whitlock more and more fell into the habit of asking Camilla to go to lunch with him or driving out to her home with her for dinner and an evening talk, and as spring drew nearer he began to talk of places he wanted her to see when the warm weather came.

Mother Chrystie, looking on, puckered her anxious brows and sighed sometimes, and wondered if this was God's best for her beloved Camilla. Wondered if Camilla understood how great a thing it was to choose the right mate for life and how wrong it was to be hasty about it. Wondered if Ralph Whitlock was not perhaps in his way as worldly as the dear bright youth who came no more to see them, nor even wrote to inquire. She sighed and wondered if she ought to warn her child yet held her peace a little longer lest she precipitate something she feared and dreaded.

And Camilla went on, sometimes breathlessly, trying not to think. Trying to take the good times that were handed to her and not question the morrow. Looking at her employer more and more in the light of a friend.

And Whitlock came to assume more and more the attitude of one who expected sometime to be even more than a friend. He assumed a kind of friendly dictatorship over Camilla, bringing her books to read, ordering her what newspaper to take, and instructing her in all things pertaining to life, almost as if he had already the right to say how she should live and move and have her being.

And yet, there was a certain point beyond which Camilla would not let him go. She would not let him grow sentimental or very personal, and she would never let him touch her, always withdrawing her hand if he took it in too close a clasp, always keeping him just a little at his distance. She did not herself know just why. She was not ready yet to ask herself questions about it. And strange to say, this attitude on her part only seemed to make him admire her more. It suited his conventional, somewhat formal character to have her so.

Camilla had attempted to probe her admirer concerning the things of life that meant most to her. She had asked him point-blank one day if he was a Christian, not realizing that her question had been half answered before she asked, by the very fact that she had to ask him, and he answered her quite readily:

"Oh, certainly! I joined the church when I was not more than fourteen, and I've been fairly faithful in attendance ever since. Of course, many things that I believed in those days have been greatly modified as I grew older and wiser, but I have always maintained that man needs religion and that the church is a valuable influence in the world and should therefore be supported by all thinking people. I have not been quite as active in the church organizations the last few years as I was when I was a lad, but, of course, a businessman has less time than a youth, and in spite of that, I have gone out of my way to accept positions on boards and so on. Just now it happens that in addition to being a trustee in the church where I hold membership, I am taking time on a special committee to work out a plan whereby our church shall be able to pay off its entire mortgage and make out a full budget for the coming year."

With this vague explanation Camilla had to be satisfied. She wished she dared ask him what he meant by not believing all that he had as a child, but there was something about him that prevented questioning of his ways. He did not suffer criticism nor suggestion, and somehow every question that Camilla tried to formulate seemed almost like a criticism of his Christian methods. So time went on, and she was still vague about his definite beliefs. Still, of course, he owned he was a Christian, and he often asked the blessing at the table when her mother asked him to. It sounded a bit cold and formal, perhaps, but still it was phrased in language that was familiar and had the right ring. She could not possibly feel that he was out of her class when he owned to being a Christian.

But sometimes Camilla wondered, and a great oppression came upon her young soul. She hadn't known him long, yet he was taking things for granted so rapidly that sometimes she was breathless and troubled.

And one night after he had gone—after having spent the evening describing at length a trip he had taken only two years before, in which he saw Paris on its most sophisticated side, an evening in which Camilla had sat almost silent in the shadow of a big lampshade, listening, looking almost troubled—her mother looked at her keenly.

"Are you going to marry that man, Camilla?" she asked suddenly.

"Oh, *Mother*! What a question! Why! Why—I don't even

know that he would want me to marry him! Why, I'm not thinking about marrying people, Mother!"

And suddenly Camilla burst into tears and buried her face in
her mother's neck.

Loving arms went around her and loving lips were laid against
her hot, wet cheek.

"There, there, dear!" soothed her mother gently. "I just thought
I ought to remind you that it is a woman's business to be aware of
such things and not let a man go too far if she does not intend to
go all the way to the altar with him! It looked to me as if he was
expecting a lot of you, my dear, and I wondered if you were ready
to choose him for life, if you were really satisfied with him. He is a
good man, I guess, but—I wondered if you were *sure*, sure beyond
the shadow of a doubt, that he is the one you want. You know, a
woman should be *sure*! That's the only thing that makes marriage
happy; it's the only thing that makes it tolerable!"

And Camilla clung to her mother, trembling, quivering in
every nerve, shot through with questionings and doubts, and trying not to remember a kiss that had gone deep into her soul. She
thought that if it only hadn't been for that kiss, she might have
been able to think more clearly.

Chapter 21

The plaything that Stephanie Varrell had found on the beach that afternoon had proved to be more than usually interesting, and before Jeffrey Wainwright's return to civilization she had used her jacinth eyes to such an extent that she was wearing a strange golden stone on her finger with a curious fire in its heart, set in workmanship of the far orient, and there was much gossip abroad, for Stephanie and her "Count" were seen constantly together.

Yet it had not been a part of her plan to have Jeff come upon them just where and how he did.

She had been accustomed to use certain tactics with Jeffrey that she found always worked. Invariably, she had been able to bring him back to her feet whenever she wished, and she had never let him drift quite so far away before.

But something had happened the night of that dinner of hers that she did not understand, and she was playing high stakes now to undo what she had dared to do in inviting Myles Meredith. There was nothing like rousing jealousy in a man's heart to bring him to terms, Stephanie firmly believed, never having read aright the fine soul of Jeff. She had never sensed that, instead of being merely jealous for himself, he was jealous for her reputation and his ideal of her, which he had made himself and cherished for genuine.

But Jeff came home just after the sun had dropped the velvet curtain of night down upon golden Florida and driven the guests of the hotel to their rooms to dress for dinner and the evening.

Then Jeff came down late to dinner, escaping a good many people whom he wasn't in a hurry to meet. He took a walk on the veranda after dinner with his mother. He sat for a while with her in the softness and darkness of the evening, talking, telling her some things about his brother Sam he thought she ought to know, how the boy was developing character and an interest in certain studies that should be fostered. He kept feeling around and wondering how he should tell her of his new experience. Was it the right time? Would she understand? In all his life he had had very little real heart conversation with his mother. She had a cold, reticent nature, taking certain things for granted, ignoring certain other things. He had a feeling that perhaps she would not approve, might perhaps think he was becoming fanatical. He greatly desired, when he did tell her, to do it so that she would be impressed with the deep reality of his new experience.

"Mother," he said at last after a long silence broken only by the regular sound of the sea breaking on the sand not far away, "I've been thinking things out while I was away in the woods, and I've made some decisions."

His mother stopped rocking in the big willow chair, with a short, sharp little sound of quietness as if she had feared something and thought it might be coming now. She wondered if it was that yellow-haired girl with the strange, sly eyes? Or was he wanting to go and kill lions in Africa? Some new sensation, of course!

"The most important decision," he went on, "is that I've become a Christian!"

He had thought it all out and had decided that this was the best way to express it to his mother. She wouldn't at all understand if he should say he had been born again. She might even resent it, as if his birth had not been good enough for him. She had a strange, deep pride of family. The word *Christian* he felt sure she would understand to a certain extent, and it was still, of course, perfectly respectable. As the world, her world, counted respectability.

His mother was still, holding the rocker motionless for a full second while she thought it over. Then she answered calmly. "That's all right with me, Jeff, just so you don't make too much of it. I'd hate to have a child with a religious complex. Of course, a little religion doesn't hurt anybody if it's kept within bounds."

Jeff sat silent for a long time after that, realizing just how little his mother would be in sympathy with his new life, yet feeling that he had no further word for her at present.

Presently Mrs. Wainwright drew her soft wrap around her shoulders with a little shiver and rose. Suddenly leaning over her son, she patted his dark head with an unaccustomed caress and said, "You always were a good boy, Jeff!"

Then after an instant, "Come, I'm going in. There's too much breeze out here for me."

He escorted her into the hotel where she settled down among a group of her kind, and with a graceful good night he left her and sauntered out to the patio again, stalking down the full length and across the sea end.

The ballroom was that way, down along the north side of the building, and dancing was going on inside, but a glance showed the patio entirely empty just then, a long stretch of darkness broken by the rectangles of light from the open windows and lit not at all except by one single lamp at the far end. Jeff strolled on, keeping out near the railing. He did not want company just then. He had some serious thinking to do. He would just walk by and glance in the windows and see who of the old crowd was there. He was suddenly beginning to realize that life was going to have some very decided changes for him in the near future. His old world was not going to recognize what had happened to him. They were not going to understand. They were not his world anymore. He had been born into a new world.

He walked slowly, quietly, the sound of the beating waves and the throb of the orchestra covering his deliberate footfalls.

Pausing an instant to glance through a window, he was startled to hear a light, familiar laugh coming from out of the shadows quite near him, and turning sharply, he saw one of the glider seats with which the place abounded, drawn slantwise into the shadow so that the occupants could get a full view of the ballroom without themselves being very visible to those inside the windows, and there they sat quite oblivious to any but themselves. They had evidently not heard his approach, for they were absorbed in each other. He could see the gold of the girl's hair, crowned with a sparkling jeweled tiara, the lifted face with the offered lips, and the gleam of her white arm as she threw it around the neck of her companion, a tall man who bent a comely head above her and embraced her passionately. Stephanie! And he had just been thinking about her!

He had just been considering that in some sort he was entangled with her, or he had at one time asked her to marry him. True, she had not answered him, had put him off time after time, laughingly. But she was capable of making trouble about it if she chose. He had been perplexing himself over it, wondering what was his duty now. For he understood himself well enough to know that she was not for him. He had been hoping that she might have gone back north, but now here she was, not three feet from him, and lying in another man's arms! If Jeffrey Wainwright had any of his former illusions left about Stephanie Varrell, they were dispelled at once. Her whole attitude, her soft, honeyed, purring tones, the caresses she was showering upon the man, made it quite plain that Stephanie was not in love with Jeffrey. And suddenly his heart leaped with a thankful throb. Here at last was absolute evidence. He had feared that perhaps, after all, he had misjudged her and that her association with other men against his protest was really as innocent as she had always declared. He did not wish to be unjust. But here was the evidence of his own eyes.

Well, what should he do now? Get away without their seeing him, of course, if it could be done. But could it? The music had stopped for the moment.

He made a quick stealthy movement with one foot, to back away, keeping his eyes upon the two on the couch. But he did not realize that someone had piled a couple of chairs in a rocker just behind where he was standing. His foot came in sharp contact with the point of the rocker, and the rocker being set in motion, the two smaller chairs came crashing down to the floor noisily.

It was all over in an instant. The two people in the porch seat sat up sharply, staring at him, and Jeff came out of the darkness and up to them at once with a grave bow.

"Sorry to intrude," he said with easy courtesy. "I did not know that anyone was here. Don't let me interrupt!" And with a significant glance at Stephanie, he turned and walked deliberately away. As he went he carried the memory of Stephanie's eyes, jacinth eyes, gleaming in the dark like cat's eyes.

He had almost rounded the sea end of the patio when he heard a scurrying sound behind him of feet running, and the two were upon him, Stephanie's light, heartless laugh ringing out.

"Jeff! Oh, Jeff! Wait!" she called, and reaching his side, she slid her arm within his own, as she had so often done before, with that soft little confiding air that had at one time meant so much to him.

"I want to tell you the news and introduce you to my fiancé," she said eagerly. "This is Count Esterhoff, Jeff, and we were just engaged tonight! He knows all about you, of course. And I want you to see my wonderful, curious ring! There isn't another like it in all the world!"

Jeff paused politely in the light of the next window to acknowledge the introduction and to survey the weird ring, whose setting of strange serpents curiously intertwined with uncanny symbols smacked of aged, pagan worlds. The newly made fiancé, who hadn't known his fate until that moment, stood there blinking and staring at the girl who had just so unexpectedly become engaged to him.

"Congratulations!" said Jeff, with a delighted grin. "That's splendid news. Delighted to meet you, Count. And say, that's some ring! An heirloom, I take it. A most unusual setting, isn't it?"

He lingered a minute or two chatting, adding a few more polite phrases, and then excused himself from the scene lest his overwhelming relief became too painfully obvious. He hurried away and disappeared by a roundabout route to his room.

He had been calmly sleeping for what seemed to him many hours when his telephone roused him, and Stephanie's voice, amazingly meek and tearful, called him from his pleasant dreams.

"Jeff, is that you? This is Stephanie, Jeff, and I'm *so* unhappy—!"

There was a silence during which Jeff got awake enough to visualize once more the scene he had witnessed on the north patio a few hours before.

"Isn't that too bad!" he said at last, a note of mocking in his voice.

"Now, Jeff, if you knew how unhappy I am you wouldn't try to be unkind," reproached the markedly humble voice at the other end of the wire.

Jeff was still, trying to think hard. Then he spoke in his clear, firm voice, with finality in its very fiber.

"I'm not trying to be unkind, Stephanie. I'm just puzzled to know what I have to do with all this. It can't be many hours since you told me you were engaged to another man, and I should think this matter of your unhappiness would be referred to him."

"But Jeff, *darling!*" She spoke the word in a tone that always used to move him deeply, and he marveled that it no longer stirred him in the least. There were sobs in her voice now and unmistakable tears. He frowned in the darkness and drew a deep breath of annoyance.

"Suppose—Jeff—" sobbed the voice softly, "that I've found I've—made—a terrible—mistake!"

"Then I would think that would be entirely up to *you!*" he answered crisply. "I certainly haven't anything to do with it."

"Yes—you have, Jeff!" went on the pleading voice. "Have you forgotten—Jeff, I know you haven't—that you asked me—to—*marry* you once? Jeff, I've seen my mistake—and—I want to tell you—b-b-before it's forever—too late! Jeff, it's *you* I love. And I'll marry you, Jeff darling, tonight, if you'll take me! I could be ready in half an hour. There's an airplane out on the field. I've chartered it, and we could go on that. And then all my troubles would be over! I should be ecstatically happy! Oh, Jeff—darling—will you go tonight? You are such a comforting person—"

"Nothing doing!" said Jeffrey. "That was all off the night of your dinner. You chose then between me and that low-life villain, Meredith Myles. And if I had needed anything else, tonight would have been the finishing touch. You'll have to go elsewhere for comfort, Stephanie. I'm going to sleep, and I don't wish to discuss this matter any further, either now or at any future time. Good night!" And Jeffrey Wainwright hung up the receiver and turned over in his bed.

But he did not go back to sleep. He held a court and judged himself. He had learned while out on that camping trip that if we would judge ourselves we should not have to be disciplined by God. So then and there he held court and found himself guilty. He looked back over his young manhood and saw himself a selfish time-waster, a chaser of every new fancy, a lazy spendthrift and good-for-nothing, and a spoiled child of luxury, playing with every toy that came his way. Of course, he had had certain standards and adhered to them fairly well, but within limits he had been determined to have whatever his fancy chose. And Stephanie had been one of those things.

That she had been dangerous he had known from the start. That she had been full of deception he had often suspected. That she could do about what she chose with him, at one time he had rather enjoyed. He had always known that she was not the kind of woman to bring into his family. That she would have to change before his mother, whom he was fond of, would ever accept her as a daughter, and before his father, whom he greatly revered and loved, would honor her. But he had blindly gone ahead, determined that she should somehow be made to conform to the Wainwright standards, convinced that when she was his, and he flung his love around her and enthroned her in his home, she would be everything that he would ask her to be.

He had known for a long time now that he was a fool to believe any such thing. The first time he saw Camilla he knew that the look in her eyes was the one he had been so long hoping to see in Stephanie's eyes. The night he dared to lay his lips to Camilla's in that precious kiss he knew that this was something rare and fine in love that he had never found in his infatuation for Stephanie. Tonight down on the hotel patio, the last shred and vestige of respect for Stephanie had vanished.

He lay a long time considering his present situation. Suddenly he snapped on the light and looked at his watch. Then he hunted a number in the telephone book and called it.

"Is that you, John? Are you still up studying? I hoped so. Well, this is Jeff. May I come out to your place tomorrow morning early and help you spray orange trees or whatever it is that you went home to do to them? I don't know how, but I'll learn, and I've got a few questions I need to ask you."

"That's great news, Jeff," came back the voice over the wire. "Bring on your questions! Wear your old clothes, and be prepared to sleep in a hammock. I'll be waiting to welcome you at the head of the lane with open arms."

Jeff wrote a note to his mother.

> *Dear Mother:*
>
> *I'm leaving early in the morning for a few days with a friend. You can reach me by phone at the above number, but please don't inform anybody else.*
>   *If Dad wires, let me know at once, and if you need me I can be back in less than an hour.*
>
> *Yours,*
> *Jeff*

Then he turned out the light and went to sleep again.

Quite early the next morning before any stray damsels were abroad, Jeff arose and went on his way to see John Saxon.

Chapter 22

Miss York duly moved in, bag and baggage, as soon as the last big snow of the season was melted and gone, and though she was still engaged on a case and was able to be there very little, it gave a comfortable family feeling to have the extra room furnished and ready for use whenever she should be able to get off for a night.

She turned up the very night after Camilla had cried on her mother's shoulder, and she announced that she had come to stay over the weekend.

They had a cheery little supper together and were anticipating a real home evening, leisurely laughing and talking as they did the dishes and suggesting how the furniture could be arranged in Miss York's room to best advantage.

And then right in the middle of it Whitlock arrived.

He had been away in New York and had attended a large political meeting and met some interesting people. He wanted to tell about it. He enjoyed telling things and liked an attentive audience.

Camilla felt a disappointment as she opened the door and saw him standing there. She had supposed he would be gone over Sunday. She was wearing a plain little old dress, expecting to help Miss York put up her curtains.

She invited him in, a constraint upon her because of what her mother had said the night before, but Whitlock was full of his experiences and did not notice her silence.

"Well," he said, taking off his overcoat and hat and hanging them on the hall rack as if he belonged there, "it is good to get back. Where's your mother? Aren't the dishes done yet?"

It was characteristic of Whitlock that he had never attempted to go into the kitchen and help, though he had several times been a guest to a meal.

"Why yes," said Camilla, "the dishes are done. Mother, here's Mr. Whitlock. Miss York, won't you come in and meet my employer?"

Camilla was a little startled at herself for calling him that. She had of late avoided calling him anything. He had told her once that his name was Ralph, but he hadn't made a point of it, and somehow she had hesitated, as if the use of it committed her to something intangible for which she was not quite ready.

"Miss York?" said Whitlock, with an annoyed frown. "Who is she? What's she doing here?"

"Why, she's a member of our family, that is, when she is not out on her job," said Camilla, with heightened color. "I guess you haven't happened to meet her before, have you? She has her room here and comes when she is not on a case."

She looked up, and there stood Miss York in the doorway, with Mrs. Chrystie just behind her. "Mr. Whitlock, this is our dear friend, Miss York!"

Miss York stood for an instant, looking at Whitlock with a sudden startled gleam in her eye as the man rose and faced her with a puzzled frown. Then the nurse spoke.

"Good evening, Mr. Whitlock. We've met before, haven't we? I've heard Camilla speak of her employer, but I hadn't an idea it was the same Mr. Whitlock."

Miss York was entirely at her ease and spoke with assurance. But Whitlock looked at her blankly.

"Miss—York, did you say? Your—ah—face does seem somewhat familiar, but I'm afraid I—I can't place you. I see so many people, of course, in the day's work."

"Yes, I suppose you do," said Miss York pleasantly, "but you'll remember me when you know who I am. I'm the nurse that took care of your wife when your baby was born. A little girl, wasn't it, and a very pretty baby if I remember rightly. I know its mother said it was the image of you, and you were as pleased as could be!"

Mrs. Chrystie gave a soft little exclamation and looked at Whitlock, and Camilla in the shadow of the hall doorway gave a startled glance at her mother and then turned to watch Whitlock, her own face still in shadow.

Over Whitlock's face had come a strange and subtle change. Every vestige of color had drained away, leaving him severely gray and tired-looking, yes, and old. Camilla was startled at the change. He seemed fairly haggard. He faced them all with miserable, cold eyes.

"Yes?" he said in his most official voice. "It seems to me I do recall a nurse. One doesn't always register faces at a time of crisis." His voice did not encourage further conversation, but Nurse York seemed not to notice. She gushed on pleasantly.

"No, I suppose not," she said. "One wouldn't be expected to remember a mere nurse at such a time. But do tell me how your wife is. She was such a sweet, dear little woman. I really fell in love with her, and that baby was one of the sweetest I ever saw. Dorothy, wasn't that her name? Dorothy Rose Whitlock. I remember thinking how well the names went together.

I suppose she has grown to be quite a girl by this time, hasn't she? Is she as pretty as she promised to be? I thought her hair was going to curl."

Mr. Whitlock fixed Miss York with a haughty stare and answered in tones so cold it was a wonder that they did not freeze into icicles.

"Miss York, I have not seen my wife for over five years now. We are separated! And I do not know anything about the child. She is with her mother!"

"Oh," chirruped Miss York blithely, "what a pity! I'm sorry I spoke of it."

He turned from her abruptly, addressing Camilla quite formally.

"I came out to see if you would mind letting me run you in to the office for a few minutes. There are a couple of letters that ought to get off tonight. I'm sorry to bother you, but they ought to be typed, and, if you're willing, why, you can go that much earlier tomorrow, you know." He tried to finish with a light laugh, but his voice sounded harsh and shaken.

"Why, of course I'll be glad to do the letters," she said heartily, "but you needn't take the trouble to drive me in to the office. I have my own typewriter here, you know, and it just happens that I brought several extra sheets of the letterhead paper out with me the other night when I brought home some other work to type."

Camilla wheeled out the little table containing her machine, drew up her stool that fitted under it so nicely, and was ready for work.

She could see that Whitlock was not much pleased with the arrangement, but there wasn't anything he could gracefully do about it, so he dropped into a chair and began to dictate in his most impersonal office voice. Miss York and Mrs. Chrystie drifted back into the kitchen, talking cheerily and moving about putting away things.

The letters proved to be very commonplace affairs, and Camilla suspected that they were a mere excuse to get her away from the house. It wasn't, of course, especially pleasant for him to be around Miss York after what had been said, but she typed away rapidly and soon had both letters written, addressed, and sealed.

"There!" she said brightly. "That was a great deal easier than going away downtown and opening up the office for just those few minutes, wasn't it?" And she smiled a bright, tense little smile. The very air seemed charged with electricity, but something had been lifted from her heart that made it lighter. She didn't stop then to question what it was; she only knew that a great relief had come upon her.

"Yes, that's very nice," said Whitlock in a dry tone that did not sound at all as if he thought it nice.

He took the letters and held them a moment, looking at them. Then, with a glance toward the kitchen where cheerful voices were still to be heard, he lowered his voice and said, "You wouldn't like to come out for a little drive, would you, Camilla?"

Camilla's breath came quickly, but she managed a bright smile.

"I couldn't, tonight, really Mr. Whitlock. Miss York can only be here for a short time, and I promised to help her put up her curtains this evening."

He stood, looking at her thoughtfully for a moment, his brows drawn in a frown. Then he lowered his voice and stepped nearer to her.

"Camilla, I want to talk to you. I have something very important to tell you. I really came over partly to tell you tonight."

"Why, of course," said Camilla, feeling her heart suddenly coming up in her throat but trying to seem brightly sympathetic. "We can sit right here and talk. Nobody will bother us. They are busy getting Miss York's room fixed up. Won't you take this big chair?" Camilla indicated the most comfortable chair in the room, well in the far corner in the shadow, and dropped into a small straight chair opposite.

Whitlock's lips were set in an unpleasant line, but he accepted the chair and sat down rigidly on its edge. He did not speak at once.

Camilla was holding herself firmly in hand. She found a tendency in her hands to tremble, but she would not let it show.

"It's about Marietta, I suppose," she said, breaking the silence. "Poor Marietta! I had hoped you felt she was doing better. But I suppose it is hard to put up with her." She felt that she must put off embarrassing topics, if possible.

"No, it's not about Marietta," said the man brusquely. "She's doing very well, far better than I supposed possible. It's all due to you, of course, and so long as you are willing to keep her on as a pupil, I'm willing to put up with her. It must be hard on you, but you are most unselfish. Camilla, you are the most unselfish person I know. That is why I have been so attracted to you."

"Oh no, I'm not unselfish," said Camilla quickly. "I'm just sorry for Marietta." She laughed lightly, hoping to avert further confidences.

But Whitlock sat gloomily across from her and looked at her, saying brusquely, "Well, it's not of Marietta I was about to speak. I was going to say that I should have told you long ago of my wife, perhaps. But I was hoping to delay until—something decisive had been done—something in the way of—divorce proceedings. Of course, it is all a very painful topic to me!"

"Of course!" said Camilla quickly in a sympathetic tone. "Please don't feel you must tell me anything more. I quite understand that it must make you very unhappy to speak of it. I am sure Miss York would not have spoken of it if she had known."

Whitlock wasn't so sure of that, but he did not say so. He

paused again painfully and then said, "No, I would rather tell you. Now that you know of her existence, you should know all about her."

"I don't see why, Mr. Whitlock. I am just your secretary. It isn't customary for businessmen to tell their private affairs to their secretaries."

She tried to turn the matter off lightly, but Whitlock persisted in watching her gloomily and went on.

"You are far more than a secretary, Camilla," he said feelingly. "You surely know that. You cannot have failed to see that. You must know what a comfort you have been to me in my loneliness—"

"Oh, Mr. Whitlock!" protested Camilla, deeply troubled by his tone and endeavoring with all her might to refuse to understand his meaning, "I'm glad if I have helped at all. I was only trying to do my duty. One doesn't know how those around us are suffering, of course."

Whitlock gave her a quick, keen glance. Was she really as dull of comprehension as she seemed?

"You see," he said, dropping his glance for a moment and placing the tips of his fine long fingers together, "my wife was a spoiled child. That was about the truth of the matter. She was determined to have her own way in everything. She had been petted and humored, and she expected me to do the same by her that her parents had done."

Something in the black look that came over his face at the memory gave Camilla a swift revelation of what it might be to live under the domination of this man, who could be so gentle and fascinating when he chose and yet so overbearing when the whim took him. She shuddered at what might have been her fate if she had gone on a little longer. Even if there had been no wife in the future, his nature would have been the same. But aloud she only said, "That was hard for you both!"

His face hardened at that.

"It was certainly hard for *me*!" he said uncompromisingly.

"It must be very hard when a home is broken up!" moralized Camilla, loathing herself for the smugness of the remark yet unable to think of anything else appropriate to say.

"Get rid of the idea that she was a martyr," said Whitlock brusquely. "She had her own way. She's living with her father in his palatial mansion. She has everything she wants. I am the one that is cast out. I have done everything that I could to make her see where she was wrong and make her come back to her home and her responsibilities, and she has refused. Now I think it is time to think of myself. I have refused to get a divorce, feeling that she might weaken, but my life is going on, and I am alone. There has been no one to understand me, no one to cheer me when I come back from a hard day!"

He paused a moment, and Camilla gazed at him in troubled silence.

"Until you came, Camilla—!" His voice softened, and he gave her suddenly one of those deep, possessive looks, those smiles that had puzzled her often before and now filled her with a new kind of alarm.

"Oh, please," she said in a distressed tone, "I'm glad if I have helped in any way. But I'm not the one to do anything much. If someone—something—could only bring you two together again! It must be so very hard for all of you. In spite of disagreement, it can't be happy for any of you to be apart! You belong together! It's what God wants—*expects* of you! And—your little girl! How dreadful for her not to have any father and for you not to see her every day and watch her grow up! My father was so much to me. I wouldn't give up the precious memory I have of him for anything!"

The man almost squirmed away from her words.

"Yes, of course, there's that," he said almost roughly. "But then, she's having every luxury, more than I could give her. She isn't really missing anything. It's I that am starved for human sympathy—until you came, and—and then I began to feel that there might still be a little brightness left for me on earth if—"

Suddenly Miss York appeared in the doorway, and her pleasant, hearty voice boomed into the atmosphere so tense and strained, seeming to clear away the morbidness and bring a fresh breath to Camilla. "Well, I just looked in to see whether you two were done with those letters. If you are, I wonder if I could get your help for a minute or two, putting up this awkward old picture. I can't seem to hang it alone. Mr. Whitlock, you used to be handy around the house, I remember. Would you mind lifting the picture while I twist the wire to shorten it? These ceilings are so low that the cord is too long."

Whitlock rose stiffly, severely, and followed the nurse into the room across the hall, doing what was asked of him without a word, his face like a thundercloud all the while, and then when it was done he turned to Camilla.

"I'll say good night," he said stiffly. "I must get these letters into the mail!" (Although Camilla knew quite well those letters weren't important at all.) "I'll see you on Monday about the rest!" he added significantly and, taking his hat and coat, departed without a word or even a glance in Miss York's direction.

"H'm!" remarked that good woman significantly. "Grumpy as ever, I see!" Then she added, "He had the sweetest little wife I ever saw, and he treated her like the very dust under his feet. I'm not surprised she couldn't stand it. But I guess he can be nice in the office, can't he?"

"Yes, he can be nice," said Camilla thoughtfully. "He has really been very kind to both of us girls in the office."

Miss York eyed her keenly and said no more, and they spent a very happy evening getting Miss York's room settled, but nothing more was said about Mr. Whitlock.

Camilla, however, was much disturbed in mind, though she managed an eager interest in Miss York's room that well covered her troubled thoughts. But when Monday morning came she went down to the office in great trepidation.

Whitlock, however, gave no sign of anything out of the ordinary. He was gravely courteous and quiet during the morning, with even more than usual of his brusque abstraction. Marietta sensed it at once when she came in and snapped into her work with a frightened vigor that warmed Camilla's worried soul.

It was not until noon when Whitlock sent Marietta out for her lunch that he unbent and spoke to Camilla.

"Now," he said, looking up with a relaxing of his grim dignity, "I want to talk to you, Camilla. Thank goodness we shan't be interrupted here, except by the telephone, for nearly an hour."

Camilla swung her swivel chair around from her desk, a startled look in her eyes, although she had been quite expecting something all the morning.

"Move your chair over here near me where you always take dictation. I don't want to have to talk very loud."

Camilla moved her chair to her usual place, innocently carrying her pad and pencil as she usually came for dictation.

She tried to look up composedly but met one of those possessive glances that had come to seem so frightening.

"Camilla," he said, "I have been utterly miserable all night." His eyes certainly attested to his words. "I haven't been able to sleep. I have thought and thought until I am nearly crazy. I felt that we should talk it over and decide what we ought to do."

"We?" said Camilla, opening her eyes wide in alarm.

"Yes, Camilla, I felt that you had the right to make the final decision."

"Decision? I don't understand, Mr. Whitlock."

"Why, decision as to how we ought to move, you and I. You know, of course, that I have been loving you all winter! And I thought that I had reason to believe that you felt the same way."

He reached out his hand and covered hers with a warm, soft, tender grasp. Camilla started out of her chair aghast and drew her hands quickly from under his clasp.

"Mr. Whitlock!" she exclaimed in no uncertain tones. "You had no right to love me! How could you have thought that I had any such feeling? How dreadful! How perfectly *terrible* for you, a married man, to feel that way!"

There were tears in Camilla's eyes, and her face was white and drawn. She turned away from the desk and stood over by the mantel.

But Whitlock got up and came over beside her. "Don't speak that way, Camilla! Don't weep. I cannot bear to see you suffer, too. You don't know how it tears my heart! You little, beautiful, lovely darling. Oh, I love you, love you, *love*—!"

"Stop!" cried Camilla. "It is disgusting to me to hear you say that! It is unholy! You humiliate me!"

"No, Camilla, you mustn't feel that way, dearest. You don't know how I love you, how I long—oh, how my hungry arms long to hold you close! Just once, Camilla, let me feel your heart against mine. We have a right to that! Just to put my lips on yours—"

His arms went out to embrace her, and there was passion in his glance, but suddenly Camilla sprang away from him and went and stood over by the door.

"Don't you dare touch me!" she cried, and her eyes flashed fire. "Mr. Whitlock, I didn't think you were a man like this! I never would have come here to work if I had known that you would dare talk to me like that! My mother would never have invited you to dinner. We thought you were simply being kind to us for the sake of our old friends at home. I thought you respected me!"

Whitlock stood white and shaken across the room from her, looking at her sternly.

"You misunderstand me," he said hoarsely. "I mean you no disrespect. I want to marry you as soon as I can get a divorce. When I said I wanted to discuss the matter with you, I merely meant whether we should go on for a while and keep our love between ourselves or whether I should come out in the open and ask my wife for a divorce. I can easily do that, you know, for it was she who left me."

"Mr. Whitlock, I don't know what you mean, keep our love between ourselves. I have no love for you, and you have no right to love me nor to tell me so. And even if I could ever care for you that way I would *never* marry a divorced man. It's not right!"

"Oh, now, Camilla," he pleaded, "don't say that! It is all right and quite respectable for people to remarry after divorce. Everybody is doing it today."

"Not Christians!" said Camilla quietly. "Not born-again ones. It would never be right in my eyes, and I do not believe it would be in God's eyes. He has given only one cause for divorce and not any for remarriage as long as both husband and wife are living. But we do not need to discuss that. Even if you had never been married and did not need a divorce to set you free, I could never marry you. I do not love you and never did. And the fact that you could say what you have just said to me this afternoon has almost made me hate you."

"What have I said, Camilla, that has made you so angry?" he pleaded, giving her a self-righteously innocent glance.

"You have confessed an unlawful love for me!" declared Camilla, her eyes flashing anew at the memory. "A love you had no right to even recognize in your heart, much less allow and foster. Oh, if I had had any such idea when you first began to show me kindness, I would never have looked at you again."

"Forgive me, Camilla," he said almost humbly, "you do not know the heart of a man when he loves."

"Well, I hope I never may know, then, if it is unholy like that. A good man would have torn it out and uprooted it and fled from anything that would have reminded him of it!" Camilla's tongue was sharp, and her tone was hard and bright. How she despised the man, and yes, despised herself, too, for not having foreseen such a possibility and guarded herself and him against it. Even if he hadn't been married, she had never really seriously considered him in the light of a lover. Not even when her mother warned her the other night had it seemed at all possible that such a thing could be. She had been to blame, perhaps, in going out with him those few times, in welcoming him to the house, and in using him as a sort of mild entertainment to keep herself from thinking of another man whose bright personality had been obsessing her. Oh, how wrong she had been! She hadn't meant to play the game of hearts the way the world was playing it.

Suddenly she lifted honest eyes to his angry, mortified ones.

"If I have inadvertently done anything to lead you on to this," she said earnestly, "I most humbly ask your pardon! I did not dream that you meant anything like this in the kindness you showed me. I am ashamed that you could even think I had cared for you that way. I *never did*!"

He was still so long that she wondered if she would have to speak first, and then he lifted his eyes again to hers.

"You didn't, Camilla," he owned. "You are a good girl. I appreciate your goodness. But you are somewhat fanatical in your ideas about divorce, you must own that. It's not your fault, of course. Your mother has trained you that way, and, of course, she's not so much to blame. It belonged to her day, and she has lived up to what she was taught. But the world has made progress today. It has gone far from narrow-minded precepts that did well enough for a former generation. What kind of a God would it be that condemned two people, utterly unmated, hating each other, making each other miserable, to live their lives out together?"

"Living their lives out apart is one thing," said Camilla, with conviction, "and either of them marrying someone else is another. Mr. Whitlock, the world may change and progress as you call it, but God is the same yesterday, today, and forever, and God's principles never change, in spite of the world's fashions. But I can't discuss this with you anymore. I wish you would go back to your work and let me go back to mine and forget all this awful hour—if we can!"

"Yes—if we *can*!" said Whitlock bitterly. "Camilla you could not talk so severely of right and wrong if you loved me as I love you. You see, this is the first time I have ever really loved a woman. I have seen in you the ideal woman of my life, and I have laid all at your feet. You could not treat me this way if you loved me as I hoped you did."

"Perhaps not!" said Camilla. "But you see, *I don't*."

He watched her furtively from beneath his half-closed lids, as she stood with her hands gripped fiercely together, her young brows knit in trouble, and her eyes dark with indignation.

Suddenly he raised his head with that motion that his young office force knew so well when he was hurried or troubled and was giving some command about work to be done. "Well, I'll *make* you love me!" he declared. "I swear I will."

Camilla laughed suddenly, a slow, amused laugh.

"That would be quite impossible!" she said in a low, controlled tone. "Not even if you were free and all things to be desired, I wouldn't love you!" And something faraway, like the memory of a dream, danced in her eyes and made them laugh.

And Ralph Whitlock stood and watched her grimly, helplessly, and suddenly knew that he had lost.

"Camilla," he asked after a long, long silence, "why? Is there someone else? Is there, Camilla?"

She looked at him steadily for a moment, startled anew, then turned her face away from him toward the window where the sun had suddenly shot out from behind a cloud, and a smile dawned in her eyes.

"Yes," she said quietly, in a clear voice, "there is!"

Chapter 23

It was growing late for the Florida season, and Mrs. Wainwright was beginning to talk about going home.

There had been no word of her husband's coming south, and she was beginning to realize that he hadn't really expected to be able to come at all. And now that the season was about over and so many were flitting to their homes, it didn't matter so much after all. She talked idly with her friends of "business" and of how hard her husband had to work in these times, and rocked and knitted.

She was distinctly glad that Stephanie Varrell had given up bombarding her with questions as to where Jeff had gone and was about to leave the hotel. Rumor had it that she had a quarrel with her latest fiancé and he had departed hastily. But recently a new adherent had arrived, a dark-browed, foreign-looking stranger who walked the patios with her and seemed to order her around as if he had the right. They were off now in an airplane, sailing over the blue sea, into the bluer sky, looking like a mosquito on a field of blue. Jeffrey Wainwright's mother profoundly hoped she would sail so far that she would never come back into her range of vision again.

Jeff, meanwhile, had been with John Saxon, doing actual physical labor and learning profound truths from the Word of God. Such fellowship and joy had come from this friendship as he had never had before and a vision of what heavenly lives could be on earth, even in a little old ramshackle shanty in the midst of a lonely Florida orange grove, waiting for the oranges to mature and pay for ordinary necessities.

One night, sitting under the Florida moon, Jeff told John about Camilla. Told him, too, that he was worried because she had not answered his letter.

John listened quietly, read between the lines, studied the speaking face of his friend, and then spoke in a tone of deep brotherly love.

"Man! If you've found a girl like that, go back and get her promised before someone else carries her off! There aren't many of them these days. Jeff, I'll be missing you, but—I'll be praying for you, old man!"

Jeff went the next day.

He found at the hotel a summons for him from his father. He would come down for a week with Jeff's mother and bring her home if Jeff would come back at once. So Jeff sent a wire and went.

His first day in the office was a busy one, for his father had left detailed directions, and Jeff carried them out conscientiously to the letter. It was late, and he was tired when he got through, but his heart was singing. He was going to see Camilla in a few minutes. God grant no other man had found her yet and carried her off. What a fool he had been to leave without telling her something, getting some definite word from her, and yet, how could he? She had definitely put a barrier between them, which he had to find out how to cross. Thank God he had found the way and crossed it, and now was free to go and tell her.

So he ate a hasty dinner and drove down to Vesey Street.

But when he reached Vesey Street, it wasn't there at all! Something had happened. It was gone entirely, dropped right out of the world. It seemed as if he were living in a fairy tale and a bad fairy had woven an enchantment. Of course, he had made some ridiculous mistake and it was there somewhere, but he couldn't find it.

He drove up a block and down a block and round several blocks and came to a standstill again right where he had thought it was, but Vesey Street had departed.

He consulted a policeman new on the beat who informed him that there were portions of an intermittent Vesey Street located erratically here and there in the neighborhood, and he canvassed them all to no purpose. It was as if 125 Vesey Street had vanished off the map.

Stephanie Varrell, sailing trackless skies to strange lands with her dark foreigner, would have laughed if she could have seen his face, utterly baffled, and so easily, by a couple of summary little telegrams. Sometimes in her thoughts she exulted over having wiped that block of Vesey Street from the face of the earth. She wondered what had become of the girl and whether she was by this time forgotten. Whether the letter, too, in ashes, had done its work. She felt, if she had no other satisfaction, at least she had that. For she hated that girl, of whose likeness to herself more than one man had dared to tell her that night.

But Jeffrey Wainwright came back at last to the heap of bricks and plaster and glass and tin that composed that portion of Vesey Street and searched until he found a boy who used to live in the row and who remembered a family by the name of Chrystie. He used to deliver them papers sometimes, he said. But they had moved away. "Suddenly," he said. "Maybe they couldn't pay their rent." He didn't know where they had gone, perhaps a long way off. "People did sometimes, when they couldn't pay their rent."

So Jeffrey went his troubled way. He tried to find out who had done the moving, but the boy didn't know. He wasn't on the spot at the time. He was delivering papers on his route. His brother might know, but he was gone away to his uncle's on a farm.

Long evenings Jeffrey Wainwright searched for Camilla, coming back each night to the empty place where Vesey Street used to be and asking anyone who passed, but nothing came of it.

He even searched out the postman on that beat, but the postman, though he remembered the Chrysties, said they had left no forwarding address. He said they never got much mail, anyway, just a letter now and then from the west. But he couldn't remember the name of the town, so that came to nothing. And the bricks and debris of Vesey Street grew daily less and less as the ground was cleared and prepared for the large building that was to go up for the gas company. Even the old wooden step where Jeffrey had stood with Camilla that night was carried away, gone, utterly gone. Only the memory of that precious kiss was left.

That night he wrote John Saxon a brief anxious letter asking him to pray hard!

One day Jeffrey remembered Miss York. Why hadn't he thought of her before? And he drove to the house where he had gone for her on that memorable night in the winter.

The snow was gone, and the grass was growing green. There was a scraggy row of daffodils blooming in the little side yard of the house where he had found the nurse, but when he knocked at the door nobody answered and, looking at the windows, he found there were no curtains and no sign of inhabitants. A query around the neighborhood brought out the fact that the folks had gone to live with their daughter instead of her coming to live with them, and the house and daffodils were for sale or rent, but no one knew what had become of the nurse!

It was a strange set of circumstances, as if some evil-minded power were playing a trick on Jeff. He thought of the kind old doctor next. He would know his patients, the Chrysties, and what had become of them. He would surely know where Nurse York was, at least.

But when he went to the doctor's house where he and Camilla went that first night they had met, he found crepe on the door. The doctor had had a stroke and died two days before, and no one around the house knew or cared where a Nurse York lived, and they had never heard of patients named Chrystie.

All day Jeffrey worked in the office, and every evening he searched for Camilla. He occasionally met acquaintances here and there in the city who invited him to their homes or asked him to go out with them, but he declined them all. He was too busy. It got around that he was at home and the telephone rang incessantly when he was there, but he told his man to say he was going out. If Stephanie Varrell called or did not call, he did not know nor care. If she was in the city, it made no difference to him. What did make a difference was that Camilla had vanished as completely as Vesey Street, and his heart was crying out to find her. The kiss upon his lips was real now and came back to him in his dreams and thrilled him. Where, oh, where was Camilla?

Chapter 24

Matters at the office had been most trying ever since that Monday talk that Camilla had had with Whitlock.

He had been in and out of the office, working hard and silently, answering everybody shortly, glaring into the telephone as if it were a human being, most irascible, even to Camilla. And as for poor Marietta, she was getting in these days all the discipline of life that she had missed when she was a child.

Camilla had time now and then to look at her proudly and encourage her with a smile, for really, Marietta was showing some of the fruits of righteousness that hard trials often bring. She was neat, and she was respectful; even in the face of faultfinding, she was humble. She did not answer back nor chew gum nor read novels, and she did her work well and more and more rapidly.

If I should have to leave, thought Camilla—and she thought it many times a day in these days—*Marietta could almost take my place!*

Camilla had not told her mother her fears. Time enough

when the blow fell if it did, but she knew enough about human nature to understand that things could not go on continually as they were doing.

But wise Nurse York was watching, and whenever she came over to the house for a few hours, which she did as often as she got a chance, she watched Camilla keenly. And she asked casual, wise questions to find out whether Whitlock was as frequent a visitor as he used to be. She had pretty well convinced herself that the Chrysties had not known about Whitlock's wife until she let it out. She did not mean to say any more about it unless she had to, to save Camilla from making a mistake, but she was taking no chances. They Chrysties were thoroughbreds and would not show their amazement, would not want her to think there had been any attention that a married man should not show. They would keep their thoughts to themselves, but nevertheless Nurse York would watch. She so loved Camilla and despised Whitlock that she would not let things go too far.

She noted the strained look around Camilla's eyes at night when she came home yet was satisfied that it was not from heartbreak, at least, and when the next weekend passed and there was no further sign of Whitlock, she drew a breath of relief and took heart of hope.

One day Whitlock came into the office about noon with a strange, desperate look on his face. He sent Marietta off to her lunch summarily, and Camilla wished she dared rise and go, too, but Marietta was scarcely out of the way before Whitlock came over and stood before her desk.

"Camilla, I'm desperate," he said. "I can't stand this any longer."

Camilla lifted up her heart in swift prayer for help and guidance. "Oh, I'm sorry," she said quickly, gently. "I know myself there are times when it seems as if there was not a soul to go to but God. But I know, too, that He can always help us through hard places."

The man looked at her strangely, his head down, his eyes lifted, piercing through her very soul as if he would probe her to find out if she was really meaning all she said, as if he would find some weak place in her armor if he could.

"How could God help me?" asked the man in a tone of scoffing.

"Nothing is worthwhile in which God cannot help," said Camilla. "You told me once, I think, that you are a Christian."

"Oh, yes, I told you that I'm a Christian. I suppose I am, perhaps; I don't know. I joined the church, but it hasn't done me much good, has it? Look what a rotten deal I've had. A marriage that was a failure and a love that came to nothing—the only woman in the world that I could ever love telling me that she hates me! Would you call that a fair deal? Would you want a God that treated you that way? Come, tell me what *you* would do about it?"

His lower jaw was out, and his eyes were flushed and angry, desperate eyes. They almost made her shudder to look into them. Camilla, if she had followed her impulse, would have turned and fled from the building and never gone back again. But something, perhaps it was the challenge from the lips of the man who was usually so calm and conservative, so absolutely correct in everything he said, made her stay and answer.

"Come, what would *you* do?" he urged. There was something in his eyes, like an angry bull about to charge.

Quietly she answered. "I think I would look into my own heart first, before I blamed God, and try to find out whether any of the trouble had been my own fault."

"What? *My* own fault?" he bellowed. "What do you know about it?"

"Nothing," said Camilla calmly. "You asked me what I would

do, and that is what I think I would do first. I would get down on my knees—on my face—and ask God to show me myself utterly. And if facing things honestly that way I found any of my trouble was my own fault, and if there was anything left to be done that I could do toward righting things, no matter if it cost me all my pride, I'd *do* it!"

He scowled down upon her, and a wave of memories rolled over him, each one bringing a deeper frown. "Right it? What do you mean, *right it*? Right my love for you?"

"Why, yes," said Camilla thoughtfully, "I suppose it would right that, too, for that was only an effect of the other, not a cause. There was something behind that or it would never have come. The first wrong was far behind that. I don't know when it came, but if you had been loving your own wife and living with her in unselfishness and happiness you would never have fancied you cared for me. It was not a natural right love, it was abnormal, and I suppose God may be trying to make you understand that."

He looked at her out of his bloodshot eyes as if he could not believe his ears.

"But I couldn't love my wife," he said, "and I don't want to live with her in happiness. There's no happiness where she is concerned."

"You thought there was when you married her," said Camilla calmly. "Perhaps I'm all wrong, and, of course, I don't know the circumstances, but there's usually wrong on both sides when things like that happen, and they never can be righted until both are willing to own it. I couldn't advise you, really, I'm too young and inexperienced. But I should think you'd talk with the Lord about it, and then you'd go and try to make up with your wife, and get your little girl's arms around your neck, and see how it feels to have her lips kissing you. I don't believe you're going to find relief in any other way. Only God can make you want things right in your life. No love that isn't right could ever bring you anything but more trouble. And now," said Camilla with a throb of great relief, "I hear Marietta coming, and I think I'd better go to lunch. I've told you everything I know to say, and if you would like me to leave the office after you have thought this over, if that will help you to do right, I'll be glad to go."

The door opened, and Marietta walked in, giving a furtive glance at the wild-eyed master and wondering if Camilla was fired at last and if *she* would come next.

But Whitlock snatched his hat and coat and hurried out of the office. Camilla smiled at Marietta out of tired, brave eyes and went out to lunch. She didn't feel equal to answering Marietta's questions just yet.

Chapter 25

Jeffrey Wainwright parked his car near the exclusive flower shop where he had been used to purchasing his flowers. The last time he was there he had brought white orchids for Camilla to wear to dinner with him. He had a yearning now to see if they had any white orchids. He did not quite know why he got out and went up to the lovely window with its marvelous display of flowers. He had a vague idea of sending his mother some Parma violets. His mother loved violets, and he had no one else now to whom he cared to send flowers. It just seemed pleasant to go there, that was all, to remember how he had gone that other night that now seemed so long ago and sent the orchids.

He locked his car and stepped across the pavement, weaving his way among the people who thronged that way always at the noon hour. It was foolish his coming there then; he could just as well have telephoned for them and saved his trouble.

He did not notice the people who stood beside the window. He stepped up and looked over the head of a woman, and there, sure enough, in the center of the window, were some lovely specimens of white orchids, their delicate forms standing out as rare faces will sometimes amid a throng.

A group of three women who had been exclaiming over a bank of brilliant yellow flowers moved on and Jeffrey took their place, where he could look more carefully at the flowers down in front. Yes, there were violets, and they looked like his mother's favorite kind. He gave one more wistful glance at the white orchids. It seemed to him he had never seen such lovely ones before, and then he turned to step behind the other window-gazer and go into the shop to order his flowers. But the woman turned also, and they were face-to-face, each trying to go in opposite directions. He lifted his hat apologetically and looked down, and then he saw her as she looked up.

"Camilla!" he cried joyously, his face lighting with a great joy, "Oh, Camilla! My dear!"

And then and there he placed a hand reverently on each of her shoulders and, bending down, he laid his lips upon hers. Right there in the throng of the street!

"Oh, Camilla, I have found you!"

And then he reached down and caught her fluttering hands.

People turned and looked, and one woman who always explained everything she saw to any companion with her said, "It's her husband! He's been away, don't you think, and he didn't expect to meet her just there? My! He looked happy, didn't he? I wonder if he'll take her in there and buy her some flowers! Wouldn't that be nice? My, I like to watch people, don't you? Yes, he's taking her in. I wonder what he'll buy her? I'd like to stop a minute and see, wouldn't you?"

"He's not her husband if he's buying her flowers!" said the other woman sourly. "They don't! She'd better enjoy them while she can. There won't be many more after they're married."

"Oh, now you don't know," said the first woman wistfully.

"See, see, I believe he's going to buy those white orchids for her. Isn't that wonderful? White orchids are awfully expensive, aren't they?"

"Yes, I guess they are. I wonder what she'll do with them," said the sour woman. "She is dressed dreadfully plain, though she's pretty. But she looks tired and worn out. She's likely his sister, and he's buying orchids for his girl. Come on, we can't stay here all day."

"No, she isn't his sister," said the first woman firmly. "Didn't you see how he kissed her? It wasn't a brotherly kiss, not that one. It was real, I tell you." And she turned away with a wistful backward look through the window.

But Camilla stood within that flower shop and watched Jeff as he bought the flowers, those very white orchids for her, and pinned them on her shabby old coat that was ten times more shabby than the last time it had white orchids pinned on it. Camilla, with her cheeks glowing rosily and her eyes alight. Camilla, trying to realize that it was herself and not a girl in a dream! Camilla, with that precious kiss stinging sweet upon her lips and the feel of Jeff's hands upon her shoulders, the hungry feel of his arms that had restrained themselves for the sake of the world that was looking from taking her close to his heart. Somehow she felt it, knew it, without a word being said about it, without the thought being even formed into phrases. It was just there, a great wonderful knowledge.

And it was all a part somehow of that word she had said in the office when Mr. Whitlock had asked her if there was anyone else, and she had answered, with such amazing quickness, knowing on the spur of the moment that it was true, "Yes, there is!"

Somehow, out of the chaos that had separated them for so many weeks, that *yes* had called him to her side.

And the strange part about it was that she had no doubts, no fears, no protests about his being of another world. Why was it that her soul was so at peace?

They went out of the shop with the lovely white orchids pinned upon her breast and her hand drawn within his arm, his eyes down upon her like a light.

"Where do we go now, Camilla?" he asked, pausing in the doorway to the immense delight of the first of the two women who had lingered before a bargain window of silk underthings just for the sole purpose of getting another glimpse of romance. "Is your car parked somewhere near, and do we have to retrieve it, or can you go in mine? And is there somewhere you must go first, or do we drive right home? And *where* is home?"

She laughed at the torrent of questions, and he laid his hand upon hers with a close, loving pressure.

"I never take my car out at noon," she managed to answer, though his eyes were looking wonders into her own. "I can go in yours, if you will be so good. It isn't far. I've had my lunch. But I must be back there in twenty minutes. My lunch time is almost over. I just came around this way—to—see the flowers!"

She bent low to look at the lovely ones she was wearing, and her face grew more rosily red than ever, for she knew by his smile that he understood that she was loving those orchids when she stood there alone window-gazing. And she knew in her heart as she looked at the delicate petals that she was also loving him, though then she had never expected to see him again. But the glorious knowledge that she loved him had so thrilled her as she acknowledged it to herself that she had had to come and look at the orchids to bear the joy of it.

All this her eyes held, and she lowered them from his gaze lest he should read it there too soon.

"Office!" he said, frowning above his smile like a sun-shower in April. "I can't spare you to an office. How long does it last? Must you go today when we have just found each other?"

"Oh yes, I must go." She laughed happily. "It lasts till five o'clock."

"Then I shall park outside the door and watch everyone who comes out. I'm running no risks of losing you again. It's been agony these last weeks since I got home and found you'd gone and taken your street away with you, root and branch."

"Oh!" said Camilla softly, her eyes glowing, and then she said, "Oh, what do you mean, 'taken the street with me'?"

"Didn't you know the street was gone? Here, I'll show you. It won't take long; we'll drive around that way so you can understand what I've been up against. I even wrote a letter and mailed it to an address that wasn't anymore, hoping somehow the post office would find you, though they had said you had left no forwarding address, and this very morning it came back to me from the dead letter office! It made me feel sick to look at it. I thought I had lost you forever. Camilla, *why* didn't you answer my letter that I wrote from Florida?"

"Letter?" said Camilla, looking up amazed. "Did you write me a letter?"

"I certainly did," he said. "And I watched every mail for an answer. I thought you had forgotten me. But you haven't, have you, Camilla?" He looked earnestly into her face.

"No, I haven't forgotten you," she said softly, "but I never got any letter, though—I often—wished—for one."

"You *dear*!" he said with that tender, wonderful look in his eyes. "Even though we were of different worlds? You looked for a letter?"

He was driving with a royal disregard of traffic laws, but perhaps because the traffic was too dense to let him go very far at a time, or because the traffic officers were looking the other way, nothing happened. And then they whirled into the open space where Vesey Street and its surroundings used to be, but neither of them realized it, for they were looking into one another's eyes, and only the angels must have guided and protected that car as it moved along in its own sweet way, certainly Jeff did not.

"But that's all over now," said Jeff with a lilt in his voice, "because, Camilla, I've been born again!" And suddenly he stopped the car and bent over and kissed her for the third time. Right in front of where the old house at number 125 Vesey Street used to be! And neither of them knew it!

Not until suddenly Camilla came to herself and realized that people were passing and looking at them.

"Oh!" she said, her voice full of great joy. "Jeffrey, we mustn't, not here! People will see us! Where are we?"

"I don't care if the whole world sees us!" He laughed. "They can't spoil our joy, anyway!"

Then he looked around him as he drew his arm away from her.

"Why, we're at Vesey Street, don't you see? And Vesey Street isn't at home! But I don't care anymore, do you? I've found you, and that's all that matters!"

Then did Camilla sit up and look around. Vesey Street? It couldn't be Vesey Street! It wasn't anywhere! And she had to look around several times before she finally identified the old church on the next street with its solemn old clock chiming out the quarter-past hour.

"Oh, I'm late!" exclaimed Camilla. "I must go at once!"

"What will they do to you, darling? Make you stay after school?" Jeffrey's eyes were laughing as he started the car.

And then he would insist on getting out and seeing her up to the office.

"I've got to know your haunts, you see," he said seriously. "How do I know but you've a way of making the office and the building and all disappear, too? Such enchantment as you carry might do almost anything. And tell me, quick, before that elevator comes, what is your new address? I'm not going to run any risks at all till I have you safe and fast for my own!"

He said these last words in a low tone in her ear just as the elevator door clanged back to let them enter, and though Camilla's cheeks were very rosy and her eyes most bright, there was no other opportunity to answer.

Whitlock stood in the hall opposite the elevator as they arrived at the office floor, his face drawn and anxious, his watch in his hand, and a look of relief came to his face as he saw her step out of the elevator.

"Oh!" he said, stepping to her side. "I was afraid you were not coming back!"

And then he saw Wainwright standing smiling beside her, he saw the orchids and Camilla's brilliant cheeks, and his face went blank suddenly.

"I'm sorry to be late," chirped Camilla blithely. "It was rather—unavoidable! Mr. Whitlock, let me introduce my friend, Mr. Wainwright!"

Whitlock turned and looked at the other man, searching his face intently, and Camilla saw that her employer's face was deadly white and stern. But he put out his hand and greeted Jeff like one who acknowledged the championship of his rival.

Then suddenly, with another look at the orchids, Whitlock raised his eyes to Camilla's, an almost humbled look of homage in them.

"I just want to tell you," he said in his usual business tone, "that I've decided to take your advice about that matter we were discussing, and I'm leaving at once. Do you think that you could get along for a few days without me in the office if I am detained?"

Camilla's face lit up, though it had seemed before that that it wouldn't be capable of shining any more brightly than it already was.

"Oh yes," she said joyously. "I'm glad! I hope you will be most—successful! I'm quite sure it's going to be all right!"

He was gone, and Jeff looked down after the elevator as it slid away and said in a pitying tone, "Poor bird! I'm sorry for him. He doesn't know what he's about to lose! But I guess he can get another secretary, and I couldn't get another Camilla in the whole wide world. She's the only one!"

Camilla laughed softly, with something moist and tender in her eyes. Sometime, perhaps, she would tell Jeff everything, but it didn't seem to matter just now, only her heart took time to be a little glad that Whitlock was going back to find his wife.

Marietta sat working away intent upon her business when they entered the office, but when she looked up and saw Camilla with those gorgeous orchids pinned to her coat and her face shining, she sat and stared, oblivious for the moment of the tall young man who loomed behind her. And when Camilla introduced him and he bowed and smiled at her, she was entirely overcome, utterly speechless.

Jeff didn't stay but a minute. He said he had an errand and would be back at five o'clock, would come up to the office and get her. "We'll drive home in your car, shall we, Camilla? And I'll have mine sent up later. I want to see what kind of a job they made of the car."

And right there before the wondering eyes of Marietta, he had the boldness to stoop and kiss Camilla on her happy lips and say, "Good-bye, Camilla, till five o'clock!"

Marietta remained speechless until the door had closed after him and Camilla had turned toward her, smiling. Then she said, "Oh, Camilla! Isn't he *swell*? Does he really *belong to you*?"

It was hard for both girls to do any work that afternoon. Marietta was fairly bursting with questions, and Camilla could not keep her thoughts from wandering back to her joy. But five o'clock came at last, and Jeff was exactly on time.

They filled Marietta with everlasting gratitude and joy by tucking her into the car and taking her home before they went on their way, but at last they were out and alone and could talk. Camilla at once became dumb. She couldn't say what was in her heart. She could only smile and look at Jeff's dear face.

But Jeff wasn't dumb. "Camilla, I've been thinking a lot while you were up there in that office. How soon can we be married? I simply can't wait a long time! We've wasted a lot of weeks already. And I've been making plans. I have a gorgeous piece of land out on the Ridge, and I thought perhaps we'd like to build and have our house just the way we plan it? How about it? Would you like that?"

But Camilla could only gasp and smile and exclaim.

"We'd want it specially arranged so that your mother could have a little suite of rooms—sitting room and dressing room and bath and so on, you know—right on the ground floor. I wasn't sure but we'd have the whole thing built long and low so we could all be together. I know it isn't good for your mother to do much climbing of stairs."

Camilla glowed. It didn't seem that any of this was real, only a dream, and therefore no answers were required of her.

"And then I was wondering if we couldn't get hold of that nurse you had. Wasn't her name York? And just get her to live with us and kind of look after us all and be someone to stay with Mother when we had to be away a few days. I thought if we arranged the rooms right it might be very pleasant, and she would take a lot of responsibility off you if any of us were sick. She seemed such a nice sort of person. Would you like that?"

On and on he went with his wild, lovely plans, and they were at the house before they realized.

Jeff insisted on going in the back door straight from the garage with Camilla.

"I want to begin to be at home right away," he said, grinning.

And then in he walked and took Mrs. Chrystie right in his arms and kissed her gently on both cheeks.

"Here I am again, Mother Chrystie," he said with his nice grin. "And you might as well make up your mind to like me, for I've come to stay. I'm going to be your son just as soon as I can pry Camilla loose from that job of hers and we can get married. I hope you don't mind, for I love you a lot already!"

"And where do I come in?" said a voice from the dining room door, and there was Nurse York just come in for a few minutes to see how they were getting along.

"Why, you come right in on the ground floor, of course," said Jeff heartily. "Camilla and I were just talking about it. We were wondering whether you would be willing to give up what you're doing and be our official nurse? We're building you a special room just as you want it, if you will, and we won't take no for an answer!"

After dinner was over and Nurse York had gone back to her patient, they sat together talking it over joyously.

"But, Mother," said Camilla, "I don't see how we're ever going to have the right kind of wedding in this tiny house with our resources. Marietta has been telling me all the afternoon what swell relatives I'm acquiring, interspersed with clippings to prove it from the newspapers, and I'm afraid they'll feel uncomfortable here. They couldn't all get in, either. And we haven't a church around here that we know well enough to feel like getting married in. I wish people could just go quietly to a minister and get married. Very poor people do that. Why can't we?"

Her troubled eyes turned toward Jeff, who met hers with a perplexed but not at all worried look.

But it was the mother who solved the problem.

"Oh, that will be easy, dear," she said sweetly. "We'll just go back home to Burbrook, and you can be married in the church where your father and I were married. The same minister is there yet. He was a young man then; he's old and retired now, but he could marry you. Then you can have a little reception right there in the church afterward; that's often done. And you know there's a new hotel there now, a lovely place, they say. That would make plenty of room for the guests who stayed overnight.

It's not so far away, only a hundred and fifty miles. Wouldn't that be all right?"

"That would be great!" said Jeff. "And now, Mother Chrystie, how soon do you think it could reasonably be? Camilla has so much devotion to that office that I can't quite trust her decision, for I'm in a hurry; I'm telling my father and mother tonight, and I'd like to announce the date. Also, I want to bring them to call tomorrow."

❁

The wedding was fixed for June and very simply planned.

Camilla went around in a daze of joy and couldn't believe it was anything but a dream until the wedding presents began to come in, and then she was almost in a panic. How could she ever live up to those wedding presents? They more than filled the little house and were more wonderful than any dream she had ever dreamed.

She said something to Jeff one day, and he put his arm around her and drew her close.

"You don't have to live up to them, sweetheart. They are only things of this world," he said, "and you and I have been born again into another world, thank God!"

But there was one wedding present that filled Camilla's heart with thanksgiving, not because of its intrinsic value, though it was beautiful and rare and costly enough, but because of the card that accompanied it, though it was only a plain engraved card. It read, "Mr. and Mrs. Ralph Whitlock," and down in the corner in a woman's fine hand was written, "In Gratitude."

The wedding was charming and the bride very lovely in her mother's wedding dress of fine embroidered organdy with bits of real, old lace. John Saxon was there, of course, and Marietta, too, the trip and a new dress being a gift from the bride.

All Jeffrey Wainwright's rich relatives were present and called the old church "quaint" and "darling" and said the bride was "rare," and wasn't it nice that she was willing to wear Jeff's grand-mother's wedding veil?

It hung around her like frost work of old silver, and Jeffrey said it made her look like an angel. She wore real orange blossoms that John Saxon had brought. But the bridal bouquet was of white orchids!

GRACE LIVINGSTON HILL (1865–1947) is known as the pioneer of Christian romance. Grace wrote over one hundred faith-inspired books during her lifetime. When her first husband died, leaving her with two daughters to raise, writing became a way to make a living, but she always recognized storytelling as a way to share her faith in God. She has touched countless lives through the years and continues to touch lives today. Her books feature moving stories, delightful characters, and love in its purest form.

Also Available from Grace Livingston Hill

Amorelle
April Gold
Ariel Custer
Astra
Beauty for Ashes
Beloved Stranger
Blue Ruin
Brentwood
Chance of a Lifetime
Christmas Bride
Coming Through the Rye
Crimson Mountain
Crimson Roses
Duskin
The Flower Brides
GI Brides
Girl of the Woods
A Girl to Come Home To
Gold Shoe
Happiness Hill
Head of the House
Honor Girl
Job's Niece
Kerry

Ladybird
Love Endures
Man of the Dessert
Matched Pearls
A New Name
Not Under the Law
Patricia
The Prodigal Girl
Rainbow Cottage
Ransom
Re-Creations
Sound of the Trumpet
Spice Box
Story of a Whim
Strange Proposal
Street of the City
The Substitute Guest
Sunrise
Tomorrow About This Time
Treasure Brides Collection
Where Two Ways Met
White Flower
White Lady

Also from Grace Livingston Hill

GI *Brides*

*Love letters unite
three couples divided
by World War II*

Available where books are sold!